SEED OF VEX

Book 2 of the Sennenwolf Series

CAPES

Seed of Vex

Published by Capas LLC 2024
www.capescreates.com

Ebook ISBN: 979-8-9863167-4-1
Print ISBN: 979-8-9863167-3-4
Copyright © 2023 by Capes. All rights reserved.
www.capescreates.com

Proofread by Brandon Fox

Cover design by Jelena Gajic
Check out her work on Instagram (@coverbookdesigns)

Illustration by Gega Dunatishvili
Check out his work on Instagram (@gegadatunashvili) or via Art Station

TOTW / INGC / TAB

PRAISE FOR SENNENWOLF SERIES

An INDIES Foreword finalist
Readers' Choice Book Awards finalist
Indies We Love selection from LoveReading

"A playful twist on the fantasy genre... Who knew witches liked to party?"
-Kirkus

"...A series worth committing to. Very highly recommend."
-Readers' Favorite

"Mutual interests give way to an unlikely alliance between a powerful wielder and the imminent Male Alpha of Velm in Capes's beautiful, romantic fantasy novel *West of Jaws*."
-Foreword

"A perfect read for fans of Witcher and similar fantasies."
-IndieReader

"A rich fantasy romance with characters you'll love and a twisting storyline that will keep you hooked."
-LoveReading

"I just want to say that I loved Helisent from the moment I first met her in West of Jaws, sprawled on the ground in the midst of a temper tantrum."
-Coralie Moss, author of *Calliope Jones* and *Sister Witches*

"The story is one of the most compelling I've ever read with such a fresh voice and unparalleled narrative."
-Erin K. Larson-Burnett, Author of *The Bear & The Rose*

THE SENNENWOLF SERIES

DEDICATION

For The Rat King (Part II)

HELLO, READERS...

I'd like to part the veil for a moment and let you know what to expect from this book. I don't want to spoil anything about the Sennenwolf Series, but I think it's fair to say that *Seed of Vex* will take our fictional friends in a... new direction. It might feel a little jarring, but it's all part of the *plan*.

I organized this series as a five-part saga from the start. The first two books focus on Helisent's development. The next two focus on our beloved boy-wolf. And the fifth... well, I guess we'll all find out together what happens then.

Enjoy!
Capes

P.S. I've added new guides to the back of the book.

After months of searching, Helisent West of Jaws and Samson 714 Afador track Oko and Anesot to the jungle capital of Alita.

Helisent wants justice for the murder of her sister, Milisent West of Jaws. Samson wants to interrogate Oko for information about his missing mother, Imperatriz 713 Afador.

In Alita, Helisent accuses Samson's father, Clearbold 554 Leofsige, of colluding with Anesot to get rid of Imperatriz. Enraged by the insinuation, Samson and Helisent argue and then part ways.

Separated, Samson hunts down Anesot. The warlock says that he has information about Imperatriz's whereabouts—but he demands that Samson shield him from Helisent in exchange for the information. Samson agrees, and Anesot admits that he marooned Imperatriz on a distant island on behalf of Clearbold. Meanwhile, Helisent hunts down Oko and forces the witch to take her to Anesot.

When she arrives, Helisent finds Samson protecting Anesot. Unwilling to hear the wolf out, Helisent kills Anesot to avenge her sister.

With Anesot dead, Samson attempts to get answers from Oko instead. He's mortally wounded in the process. Terrified to lose him, Helisent wields a healing spell that's powerful enough to save Samson's life—but it also wipes all memory of the last four years from both of their minds.

Seed of Vex starts eight months later.

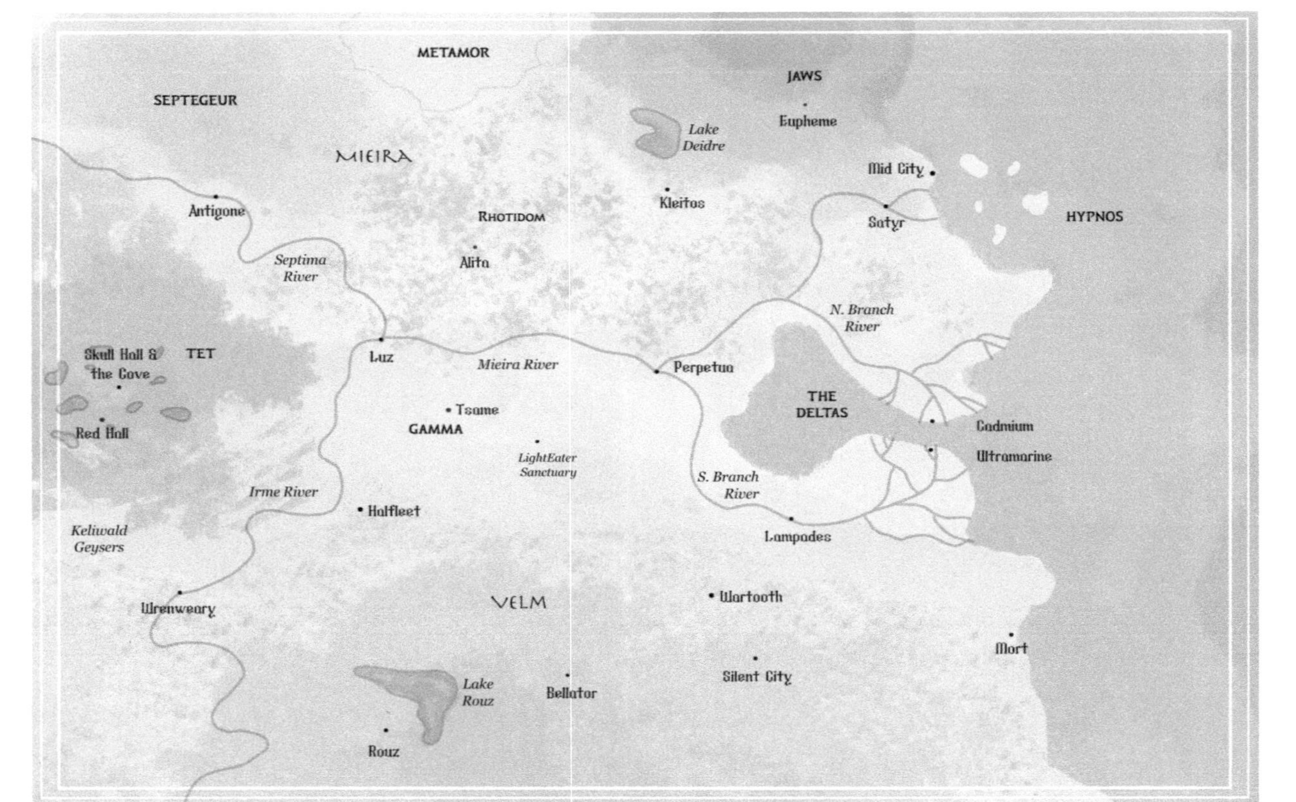

METAMOR
SEPTEGEUR
JAWS
MIEIRA
Lake Deidre
Eupheme
Mid City
Antigone
RHOTIDOM
Kleitos
Satyr
HYPNOS
Septima River
Alita
N. Branch River
Skull Hall & the Cove
TET
Luz
Mieira River
Perpetua
THE DELTAS
Red Hall
Tsome
GAMMA
Cadmium
Ultramarine
LightEater Sanctuary
S. Branch River
Irme River
Keliwald Geysers
Halfleet
Lampades
Wrenweary
VELM
Wartooth
Lake Rouz
Bellator
Silent City
Mort
Rouz

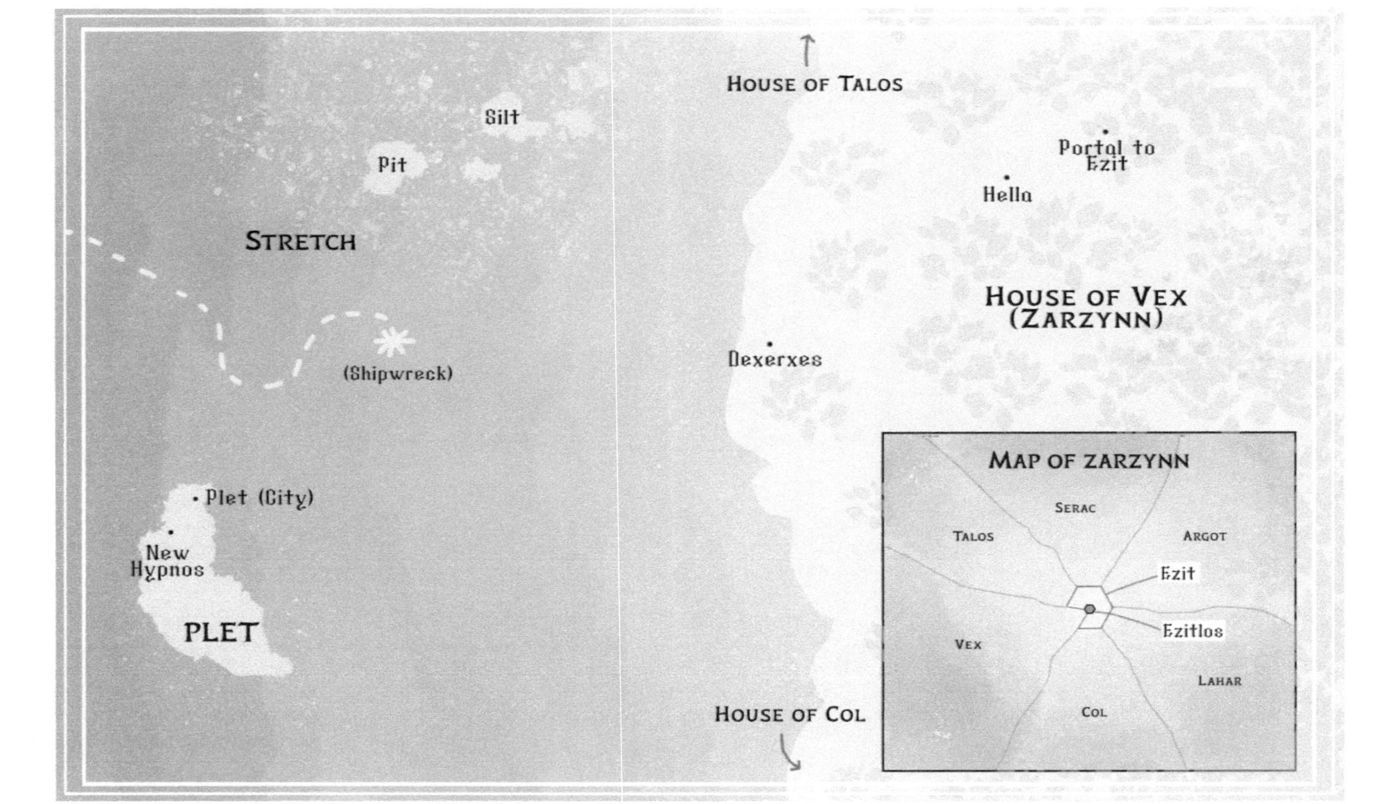

Silt
Pit
STRETCH
(Shipwreck)
Plet (City)
New Hypnos
PLET
HOUSE OF TALOS
Portal to Ezit
Hella
HOUSE OF VEX
(ZARZYNN)
Dexerxes
HOUSE OF COL
MAP OF ZARZYNN
SERAC
TALOS
ARGOT
Ezit
Ezitlos
VEX
LAHAR
COL

CONTENTS

VIGNETTES

INTERLUDE I
(DON'T DO IT, HELISENT)

I stare down at my bed.

Onesimos rests on his side, facing the rough black wall my bed is pushed up against. His wiry vermillion hair is matted on one side from laying the same way every morning. Esclamonde lays on the other side of the bed, arms outstretched like she's prepared to catch him from a nightmare. Her foot twitches. Onesimos snores. A tattered blanket lies pooled between them.

I stare at them, standing in the center of the room.

I turn and glance out the front door, which hangs open.

Sunlight blankets the uneven horizon of volcanic cones beyond my hovel.

Don't do it, Helisent.

I blink at the world that waits past the front door. "I'm going to do it."

Already, my stomach is in knots. I change my mind—

I turn back and kneel on the edge of the bed, knees sinking into the mattress. I stare at the space between the witchling and the oread. I try to force myself into the bed like I have for the last eight months.

It doesn't work this morning.

I change my mind again.

I step away from the bed. As though moving of their own accord, my feet backtrack to the opened door. My bottomless bag waits on a square table beside it.

I open the faded leather bag's clip, then reach inside.

I look at the bright light spanning the Jawsic countryside, the cloudless sky above.

Don't do it, Helisent.

I flick my fingers, casting collecting magic into my bag. Its contents flutter upward toward my hand. Carefully, I divest the bag of its contents. They stack in teetering piles on the table; a notebook, a bracelet, the tattered remains of notes my father writes me. I don't watch the items collect.

I look out the door again. Grass rises from the hill-like cones in narrow seams, crawling over them like veins. On and on, the hilly cones roll westward—eventually, they end in freedom.

In the ocean.

In Hypnos.

The knots in my stomach tighten as the bag's contents clatter and stack. A few shoes, an extra pillow, and a series of empty bottles find a place. A brown suede pouch is the last item to float free of the bag.

I've done this before: emptied my bottomless bag with my eyes locked on the eastern horizon. I've done this before: toyed with the brown suede pouch and the strange object it holds.

Inside is a circular white marble piece, which looks like a wheel.

I sniff the marble, then bite it. It's hard and scentless.

And obviously Velmic. I hold onto the white marble, then I search my pile of belongings for a letter.

In one hand, I hold the marble piece. In the other, I reread the letter sent to me last month. The words don't actually matter. My tracking magic will lead me to the letter's writer.

Some okeanid-witch named Butter.

I really only need Butter's note to find her in Hypnos, but the marble piece...

I don't know why I can't leave it behind. Maybe I've never been good at letting go of things I hate.

I hold it in my hand beside the letter from Butter, then use fire magic to send my pile of belongings up into flames. I cast smothering magic to shelter Onesimos and Esteban from the sounds and scent.

Firelight wheels around the room, glinting off the dim lava stone walls like lightning.

Onesimos snores while flames consume the items, crunching and lashing.

Esteban's foot kicks again.

Maybe if I remembered them, I'd stay.

Maybe their devotion to me would mean more if I could recall the last four years of my life.

When the flames simmer and die, uneven piles of ash remain; the world will have nothing to track me with but scattered ash.

I turn toward the door.

Don't do it, Helisent.

You are banished.

Lay low and the Class will free you soon.

I take a step away from the piles of ash and my sleeping friends. I look down at the white marble piece, then at the letter from Butter. I push the door all the way open, then step from the threshold.

I flinch from the light, raising a hand to block the sun. "Okay." I clear my throat, trudging westward. "Here I go."

INTERLUDE II
(THEY'RE JUST NIGHTMARES, SAMSON)

A warm hand wakes me by the shoulder.

With a gasp, I open my eyes.

A nightmare hangs in my mind like smoke from a fire. As though imprinted by a flash of light, I see a witchling in a yew tree.

I blink away the image slowly.

"Good morning, Lapsi." Brutatalika strokes my cheek. "You had another nightmare, but at least you slept in."

I take a few deep breaths and open my eyes, legs tangled in my sheet. Brutatalika lays next to me, head propped in her palm. Her blue-black eyes scan me while her finger traces my cheek, my jaw, my hairline.

I know what her doting eyes tell me:

They're just nightmares, Samson.

Just a trick the red witch uses to punish you.

I close my eyes. The witchling watches me from the threshold of the dream; her cape is bloodred, just like her irises and the yew's berries. In most nightmares, the witchling, aged around twelve or thirteen, waits for me in the canopy. She stares down, giggling and trying to direct my attention to something higher in the tree.

Her hands are full of red strings; some are already tied around my arms and wrists in the dreams, like an animal slowly being fettered.

It's just a witchling in a tree. Just a few red strings, light as twine.

I don't know why I can't let it go.

I open my eyes and stare at the ceiling.

Brutatalika runs a hand through my hair. Unlike me, my wife is fully dressed and ready for the day. She lounges across the blanket, shined torcs catching the light from the window. It glints off the golden studs in her lobes; my wedding gift to her.

"You have driproot, right?" She looks over her shoulder toward the door. My satchel sits beside hers, both full and neatly packed and ready for months on the road.

I sit up and she mirrors me. "I do. Thanks for waking me."

I lean toward Brutatalika, wrapping my fingers around her arm. With a quick smile, she leans back to kiss me. I close my eyes and take all the comfort I can from the touch.

I still have nightmares about the red witch—

But Helisent West of Jaws didn't destroy me, like she intended.

I survived my brush with death in Alita, then went on to have my wedding in Silent City. Despite the witch's plans to end me, Sutnazzar 712 Afador carved my name into a pillar above Imperatriz 713 Afador's. And then she carved Brutatalika 567 Sigivald's name next to mine.

I like to think things have been normal since that day two months ago.

Like we have most mornings since our wedding, Brutatalika and I get ready for the day side by side. Since she's already dressed and packed, she helps brush my hair, then tugs it into a bun, then slides my torcs into place on my upper arms.

I tighten the straps of my satchel, then sling it over my shoulder. Brutatalika does the same at my side. I slide the door open, then she steps in front of me, blocking my path with sparkling eyes.

I slide my thumb over her pink lips, scanning her features and filling my lungs with her ala. It's imprinted in my psyche now; not just as the ala of a loved one, but as a critical extension of myself. After two months spent together, our alas are layered at all times.

She smells like rosemary, like the birch logs the winter fires slowly consume.

Brutatalika takes a deep breath and sets her forehead against mine.

She's much more affectionate than I would have imagined. And

I'm much more receptive to that softness than I would have thought, too. I lean forward, lifting my chin for another kiss.

"Be safe, Lapsi," she whispers against my lips.

"Be safe, Tali," I whisper back.

"I mean it. You're heading north—and she's still in Jaws."

"I know where the witch is. I'll be careful." My heart thumps in my chest. I fear the red witch... but I fear my own people, too. "I'm more worried about you. Malachai has been camped out in Mort since the wedding. I heard there's a new symbol in the city."

A letter arrived two days ago outlining the symbol's design and where it's been carved around the coastal city—near the river where elders wash clothes, where the merchants drink at night, where the children play after school.

Brutatalika presses her lips against mine. "I read the letter, Samson. I'll be mindful." She sighs again. "Are you sure we should part ways? Why don't we travel together? It can't be unprecedented to stay side by side for the grand tour."

I smile faintly; it's good for the Female Alpha to want to stay close to the Male Alpha. Still... "Newly married Alphas do their tours separately. The public has seen us together. Now, they want a look at our courts separately. And speaking of courts..."

I imagine my packmates are waiting in line at Cadmium's northern streets, prepared for the journey to Satyr. I imagine Brutatalika's court waits in a similar formation at the city's southern port, prepared for the journey to Ultramarine.

Brutatalika's response is a tsk. She turns away from me and guides us into the hallway.

I follow, a knot building in my stomach as we head for the Cadmium Estate's front gate.

They're just nightmares.

Just a trick she uses to punish you.

But I can still see the red witchling from the nightmare this morning. I can see the threads of crimson woven through her irises; they're the same color as those tied around my arms, my wrists—even my ankles. I can hear the exact tone of her high-pitched cackle when she leaned down to sneer at me.

I remember what she said, too.

"I'm free now, boy-wolf."

CHAPTER 1

THERE'S ONE
FOR EACH OF YOU

HELISENT

Honey Baby,
I taught you to follow your bliss because I wasn't good at much else myself. But
maybe you are. Sometimes, the only thing over the next horizon is another
horizon.
Papa P.

I stomp through the ragged forest and wish I wouldn't have burned my lilith with everything else in my bottomless bag.

These legs are not made for walking.

I'm also *ruining* my white suede boots. (They're beige now.)

But all that's left in my bottomless bag is the Velmic talisman and a note that's leading me to Butter. I'd considered keeping my lilith, but the cushion wasn't nearly as impressive without its dangling metal ornaments.

And the Class took off with most of them after the incident in Alita.

One member even insinuated that I used the largest rod to impale the Kulapsifang of Velm. Samson 700-whatever Afador.

With each step, my mood worsens.

I'm exhausted after spending the morning wandering the coastal forests of Hypnos. My white hair is tangled from the wind, my brown skin dry and sunburned, my dress littered with twigs and dirt. And my white boots are now beige.

I'm on the edge of hopeless after a week of lonely and suspicious travel.

How far away can the ocean be?

With a sigh, I lean against a short fig tree. The curved leaves offer little shelter from the sun, but with the windy winter whipping through Mieira, I don't mind. I wipe the hair from my eyes.

I just need to figure out where I am...

I've been heading southeast blindly in search of the beach. Two days ago, I passed through Satyr—and haven't seen civilization since.

I swear I can *smell* the briny ocean...

Somewhere over the next horizon.

Somewhere Onesimos and Esteban and the rest of the world won't find me. At least, not anytime soon.

To my left, someone snorts. "I can't fucking believe you did it."

I turn to find a strange-looking woman beelining for me. I scan her twice, confused by her features. Her loose curls are white, tinged at the ends with cerulean. Her soft skin is a few shades darker than mine, while her eyes glitter with gold and turquoise.

Neither okeanid nor witch... unless she's both.

Hello, Butter.

She stops before me, holding aside a branch. Her smile is broad, almost unbelieving. Her features are smooth and flat, aglow with a promising youth I can pinpoint now that I'm leaving it behind.

The okeanid-witch snorts again. "You look like shit. Have they been starving you in Jaws?"

Compared to her, I probably look worse than shit. She wears a long and flowing robe; the orange dye is faded, but the fabric is impeccably clean. It even matches her bottomless bag, which has dusky yellow sequins.

Like I annoy her, she goes on, "And why have you let the Class keep you in Jaws for this long? They can't enforce anything. Especially not against you."

I blink, surprised by her argument.

Onesimos had begged me to respect the banishment in hopes of a better future; witches are long-lived, after all. Esteban said not to think about it; then she'd hand me some dextro.

Rather than respond, I narrow my eyes and reach into my bag.

I pull out the folded letter, then clear my throat. "'Hey, come meet me in Mid City. Half the beings here are banished. No one will notice you. Except me. I'll keep a lookout for you. We were friends, by the way. I'm Butter. Did anyone tell you about me?'" I study her orange robe, her bare feet and relaxed stance, her magenta lips. "I thought you'd look different."

She rolls her eyes. "Sorry to disappoint."

I glance around to make sure we're alone.

Near the coastline, the towering giants common to Rhotidom give way to squat pines and gnarled fruit trees. Dry leaves and broken branches litter the ground, tumbling in the wind. I don't see anyone spying from the other side of a trunk.

"Are we close to Mid City?" I ask. "I'm not much of a traveler."

"It's an hour away. Come on." Butter takes off with a wave of her hand, and I follow at her side. Unlike me, she doesn't trudge. She looks... hopeful as she waltzes into our future. "I would have thought you'd like the traveling after spending eight months trapped in rural Jaws."

I shrug. "Maybe you didn't know me that well, after all."

(Which is fine. I don't really know myself that well anymore.)

I glance sideways, studying Butter's features. "Do you want some help with your hair? You need to pick a lane here. Is it white like a wielder or... blue...? And why blue?"

Butter throws an arm around my shoulders and tugs me closer. I awkwardly try to keep up; she's a few inches taller than me. Her curls fall across my face, itching and blinding me.

"This is my real fucking hair, sweetheart. I figured you would have told Onesimos or Esclamonde about me. Or at least about the letter. Wow, okay—let's catch you up on our friendship.

"Last year, you came to Ultramarine to speak with my grandmother, Kierkeline Ultramarine. I led you to her, which is how we met. My grandmother sent you in search of Mieira's other Ghost-Eater. The other one lives in Alita—in case you were wondering why you ended up there.

"There's something else you should know, too. I guess you had bartered a look at your form with Kierkeline. My grandmother has told everyone in Ultramarine that you have six bloodred horns. Like ram-sized horns. The cat's out of the bag.

"Oh! And about my hair. Aside from my grandmother Kierkeline's blood, from my mother's line, I'm all okeanid. That's why my hair is white and blue and whatever it wants to be. Nymph magic, baby."

I weigh her revelations as we crest a low hill. She unslings her arm from my shoulders, glancing at me as she waits for a response.

She's not the first being to hand me a series of wildly interesting and deeply empty details about a life I don't remember.

The realization that Ultramarine knows about my bloodred horns is particularly novel, but I don't know if I feel shy about it.

More and more, I like the idea of the world knowing about my horns. I don't want them to fear me, but I need the world to know that banishing me is idiotic.

That controlling me is impossible.

Still... using brute force to convince others I crave peace won't fix my problems.

I chew on Butter's words as we pause on the hilltop. A few thatched huts come into view amid the distant horizon of sparse, rolling forest. Sunlight twinkles in a cloudless sky.

"Tell your sweet grandmother to be careful talking about my horns. There are too many wolves in Ultramarine for that. The last thing I need is another indictment from Velm."

I don't actually care about Velm—

I just want Velm to stop caring about me.

Butter reaches into her bottomless bag, hidden in the folds of her loose cloak, and pulls out a small packet wrapped in a faded green leaf. As we get moving down the hill, she packs it between her teeth and cheeks.

"Want one?" she asks. "It's betel nut."

I narrow my eyes. "Sure."

"I was kidding. You hate it."

"Oh."

We walk for the next few minutes in silence. Eventually, she reasons, "She talks about your horns to give you glory, not to make you sound dangerous."

I tsk as the wind whips my hair. "Sure, but the wolves fear me even at my most *glorious*. If you know what I mean."

Butter spits to one side, then she stares ahead. "My grandmother is working on a memory-restoring potion for you and Samson 714 Afador. She hasn't stopped working on it since she heard panic magic wiped both of your memories in Alita. Before she was a GhostEater, she was a healer. I guess there's a psychological element to healing—she's using what she knows about that to brew the potion."

I keep my eyes on the horizon.

I let Butter work through her memories of me. It's probably more taxing on her than it is on me at this point.

Eight months ago, I would have hunted down the GhostEater, desperate to remember what happened in Alita to prove (with grimoire) that I never hurt the Kulapsifang.

And now...

"I guess that's nice of her. Kind of weird she cares so much about my honor." I tuck Butter's letter away, then adjust the strap of my bag. "I'm tired of convincing the world I'm not dangerous."

I'm tired of convincing *myself* I'm not dangerous.

Maybe I am.

Butter keeps quiet for another stretch. She keeps spitting reddish saliva as we shuffle through the dry leaves. "Is that why you left Jaws? The first time I wrote to you, you responded saying you'd wait until you remembered everything—which doesn't make any sense. Kierke-line ignores the mandates from the Head Witch and Warlock of Ultramarine all the time. They still let her sponsor the city. So—why did you let them? Eight months is a long time."

I take a deep breath.

The answer is so pitiful; I bury it inside of me rather than admit it to Butter right now.

Because I wanted them to like me.

To approve of me.

To let me belong.

I wanted them to know I'm not dangerous. And now...

That neediness has hardened—and I'm not sure into *what*.

I exhale the long breath I drew in. "I guess I was having fun with Onesimos and Esteban. Jaws specializes in dextro and wine."

Butter cackles loudly. "Well, there's even more in Mid City. I hope you aren't tired of partying. Oh, and you don't need to worry about disguising yourself. Feel free to bust out the velvet robe. I meant what I wrote in my letter. Mid City is full of banished beings."

"Ah, the velvet robe..." I muse. "I've heard many tales of a velvet robe. I have zero memory of its existence and no idea where it might be today."

Butter's eyebrows bunch. "Someone stole your velvet robe?"

I nod. "It's one of the thousands of indignities that have befallen me since Alita."

Past the thatched huts on the horizon, the glittering ocean comes into view. I'd forgotten about this type of blue; a base of indigo that bubbles into a stretch of candied cerulean. Dark brown boats float on the shallow beach, casting their black shadows onto the sandy bottom.

I pick up my pace, desperate to set my feet in the ocean's warm currents.

Butter keeps up at my side.

Neither of us brings up the robe again.

When we pass the first cluster of huts, I ask, "Can you actually change the tides like the rest of the okeanids? Or is most of your magic from grandmother GhostEater?"

Butter snorts proudly. "I can do it all. That's why I look like a witch and an okeanid. I'm the best of both worlds."

She chatters on—and it's just enough to distract me.

Distract me from the fact that this fucking beach probably isn't the answer I've been searching for; it must linger on the next horizon.

Part of me knows I'm running from something I can't escape.

Something that's in my mind.

It's like the last four years are a pitched black room, and I can run my hands over everything in the room to feel the shape of those memories, but I can't open the shutters to let in the light and see what's stored there.

There is something very important in that room.

Standing in the center, taking up a lot of space. Silently.

Sometimes, I wonder if it's alive. Sometimes, I swear I can hear it breathing deeply and calmly.

"I have a little hut on the beach that we can share. Everyone in Hypnos needs dove, so we can barter and live like queens here. Oh! And speaking of queens, an okeanid demigod just brought Hypnos's latest monarch. Her name is Otrera. Have you ever seen an okeanid demigod? They're *beautiful*. Bluer than the rest. And I think…"

My ear twitches now and then, tallying Butter's words as she keeps explaining things I never asked about.

But mostly, I'm stumbling through a dark room where my dead memories sit like stacked shoeboxes.

I'm staring at the horizon and wondering what the fuck comes next.

The next few days pass in an *exceptional* stupor.

I was wrong to doubt Butter. I was wrong to be upset about the white boots turning beige. Who cares about the velvet robe, either?

It's almost enough to erase the guilt of leaving Onesimos and Esteban in Jaws.

I'm sure they'll track me to Hypnos soon—assuming they can be bothered with my existence anymore.

I'll have a few months here until Butter tires of me.

For now, she and I keep things simple.

She didn't lie; she has a thatched hut on the beach. Its woven walls are starting to disintegrate, but we don't care about privacy.

In the early afternoon, we wake up sticky and unkempt inside its sandy, salty walls. We stumble into the daylight and stagger toward the shallow water. The low tides turn the beach into a warm bath, even in the last weeks of the windy winter. And, for whatever reason, I'm not nearly as prone to drowning as I once was.

Our frolicking usually wakes the neighbors. They come outside with their drinks, and then we assemble a basic meal. Sometimes that meal is only dextro and powdered sassafras. Other times, it's dextro and a few magical mushrooms plucked from the cow shit that dots the coastline. Much like us, the lazy cows wade into the calm water before shuffling back onto land to eat and sleep and huff.

By nightfall, me and Butter are flying.

We make many friends.

And no one recognizes me as the dangerous red witch who was banished to Jaws for wounding the Kulapsifang of Velm.

Even when Butter introduces me to the okeanid queen, who shouts and laughs most nights in Mid City's single tavern, she doesn't bat an eye. The Hypnotic Queen's blue eyes are darker than the rest of the brown and black-skinned okeanids. Her thick, soft hair is half pulled back into a puff style, layered with sparkling lapis lazuli gems and aquamarine quartz.

By sunrise, Butter and I stagger back to our thatched hut. Some nights, she goes home with one of the okeanids who lives to our left. Some nights, I go home with one of the dryads who lives to our right.

One morning, dawn tangles on the eastern horizon of ocean. Rather than head inside the hut or to one of our neighbor's, we shuffle into the water and finish our drinks.

A black silhouette looms on the ocean near Mid City's five or six streets. The vessel is ten times the size of the rowboats the fishers push into the waves in the mornings. I squint, wondering if it's a boat at all—or maybe a house on the water.

Butter hiccups at my side. "See that? It's a proper ship. A weird hesperide sails up here from Cadmium every now and then. He's a merchant. Once he's bartered all his goods, he throws parties onboard —and I heard he bartered everything a few days ago."

She hands me her half-drank ale.

The goblet is heavy, teetering. "Butter, why haven't you just switched to brandy yet? You hand me a half-drank ale every morning. Will Queen Otrera be at the party on the boat? I want to make her my friend. Like a proper friend, not just someone we get fucked up with."

She leans back to stretch. "Because brandy makes me act crazy. And it's a *ship*—not a boat."

As sunlight leeches into the sky from the east, more of the ship's hulking shape comes into focus. I've never seen anything like it. At least, not that I can remember.

"Yeah, of course," Butter says. "The hesperide lets anyone onboard. And he loves okeanids, so Queen Otrera is a shoo-in."

Maybe a life at sea would be freeing—the ship certainly looks spacious enough. Larger than my hovel in Jaws, larger than the hut I share with Butter. Three poles shoot up from its deck, slack fabric collected against each. It looks like one hundred beings could fit on board.

Butter yawns, then she hooks her arm through mine. "Come on. Let's go to sleep."

I pour the rest of her warm ale into the waves as we amble onto the shore. Our feet sink into the sand and salt water pinches our skin as it dries on our legs. Our shack sits just past the beach, sheltered beneath a pine and palm tree that look at odds with each other. Inside, cool sand dusts the woven mats. I use sweeping magic to clean it before we lay down.

Butter falls onto her bed mat and settles in, tugging her blanket over her shoulders.

On the other side of the square room, I take off my bundled necklace and hang it from a nail on the wall.

The salt water has started to decay a few of the metallic pieces.

I snap my fingers to lift the hiding magic that disguises the colorful thread and dangling pieces. Though once vibrant, dark brown goo coats the strands. I know it's blood, but I can't remember how the necklaces came to be soaked—*and whose blood is it?*

The answer is in the black room of memories.

I settle onto my bed mat as Butter starts snoring. I set my head on my folded arm and stare at the necklace. I study the stained thread, the goo wedged into the crevices of the metal charms.

"Helisent West of Jaws," I whisper, "what happened to you?"

The ship is fucking awful, but I stick around in the hopes of impressing Queen Otrera.

She wears pale blue layers with white embroidery. Beads of lapis lazuli layer her half-pulled-back hair once again, nestled into her soft, tightly packed curls. Other shined decals dot her earrings and necklaces, glinting with moonslight.

It's hard to look away from Otrera—and not just because I'd like to make nice with the queen. It's her smile. I've never seen a person *smile* so fully or so often. I keep glancing over my shoulder, expecting to see a blue-hued okeanid demigod peeking over the ship's railing and drinking in our desita—nothing.

I'm surrounded by a reeling crowd instead.

They make it impossible to approach Otrera.

The queen doesn't walk around, instead shifting to direct her smile toward the next being who approaches her; they offer her drinks, small treats, more twinkling jewelry. And rather than rush forward, she stays planted in the same place, nodding and offering a few words.

Rowdy nymphs and wielders (even a few wolves) wander onto the ship from its slanted gangplank, each louder and drunker than the last. Most beeline for the queen.

After eight months of parties for three, it's a disorienting madness.

With each passing moment, I find it less appealing.

The deck tilts as the ship bobs in the water. Stars glitter against the black ocean past the ship's wooden banister. Overhead, all three moons wane toward slender crescents. Even Marama's massive pink-gray face trickles down dainty, faded hues. Firelight sconces provide most of the light, flashing over sweaty limbs and crazed smiles.

I steady myself on the deck's banister before finally making my way to the queen.

I don't have drinks or treats or jewelry to offer—just the promise to give Mid City all the dove it needs. I've also prepared a short list to flesh out exactly what my dove could do here. (It starts with a sewage system and ends with a dancehall.)

Before I reach Otrera, she breaks away from a doting group and heads below deck. I follow her, ducking and slipping around the wayward crowd. As I take the stairs to the lower deck, I catch Butter heading back upstairs.

I grab the okeanid-witch's shoulders and redirect her. "Come with me. I want to talk to Otrera. Now's our chance."

Butter giggles as I turn her around, falling against the wall. "Careful!"

We rush down the stairs. The queen's pale layers float behind her as though caught in a tide. She heads into one of the square storage rooms and we follow her, almost running into two hesperides in the doorway.

The men back up; we apologize to them as they apologize to us.

The nymphs wear clean leather layers and wide-brimmed hats. Dark spots speckle their fair skin, along with a few pale scars. Their brown hair sits tangled to their chests near their silver captains' badges.

It must be their ship.

One of the men smiles. The other watches Butter and I step into the room with a frown. We head toward Otrera, who takes a seat on one of the barrels lining the walls. It looks like the dark wooden barrels were used to transport goods up and down the coast. They smell old, slightly rotten.

I look back at the hesperides, prepared to ask for a moment alone with the queen. Then I realize how strange it is that two hesperides command the ship.

Wouldn't an okeanid have an easier time navigating currents and facing wild seas?

And what kind of sailors wear leather?

I brush off the details.

I know even less about tidal currents than I do about the skills it takes to sail ships. About what clothes sailors should be wearing.

"Butter! Come here." With a smile, Otrera beckons my friend over to her.

The hesperides stand aside as though suddenly shy or uncertain. I glance at the doorway, expecting them to leave.

Butter takes a seat next to the queen on one of the wooden barrels. It's large enough that neither woman's feet touch the ground. They dangle like children's legs, mirroring the innocent smiles on their lips.

Otrera nods toward the hesperides. "These dear nymphs captain this ship. They just came from the Deltas—and they say they have a gift for me."

The men offer unenthused smiles to me and Butter. One does a double-take when his eyes meet mine. He takes a quick step away from us, tucking his arms behind his back; I can't tell if he's nervous or surprised to see me.

He's younger than his cohort, and a bit plain. His eyes flash toward me again, then lower. "Hello."

I offer a quick wave to the hesperides, then take my place next to Butter and Otrera on the barrels.

The younger hesperide clears his throat as he watches me. "You don't remember me? From Cadmium?"

I roll my eyes—so that's what his weird behavior is about. We must have slept together at some point. "I don't remember the last four years, my dear hesperide. Give me another month or two. I'm sure your face will be the first thing that comes back to me."

The older hesperide looks at his companion; they stare at one another, but I can't tell what they're communicating between their widening eyes.

As though he suddenly understands, the elder hesperide gapes at me. "*You're* the red witch who lost her memory in Alita?"

I suck in a breath, sliding a glance toward Otrera to see how she's handling the revelation.

The Hypnotic Queen raises her eyebrows, returning my gaze as though expecting an explanation. She may not have batted a lash at my real name, but pretty much everyone in Mieira has heard about *the red witch in Alita* and what she (allegedly) did to Samson 714 Afador.

I toss a dirty look to the hesperides. "You can call me Helisent, thank you." I clear my throat and turn back to the queen. "It's a misunderstanding with the wolf. I wasn't banished by any nymphs or demigods—just the Class. I'm only in Mid City for a little vacation. I swear not to do anything you wouldn't do."

Otrera looks unconvinced, but the younger hesperide claps his hands together before she can respond. He steps forward and brandishes a wide, hopeful smile at us. He raises his square hands; three necklaces dangle and twist where they're strung between his fingers.

Clunky, pinkish stones line their threads.

They almost look like chunks of Marama, slightly aglow and alluring like moonslight.

"There's one for each of you," the hesperide coos.

He sweeps one over my head, another over Butter's disheveled curls, and then the last over Otrera's tightly packed curls.

I glance down to see if the necklace looks good on me; it's sort of pretty. To my left, Butter and the queen do the same.

That's when everything starts to feel weird.

Really weird.

Bad weird.

The women at my side don't lift their heads back up.

The pair slump forward as though on the verge of passing out.

The younger hesperide faces me. He keeps smiling, his cheeks dimpled.

Why am I so tired?

I look back to the women. The older hesperide steps forward and lifts both hands to cup their foreheads, preventing them from falling forward. The queen's eyes are fully closed, her lips parted and slack like she's been asleep for hours.

Butter doesn't conk out quite so quickly.

She looks at me, eyes squeezed as though she's fighting sleep.

Her lips twitch like she's trying to say something.

Then her shoulders slump as she passes out with the same totality as Otrera. The hesperide shifts his weight to keep the women upright. His arms flex as he grunts, shuffling the women up into a sitting position.

I try to move, try to sit back, try to figure out if the younger hesperide is still smiling at me; he is.

Bad—bad—bad—

Where is my panic magic?

My fingers flex, anticipating some kind of show.

Nothing.

The younger hesperide isn't smiling anymore.

His narrow eyebrows tug together and his lips press into a line. "This is going to be really unpleasant. For me, too—your magic is in my blood now. But that's how it goes. Ezit will give us *anything* if we pass you off alive."

I suck down a deep breath and try to cast magic.

Again, nothing.

With each passing second, a heavy and unpleasant hum emanates from the pink stones that press against my shoulders and collar and back. Every thread of magic I attempt to cast floats back to the pale, pinkish stones.

The older hesperide shifts away from Otrera and Butter. He stares at me for a moment. Then his broad hands take mine where they're slack in my lap.

Terror spreads through me like a white-hot flood.

Bad—bad—bad—

Not my hands—

Where the fuck is my panic magic?

His pointer fingers slide under my wrists, his thumbs pressing down on top of them.

My slack body follows his momentum as I slump atop the wooden barrel.

Revelers start a chant on the deck above.

Even if I had the energy and sense to scream, they wouldn't hear me.

The younger hesperide turns away from us and pulls a strange box from a wooden crate.

It's not a *box*, necessarily, just a frame made of the same pink stones that encircle my neck. In the center of the boxed frame is a single rod of the same stone.

The younger nymph holds the box while the elder arranges my hands inside of it. As soon as my palms touch the cylindrical bar in its center, red light fills the room, leeching from my eyes.

The hesperides freeze.

My heartbeat flutters as I wait for them to back off; I'm in my form, and they should know not to trifle with a seven-horn.

But I don't feel any spark of panic magic.

I can't even wield the instinctual magic that hides my form anymore.

My heavy horns drive my head forward. My body follows their momentum as they fall toward my hands and the box. The elder hesperide curses and grabs one of my horns to keep me from toppling over. My neck bends as my head lifts at an awkward angle.

That's when I finally admit what's happening.

In a few seconds, it all takes shape: they're going to break my hands and then they'll hand me over to...

What did they say?

Who wants me alive?

The men force my fingers around the cool cylindrical bar, fitting them tighter. All I can see is the ground and a sliver of the pink-stoned frame that the nymphs hold in front of me.

"Do it now," one of them says.

"No—make sure she's out first. We can't risk it if her magic is still awake."

"Just break her hands. There's no way we're taking the fucking Vexen to Zarzynn with her hands intact."

"She's my familiar."

"She's the last Vexen. Move."

"Jen, we're not—"

"Pel, the rosarium won't be enough to keep her quiet until we get to Pit. Move. *Now.*"

I try to take in enough air to yell—either for help or to beg them not to do this.

It would be a lot scarier if I were more cognizant.

"Okay. I really am sorry about this."

Bad—bad—bad—

No—no—no—

There's a black room where all my forgotten memories await me.

That's where I go now when the hesperides break my hands against the cylinder.

That's where I go to lay down and die just like everything in my mind.

CHAPTER 2

ACROSS—ACROSS—ACROSS—

SAMSON

My grandson,
Your mother was never one for patience. Wherever she is now, I like to think
she's learning that lesson. And so are you, my Kulsapsifang. But life can be
unkind, and sometimes, patience yields nothing.

I scoot to the edge of my bed and massage the scar tissue on my chest.

Since the scar healed last autumn, I've taken to prodding it—more out of habit than anything else.

This morning, the scar sends shooting pains through my chest with every breath. I gasp with each intake, paranoid about the pain. The scar didn't hurt like this even when it was still open and unhealed.

Instead, the shooting pain concentrates around my chest.

My heart.

Something is *very* wrong.

I lean forward, then glance around my quiet room in Satyr. There's no sign of a break-in. No sign that the red witch found me in the night.

Am I having a heart attack?

Desperate for insight, I search through the endless pit where my memories of the last four years lay in darkness. I even search for the recollection of a nightmare—*maybe the witchling in the yew tree had something to say to me before I woke up?*

I remember suddenly—

Last night I dreamed for the first time of red strings—without the witching present.

I'd been sitting in the canopy of the yew tree, precariously balanced. I'd looked around, expecting to see the witching with her hands full of bright red string.

Instead, there was a woman nearby. Seated on the other side of the yew's trunk, I couldn't quite see her face or make out her features. She had white hair, she was an adult, and she was staring in the opposite direction as me.

I didn't want her to see me. I could sense that she loathed me, that she wanted to harm me—

With a gasp, I looked down to find myself covered in red strings. Unlike my dreams with the witching, the strings weren't loosely roped around my limbs. Instead, they were smothering, taut, and tightening quickly.

The witch had turned to face me—and rather than meet her gaze, I'd woken up with a lash of pain to my chest...

More and more, I've started to wonder if the dreams might not be dreams.

If they could be...

If the witch is still...

No.

It's too early for those thoughts.

I glance at the door. Though the blush of morning light brightens with each minute, the street outside my rented room is quiet. I listen for any sounds of life from the rooms surrounding mine; my pack-mates are sleeping close by. A few weeks into our tour of Mieira, we're all happy for the chance to sleep on a mattress.

I settle in where I'm seated on the edge of mine.

One of my packmates will wake up soon and I can call out for help —though I'm not sure what sort of help they can offer.

Until then...

I try not to move. Try not to die.

At least Brutatalika isn't here. She's understanding about my night-mares, but a physical deficiency is harder to ignore than a psycholog-ical one.

What started as a political marriage two months ago slowly turned into a genuine friendship—and, in the last month, a fledgling love. It's a promising start to my future as Alpha, but I'm still curating the man my wife thinks I am.

I don't even want to show this weakness to my pack, and I hand-selected each member based on their devotion to me and to Velm.

I reach for the cup of water at my bedside.

It shakes as I bring it to my lips.

I pat my chest with my other hand, laid flat on my peck. "Don't fail me now."

Once, I'd thought marrying the Female Alpha would solidify my place in Bellator Palace.

But my father, Clearbold 554 Leofsige, Male Alpha of Velm, married a stand-in Female Alpha when my mother disappeared seventeen years ago. They produced a spare heir, Malachai 555 Leofsige.

Malachai and his mother didn't attend my wedding.

They stayed in Mort, chipping away at my reputation in Velm's southeast. Crafting a new symbol to replace that of Afador, of Velm. Several villages south of Mort didn't raise the black ribbons in celebration of my marriage. Instead, word has spread of white ribbons.

White ribbons with a new symbol painted at their fluttering ends.

I carry my mother, Imperatriz 713 Afador, Kulapsifang of Velm and its rightful Female Alpha, in my blood. I carry her legacy in my body.

In this fragile heart.

I groan with pain, trying not to hate myself for what happened in Alita. For whatever foolish reason drove me toward the red witch and, invariably, this chest pain right now.

When the ache doesn't lessen, I stand and stagger to the window.

I pull open the shutters and drink in the cool morning air. Pale light falls across the empty dirt road passing through Satyr's city center. With less than three thousand residents, there's no local estate for wolves. And while the pack leader invited us into his home when we arrived last night, five grown wolves require too much space, food, and resources for comfort.

I led my pack to one of the city's empty hostels instead.

Bordering the wild jungle of Rhotidom, the wasted cones of Jaws, and the sleepy beaches of Hypnos, Satyr sits at a dreamy crossroad. Oreads from Jaws, okeanids from Hypnos, and dryads from Rhotidom outnumber the small wolf and wielder populations.

Across the street, an oread splits open an orange. His vermillion hair sits in thin, even locks. Two more hang from the fuzzy beard hugging his chin.

He smiles and waves when he notices me, seated on a short stepping ladder. "A big commotion just came into town. They'll get here soon. It's Hypnos—I'd bet anything. Another ship came in, then it left."

The farther north I travel with my pack, the more oreads we've met.

They confound me.

The rest of the nymphs' elemental powers are easy enough to quantify; an okeanid controls coastal tides, a naiad manipulates freshwater, a hesperide summons wind and seedlings, a dryad can sniff out anything in the forest.

Aside from being able to start small fires, which seems vague enough, oreads also have elemental powers tied to metal and stone.

I've noticed a few shifting their feet in places where I can smell high levels of iron, magnesium, and calcium in the soil. Satyr's unpaved streets are rich in all three.

I leave the oread to his cryptic musing. I turn and dress, pausing to groan and hold my chest and curse the red witch.

By the time I'm presentable, I hear Berevald and Rex stir in their rooms near mine. Water splashes from one, a yawn echoes from another.

Then a ruckus kicks up on the street.

I leave my room and shut the door behind me. The oread on the step ladder looks from me to the City Council that hustles my way.

In the center of the group walks the local male pack leader. The nymph authorities surround him: an elder okeanid and oread, along with a middle-aged dryad.

I walk into the center of the street. With each step, I grit my teeth to avoid flinching from the lashing chest pain.

"Samson 714 Afador," the wolf starts. "Did you sleep well?"

It's a polite question. The group's eyes glitter with urgent news, their features twisted with tension.

"I slept well." I stand at an awkward angle to hide my discomfort. "I am here. What happened?"

The elder okeanid steps forward. Her eyes are clear like the crystal beaches east of Satyr, her voice steady and deep. "Word arrived of another kidnapping in Mid City. They took a Hypnotic Queen, Samson 714 Afador. And a powerful witch. *We must sail—*"

"We must *convene* in Mid City to decide on a solution," the wolf cuts in. "There must be a response to these abductions, Kulapsifang."

These abductions?

Clearbold hadn't mentioned any disappearances in Hypnos when we parted ways in Silent City. And we spent the last day there hashing out Velm's most pressing issues.

The oread sets a hand on the okeanid's shoulder. He squeezes in commiseration, then looks at me. "How many ships will we watch disappear on the horizon?"

Does Clearbold not know?

The gears in my mind start turning. I need to send word to Bellator, to the pack leaders in Mort, in Cadmium, in Ultramarine, in Eupheme—all the cities on or near the coastline.

The urgency of this news helps quiet my chest pain. It doesn't alter the numbing ache—just distracts me from its presence.

"An okeanid demigod selected Queen Otrera two weeks ago," the dryad chimes in. "They *cannot* have our queen, Samson 714 Afador."

To my right, Berevald and Rex step into the street. Like me, they wear freshly cleaned tunics and harem pants, along with shined torcs on their upper arms and necks. Dark rings hang under their eyes, stark against their pale skin. We arrived late last night, and dawn has barely broken.

"Did you unpack?" I ask the pair.

Berevald and Rex shake their heads as they approach.

Compared to my other two packmates, Rex and Berevald are eager to be useful to me. Though the others respect their roles as part of the Alpha's pack, both have left behind wives to join me in establishing diplomatic ties across Mieira.

I can appreciate how unideal that setup is now that I've been away from Brutatalika for a few weeks. Her ala has started to fade from the items I keep hidden in my satchel; her hair tie and a small leather pouch she used to store herbs.

Rex studies the City Council, then glances at me with a glint in his eyes. Unlike the rest of the group, Rex can read my current state. As one of my primary caretakers after my injury in Alita, he's probably already registered my off-kilter stance.

Berevald 522 Firstin doesn't notice. Though a critical thinker, Bere is often hung up on all the wrong details. Right now, he seems to be focused on the oread who digs into his second orange on the stepladder across the street.

"We're going to Mid City," I explain. "Leave a note for Pietrangelo and Riordon to wait here for our return. We haven't rested since we left Cadmium. They can take a few days off."

Berevald spares one last glance at the nymph before turning and following Rex back to their rooms. Unlike Rex and I, he hasn't pulled his hair into a bun. It dangles to his belly button, soft and puffy from its morning brushing.

The City Council watches the exchange, eyes flitting from me to my pack.

The okeanid takes another step forward to set her palm on my arm. "You'll go to Mid City even though no wolves were taken?"

I nod, trying not to glance at her hand. Nymphs always forget not to touch. "Wolves live in Hypnos. Their well-being is my responsibility, too."

The nymph's hand tightens on my arm. "Good. They killed sheep for you last night. We will eat before you leave. Mid City is three days' walking from here—you need to move quickly. The locals in Mid City are preparing a ship. They want to follow the kidnappers this time. We will send word for them to wait for the Kulapsifang."

The council parts ways, but the wolf stands at attention in the middle of the street.

I hold my place, forcing breaths in and out of my lungs at a measured pace. I need the respect of every pack leader I meet during this journey—and physical weakness won't help me foster that.

"Thank you, Samson," he says.

His appreciation is noted, but behind it lies surprise.

Had he expected me to say no?

The wolf goes on, "Clearbold avoided the conflicts in Hypnos. He said it was a wasteland of drunken wielders and lazy nymphs."

He sweeps his hands behind his back. For a long moment, he studies me, but I can't think of the right words. Clearbold's response seems underwhelming, if not outright suspicious.

My Alpha taught me that wolves don't live free of nymph and wielder trials. The okeanids, in particular, have a longstanding relationship with Velm. We trade goods, food, crafts, and more—and that trade is facilitated along the coastlines where okeanids manipulate the tides.

Okeanids notwithstanding, there are wolves in Hypnos. Maybe not many, but even if it were only one wolf, he or she would be afforded protection as my ward.

(A wolf's blood belongs to Velm; to Hetnazzar; to me.)

"I was born in Mid City seventy-two years ago." The wolf raises his chin. "Locals call it Sunrise because sunlight blinds the village every morning it wakes, and we'd give our sight to be bathed in it. I never once thought of it as a wasteland."

After my wedding, my wife and I stood in the snow outside Rouz. We decided on a list of simple agreements that would dictate our marriage.

The first was to live and lead as our own authorities.

Not as descendants or heirs to Clearbold. Certainly not to Emerel.

But to Velm. To each other. To the Afador line and to Brutatalika's Sigivald heritage.

This isn't the first mess of Clearbold's that I've run into since beginning my tour in Cadmium. I can sense it won't be the last, either.

I meet the pack leader's gaze. I hope he sees an Alpha who is worthy of his loyalty, but I can never quite discern the twinkle in the eyes of the pack leaders who stand before me. Not yet, at least.

"I understand." I bow my head, then turn back to my room and collect my bag.

We make it to Mid City in two days.

By then, our cheeks are pinched with sunburns. Just like the forest thins and the trees shorten, the clouds also seem to disappear. And though my pack once traveled to these same beaches while in our first war band, that was over ten years ago.

I don't remember the constant sunlight or the nauseating scent of the salty ocean.

Our only saving grace is the cool breeze that shivers through the trees and dry grass.

Along with the dryad and male pack leader from Satyr, we've pushed our bodies to make it to Mid City before the locals sail after the kidnappers.

We arrive just in time.

They guide us to the village's center. A wide lane runs between a few single-story wooden buildings with thatched roofs and sand-blasted floors. Scraggly plants climb across the wooden panels, their pink flowers shivering in the breeze.

A raucous mob mills where the lane ends at a low dune. Just beyond it sprawls the broad, endless beach.

Unintelligible shouting heightens as we wander closer. Most of the group has the dark skin of okeanids and oreads, interspersed with the rich olive of wielders and their stark white hair. I tally a few wolves, one of which is unnumbered, and a few naiads with flat brown curls and skin almost as pale as mine.

The mob seems to be haranguing two individuals. The first is a warlock with a skinny frame and a boyish face. He wears a long white cape reminiscent of the Class. The second is a regal dryad with luscious locks of emerald hair and a flowing lilac cloak. His broad, smooth features are handsome, his eyes twinkling with calm certainty despite the noisy madness around him. I can't tell if he's broad-chested or prefers to stand in a way that makes him seem imposing.

I filter through their alas; the white-cloaked warlock smells famil-iar. While Samson doesn't remember anything from the last four years, my fangself isn't quite as helpless.

He's gained authority since I woke in Alita, invigorated by a strength I can't fathom or see. My body was weakened after the witch maimed me, starting with this mark on my heart, but Samsonfang grew stronger.

Though the moons aren't nearing full, Samsonfang peeks through my thoughts.

He whispers, **You have met this warlock before. You don't remember, but I do.**

I study the lanky warlock. His bright golden eyes dart around the crowd, lips parted like he's ready to speak. Though his cheeks are full, his face almost cherub-like, his busy eyes betray any notion of innocence.

The dryad with the flowing lilac cloak next to him has the pungent ala of a king. In appearance, nymph royalty doesn't stand out. It's only their alas, tangled with the rich notes of a demigod, that differentiate them.

The pair widen their eyes when they see me approaching with my small group.

The warlock throws his hands up in my direction, as though relieved. "Samson 714 Afador! They sent word that you were coming but I thought it was a joke."

The mob standing around the warlock and king turn to face us.

Two dozen nymphs, wielders, and wolves study me, Rex, and Berevald with crooked, unimpressed expressions. A few open their mouths, as though preparing to start shouting in our direction.

Their alas come into general focus; most have traces of adrenaline in their systems, along with plenty of cortisol. Exhaustion and fright hang in the air, just as palpable as the ocean's salt water.

The king seizes the momentary silence to address the crowd. "Please, leave us in peace to decide on a solution. We have heard your qualms—give us time to rest and debate."

The white-caped warlock shuffles past the king to intercept me.

The dryad hangs back to listen to a few more comments; one okeanid seizes his lilac cape, sobbing loudly.

When he reaches me and my packmates, the warlock wraps his hand around the back of my elbow, directing me toward the beach. Satyr's City Council hangs back amid the crowd.

I don't appreciate the touch—or warlocks in general—but the wielder at least starts a breakneck explanation as he leads us into the sand.

"Hello, Samson 714 Afador. My name is Absalom Metamor—I'm sure you don't remember me. I was the Head Warlock of Luz until recently. That's where we met." He cranes his neck to glance behind us; Rex and Berevald follow close at our heels. "Who are they? Is this your pack? I heard you got married—congratulations. You're doing your little tour now, right?"

I glance where his tapered fingers still clutch me.

My feet sink into the sand as Absalom leads us toward a bare shelter near the calm tides. Four poles support a thatched roof, which provides a square patch of thin shade. A large jug of water awaits us, along with wooden cups.

"Thank you. And this is only half my pack. That's Rex and Berevald." I study the warlock's tense expression. "Aren't you a bit far from Luz as Head Warlock?"

"I said I *was* the Head Warlock of Luz. Now I take care of... other things for the Class. I was north of Satyr when I heard Helisent West of Jaws went missing—I came here looking for her. I made it to Sunrise the morning after the kidnapping."

The ache in my chest flares at his mention of the witch's name.

Though the pain that first woke me in Satyr has lessened, the witch hasn't wandered far from my mind. At least once an hour, the pain spikes, as though she's wielding one last spell against me from afar.

And this warlock thinks she was kidnapped *with the others?*

Absalom unhands me once we reach the shade. He looks over Rex and Berevald, then checks behind us as though making sure we're alone. Back in the village, the wolf and the dryad from Satyr are occupied with the crowd, hands gesturing as they stand between the locals and where we sit on the beach.

Absalom points to the massive jug and stack of wooden cups. "There's freshwater." He sits down, gathering his robe.

I sit down; Rex and Berevald mirror me. I reach and fill the first cup of water, passing one to Rex and a second to Berevald. "Do you think the red witch had something to do with the disappearances?"

Absalom flinches, leaning back while his eyes dart over me. "What? No. What are you talking about? A whole ship of okeanids was taken—Helisent included. Apparently, the ship belonged to a hesperide merchant and his apprentice. The locals have known them for a few years. They don't have any useful information to share on either."

I sip on the water and wonder how a being as powerful as the red witch gets *taken* anywhere against her will.

The dryad king ducks into the shelter and sits next to Absalom. He smooths the emerald waves of his thick, shoulder-length hair as he studies us. His small eyes, pitted with amber irises, flit across me. I can smell his jacaranda jewelry: rings, earrings, and a beaded necklace.

"Samson 714 Afador." The king bows his head. With a deep sigh, his puffed-out chest recedes to an exhausted slump. "I greet you and your packmates on behalf of my demigod in Rhotidom. My name is Hemlock East of Alita. Did Absalom tell you what happened?"

"We've heard different accounts of the kidnapping over the last few days." I nod in confirmation. "What I don't understand is how any being could *kidnap* Helisent West of Jaws. According to a Ghost-Eater named Kierkeline Ultramarine, she has very large horns. There's no controlling the witch—certainly no kidnapping her."

Absalom looks at the Rhotidic King. Hemlock looks back at him.

Then the nymph turns to me and raises his eyebrows. "It's a pretty terrifying thought, isn't it? That something *more powerful* than the witch took her."

"Is it scarier than the possibility that the witch is out of control?" I ask. "That no banishment or law could bind her? There was nothing stopping Helisent West of Jaws from leaving Jaws. And there's nothing stopping her from—"

"Oh, *watch your fucking mouth*, boy-wolf," someone shouts.

Past Absalom and Hemlock, a warlock steps into the sand from a grassy dune.

The squat man is led by a round, healthy belly. Two well-built warlocks flank him, a full head taller; their alas tell me the men are related. Father and sons—twins, in fact. The twins have thin faces with large eyes and neat, pulled-back hair. Their father has rounder and softer features—though his eyes are just as bulbous.

They're reddened, too, like his nose.

Salty tears smear his cheeks. His heart ratchets in his chest, flitting like a desperate bird. His golden eyes dart around the shelter as he and his sons approach.

You met these warlocks, too, Samsonfang coos. ***You don't remember, but I do.***

Absalom licks his lips and inches closer to me and my pack. He turns, as though afraid to keep his back to the trio of warlocks.

The elder warlock focuses on me. His features bunch with anger. "You're worried the witch is out of control? Let me tell you something, she was born out of control. They all were!

"One rainy spring, my four children took me hostage. And there was no mercy for their papa. I was tied up by the ankle with a magical rope and left to rot in a pit. They said they wanted to train me to dance so we could all join the circus."

He raises a finger, baring it at Absalom. "My sons took no pity on me—look at their faces! *No pity.* Milisent West of Jaws also showed me no pity. I spent seven nights imprisoned in that pit. But Helisent came to me. She gave me wine and scraps of pancakes. She sang me songs and made me a roof out of broken tiles."

I take a deep breath as the wielder's shouting echoes around me.

The father and sons stand in a triangular formation. Absalom continues inching a safe distance away from them, chin lowered. The twins switch their gazes from Absalom to me often, as though unsure who to address first.

The eldest keeps chattering in the meantime, hands flying around. "And that *frightens you?* Ha! You should thank the moons Yngvi and Yves don't have her power. You should thank the moons my first daughter isn't alive to witness this. The Class has *fucked it* on this one, Absalom! I told you a banishment would *do nothing.*"

Absalom's nostrils flare as he takes in a steadying breath. He doesn't look prepared to act—just to endure. "I realize that, Parsifal."

The elder warlock lowers his voice. "So, you knew that Helisent's banishment would do nothing? And yet you still lingered around Jaws keeping tabs on Honey Baby and reporting back to the Class like *a sniveling pervert?*"

Absalom's jaw clenches. "I told them it was useless to punish someone they couldn't control."

Helisent's father, Parsifal, takes a deep breath. He rubs his temples, gritting out, "Then why does the Class hurt the things it fears? Why does the Class accept my daughter's dove and reject the witch who provides it—even after they refused to bring Anesot and Oko to justice for Milisent's death?"

Parsifal's head angles, eyes twinkling with a tendril of infrasound. I swear the sand beneath us shakes, shivering and fizzing.

His voice drops to a growl. "You may think nothing of me, Absalom Metamor, but you would do well to remember who mothered my witches. Andromeda North of Skull is watching us from death. And she will wait for you at its threshold, *you slimy fuck.*"

Parsifal looks toward the glittering ocean. Almost wistfully, he says, "The Class is to blame for my daughter fleeing her banishment in Jaws. The Class is to blame for whatever took Honey across—across—across—"

With deceptive speed, the warlock bolts from the shelter. He rushes past where Absalom stands with his shoulders slumped, hustling into the wet sand and balling his hands into fists.

With what looks to be all his might, Parsifal screams, "Helisent!"

I sit back, gut clenching.

His voice fills my mind with doom.

The pain in my chest ratchets.

"Helisent!" the warlock shouts again. He collapses into the sand and leans forward onto his hands. He sobs loudly, body shaking.

For a split second, I'm looking into the past.

For a split second, I remember doing something similar outside of Mort.

I was twelve years old. I had just arrived on the coast after hearing of Imperatriz's disappearance. I knew I was far from where she had disappeared in Hypnos; farther from whatever place she had gone. Mindless with fear, anxiety, and doom, I had bellowed her name into the unhearing waves. Again and again. Until I fell with wearied exhaustion.

(And even then, I'd hiccuped the word *mama*. Even if she didn't respond to her name, I knew she'd respond to that call. I knew that call connected us like a trunk bridges roots to branches. I knew it as a type of magic. One that failed.)

One of the twins heads to his father. He sinks into the sand at Parsifal's side, murmuring small words of comfort.

The other twin stares at me from the other side of the shelter.

According to Samsonfang, I once knew this warlock.

Now, we watch one another with suspicion and antipathy.

He takes a step forward to squat in front of me so we're at eye level. "Watch your fucking mouth when you speak about my sister. She's the only one we have left." He angles his chin, nose curling with loathing. "You have no idea how fucking *stupid* you're going to feel about this one day."

I already feel stupid. I shouldn't have brought Rex and Berevald here. The only thing more ill-advised than entangling myself in another affair with Helisent West of Jaws would be *sailing away* from Mieira and Velm to do so.

The warlock stands and turns away.

He joins his family in the sand. The father continues to weep, shouting theatrical nonsense toward the waves every now and then.

Absalom returns to his place next to Hemlock East of Alita. With a sigh, he glances at the hunched trio.

"I'll save us all a bit of discomfort here," the king says with a strange smile. "I don't particularly believe Helisent would have had a reason to hurt you in Alita, Samson 714 Afador. You will find this is a sentiment shared by many in Mieira; the witch was a sponsor to quite a few cities. Her dove has been missed *dearly*. And please remember, she is a friend of the nymphs. The demigods have not banished her.

"Only wolves and wielders.

"However, I will wait until either you or Helisent remembers the last four years before making any more conclusions. Please understand that my interest in chasing that ship is to find and return *all* Mieirans —even those currently banished by your and Absalom's people."

I nod, relieved by the simple explanation even if it's laced with quiet condemnation.

I study Absalom next. He finally tears his eyes away from the trio on the beach. "Before the incident in Alita, I knew you and Helisent as partners in some sort of mutual endeavor. I won't waste my breath with what I think that mission was. I'll only tell you that I'm going to sail after the kidnapped okeanids for the same reason as Hemlock. And so long as I represent the Class, Helisent's well-being is my problem."

Absalom brushes the hair from his face, golden eyes burning into mine. "And I understand if you want nothing to do with this on account of what happened in Alita. With Helisent. Hemlock and I will spread the word that you arrived and offered us thoughtful counsel on behalf of Velm."

I glance toward the ocean.

For a split second, it's all very familiar again.

I remember staring into the ocean outside of Mort and wondering desperately what awaited me on its far side. Wondering where my mother had gone. Wondering when I'd also leave the shore to find her.

I'm keenly aware that these are the same beaches where Imperatriz disappeared seventeen years ago.

And yet...

I look from the warlock to the king. "I'm sure both of you understand that I won't participate in any cause that involves Helisent West of Jaws."

I set my hand on my chest. Pain sparks and then slowly fades, like a dying heartbeat. Aside from fearing the witch might kill me once and for all, I know Malachai will make power grabs in my absence; he's making them now in my presence.

The redrawing of the Afador symbol in Mort is only one of three pressing incidents that mark a coming change in Velm.

I clarify, "I *can't*. We will find lodging tonight and stay until morning. Feel free to call on me and my packmates."

Absalom nods, offering a weak smile.

The Rhotidic King looks less accepting. His brow scrunches as I stand, and my pack follows suit. He doesn't say goodbye, just slowly crosses his arms as we turn and leave the shelter.

He thinks I can't hear him as we walk away. "What did I tell you, Absalom? Velm has a *border*, and it moves farther south each year."

I wake in the middle of the night, groaning as I sit up and clutch my chest.

The pain that started in Satyr rattles my chest and shakes my bones. I gasp for breath and force myself to sit up in the tiny, thatched hut.

My feet nearly graze its far end where a doorless entrance leads to the beach.

Beyond the sound of the gentle waves, I hear whispering. My nostrils flare as I catch the alas of Rex and the warlocks from earlier; the weeping father, the livid twins. And past theirs is a witch's ala— the GhostEater from Ultramarine.

I'd met her briefly when passing through the city, at which time she'd cornered me in a tavern and attempted to speak with me about the red witch.

Her name is Kierkeline.

What is she doing here?

"We'll ask him in the morning," Rex whispers. "Give him time to—"

"There is no time," the GhostEater hisses. "They're going to sail tomorrow morning. My granddaughter was also on that ship, my dear wolf. I won't let them delay leaving."

"We do it now," Parsifal says. "Just wait until he—"

"*Shh*," Rex cuts in.

He must have noticed the shift in my breathing pattern.

I've barely stirred; I sit frozen on my bed mat, one hand on my chest and the other on the ground.

I stand with a groan and head for the door. I ignore the lashing pain in my chest, which extends to my back and down into my abdomen. For the first time, I can sense a slight hum within my body, like the shivering bass of infrasound.

What the fuck is inside of me?

I push away that nightmarish thought for another time.

I need to figure out how to breathe—how to ease this pain—

I stagger one step toward the hut's entrance. Rex's large frame blocks the moonslight as he steps in front of me. He flattens a hand against my solar plexus to stop me from advancing.

I fall still. I'm still half-asleep, but now warming to the notion that Rex might have been colluding with the wielders outside of my hut.

"Samson," he says. "Are you well?"

My back hunches as I try to alleviate my aching. I search the air for the wielders' alas, trying to figure out which direction they scampered off in. Heavy shadows fill the gaps between the huts and trees.

"My chest," I manage. Sweat dampens my skin. My breaths come ragged the longer I stand before Rex. "Who were you speaking with?"

"Do you trust me?"

My nostrils flare as Rex's hand flexes against me, goading me back into the hut.

He's never given me a reason to distrust him—but he's also never asked me such a pointed question at such a dubious hour. And not when I felt physically weak.

Not with the Leofsige line carving new symbols into the marble of Mort.

My adrenaline kicks in. "Rex—"

"Do you trust me, Samson? Yes or no."

"Yes. Why were you speaking with—"

"I need you to drink the memory-giving potion the GhostEater offered you in Ultramarine. Kierkeline is here. Her granddaughter was one of the beings kidnapped. I believe we can trust her. I need you to take the potion."

I narrow my eyes. His voice is low, his tone calm and direct.

I zero in on each of his words. I didn't tell him, or anyone, about the offer Kierkeline made me in Ultramarine.

I definitely didn't tell anyone her name.

When did she find Rex? What did she tell him just now?

"Then accept the potion from her. I won't take it now—I'll take it when I'm ready, Rex. On my own time." And when I don't feel like I'm on the verge of a heart attack. "I need air. Move."

But my packmate doesn't shift.

Parsifal takes a step into the moonslight to my left and looks up at me. Unlike this afternoon, he looks both lethally calm and pointedly unhinged.

"Did it start three mornings ago, Samson?" the warlock asks. "The chest pain?"

It did, but I don't tell him that.

I shift my weight onto my back leg, trying to straighten my spine.

Beneath the aching, I can feel a deep buzzing...

Of infrasound.

The warlock goes on, "Even if a wielder doesn't know healing magic, their panic magic can... fill in the gaps. It rarely pans out well in the long term. And I wonder..." Parsifal's golden eyes linger on my chest, near where Rex keeps his hand pressed flat. "If my daughter was helping you instead of hurting you, like I believe, there may be a little seed of her magic inside of you, Samson 714 Afador."

The thought almost sends me into hysterics.

If the red witch cast some sort of lasting spell on me, then my life just got infinitely more difficult.

More *fucked*.

"What?" is all I manage.

My patience snaps, temper unrolling as I realize the gravity of every bad decision I made last year. The chest wound is only the beginning if what the warlock says is correct. If the witch implanted her magic into me like poison.

What if this follows me for the rest of my life?

What the fuck do I tell Brutatalika?

The warlock opens his hands to me. "My daughter's magic—"

"Get away from my hut."

Parsifal takes a quick step back. I grab Rex's wrist so I can move and charge onto the beach—I need air, need to breathe, need to find some comfortable position to ride out this pain and the realization that I may be cursed with Helisent's magic.

But Rex digs his heels into the sand. He braces his hand. "Samson—Samson, *you need to trust me*—"

"Get out of my way," I growl.

I push against his hand, then against his chest. As soon as I attempt to exert any force, I buckle at the waist, pain ratcheting through my chest and ribcage and spine.

With a single step, Rex forces me back into the hut.

He pulls me close to him with a fistful of my tunic. He whispers into my ear, words hot and quick, "I found your bag when I picked you up in Alita to take you back to Bellator. Inside, you had a note that was written for Imperatriz. She was in Hypnos searching for a witch named Oko when she disappeared—the witch you were hunting with Helisent West of Jaws.

"Forget the witch for ten seconds—focus on Imperatriz. What if you learned something useful about her disappearance? They found Oko dead alongside Anesot. Maybe she told you what she knew about our Alpha's disappearance before you were injured."

I stagger back as he releases my tunic.

My mouth falls open. For a split second, my mind focuses solely on the possibility Rex just presented.

Just like I have no memory of what happened in Alita, I have no clue what motivated me to work with the red witch. (I don't know what she looks like, whether the witchling I see in my dreams is a figment of my imagination or partly real. I can't fathom who the grown witch is, either.) Clearbold told me he didn't know what Helisent and I were doing journeying across Mieira.

Of all the possibilities I had considered, something as dire as my mother's disappearance seemed too unlikely. Too important to trust with a witch like Helisent. With a witch at all.

But Rex wouldn't lie, especially not for a wielder.

He lowers his chin, studying me as I stand motionless in the center of the hut. He clears his throat. "And I'm sorry about this."

I almost ask him what he's sorry about. Then he rushes forward.

Rex lowers his body to sweep my legs out from under me. I clench my eyes as I land on my back, exclaiming from the pain before Rex positions himself over me and uses his large hand to cover my mouth.

I raise my knees to struggle, but his weight pins my abdomen. The hand covering my mouth presses my head back against the bed mat. At the same time, his legs lock mine—and then two more large, shifting masses pin my arms.

I suck in a breath through my nose to study their alas; the twins from the beach. Each warlock pins one of my arms, bearing their weight at my elbows.

I jerk and writhe, managing to displace Rex for a second—

I freeze when someone grabs my balls.

Fingers wrap around one of my testicles. Another set of fingers pinches the skin attaching them to my body.

Holy fucking shit. Samsonfang stampedes into my mind and assesses the situation. ***Stop moving.***

My stomach clenches as my temper spirals, gaining momentum as I start to tally the exact weight and strength of the beings that keep me pinned. The discomfort in my chest hasn't stopped, but my adrenaline cloaks it well. It sends unfathomable energy throughout my body.

"Once I told you I have less reason with each I lose! Do you believe me now?" shouts Parsifal, hidden behind Rex; he's the one holding my balls. "Just hold still, my bucking bronco."

I will break the warlock's teeth for holding me like this—

I will beat his sons, wait until they have children, then beat them, too—

Rex strains to keep me pinned. Even though I'm no longer fighting, it wouldn't take much to incite more chaos. He pants as he stares down at me. "I'm going to move my hand. Don't shout or the Ghost-Eater will do magic on you. She's not fucking around, Samson. *You need to drink the potion.* Just do it, okay? Just *trust me.*"

I start thinking about what I'll do to Rex for spearheading this offense.

I'll cut him out of my inner circle, then challenge him to a waricon.

I'll find my own warlocks to pin his arms and manhandle his testicles.

You're outnumbered. Think fast, Samson.

Rex lifts his hand and something moves toward my lips. A cold, bitter liquid falls straight into my mouth, sliding down the back of my tongue and forcing me to either swallow or choke. On instinct, I fight as I suck down a breath.

I cough, body buckling as the pinning forces slide off of me.

I roll onto my side as horrible pressure mounts in my head.

Memories begin to filter through my mind, too fast to hold onto.

I can feel myself in the hut, braced against the sandy bed mat as a cool breeze passes over me. But all of my attention is focused internally, on each memory that finds its way back into my psyche.

I lay on the floor, in the hut and not in the hut, as someone holds my head in their lap.

Adrenaline shivers through me as the memories take shape. Panic mounts, along with pain—

I shift onto my side, grappling with something—

Something is caught inside of my breast bone, lodged and unnatural—

A copper metal piece juts from my chest, coated in hot blood— I'm dying—I'm dying in a memory—

And there's a witch here beside me. Her face is round, her cheekbones high. Tears fill her eyes as she hovers over me on her knees. Blood coats her hands, droplets sprayed across her chest and face.

She's killing me.

I'm dying in this memory.

Unless—

Is this really—

And that's her—

Lekeli Kelnazzar—

This isn't what I thought—

She must love jewelry.

I wake to bickering.

My head rests against a soft thigh, my cheek against a sturdy calf. Sweat coats my hair, clinging to my forehead. My mouth is dry and my tongue swollen.

Someone wipes a strand of hair from my brow.

"Stop touching him," Rex says.

"You're touching him, too," Yngvi says.

"I'm part of his pack," Rex says. "He's my Alpha."

"Yeah, but now he's going to remember me. I'm basically part of his pack, too."

"No, you're not. Not even close."

"I ate dinner with him in Alita. And he had a close relationship with my sister. I'm owed special allowances. And what are you owed, Sweet Roxanna?"

"My name is Rex."

"You look like a Roxanna."

"And which one are you again?"

"Yngvi. I'm the eldest."

"You talk too much."

"Look, I'm actually on my best behavior right now, so if you think this is me talking too much, then we'll never be friends."

"Was that actually something you thought would happen?"

"Well, me and Samson are friends. I figured I'd be friends with his whole pack. Or are you guys grandfathered in based on generational count? What's yours again? 300-something?"

"563, thank you." My head shifts as someone moves; then I hear a gentle slap. "I said stop touching him."

"Were you this fussy when he was with Helisent? If you think I'm touchy, you should spend more time around—"

"I'm well aware."

"We should probably wake him up. They're going to start loading the ship soon."

"He needs rest. Give him another hour."

I lick my lips and open my eyes. Bright light floods the hut from the entrance near my feet. My head rests in Rex's lap, his legs folded together. To my right, Yngvi sits cross-legged, staring at me with shadows beneath his eyes. Yves lies at my side, asleep with his head in his brother's lap like Rex and I. All I see is a mess of Yves' white hair, half-freed from its hair tie.

Rex leans forward to meet my eyes. His jaw and brow pinch guiltily. "Are you okay?"

Yngvi looks just as uncertain. He glances at Yves, then the entryway. "I didn't touch your nuts. I swear to the moons."

I can't fathom their banter yet.

The last four years stew in my mind.

A lump swells in my throat.

I groan as I sit up. Pain flares around my scar, though it's more manageable than last night.

Rex helps me, bracing his arms against my shoulders and back. The coarse sand clings to my damp body as I adjust to a sitting position. I look down and realize my pants are soaked to the knees, the sand beneath me just as wet. The scent of urine fills the thatched walls, dense enough that I imagine even Yngvi can smell it.

I barely register the mess.

I stare past the entrance and into the ocean.

I have no idea how long I laid in a stupor, at which point I pissed myself, whether I slept after my memories found their places in my mind.

But it's all there now.

I see it all.

I *feel* it all; it begins with wrath and helplessness, then spirals to encompass a fuller range of emotions. Love, anguish, terror, regret, hope, denial, and that unwavering drive to claim and possess and protect the things that are *mine*.

These are the bare facts:

I betrayed Helisent in Alita to protect Anesot and she spent her magic saving me after I failed to interrogate Oko. Helisent was banished for this; I returned home to a palace.

And then I married Brutatalika.

(I *married* Brutatalika. I am *married*. I have a *wife*.)

And then... then someone took...

My breaths come faster as reality settles into a more comprehensible shape.

Yngvi leans onto his elbow to meet my eyes. "So, do you remember everything or what?"

I can't find my voice to confirm that I do.

But I do—

These are the rest of the bare facts:

Anesot came from a world called Zarzynn where breath is more important than love. He is responsible for launching the kidnapping of okeanids on Mieira's coasts, who are turned into necromancers by something called a vampire in Zarzynn.

To pave the way for this trade, and to please Clearbold 554 Leofsige, Anesot lured Imperatriz 713 Afador onto a ship in Hypnos. This ship sailed to a place called Stretch and stranded my mother on an island called Pit.

Her disappearance gave Clearbold the chance to replace the Afador line with the Leofsige line. And when Imperatriz was gone, my father sent me to kill the wooly hoping I would die. He provided Velm a spare heir not out of caution, but as part of a long-term plan.

Clearbold knew that Helisent and I were searching for Oko last year; I told him myself what we were doing in Luz. He has pretended for eight months not to know.

Clearbold has lied to me; often, repeatedly, and with great care.

Clearbold has hurt my Female Alpha, my Kulapsifang.

My mother.

(These are the easy facts.)

Past the entrance to the thatched hut, the shallow beach glitters, pale and fragile as dawn breaks on the horizon.

With a groan, I roll forward onto my knees, then brace my hands to rise to my feet. I stagger into the light, dragging my feet through the cool sand until I reach the ocean.

I keep walking until the water reaches my belly button.

I set my hand on my chest where my scar aches with a low, endless agony. I pat the area twice—not to alleviate the pain, but with the hope that Helisent's magic will feel my touch wherever she was taken.

These are the last bare facts:

I belong to Helisent West of Jaws how Velm belongs to the moons.

And someone took...

Someone took...

I set my hand flat on my scar.

I can't face that thought just yet—

That if Helisent's magic resides in my chest, then the pain I feel is a reflection of some harm being done to her.

And that's because...

Someone took Helisent West of Jaws from Hypnos.

And she is not the first woman I have lost on these shores.

I remember the scent of her ala and her perfumes, the cadence of her laughter and snoring. Her red irises catch my attention like her bright jewelry, like the poisonous berries of the yew tree.

I remember the taste of her pussy, of her skin, of her brandy.

Memories of her float through my mind like clouds, overlapping and disappearing before taking form again.

Samsonfang floods my mind with each.

Find her.

Again and again.

Find her.

I close my eyes.

In my mind, I see Helisent staring at me where she lies nestled in my bed in the Luzian Estate. Her white hair is messy and strewn across the pillow, her shoulders bare and soft where they poke above the sheet. Our alas are layered in the room, complex and intertwined. She smiles as she stretches out and sighs.

I can hear her voice with clear precision, can see the exact twinkle in her fake golden irises when she says, "Good morning, sweet wolf."

Find her.

I take a deep breath and try to let go of the memory.

I open my eyes and stare into the horizon of azure ocean and blinding sunlight.

"I am coming to find you, little bird," I swear into the dawn. "And I am going to fucking kill whoever did this."

CHAPTER 3

GOAT-MAN

HELISENT

Honey Baby,
You don't remember the first time a demigod sensed your power. (You weren't
walking yet.) But I remember. It found us near an oak tree, poked your little
belly, then you farted and laughed, and I knew you were destined for glory.
Papa P.

I'm not positive about what's happening at any given moment.

Only a handful of certainties.

First, everything keeps moving. The hesperide's ship once bobbed evenly in Hypnos' shallow water. Now, it shifts back and forth with violent lurches, rocking my body. The box holding my broken hands, too. I throw up, but quickly run out of fluids to expel. Then comes dry heaving.

Second, I'm not really awake. The pink stones circling my neck and the box frame encasing my hands subsume my magic, as well as my energy. I'm in a fever dream, with half-real images drifting around me. I'm laid flat on a hard surface on my side with my hands extended in front of me, trapped in the frame. I remain in my form; red light soaks my vision when I manage to open my eyes.

Third, I'm not alone. Past my mangled hands, Butter lies on the ground. She's on her back, she looks asleep. We're in a larger room than where the hesperides put the necklaces around us. I think there are others, too, laid just out of sight. When the thrashing waves lessen and there's a precious moment of calm, I can hear all of us breathing, sucking in breaths before groaning them out.

Sometimes, someone squats near my head with a bucket and lifts my head to spoon water into my mouth. I see pale, thick fingers as they hold my face and tilt a wooden ladle. I'm vaguely aware of my mounting hunger, along with a nauseating scent that hangs in the room. My groin is damp and sticky.

The room where my memories lay stacked in darkness becomes my haven.

I stay hidden there.

Over the last eight months, I've come to fear the nothingness that dwells in this room.

Now, it's the only thing keeping me sane. Alive.

I try to count the days at certain intervals, but I can't see daylight or the moons.

It feels like days. Weeks.

A lifetime.

I open my eyes when I hear dragging and grunting.

My teeth are dry bones, my tongue swollen, eyes stinging. The pale fingers that fed me water now seize Butter by her stained cloaks. Even her hair is grayish with filth.

The hesperide grunts as he drags her, step by step, from her collar.

I can't move my head, so I stare ahead.

"Butter," I whisper.

Her slack arms and legs shift as the nymph grapples with her weight.

Inch by inch, he pulls her out of view.

"Butter," I try again.

I roll my eyes above and below; I don't hear any others breathing.

The boat rocks gently rather than tossing back and forth.

Is it over?

Then I can't hear anyone dragging Butter away.

I try to shift my weight onto my elbows and raise my head, but any movement causes my hands to adjust, sending searing pain up to my shoulders. My horns don't help; they weigh me down. My neck aches from the angle at which my head rests. I never got used to living in my form, nor how to lay comfortably in it.

After a few seconds of exertion, I slump back onto the hard floor. Nausea pools in my gut as my head throbs.

Then I hear the hesperides speaking, faint and echoing from another room.

The first says, "Fine. We'll pass the okeanids to Ezit, then we'll go to Plet and lay low for as long as possible. If we leave now, we'll have the okeanids sorted in a few days. We can sail for Plet right after."

The second says, "And do what with the witch? *Leave her on the ship?*"

"We're on Pit, Jen. Who would bother with her?"

"The wolf lives on this side of the island."

"We'll put wolfbane on the rosarium box. She won't be able to do a thing."

"She'll come onto the ship. She's been trying to stow away since she got here. I'm not going to let that fall on my head. The House of Serac wants her kept here."

The first tsks. "Then what do we do with the witch? Do you *really* want to offer her to Ezit now? Think about it. If we play this right, they'll hand over *whatever we ask for*. Maybe even freedom, Jen. We leave the Vexen on the ship, we hand over the okeanids, and then we come back."

The words add up to something conclusive.

But I can't take reality with me into the dark room of oblivion.

And I really need that room right now.

As nice as it is the hesperides just handed me this information, I'm beaten.

Well and truly nullified where I lay on the floor.

Alone.

The hesperides leave; no one spoon-feeds me water.

The ship rocks gently.

The muck covering my robes dries.

Opening my eyes gets harder.

My body fevers. My agony simmers into an empty nothingness. In the dark room, I can't feel my hands at all.

I prepare for death in that room.

I wait for it; death isn't so empty for me.

Milisent West of Jaws is waiting for me on the other side of this endless suffering.

Andromeda North of Skull, too.

Someone is touching me.

I manage to lift my eyelids once; I see a blur of dark hair, of pale features.

How long have I been here?

Cool water trickles into my mouth. Someone touches my neck; I think they're trying to help me drink. I try to swallow, but my diaphragm locks. Slowly, the water slides down my throat. The first drink is the hardest; the rest of the sips are more manageable.

Then my body shifts.

Pain and relief shoot through my limbs. What starts with more discomfort eventually becomes relaxing. It feels like my legs are slightly raised.

Who is touching me?

I know it isn't the hesperides. This touch is too comforting, too gentle. My helper speaks sometimes, too. I can't tell if it's a man or a woman, but their voice is reassuring. Soft, cool rags run along my feet, then my calves. I fight on instinct when the hands tug my cloak and dress up around my waist, leaving me exposed.

The hands stop moving.

A warm palm cups my shoulder, then I hear the stranger's voice clearly for the first time.

It's a woman; she doesn't sound afraid. "Be still, daughter of Andromeda. You need to be cleaned."

I go back to the dark room for a while longer.

I hear the voice.

I can't understand her.

Being clean and drinking water doesn't give me the strength to rally, just to weep.

The stranger doesn't leave.

I sleep.

Sometime later, they feed me a bland paste.

I spit out the first few bites, wary of the taste and texture and a future of vomiting. I don't have the strength for any of it. But the stranger slides a tiny morsel onto my tongue, then a few more.

"They put wolfbane on the rosarium," she tells me. "I can't take off the necklace or get rid of the box."

She waits between feeding me bites. As my stomach absorbs the food, my strength grows. It's just enough to drag me out of the black room of nothingness.

"The vampires will return soon," she goes on. "They will take you to a place called Plet, then onto the mainland to a city called Ezit. Survive until then, daughter of Andromeda, and you will live to see your vengeance. Keep hope and strength."

Something tugs around my upper arm. "Don't forget me." Something tugs around my other arm, and then my neck. "Come back for me, daughter of Andromeda."

The stranger's warmth pulls away from me. My gut clenches, terrified of losing her kindness and facing another hellish bout of neglect.

"Heli..." I want to tell her my name—want to separate myself slightly from this degraded heap on the floor.

Her hand cups my shoulder again. "What are you saying?"

"Helisent."

"Helisent. My name is Imperatriz." It sounds familiar—*really* familiar. "Don't forget me. Don't remove the braids I tied around you. Take them to Samson 714 Afador. To Velm."

I try to thank her, try to tell her that I will try to live, to return home, to take the fabric tied around my arms to Velm and someone named Samson. But my brain can't keep up, no matter how much the portion of food helped.

All I get out is, "Imperatriz."

She sighs. "Be strong."

Then I hear footsteps drift away from me.

I try to be brave. Try to rally more thoughts now that I have some degree of strength. Try to remember why I know the name Imperatriz.

I don't make it far before I sink back into the room of nothing.

The thing I once sensed looming in the center of the room comforts me. I lean into its shape; it is warm, it is breathing, it is more alive than I am right now.

I don't hear or see the hesperides anymore.

I only know we're moving again based on the ship's awful rocking.

Soon, I'm covered in vomit and my own mess again. Soon, I forget what the stranger's name was, whether they were male or female, why they helped me.

Whether they were real at all.

The more time I spend in the dark room, the less real everything else becomes.

And I'm fine with that.

The ship settles once more into a peaceful rhythm. It's the only way to know whether time is passing or I'm trapped between worlds with an empty stomach, broken hands, aching bones, wet layers.

I hear the hesperides again.

The first says, "You stay with the witch. I'll handle him."

A second says, *"Handle a four-horn?* We'll both stay here. He can't make a play for us and the witch at the same time."

"I told you we should have handed her off on Pit—"

"Just keep your wits."

Then the boat moves again; it doesn't rock but shakes and vibrates as though someone wields magic against it. My body and horns rattle against the wooden floor, setting me alight with pain.

Frigid salt water starts to leak between the floorboards. It rises, lifting my numb body from where it has laid against the wood. What starts as a relief soon spirals into panic; the box frame binding my hands doesn't move.

I angle my head to keep my lips above the water.

It rises quickly.

Very quickly.

I exhale forcefully to spit the water out of my mouth before sucking in a breath.

Soon, I cough on the salt water. I try to flee, but my hands are trapped in the box, and the box is fixed to the floorboards.

I go back to the dark room and seize the warm, breathing thing.

I tell it, "I'm dying. I'm dying. This is it—take the pain away."

Then unfathomable pain shoots through my hands like they're being broken all over again. I shriek loudly—once, twice—and realize I'm not gulping water anymore. I open my eyes to a dizzying flurry of raging ocean, white foam, and white hair.

Someone is carrying me.

Their body is warm; they're breathing.

I think they're speaking with a heavy, strange accent.

"Do not hurt me, Vexen."

Am I in the dark room?

Did the thing in there pick me up?

Or am I dead?

All I know is that I'm more comfortable now.

If this is death, I am happy, at last.

I wake up in a comfortable bed.

A heavy, plush blanket covers me. Feather-filled pillows support my neck, surrounding my head like a halo.

With a long sigh, I turn over and stretch out. I grab the edge of the blanket and tug it over my head to block out the bright light from a wide window to my left. I adjust the pillow under my head, then snuggle into its cool side.

I lay half-asleep for a while; it's a perfect morning. I dream of tart brandy and pliant men.

Comfy, comfy, comfy.

Eventually, I realize the pillow smells... unfamiliar.

So does the blanket.

I should be asleep on a sandy bed mat in Hypnos with Butter at my side...

I sit up and stare around a room I've never seen before.

Don't worry, Helisent. This has happened before.

Butter isn't here. The air isn't cool and humid or scented of the salty ocean. I squint out the window to my left and see a plain city built on a steep cliff. In the distance, the ocean wavers like a navy shadow.

I blink, confused.

It looks like Ultramarine or Cadmium, but the buildings aren't white and square. Instead, they're mismatched with different types of pale and dark wood, thick planks and twigs alike. Glass windows reflect the pale light like blocks of gray. The cliffs beyond the city are steep and plummeting; the ocean looks too wild for the Mieiran coast.

I filter back through my memories—

With a gasp, I shove aside the blanket and look around.

Fuck.

The room is narrow and thin. The mattress takes up most of the space, pushed against a huge window. Shelves with books, jars, and other small knickknacks cover the walls. A basin with water sits on a stool at my bedside, along with a bowl of apples.

Where the fuck am I?

I look down at my hands. I turn them over and wonder who healed me, and when, and how they were able to fix such serious breaks so quickly. I'd never had my hands broken before, but it didn't seem like minimal damage.

I lick my lips to rally my courage, then shiver into my form.

My brown skin hides the scars, just like they do my bright red skin, my bloodred horns, and my tail. But in my form, pale scars mark the places where my skin was broken. Knotted dots highlight which wounds needed stitching—a few near my wrist, another at the knuckle of my middle finger, another on my palm.

I hide my form, trading my red tone for brown, my scars for smoothed skin.

It's both disconcerting and comforting to hide them. If it weren't for the scars, I don't know if I'd trust my memory.

All it gives me now are a few unfathomable images and feelings: my broken hands, the pink necklaces, someone dragging Butter away, someone cleaning me, and then, the grand climax, drowning.

I study the cityscape beyond the clean window.

The buildings are stacked in uneven grids. Some tower into the sky with seven or eight stories. Clothes and flags hang from windows and lines strung between the rickety wooden buildings, but they all seem... foreign. The clothes have too many layers, while the flags have strange designs and faded colors.

Large birds with white feathers and bright orange beaks as large as my arm sail below the cloudy sky. They squawk and scream, circling and swooping. I have never seen these awful birds before.

A gentle knock sounds to my right.

It takes me a second to notice the doorframe in the wall. It's hidden seamlessly in the wood-paneled partition, everything painted eggshell white.

It slides open a few inches and someone stares at me from a dark room.

A *horned* someone.

All I can see is a purple-hued eye, slightly aglow, and the outline of one large horn as it curves back from the wielder's temple. Their white hair is short and their skin violet, almost as dark as the ocean beneath the city built on the cliff.

A *purple* wielder?

Where the fuck am I?

"You are awake," the warlock says. He speaks with a strange accent, even more pronounced than the wolves who come from deep within Velm. "Can I come in?"

"*I don't think so, motherfucker.*" I raise my hand and extend it toward the door. I don't actually want to start a fight right now. I'm too tired, too weak, too confused—and very aware of how large the warlock's horns look from where he peeks in.

But I want to get the fuck out of this awful place.

The door slides shut quickly. From the other side, the warlock continues, "Degivampires took you. I saved you three days ago. You have slept."

A degivampire? What the fuck *is that?*

"Who healed me?" I ask, unsure where to start. "Who took me here? And *why*?"

"I healed you. And degivampires from House of Col took you. They wanted to sell you to Ezit."

"*Sell?* What is *sell*?"

"We do not barter here. We trade with coins. It is different."

No idea what that means. "Right. What the fuck is Ezit? Where are we now? Where are the rest of the okeanids?"

"Ezit is the biggest city in Zarzynn. It is far away. You are on Stretch, a chain of islands. This island is Plet, this city is also called Plet. And the okeanids are in Ezit. The degivampires wanted to sell you for a high price—later."

Whatever it is, *selling* sounds bad. *Degivampire*, too.

I sink back into the pillows and set my hands over my face.

The warlock's explanation isn't nearly as simple as I'd hoped.

"Do you have any grimoire?" I ask.

"Grimoire?" He can barely pronounce the word. "I do not understand."

"Grimoire—you know, the powder. Sort of white. Used to root out liars."

"I do not know grimoire."

"Fuck." I fill my lungs and shout the word. "Fuck!"

I massage my temples and try to figure out what to do with the stranger behind the sliding door. "Look, I need you to take me home. Just tell me what you want in exchange. I'm guessing you saw my horns. Just tell me what you want, then get me *the fuck* out of here."

"If I knew the way to Mieira, I would leave now." The warlock's voice lowers, "I am sorry, Vexen, for what happened on the ship."

"That's not my name." I sigh. "So, what the fuck is Ezit? Why do they want me and the okeanids?"

"I know it is not your name. It is what you are—Vexen. Maybe the last." He takes a deep breath. The door groans; I can see the outline of his shoulder leaning against it through the thin partition. "And Ezit is the biggest city in Zarzynn, like I told you. Ezit is where the six Houses meet to rule Zarzynn together. They need the okeanids because they want necromancers. Only an okeanid can become a necromancer. And they wanted you because you are Vexen. Maybe the last."

I review all of his simple, clear explanations. Despite his heavy accent, I understand each word.

"Hey, that sounds really fucking cool. Do you understand sarcasm? I'm fucking with you. What's your name? And do you happen to have a suspiciously large amount of booze with you?"

"My name is Halcyon. I was born into the House of Serac, but I am from Plet. And I do not know what *booze* is. What does it look like?"

"House of Serac? Sure. Whatever. And booze is alcohol. Something that will get me drunk—quickly."

"I have many things. There is wine. Can I come in?"

I want the wine; I'm less welcoming to the idea of a stranger joining me in this tiny room. I'm too tired and frazzled to be quick on my feet, magically or physically.

I prepare halting magic before asking, "And why are your horns out right now? I saw them when you opened the door."

"My horns?"

"Yeah." Four horns or not, Halcyon seems to be tolerant of me. I lean into that, testing how far he'll bend. "Put them away. Or do you not know what horns are?"

"I know what horns are." He pauses. "Put them *where?*"

"Hide them with your magic." I squint, wondering whether wielders on Plet bother hiding their forms. "Do you know how?"

For the first time, the warlock sounds curt. "Fine. My horns are gone. Can I come in?"

He's starting to sound suspiciously good. "Yeah... but why are you helping me? Tell me that first."

A long sigh sounds from the other side of the door. "One, because what the degivampires do is wrong. Sometimes, their ships stop here before going to Zarzynn. We free okeanids if we can. That is how I learned your language. I am a friend of the nymphs who live nearby.

"Two, your hands were inside a rosarium box. They were broken. I know this is very unpleasant.

"Three, because you are Vexen, maybe the last, and you do not know a lot about magic. You need to learn fast if you want to survive in Zarzynn.

"Four, because I... want something. From you."

Halcyon.

I can work with this—I think.

"And what might that be?" I ask.

"I told you I would go to Mieira now if I could. If you learn how to wield powerful magic, you can find your way home. You can find a way for me, too."

I snort, relieved by his last point. It's a fair barter for everything I'll make him do for me. (I don't know what I'll make him do yet, but something tells me I'll need a willing sidekick.)

"Fine. You can come in."

The door slides open slowly.

A warlock with a strange cut of white hair steps into the room. It's cut short on the sides, but the strands at the top are longer; one thick tuft hangs along his jawline. Like me, his skin is a deep brown—uncolored—and no horns stick out from his forehead or scalp.

Despite his youthful voice, he looks to be a decade older than me. His nose is straight—not arched like mine. His upper lip is slightly larger than the lower, stuck in a pout. He has a scar near his left eye, shaped almost like a star and placed perfectly to catch a falling tear.

The only hint that he's a purple wielder are his deep, uneven irises. They're colored like the bruised plums that fall from the trees where I grew up west of Jaws.

He wears fitted layers of dark gray, which includes a hard-looking collar that rises halfway up his neck. They hug his average frame. A loose cloak, paler than his gray layers, clings to his shoulders.

It reminds me of the tailored pieces Anesot preferred.

The thought spirals, catching like a flame on a wick.

Anesot told stories of a world across the sea...

A cruel world where he was born, then escaped...

I try to separate Anesot's memory from Halcyon, who steps into the room and stops at the end of the bed. Without taking his eyes off me, he sinks onto the edge of the mattress with a wooden tray in his grip.

The tray carries two exact portions of water, wine, nuts, and glass vials of white liquid.

I study each of his movements, hands braced beneath the blanket at the ready.

Halcyon ignores my suspicious staring. He balances the tray in his lap.

He offers me the mug first. "It is dark wine. We grow grapes."

I bring it to my lips and gulp it down. It's sweeter than any wine I've ever tasted, and more acidic. Halcyon barely takes a sip of his.

He hands me the small bowl with nuts next. As with the wine, he eats while I eat. He stops when I finish the bowl of nuts, then offers me the rest of his. I eat them quickly as my appetite grows.

He hands me the water once the wine is done, and drinks it as I do —once again, at a slower pace. He watches me with each movement, looking more fascinated than suspicious.

Soon, there's only the bowl of off-white, goopy liquid.

I raise my eyebrows. "What the fuck is that?"

"It is for your skin. You have dry skin. You have some rashes."

I narrow my eyes. "I didn't ask why it's here, I asked what it was."

"It is a mix of beeswax, and... the brown fruit with white insides... and the green plant with spikes. I do not know their names in Mieiran."

"Fine." I pick up the small vial, then pause. "Rashes? Where?" I look down and realize I'm in unfamiliar layers. Specifically, a white pair of linen pants. "Who *the fuck* put me in pants?"

Halcyon goes still. "Two witches washed you and put you in these clothes. They are close to me. They will keep your secret. We have what you wore on the ship. And you can find the rashes. I will take my portion with me."

"Okay." I stare at the warlock, eyebrows bunching. "What secret are you talking about?"

He raises his eyebrows; now, he looks a bit more suspicious. "You are the secret... six Houses control Zarzynn from the city of Ezit. You are from the House of Vex. The Vexen, *your* people, left Zarzynn a long time ago. Your horns are large. You have a lot of magic. That means there are not many of you left."

I blink at him, searching his features for something familiar or comprehensible.

Houses?

Halcyon has already mentioned the House of Serac and the House of Col.

House of Vex.

It doesn't sound entirely unfamiliar from the Class's long lineage of dynastic families who rule Septegeur and Antigone. "Why is that a secret?"

Halcyon blinks at me for a long moment.

I stare back at him, waiting.

Eventually, he says, "*I told you*—you do not know a lot about magic. And if the other Houses know this, they will hurt you again. You survived the ship. You understand their evil. They will use you or they will kill you.

"And... when I took you from the ship, I killed one degi. But the other degivampire named Pel lives. He works for the House of Col. He will tell them that he lost you—that you are alive and free. The vampires will hear. The gorgons will, too. Everyone will know you are here in Plet."

As his words settle in, my hands start to shake. My body registers my panic before my mind does. By the time it all adds up, my body is cold and clammy, pitted with the urge to flee or just die.

I drag down a breath and look away from the strange warlock. I search for the sea past the stacked, wooden city.

Halcyon is right.

I can't use my magic to its full capacity—maybe not even half. Or a fourth.

My mother Andromeda died before she could teach me or Milisent the extent of our power. And Milisent died right as we were beginning to refine our spellwork in Antigone.

I am... alone.

And things are different now.

In Mieira, I feared trickery and manipulations because I knew the Class could never hope to overpower me. I feared being centerheart. Feared emotional things.

Now, I'm in a foreign land. I don't know what the fuck a vampire or a degi is. Or a gorgon.

And had I obeyed the Class, I would not be here right now.

(That's the most fucked up part.)

"There is hope, Vexen." Halcyon tilts his head, catching my attention. His gaze is soft, his eyes aglow with the cloudy light. "In Zarzynn, magic comes from Landmarks. Your magic is still alive in Zarzynn, on the mainland. I can take you there—we can go as soon as you are ready. But, to do this, we will have to travel onto mainland Zarzynn."

I set my head in my hands.

Halcyon's optimistic proposal sends me tilting back toward the dark room in my mind. I check back on the comforting shadow of forgotten things. I step inside the room to lean against the looming, breathing thing standing in its center.

I rub my cheeks as tears sting my eyes.

I'm in way over my head.

But I guess that doesn't really matter anymore; I've been in over my head since I was taken from Hypnos weeks ago.

Halcyon goes on in a soothing tone, "Promise that you will take me to Mieira when you go back—me and four others. Five total. Promise that, and I will do anything, Vexen. I am Pleten, but I am not weak. I have four horns; my magic will help you."

I am clean, safe, and healthy in this small room, thanks to this warlock.

And trust doesn't seem out of the question given he and four others need me for passage to Mieira someday.

Someday...

And how far away will that day be?

I pull my head from my hands. I sniffle, wipe my eyes, and stare at Halcyon. At least he looks appropriately wary, white eyebrows tangled and jaw clenched.

With a long sigh, I stare into the face that now represents my only hope of getting home. I study the star-shaped scar near his left eye; it's endearing enough. "Fine."

"Do you promise?" he asks. "If you want more time, you can take it. You can stay here and rest. I will leave so you can be alone."

I look at the half-hidden door. I almost drop the vial of goopy cream as I reach out to grab his wrist. "Leave? Where will you go?"

Halcyon clears his throat. "To the other room. This is not my home. It belongs to a witch. We can stay here until you feel better."

"I don't want to be alone." A few more tears slip down my cheeks. I stare out the window, clinging to the stranger's wrist and pretending he's not here while also desperate for his company and the sense of safety it brings me. "Not yet."

I weep gently.

Halcyon stares out the window, like I do. He glances at me now and then, as though waiting for the right time to excuse himself. Eventually, with a sigh, he takes the vial of white goop out of my free hand, sets it back on the tray, then uses magic to move it to the floor.

He scoots into a more comfortable position on the end of the bed. He rests against the windowed wall near my feet. All the while, he stays half-leaned toward me so the wrist I cling to doesn't shift too much. After a long stretch of crying and wrist-holding, I shift my fingers toward his palm, then intertwine our hands. His warm fingers are long and sturdy, surrounding mine.

If he thinks it's weird, he doesn't say anything.

But I think it might be more familiar to him than it is to me.

What did he say earlier?

I am a friend of the nymphs.

Maybe he has done this before with other okeanids who were just as wordless and rattled as me.

I stay in the room for the next few days.

I leave only to eat in a cramped kitchen, then use the tiny washroom. The apartment is wooden and confined; I can hear others living behind its thin walls. I hear them wash, argue, make love, and yawn in the mornings and at night.

The sounds of life comfort me—distract me.

I sit in the bed and stare out the window. I study the city, named Plet, and its inhabitants. Like Halcyon, the beings here don't hide their forms. From my view, I count wielders of varying colors and horn sizes.

Sometimes, Halcyon sits at my side and points them out. House of Col; jade. House of Serac; indigo. House of Lahar; burnt orange. House of Argot; white. House of Talos; gold, just like my papa and brothers.

I don't see any red wielders; House of Vex.

Other days, I wander the apartment's few rooms. The wooden floorboards groan and spew an ancient, musky scent. Along with the apartment's frigid temperature, the planks remind me of the ship. Even the wind that howls against the walls takes me back to that stint.

The window lining the bed is safe.

Halcyon brings my meals on the wooden tray. I've never eaten so many types of fish in my life. Small, salty fried fish; dried strips of smokey fish; large, buttery white fish; fish heads in rich broth; fish skins fried in batter. The noodles are a safe choice, which Halcyon prepares each morning and night.

Like he did the first day we met, he eats and drinks in proportion to me and at the same time. When I ask why, he says, "It is respectful. We will be bound."

He is mostly quiet, and observant, and patient.

When he hears me crying in the bedroom or the washroom, he knocks on the door, then tells me a story that has nothing to do with anything.

This morning, it was, "Vexen, there is a mollusk you should eat. Only the okeanids from Mieira like it. It is bitter and slimy. I will bring you the mollusk today—everyone at the market will laugh at me for buying this mollusk. You will watch me cook. It is disgusting."

Yesterday afternoon, it was, "Vexen, did you know that the islands of Stretch were created by a bird? You call them phoenixes, we call them firebirds. They flew between Mieira and Zarzynn, where the ocean is dangerous. They got tired—the journey is long.

"The firebirds filled their beaks with dirt and seedlings and rocks before they flew. They spit it out in this spot when they flew from Zarzynn to Mieira. Slowly, the islands grew. If you feel sad, then look at the land. What you see may be from Mieira, left by a firebird."

By the time he's done rambling, my tears have dried.

By the end of the week, I'm comfortable thinking of the future again.

We sit in the kitchen at a square table with dinner between us. Nearby, a window faces the ocean. A storm brews overhead, churning the waves below. I can't see where they crash against the dark cliffs, but now and then I can hear their roaring drift up from far below.

I poke at the mollusks on my plate. I like their flavor like Halcyon predicted, but tugging them free of their shells feels a bit violent.

And my mind is elsewhere.

I stare out the window at the ocean. "You said magic comes from Landmarks in Zarzynn." It's not entirely unfamiliar from the nymphs and their demigods; both wield elemental power that's tied to a geographic region. "How long would it take us to get there? And do you think the magic would... recognize me?"

What I need are resources.

Not just an unfathomable depth of magic power, but spells to harness it. (I don't know how a Landmark teaches me spellcasting, but that's a question for another day.)

Halcyon glances out the window, too. "The magic is yours, Vexen. It will know you. The okeanids who live here tell stories about wielders in Mieira. They say you have panic magic. We call this ejima —raw magic. You must control the magic instead of letting it control you."

"And... you learned to control your ejima by going to Zarzynn? To your House—House of Serac."

Halcyon sighs. "I have never gone to mainland Zarzynn. I learned to control my ejima from a warlock here in Plet."

Control my ejima...

I haven't asked many questions over the last week. Almost exclusively, my inquiries have covered mundane topics like how to draw water in the bathroom.

Now, I feel a bit more prepared to dissect Zarzynn.

I take a sip of my wine, happy that there's plenty left in my glass. Other nights, our bottles have run dry; things run out quickly in Plet, it seems. "Right. I think it's time you tell me about Zarzynn. About what it means to be Vexen."

Halcyon also reaches for his wine. "I want my horns."

"I've never seen a *purple* wielder before."

His nose scrunches; he doesn't like naming wielders by color. "I am from the *House of Serac*. Even if I am not from Zarzynn or Ezit, my blood is Seracyd."

I try not to roll my eyes again. "You say that the okeanids tell stories about life in Mieira. Didn't they tell you wielders don't wear their horns? The nymphs and wolves see it as a threat. There was a war—it changed how they see us."

Halcyon tsks. "How ugly. Horns are beautiful. They are safe."

My chair creaks as I sit back.

That thought had literally never occurred to me before.

Are they?

Before I can stutter a response, Halcyon's form ripples across his body. Unlike the first time we met, the warlock wears loose linen pants and a tidy gray shirt, which leaves his arms and collar bare. Like his eyes, his skin is a mix of plum and orchid hues, while his lips are indigo.

The only other wielders I've seen in their forms are Mieira's golden wielders. Their golden hue gave their brown skin a glowing quality rather than a new shade. When Milisent was alive, my red coloring was fainter, like an overlay of strawberry on my olive skin. It's similar to Halcyon's current shade of violet, which is distinct enough for multiple hues.

And, like mine, his horns are large.

Light from the window casts a milky hue over them, drawing out every detail.

Most golden wielders have two semi-developed horns that jut from their foreheads and curl upward. Like me, Halcyon's forehead horns are the length of a hand. And, like me, Halcyon has two more horns that start at his hairline. They grow back along his scalp before curling forward. Though thick as my wrists, his secondary horns aren't as broad as mine.

And the warlock doesn't have a third set like I do. My third set curls back near my ears like ram horns.

Still, the size and girth of Halcyon's violet horns impress me; I've never seen any this large on another wielder aside from Milisent.

I've also never seen a tail out. Even when Mint and I interacted in our forms, we left our tails curled around our bellies.

Halcyon's spade-shaped tail flicks back and forth behind him. After swinging a few times behind his stool, it curls forward and drapes across his lap.

He's terrifying, beautiful, wild, unknown; the same.

Everything in myself I could never quite face.

"You can do it, too," he says.

"No, thanks." I clear my throat. "You can tell the story now."

I force my eyes back to the mollusks, nervous I'm studying him too closely.

Halcyon has been exceedingly pliant. The handholding has become more comfortable and routine, but I'd hate for him to see it as an invitation. In another life, in a place like Hypnos, I would have made a lover of Halcyon.

Now, I need a guardian more than an orgasm.

(I mean, I also want the orgasm, but I'll take survival first.)

Halcyon folds his hands in his lap. "In Zarzynn, magic is tied to Landmarks. To *six* Landmarks, specifically. We call these Landmarks and their wielders Houses. You are from House of Vex. Your magic comes from caves, Vexen. In House of Serac, where my people live, magic lives inside glaciers. House of Talos from waterfalls; House of Col from cliffs; House of Lahar from... I do not know the word. A mountain. A mountain full of fire. And House of Argot from... I also do not know. Hot jumping water."

I nod, so Halcyon knows I'm trying to follow along.

I set the other Houses aside for a moment, focusing on my own.

House of Vex.

Halcyon goes on, "A long time ago, wielders learned to create spells from the magic born in these places. This is how the Houses formed—with the Landmarks that gave wielders power. And, like you say, color. These Landmarks are spread out across the mainland... but all the Houses meet in one location, right in the heart of Zarzynn.

"We call this city Ezit.

"Wielders built the city along with vampires and gorgons. Life was peaceful and—"

"What are gorgons and vampires?" It seems like a degi is a type of vampire. "You said the men who took me were vampires, but they looked like nymphs to me."

Most troubling of all, one of the vampires knew me.

And I have no memory of whether or not I knew what he was the first time we met.

Halcyon unfolds his hands, pausing now and then as he explains, "Vampires drink blood to survive. They don't have horns. Sunlight burns them; they only move by night. They have sharp teeth." He taps his upper and lower incisors. "They don't wield magic, but they can... become strong. Very strong. Their bodies, I mean.

"And the gorgons are... hard to explain. They also have no horns. They do not wield magic. They live a very long time—to two hundred and fifty years. If you look them in the eye, you will turn into stone. *Stone*, Vexen. Your body stops moving, then you die quickly. In seconds. They build walls around their villages. They do not live in Stretch. Only the mainland."

Halcyon lowers his chin, explaining with great care, "If you see a wall on the mainland, do not cross the wall. If you *must* cross the wall, wear a tie over your eyes. It is gorgon land. You *must* hide your eyes. Inside the walls, they do not hide theirs."

I poke at the mollusk shells, hand twitching. "Gorgons turn people into stone through eye contact? What kind of stone?"

"I do not know." Halcyon glances out the window, features bunching. "I... do not know about stone. About kinds of stone."

"But it's not the pink stone, right?" Even thinking about the chunky, shiny stones from the ship makes my palms sweat and my throat lock up. "The kind the vampires put around my neck in Hypnos."

"That is different. The pink stones are called rosarium. They come from Zarzynn—from deep inside the ground. And those men were not ordinary vampires. Those are *degivampires*."

Halcyon's hands twitch like mine did a moment before.

He also has a few conspicuous scars that mark his knuckles, palms, and wrists. When I first woke up, he said having my hands broken must have been unpleasant; I didn't realize he knew that on a personal level.

Before I can ask about the difference between vampires and degivampires, he clears his throat and goes on, "So, wielders created Ezit with the magic from their Landmarks. Vampires and gorgons also built the city. For many years, there was peace. But... the Landmarks gave wielders great power through magic.

"And they liked this power. They wanted more. They took every drop of magic they could from their Landmarks.

"It meant that no one could stop them if they broke promises. If they stole. If they lied. The vampires and gorgons suffered greatly; Ezit's wielders controlled them with violence. With threats. With killing spells, with torturing spells, with confusing spells. Naturally, the vampires and gorgons wanted to leave.

"The gorgons took off their eye covers. They left Ezit. Some gorgons are born with... I do not know the word. Magic does not work against them—the older the gorgon, the less magic works against them."

I sit at the edge of my seat, hanging on to every word. "Immunity. They are immune to magic."

"Yes—immune." Halcyon scratches his chin. "But the vampires do not have this. They could not leave. I told you, sunlight burns them. They sleep together when it is daytime, then leave at night to eat. The Houses understand this—they used this to control vampires.

"They made them *degivampires*.

"*Degi* comes from Zarzyd, my language. It means below. It is a part of Ezit—the city below the city. To be degi is to live there. To be bound to a House of wielders and live below them.

"Degivampires serve three purposes. Some handle normal tasks, like a messenger or a clerk. Others defend the Houses and their wealth. These vampires are taught to fight. They are... warriors, I guess. The third type of degivampire creates necromancers.

"The art of necromancy is very new. It started around fifteen years ago. That is when news reached Plet—that a warlock from here and his witch sidekick went to Mieira. They had been banished first from Ezit, then from Plet. Their plan to undo their banishment from Ezit was necromancy. They wanted to offer the Houses something they would want—and need.

"Necromancers can communicate with the dead. Maybe your people have never heard of them. But that is why Zarzynn kidnaps your okeanids. To speak with the dead in Ezit.

"Pel and Jen, the men who kidnapped you, are not nymphs. They are degivampires—a degi, for short. They are bound to the House of Col, who sends them across the sea to kidnap okeanids. They take them to Ezit. They change them with ritual magic."

Halcyon slaps his thighs with a sigh. "So, this is Zarzynn."

I stare at him, trying to find a light at the end of this moons-awful tunnel.

Degi.

I don't have the strength to deal with that. To imagine an existence in the sewers of Ezit similar to what I endured on the ship.

I move to a different topic. "And what happened to the House of Vex? You said that I might be the last. Where are the rest of my people, if they aren't on the mainland?"

Halcyon takes a deep breath. "There was a war. A great war.

"Not every House wanted to control vampires and gorgons. The Houses of Vex and Talos wanted to live with gorgons and vampires in peace. This was the natural state of Zarzynn for thousands of years—prosperity, harmony.

"But the other Houses did not want to lose their degis—or the Houses of Vex and Talos. They needed the magic and labor of these Houses and vampires. They fought to keep them within the walls of Ezit."

My eyes wander back to Halcyon's horns. They gleam spotlessly, as though smoothed and then shined.

He is from the House of Serac. His magic comes from a glacier.

And his ancestors wanted to kill mine.

"What happened next?" I push.

Halcyon nudges my mug of wine toward me. He drinks from his cup as I drink from mine. "Vexen and Talosen wielders died. So did many vampires." He gestures to my cup, then to my hand, which rests on the table nearby. "The coasts of Vex and Talos are near Stretch. Like this."

Halcyon creates a rudimentary map of the table's few items. According to the description, Stretch's islands sit between Hypnos to the west and Vex and Talos to the east, on mainland Zarzynn.

"Hundreds of years ago, war started in Ezit. Vex and Talos lost quickly. They retreated from the city toward the coasts. They were trapped on the coasts, so they began to make ships. When Ezit's army came, Vexen, Talosens, and vampires sailed away from their Landmarks. Away from the mainland.

"They sailed to the islands of Stretch. And after founding Plet, some kept sailing westward. They wanted to find a *larger* new world."

I sit up straight as his words start to paint a picture; Halcyon's tale accounts for the wielders who showed up on Metamor centuries ago. According to nymph legends, the first wielders spoke a foreign tongue, they were demigodless with a penchant for hoarding and violence.

A smile plays on Halcyon's lips. "This is why you know the *golden* wielders, as you call them. There must be many from the House of Talos in Mieira."

I nod. "All of the wielders in Mieira have golden horns."

I clench my jaw, immediately regretting the statement. While I *think* I trust Halcyon based on our barter, I don't want to hand over information on Mieira. On safe, beautiful, peaceful Mieira.

Halcyon doesn't bat a lash. "House of Talos has thousands of wielders. There are too many—their magic is weak. A Landmark does not have infinite magic to share; there is not much left for each Talosen wielder.

"But I don't feel bad for Talos. You will see why.

"Over time, thousands from the Houses of Vex and Talos sailed to Mieira. Thousands more stayed here in Plet. But... not all wanted to search for a new world. The vampires refused to leave. To admit defeat. And many from the House of Talos wanted to return to their waterfalls, their Landmark.

"Eventually, the House of Talos made a deal. A deal that let them return to Ezit and trade again.

"But the Vexen... the Vexen did not make a deal with Ezit.

"Around six hundred years ago, they left the mainland for good. There was a great battle in the caves, then their ships arrived in Plet. In them were the last of the Vexen."

Around six hundred years ago...

Around that time, the Vexen who had found their way to Metamor and Septegeur would have started fighting the wolves in western Mieira during the War Years.

I sit back in my chair with a sigh.

After dying in hordes in Zarzynn, the Vexen fled to Mieira to do the same.

Halcyon goes on, "The Landmark is still alive, Helisent. Sailors still tell stories of the red stone they see on the coasts of Vex. Pine barrens cover most of the land. Beneath them are caves."

I poke at the mollusks on my plate. They're cold, the clear sauce congealing.

Halcyon reaches for his wine, making sure to slide mine toward me first. "But no one has seen or heard of a Vexen wielder in centuries."

He finishes the mug, gulping quickly.

He stares at me, blinking his glowing eyes as though suddenly shy. "Not until last week, at least. I saw Pel and Jen dock a ship outside Plet. We know where they go, death goes. I went onto the ship and I found you. A Vexen."

We stare at one another for a long time.

Waves crash against the cliffs outside while orange-beaked raptors soar through the air, screeching.

I rub my face with a sigh. "How do I learn magic from a cave, Halcyon? And you're sure that you know how to get there?"

"No one lives in Vex aside from a gorgon settlement and a few free vampire dens. They keep many legends about Vex. I know sailors who will take us to the mainland. We can ask for directions at the gorgon settlement, then hope for the best."

I snort, ready to pick apart such a horribly vague plan.

But Halcyon goes on before I can interrupt, "And how long until your people come for you? We can wait for them in Plet."

The question is like a punch in the gut.

I'm officially cut loose from anything I've ever known.

I shrug, then look back to Halcyon. "They won't."

He raises his eyebrows. He doesn't look suspicious, just confused. "No one will come for you? A Vexen with six horns?"

Seven horns, my dear warlock. Or do they not count tail horns here?

"I was banished when I was taken." I swallow the lump in my throat. "My disappearance isn't really a problem for wielders in Mieira. It's more like a solution."

"Banished?"

I slump toward my plate. "*Banished.* So, when can we leave for the cave?"

Halcyon still looks hung up on the banishment comment. Eventually, he shrugs. "When you are ready to sail again. On a ship."

I chew on my lip and glance out the window again.

The sea is ablaze with foam.

With each day, I remember less of my time on the ship. I keep shoving those awful images into the black room where my memories are dead; the longer I stay in Plet with Halcyon, the less I go back to the room. The thicker its walls become, protecting me from everything stored within.

"Let's go tomorrow." I study Halcyon's horns, study the patient pit of black in the center of his plum eyes. "And when we're back from Vex, I'll take you and four others to Mieira with me."

"I see." He sits back on his stool, tail curling behind him like a sultry cat. He crosses his arms as he studies me with a growing smirk.

I pat my hair, making sure no strands are out of place, then run my tongue over my teeth. I can't find anything in my appearance worth studying so intently.

His expressions have become increasingly playful; I'm not sure how I feel about it.

"*What*, Halcyon?"

"I remember your horns. They were not polished. It is normal that the more attitude a witch has, the more she cares for her horns. For you, it is the opposite. A lot of attitude—and rough horns."

My mouth falls open. "Stop thinking about my horns. It's *very* forward."

"The memory is mine." He taps his temple with his pointer finger. His vague smile grows. "You have horns like an animal."

I cross my arms. "You look like the prettiest little goat in a livestock fair. The nymphs shine their horns to impress the crowds."

Now, his mouth falls open. "A *goat?*"

For the first time since waking in Plet, a full smile spreads across my cheeks. "Exactly. A *goat.*" I glance out the window, extending my hand toward the northeast. "Take me to the cave across the sea, goatman. I'm ready."

His nostrils flare as he studies me; he looks amused, then slightly annoyed that he's amused. "Right away."

CHAPTER 4

EVEN IF I DIE AGAIN

SAMSON

My grandson,
You will know two extremes. The first is maintaining Velm's culture and tradition. The second is delving into the future and its uncertain outcomes. You are our people's catalyst for change; trust yourself, Samson.

I stare at the folded note pinched between my fingers.

Absalom stands next to me on the upper deck, staring into the calm sea. Everyone onboard the massive wooden ship is prone to similar bouts of mindless staring, fixed on the endless horizon of ocean and sky.

I haven't seen land since the coast of Hypnos fell out of view just over two weeks ago.

I glance at the warlock. His short white hair and his long white cloak whip in the wind. He looks... at peace.

I unfold the note in my hand and skim the words one last time.

Brutatalika,
I promise to explain everything in detail when we meet again. For now, I can only cover the bare facts. When my pack went to Satyr, we heard of a kidnapping in Mid City. Okeanids were taken, including a Hypnotic Queen and the grandchild of Ultramarine's GhostEater. Helisent West of Jaws was also taken.

Rex and Berevald set sail with me in pursuit of the kidnapped beings. We've spent two weeks at sea, sailing east with the guidance of two powerful okeanids. I'm hopeful we will find more information about the missing nymphs soon. I'm also hopeful I'll learn more about Imperatriz 713 Afador's disappearance.

I hope this note finds you well. The former Head Warlock of Luz, Absalom Metamor, sent it to you on my behalf.

Samson 714 Afador

My hand itches with the urge to give Brutatalika more information.

If I shove everything else away—my love for Helisent, my drive to find Imperatriz, my need to destroy Clearbold and ruin his pup—my trust in Brutatalika remains.

And now that I remember Clearbold and Anesot's collusion, and understand my father's ultimate plan with his second heir, I'm more afraid for my wife than ever before. For what could happen when I'm not there to stand between her and Clearbold.

Her and Malachai.

And why I might not be there to do that.

Though I don't know what my future holds in relation to Helisent West of Jaws, I won't let her disappear like my mother did seventeen years ago.

I'm no longer a twelve-year-old boy; what the world takes from me now it will pry from my cold, dead hands.

I refold the note with a sigh.

As though he's been watching from his periphery, Absalom opens his hand to me without looking away from the horizon.

He looks up at me when I hand it off. "What should I use to track her?"

I take the cigarette behind my ear, then pull at my hair tie and the tidy bun it holds. My hair falls loose, tickling my shoulders and back. Like many of my layers, my tunic is hanging damp in my cramped cabin below. The chill is preferable to the wet.

I hold up the navy blue hair tie, but don't set it in Absalom's waiting hand. "I'd prefer if you didn't touch it."

He raises his eyebrows. "Fine. That's what the other ones said, too."

The other ones. Absalom isn't the only being on the ship to refer to Rex and Berevald in diminutive terms.

The warlock taps one of the letter's folded corners against the hair tie. He murmurs something under his breath; even though I stand near him, the wind howls and all I hear is, "...swiftly right now."

He retracts his hand from mine, then the square note lifts into the air.

It flutters through the strong gusts, rising high above the ship's deck and into the sky. Soon, it disappears amid the piercing rays of sunlight. As the clouds overhead darken with night, a blinding seam of light wavers on the western horizon.

The rut in my gut deepens.

I'm *very* far from Velm.

Far from my wife, my responsibilities, and the destabilizing havoc of the Leofsiges.

Shortly after my wedding, Sutnazzar 712 Afador, my grand-Alpha and the Kulapsifang who birthed my mother, wrote to me about the new symbol carved around Mort. Only a week later, Berevald wrote to me about a village on the border with Gamma that lynched a warlock. One week after that, a third letter came.

A pack leader named Invidio 499 Kelberg, who I now remember distinctly, drove out the nymphs and wielders who lived in his village. Apparently, he did so with great violence and zeal.

As I watch the letter soar back toward Mieira, I push Velm away from my mind.

Worrying about it won't help me now.

So long as I bring back Imperatriz or information about her whereabouts, I'll be welcomed home.

I turn, sensing Absalom's gaze. He crosses his arms as he faces me. "So, you drank the potion from Kierkeline. She told me a few days ago. And what do you think could've taken Helisent? Along with Parsifal, you know the witch. I'm sure you understand her weaknesses."

Two weeks into our journey at sea, the unbearable pain in my chest suddenly gave way. I woke to a permeating relief, like I'd been held beneath the water only to be plunged into the air again. Each breath was freedom and hope—

That maybe the worst of Helisent's agony is over, wherever she is.

But part of me misses the pain.

It felt... cathartic, at least.

Something that I deserved to feel.

I study Absalom's boyish, unlined features.

I'm sure you understand her weaknesses.

I do.

Love is her weakness as a centerheart; for all of her unmatched power, Helisent West of Jaws can't wield magic against those she loves. Not unless it serves their highest will.

And I wielded this knowledge, and her love for me, like a throwing axe against her.

I did it for a chance to find Imperatriz—*but what will that change for Helisent?*

And even if she can see past my decision to defend Anesot, she and I never hashed out what would happen after I married the Female Alpha in winter.

I glare at Absalom. He watches me with a smug bend to his eyebrows.

I have no idea who took Helisent. I have no idea how they gained control of her, or why, or how that may have worked out.

But I don't explain that to Absalom.

I ask, "Can you light this?"

Absalom blinks at me. "Maybe. Are you asking me to light it?"

I turn away with a task, then head for the ship's rear rather than beg the warlock for a light.

On my way to the staircase, I pass Eos and Aura. The okeanids sit at the ready on either side of the ship's broad deck, preparing their current-shifting magic in case of another storm. So far, the women have managed to keep the ship afloat through gales that bred waves twice the height of our vessel.

Aura keeps her black hair shaved low; a diadem of turquoise wraps around her forehead, along with dangling earrings that look like droplets of water. Eos stands a few inches taller than her partner. She has narrow, black locks that drift to her shoulders. Shined turquoise gems dangle from a few; I'd wager they were gifts from Aura.

Hemlock East of Alita, a king of Rhotidom, sits near the okeanids with Kierkeline at his side. The pair prop their feet up on barrels, sharing sips from a bottle of cider and trading stories so the okeanids don't get bored at their posts.

The nymphs don't look up as I pass.

Kierkeline spares me a glance. We haven't spoken aside from a brief thanks for the memory potion. The witch sits in a heap, her knobby limbs poking from within her long robe. Her wrinkled face and hands denote wisdom born from age—but her round and ever-twinkling golden eyes stir with something timeless and cruel—something on the hunt for its granddaughter. Even her bronze and copper rings and necklaces shimmer with something clandestine and lethal.

Since setting sail, the formal rapport between the three nymphs, three wielders, and three wolves has become more casual. Hemlock and the two okeanids handle their own routines separate from the three wielders. The same goes for me, Rex, and Berevald.

For the most part, at least.

I duck as I take the stairs. Okeanids built the ship; I have to hunch to get around, even in the tallest storage room that Rex, Berevald, and I share.

The lower deck already smells like an unideal mix; mounds of grains and nuts, dried fruit and meat, barrels of fresh water, and the musky tendrils of every being's ala. Without a consistent source of fresh air, I can smell traces of sweat, oil, and mucous from everyone.

As I head for our door, Rex exits.

Rather than keep the door open, he jerks his chin back in the direction I came. Before the door to our shared room closes, I catch Bere's sickly ala. His stomach has yet to acclimate to the waves. At best, he keeps down water twice a day and a meal once. What started with a visage of sunken cheeks has escalated into a worrying loss of body mass.

I turn and head for the private office at Rex's request. Closer, I make out Parsifal's ala as it seeps past the doorway. Since the warlock and Rex forced me to drink Kierkeline's memory-giving potion in Mid City, they've grown closer. I've found them chatting in the office several times. Laughing, too.

When we left Alita, Clearbold claimed not to know why I had colluded with Helisent. But Rex knew better. My packmate had found a copy of Imperatriz's letter in my satchel. And for eight months, Rex had waited at my side for the right time to present me with Clear-bold's lies.

In Mid City, Rex confided in Parsifal that he knew Clearbold was lying.

And in response, Parsifal pulled out a foreign item he had found in Helisent's bottomless bag; a snowflake that I had carved and polished from white marble.

Both pieces hinted at what both men already knew to be true: Helisent and I had been allies, not enemies, in Alita.

Still, I find the budding friendship between Rex and Parsifal surprising for a thousand reasons—starting with my tangled history with Rex and ending with my packmate's suspicion of magic and warlocks and hedonism.

Rex picks up his pace, prodding me toward the office. Inside, Parsifal stares at the desk with his chin propped in his palms. He snif-fles, filling the room with the scent of tears.

The sight of his despondence has become less upsetting. He no longer screams and bawls like on the beaches of Hypnos; it's mostly silent weeping now.

He turns when he sees us. His cheeks wrinkle with a smile as he wipes them clean. Rex and I take a seat at the sturdy table that takes up most of the room, surrounded by small, oval windows.

Parsifal stares at my chest as we shuffle into our seats.

I sit down and study his face, picking out all the features that make me feel close to Helisent, and he stares at the scar on my left peck where Helisent's magic toils in my heart like dove in a city processor.

He leans over to pat the scar. "Good evening, Honey Baby—we're still looking for you. Where are you? No playing coy."

Just like I've taken to patting the scar, Parsifal has taken to speaking to it. It's a reminder—

So long as her magic lingers in my chest, its infrasound faint but palpable, she is alive.

So long as I don't feel shooting pains, she is free of torture.

Parsifal smiles, looking from me to Rex. "How are you, boys? You didn't happen to see a fluffy canopy on the horizon? A mountain or a beach or a waterfall? Maybe the end of the world instead? I'm terrified it's going to be a cliff. I hate that feeling when your stomach drops."

"No signs of land." Rex folds his hands on the table. "But tomorrow is a new day. Did you send a note back to the twins?"

Parsifal nods, glancing at my chest again; it's part of the reason I've remained shirtless for most of the trip. He stares at the scar often, brow bunching into a look of anxiety.

"I did. I told Yngvi and Yves what to do if it all goes to shit." Parsifal sighs and runs his hands through his hair. Like Helisent's, it's a wayward mess—and thinning. Tangled with the salty air, his white hair stands at odd angles most of the day. "But I think it's time we have the conversation about what *you two* do if it all goes to shit. Samson, you didn't happen to mention anything about your father's... decisions... when you wrote to Brutatalika, did you?"

"No." I sit back in my chair with a sigh. "It's too sensitive to trust with a letter—and definitely to trust handing over to Absalom."

Nobody would believe it, either.

If that letter were intercepted, it would look like I was making wild claims in an attempt to destabilize Clearbold.

I need *proof*. Irrefutable *proof* of what my Alpha did.

Rex and Parsifal nod. They stare in opposite directions, deep in thought.

Eventually, Parsifal says, "You need to write that letter, my dear Afador. I've been... less vigilant than I ought to be. Andromeda North of Skull gave me two daughters and the world two red witches.

"I used to tell my boys to bury me naked because the first thing I was going to do in the afterlife was climb that witch like a tree. Now... I think Andromeda's going to beat me to death for losing our daughters—she's a powerful witch, she'll figure out how to command my death twice. I have no doubt."

He leans onto his elbows and rubs his face again. "We called her Amaro. She wasn't like Mint and definitely not like Honey Baby. That's how bitter she was."

When he looks up, tears rim his red eyes. "But that's my fate. What I'm more concerned about is making sure you two get out of this alive. Samson, you need to steer the wolves back north. You said you trust your wife, and Rex said she seems to trust you—so why wouldn't you explain what Clearbold has done?

"That secret dies with you, my boy," Parsifal continues. "It already disappeared for the last eight months. If you don't want Absalom to send the note, that's fine—I'm a warlock, after all. A red witch won't make you more powerful, but she will teach you a lot of useful tricks. I can send your letter with confidence. I sent my own earlier—I gave Absalom a fake one. Little fucker."

I turn to Rex, who is already looking at me.

My packmate says, "I agree. But I think we should keep this information hidden until we have indisputable proof of what Clearbold did. The wolves will demand evidence."

I nod at Parsifal, confirming Rex's theory. "The only evidence I had was my mother's hair tie, and that was burned to ash alongside Anesot. Without the hair tie, there's no proof that she still exists."

"Sure, but you're the Kulapsifang." Parsifal narrows his eyes. "Doesn't your word mean more than Clearbold's? *You* are the Afador. Clearbold is just another wolf—no offense, Rex."

"I understand." Rex levels his gaze at me again, a knowing glint in his blue-black eyes.

I stare out one of the circular windows. Outside, sunset leaves the ocean a shifting mass of shadow. Droplets spray against the windows like flecks of black ink. The waves stir with the night; already, the ship lurches back and forth.

With a snap of his fingers, Parsifal lights the wicks of the candles on the table's rusty candelabra. "Well, Samson?"

"I wish my word meant more." I stare at the flames whipping back and forth atop the candlesticks. With a sigh, I lean forward and light my cigarette. "It would mean more if I'd... Parsifal, I'm sure Rex has already clued you in, but after Imperatriz disappeared, Clearbold sent me to kill a wooly outside Bellator.

"The rite of passage is for fifteen-year-olds, not twelve-year-olds. I wasn't supposed to survive, and I wouldn't have—but Hetnazzar stepped in. My demigod saved me and," I hate admitting this part to myself, nonetheless to others, "I didn't tell anyone. If I told my people now, they would also demand proof."

Parsifal blinks at me for a moment. "Well, at least your demigod understands timing." With a sigh, the warlock reaches into his peridot cloak and pulls out a scrap of parchment. He lays it on the table, then reaches for the quill and ink sitting near the candelabra. "Let's write a letter telling *someone*, at least, that Clearbold is full of shit and dangerous. We'll figure out where to send it later."

He looks from me to Rex.

I wait for him to start writing the letter as he adjusts the quill in his pudgy hand.

Then Parsifal hands it to me. "Actually, it should be in your handwriting."

I take the dark feather as he slides the paper toward me.

I stare down at the empty page, taking a long drag of the cigarette.

Rex and Parsifal squint at the paper as though at a loss.

I begin, "I'll start with finding my mother's letter in Rouz, then the journey to find Oko. I guess... from there, the selkie's prophecies are important. The selkie knew the truth about the okeanids and Clearbold before we did."

Rex nods. "And Helisent getting bitten by the vampire in Cadmium. That proves that the selkie was right."

"No," Parsifal interjects. "You have to start before that. You have to explain why Helisent was after Oko in the first place."

Each time someone says her name, my ears pull back and my lungs suck in a huge breath; I'm straining for the sound of her voice or a trace of her ala.

I haven't spoken her name since I drank Kierkeline's potion.

My mind keeps skating around her name, around any explanation that would require me to say it. Parsifal feels that he failed his daughter, but I'm the one who decided not to believe Helisent when she hypothesized Clearbold was working with Anesot.

And it was my own caprice that led to Oko maiming me. That led to Helisent spending her magic and our memories to save me.

My fingers shift the quill into position. "I'll start with Anesot, then?"

Parsifal taps the parchment. "Exactly. It started with him—he got his hooks into Clearbold first, and then he went after Honey Baby."

Rex nods. He lifts the candelabra and shifts it closer to me, offering more light. "And Zarzynn. Write that he came to our land from another place. Then we'll go through the main points. We'll keep it simple."

Parsifal wags a finger at Rex. "Keep this guy around. He's smart."

"I'm already in his pack," Rex says with an understated smile. "You don't have to put in a good word for me, Parsifal."

"Maybe I want *you* to put in a good word for *me*, Rex."

"We don't have any extra liquor hidden. No need for cajoling."

"Oh, let me cajole a bit. If I can't have the liquor, at least let me have my laughter."

I take a deep breath, ignoring the pair's banter.

I write, *Even if I die again, this truth must survive...*

Three nights later, I cling to the doorframe below deck and thank the moons that Parsifal sent my last letter to my bedroom in Rouz.

I don't know that Brutatalika will find it before Clearbold or Malachai if I die, but I'm relieved the note is safe—far from the raging storm that shoves the ship back and forth in the dead of night.

Rex clings to my waist, while Berevald clings to his.

My shoulder crashes into the doorframe as I'm knocked back. The magical lamps around us extinguish with the impact. I drag Rex into the hallway as I fall, fingertips slipping on the wood in total darkness. Berevald grunts and curses someplace nearby.

Though I'd originally gotten up to claw my way to Parsifal's room to check on him, I'm now fighting to keep track of which way is up in the reeling darkness. Water batters the ship like pounding thunder.

It's like being trapped in a barrel that's rolling downhill.

A wave crashes into the deck above and blasts through the wooden ceiling.

Frigid water and debris crash into the blacked-out gulf; the flash flood that almost drowned me and Helisent in Skull was a rain shower compared to this madness. I start swimming, seizing Rex, who holds onto Berevald, so we don't get separated.

Shouting kicks up from the other rooms as the ship's wooden walls start to splinter and pull apart.

"Get Parsifal!" Rex bellows. Though right next to me, I barely hear him through the croak of tearing wood, the crash of heavy waves, the bellow of thunder overhead, the mindless cries from the nymphs and wielders. "I have Bere!"

I take off toward Parsifal's shouting, but I can't see a thing—

Only a brief flash of lightning guides me. It traces the outline of the upper deck, now a heap of shredded planks that fall below. I scramble over the wooden scraps.

"Parsifal!" I scream into the pitched blackness. "Where are you?"

I doubt the warlock can swim—I just hope he flails better than his daughter until I can find him.

I swim and slip and stagger, leaping across wooden surfaces and shrapnel without any reference. I cough as salt water fills my mouth, then I slip below into its cold reaches.

My hand knocks against wood and I pull myself toward the surface—

Toward what I think is the surface.

But below is black, above is black, right now is black—

Salt water slides down my throat and into my lungs.

My gut clenches as I fight the urge to suck in a breath and cough.

I trade the search for Parsifal for my immediate survival—for a breath of air—

And then I'm floating.

Salt water falls around me as I curl weightless in the air, gasping for breath while my arms flail.

I recognize the feeling of floating magic from my time with Helisent. The ship disappears around me as I hover upward. Wind and rain lash against me like icicles, but my body doesn't shift under their momentum.

A flash of lightning gives me another second's reprieve.

I see an inconceivable sight, a thing I'll never forget no matter how long I live.

The roiling ocean below is black, crossed with flushes of white foam. Waves the size of small mountains extend in each direction, hovering around us as they break and reform in pyramidal shapes—on and on and on until the horizon fades into black rainclouds and water.

Cleaved in two, our ship falls apart. The ocean's maw unhinges to swallow its front whole, already half-submerged in a wave. The back portion shifts in a freefall toward a trough of foam and death.

And thirty feet above the surging waves and the shattered ship, nine beings float to safety.

Phantom-like orbs of blue light surround the others. They shelter us from the wind and rain. I catch a glimpse of Parsifal's white hair and green cloak; of Rex and Berevald, still clinging to one another. We rise at the same height, as though controlled by the same spell.

I look for the GhostEater next—

It must be her magic saving us.

But I don't see the hunched, ancient witch before the lightning disappears.

I cough as rain and seawater fill my mouth. Though safe from certain torturous death, I can't control my body. One second, I'm upside down. The next, I'm curled in a ball, attempting to reach out and steady myself. My stomach twists and rolls. I clench my stinging eyes shut.

Eventually, I see more blue light.

I can't tell if it's pooling below the ocean's surface or within the thick clouds above.

All I know is there's a blueish light that gets larger, comes closer.

And then it's reaching; I see five rods. They curl; they're fingers.

I realize it's a blue-hued hand...

I open my eyes fully, braving the sting of salt water. I see something else I'll never forget: an okeanid demigod rising from the waves, glowing with sapphire light. It stands amid the rushing surface of blackened ocean, unmoving like a mountain amid a windstorm. The being's blue features are obscured by the dense gales, but I can clearly make out a head, a symmetrical afro, a flat chest and broad shoulders, and two arms.

And two hands, one of which reaches for me.

With a roll, I land on my shoulder in the steady palm. I rise, still gasping for breath, and make room for the rest of the beings the demigod plucks from the sky. First is Hemlock East of Alita. Then Parsifal, who screams mindless nonsense about Amaro, about Mint, about Honey, about The Boys. Last are Eos and Aura, both okeanids passed out and half-aglow with their demigod's power.

Hemlock and I leave Parsifal to his shock. We tug the okeanids into stable positions, clinging to them. Though the demigod's cupped hand is large and stable, the women could slip through its fingers easily.

When they're secure, Hemlock and I calm Parsifal into a more relaxed state. He helps us toss away the water that pools between the demigod's fleshly palm and curled fingers. He offers us a bit of warming magic, which lessens our shivering.

Then we wait.

Relying on intermittent flashes of lightning, we spy past the demigod's thumb to make sure the rest of our group is safe in its other hand.

Please let Rex be safe.

Please let Berevald be safe.

Please let me be a worthy Alpha.

Hours pass before the wind-whipped night lightens. I stay slumped with exhaustion and fear. Eventually, a hopeful periwinkle eats the sky's darkness. The air warms and the wind calms enough that I can smell Rex and Berevald's alas, drenched in testosterone and cortisol and salt water.

And then comes the sound of a bird cawing.

The blue-tinted fingers around us unfurl.

Like Parsifal and the nymphs, now woken and groggy, I stare wordlessly at the eastern horizon.

Navy blue clouds clog the sky like a bruise. Beneath them stretches a coastline of pale and coarse rock. Beyond the piles of uneven boulders sits an emerald tree line, tall and proud like the jungle of Rhotidom but filled with evergreens. I can smell their dry needles on the flaky rock. Small dark birds and massive white birds cruise through the air, each louder than the last.

Where are we?

My abdomen pumps to pull in breaths.

I search the wind for Helisent's ala as the demigod approaches the coast. I search for Imperatriz's, too. This could be Stretch, or Pit, or Zarzynn—

Or someplace totally different.

I smell nothing familiar. The trees are coniferous and full of sweet sap. The bushes that line the ground are flaky and tough, their leaves small and dark. The birds' feathers and scat are familiar enough to the seagulls of the Deltas and pelicans of Velm, but I've never seen their curved bills or bright blue plumage.

Even the boulders are unknown; the pale stone smells like calcium, like dolomite. Not like sandstone, not like marble, not like granite.

It almost...

It almost reminds me of Helisent. Not her normal ala, but her form's ala. It was cold, ancient, bitter—imprinted in my mind since she briefly wore her form once in Rhotidom.

The rocky coastline stretches on and on to the north and south. With steady steps, the demigod wades toward the boulders. It bends at the waist and unfurls its hands, creating a bridge of fingers that leads onto land. We scramble over, then tiptoe atop the mossy rocks, full of dark-shelled mollusks.

Rex keeps an arm slung around Berevald. They slip on the rocks, Berevald curling toward the ground. His skin is colorless, his lips white. His blue-black hair is tangled in a braid that clings to his back.

I almost run into Hemlock as I beeline for my pack.

The Rhotidic King sinks to his knees and stares up at the okeanid demigod.

I also glance up at our savior. The great being looks just like any okeanid living in Hypnos or the Deltas: thick and dense curls, wide and pleasant facial features, eyes that twinkle like lapis lazuli, and a sturdy bearing. It stands to its waist in the ocean, which now pales to a friendlier, cerulean blue. The waves also smoothen, washing against the shore like whispers.

The okeanid demigod stares at us with an unreadable expression.

I can never quite tell what the demigods mean to communicate—

But I know this one isn't here to drink in our desita.

Without any farewell or even a curt smile, the demigod turns around and walks back into the waves. Each step lowers the demigod's height, as though strolling along the deepening ocean floor.

I turn and rush toward Rex and Berevald, legs weak and shaking. Rex manages to haul Berevald off the rocks and onto a stretch of grassy sand. Berevald collapses onto his back, body heaving with each breath.

Rex's eyes widen when he sees me. "I can't get his attention—he's out of it."

Berevald looks half the size he was when we left Hypnos. His cheeks are sunken, his features colorless. Even his hair looks limp, tangled in the sand.

I turn around, zeroing in on Kierkeline; someone mentioned the witch was a healer before she became a GhostEater.

And by some miracle, she survived the storm. Atop the rocks, Kierkeline straightens her bright blue robe. Given her size, I doubted the witch's capacity to survive even a peaceful journey.

Now, she waves her hand to set her ultramarine robe in order and rebraid her thin white hair. It curls atop her head into an elegant bun as she tiptoes across the rocks with patience.

She's already watching me, Rex, and Berevald.

"Well, Samson?" she barks, pointing at Berevald. "This one refused my help onboard the ship. He will die if he denies it now. What will you do, Kulapsifang?"

I prepare to ask for her intervention, but she doesn't give me the chance. She stops before us and gestures to Berevald again. This time, she tsks. "Wolves eat too much. You're too large. You require too much food, too much energy. It's nonsense for you to survive in a place where there aren't large animals to eat and large loaves of bread baking in large ovens."

Once, I would have scoffed at someone offering help after an insult. I would have preferred to figure things out myself—

But survival is the true master of Velm. And, apparently, it's the true master of wherever we are now.

I bow my head to the GhostEater. "Do what you must to save him, Kiekerline Ultramarine."

Though Berevald shied from the witch's hands while on the ship, he doesn't notice her kneeling beside him now with a smirk. He doesn't lift an eyelid as she raises her hands and lays them palm-down a foot above his chest.

"I can't save him forever, Samson 714 Afador." Kierkeline takes a deep breath, which raises her shoulders as her wrinkled hands hover aloft. "He needs protein and vitamins, and plenty of rest. Most importantly, my dear wolf, he needs potable water—jugs of it. He's dehydrated."

With a sigh, she leans over his chest and sets her palms around his ears; once again, Bere doesn't notice as he toils for breath.

With a satisfied huff, the GhostEater sits back. "His sickness was born in his ears. You would have never figured that out."

Berevald gasps for air and then sighs. His heaving breaths calm after that, picking up a steady rhythm.

I glance at Rex. Like me, he slowly sinks into the sand, slumping with exertion. Kierkeline keeps her hands raised, peppering her miracle with a series of lighthearted insults.

The GhostEater's genius continues to stun me.

On our journey, she divested a *huge* portion of food from the ship's supply barrels and stowed them in her bottomless bag. She admits freely the idea was originally born from greed, which dismays Hemlock and enrages the okeanids, then argues it became a strategy to protect our supplies from destruction in a storm or plain old rot.

Hemlock stops complaining when she pulls out handfuls of dried fruit, dried fish, and loose barley grains. Buckets of freshwater, too. It's enough to keep us all fat and happy for at least ten days—me and my two packmates included.

We take shelter beneath the skinny, looming pines that border the beach, then eat in ravenous silence. By the time night falls, everyone, even Berevald, rests in comfort.

Before we tire, Rex and I volunteer to keep guard. Though the nymphs and wielders also offer, wolf noses are our best bet at defense.

Rather than switch turns, Rex and I spend the night flinching at every sound, passing cigarettes back and forth, and generously marking our camp with urine.

We survive until dawn.

After a quick nap, Rex and I prepare to explore the forest. Aura volunteers to join us, which leaves the rest of the group to prepare breakfast and tally our supplies to map out future meals.

Eos walks beside Aura for the first stretch, holding her partner's wrist. When I first saw the pair wooing tides back and forth on the ship's upper deck, I wondered if they were lifelong friends. Since then, they've chattered about their all-female warren enough to flesh out a very clear picture of their relationship.

Eos summed it up best, "Me and Aura are Alphas. Not of a pack or a family, but our warren."

Like Alphas, the women walk ahead of Rex and me, leading the way into the forest without looking back.

Before we lose sight of the camp, they stop. Eos and Aura kiss each other's palms, then lips, then both of them look up at me.

Aura raises her eyebrows. "Eos is going to stay behind and fish."

Eos gives me the once-over, brushing her locs from her face. "Make sure to bring Aura back."

Aura switches her gaze to Rex, then back to me. She raises her chin and emphasizes, "I expect to be brought back."

I slide my eyes to Rex. He returns my confused gaze. Hoping to offer the women a measure of security, I set my hand over my heart. "Aura, you will come back to camp with us."

I can't actually guarantee that, but my promise satisfies the okeanids.

Without delay, Aura turns back into the forest; Eos heads toward camp with a heavy sigh.

We walk westward, staring past Aura's turquoise-dotted diadem. The forest is unfamiliar; I don't recognize the exact type of pine trees or the mammals and their fur or the birds and their feathers. And still, for the most part, it looks like the woods common to Velm and Septegeur and Rhotidom; a forest is still a forest.

Until we see a wall between the trees.

Pale stones from the beach are cobbled high, extending a full two heads taller than me and Rex.

We stare at the wall; it was built by either hands or magic, without mistake.

Aura tsks as she runs a finger along the stone. "Nymphs don't use walls." She looks up at Rex and me. "But the wolves do."

Nymphs have never understood our usage of walls. In Mieira, hoarding resources like grains or gold or brandy is considered an affront to the demigods and their bounty. And they see walls as ways to hoard the land, to pen in the demigods like chattel.

But nymphs don't live with blood feuds. With the brutality of Night.

I explain, "Some packs build walls in territories where populations don't mix well. They're designed for safety. If that's the case here, we should look for a gate."

With a huff, Aura takes an orange bandana from her bag and ties it to a branch. Then we start to round the wall, moving slowly so I can smell and listen for threats. The wall curves farther inland, away from the beach. We walk for long enough that I wonder if we'll loop back to where the orange bandana flutters from a branch.

Then a breeze carrying dozens of alas crosses our path—

Like I was once certain outside of Cadmium that I'd smelled a vampire's scent, a *fifth* scent, I'm certain this is another being. A *sixth* scent, just as distinct as a wielder or a nymph or a wolf or a vampire.

Rex also stops, chest expanding with a large breath. "What the *fuck* is that?"

Aura pauses, looking from me to Rex as we pull in short breaths to investigate.

I flare my nostrils; the beings are inside the wall. There are many —hundreds. Their alas pool and condense and layer; this is where they live. I catch a few more vague hints of civilization; food I don't recognize, textiles like leather and something similar to cotton, livestock like chicken and goats and something that smells like a rodent, then smoke from fires. I also smell more of the stone wall, as though the village inside is built from it.

Aura pokes my abdomen. "Say something. Do you smell the okeanids? Helisent?"

I shake my head. "No—neither. It's a new being. Something that doesn't live in Mieira. There's a settlement inside the walls. A few hundred live here."

"Beings..." Aura sucks on her teeth. She runs a finger down the wall once again. "Like a demigod or a sable or—"

"Like us," I explain. "Not an animal and not a demigod. I smell fire and food and clothes, if that paints a better picture."

She nods. "Do you smell blood?"

"Good question," Rex says.

Like him, I suck in another large breath, searching for a trace of blood. I don't find any alarming amounts of sickly-scented iron. "Nothing out of the ordinary."

"Shall we continue, then?" Aura doesn't wait for a response before she continues along the wall.

As we advance, I focus on the alas; they split and become more complex. These beings have two distinct genders, but they seem to be divided by age. I smell children along with elders and adults—but they seem to be evenly numbered. As though there's no majority population in terms of children, adolescents, adults, and elders. Each age group has a startlingly similar population.

Only one ala smells different from the rest—and that's because it's alone.

"I think we're close to the gate," I warn Aura. "And whoever is guarding it."

She turns back with a tsk. I wait for her to register the possibility of danger, but she rolls her blue eyes instead. "We forgot to bring a gift."

Once again, Rex and I glance at one another.

Adrenaline lingers in my veins, waiting.

My entire being is focused on the possibility of finding my mother or my witch; the only gift I'm prepared to offer the guard is a fucking swing from my throwing axe.

I take a calming breath as we near the male.

The adult comes into view a moment later along the wall's gradual curve.

Though not as tall and broad as a wolf, the man is twice the size of nymphs like Aura. He's also in his prime, with thick muscles banding his arms and legs. His skin is rich brown like the dryads found in Rhotidom—but heavily freckled along his shoulders, his cheeks, his chest, his arms. His dark brown hair is cropped short, dangling near his ears.

He wears long beige layers tied around his shoulders and his hips. The fabric dangles around him, thin and opaque. He holds a spear with a sharpened tip, which stands taller than me.

The guard shifts to face us, keeping his back to the wooden gate behind him—

Which is impressive, because he wears a thick blindfold, the same material as his light layers.

He doesn't look afraid or uncomfortable as we shuffle to a stop.

He tilts his head, nose twitching like he's studying our scents.

Then he addresses us in a loud tone. While he doesn't sound threatening, he's certainly speaking directly. And I have no idea what he says. Each syllable is stranger than the last, jumping in pitch.

I look at Rex, then Aura. The three of us stare at one another. Eventually, Aura raises a hand, as though accepting the role of speaker. I shift my hand toward the throwing axe at my hip.

Aura clears her throat, taking one step ahead of us. "Hello, dear friend across the sea. My name is Aura Hypnos. What is your name? Where is your demigod?"

The being tilts his head, then offers a long response; I can't tell if he's stating something, asking something, or hinting at something. Maybe none. Maybe all three.

Aura looks over her shoulder at me. "Want to try in Velmic? Just in case?"

Only wolves speak Velmic, but it can't hurt. "Sure."

I ask for the man's name. We're met once again with a foreign response—though I guess it's good he responds at all.

After a moment, he steps toward us.

I watch his hands, then his feet, to see if he means to charge. The spear's tip faces the sky, its end set on the ground.

Slowly, the man bends his knees. He shifts the spear to lay it horizontally in the dirt, careful not to direct its tip at us. With the spear separating us from him, the guard backs toward the gate. Then he turns and slides open the thick, wooden panel with a grunt. He slips into its narrow opening, then hauls it shut behind him.

We wait in silence as a commotion kicks up past the wall.

Gasps precede a few shouts from children. Then comes the familiar sound of chiding, the familiar sound of disappointed sighs. Low conversations echo over to us next.

Eventually, the gate creaks open.

The male guard leads four elders toward us. Each wears a blindfold that matches their tan layers, light-colored and opaque and tidy. The only notable difference is the number of freckles. As though they multiply with age, the elders have dark freckles spanning their bodies; unlike the guard, they have black freckles on their legs and ankles, too.

Though all are elderly, they're separated into two distinct generations. The first is so old that I keep sucking in their alas with disbelief; a male and a female somewhere past their 200th birthday. The next gendered pair, who trail their elders, aren't far behind.

The guard, who leads the four elders forward, wears a different blindfold. Rather than a soft piece of fabric tied flat over his eyes, he wears a rigid, angular piece. It looks like it confines his eyesight to a narrow seam pointed at the ground.

Aura takes a step back. She glances up at me and Rex. "It seems like they don't want us to make eye contact with them—that's why they built the wall and why they wear the blindfolds. Let's be careful if they come off."

"Agreed," I say.

Rex nods.

The guard helps the oldest couple sit near the spear; the eldest pair face us, then the second-eldest pair sit right behind them. As though the elders have no problem identifying where we stand, they raise their chins toward us.

The guard sits beside the group. He reaches over the spear's wooden shaft to pat the open space opposite them.

"We should sit down," Aura whispers.

She takes the first step, then pauses. In response, the guard taps the dirt again—it looks like a pretty clear invitation. Rex and I follow Aura; I watch the spear, while Rex watches the guard.

We shuffle into a row.

One of the elders speaks. When she stops, the guard leans forward to draw an oval in the dirt before us. His finger jumps around until we're staring at a rudimentary drawing of a face: two eyes, one nose, one mouth, and a scalp of hair.

Then the guard gestures from his chest to the hand-drawn face.

"That's what we look like, too," Aura says.

Before I can ask if she's certain about what the guard is communicating, the okeanid leans forward and draws a face beside the first. Her sketch faces the guard, who lifts his chin as he studies it.

He extends his hand and sets it over his drawing. Then Aura does the same with hers.

Slowly, the guard's hand approaches the okeanid's.

She tenses, looking at me as though uncertain what to do. I lean closer to her, prepared to intervene.

Gently, the guard's broad hand cradles hers. He brings it slightly closer to him, then he leans forward to close the distance between his face and her hand. I watch his lips in case he decides to bite—but he only inhales a large breath.

He sighs, then says something.

He repeats the word, letting go of Aura's small hand.

I set my hand over the face she drew next. The guard takes my hand in his, then smells it like he did with the nymph. He says a different word this time.

Suddenly, the group of elders starts to chatter.

They speak freely, barking at one another and cutting each other off. It sounds aggressive, but their body language doesn't hint at any discord. Their shoulders are relaxed, their hands resting on their folded legs. The eldest woman even hisses a laugh a few times. Eventually, she throws a hand back toward the walled village.

The guard stands in response, then scampers to open the gate and hustle back inside the walls.

"Well, they clearly trust us," Rex grunts, looking from the abandoned spear to the group of elders.

"Because we're outmatched," Aura murmurs.

Like me, Rex stares at her.

"Is there something you know that we don't?" I ask.

Aura raises her eyebrows. "No, but I'm a nymph. I trust first and ask questions later. And I can tell you that these beings aren't dangerous. They're *curious*."

"You just said it could be dangerous if we make eye contact with them," I counter.

As we speak, the four elders sitting before us twitch their heads. They flit between us in perfect unison, as though the group is following the conversation as we take turns speaking.

"Their eyes are dangerous," Aura explains, "but they aren't. Does that make sense? They wouldn't *mean* to hurt us. That's why they built the wall. Not to keep people out, but to mark their home."

"Let's hope so," Rex whispers.

I can almost hear what he's thinking...

Let these be the beings who took Helisent, who took the okeanids, who took Imperatriz.

We will take all of this trust and hand them vengeance.

The guard hustles past the gate, slides it shut, then takes his seat again. He carries a handful of bright red berries in one hand. He extends his empty hand toward us, leaning over the spear to hold it above the faces drawn in the dirt.

The guard waits, as though expecting us to hand him something.

He says a word. He repeats the word, moving his opened hand.

Rex extends his hand in offering. The guard says something, then gently moves his hand away. I offer mine next, which he also pushes back. Lastly, Aura sets her hand in his.

Rather than lean to smell her again, he takes the berries in his other hand and sets them in her palm. Then the guard closes her hand, smashing the berries between her fingers.

"What the fuck..." Aura murmurs.

The small fruits break, skin tearing and insides spreading into a bright red goop.

The guard smears the residue across the pale skin of her palm, then onto her fingers and up her wrist.

He says another word.

He repeats the word again and again, shaking Aura's berry-stained hand like he wants to make sure we can see it.

The word sounds like, "Vexa."

He uses his clean hand to gesture northward. He digs into the dirt with a finger. He scoops the dirt, carving a small hole, then gestures to the north again.

"Vexa."

He drags Aura's hand toward the hole in the dirt.

"Vexa."

"Any ideas, Aura?" Rex asks.

She sighs. "No. Let's give him a minute. Moons know he's trying to help."

Then it clicks; the beings are using their noses like wolves.

He used a different word after touching Aura. I thought maybe it represented nymphs, but maybe it represented the fact that she's a woman.

And why spread the berries on her hands?

Red berries.

It clicks again—*what are the chances?*

"Helisent," I whisper. "He knows we're looking for a red witch— she must have shown up here. They wouldn't have forgotten someone as foreign as us—and they'd remember what Mieiran sounds like if she spoke it around them."

Maybe I'm just desperate. Maybe I'm making a connection where this isn't one.

And maybe not.

I reach toward the face that Aura drew, extending my finger. The guard releases her berry-riddled hand to watch me add to the drawing.

I try to imagine what Helisent's horns looked like based on touching them one morning while traveling deep in Rhotidom. What I remember most was her scent—something akin to these pale rocks —and the fact that I could sense enough dove in her form to level Bellator.

The coarse husk of her horns, like a secret the groomed witch kept from herself.

I draw six rudimentary, off-scale horns jutting out from the drawing's scalp.

The guard stares down at my work. For the first time, he laughs, deep and satisfied.

"Vexa."

He smiles, then gestures northward again.

CHAPTER 5

A FUCKING FULL-GROWN ADULT

HELISENT

Honey Baby,
Do you remember the make-believe world you created with Mint? You called it
Gooseworld. Before you discovered brandy, you two had big plans for Mieira.
Beautiful plans. Sometimes, I wonder if you remember them.
Papa P.

I stare around the scrubby forest.

We're getting closer to something...

I can't put my finger on how I know that, but my certainty helps lift my exhaustion.

Since leaving the gorgon village, named Dexerxes, Halcyon and I have wandered north.

During our two-night stay, the gorgons ferried us around their village with blindfolds over our eyes. The blindfolds are linen like the rest of their flowing layers—a textile made from flax seeds.

During certain meals and discussions, we traded blindfolds with the gorgons so we could look around freely.

Black freckles dotted their brown skin, denser atop their shoulders and cheeks and hands. The beings look like a bulky mix between a wolf and a hesperide. They were curious like nymphs and direct-speaking like wolves.

After sailing to the mainland with Halcyon and a gaggle of sailors,

Zarzyd's jumping syllables felt a bit more familiar. Through Halcyon, the gorgons asked questions.

About nymphs, about wolves, about demigods, about saigas, about mountains—

But they didn't want information. They wanted stories. I described what a saiga was, and the gorgon's head matriarch, Accra, had tsked with dissatisfaction. She wanted to know *how* a saiga was. What it does. Why it does those things.

Before I go home, I'll return to Dexerxes. I'll tell her myself—without asking Halcyon to translate.

I try out a few Zarzyd words now. "*I walk with you.*"

Halcyon flashes me a quick smile where he walks at my side. "You walk with me. Good." Slowly, he asks me something in Zarzyd.

I narrow my eyes. He said something about food. I think. I respond with, "*I'm hungry.*"

"I asked if you feel anything," Halcyon says with another smile. "In the forest."

With each day we journey north, the foliage grows thinner and taller. Narrow pine trees crane toward the sky, straight as arrows. Drooping moss covers the lowest branches. The rest condense high above in the canopy, gobbling the light with their rigid needles.

Like the coastline, the forest is intercut with pale outcroppings of limestone. Vibrant green moss clings to most of the boulders, sticking out like poison in the dark emerald forest.

Halcyon walks confidently in his form, just like he has since we left Plet. The sight of his gleaming horns no longer makes me uncomfortable or shy, nor his slightly aglow eyes, nor his thick fingernails.

What started with hand-holding sessions in Plet evolved into full-on clinging when we sailed to Vex. And what started with terrified clinging turned into something much more... investigatory and naughty.

To be fair, I had to be distracted, and Halcyon is a man, and I'm a woman, and there were only so many fucking table games and puzzles I could sit through.

So far, our sex life has been fruitful; there's a reason I've started picking up Zarzyd and Halcyon's Mieiran has improved. Sex magic, sympathetic magic, or, as Halcyon calls it, ejima-touch.

Aside from introducing me to Zarzyd, a few extra orgasms have also helped keep my spirit up as we search Vex for its red cave system. My *Landmark*.

"I can feel that we're getting closer…" I murmur. "But I don't know *how* I know that."

Halcyon doesn't seem perturbed by my vague confirmation. He just nods and carries on walking.

I've started to wonder how a powerful warlock like him ended up on Plet.

So far, he's mentioned it's a haven for outcasts; he doesn't seem like much of an outcast. Part of me is hopeful he's banished, just like me.

Maybe we can be outcasts together. Maybe we already are.

That's when I see the strangest thing.

Not in the forest—in my mind's eye.

I see a bottle of brandy. It's laying flat on a floor; my heart pangs when I realize it's empty. And it's spinning. Spinning slowly in a circle on a wooden floor.

It's vivid enough that I fall still.

The bottle spins and spins—

It's almost like a waking dream, like a mirage or a hallucination or an invasive thought—

My hands raise, as though I could pause the vision long enough to gain clarity. *Is this thought mine? Is it normal to wonder if a thought is mine?*

At my side, Halcyon also falls still. He stares at the forest with his hands flexed at the ready.

Animals shuffle in the dry canopy. A bird coos. Sunlight pools on the ground in golden puddles.

The bottle starts to slow down, its green glass catching the light.

"Halcyon…"

He barely spares a look at me as his eyes jump from shadow to shadow. "What do you sense?"

Am I going crazy?

"It's… a vision?"

This time, Halcyon sidesteps to press our backs together. "Tell me what you sense—is it an ambush? What do you see in your vision?"

"An *ambush*?" I raise my hands further, this time in anticipation of an attack. I study the forest as Halcyon's butt presses against my lower back. Once again, I don't see or hear anything out of place. The brandy bottle spins in my mind's eye, slowing more with each turn. "Should we be preparing for an *ambush*? I thought you said no one came to Vex anymore?"

"Vexen—tell me what you see in your mind."

My heart thumps in my chest. "It's a bottle of brandy—an *empty* bottle. It's spinning. I swear—this isn't *my* thought."

With a scrape of glass against the floor, it finally eases to a halt.

I stand at the ready, knees bent into a half-crouch.

With a snort, Halcyon straightens and turns toward me. His hands hold his hips, weight set back on one leg as he watches me.

"Then maybe it is Vex's vision."

My jaw clenches. "Don't mock me."

I try to walk myself through what's happening.

I've always considered my magic to be a twin—

I didn't realize it could... make me see things in my mind.

The bottle remains stationary, pointing toward the northeast. I pivot toward Halcyon; the bottle shifts again. Its narrow neck moves as I do so the bottle points in the same direction.

"I'm not mocking you," Halcyon says. "There are legends that the Landmarks speak directly to their Hosts if their ejima is strong enough. Maybe it is showing you an image. Using an image like a word."

Good fucking moons. The Landmark is communicating to me through brandy bottles.

And, as with most other things in Zarzynn, I have little choice but to believe the warlock.

I gulp, returning Halcyon's steady gaze. "I think it wants us to go that way." I point to the northeast. "And don't tell anyone about the bottle."

"I will not. It means something to you?"

"Sure. Whatever." I clear my throat. "How... does Vex know what matters to me?"

"In Mieira, you call raw magic *dove*," Halcyon explains with a nod. It's a gesture he picked up from the okeanids in Stretch, but he doesn't nod in confirmation—just to emphasize his ideas. It's confusing. "In Zarzynn, we call it ejima. And ejima isn't *just* dove. Ejima is also the *intelligence* of that raw magic."

I narrow my eyes. "So, it's smart?"

Halcyon keeps nodding. He also presses his palms together; he does this anytime he finds my ignorance especially problematic. "Your magic learns from you. You speak Mieiran, so Vex knows how to speak Mieiran, too. That's why I speak Mieiran better—because Vex's ejima taught it to my ejima."

It slowly clicks into place.

Vex is my magical twin—and it knows many things.

Including how much I love brandy. How much I miss it.

I study the limestone boulders around us, searching for an entrance or a grotto. "Right, well, Vex—my dear Landmark—I hope you're leading us to a cave. By nightfall, preferably. I'm here to... to learn how to wield great magic."

Even I doubt myself by the end of that sentence. If Vex knows everything I know, then it knows that I got myself kidnapped by a pair of degivampires—which I can't imagine comes off as impressive.

With a sigh, I trudge onward, following the empty brandy bottle that points to the northeast.

As we wander, the image morphs.

What began with a sterile image transforms into something... something like intuition. The image of the bottle drifts in and out of my mind as we walk.

It feels like I'm remembering something from long ago; the name of a friend, the scent of a certain type of soap, a melody sung to me as a child.

I stare toward the northeast.

Something invisible and yet mammoth is... calling to me. Without words. Without a voice.

And I know what it is.

It's a cave. It's much larger than I thought it would be. It has a name, too.

My feet move faster.

This isn't how I thought it would be—

I thought I was seeking the cave; I think the cave is seeking me, instead.

I walk toward it without a second thought or qualm or question.

Like a bee finding its nest; a swallow finding its colony; a saiga rejoining its herd.

Maybe because my magic does not belong to *me*.

I belong to *it*.

To Vex.

Like a demigod.

The closer we get, the quicker my feet move. Halcyon trails me wordlessly for hours. Dusk falls, sending gilded light and shadows into the forest.

Ahead of us, the forest finally clears, giving way to pale stone.

A few grassy patches dot the limestone glade, bordered by pine trees that crane skyward. Moss and lichen riddle the pale, green-yellow rocks. And there, in the center of the vast clearing, sits an empty gulf of shadows.

An entrance to a cave.

My head tilts as a word pops into my head—

Hella.

"Hella..."

I rush toward it, heart leaping in my throat.

The bottle in my mind's eye stops frothing. The bubbles flatten near its opened top, leaving a puddle on the wooden floor. As though shivering with infrasound, the bottle rattles against the ground.

I stare over the ledge, then turn to Halcyon. He stares at me as he wanders to peek over.

The last of the sun's golden light trickles into the cave.

My lips part as I stare below.

I squint as I pick out angled rooftops and buildings.

Not a cave—a city, almost the size of Luz.

In the center of the forgotten city is a circular stone shape, which looks like it might have been a fountain. Road-sized gaps lace between the round buildings, but I don't see anything left behind that hints at civilization; no carts, no sculptures, no merchant stalls, no pools of freshwater, no pottery, no furniture, no flags.

Only curved walls of seamless limestone—but not cobbled like the gorgon's village wall. It's as though the city was carved straight from the earth, and then left behind to be consumed by the forest.

Hella.

Vex's Landmark.

I can make out crimson tiles and painted walls, just as bloodred as my horns. The accents make Hella look slightly more welcoming, if a bit larger and colder.

Meanwhile, the empty bottle in my mind keeps shaking. The glass rattles against the wooden floorboards, loud enough that I can't shake it from my mind—not the image, not its sounds.

The glass is going to break... the bottle will explode into shards...

I stare below.

Halcyon leans over the ledge to study the city. With a wary expression, he levels his glowing indigo eyes at me. "It's clean."

I blink at him.

It seems very obvious now; Vex knew we were coming. Vex has sensed my presence here since I stepped foot onto the mainland.

But before I can reply, another vision of a brandy bottle grips my attention.

I gasp, stepping back.

In my mind's eye, I see someone grab the empty bottle by its neck and, with a swift and brutal movement, raise it up and then slam it down. The green glass shatters against the floor, the bubbles spraying onto the jagged shards.

My heart pumps in my throat.

It was so sudden. So violent.

And I recognized the hands that took hold of the bottle.

I clear my throat. I look down at my hands, opening my palms to check for glass or blood.

Nothing.

I'm standing here above Hella with a confused warlock at my side.

I ignore my shaking hands. The confusion and panic that settles in my mind after the vision's abrupt and violent end. Below it is a conversely peaceful intuition that connects me to Vex.

I take a deep breath, then release it.

I take a step off the limestone and into the air above Hella. "Let's go." I turn back to offer my hand to Halcyon.

His jaw tenses, eyes flitting from me to the shadowy city below.

"Are you scared?"

He bunches his eyebrows in the waning light. "No, but..."

I glance below again, wondering if this is the part where he betrays me. It's all gone swimmingly up until this point—a little too swimmingly, considering how I ended up here.

"But what?"

He studies my outstretched hand. "But I am from House of Serac. Maybe I am not welcome inside the cave."

I wiggle my fingers; I don't want to beg him to come with me, but I need him at my side. I might belong to Vex... but this is all very new. Very foreign. And I can still see the shards of glass shattered in my mind's eye; it scares me almost as much as the room of blackened memories.

I offer him a small smile and hope I don't sound as nervous as I feel. "I'm inviting you inside right now, Halcyon."

The warlock inhales, long and deep. He kneels to touch the grotto's lip and murmurs something in Zarzyd. Then he stands and takes my hand without looking back. With one swift step, he leaves the limestone to stand in the air with me, hand crushing mine.

I send us floating slowly downward, into Hella's shadows.

From above, the city looks easy to navigate. Streets weave through the buildings, while a few plazas break up the endless span of one-story and two-story halls and dwellings. Most are rounded. Some stretches look entirely bathed in red color—though I can't tell if it's paint or tiles.

"So, this is pretty fucking cool, right?" No part of me thinks this is cool. At best, it's interesting; at worst, I'm floating to my death.

Halcyon joins my little act. As though nauseated, he stares past his boots and studies the snaking streets. "Yes. Of course. I love this."

Aside from my father and brothers, no beings have relied on me for safety before.

Except for Halcyon.

He slayed the degivampire named Jen to free me from the ship. He brought me to the mainland into the House of Vex. He navigated a run-in with a gorgon village.

But he jumps at each shadow in Hella as I lead us to an empty dwelling. He lingers close, one hand holding my waist and the other gripping my shoulder.

He keeps holding tight as I prepare an abandoned room near the city center.

The single-story structure has white-tiled floors and walls, strewn with delightful red accents. The curved walls are a little odd, but once I set up a sleeping space and sort our supplies by the bedside, the setup feels familiar. So does the candlelight and the scent of incense Halcyon likes to burn at night.

When he finally lets go of me, he stands at the room's far end and looks from the doorway to the window beside it. He sets his hands on his hips with a sigh. "Vex is okay? I do not have to stay inside Hella. I will give Vex respect."

In Mieira, others expected unpredictability from me—not security.

But as with my brothers and father, Halcyon expects my protection and guidance. And the more he relies on *me* for leadership, the easier it becomes.

I offer him a smile. "If Vex knows everything about me, then it knows that you saved me from the ship, Halcyon."

His head tilts as he considers the idea. For the first time, he nods at the correct interval. "I think that is true."

With a sigh, he gets comfortable.

Like Mieiran wielders, Zarzynnians use bottomless bags. But rather than a respectable purse, outcasts who live in Plet use socks and other articles of clothing for storage. It makes them more difficult to rob—it forces a thief to decide if something is a dirty sock or a cache of goods.

Halcyon uses multiple articles for storage. He claims to have some items so well-hidden that he hasn't seen them in years. But his favorite is a dingy gray sock.

Tonight, he shoves his hand into the sock's opening. He sinks onto the bed I laid out, fishing around inside the fabric. I head over to his side.

I recognize the gray sock. It holds the ceramic jug of clear liquor the gorgons gave us.

With a grunt, Halcyon pulls the round container from the sock's narrow top. "I will drink a lot now."

I clap my hands together and scurry closer. He hands me the jug, then reaches back inside the sock to pull out a bundle of red berries. We've taken mixing in the dried berries, which makes it easier to sip.

We relax and let the day dissolve, taking turns shooting the liquor.

Then we tumble across the bed and Halcyon does what he does best: gets me into my form. The first time we had sex, he said that he had a gift for me. I had rolled my eyes with the realization that men in foreign lands aren't different at all. To my great surprise, that gift was not his cock, but a certain type of magic that makes his fingers vibrate.

He says it doesn't feel like much for men, but the sensation was highly stimulating for me.

I have never cum so hard in my (remembered) life. So hard my horns came out.

Since that first form-gasm, Halcyon has treated my pleasure like a special challenge, attempting to find another way to startle me with an orgasm and free my horns. And I sometimes walk around half-naked in challenge.

He's too skittish for a longer performance tonight, but I don't mind.

When we lay in bed later, he reads from a book filled with short romances penned by the okeanids who escaped to Plet. He quickly tires of the stories, then hands me the book so he can peruse his own about myths and legends. We snuggle into our flat bedding, books held close to our faces and the ceramic jug of vodka nestled between us.

Before I slip into sleep, Halcyon lowers his book. He lays it flat on his belly with a sigh.

With a shuffle, he turns to face me. "Vexen, I have a question."

I glance at him, wondering if I should stop reading. (*Is this the part where he betrays me?* Just in case it is, I put down the book.) "Okay."

On his side, he sets his hand on his horn to prop his head up. "You are banished. I do not understand the word in your language. It is very, very serious in my world. What does it mean to you?"

I pick at my book's faded spine, trying to decide how much to tell him. "Well, a being can be banished from a city or a region. I was banished by the wolves and the wielders. That means I can't go into larger cities in Mieira. And I can't go to Velm at all." I roll my eyes and wonder if this will change how Halcyon thinks about me. "It was because I did something violent in response to... to something else. To another violence done to me. To my sister."

I lick my lips and stare up at the limestone ceiling. I wait for Halcyon to grow suspicious.

Instead, "You do not want to talk about it?"

"I don't mind talking about it." I shift into the same position, laying on my side and resting my head in my hand. "But if I tell you, then you have to tell me why you're in Plet."

I finish my vodka.

As much as I'd like to deepen our bond, I'm afraid of learning who the warlock really is.

I don't want a reason to start hating Halcyon. Not now. Not when I need him here.

When I turn back around, he doesn't look doubtful. He looks... patient. Very mature. "We are bound now, Vexen. I will take care of you while you learn magic here. Then you will take me and four more to Mieira. We are *bound*."

From the little I know of Plet, *being bound* equates to trust. It's a way of building trust—but it means nothing to me. Once, a warlock told me that trust is what the weak cling to when their shaking hands can't hold more.

I wish it didn't ring so true.

I stare at the muddled glow of Halcyon's purple eyes, the indigo curve of his lips, the stern set of his brow. "I'm not very trusting. Except for the nymphs, others have taken more from me than they've given back, and I'm not the warm witchling I once was.

"Tell me how you ended up in Plet. Tell me who you're risking everything for right now. Then I'll tell you how I ended up banished."

Like with most other things, Halcyon takes my proposal in stride. With a long sigh, he sits up and crosses his legs. He reaches for the liquor, setting the jug in his lap. "As you prefer, Vexen."

I mirror his position, then I hold out my empty mug for another serving. I've started to mirror him more and more, just like he did when I first awoke in Plet. He said it's a show of respect in Stretch; a sign of equality.

We take turns sipping.

I sum up my story in my head; I imagine he's doing the same.

When Halcyon's shoulders slump, I prepare myself once again for some sort of betrayal. Or, at best, an unpleasant surprise. He glances at me, chin lowered. "The Houses in Ezit are careful about children. Powerful families in every House have to be careful..." He opens his hand to me. "What is the word for being at the top of a group?"

"Hierarchy?"

"Yes—exactly. Each House has a hierarchy. Married couples at the top are careful to have one son and one daughter. No more and no less. This is important. If they have more children, their Landmark's power will spread out. The more bodies magic lives inside, the less power each body can wield.

"Serac is a powerful House. There are not many Seracyd wielders—and those who are born tend to be cruel. Their power makes them cold and unfeeling. In fact, the first necromancers were created under the command of a desperate Seracyd warlock. Necromancy was an experiment... an experiment from a Seracyd wielder."

Halcyon explained the magical art to me on the way to the mainland.

What a necromancer is. How an okeanid can interact with a special type of mirror and call the dead into its pane. Halcyon hasn't seen it himself, so he doesn't understand how it works. How long the dead stay alive, whether they can talk, whether they understand what's happening when they're pulled back to life through a mirror.

"But that is another story," he sighs. "Like I said, powerful wielders have one son and one daughter. If they have a second son or daughter, they kill them.

"My father is Seracyd. He is at the top of the hierarchy. I know his name. Suleiman. I do not know my mother's name. My father is very important... and he had two sons."

I reach out and set my hand on Halcyon's wrist. He looks up as though surprised by the touch; his gaze is heavy and withdrawn.

Before I can guess that he was the second son, saved by his mother from infanticide and shipped off to Plet, he murmurs, "A powerful warlock with two sons is a problem. But my father loved many women. One was my mother. And she had me—a third son."

My stomach clenches. I sip from my mug, unsure of where to look.

I glance at the door, at the silent stretch of shadow on the pale stone that fills the cave.

He's on the run from Ezit.

From Serac.

From a very powerful family.

Fine—I can deal with that.

I think?

"My mother went to Plet to have me. My father found us in Plet— my mother knew that he would. My mother made a plan for me. The plan was to disappear. There are many in Plet who hide from Ezit. We are good at it."

He nods. Once again, it's at the wrong interval, but I nod back so he doesn't realize that.

Halcyon looks away from me, toward one of the magical lanterns. The golden light traces, the star-shaped scar below his left eye. "The plan was to disappear with a warlock. The warlock was like a father to me. I think my mother met this warlock in Ezit before he was banished to Plet. That is why I ask about your banishment... Ezit is evil. When Ezit *banishes* a wielder, it is because they are very evil. *More* evil than the rest."

His eyes flash to meet mine. "You do not seem evil, Vexen."

"But this warlock was evil. The one who became my father. He was banished for trying to replace Serac's Hosts. A House's Hosts are its most powerful wielding couple. This is very difficult to do—but not impossible. For this, he was exiled to Plet. I did not like being a child—it was difficult. But he taught me things that have kept me alive. I do not complain about breath—breath is more important than love in Zarzynn."

Halcyon tilts his head back to shoot his vodka.

I stare at him, gut clenched.

Breath is more important than love.

Those were the same words Anesot once used to describe his own childhood.

For the second time in Halcyon's presence, I'm reminded of Anesot.

Did Anesot grow up in Plet, too?

I try to push him out of my mind—far away from the warlock sitting before me. "I'm sorry, Halcyon. For all the bullshit I've ever gone through, I had a safe childhood." I stroke his wrist, dragging it toward me. I'm not sure what to say. How to console him. I try to keep things moving. "So, who do you want to bring to Mieira if you have no family?"

He pulls back to refill my mug. I don't take his hand again, sensing he doesn't want to be touched right now. "Do you feel okay about me?"

I lift a shoulder; it's an odd question. "Sure."

"I am happy. My life was not always bad." Halcyon raises his eyebrows, as though emphasizing that point. "I am very lucky in many ways. I lived in Plet, and there was a witch who lived on the far end of the island. We met by accident one day, then wrote letters. We fell in love through the letters. One day, we made a plan to meet again. It was dangerous and difficult. Her name is Ceyx."

My head tilts. "Ceyx." I'm relieved he used the present tense.

Halcyon scratches his temple, staring at the sheet bunched between us. "Ceyx. Yes. We made a plan to meet. We... had a very good night. She wrote more letters. One day, I opened my door in Plet and Ceyx was there. And she was pregnant. We were very young. Nineteen."

Silence fills the cave. The only interruption is Halcyon sipping his liquor.

Eventually, I croak out, "*What?*"

I sit back, staring at Halcyon in a new light.

He shrinks further into himself, head hanging and shoulders buckled.

I prod one of his horns with my finger. "You're a fucking *father?*"

This is fine.

I think?

I imagine my papa and his wrinkled face and thinning beard. Halcyon, in comparison, seems so *young*. So much like *me*, a being who certainly could *not* take care of a child.

Halcyon takes a deep breath. "Yes. Ceyx had our son. He lives in Plet."

I narrow my eyes as the information settles in. "Right. Okay. So this child is a fucking full-grown adult? How old are you? How old is he?"

"I am forty-two years old. My son will be twenty-three later this year."

It's too much.

I let out a long yelp, which dwindles into a wild laugh. "What the *fuck*, Halcyon—look, I'm not freaking out in a bad way. I'm just freaking out in general. You're a *father*. You literally had a baby before I ever took a man to bed."

Halcyon winces. "Okay."

I go still. "Why do you feel so weird telling me this? Children happen. It's not your fault. Or do Ceyx and your son hate you...?"

His eyes shift across my face. I can't tell what emotion he's feeling, but it looks highly uncomfortable. "Because I did something bad. I made a bad decision, Vexen. It is dangerous. I am the third son of the Male Host of Serac. Do you see? My father came to Plet to find us. To kill me and to kill my son."

All my mirth boils into fear.

In my mind, I don't see my papa anymore. I see Halcyon, aged nineteen with another nineteen-year-old at his side, trying to figure out things like nappies and breastfeeding while outwitting one of the most powerful warlocks in Zarzynn.

I lean forward and set my hand on his wrist again.

He glances up at me before going on. "We left the city. We lived on the coast in Plet. Life on the island is hard... but with Ceyx and our son, I was happy.

"We had fun. My son... well, he is very smart. He gave me pure love, Vexen. He was the first to give me pure love in my life. To him, I was strong. And it made me better to know that.

"Me and Ceyx were young. We were happy for a long time, but she wanted to be free. With each year, we became more powerful. We *could* be free. Do you understand? In Stretch, you have to be smart. Powerful. We had that together. One day, we also had it alone. She could be free alone, and be safe. And I wanted her to be happy."

Halcyon takes another shot of liquor, then rubs his cheeks. I wait patiently, drinking from my cup while he searches for the words. For now, I suspend my reactions; his story has already taken multiple unexpected turns.

The warlock goes on, "Ceyx has a sister, Cleo." Also present-tense; also good. "When Ceyx was gone, Cleo and I drank wine. My son was with his mother... so..."

Halcyon winces, staring at me.

I blink—*is he baiting me right now?* With disbelief in each word, I ask, "And... did you... also get Cleo pregnant?"

Halcyon presses his lips together. He blinks at the wall just past my shoulder. "My father has three sons. I have two. We have a talent for making warlocks."

I swing swiftly back to mirth, then back to heartbreak, then back to adoration.

Halcyon is ten thousand times more complex than I thought.

And dangerously fertile.

I try for humor as he slumps with defeat again. "Look, it has to be better than raising witchlings. We're a disaster when we're young."

He stares into the jug. "Maybe."

"So... your second son?"

He sighs. "He is a quiet genius. He is thirteen years old. The place where you woke up in Plet is his bedroom. It is where my second-born and Cleo live. Ceyx and our first-born live above. They stayed together while we stayed below."

I think back to the clean, white room. To the tailored clothes I woke up wearing. Halcyon mentioned that trusted witches had tended to me. "Ceyx and Cleo healed me, then?"

Halcyon nods. "Ceyx is a powerful healer. Cleo is still learning. They reset your bones, stitched you, and washed you. They have your items, too. What you wore on the ship. I do not know if those things mean anything to you."

I squeeze his wrist. I'm no longer thinking about the apartment or the clean layers, but the birth of Halcyon's second son. "Did your father come back?"

"He comes back every few years. But we know how to disappear." Halcyon raises his chin, jaw clenching. "My wives are clever. And our sons are brave."

Wives.

I slowly extract my hand from his wrist. This is the betrayal I had anticipated before; Halcyon is using me for safe passage to Mieira, and his affection is a manipulation to get him there, and I've just been letting him see my horns because his fingers vibrate.

Wooooooooow, Helisent.

I try not to sound as livid as I feel. "And what do your *wives* think about our... little adventure?"

He taps the lip of the jug. "They worry I will upset you. You are the most powerful wielder in the world. They worry you will hurt our sons because I upset you." He stares at the wall and clears his throat. "They live in danger because of me, Vexen. Because of who my father is."

"That's great, but I was thinking about your cock and the places it goes." I roll my eyes. "It doesn't bother them?"

He looks at me, tilting his head. "My cock and the places it goes? Does it... not go in the right places?"

I blink at him; he's being serious. "Let's go back for a second. You said Ceyx and Cleo are your *wives*. So, what does that mean in Plet? In Mieira, marriage is rare, but it's *monogamous*. The same in Velm."

His eyes narrow. He leans closer to me. "What is *monogamous*?"

"It means two people belong to each other. They don't have sex with other people. I think some emotional topics are also off-limits." I wave a hand. "I'm not monogamous, so I don't understand it."

Halcyon stares at me for a long moment. With sudden realization, he rocks back. "No, no, no. I am not monogamous. My wives are not, either." He says it like *monogomoose*. "Ceyx and Cleo are my wives because of our sons. We are *bound* together. Forever. I help them, and they help me. No questions. Maybe I do not understand marriage. An okeanid explained it to us."

I snort. "That makes sense. Nymphs don't get married."

"And what is Velm? You are banished from Velm, but the okeanids only tell us about Mieira."

"Oh, right—well, it's where the wolves live." I lick my lips, then finish my liquor. "Is it my turn, now?"

"Yes." He refills my cup, glancing up at me. "Do you have questions?"

"Maybe tomorrow. For now, no."

I shoot the liquor again. And then I tell my story before I can second-guess what's happening in this quiet room right now. (No betrayals so far.)

I go through everything in horrible detail, starting with Andromeda North of Skull and the murderous triplemoon on which I was born. I end the tale with my banishment in Jaws after slaughtering the warlock and witch who killed Milisent West of Jaws, then slowly losing my mind during my banishment and slipping away to join Butter in Hypnos.

That's when the bad images start to filter in; the door to the dark room creaks open, and no matter of pushing shuts it.

Butter—

What happened to Butter?

When was the last time I saw her?

I think I know; I think I'm about to see reality in that dark room, and then I shut my eyes. I keep my head bent, eyes clenched. Halcyon's hand encircles my wrist just like mine did with his.

Face hidden, I tell him, "There's something you should know about me. I don't remember the last four years or my time on the ship. Not really... Panic magic wiped my memory clear when I killed Anesot, and something must have happened—"

"*Anesot?*"

I open my eyes and look up.

Halcyon stares at me with widened eyes, tail frozen where it's half-curled behind him. "*You killed Anesot?*"

I return his stunned look—*Halcyon knew Anesot?*

I clear my throat. "That's the warlock I was telling you about. The one who killed Milisent. I don't like saying his name. He must have been from Zarzynn, but he kept his horns hidden so I never—"

"He was born in Ezit to House of Serac... before he was banished to Plet for plotting to overthrow his Hosts. He met another exiled wielder—a witch from Col in Plet. Her name was Oko."

My gut clenches as the world goes still.

He doesn't notice. Halcyon huffs indignantly, adjusting the jug in his lap. "Plet is full of outcasts like them. But not everyone in Plet is happy to start over. Anesot and Oko wanted to go back to Ezit. And they slaughtered for it... they worked with the worst of the vampires and wielders to try to wriggle their way back into Ezit. Until, eventually, Plet banished them, too. The last time I saw them, they were sailing west with a group of vampires."

Halcyon stares at his hands like he's stewing on something. He goes on, "Before, I told you about a Seracyd warlock. The one who invented necromancy."

I sigh, emptying my lungs, as the pieces fit into place.

It's a lot to process.

After being banished from Plet, Anesot and Oko must have found their way to Mieira.

To the okeanids in Hypnos.

Eventually, I ask, "So, you knew him from Plet? Did you know him well?"

Halcyon's eyes burn as he looks at me. "You could say that. Anesot is the warlock who took me in when Suleiman killed my mother."

For a long moment, Halcyon and I look at one another.

My stomach flips when I realize Anesot's long-term plans for me likely rested in Ezit rather than Mieira.

And what else didn't I realize about the warlock?

I'll think about that later—maybe never.

"When did the first necromancer show up in Ezit? Do you know?" Almost seven years ago, Oko killed my sister to consolidate my power. Almost seven years ago, Anesot escaped his first brush with death at my hands.

Halcyon sighs. "We heard about them around fifteen years ago. They started escaping Ezit and showing up in Plet around ten years ago—maybe a bit before. That's when New Hypnos was formed."

That means Anesot tried his luck with necromancers first. That was his original plan to worm his way back into Ezit—necromancy. I was his second ticket back into Ezit: the last Vexen. A second attempt after his first failed.

I close my eyes and wish I could remember Anesot's death. Wish it could give me some measure of comfort. "Well, in that case, you're welcome. It sounds like you also wanted him dead. It would be nice to be known as *Helisent the Savior* someplace."

"I hope he died slowly."

While I battle nausea, Halcyon smiles and takes another drink. The smile lingers; he looks emptily over my shoulder. With each second, his expression lightens. His grin widens.

He takes a deep breath, then leans forward and kisses me. The unexpected touch is tender, lips caressing mine with lingering pressure.

He whispers into them, "Thank you, Helisent. My wives and my sons are safer because of you."

I smile.

Safer?

Because of me?

I like the idea of saving Halcyon. Of taking him and his wives and their sons to a place where they can't be hurt. (Does this mean we're all *bound*? Or am I orbiting a family of five?)

I kiss Halcyon back, setting aside my mug to run my fingers up his cheeks, into his soft white hair, against his sleek horns.

"You called me Helisent," I realize, eyes popping open. "Why? I like it when you call me Vexen."

He raises his eyebrows, staring at my lips. "You never told me your name. Not until now."

"*What?*" In the next breath, I caw with laughter, falling away from his touch.

I hadn't realized I hadn't told him my name—it wasn't a conscious omission.

Halcyon follows as I tumble backward, toppling over me.

"It's very nice to meet you," he chuckles.

I wake up to an image of a spinning bottle.

Relief floods me—

The last time I saw it yesterday, it laid in frothy shards on the floor.

Whatever that awful vision was, it wasn't permanent.

The bottle is beautifully whole; its uncorked top points in a different direction now.

Vex, feel free to pick another image. I'm starting to crave brandy constantly.

With a yawn, I open my eyes; Halcyon lays half-draped over me, graciously cradling one of my breasts as he snores.

I squint into the milky light filling our circular room. Past the door and the square window beside it, Hella sits in stark detail. Birds sing inside the cave, filling its cool walls with delightful echoes. I can even hear the sound of running water, as though the fountain in the city center is full now.

I sit up with a sigh. Halcyon adjusts, turning into his pillow.

I rub the sleep from my face, then slip out of bed. I don't want to wake Halcyon; he needs the rest, and I wouldn't mind a moment of privacy with Vex.

I head toward one of our neat stacks of supplies. With only tailored shirts and *pants* on offer from the clothiers in Plet, I've taken to wearing long strips of tan linen from the gorgons. One length ties at my hips to form a loincloth, while another fits around my collar and chest.

While I'm comfortable in the linen fabric, I imagine I look like a degenerate to Zarzynnians. The wielders I saw in Plet wore tidy and tailored layers like Halcyon, dyed a range of grays, violets, oranges, and blues. The gorgons on the mainland wore their linen strips in layers, which drifted in their wake like separate cloaks.

I glance down when I'm done.

It's a bit brisk, but I have a sentient cave to worry about—

I head to the door and glance back. Halcyon has claimed the bed in my absence, his legs and arms sprawled out.

I snort. I wonder what his kids look like. His wives.

Then I step out of the room and stare around in wonder.

In the morning light, the subterranean and bowl-like cave looks clean, hopeful, vast. Drenched in light from above, I can make out more buildings than when we arrived yesterday evening. Like I suspected, the circular buildings continue into the cave's deepest shadows where Hella's slanted walls curve upward.

Sure enough, clear water now fills the central fountain. A broad and shallow bowl sits atop a narrow pole in its center; water trickles downward as it overflows.

I pause to let the vision of the bottle return. I shift to follow where its narrow neck faces this time.

Northward. I take off.

As I pass the empty streets, a lump lodges in my throat. I wonder about all the happy sounds of life that must have once layered this silence. These shops were where the Vexen traded and gossiped; these homes were where the Vexen made love, where their littlelings slept, where they washed dishes.

I pause multiple times to study the rococo decorations that line the windowsills, the doorframes, the molding on the ceilings. Red tiles litter the streets and walls, catching the light and gleaming like someone shined them with wax. They glimmer in crimson, in vermillion, in scarlet, in garnet. Tiles run from one building to the next; some expand into mosaics of portraits and still-life images.

One building depicts the cutting of grain. Another wall shows a group seated in a circle. *Wielders* seated in a circle, horns dense and proud, tails curved behind them.

Not just *wielders*, but Vexen.

They're larger than me. They look wiser too, their expressions demure and placid and cunning all at once.

Eventually, the broad avenue that leads away from the central fountain splits into three separate paths. I stare down the middle path where red tiles dot the smooth street; they cluster and multiply, leading to a long hall.

I follow them to the vast, empty structure.

Tiles cover the doorframe, the windows, the floor, the ceiling—every single surface. But they aren't laid in a uniform pattern. They frame the room's center point where a slab of limestone juts from the ground. The tiles fan out around the slab in an asymmetrical circle, rippling outward across the floor, like a droplet hitting a still body of water, before moving up the walls and onto the arched ceiling.

My eyes lock immediately on the limestone shape.

It arches up from the ground, as thick as my leg, and then curves like a chunk of hardened lightning. It isn't gray and green like the rest of the limestone in Vex.

This stone is bloodred, pulsing with an unmistakable and low hum.

I take a step into the room. When I do, my illusory appearance of brown skin and a hornless scalp fade. In its place comes my form—my crimson skin, my seven horns, my curling tail.

If this cave is my Landmark, then this is its heart.

The Hellastone, I decide to call it.

Once again, intuition guides me.

I approach the stone like a sleepwalker. I sink onto my knees before it. My hand raises, palm shivering with anticipation as I reach toward the bloodred stone and fit my hand against its coarse grain.

Like a set of tipped dominoes, my thoughts lead from one to the next—I start to graze truths no one taught me—this must be how a cave teaches me magic.

The abstract concepts I've been learning from Halcyon click into place.

The Hellastone, as the Landmark's core, contains the highest concentration of Vex's ejima. Not just dove, but *intelligent* dove.

I can feel it humming inside the stone, a deep and comforting pulse of infrasound. It contains every spell known to my magic.

I raise my other hand and set it against the coarse stone.

"Show me," I whisper to Vex. "Show me how."

Magic roils in the stone; I can feel it concentrate around my palms. The infrasound heightens, then dulls. I pull my hands off the stone.

Two tendrils of red fog lift and follow my palms, concentrated into small, string-like forms.

This, at least, isn't entirely unfamiliar.

Years ago, Anesot taught me and Milisent to store our dove in glass cylinders so it could be used to power cities. Like all dove in Mieira, Milisent and I packaged ours in a golden color, like liquid starlight.

But that was one of many lies I've told.

Because our dove was bloodred like the magic that threads my palms to the Hellastone.

I sit back, my body shaking.

I stare at the threads in wonder as they lengthen and droop, as though heavy.

Without a second thought, I tilt my head and reach up to wrap one of the threads around one of my horns. It takes a few quick loops of my hand before the string disappears, then I do the same with the second strand.

With little more than a croon of bass, the threads tighten around my horns. I reach up a second later, but can't feel either encircling them, as though absorbed.

Still moving like a sleepwalker, I set my palms against the Hellastone again.

The air eddies from my lungs as more realizations start to filter in.

These caves store raw magic; so do my horns. My horns are stronger and denser than my flesh, my blood, my sinew. My horns, like these limestone caves, can retain enormous amounts of magic.

It coalesces within me, and all around me, waiting for animation. Like my horns, my coarse, thick fingernails store more; cast more.

I lean forward and set my forehead against the Hellastone.

Here I am.

Vex's only living wielder; its greatest spell, its greatest activation, its only channel to the world.

Gratitude floods my heart. I have known evil; I have survived death; and maybe it's all been worth it. I might still become someone. I might still be worthy.

I like that thought.

I see the bottle again—it's full this time. It sits upright, sweating with beads of condensation.

There, next to it, sits another bottle. This one is miniature; shaped precisely like the larger green bottle, but shrunken to one-fifth its size.

I study the second bottle. Unlike the original, it looks to have only a few precious drops of brandy wetting its bottom.

I jolt up, back straightening. I lift my hands from the Hellastone.

Like the bottle pointed me onward, I can sense a hidden message in this vision.

I close my eyes, reviewing the strange image.

Two bottles? And why is the second so small?

I open my eyes again—I understand.

The brandy is my magic, the bottle my body.

Which means the second bottle...

Someone else has access to my magic?

I look around, expecting to see another wielder in the hall with me.

No one else should have any access to Vex's magic—not with my mother and sister long dead.

The hall is empty, silent, glittering with red tiles.

Where is the fuck is the rest of my Landmark's magic, then?

CHAPTER 6

WELCOME TO ZARZYNN

SAMSON

My grandson,
As a Kulapsifang, I have often been confused by the known and the unknown. I
find them hidden inside each other. This used to distress me; now it gives me
hope.

We follow the forest northward.

Thick moss covers the limestone boulders, which litter the ground beneath the tall pines. The tree's lowest branches have broken free; the forest's canopy doesn't start for another thirty feet overhead, thickening to block most of the sunlight. Birds flutter along the flaky branches; their bright colors are as foreign as their songs.

Slender pockets of sunlight dot the needle-ridden floor, reflecting off the still water collected atop the pale outcroppings.

I count the pools of light.

I tally the scents of the birds overhead; I count eight distinct species.

It helps distract me from our growing unease. Doubt whirls between our silent ranks. It has since we set foot on the ship in Hypnos, but it's tripled since our run-in with the strange beings inside the walled village.

The blindfolded elders had directed us northward. Though we can't be certain, it seems like they called themselves 'gorragons'.

What they directed us toward, we can only guess. Ideally, it's the six-horned red witch we traded messages about.

Hemlock and Parsifal guide us through the pine barren. In Rhotidom, Hemlock's elemental powers give him a keen sense of direction—toward fruit-bearing trees, freshwater springs, and sheltering caves. Here, he looks just as lost as the warlock.

They turn their heads at the slightest sound, as though expecting to find Helisent or a group of wandering okeanids.

I take a quieter approach to my mounting unease.

I fill my lungs with each step, searching for Helisent, Imperatriz, or an okeanid with enough force and frequency that my ribs hurt by dusk.

There's no trace of their alas. Just dry limestone, flaking pines, flowers that rotted in their buds before blooming, and lifeless soil interspersed with stone and tepid water.

Still, there is...

A feeling in this forest.

It is ancient, infertile, and forgotten—but in every shadowy grotto, in the black eyes of the birds that watch us from the trees, I can feel the delicate hum of infrasound.

I glance at Rex, who walks at my side at the group's back. He doesn't seem to notice anything. I study the GhostEater in her bright blue robe next. She also doesn't seem to notice the forest is alive.

The witch floats on an ultramarine lilith at Berevald's side. Since healing him on the beach two weeks ago, she's offered other boons to us wolves. First, she prioritizes our size when splitting the group's food supplies, making sure to dole out proportionate servings for us. Second, she clears the scents that encroach on our campsites; not everyone settles for bathrooms a suitable distance away. Third, she sticks beside Berevald, checking on his vitals and harassing him intermittently.

Kierkeline prods Berevald's elbow today, chiding him about his diet.

Her voice fades as Samsonfang pads into my mind.

This forest is alive, he says.

At least he's also aware.

I slow to a stop, glancing around for any deviation that might clarify how, exactly, it's alive. Nothing looks out of place.

Rex waits for me. He doesn't say anything, just raises his eyebrows in silent question. Dark rings hang around his eyes. His cheeks are sunken, too—not just from the sudden change in diet, but from our arduous journey and a piling series of unknowns.

We have no ship to take us home.

We have nothing but vague directions from a group of blindfolded strangers.

We have less food by the day. Less spirit by the hour.

I run a hand through my hair. Despite the warm temperature, I keep it down. It sways to my chest, spreading my ala through the forest with each breeze.

With the group far enough ahead, I whisper a response to Samsonfang, "The forest is alive with what?"

With magic. It lives in the stone.

I take a deep breath and close my eyes.

Samsonfang hasn't spoken to me since I left Hypnos—I've wondered whether he *could* connect to me this far from Velm. If my fangself is tied to my demigod, then I figured the distance would cut me off from Hetnazzar and Samsonfang—possibly even make me pith from distance like a nymph.

I keep my voice low. "Whose magic is it?"

Please say Helisent's.

It belongs to Vex.

My heart thumps—not out of nervousness or apprehension, but in reaction.

Like someone touched it.

In my mind's eye, I see a massive clearing. It stands out like a pale smear between the thin and straight trees. An unfathomable hum boils inside the earth...

I open my eyes and look to my right.

The clearing is over there—somewhere vague, in the distance, waiting.

I'm not sure *how* I know that, but the sensation doesn't come from my own mind or gut. It comes from Samsonfang, just as insistent and intuitive as the urge to mark my campsite, to separate my food from the group's, to howl at the full moons.

I shift to the right, prepared to take off.

"*Samson.*" Rex grabs my arm.

I ignore him, blinking into the tangle of forest. I can't see a clearing between the trees, but I'm convinced it's there.

Rex lets go of my arm, then pits himself between me and the rest of the group. They walk on, drifting out of sight between the thin pines. "What's going on?"

I set my hand on my heart. "I can feel magic. It's... called Vex."

Rex's eyes narrow. "Vex? What is that? How do you know?"

I still haven't explained how magic works to Rex; he hasn't asked. And I shy away from talking about Helisent at every turn. But I wonder...

'Remember when I told you magic is like a twin?' I can hear Helisent in a memory. In a canopy high in Rhotidom. *'Well, my magic knows about you now. It knows what you like and don't like. It pays attention, Samson.'*

Helisent said magic is a living thing that learns, and understands, and has its own willpower—like a twin.

If she was right, then her twin may be whispering to me right now—

Not to *me*, necessarily.

The witch is mine, Samsonfang explains in response.

Before I can figure out what to do with that statement, Rex reaches out and sets his hand on my chest. He prods the bundle of scar tissue tangled above my heart.

It isn't flesh-colored anymore; it's bright red.

Rex pulls his hand away, checking his fingers for blood.

I do the same. But the scar isn't bleeding—and it doesn't feel any different when I touch it. Still, the scar, around the size of my thumb, gleams a stark crimson.

Rex looks at me and I stare back. My lips part as I think of a response—of any kind of explanation. We've toyed with the idea that Helisent's magic may be keeping me alive, but the idea that the witch's *form* has spread to my body is a fresh mystery.

One that makes me terrified of loving her.

For now, I choose to interpret the bloodred scar as a sign that we're getting closer to Helisent. I push every other conclusion to the back of my mind.

Rex pulls my tunic where it hangs from the waistline of my pants.

He shoves it into my abdomen and I get to work pulling the shirt on. Then he swivels back to the group and calls out, "Samson smells something." He nods to the right where I originally turned to pursue Vex's magic. "That way."

Parsifal shouts Helisent's name as he loops back toward us, then asks which direction we should head. Rex mentions that it was a *possible* lead, hoping to keep the group from asking too many questions.

They trail me and Rex as instinct compels me to the clearing.

If magic lives in the stone, then we're waltzing toward its rocky core.

But hours pass before we reach the rocky dell I saw in my mind. I'm both relieved and terrified when the slanted field of limestone stretches before us, dipping and piling like the uneven faces of the moons.

In its center sits a plummeting gap as large as Luz's temple district.

Parsifal sprints toward the hole, Kierkeline zooming at his side on her lilith. Eos and Aura also take off, leaping over the gaps between rocks with their hands clasped together.

Maybe Vex will lead to Helisent—

I also waltz forward, chest pumping with hope and fear.

Parsifal stops at the ledge and cranes over it, staring below. "Holy moons—holy, holy moons."

Kiekerline turns back, stretching her hand to beckon me toward them. "Samson—please—what do you smell?"

I stop at her side and peer below.

Past the crumbling filament of pale limestone sits an empty and pristine city. Wide streets divide the circular buildings, which don't look to have any seams or angles. Like they were carved out from the ground rather than stacked. Red tiles dot the city in differing shades; each closely mirrors the stark color of my scar. Pale water fills a few circular fountains, littered with sunny reflections.

Though spotless, I don't see any signs of life.

I bend to squat, angling my head into the cave.

I suck in a breath—

And then I smell Helisent.

Helisent West of Jaws.

Her scent tells me she is safe and whole—but her ala is markedly different from when I smelled it last in Alita almost a year ago. Then, her ala had consisted of notes of metallic jewelry, potent perfumes, a touch of brandy, a touch of bitterroot. Now, it's bereft of these four primary accents.

In their place is the ala of a warlock, a clear liquor I recognize from the blindfolded village, and foreign textiles I also recognize from the village. From this distance, I can't gauge her physical health from her ala—only that she's not wounded or dying.

I focus on the warlock instead. I can smell his large horns from here; dry and fibrous bone. I can also smell his clothing, made from flax like the other layers.

Is his name Vex?

Are we surrounded by his magic right now?

I rise with a long sigh, preparing myself for what I'll find below. I've summarized my misfortune into two simple statements over the last month, which I repeat often.

First: *Helisent does not remember you, but one day she will.*

Second: *It is possible she will still love you when that day comes, so keep hope until then.*

I quickly add a third: *Don't maul her lovers in the meantime.*

"Samson, Samson, Samson!" Parsifal shuffles past Kierkeline and her lilith. He looks from me to the cave. "Do you smell her? Is Honey Baby down there?"

I nod. "Yes, she's safe. She isn't alone. There's a warlock, too."

Kierkeline's eyes glimmer as she looks up at me. "No okeanids?"

I shake my head. "No, just Helisent and a warlock."

Over a month of grueling travel and multiple brushes with death have brought me here. But I suddenly shy away from the reality of what it will be like to see Helisent and not be able to touch her. Not be able to smell her hair or cradle her face or pull her against my chest.

Not be able to apologize for the wrong I did in Alita.

"Let's get down there! You heard him!" Parsifal waves at Rex, gesturing for the wolf to take his other side. Then the warlock worms his sweaty hands between ours. He glances up at Rex. "Close your eyes. You think you trust me, but you don't."

Nearby, Kierkeline takes Berevald's hand, then waits for Hemlock to take the other. Aura and Eos line up at either side of Absalom, poking their heads over the ledge to stare below.

"Wait." Absalom holds up a hand before we start floating. "I'll handle any aggressive spells in the event things go poorly. Parsifal, if that happens, can you and Kierkeline take the wolves and the nymphs to safety?"

Parsifal blinks at the white-cloaked warlock for a long moment. "Are you being serious?" He glances down our ranks. "I'm prepared to let every single one of you die a horrible death if it means I can take Helisent home."

With each word, Absalom's expression falls. He redirects his gaze at Kiekerline next. "And you, GhostEater? If I handle a threat, can you take the group to safety?"

Kiekerline bares a violent smile at him. "It seems Parsifal and I have a lot in common. I also won't be going anywhere without Calypso. Or Helisent, so long as she can take me to my granddaughter."

Absalom rises to his full height. His jaw clicks as he looks between his fellow wielders. "I understand that—"

"*Stop blathering,*" Parsifal shouts.

His hand tightens on mine, then the slight hum of magic fizzles around me. I close my eyes, body tensing, as the limestone disappears beneath my feet.

Rex seethes, "*Lekeli Kelnazzar.*" He curses Parsifal, he curses me, he curses life.

I understand why.

When Helisent took me into her nest, I didn't even notice I wasn't standing until my butt hit the birch twigs. With Parsifal, we float downward in a series of tiny freefalls. I clench my jaw and try not to lose faith in Parsifal while Rex spews foul words in Velmic.

I open my eyes when my boots scrape rock.

Parsifal gives Rex a spank as he straightens on his feet. "Chin up, Roxanna."

Rex swats at his hand. "No touching."

I stare around at the bowl-like city that fills the cave from crooked wall to crooked wall. It reminds me of the narrow valleys common in Velm, sheltered by the vertical mountains.

Except it's much brighter.

The limestone is beige and gray, glittering with lines of quartz. The red accents are striking, reflecting the sunlight that falls into the cave in rigid beams.

Like the walls, the structures are built of limestone. Circular buildings pile on one another unevenly. Closer up, I realize the red tiles aren't just for decoration. Mosaic murals cover the walls, depicting mundane scenes from daily life. Grand statues jut from rooftops and fountains, buried in minute details from fluttering capes to ornate jewelry.

They're all horned. Most of the wielders depicted have two large horns, while others have four.

And like a shadow overlaying the city, I can sense a pitch of infrasound, a heavy ala.

I associate both with Helisent. When in her form in Rhotidom, she smelled like the ancient and tepid limestone that fills this cave. And her pulsing infrasound buzzed at a similar pitch as this city.

I track Helisent and the warlock's alas to one of the rooms near the city's central plaza, which encircles a massive fountain. I beeline toward the single-story building, the group at my heels.

I can smell that Helisent isn't inside—neither is the warlock. But with each step, her ala comes into clearer focus, filling my lungs and my mind and commanding my full attention.

I'm close to her—I haven't lost her—she is someplace close by—she is alive—

I reach the empty doorframe and stare into the plain room. A padded bed sits along the far wall. Nearby are piles of supplies; food and dining materials, booze, freshwater, books and writing devices, folded linen clothes, and grooming supplies.

And, of course, all the scents that come with domestic life.

I study her physical health first; she's weak, but not from an injury like a wound or a broken limb. It's a frailty that typically follows a sickness, birth, or difficult journey when a being requires more hydration, vitamins, and minerals.

Helisent's white hair tangles in the sheets and blankets and linen clothes. The warlock's hair is tangled in the same places. Helisent's intimate ala is tousled in the sheets and blankets and linen clothes. The warlock's, too.

He is older than her, and healthier. He is powerful.

I can smell the husk of his horns nestled into the fibers of his pillow.

And while I'm not at all surprised that she's acquired another lover so quickly, jealousy stirs in me.

Parsifal's elbow rams into my gut as he rushes past me. His head twitches as he studies the rudimentary bedroom. "Helisent!" He rushes to its far side and looks across the supplies stacked in piles. He whips his head toward me. "Where is she? Where does her scent go? This is her room, right?"

"It's her room, but I don't know where she is right now." I take a few steps away so the rest of the group can investigate.

My jaw tenses as Rex and Bere poke their heads inside. I don't like that they can smell Helisent's ala so closely, especially the traces of her sexual ala. I'm not sure if they can pick it out since they don't have a memory of it, but they're both well past their 500th generation; their noses are almost as strong as mine.

As the nymphs and wielders poke around, I clarify, "I can't track her scent. It's not dense enough. I should be able to smell her when she's coming back."

Kierkeline stands at the foot of the bed, her hands wrought together. She glances across the stacks of supplies. "And you can't smell any trace of the okeanids she was with? Not even on her belongings?"

I study the tidy piles; none of it smells familiar. Only a once-strange spice that I had scented on Anesot but now associate with Zarzynn. Or wherever we are.

I shake my head. "No. I'm sorry, Kierkeline."

Eos slips her hand into Aura's. The women glance from Kierkeline to me.

The turquoise gems in Eos's hair jangle together as she shakes her head. "Why separate Helisent from the okeanids?"

Aura sighs, head resting on Eos's shoulder. "Maybe that's why she and the warlock are here. They're looking for them."

Eos swallows. "Yes, of course. Helisent wouldn't forget them. She was a friend of the nymphs."

I back away from the doorway as Parsifal exits the room and turns back toward the fountain where we entered. He clambers onto its wide lip and rears back. With all his might, he yells, "Helisent West of Jaws! Come to your papa! Right now!"

The same instinct that compelled me toward the cave now turns my head northward.

There, Samsonfang confirms. ***She's there.***

I stand beside Parsifal as he spins in a circle on the fountain and searches the streets. I glance across the sloped rooftops to the north, but nothing stands out about them.

Until the breeze shifts southward and sends a warlock's scent toward us. His ala clogs the wind; I can sense Helisent's behind his, as though he's standing between us and her.

My heart pumps in my chest as I square up to the street where I smell him. I try to calm the rage that churns in my gut; every uncertainty at this moment propels me toward loaded violence.

(It would be easier to get rid of this warlock than to try to understand him. He is a problem, and I have thousands of problems right now, and I desperately want the relief of eliminating just one of them.)

I force down a calming breath. I reason that, unpleasant as their alas are tangled together, it doesn't seem like he has caused her physical harm.

Parsifal swivels to face the same direction as me. "What do you smell, my bucking bronco?"

"The warlock and Helisent are that way. Helisent is farther away than he is." I spare a glance at him. "And stop calling me that."

Parsifal reels back far enough to throw his peridot cloak swinging. "*Warlock*! Come here! *Now*! Bring the witch!"

My gut steels when I see a flicking tail on a rooftop. It curls back and forth near a spire atop a three-story building. Though I've seen the horns of a few golden warlocks, and Helisent once graciously shoved her tail horn into my mouth, I've yet to see a tail in use.

It moves just like a cat's, sultry and investigatory.

The rest of the group gathers around us. Like me, Rex and Berevald quickly pick out the warlock near the spire. Rex makes a low unhappy sound, while Berevald pivots like I did to square up to his position.

Parsifal points at Hemlock. "You talk to him. You're a king."

With a sigh, the nymph fixes his lilac robe and smooths his

emerald beard. "Certainly. Though I don't know if this warlock will recognize my authority, Parsifal."

Parsifal laughs, low and humorless. "Hemlock, my dear nymph, just ask him to come here *before I make him come here.*"

With each second, I start to wonder what an offensive from Parsifal would look like. Whether he'd have the gall to attack the warlock and whether I'd have the self-control to stop from joining in if a rampage starts.

With a slight shuffle, Hemlock puffs his chest out, barring his jacaranda jewelry. He cups his hands around his mouth to shout, "Good evening, my dear warlock. My name is Hemlock East of Alita. We're here for Helisent West of Jaws. As you can see, her papa is a bit hysterical."

In silence, we stare at the spire where the warlock crouches. His tail flickers, but he doesn't move otherwise.

In his ongoing silence, Parsifal looks at me. "Use that big scary voice, Samson. How close is—"

"What is a *papa?*" The warlock's deep voice booms from the rooftops with the help of magic.

He steps into view from the spire. His indigo skin blends into the shadows at his back like a thread of impending night, like the last trace of dusk before the stars come alive.

He walks across the rooftops toward us, swift and calm and direct.

Like his tail, his horns are on full display. Unlike Helisent's, they're smoothed and polished like Velm's marble cities. All four are large; one pair juts from his forehead and the second curves back along his scalp before doubling back.

If I hadn't felt Helisent's, I would be intimidated by their size.

He wears fitted layers of gray linen and a dark cloak, which flares as he walks down one final sloped roof. Without taking his eyes off the group, he steps into the air from a rooftop bordering the central plaza. As though taking an invisible set of stairs, he descends toward where we stand around the fountain.

His purple-glowing eyes glance over our ranks quickly.

The hairs on the back of my neck stand up; his expression is serious, his eyes searching for quick movement, his hands ready.

We wait tensed, our breaths silent, suspended.

Adrenaline pools in my core.

The warlock stops mid-air on his invisible steps, still out of reach. He focuses on Parsifal, his expression calm and unreadable. "A *papa* is a father?" His Mieiran is accented, but it's not difficult to understand him.

Parsifal throws his arms out. "What, you don't see the family resemblance?"

The warlock blinks at him. "I do, but—"

"*Then where is my daughter?*" Parsifal bellows.

The warlock doesn't look phased by his temper. He tucks his hands behind his back as a breeze sends his cloak into the air. "She is with the Hellastone." He looks past Parsifal to study the rest of us again. "I know what an okeanid is, but the rest of you are strangers to me. Helisent is banished. She said that her people would not come looking for her. So, who are you?"

Parsifal flinches at the warlock's words. They hit me like a physical blow, knocking the air from my lungs.

She didn't think anyone would come for her?

And... is that what Imperatriz thinks, wherever she is?

I've been kicking myself for coming here—for putting my pack in danger, for leaving Velm, for realizing I would have to contend with Helisent's lovers and ill will. Now, I can't believe it's taken so long to leave my world behind.

If not for the witch, then for my mother.

My Alpha.

Hemlock finds his voice first. "Helisent West of Jaws was not banished by the nymphs. She is a friend of my people. She is one of hundreds who we're looking for."

"We're in search of the okeanids, too," Eos chimes in.

Aura goes on, "Helisent was kidnapped with others of our kind. Do you know where they are? Are they safe? They took our Queen Otrera, my dear warlock. She's an okeanid, like us."

The indigo warlock stares down at us. Doom hangs in his eyes; it's answer enough.

The okeanids aren't here. Wherever they are, they aren't doing well.

Kierkeline steps forward. Her copper and bronze rings clank as she wrings her hands again. "Where are the okeanids, warlock? We've come a very long way. We won't be leaving without them or Helisent."

With a long sigh, the warlock continues down the invisible set of stairs. "My name is Halcyon. Your okeanids are in Ezit. It is a two week journey from Hella."

Hella? Is that the name of this city?

And if this warlock's name is Halcyon, then who is Vex?

I glance to the north where I can sense Helisent's ala, Helisent's magic.

Halcyon shifts to meet my gaze; he notices that I notice that part of the cave. His body pivots, as though ready to stand between me and her.

"I will meet your vague words with violence, warlock." Kierkeline's voice lowers. "Tell me why Ezit took my granddaughter. Tell me where to find her *immediately*."

In a less reasonable tone, Parsifal tells the warlock, "I'm going to lose my shit if you don't explain what is happening. Right now."

Halcyon's features come into closer view; he reminds me of Anesot with small, twinkling eyes and a strange crop of short hair. He sighs as he studies Parsifal. "I understand, but—"

"*Right now*," the warlock grits out. "I want to see my daughter."

Halcyon glances once more toward the north, then levels a hard gaze at Parsifal. "It is better not to interrupt. Helisent is the last Vexen. Before she can go home to Mieira, she must learn from Vex. She is the last Vexen. Do you understand? There are six Houses—and your daughter is the *only* wielder in the House of Vex."

House of Vex?

Not a being, but a place.

I glance around, wondering how a place becomes a being.

Halcyon's boots hit the ground. He keeps his eyes on us as he rounds toward the room that he shares with Helisent. Soft light reflects off his horns as he moves.

He looks from Absalom to Kierkeline. "You are from the House of Talos. What Helisent calls a golden wielder. I am from the House of Serac."

We linger near the fountain as he disappears into the room. He comes out a second later with a ceramic jug that I recognize from the blindfolded settlement; a familiar bitter liquor sloshes inside.

The warlock takes a long drink, wipes his mouth, then looks at Kierkeline. "Ezit has your granddaughter. They want her to become a necromancer. A necromancer can communicate with the dead. And only degivampires can turn an okeanid into a necromancer." He raises his eyebrows. "They are valuable in Ezit. Everyone wants to speak with the dead."

"And Helisent..." Absalom narrows his eyes as he phrases the question. "Why did they take Helisent if they need okeanids?"

The warlock sighs. "I told you. Helisent is the last Vexen."

Aura seizes Eos's hand, and the pair take a step toward Halcyon. Both look prepared to curse him, their shoulders pulled back and raised.

"So, why are *you* here?" Eos pushes, lips pulling back from her teeth.

"Who are you loyal to?" Aura asks.

The warlock narrows his eyes into seams of glowing indigo. "We are *here* so that Vex can teach Helisent. I am not *here* for the okeanids. I told you, they are in Ezit. They are *without hope*."

Aura and Eos take another step closer to the warlock. Eos whispers the word, "No."

Halcyon takes a step away from them and clears his throat. "I am sorry."

"Helisent would not have left Butter behind. Both are savvy wielders, but you want me to believe that someone overcame the women. Perhaps it is possible—but only if the women were separated. Not if they were together." Kierkeline's ultramarine robe undulates, picked up in a wind no one can feel or hear. "You are not speaking the truth, warlock. *Speak it*."

For a split second, that's the last thing I want.

Because I know a zhuzh when I hear one.

The warlock is obscuring the truth—and for a reason.

"The truth..." Halcyon drinks from the jug again, then levels a hateful gaze at the witch. It wavers when he looks at Aura and Eos, at Parsifal. "The *truth* is that Helisent was alone on the ship when I found her. She did not leave the okeanids behind. The degis sold the okeanids to the House of Col—that was their goal, their mission. To sell the okeanids so they can be turned into necromancers in Ezit.

"Helisent, as you said, did not want to leave the okeanids behind. I found her before the degis sold her in a separate deal." He looks away from Parsifal. He looks at the ground, at the jug, then back toward the northern streets. "I am very sorry, but the *truth*… this was a very cruel affair. In Zarzynn, there is a stone called rosarium, and no wielder or nymph can overcome its power. Not even the last Vexen. An okeanid goes to sleep when they lay rosarium on them. But witches don't.

"So they broke her hands and then they starved her. There is your *truth*. That is why the women could not save themselves or the others. Because they had no access to magic—not okeanid magic, not Vexen magic."

My mind tries and fails to weigh and accept those statements. My body also reacts; I take a step back, set my hands on my hips, and look up at the sunny span beyond the cave.

I blink at the pale sky as dark birds shoot across it.

Samson can do little about these things; they have already passed. And I have no idea what it is to sell something for a price.

But Samsonfang isn't bound to reality with quite the same rigidity. These things have already happened, but they can be undone with collateral damage.

Samsonfang will make the world regret it. Samsonfang will destroy Zarzynn's present so thoroughly that the past is lost.

I take a deep breath as I stare into the sky.

I will wage war for this, and you will not stop me.

I release my breath and look back at the indigo warlock.

Halcyon goes on, "Degivampries kidnap the okeanids from Mieira and sell them to the Houses on an island called Pit. The House of Col has control of them now."

He gestures toward the east. "Ezit is that way if you want to go. You won't survive it."

Pit?

That's where Anesot said my mother was taken.

Does this warlock know the way there?

Parsifal stares at the ground at my side. He glances at the northern streets now and then. I shift closer to him; his vitals are lagging like he's going into shock. His heart rattles in his chest, blood sugar dropping with each breath.

Halcyon's tone softens as he faces Eos and Aura. "Some okeanids escape. A community lives on Plet, just outside the city. There are over one hundred okeanids and their descendants living there. That is where your hope lies. In New Hypnos—not in Ezit."

Aura and Eos glance eastward, like they're considering walking to Ezit.

Kierkeline does the same, looking at the okeanids, then at Hella's cavernous opening overhead.

Halcyon studies our ranks. He sighs what sounds like a curse, foreign and heartfelt. "Helisent will come back later. For now, I will tell you about the mainland. That's where you are now. On mainland Zarzynn, in the House of Vex." He sits on the fountain's ledge. He takes one last drink before starting, "And here, very long ago, magic was born from the land..."

We shuffle into sitting positions around the fountain. The nymphs sit closest to the warlock, while the wielders and wolves keep our distance. Parsifal sits farthest away, watching the northern streets over his shoulder.

Halcyon outlines a long and horrifying tale about this world.

He describes the six Houses that split Zarzynn and their collusion in the mega-city of Ezit. He tells us about a civil war that saw the Houses of Vex and Talos, home to red and golden wielders, flee overseas to our world.

He describes the degivampires controlled by the Houses. About Anesot's plans to use necromancers to weasel his way back into Ezit. How the Houses use necromancers like a currency, selling their services to those desperate to contact the dead.

This brings us to the topic of money—of currency, prices, selling. Instead of bartering, they trade tiny coins that look like jewelry. Halcyon shows us three different types: bronze, copper, and iron. But the coins are useless on their own—they won't feed anyone, won't shelter them, won't clothe them. They're collectibles, as far as I can tell.

Then Halcyon describes Stretch, a string of islands and a wasteland for Ezit's unwanted and a haven for those targeted by the city's madness. He goes on to describe vampires in greater detail, how they survive on blood, and then finally the gorgons, their blindfolds, their walled settlements. How eye contact with a gorgon turns beings into stone.

And when the story ends with us discovering him and Helisent in Hella, Halcyons slaps his thighs. "So, welcome to Zarzynn. You really should not have come."

Later that night, Rex and I wait for sleep while Berevald snores in our shared room.

A spare light sits in the center of the room, aglow with Absalom's dove. The domestic shuffle of bedtime sounds beyond the doorless frame. Parsifal chats with Halcyon, while Eos and Aura deliberate about what to do about Ezit.

I sort through my supplies on my bed mat. I glance at the door every other minute, hoping for a sign of Helisent's return. I'm also fighting the instinct to mark our dwelling—to mark the entire cave with my scent.

Across the room, Rex points to his chest. "Is it still there?"

I tug down my tunic to stare at the scar. It's just as bloodred as before.

"Tell Parsifal," Rex goes on.

I prod the scar again; it still feels normal.

"What if he was right and... you're *tied* to her magic now? *Permanently?*" he asks. "We need to know what that's going to change for you. For Velm."

I gesture at nothing, frustrated he brought it up. I'd just managed to shake the implications from my mind. "I'll know more when she comes back."

"Helisent isn't going to remember you—which means she's probably going to hate you. If you show her that scar before she remembers the last four years, it might not pan out well. I hope she takes Kierkeline's potion for your sake... but we came here to find Imperatriz." He pauses, letting that sink in. "We need to be yielding with Helisent—if that ship stopped in Pit, then she might remember something about our Alpha."

I can hear his silent insinuation: *And that's more important than your affair.*

A twinge of guilt flickers in my gut.

My thoughts have dwelled on Helisent more than Imperatriz since we entered Hella.

Possibly since I took the potion in Hypnos.

I rub my face with a long sigh. "I need to be careful with Halcyon, too. Stretch includes Pit, based on what he said. He might be our best bet at finding it." I raise my head, happy that Berevald is asleep and I can share my full thoughts with Rex. "But you need to step in if I start to..."

Rex raises his eyebrows. "Start to treat the warlock how you *want* to treat the warlock?"

I gesture at nothing again; it's the most reasonable reaction I feel capable of.

Still, my anxiety lessens slightly with the knowledge that we're on the same page. "I'll find the right time to ask Halcyon about Imperatriz. If we're lucky, she's found her way to New Hypnos by now."

On instinct, I reach for my tobacco packet; it's running dangerously low. For three days, I've kept enough shreds for a final cigarette, but haven't let myself roll one yet.

Rex eyes me and my bed mat. I haven't unrolled my blanket or fluffed my small pillow. "Will you sleep?"

I study his features from across the room, comforted by his presence and steady gaze. Everything else my senses collect now is foreign and cold and scented of limestone.

I was going to try, but I know I'll just stare at the door, waiting, toiling, wondering. I stand with a groan. "No. I'll wait with Parsifal."

Rex glances at the door. "Don't let him drink too much. Did you hear his heart earlier?"

Like Rex, I've checked on Parsifal throughout the evening. Though he seems to have skated by his brush with shock, he might not handle the next surprise so well.

"I noticed. I'll keep him calm."

Rex nods. "Be careful."

I head for the door but turn back at the entrance. Rex looks ready for bed, from his loose hair to his clean face to his tidy bedside arrangement. But I can tell by his bunched eyebrows that he's just as stressed as I am.

I meet his eyes. "You need to rest. I'll sleep in tomorrow if I need it. But you need to be up early."

He snorts. "We're in a magical cave in an unknown land. Don't tell me to go to sleep, Samson."

In my mind, I see Rex from twelve years ago. He's sitting on his bed mat like he is now, only smaller-framed and shorter-haired. His pout was even more vibrant because he hadn't grown into his full lips yet. Instead of a magical cave in a foreign land, we were on our first war band tour near Mort. He wasn't lamenting the vague dangers surrounding us, but how far from home we'd ventured to become men.

Like I did twelve years ago in that camp outside Mort, I go to Rex's bedside.

Like I did twelve years ago, I kneel and pull Rex toward me, leaning back so his weight falls against my chest and abdomen. And like he did twelve years ago, also with Berevald snoring nearby, Rex leans into the embrace and lets me hold him; for one heartbeat, two heartbeats, three.

We slump back onto our knees, heads resting on the other's neck.

We pull in long breaths.

Rex looks at me when I sit back; he's still pouting.

"We survived Mort. We'll survive Zarzynn." I stand and back toward the door.

Rex doesn't say anything. He shuffles back onto his bed mat, tugging his blanket up and reaching back for his pillow.

I leave the quiet room, then pass the row of plain, doorless lodgings where the others have paired off for sleep.

I knock on the frame of Helisent's room. Halcyon and Parsifal sit cross-legged on the bed, a jug of liquor set between them.

Parsifal smiles when he sees me, while Halcyon watches me with narrowed eyes. The elder's free smile doesn't seem to put him at ease.

Parsifal pats the free space near them on the bed. I look at the bunched blankets close to the pillows. I'm unenthused by the idea of standing in the room where Helisent's ala is tangled with the warlock's —to say nothing of sitting on their bed.

Why don't wielders wash the sheets? Ever?

I direct my attention toward Parsifal. "I think we should speak."

Halcyon cuts in, "I think *we* should speak." His look of disdain shifts into something coyer. Amusement dances in his eyes. "Please, come in."

Parsifal leans onto a hand to look past me. I glance outside; the street is quiet and empty, half aglow with magical light.

"Just making sure." The warlock sits back and explains, "Absalom was lingering before. I think he wants to catch a glimpse of Helisent in her form. Halcyon says that she goes into her form when she works with the Hellastone, and I was just telling him that Honey Baby will *blind* Absalom if she finds out he saw her horns."

Halcyon glances at the door. "Then we should blind him now. It will save her the trouble."

Parsifal wags a finger at the warlock. "Careful. Wielders only play violent in Mieira. *Play* violent, Halcyon."

"Well." Halcyon scratches his chin. "You are Talosen, after all."

"I'm a *golden* wielder. And if I'm any House, it's House of Andromeda. Thank you *very* much." Parsifal turns to me and beckons toward the bed again. "Come, my dear Afador. Halcyon cast a spell around the walls—we can speak freely."

I take one step inside the room. I lean against the wall next to the door and cross my arms, determined not to go anywhere near the bed.

Parsifal seems satisfied with my entrance. "Halcyon, you can trust Samson here—even if Helisent... if Helisent doesn't remember him. You see, she doesn't remember the last four years. Samson does. He took a memory potion from Kierkeline. If I can't answer your questions, maybe he can."

Absolutely not.

I level my gaze at the warlock and hope his glowing eyes can read my mind.

Don't you fucking dare.

The warlock looks away from Parsifal, narrowing his eyes as he stares at me. "She said she lost her memory. And you did, too?"

Parsifal takes a long swig from the jug of liquor, then dries his beard with his peridot cloak. "Well, she wiped *both* of their memories. Samson had been mortally wounded, and Honey Baby doesn't know healing magic so... her magic did what it needed to save him. She might hate him now, but they were close at the time. How do I explain this..."

Parsifal looks up at me. He presses his lips together, then his fingertips.

I'm not sure how to explain my and Helisent's predicament either, though I appreciate Parsifal is trying.

I glance at Halcyon. I can feel the words taking shape...

You only have the witch because she doesn't remember me.

And she will leave you when she does.

But... even if Helisent chooses to take Kierkelin's potion, she might not leave Halcyon.

She might not ever want to look at me again.

Halcyon doesn't look phased or perplexed despite Parsifal's vague start.

He slides his eyes past me, toward the open door again. He directs his gaze toward the north. To Parsifal, it probably looks like a vacant stare—but I know exactly where Halcyon is looking.

The Hellastone. Where Helisent communicates with Vex. (In her form.)

Halcyon looks back at me. "You know where she is. You've sensed it since you got here. So... I think we can be honest with each other."

For a long time, I stare at the indigo-eyed warlock. In the well-lit room, I can make out tiny knicks on his shined horns, the pale scars that mark his wrists, his knuckles, his fingers. A star-shaped scar near his left eye.

He looks like he's already survived more than a few brushes with death.

Maybe even a brush with Pit, if I'm lucky.

I don't have time to play everything right in this cave, in this awful land. But it seems the warlock is on his best behavior—maybe for Parsifal.

Without second-guessing myself, I push off the wall and squat near the warlocks. I tug my tunic over my head and pivot my body away from the windows so the warlocks can see my chest clearly.

Both of their eyes shoot to the red mark over my heart.

Parsifal coughs on a sip of the liquor. "Good fucking *moons*."

At least he's seen this shade of red skin before.

Halcyon doesn't look nearly as shocked. He leans toward me, eyes pinching as he studies the mark. He raises a hand as though about to prod me with a finger. Thankfully, he pulls back.

With an anxious sigh, Halcyon sits back. "In Zarzynn, we don't have a word for panic magic. The type of magic that wiped your memories. You call raw magic dove. You store it to use for simple spells—Helisent told me about city processors.

"But here we call it ejima. And ejima isn't just the raw power of that magic, but it's intelligence. It's *willpower*." Helisent's twin. "We learn different spellwork and we train our ejima from a young age so that it does not cast... its own magic. We don't allow panic magic to happen. Do you understand? Ejima should not be making... making decisions..."

Like me, Parsifal leans closer to the warlock.

But Halcyon doesn't go on. He pulls the jug from Parsifal's hands, then sips from it, looking at my chest all the while.

I shake my head. "What the fuck does that have to do with the scar?"

Halcyon takes another drink, then clears his throat. "Ejima knows more than a wielder does. It's the intelligent aspect of magic. And that intelligent aspect of magic comes from the Landmark. So, it comes from these caves. From Vex."

Parsifal's wide eyes flit from my chest to the jug of liquor to Halcyon. "So... panic magic is when our ejima decides what to do. And if panic magic cast that spell... then... Vex?"

I'm not following. "Then Vex *what*?"

"Vex cast that spell." Halcyon lowers his chin to clarify. "Not Helisent—because Helisent doesn't know healing magic. Vex does, though. Vex remembers every spell it was ever cast into."

My heart thuds in my chest as I stare down at the bright mark.

I guess that explains how Samsonfang knew where she was. Knew what we were looking for in the forest above and in this cave below. It's not a connection to Helisent's magic, necessarily, but to this land, these caves, a Landmark.

Panic brushes my mind just like it did on the beach in Hypnos; how will this affect the next Kulapsifang born to the Afador line? It's quickly replaced with a satisfying vindication; now, Helisent and I will be intertwined forever, no matter where our destinies take us.

Parsifal hands me the jug of liquor. Quietly, he explains, "Samson was in pain when Helisent was taken."

Halcyon sighs. "It makes sense. Vex connects them. Vex was telling him."

I take a long drink of the bitter liquor, then hand it back to Parsifal. I tug the tunic back over my shoulders, pacing a few steps.

It maddens me to think that Helisent was in pain all that time that I was. That the discomfort I felt was only a sliver of the torture she faced.

I'd planned to ask when Parsifal wasn't around, but I still don't know if I trust the warlock when he isn't behaving well for Helisent's father.

"Who broke her hands?" It's only half the question I want to ask. *And did they cause her any other harm?*

I'm desperate for Helisent to return and tell us what happened. My mind breeds darker and darker scenarios the longer I have to stew.

"Pel and Jen are the degivampires who took her. They are both evil. I killed Jen, but Pel is alive." Halcyon pivots away from Parsifal slightly, toward me. "And I don't know who broke her hands. I haven't asked any questions about the ship. She said that she doesn't remember it. Some okeanids in Stretch also forget what happened. Maybe it is better like that."

Parsifal rubs his face. "Okay, okay, okay. That's all I can handle for today. Thank you."

I try to let it go, but I can't. And even if I could, I can hear Samsonfang growling in the back of my mind. Can hear him taking in long breaths, searching for an ala.

When I can't let it go, I switch topics. I tuck my hands behind my back and offer my most neutral expression to Halcyon. "I would appreciate your discretion. No one can know about the mark of ejima."

Halcyon waves a hand. "Fine. It doesn't matter to me."

Parsifal shoves the jug back toward me. "And have you seen Helisent in her form yet, my dear wolf? Maybe you should go back to your room for the night. She might also blind you if she finds out you saw her horns."

Halcyon stares at me as he awaits an answer; the coy amusement has returned to his eyes.

Has he... has he seen Helisent's horns?

Samsonfang's growling doubles. **Get him, Samson**.

No. No getting.

Deep breaths.

It dawns on me that this warlock has possibly even touched them. May have smoothed and shined her horns into a state similar to his. The only time I touched Helisent's horns, they were as coarse as a wooly's husk.

I slide my eyes toward Parsifal. "Do you think she would be *able* to blind me?"

I'm not sure how being centerheart works if a wielder doesn't remember being in love.

And I'm hoping Halcyon hasn't realized she's a centerheart; I remember Anesot mentioning that centerhearts don't exist in Zarzynn.

Parsifal presses his fingertips together again. "What a wonderful and dangerous question..." He looks at Halcyon with narrowed eyes, then back to me. "Why don't we ruminate on that in private, Samson? For now, tell me about this booze the gorgons handed over. What's it called again? Latke? Bobcia?"

Halcyon pinches his lips to hide a smile. "It's *vodka*. It's made from potatoes."

"My *moons*. What an impressive feat for a potato."

"Yes."

With a yawn that fizzles into a burp, Parsifal reclines across the bedding. He keeps the jug of vodka close to him, then nestles his face into a pillow.

The warlock studies Halcyon. "Have you thought about where you're going to sleep tonight, my dear warlock? I don't know if all three of us are going to fit in the bed, and I wouldn't hold out on Samson sharing his mat with you."

Halcyon doesn't balk. "I have extra bedding with me. I will make another bed."

"Good. So, what's my Honey Baby been doing since she got here? Tell me something *nice*. This journey has been, and I cannot understate this, a bummer."

Halcyon wags his head back and forth. "Well, she loves the vodka."

Parsifal cackles, kicking his tiny feet with delight. "She's a good girl, isn't she, Halcyon?"

It's easy to hate Halcyon.

Even easier to be jealous of his straightforward demeanor.

But the longer I stay in the room and listen to his simple observations, devoid of possessiveness and suspicion, the freer I feel to study his shined horns, his plum-colored skin, his pale scars.

By the time I return to my room and stoop to sleep, I'm certain of three simple facts.

Halcyon is not bad.

And it's good he is here.

But I still hate him.

That night, I dream of Helisent.

Not Helisent the witchling, aged twelve years and tangled in her red cloak. This is Helisent the witch, with a full bosom that fills out her strapless dress and enough jewelry to outfit a village. Her silky white hair catches against the sticky yew branches, tangled with stubby, emerald needles.

I watch her from the ground below. She adjusts on a thick branch as she clings to one overhead, steadying herself. Her eyebrows bunch with concentration. She bites her lip as she extends her leg toward an adjacent branch.

Before I can call out to her, I realize I'm not alone on the ground.

I see a witch—the same faceless witch who has appeared in the seething dreams before. She faces away from me, seated on the ground on the opposite side of the yew's trunk.

She wears a modest robe, its fibers torn and thick. I can't see her hands, which are set in her lap, but I imagine they're full of red string; a single red twine trails along the ground from her to me.

I'm afraid again.

My heart thumps in my chest—

Helisent is in the tree above; I do not trust whoever is with me on the ground.

One of her arms moves, elbow shooting to the side.

The strings looped around my limbs tighten. I stagger, catching myself on the tree's trunk as adrenaline soars into my veins; the strings are too tight, and they seem to be humming with infrasound, and I can see something moving in my periphery.

I back myself against the tree's trunk. My vertebrae press against the sturdy bark; apprehension snakes up my spine like frost on freezing water.

In a split-second, I can't decide what to do—*should I call out to Helisent for help? Will she remember me in the dreams? Will she help me?*

"Once my papa told me that for every child the wolves slaughtered during the War Years, a tree grew in your forests," Helisent's voice echoes from above. "That's why Velm is covered in emerald woods. We gave your people a death *full of life.*"

My heart pumps in my chest.

When I look up to ask her for mercy, something in my periphery catches my attention.

The witch sitting on the ground turns her head; she sees it, too.

A wolf watches me from the crest of a hillock nearby.

It has blue-black fur and triangular ears. Its blazing eyes, the color of night between the stars, twinkle. White fangs poke from its maw.

I lock eyes with Hetnazzar.

I haven't seen my demigod since I was twelve years old.

Now, it stares at me in a dream.

Red strings tangle around its neck and ears, half-invisible where they're tucked beneath its thick fur. My demigod blinks at me.

It doesn't look afraid.

CHAPTER 7

I WILL BEG MORE
THOROUGHLY IN PRIVATE

HELISENT

Honey Baby,
There was a rumor in Antigone that your mother's mother, Pereline, had a
penchant for lacing the city's water supply with magical nightmares. I'm not
sure if it's for the better or worse that you never met her.
Papa P.

I look at the sleeping wolf.

His lips and eyelids twitch, as though engulfed in a dream.

Wow, what a massive lump of shit.

I clench the bucket of freezing water and rear back to scream with all my might, "Get the *fuck* out of my cave!"

Then I empty it on Samson 714 Afador and his bed mat as he jolts awake.

He sits up, eyes opening and hands splaying like he's ready to grab something. His chest rises and falls with quick breaths as he wipes cold water off his face. His shirt, hair, and bed mat are soaked. So are most of the items at his bedside.

I adjust the bucket; there's still some water left.

I raise my chin and clear my throat.

Two more wolves watch me from their bed mats. I ignore their livid stares, their frozen positions.

The Kulapsifang's eyes flit to me, studying me like he's going one limb at a time. He sits frozen, his hands hovering near his face like he's prepared to shield himself from another splash—which he's right to do.

I slosh the rest of the water across him. Samson barely flinches, then starts to wipe his face dry again.

I tsk. I was expecting a *bigger* reaction when I woke up twenty minutes ago with my papa at my bedside.

He quickly caught me up on the fact that Mieirans are here in Hella. That nymphs and wielders and *wolves* followed the ship that kidnapped me to Zarzynn. That Samson brought two of his pack-mates with him and was sleeping peacefully just down the street from me.

In my cave.

In my *Landmark*.

"Excuse me, boy-wolf," I seethe, "you are *banished* from Vex."

This feels *really* good.

They never say life is fair, just that it will all be worth it in the end.

I squat onto my haunches to get a better look at Samson.

I study the carbon copy of the Male Alpha of Velm. With only the first light of dawn filling Hella, his fair skin looks richer. His dark hair is loose around his shoulders, thick and wavy. His deep-set eyes twinkle with an unwavering intensity.

Even though I don't remember the last four years, his features strike me as familiar. When I first laid eyes on him a few minutes ago, my rage tripled as I saw his face and was reminded of Clearbold. The one who banished *me*—

Now I see the slight differences in Samson's features. His are softer, kinder. They don't deviate as he stares at me. Only his lips part —slowly, with shock.

My nose curls. I can't believe he isn't giving me any kind of reaction. *"Pack your shit."*

I'd wanted a big affair when I stomped into the room. Now, I doubt he'll give me the chance.

He glances over me from head to toe again.

When he looks like he's about to speak, I cut him off. "Good luck in Zarzynn. It's *crazy* out there." I lift the empty bucket and gesture to the other wolves. One watches me with a twisted brow, while the other half-smiles in disbelief. "I'm going to fill this up. Be gone before I'm back."

I stand and turn, lifting my chin as I stomp out of the room.

Halcyon and Parsifal wait for me in the middle of the street with their hands behind their backs. Both tried to stop me from banishing Samson and his wolves when I woke up from a long night spent in the Hellastone's trance; both failed.

It looks like my episode woke up the rest of the group. Two short okeanids watch me from a doorway next to the wolves' lodging, expressions drawn and eyes wide. A kingly dryad stands next to a skinny warlock who wears the Class's white robes. Last is a sleepy old witch who stares with her ultramarine cloak drawn tight over her narrow shoulders.

Their eyes scan me in silence. I don't recognize any of them, which only spurs my foul mood.

I've liked who I am in this cave, with Halcyon...

These people don't like who I am. They don't know who I am.

Who I'm on the *cusp* of becoming.

The wielders didn't care about my well-being, and neither did the wolves. I can't fathom why they followed the nymphs here in search of me and the okeanids.

And I'm already panicking at the prospect of recounting my kidnapping.

They're going to have a lot of questions; I can see them boiling in their eyes.

Not even me and Halcyon have spoken of it. He listens closely anytime I speak of my time on the ship, but he has yet to ask a single question.

Quietly, the warlock whispers to me now, "The wolves will die if you banish them."

Dark rings hang below his glowing eyes. Usually, he looks brightest in the morning, but now he looks just as exhausted as my papa.

Parsifal nods at his side. His unbrushed hair sticks up at odd angles. He didn't sling on his peridot cloak and stands in a long tunic that shifts dangerously in the morning breeze. "They came to find you, Honey Baby. Just give them one day to change your mind."

I turn when I hear footsteps shuffling across the stone.

Samson stands in the doorframe looking slightly more awake. He wears his golden torcs and his hair is pulled back into a bun. He scratches his arm, glancing from me to my papa and Halcyon. Slowly, he approaches us, then stops like he's facing a council's verdict.

I cross my arms. Given I only stand to his chest, I have to settle for dramatics to compensate. "If you'd like to avoid a banishment that means certain death, I'd start begging. *Now*."

I point at the cold limestone at my feet, suggesting he start there.

Samson's expression stirs my anger; once again, each feature stills into something unreadable. He raises his eyebrows. "I will beg you to spare us *in private*."

I wag my finger, pointing at the ground. "*No*, you will beg *in public*."

He raises his chin an inch. "I will beg more thoroughly in private. You will enjoy it more."

I try not to flinch at his unexpected words, from how unbelievably self-assured that statement was.

(And he's right—the idea of him begging *thoroughly* pleases me greatly.)

Unfortunately, I'm already pointing at the ground. I would look stupid capitulating so quickly—especially with an audience watching us from the windows.

But I guess it's like Halcyon told me when I first started absorbing Vex's dove from the Hellastone. '*Remember that all leaders have to make sacrifices. The best know how to cash in on those sacrifices.*' It led to a long discussion on cash, which I still don't understand.

I think Halcyon meant that I'll have to make sacrifices, but these sacrifices are part of a larger, more complex barter.

I lift my finger and turn. I don't spare a glance at Halcyon or Parsifal, nor the spies who stare on from nearby windows and doorways.

I clench my jaw and try to focus on being a leader. A *good* one. "Fine, boy-wolf. Follow me."

I lead us past the circular fountain. I listen closely to Samson's steady footsteps, determined not to look behind me.

His hands are *huge*. With an expanding repertoire of spells that I pull from the Hellastone like string from a spindle, I'm less afraid of the world than ever before—wolves and their hands included.

Still... I don't trust wolves.

Especially not Alphas.

Muscle memory takes me northward. The closer I am to the Hellastone, the more comfortable and powerful I feel.

I set my grooming magic in motion. It tidies my hair and cinches my tan linen layers. I didn't have time to get ready—I just woke up and started filling a bucket with cold water, red rage stewing in my mind.

I lose my nerve halfway and peek over my shoulder. Samson meets my eye like he'd been watching me, then opens his mouth like he's going to say something.

I turn around before he can.

When we reach a square plaza with another water-filled fountain, only four blocks from the Hellastone, I turn around. I set my hands on my hips and wait for Samson to sink to his knees.

Instead, he glances around the plaza. I've taken to liking the open area. A mosaic depicts a formation of soaring, large-beaked birds. The small fountain is also covered in fingernail-sized tiles, each an off-shade of crimson. It turns the water within into an illusion that looks like blood.

Samson stares at the water, then swivels to study the walls.

I clear my throat to get his attention. "I'm waiting."

He turns to face me, expression once again unreadable.

"And stop looking at me like that. What the *fuck* are you doing here? Did you run out of wolves willing to listen to how dangerous I am? Are you here to start spreading the word throughout Zarzynn, too?"

That finally hardens his features. "I came to help find you." He gulps, voice lowering. "We were... friends. Not enemies."

Each steady word feels like a secret whispered into my ear.

I blink at him, waiting for a cruel retort to pop into my head.

Nothing.

This motherfucker really thinks we were friends?

I've done a lot of dumb shit in my life, but I sincerely doubt befriending Samson was one of those mistakes. If anything, I must have manipulated the wolf into thinking we were allies. It would have been a solid move.

In my silence, he goes on, "I know you're innocent. You never hurt me, Helisent West of Jaws. Kierkeline Ultramarine gave me a potion.

I remember everything." He pauses, blinking at me like he's not sure what else to say. Eventually, "I will clear your name in Velm as soon as I return. I've already told the group that you're innocent."

He's not *begging*, but he's at least taking responsibility. And he seems to be serious about my innocence.

Still, it's hard to nudge my anger. It's lodged in me like a splinter.

I glance past him, studying the mosaic wall when his gaze starts to feel too heavy. "I don't know who Kierkeline is." I cross my arms. "And I'm not sure I believe you're actually here *because we were friends*. I'm sure you have other friends. More important friends."

He runs a hand over his scalp, down his smoothed hair. "I'm also here to search for information about Imperatriz 713 Afador. She went missing from the coasts of Hypnos seventeen years ago. More like eighteen years now." Samson gestures at nothing. "I know it must be difficult to believe me, but we *were* friends. And..."

"You're right," I huff. "It is hard to believe."

But...

Already, Samson has capitulated more than I ever thought he would. And it makes me wonder if everything else I've assumed about the last four years might be... different than what I imagine.

If I hadn't been kidnapped, if I didn't sit in this cave with so many unfathomable uncertainties, maybe I would investigate that more.

Instead, I point at the ground, finger twitching. "Time to beg, Samson."

Voice wavering, he says, "You were saving my life in Alita."

A lump forms in my throat. "Well, we all make mistakes."

I keep my finger pointed at the limestone.

With a long sigh, Samson turns and looks over his shoulder. He even looks up, as though searching for onlookers in the windows and alleys. He makes a low, unhappy sound. *"Lekeli Kelnazzar."* He turns back to check once more, then slowly squats.

With another whispered curse, he shifts onto his knees.

"Go on, then."

He looks up at me, eyebrows bunched. "Clearbold wrongfully banished you from Velm; I beg you to let me right this. I am the Afador, the Kulapsifang. Soon, I will rectify Clearbold's mistakes.

"The wolves of Velm should have thanked you for saving me, not banished you under the assumption that you hurt me. I beg you to forgive my people; they have been misled by Clearbold. I beg you to follow *my* example, Helisent, and that set by Rex and Berevald."

I study his expression, waiting for a moment of deviation.

Memories rattle through my mind, half-formed, half-real. I smell tobacco; someone is brushing my hair; my lilith's ornaments are jingling.

The taste of brandy fills my mouth.

This man is a pussy-sniffer.

I have no idea where that thought comes from—

It's jarring enough that I lift my hand.

Samson stares up at me from his knees as I tell him, "We aren't in Velm, so you have to listen to *me*. This is my cave, my Landmark, my territory—all of it. So long as you're in Vex, you live under my rule."

His eyebrows lift with shock. "Okay."

I flick my hair over my shoulder. "Fine. Get up. You look pitiful."

I turn and head back toward camp. Samson sighs, then I hear him shuffling behind me.

I waltz back onto the main avenue that leads to the fountain at Hella's center. I make it one block before Samson calls from behind me, "Do I have to walk ten paces behind you?"

I turn to shout over my shoulder, "You could walk ten paces off a fucking cliff for all I care. Stop talking to me like we're friends. I don't remember any of it."

And I won't believe it until I do.

Samson makes a long sound. I can't tell if it's a sigh or a groan.

I spend the rest of the morning in silence.

Halcyon guides the group through making a large meal with the food harvested in the forest above. Most of the tubers, nuts, and fruits are foreign to us Mieirans. Though not entirely different from our diet, some are prepared differently. Here, they pull potatoes from the dirt—not cassava. The same goes for the farro and millet, which look like wheat but require different treatment and processing.

I sit on the fountain with my papa and try to ignore the curious stares from the others.

Halcyon sits nearby, getting up now and then to review the group's work cooking and storing supplies.

"I don't *remember* any of them, papa," I whisper. "It feels weird. They keep staring at me."

"That's okay, Honey Baby." He pats my leg with a wide smile. Like many of his smiles today, it looks strained. "It's because the hopelessness is starting to exhaust everyone. And Kierkeline has the memory potion. In case you want to remember."

I also ignore his mentions of the potion Samson took in Hypnos.

The last four years might not be enough to break me, but I'd rather keep my time from the ship tucked in total darkness—at least until I'm safely back home. I fear the potion would drag those days back into the light.

"Kierkeline is the old witch, right? How the fuck did *she* survive the trip?" I watch the ancient wielder as she sits to eat her meal with the wolves. She's touched one of them a few times, prodding him like he's a naughty grandchild with her ringed fingers.

The wolf, who had looked ready to fight me this morning, has long and twisted hair. Unlike Samson and the other one, he doesn't keep it tied back. He's also leaner than his packmates, with a longer neck and larger hands.

"Well, she's a GhostEater. Extremely powerful. And she's after one of the okeanids who was taken with you." Parsifal nudges the plate in my hand. "Finish your meal, Helisent."

"I'm not hungry. And what about the warlock in the white? He must be with the Class. He looks like an asshole."

Parsifal studies the warlock with an unhappy grunt. "That's Absalom Metamor. He knew you in Luz. I think the Class had him keeping tabs on you in Jaws."

I snort a laugh at that thought. The warlock, half-buried in his too-white robes, turns his head at each sound, as though expecting something to step out of the shadows. "How are Yves and Yngvi?"

My papa takes a big bite of faro, then chatters as he chews. "Oh, they're the same as ever. Yves keeps talking like he wants a littleling with Kiki Red Tier, then Yngvi brings up how difficult littlelings are and gets him to back down. Do you remember Kiki? Yves brought her to visit you in Luz... oh, wait. Never mind."

I log Kiki Red Tier as another face from another life.

I stop asking questions after that.

I turn back to my meal, shoveling in bite after bite even though

I'm not hungry. Now and then, Parsifal offers me compliments. He says I look nice in my linen clothes. He says Halcyon is a worthy ally. He says I'm a capable witch who will leave Hella a master.

Still...

I study the group with mounting uncertainty. Halcyon already caught them up on how I ended up here, and he caught me up on how they ended up here. It spares me the discomfort of reliving my time on the ship... but I'd want every last detail if I'd come as far as them.

As we finish our breakfast, I prepare for what comes next.

The questions.

The horrible, awful questions that they wouldn't have felt comfortable asking Halcyon. That he wouldn't have been able to answer.

I sit on the lip of the fountain and prepare myself, my papa on one side and Halcyon on the other. The okeanids sit at our feet, Kierke-line and Hemlock and Absalom right behind the pair. Samson and the wolves stand behind them.

Then the trio swivels, turning toward the cave's southern entrance. Samson wanders away from the group to stand in the middle of the street.

I follow his gaze; he stares in the direction of one of Hella's underground entrances. Though Halcyon and I descended into the cave from above, he's since found three subterranean passages. They lead to different spots in the forest; one near the fruit groves, one near the pastures where the alpacas graze, and one to a field where wild millet grows.

But the Mieirans haven't found these tunnels yet—and Halcyon wouldn't have revealed their locations without consulting me.

I watch the wolves. Before I can ask them what they smell, I sense it myself.

Since spending more time with the Hellastone, I've started to understand the flushes of intuition that Vex uses to communicate with me.

Four beings are stepping into Hella. They are not strangers.

Samson turns to me. "The gorgons are here. Four elders. All female." His dark eyes flash to Halcyon. "We couldn't communicate with them when we found their village. We don't know their names or understand their hierarchy."

Halcyon had mentioned the Mieirans were directed to Hella by the gorgons in Dexerxes, just like us. But I hadn't expected a visit from the gorgons quite so fast—*did they follow the Mieirans here?*

Maybe they also mistrust my people.

Halcyon, at least, doesn't seem surprised. He looks past the wolves, down the empty street. "Helisent invited them to visit." He glances at me. "What is hierarchy?" He pronounces it like *hair-arky*. "Being at the top of the group?"

I nod, then gesture to Hemlock. In the morning light, his lilac cloak and shimmering emerald hair give him the air of a regal blossom. "Exactly. Hemlock is a King of Rhotidom, so he's close to the top of nymph hierarchy."

Hemlock beams a smile at the warlock, his sturdy features melting. "Second only to the Rhotidic Demigod who grants me my title and power."

Halcyon bares a bland, political smile at him before turning back to Samson. "Gorgon hierarchy comes from age. Each generation has its own male and female leader. Their village only has two names—and they're for the elders. Accra is close to two hundred and fifty years old. She will come today—and probably the next three after her. Her Accras-in-waiting."

He had explained this when we were in the village, but I hadn't exactly come to my senses yet. I was more preoccupied with the gorgon's blindfolds than their names.

Soon, I hear their dragging footsteps. The wolves' shift where they stand, noses twitching and chins raised. The nymphs and wielders stand up and dust themselves off, preparing to meet our visitors.

Halcyon elbows me.

Right—it's my cave.

I stand up and scurry down the street. "Everyone close your eyes! I'll talk to them first." Halcyon trails me at a more relaxed pace.

I'd like to impress Accra—to show the gorgons that I was worthy of their help. When we first met, I was a silent and frightened thing, suspicious of every shadow, every snapped twig in the night.

Weeks later, I'm not so helpless.

I rush toward their shuffling where it echoes from a side street. I call out in Zarzyd, thrilled to communicate with the women directly. "Hello, my dear gorgons! Welcome to Hella! I'm coming to get you!"

The group of four steps into the light at the far end of the street. Accra leads the way with a strip of linen around her eyes; it's a rigid piece. The specialized blindfolds are designed for travel outside the village walls. They let the gorgons direct their gaze downward so they can watch their step and study their immediate surroundings.

It also helps them walk in perfect tandem.

They move like a single being, depicted in four distinct eras.

The women's linen layers drift around them, giving them a touch of refinery and feebleness that doesn't match their brawny builds, their deep voices, their direct questions.

Accra stands nearly as tall as a wolf and almost as wide. Like all the gorgons, black freckles cover her brown skin. They multiply around her cheeks and hands and jawline. Gray segments lighten portions of Accra's black hair, which is neatly pinned down. The youngest gorgon, who stands at the group's rear, still has a glossy mane of black.

I expect them to stop or smile at my voice, but they don't miss a step as they continue approaching.

I clear my throat. "And I speak Zarzyd now. Halcyon and Vex have been teaching me. Every morning, I wake up with a few new words. Halcyon says I speak like an old man, but..."

Finally, the group of four stops. They stand a full head taller than me.

The corners of Accra's lips tug upward. "That is good. We come bearing gifts; the gifts are stories. Without language, the gifts are only ideas. And ideas will not help you now, Vexen. But surely, you have realized that already."

"Totally. Thank you." (I hadn't thought of any of that. And if I had, I wouldn't have thought a story could help me more than an idea.)

"Halcyon, we brought more vodka," Accra goes on. She shifts her head to face the warlock, a few feet behind me. "We left it above the cave in the shadow of the gum tree. You may collect it when we leave. Cover your eyes now, both of you. We would like to see the dead city."

I call over to the rest of the group, safe a few blocks away, and ask them to close their eyes. Then I press my shoulder against Halcyon's, twine our hands, and close mine.

All I hear is a faint shuffle of fabric and boots on the ground, followed by a few unimpressed tuts.

"I was right." Accra sighs. "The city will remain dead."

When Halcyon first led me to the gorgon village, I had been enamored by the thoughtful beings. Now, I can appreciate that my first interpretation was romantic.

Accra sounds like a tough crowd.

She also seems to be spewing prophecies.

"Our eyes are closed," she says.

I open mine. "Right. Are you hungry? Or thirsty? We're finishing breakfast. The other Mieirans are here. They found us thanks to your help."

I step forward, uncertain how to guide Accra. When we met in the village, she gave us a smooth paddle that we held onto, following her with our eyes blindfolded.

I open my hand and extend it toward Accra. A foot away from her, I assume it's visible from the confines of the rigid blindfold. "I can guide you."

She grabs my hand like it's a piece of fabric, holding it beneath her palm and fingers. My hand folds awkwardly beneath, fingers tangled.

Has she never held hands before?

"We are more than capable of following your footsteps." She tugs my hand closer to her, toward the blindfold. I concede a step with a shuffle. "You hide your form still. Why?"

I take off toward the group at the fountain. "I only showed you as an act of good will. Where I come from, we hide our forms. "

"This is where you came from; where you stand right now."

"I mean where I was born." Halcyon sticks close by, dragging his feet with added laziness. He doesn't need to; Accra keeps her stranglehold on my hand. "In Mieira."

"Mieira is the place you were born, but this is your home," Accra announces cryptically. "It is where your magic returns when it gets lost. Tell me what defines a home better than that?"

I walk at a quick pace, aware of how much longer the gorgons' legs are than mine. I watch the other three women, waiting for one of them to talk. Like in the village, only the elder speaks; the others don't seem to mind. They walk with their hands behind their backs in close ranks, their linen layers tangling as they step.

"Have you made Halcyon your Host?" Accra asks.

"A Host?" I ask.

At the same time, Halcyon says, "*No.*"

"But you will soon, Helisent," Accra goes on. "Every House needs two Hosts. Halcyon is the only reason you're alive; your magic and life are owed to him. You will fight and fail to find a better Host. One should present itself just as he did. Fate always meets us halfway, Vexen."

I glance at Halcyon. He shakes his head with wide eyes, as though denying involvement in the idea.

I don't know what to say to Accra; I don't know what a Host is. I know I've heard it before in reference to Houses, but its meaning is complex. The word has a loose equivalent in Mieiran. It's like a host, as in someone who serves guests. And it's also similar to matriarch and patriarch, relating specifically to a hierarchy. In Zarzyd, a *host* is at the top of this hierarchy, but they aren't alone.

I slide my eyes toward Halcyon, who looks like he might be blushing.

"We can discuss this later, my dear Accra," I say. "Would you like anything to eat or drink before you tell your stories?"

The Mieirans wait for us in silence, scattered around the fountain like curious schoolchildren. Dirty plates and cups sit stacked near our makeshift kitchen, arranged in a single-story building nearby.

Accra's nose twitches as we reach the fountain. "I would like to sit down. We have walked for days to reach the dead city. And then I would like water; our mouths will dry from telling our stories. You will sit above us when we tell them. It is bad for the neck to always look down with these blindfolds on."

I lean away from Accra to get her water, but her hand tightens on mine.

"These gifts are for the last Vexen, not the Mieirans. We will tell our stories in private, Helisent."

Like me, Halcyon glances at the expectant and curious expressions from the wielders, nymphs, and wolves. They stand at the ready, unable to understand our exchange.

I offer Halcyon a guilty smile, hunching my shoulders, "Do you mind...?"

He blinks a few times, as though trying to find a way to tell me that he does mind.

He and I are bound by an agreement; babysitting a group of help-less Mieirans was never part of the deal.

But he swore to be helpful.

"I'll show them the tunnels and the foot paths outside. Here." Halcyon hands me a stack of cups—it takes me a second to remember the gorgons requested water.

I lean away from where Accra keeps holding my hand. I whisper to Halcyon in Zarzyd, "I won't go far. We'll be back soon."

Halcyon lowers his voice to respond, "You need to tell them some-thing after. You need to take control of this situation, Helisent. The Mieirans are getting nervous—I would be, too. They need a *plan*."

I growl, frustrated that I'm once again responsible for the Mieirans.

Navigating my role as the last Vexen was hard enough when I was alone and concerned for my and Halcyon's survival.

Now, I'm saddled with whatever brought the nymphs, wielders, and wolves here, and I'm guessing its the okeanids—not me.

"Yeah, okay." I turn away from the warlock. I glance northward, thinking of the plaza where I took Samson a few hours ago. "This way, Accra. Halcyon will stay with the Mieirans."

My hand starts to go numb between Accra's strong fingers. I take off, glancing back once. Much to my discomfort, the group of Mieirans watch us go with disgruntled expressions. Parsifal stands a few feet ahead of the group, as though prepared to trail us.

I use whispering magic to explain to my papa, "They know things about Vex. I need to learn from them. I'll be back as soon as I can. Okay?"

Parsifal takes another step toward me, expression tensed. To my surprise, one of the wolves approaches him. The handsome one with pouty lips sets a hand on my papa's back—and Parsifal turns to follow him with a sigh.

Are they worried about my safety?

Or do they doubt my ability to represent Mieira and Velm to the gorgons?

Probably the latter.

Once we're in the square, I guide the matriarchs to a smooth patch of limestone. I clean it with a spell, then the women sit down. Like they walk, the gorgons also use minimal movements to find a comfortable position. I fill the cups with water, then hand them out.

They sip for a few minutes, resting. When they set the cups down, I close my eyes and extend my hand. "Okay, you can take off your blindfolds. If you wouldn't mind lending me one..."

A piece of fabric falls into my hand. I use magic to tie it tight around my eyes.

With only a seam of light below, I nod. "Ready."

In the distance, I make out the faint chatter from the group. It sounds calm, at least.

Then Accra clears her throat, and then I hear drumming—not the pounding drums common to wolves or the frenetic drumming common to nymphs. This is quiet and steady as a heartbeat, rhythmic and peaceful; it must be a single, small hand drum.

Accra speaks over the gentle beating. "Long ago, the Vexen traded my people flax, and we traded back linen. We traded them felled trees, and they traded back furniture. Our villages were made strong by these trades."

Like Halcyon, Accra uses fewer words and annunciates each. Compared to how she speaks to Halcyon, the matriarch draws out her Zarzyd for my benefit.

"We traded in goods, in deeds, in spells; sometimes, we traded in love.

"You traveled to my village, Dexerxes. The limestone walls are sturdy; we built them centuries ago. We built them after my great-great-great-grandmother entered Hella.

"She spent her days in the cave with her eyes cast to the ground; the Vexen spread the word of her arrival. The strangers in this city were kind. They fed her. They guided her to sculptures, to plazas, to a small room where she could sleep.

"When the Male Host of Vex heard a gorgon lived in Hella, he came to meet her.

"He commanded all residents to wear blindfolds. My great-great-great-grandmother opened her eyes for the first time in this city; she saw Vex's Male Host first.

"She had never seen such large horns; they were the color of life that bled between her legs, the color of life that spilled from the throats of the animals, the color of the cranberries distilled in liquor for winter.

"The Male Host visited her at night. She could never meet his eyes, but in the darkness, they glowed red. They were bright enough for her to sense beyond her blindfold. When he left her room, she dreamed in red.

"One day, my great-great-great-grandmother left Hella to return to her small village. Though she loved the cave-city, she missed her home. The Male Host followed her; once again, he wore a blindfold."

My mind buzzes as it struggles to invent an image of a *male* Vexen. No one has seen one in centuries—the only male Vexen I've heard of were whispered legends in Antigone's seediest taverns.

A *warlock* with red skin, with horns thick and wide, with the large eyes of the red line.

A Male *Host*.

Accra's words from before suddenly fit into place—she was talking about finding a warlock to carry on the red line. More specifically, she was talking about *Halcyon* assuming this position. *Halcyon* fathering the future littlelings of Vex.

Red fills my cheeks at the thought. This is the first time I've deeply considered my responsibility of bearing red wielders.

But magic passes down according to gender for wielders. Any warlocks born from a union with Halcyon would take after him; indigo, Seracyd.

I can't fathom how I'd go about producing a *male* Vexen without a red warlock at my side.

The matriarch goes on, "When the villagers finished building the limestone walls, the Male Host of Vex wielded magic to build a lasting gate. When he shut the gate, he stood inside the limestone walls. Dexa was his name; Xerxes was my great-great-great-grandmother's.

"Our village, Dexerxes, carries their names. The story has not been lost; we live within its bounds still.

"This is the wisdom I pass onto you, Helisent: the Vexen have never been insular like the other Houses.

"This knowledge is yours again."

Someone pounds the drum four times, then silence fills the air.

Just as detailed and realistic as the bottle of brandy, I now see a man in my mind's eye, like a memory waiting to be recalled.

Dexa.

His four horns are almost as large as mine, his white hair longer.

He grins, as though drunk and foolish. His teeth are straight, his eyes large enough that they still glitter when he smiles.

In his large red eyes, a light glows—a light like love, like passion, like reckless and fulfilled abandon. Red clouds hang around him as Dexa directs that wild gaze at me.

The drum starts to beat again; its rhythm quickens.

Dexa's face doesn't wander from my mind.

It feels like he's sitting beside me, listening to these stories, sliding sly glances at me.

Another gorgon speaks, deeper and quieter than Accra. I strain forward to hear her clearly. "The baby's mother named her Bathsheba. She was born three blocks from where we sit now. After her birth, the witch traveled to her mother's village to present the witchling to her elders. But the mother died in a sudden tragedy during the journey.

"Bathsheba, too young to speak or walk, cried. Vex's ejima provided her with the tools for survival, but no infant survives their third night alone—with or without magic.

"Vampires heard Bathsheba crying when they woke at dusk. They crept toward its sound. They beheld the tiny Bathsheba, her skin as red as fresh blood. A female vampire, also a new mother, put Bathsheba to her breast. The witchling drank.

"And drank.

"And drank.

"The vampire liked how it felt when Bathsheba's short horns grazed her chest. The infant was strong in spirit and in body. The vampire took the baby Vexen home to her den; the child slept through the days and woke at dusk. The child ate berries and meat; she also drank blood."

I go still.

I ignore the rakish smile Dexa bares at me in my mind's eyes.

Was Bathsheba Zarzynn's Bloody Betty, hundreds of years before the wolves conceived the same devilish plan to end the War Years?

Is this my second lesson? That the Vexen are easily manipulated?

The second gorgon goes on, "Bathsheba came to power when Ezit took the first degivampires. Bathsheba rode to war under the moons with vampires. She drank the blood of her enemies; she wore the pale furs of vampires; wore the soft feathers of blood-drinkers.

"One day, she met other Vexen on the battlefield. They stopped when they saw Bathsheba. There was blood on her red skin, dried to black near her mouth and staining the ends of her white hair. The Vexen knelt when they saw Bathsheba fell her enemies; though the battle was won, the war would be difficult.

"They would need Bathsheba.

"They took the witch to Hella; they took the vampires who walked in her shadow. Here, they joined forces under Bathsheba. Here, in these fountains, the Vexen pooled blood for their guests to drink freely.

"This is the wisdom I pass onto you, Helisent: the Vexen did not fear blood or power. They did not fear it within their own kind. They did not fear it in others.

"This knowledge is yours again."

Vex's magic reaches into my mind; the red clouds shake and reform.

Dexa's naughty smile doubles in size as Bathsheba's face comes into focus. She closely resembles Dexa, though her face isn't quite as broad and her nose not quite as flat. Still, she shares his devilish and unrepentant gaze. She doesn't smile like Dexa; she keeps her mirth hidden in an insatiable glow that pits her pupils.

Once more, the drumming stops.

Within a few seconds, it picks up at a quicker pace.

The third gorgon speaks. "A powerful witch birthed a warlock named Axerxa. You sleep in his room, Helisent, where the most powerful Vexen warlock once slept.

"War filled his life. He spent his childhood in fear, he took solace in nightmares, he lived in shadows until he could hear their secrets. He grew knowing his fate—death.

"When Axerxa was grown, he walked to the coasts and packed the longships with supplies; he helped the elders and the children aboard; he kissed his mother and he kissed his beloved witches. He bent to kiss the stomachs of the witches who were pregnant; each prayed for warlocklings.

"The armies of Serac, Argot, Col, and Lahar were coming from Ezit. They would destroy the last of the Vexen, and then Vex itself.

"Axerxa stood on the shore as the ships sailed into the horizon.

"Then he walked alone back to Hella; by then, the city was dead. Dead is it is now.

"Here, he waited.

"Here, he fought to his last breath. Not to defeat the armies of Ezit, but to defy their wish that he would disappear. That he would capitulate.

"This is the wisdom I pass onto you, Helisent: the Vexen accepted annihilation before they accepted coercion.

"This knowledge is now yours."

Goosebumps line my skin.

A deep sense of grief, pride, and curiosity whirl inside of me.

The Vexen have never been insular.

The Vexen do not fear blood or power.

The Vexen accepted annihilation before they accepted coercion.

I can still see Dexa and Bathsheba in my mind's eye. They sit in static places as though listening; and now, they look to my right, where another Vexen comes into focus. He has the same broad face and large eyes as me. The same pointed chin and arched nose.

The love that burns in Dexa and Bathsheba's eyes fizzles and crackles like a weapon in his.

Of the three ghosts, Axerxa feels most alive.

Dexa reaches out and sets his hand on Bathsheba's shoulder. Like a proud father, he nods at Bathsheba; and Bathsheba does the same when she turns to look at Axerxa. Though separated by centuries, it's obvious that they're familiar.

My blood goes still as I understand—

Axerxa was the last Vexen to live here on the mainland where our magic was born.

And he died here to ensure his pregnant witches would carry the Vexen line to Plet, and then on to Mieira.

Eventually, hundreds of years later and thousands of miles away, that line led to me.

Axerxa holds out his hand toward me. His broad palm waits, fingers still. His features break with a hesitant smile.

Holy shit.

Like a severed tether becoming one again, I reach into the red fog in my mind's eye and set my hand in Axerxa's sturdy grip.

He looks like he's going to say something.

I wait, body rigid.

The drum kicks up for a fourth time, jarring me.

The last Accra-in-waiting is the loudest, the most melodic. "The last Vexen was born across the sea, far from her home and her Landmark. A degivampire laid rosarium over her to put her magic to sleep, then took her back to Zarzynn. A Seracyd rescued the last Vexen and killed one of her captors. But the other escaped...

"The degi named Pel tells Ezit of her presence in Vex. The degi named Pel knows of the Vexen's magic; it runs in his veins. He is the only living vampire to have drank Vexen blood."

What?

When I first touched the Hellastone, I realized I wasn't the total sum of Vex's magic.

That's where the rest of my magic is—with one of my captors?

I raise my hands, prepared to pull off my blindfold and scream with all my might.

"The Seracyd dwells with her now in Hella; where Dexa was born, where Bathsheba was born, where Axerxa was born.

"This is the wisdom I pass onto you, Helisent: the future of Vex lies in your hands.

"This knowledge is yours to do with as you see fit."

The story ends with three quick drumbeats.

Then I'm on my feet, tugging off the blindfold as panic shoots into my veins. I turn away from the gorgons immediately—I have at least that much sense.

"He bit me?" I shout into the plaza. My words echo off the walls. "When the *fuck* did he bite me?"

"Put your blindfold back on," Accra chastises. "Control yourself."

Suddenly, it clicks—

My memories from the ship are shrouded in darkness—but I vaguely remember the party that preceded that hell. I remember following Butter downstairs... and I remember a weird-looking hesperide—

He knew me.

'You don't remember me?' he'd asked. *'From Cadmium?'*

I reel back and scream as loudly as I can. I set my hands on my hips and pace, pivoting on my heels. I ignore the clump of gorgon shapes in my periphery.

"The degi can't cast your magic, Helisent. *Control yourself.*" I can't tell if Accra's tone is amused or impatient. "When a vampire drinks your blood, you become their familiar. They can sense things about you, like where you are and whether you're healthy. Nothing more."

I cover my face with my hands, forgetting the blindfold that's caught between my fingers. I face the gorgons and try to lower my voice. "Then he can find me here, Accra. The House of Col controls him. He's a degivampire. He'll lead them *straight here*."

Accra makes a pensive sound. "Ezit knows these caves. They've never forgotten where Vex's Landmark is. They would have figured out you were here whether Pel survived to tell them or not. Why do you panic? They will offer gifts before they attack. There is no need to prepare for war right now."

Right now...

But eventually.

I rub my face, then angle it upward. I open my eyes and stare at Hella's pitted entrance where sunlight streams below. For a split second, the cave-city feels like a quiet tomb.

I let out a long breath and try to calm down for Accra's sake. "I'm just..."

Just freaking the fuck out.

Axerxa didn't survive this... how will I? I don't know that I would choose annihilation over coercion.

I shuffle back toward the gorgons, ram a knee into the stone fountain with a curse, then use its circular border to guide me back to where the women sit with my eyes clamped shut. I hand off the blindfold, extending my arm.

My breaths stutter in my chest, palms sweating as the gorgons refit their blindfolds.

When Halcyon and I arrived in Hella, our focus was on developing my skills as a witch—quickly, to avoid any conflict or run-ins with Ezit. Now, there's a group of expectant Mieirans below. I haven't addressed them yet, but it's not hard to imagine why they're here.

They want the okeanids.

"Accra," I whisper, "can I ask you something?"

"Many call upon Accra and Acet for their foresight; you may request our wisdom now."

Acet; that's the male counterpart to Accra and the matriarchs. "I don't need any foresight—just your opinion. I mean, you're long-lived in Vex. If I go... if I go to Ezit... and try to save the okeanids... even though I'm just me... what happens?"

She makes a low noise. "I will share with you the wisdom of Accra: what comes next will destroy you, Vexen."

The matriarchs sit before me with their blindfolds in place. Their chins are raised, their jaws aligned perfectly in my direction.

'What comes next will destroy you.'

Before I can curse Accra for cursing me, she goes on, "Like I said, Vexen, fate meets us halfway."

And then she smiles, wide and genuine. The Accras-in-waiting do the same, but I have no idea which of the matriarch's cryptic words they find amusing.

I stare at Accra, features bunching with distress.

Panic drums through my body.

"Halcyon says the okeanids in Ezit can't be saved," I reason. "And if you say that what comes next destroys me... then it would be stupid to go to the city."

Talk me out of it, Accra. I'm begging you.

Instead, she says, "When your people died, my people kept these words alive. When there were no Vexen left, we told the stories so that, someday, Vex could take form again." Accra raises her eyebrows. "The okeanids are beings of light. We have met many before. We tell their stories, too. In case there are no more left one day."

I clear my throat.

Suddenly, I realize why the gorgons came.

They aren't here to check in on the Mieirans or make sure that I found Hella.

They're here to gauge what I'll do now that I've been reacquainted with Vex. Now that the final Vexen has returned after being driven out hundreds of years before.

Fuck. Fuck, fuck, fuck.

My body tells me I can't go to Ezit; my hands shake, my palms sweat, my heart leaps into my throat. My body understands the risks immediately—right in this plaza, hundreds of miles from the nearest threat.

And my mind is a blackened chamber full of stacked, forgotten memories. My mind is happy to stay shrouded in darkness.

I stare at Accra, jaw clenching.

The truths start piling up quickly, and I hate each more than the last.

Clearbold banished me from Velm after the incident in Alita. The Class marooned me in some outpost in Jaws. But the nymphs didn't banish me. The local nymphs bartered with me and Onesimos and Esclamonde; some even brought gifts.

And before that, throughout my life, I've been sought out by demigods. My papa said the first one greeted me before I could walk. They offered gifts for all they sought from me; even-handed gifts. Rubies, on one occasion.

Could I really turn away from the okeanids?

Especially when I'm the only Mieiran here who understands Ezit's evil on a personal level.

When I'm already so close to where they're being held.

When I'm their only chance at escape.

Like she can hear my internal capitulation, Accra goes on, "I've already done you a great service in writing to Vic and Zeu the Chosen. I wrote the news of your return. Vic and Zeu lead the most powerful vampire dens in Zarzynn, free of Ezit. They will have advice for you. Expect their arrival with the dusk. Listen for drums and chanting."

I scratch my previous theory—Accra isn't here to see what I'll do.

It sounds like she already knew what I'd say.

(And to think I used to fear the prophecies of selkies.)

With a grunt, Accra shifts to put her hands on her knees. "Help me stand. My back hurts."

I help Accra rise, then stoop to help the rest of the matriarchs back onto their feet. I cast a spell to dust them clean like I saw Halcyon do in the village. Like then, they don't bat a lash at the graze of magic.

I take Accra's hand. This time, I hold *hers* in the hopes of demonstrating an appropriate arrangement. "Will you stay and rest?"

"We will stay for a week." Accra adjusts our hands as we head back toward the city center. Given I'm outmatched in terms of size and strength, my fingers are swiftly crushed again.

"Okay. I'll help you get settled... but I need to talk with my people first. I spoke with you before I spoke with them. Can you and your Accras-in-waiting manage on your own?"

Accra grunts. "Take your people into a room without windows, and we will be free to find our own arrangements in Hella."

"Fine. Anything else, my dear gorgon?"

She makes a pensive noise. "You didn't react to my prophecy. So you must already know there are two types of fate."

Two types of fate? I can barely handle the regular type. "Let's pretend there's only one type of fate I need to worry about for now, Accra. At least until I have a drink."

She smiles keenly. "The vodka helps, doesn't it?"

"Not nearly enough. Not anymore."

Especially not if I have two separate fates to contend with.

CHAPTER 8

QUEEN OF NIGHT

SAMSON

My grandson,
There is one part of my soul that has never sought guidance. What does
Samsonfang tell you? Sutnazzarfang thinks she's the true Afador. Sometimes, I
think she's right.

Helisent paces in front of us in an empty hall.

Her hands clench her hips as she stares at the ground, pivoting back and forth.

Three tiers of limestone benches line half the room, but they're mostly vacant. Only Eos and Aura sit down beside Rex and Berevald in the windowless hall where the witch led us a few minutes ago.

The rest of us loiter around, waiting for her to speak. Her linen layers float behind her; one near her hip and another at her back. The strips of fabric leave part of her belly exposed, along with her arms and collar and most of her legs. Her ala drifts around the room, distracting me.

It's hard not to stare at her.

Not to go up and smell her hair behind her ear.

Part of me isn't really scared of the consequences; I'd gladly trade a sturdy slap for a proper sniff. Then there's her face. I want to run my finger down the high arch of her nose, kiss her round cheeks, her soft lips.

I study the walls to distract myself.

Like most locations in Hella, red tiles partly cover them. They form clouds where the walls curve into the sloped ceiling.

The red witch paces beneath them, looking conflicted.

She hasn't said much since the gorgons shuffled down an alleyway twenty minutes ago. She and Halcyon exchanged a few tense words in Zarzyd outside. At first, I'd been flabbergasted that Helisent had picked up on the language during her brief time here.

Then I remembered a story about an oread named Onesimos teaching Helisent fire magic. Through something called sympathetic magic, also known as sex magic.

I cross my arms, staring between the witch and her lover.

The warlock stares at Helisent with displeasure. His jaw clicks, brow bending with each passing second.

Helisent stops pacing in the middle of the room. She brushes her hair out of her face, glancing across the row of Mieirans. "Welcome to Vex, everyone. Just so we're on the same page, *Vex is mine*. The Class's authority means nothing here. Neither does the Kulapsifang's." She shrugs, glancing at Hemlock. "I won't curse the nymphs or their demigods. We're in good standing still."

The witch already clarified that I'm in *her* realm this morning. Sliding onto my knees to beg her to lift the banishment violated every instinct in me; Alphas don't bow, don't stoop, don't kneel. But Helisent exercising her power over me felt ...

I don't know what it felt like, but it was a good feeling.

Relief, maybe.

It floods me again now.

Take charge, Helisent.

"I know you're here for the okeanids." The witch's eyes dart across the group. "So, here's what's going to happen next. Halcyon and I have made a binding agreement that he and four others will receive passage to Mieira. Don't ask who he's bringing. It's none of your business."

She pivots toward Halcyon, who still frowns. "And Halcyon, you will order four *large* ships to be built in Plet. Whatever magical resources you need to make that happen, ask."

"We don't barter dove," the warlock quips. "I need *coins*."

Helisent rolls her eyes. "How many?"

"Thousands. And then, we'll need to pay more in bribes so the builders keep our secret. If word gets out that there's a fleet of ships going to Mieira, half the island will try to board them."

"Fine. I'll get you a million coins." She turns away from the warlock and looks at Hemlock. "I don't know if Halcyon broke the good news, but a bunch of okeanids have escaped Ezit. They started their own settlement in Stretch called New Hypnos. We'll sail them home with us, too.

"Halcyon says the journey to Meira can only be taken via phoenix light. But we don't really have time to find a phoenix and wait for it to fly back home. My papa said an okeanid demigod saved you—so, maybe we'll get lucky on the way back, too.

"If not, I'll make phoenix light. I'll find our way back."

She takes a deep breath. "Halcyon already told you about the other five Houses in Zarzynn. They want me for a variety of reasons. Lucky for us, Accra thinks the Houses aren't going to wage war with me immediately, which means we have some time."

Halcyon buries his face in his hands. He seethes something at Helisent in Zarzyd.

I stare at him, my anger boiling.

I'd liked him enough last night—

Now, he seems extremely displeased and unpleasant. *What happened with the gorgons? What did Helisent tell him outside?*

Parsifal also studies Halcyon from the corner of his eye. "Have time for what, Honey Baby?"

Helisent shrugs. "To figure out what to do to Ezit. How to get the nymphs. That's what everyone wants, isn't it? The precious okeanids. So, we'll go get them, then we'll pick up the nymphs in New Hypnos, and then we'll go home." She raises a hand when Kiekerline, Hemlock, and I step forward with questions. "And *when we get home*, I'll be expecting *full pardons* from Velm and the Class."

"You *cannot go to Ezit*," Halcyon cuts in with lethal calm. Instead of looking at Helisent, he turns to Parsifal. "There are tens of thousands of wielders there. The leaders of Ezit control their House's spellwork and they train their whole lives in the art of killing. *Your daughter will not come back from Ezit.*"

Parsifal looks at Halcyon, throat bobbing.

Though his words are enough to make me reconsider our goals in Zarzynn, Helisent doesn't look frightened. Instead, the witch's eyes bleed with red light. Her olive-brown skin doesn't deviate in color, but I know she must be hitting a high emotional level if her eyes are glowing.

They almost cross as she hisses, "I have been half-dead before. Full death won't be nearly as unpleasant. The nymphs are coming home with *me*. And if Ezit does not hand them over," her voice raises to a shout, "I will break their hands and slit their throats and *take what is mine*. It is all *mine*."

I can't tell if I'm afraid or enamored. Likely both. Afraid for Ezit, afraid for the witch, for all of us tangled in this game. I'm enamored by her raw power, her wrath, her stubborn unwillingness to let Halcyon influence her.

How she puts her hand on her hip. How soft her hair looks.

I want her to make me beg for—

Focus, Samson.

Kierkeline laughs, low and cool. "I will go to Ezit with you. I am willing to die, Helisent West of Jaws, so long as you give me your word that you will take Butter back to Ultramarine. To my daughter, Eleve-nine Ultramarine."

Helisent raises her eyebrows; the red from her eyes starts to fade gradually. "I'll take all of them home."

Hemlock jumps in next, puffing his chest out and gesturing with a hand. "As you've heard, the okeanid demigod saved our ship on the way here. But in the event it's gone home, how will your magic save our ship?"

Helisent purses her lips while she considers the question. "I'll carry the ships above the clouds and we'll sail the sky home. A cloud is water, too. How does that sound?"

Hemlock raises his burly, emerald eyebrows. "It's certainly imagi-native. I'll try to come up with a few spare ideas."

Halcyon tries one more time. "You are the *last* Vexen, you *cannot*—"

Helisent barks something back in Zarzyd, and the warlock goes silent.

She directs her feral gaze at me next; my insides melt with anxiety and adoration. "And what about the wolves? Will you help us free the okeanids from Ezit?"

I promised to make Ezit regret hurting Helisent; I can only do that inside the city. But... "As wolves, we would be more helpful on a triplemoon."

Otherwise, I'm just a man with a throwing axe and a good sense of smell—still very passionate and focused, if less deadly.

Helisent huffs, a cruel smile on her lips. "You'll also be a wild animal on the full moon. That wouldn't be very helpful, would it?"

A wild animal?

My facial features tighten as a thousand insults flood my mind.

Her stupid little hand on her hip. Dumb hair. Least intimidating glare on the planet.

A wild animal—really?

Rude.

She moves on without a second glance in my direction. "Accra said she sent word to the vampires that I'm here. There are two dens that live in Vex, free of Ezit. One belongs to Vic the Chosen. The other belongs to Zeu the Chosen. Halcyon says the free vampires hate the degivampires and Ezit. I'm sure they'll help us free the okeanids. Like I said, we have time.

"My magic isn't strong enough for me to waltz into Ezit. Not quite yet. So, get comfortable. I need a few more weeks. You guys can hash out a plan in the meantime."

The triplemoon is in six and a half weeks.

I'll make sure she waits until then; I even have a doublemoon beforehand to endear her to Samsonfang and convince her (for a second time) that he isn't a wild animal.

But I don't tell Helisent that. I hold my tongue while the witch studies us.

She asks, "Anything else?"

Though our silence is heavy, it doesn't feel defeated.

And it seems we finally have a clear leader in our ranks.

She turns her chin up and waltzes from the long hall, her papa trailing her. Aura and Eos are close behind, vicious smiles on their lips.

And then there's Kierkeline and her equally cruel visage; instead of following Helisent and the okeanids, she directs her sneer at Halcyon.

Over the next week, life in Hella grows easier.

Like we did on the ship, the group finds a rhythm between responsibilities and leisure. The gorgons speak a bit of Mieiran, which helps us battle the long nights with stories—and the gorgons enjoy these exchanges. Eos and Aura quickly find their place with the women, listening to and telling tales in equal measure.

Meanwhile, Halcyon's only acknowledgment that the group will be going to Ezit is teaching Kiekerline, Absalom, and Parsifal the forms of killing magic that he knows. They work in Hella's eastern streets where their infrasound won't disturb me, Rex, and Berevald.

Like me and my packmates, Hemlock spends most of his time in the woods above Hella.

The living forest starts to feel more familiar. Within one week, our footpaths and alas riddle the forest. Me and my packmates have left our scents around the cave; the territory has been marked thoroughly, which helps us rest easier.

I know where the animals roost and graze; I even know their names.

Alpacas are the long-necked relatives of saigas.

Raccoons are striped cousins of sables.

The badgers are identical in ala and bearing.

Hemlock doesn't hunt the creatures with throwing axes like Rex, Berevald, and I. Instead, he makes his own paths between the trees, which lead to fruit and nut groves, to freshwater streams, to pines with enough kindling needles to burn down the world.

Though his demigod lives far away in Rhotidom, Hemlock soon learns the rhythm of Vex's forest. He even stumbles upon a midden of fig trees ready for harvest, which he and the okeanids collect to start distilling into fruit wine.

But the king keeps to himself.

And I do the same.

For the first few days in Vex, I stay with Rex and Berevald. We explore the pine barrens; we lament the seeming lack of tobacco growing here.

But hunting in a pack is always more difficult, and soon we want our own space; wolves roam a great territory.

I'm happy to be alone with my thoughts most days.

With my daydreams of the red witch.

One afternoon, I realize I'm not alone in the forest.

I duck behind a boulder, peeking out to see what's coming and whether I can kill it, skin it, and roast it. With so many loose limestone pebbles and fallen branches, only Vex's birds are safe from my axe.

I tighten my grip on the leather handle of my weapon.

I shift my stance to prepare to sling it toward my prey.

I wait for a long time; I don't hear another sound, even though I swear I heard footsteps. I cross deeper into the shadow that falls from the limestone boulder.

Until the shadow starts to fizzle with infrasound; it almost feels like boiling water.

I back away, staring at the shadow cast by the mossy limestone.

I jolt backward, my shoulder blades hitting an adjacent boulder as something steps out of the shadow. The darkness parts as though it were a doorway with a black curtain hanging across it.

I don't know how to describe it—

Just that I'm staring at a shadow, and then a being is stepping out of the shadow, and that being is Helisent West of Jaws.

She bellows when she sees me, opening her mouth wide enough that I could count her teeth. She staggers backward as we lock eyes.

Her gaze flashes to the axe in my hand. "Put that thing down, you psycho!"

It slips from my hand and clatters on the limestone at my feet. *"Holy shit."*

How did she do that?

My spine straightens with total shock.

Helisent blinks up at me, just as startled. Her hair drifts to her waist, where one of the linen strips hugs her skin. The strips hold her ala well, sending it around the cave to haunt me day and night.

"Where did you—*how?*" I stutter.

At the same time, she says, "My *moons*, why are you so large and violent?" She looks from my axe to my face, then back again.

She breaks my heart with similar insults at least once a day, but part of me is thankful. At least she's spirited as ever. Whatever happened on that ship didn't break her.

It was the first thing I thought when I woke up to her throwing cold water over me—

At least she's still *her*.

"I'm hunting." I'm not sure how to hold myself. We're standing between tall boulders, which seal us into a tight space. A space I know Helisent would have found threatening when we first met last year.

I keep my back pressed against the rocks. She floats to take a seat on the outcropping. It puts her just a bit taller than me.

"Right." She studies her nails after sitting down, then clears her throat. "There are some things I don't remember that I thought you might remember. You know, since you claim we were friends." She tosses her hair over her shoulder. "It's about a vampire."

My gut clenches.

"*Tell me.*" She levels one of her pointers at me. "I can see it in your beady little eyes—you know something."

I try to find the words, picking at flakes of moss on the boulder.

"One of the Accras-in-waiting said there's a vampire with my magic in Ezit. And... one of them knew me. One of the vampires from the ship. I guess that means he bit me—but I can't—I mean—I don't remember when it happened. I also don't seem to have any bite marks..."

"He bit you in Cadmium." I force the words out so she won't keep rambling about being bitten. (I'll make Ezit regret that, too.)

Her gaze falls. She clears her throat. "Did he look like a hesperide? That's how he looked on the ship."

I take a deep breath. I study the canopy, the tangle of pine barren around us. It's easier than meeting her eyes and dwelling on what happened. "Exactly. He disguised himself as a hesperide."

I'm not sure how much she wants to know.

"And what? He jumped out of nowhere and bit me?"

"No. You took him home and into your bed. He asked to bite you, and you said yes. He didn't tell you that he was going to drink your blood. You thought that he meant it in a more... casual sense."

The witch stares blankly into the distance. With each second, her face scrunches into a mask of rage. Soon, red light trickles from her glowing eyes, just like the other day in Hella. I study the red of her irises, the exact shade that oozes light into the forest.

I go on, "A selkie had warned us about an unknown being in Mieira. We hadn't realized it was a vampire. We didn't know what they were at the time—just that you'd been bitten by something that drank blood."

"My necklace..." she murmurs, finger pressed against her lip.

I nod. "It was covered in blood."

Her eyes flash to mine. She nods back.

I remember how baffling it was to heal after Alita and tend to a wound whose infliction I couldn't recall. How disturbing it was to not remember the violence done to me.

Helisent sighs as the red light from her eyes slowly dissolves. "And I told you what happened with the vampire?"

I'm happy she seems to trust me, even if I wish we could talk about anything else. With each second, her bearing becomes more relaxed. Her shoulders slump and she tugs one of her linen layers into her lap.

"You did. I cleaned the wound. You couldn't do it yourself because it was on your neck where you couldn't see."

She scratches her chin. "And we ran into a selkie on our little... adventure?"

"We did. You didn't like her very much."

"Because they're whores and liars."

For the first time since we arrived, I let myself smile. "Exactly."

As soon as I smile, Helisent frowns. With a sigh, she floats back down between the boulders to stand before me. I glance at the shadow, wondering if she's going to disappear into the same place she appeared.

What the fuck kind of spell is that?

She sets her hand on her hip. "You should be careful out here, you know. Vic the Chosen sent a reply to Accra. She's bringing her den to Hella. They're going to Ezit with us."

I study the golden light that falls in beams from the canopy. Tiny flecks of dust float through them, suspended like stars in the sky. "I thought they were allergic to the sun."

"Who knows?" Helisent raises her chin like she's threatening me. "Maybe that's just what they want us to think."

She takes a step back toward the shadow. She looks at the axe at my feet, then into my eyes.

She backs into the shadow before I can ask another question.

I stare at the black gulf sheltered between the limestone boulders.

I reach into it. My fingers knock into the boulder's cool and flaky surface. I pull back and stare at them.

One week later, Accra and her matriarchs-in-waiting wander toward us with full satchels slung over their backs.

We loiter around the freshwater fountain. A spread of fruit, honeyed millet, and fried fat sits on large wooden platters between us. We've started to opt for smaller meals throughout the day given our fluctuating food supplies. Between our hunting and foraging, our stockpile has grown—but not nearly enough for comfort.

As late afternoon turns into evening, we sit down for what Berevald calls Dinner One. Some nights, we make it all the way to Dinner Three... though that's usually a private meal for the wolves. And, if he hasn't guzzled himself to sleep, Parsifal.

Accra and the three Accras-in-waiting stop ten feet from our meal. Over the last week, they've shuffled into our circle and taken a place eating alongside the nymphs.

They seem disproportionately familiar given the short stint of time. Part of me chalks it up to their quiet and thoughtful demeanor, another part to the language barrier; it's hard to disagree when we can't communicate easily.

Accra opens her hand toward Halcyon. She barks a word at him, which gets the warlock stepping away from his meal of millet and fruit. Accra hands him her bag, then Halcyon takes it to our spread of food.

He squats and pulls linen strips from Accra's satchel, which he uses to bundle away most of the meal. Berevald watches at my side with a tsk, which Rex quickly mirrors. (I haven't filled my plate, but I've been eyeing which pieces I want to claim.)

Halcyon slides his eyes toward us three. "The gorgons are returning to Dexerxes. They'll get hungry along the way."

Eos and Aura lean toward Halcyon and offer the rest of their untouched figs and grapes. With a gracious smile, he accepts the fruit and tucks it into Accra's sturdy bag.

Helisent, recently returned from a day with the Hellastone, eats alone away from the group. She lounges on her back, one leg hiked over the other as she stares into Hella's pitted entrance above. Outside, the cerulean sky darkens. She munches on small, dark figs, licking her fingers and sighing.

When she turns her head, I immediately look down at my meal.

'I can see it in your beady little eyes.'

The witch looks past me, toward Halcyon. She gestures toward the cave's eastern network of tunnels where the gorgons entered last week. "I already said goodbye to the Accras. I gave them gifts, too. I'm going back to the Hellastone in a minute."

I eye the gorgons' bags. The other evening during a particularly chatty dinner, we exchanged gifts with the women. We handed over the few items salvaged from our wrecked ship, including Mieiran paintings and jewelry. On behalf of Velm, I offered Accra four pieces of carved marble. I'd brought them north on my tour to offer as gifts to important acquaintances I made with my pack; I'd brought them across the sea with a similar purpose in mind.

Halcyon glances at Helisent where she lounges; he doesn't respond. He finishes packing Accra's bag, stands up, and hooks his arm through the matriarch's. Without a glance back at the fountain, he steers the women toward Hella's closest exit.

Since Helisent announced her plans to rescue the okeanids from Ezit, the pair don't seem as close. They stand farther apart, they speak in neutral tones, and their alas aren't nearly as layered when they drift from their shared room.

Unless that's just hopeful thinking on my part.

Accra turns back once and offers one of her loaded, knowing smiles. The rest of the matriarchs follow suit with spooky precision. "Goodbye, Vexen," the gorgons say.

Helisent shouts a goodbye. Then the women turn to follow Halcyon. The gorgons shuffle behind him, a few inches taller than the apex of his curved horns.

I realize it's my chance to catch him alone.

I hand my plate to Rex. "I'll be right back."

Rex shifts, as though prepared to stand and follow me. "Where?"

Berevald glances over his shoulder toward the warlock and the gorgons. "Why?"

"I have a few questions," I whisper.

The pair blink at me, baffled. Near the rest of the group, I don't want to say I plan on cornering Halcyon to ask him about the possibility of Imperatriz being on Plet. To see if he knows how to get to Pit if she isn't.

Berevald gets it first. "*Oh*. Got it. I'll explain to Rex."

I nod, then hustle after the warlock and the gorgons. By the time they come into view, the group is almost to Hella's portal.

Like the rest of the subterranean passages, this tunnel sits inside a grand, single-story building. The vestibule matches the rest of the street, with tall window frames and red tiles—except that it ends in a single gulf of shadow.

Though shaped like a door, the frame is filled with a darkness that deposits us in the forest above with a brush of magic. I imagine it's the same form of magic that allows Helisent to leap into one shadow and out of another.

Halcyon's expression falls with obvious disdain when he notices my approach, but Accra's lips pull into another signature smile. The smile intimates that she knew this moment was coming; that she knows what's about to happen next.

That she might have orchestrated this moment to be in the right place at the right time.

(And maybe none of that is true. Maybe Accra just likes to smile.)

Halcyon scans me from head to toe. "I hope you're not coming to ask them to return a gift."

I brandish a plain smile, trying not to be offended. "Of course not. I'd like to speak with you alone. I'll help you see the gorgons off."

To my great pleasure, Accra lifts her hand from Halcyon's forearm as I meet the group outside the portal room. The matriarch reaches toward me, and I extend my arm to oblige.

Halcyon continues forward. "Wonderful." He leads us into the vestibule. Red tiles surround the door-shaped gulf, bleeding outward onto the pale limestone.

We step into the hum of infrasound. In a single stride, the shadow surrounds us, grazing my body like a breathy sigh.

And then we're staring at a mossy pine barren where the last traces of light filter through the canopy.

I step onto the grass, littered with limestone pebbles, and head toward the dirt path to our left. Accra lifts her chin as we move southward in the direction of Dexerxes.

Her thick fingers tap my forearm. "Thank you, Samson."

I wish I knew enough Zarzyd to respond in her tongue. "You are welcome, Accra."

The youngest Accra calls to Halcyon in Zarzyd, then gestures to a twisted gum tree ten feet away. The warlock lets out a sound of delight as he heads toward the three clay jugs nestled in the grass at the base of the trunk.

He makes a comment that goads laughter from all four Accras. The women link arms and adjust their full satchels, smiles lingering. Then they line up on the dirt path that heads south, falling in line and walking in tandem.

Without another word, they set off.

As the sun sinks into the horizon, a breeze breaks the humid air, sending the leaves and grass shivering. Gold from the gilded sunset twinkles on the ground between the shadows of the pine trees. Cicadas start their nightly chorus, accented by the grasshoppers hiding in the brush.

Halcyon lifts one of the jugs, tugs off its fabric top, then tilts his head back to drink. He sets it down with a happy sigh, then wipes his mouth with the collar of his gray tunic.

He leans back against the tree's trunk to study me.

Beneath the shadow of the gum tree, his indigo skin has never looked more foreign or vibrant.

I can tell by how he speaks to Parsifal that he's worried about Helisent's safety. I can tell by how he speaks to the witch that he thinks she's in over her head. And I can tell by how he avoids the rest of us that he doesn't trust Mieirans.

But he spends his days teaching Absalom, Kiekerline, and Parsifal killing magic. He spends the evenings telling the okeanids about New Hypnos, about the okeanid-wielder children that populate the island more each year. He wakes in the mornings and sits quietly near the fountain, staring around in wonder like this experience might be novel and slightly terrifying for him, too.

(He isn't bad, and it's good he's here, and I still hate him.)

As I prepare to ask about Plet and Imperatriz, he narrows his eyes at me. "I wouldn't worry about it, Samson. I'm not interested in *the possibility*."

I glance at the gorgons; Accra's salt-and-pepper hair slips out of view amid the trees. Even if they understood basic Mieiran, they wouldn't be able to hear our conversation from the distance.

I turn back to Halcyon and give him the once-over. "The possibility of what?"

He stoops to pick up the jug and drink again. This time, he doesn't set it back in the grass. "The Male Host. *Helisent's* Male Host. Aren't you here to threaten me?"

I blink at him, confused. "What?"

The last thing I want is a rift between us. At least, for now. (In the future, I might welcome it with gusto.)

The warlock tilts his head, as though just as bewildered as me. "You're in love with Helisent. I'm not stupid."

I figured he'd put that much together the first night we spoke. Parsifal and Rex are the only beings whom I've told, but I imagine that Kierkeline, Absalom, and Berevald all suspect something romantic happened between me and Helisent last year.

'The Male Host.'

He's talking about the fact that Helisent must continue the Vexen line.

I glance at the jugs at his feet, desperate for a drink.

Though I hate to admit it, I say, "You'd probably be a good choice compared to her other options."

Halcyon knows killing magic. His scars and scuffed horns hint that he knows how to survive. And he was the one who freed Helisent from the ship where she laid with broken hands.

Not me.

In my silence, Halcyon goes on in a low, direct tone. "I *can't*, Samson. It's impossible."

I narrow my eyes. It would be a little forward to tell him I've smelled his semen on several occasions—but I don't really understand how infertility works. I suppose a man can still produce semen and be infertile.

"You... *can't?*" I ask.

His chin lowers—not with shame but for the sake of clarity. "*Impossible*, Samson."

I bite back a smile. I also won't be fathering Helisent's babies, but at least I *could.*

"No need to threaten me. Save it for another warlock—or for Zeu the Chosen. His mother was named Heb, you know. Short for Bathsheba." Then he smiles, wide and fake.

I set my hands on my hips. *Save it for Zeu the Chosen? What does the name Heb mean—and who is Bathsheba?*

I shake my head—I'll worry about that later. "I wanted to talk to you about something else."

I clear my throat, trying to phrase my appeal about Imperatriz and New Hypnos. Multiple starts pop into my head, but none seem right. I guess they won't, considering I don't trust or understand Halcyon, and don't have the time for a more diplomatic approach.

To my surprise, the warlock capitulates. "If you aren't going to threaten me, you can have a drink."

He picks up one of the jugs, then backs away from the gum tree. He goes straight to a slanted rock and sits down. He jerks his chin toward the remaining containers, nestled in the grass.

I head to the gum tree and take a large gulp of the bitter liquor. Though the flavor is better than Velmic moonshine, it still bites.

It gives me the courage to start this conversation.

"Have you been to New Hypnos—often?" I ask.

He taps the ceramic jug and nods. It's the first time I've seen him nod at the correct time. "Yes. It's close to the city. I work with sailors, and sailors work with the okeanids in New Hypnos. It's how I know the vampires, too. Zeu the Chosen frees okeanids, then we take them to New Hypnos. I've met him and Vic before—many times."

"But the actual settlement of New Hypnos... have you been there a lot?" I clarify, "I'm asking if you know the residents who live there."

"I learned Mieiran in New Hypnos, which took a while. And I have friends who settled down with an okeanid. They share children. Wielders and okeanids move freely between the city and New Hypnos." He shifts, eyebrows bunching. "Why do you ask?"

"I'm asking about a wolf, Halcyon. Not an okeanid. Her name is Imperatriz." I clear my throat. "She's my mother."

He sits back on the boulder. Once again, he surprises me. Rather than dangle the information over my head, his features fall. "I have never seen any being like you or Rex or Berevald. I would remember that. And New Hypnos isn't home to many. No one gets lost living there. As far as I know, there are no others who look like your kind in Zarzynn." He looks away, then glances back at me. "But that doesn't mean she isn't somewhere else in Stretch. There are dozens of islands. The largest is Plet, then Silt, then Pit.

"Silt and Pit sit hidden in massive gulfs of fog. No one knows how to find them, aside from a select few degis and wielders. But that's the thing about Plet. It's full of spies, and mercenaries, and outcasts alike. Some find their way back into a House's good graces—and some sail to Stretch's smaller islands to be of service to them."

He sighs, chewing on his words. "What I'm telling you, Samson, is that maybe someone saw a wolf. If not on Plet, then on Silt or Pit. Almost everyone has a price in Plet. Loyalty can be bought and sold— with coins. The coins we use as money. For the right price... maybe someone would take you to the other islands."

My heart sinks.

I take another drink, trying to rein in my sudden hopelessness. I can't explain why it returns so strongly; Rex, Berevald, and I assumed Imperatriz would be on Pit, like Anesot said in Alita.

Hoping she had made it to Plet was a pipe dream.

But to have come this far... and to still be so disconnected from her...

Seventeen years will soon become eighteen.

"I can ask someone to look for information about her," Halcyon suggests quietly. "If you like."

"No. I agree—you would remember. Someone would remember." I force down a deep breath. Though I appreciate his offer, I don't want anyone whose loyalty can be traded like a coin involved in this search. "One of the wielders responsible for kidnapping her was named Anesot. He told me she was on Pit, but Helisent killed him before I could make a deal for her freedom. That's why I came to Zarzynn. I need to find a way to that island, Halcyon."

Halcyon's nose curls. "*Anesot* kidnapped your mother?"

It boils my blood. I *hate* the warlock for manipulating me in Alita; I hate myself for bowing to his maneuvering. "The warlock has committed many crimes in Mieira and Velm."

Halcyon leans toward me. "Then why banish the witch for killing him? Why not banish *Anesot* for his crimes?"

"Because my *father* is the Male Alpha of Velm. I'm not the one who banishes wielders and nymphs. Not for another twenty years."

Halcyon makes a low noise. For a long time, he studies me through narrowed eyes. We sip from the jugs as birds hoot overhead, as the cicadas and grasshoppers sing on. Part of me wants to ask how he knows Anesot; the rest of me would rather not know.

Eventually, he says, "Well, no man is his father. And why did

Anesot kidnap your mother? Why isn't your father here looking for her?"

Because my father wants to destroy the Afador line and replace it with his own name.

Leofsige.

I scratch my chin. "It's complicated."

Halcyon smiles without humor. "Everything is complicated now, isn't it?"

For the first time, I wonder if Halcyon is entangled in this situation for a higher goal than Helisent's love. I know she promised him passage to Mieira with four others, who I assume are his immediate family. But I have no idea who he is or what his life has been like up until this point.

If he *isn't* here to prove his worth as a potential Male Host for Vex, then...

All the conclusions I've been building in my mind no longer apply.

Halcyon slides off the slanted rock and stands up. "Grab the other jugs. Let's pretend they left one for the group. I won't ask where you take yours."

He turns for the portal while I stoop to grab the third jug. From the forest, the passage looks like little more than a shadowy pit tucked inside a hillock of limestone boulders. A tangle of dry vines half-obscures the entrance, which spews gusts of cold air straight from the streets below.

I trail the warlock to the portal.

He pauses at the last second and looks over his shoulder at me. In a hushed tone, he tells me, "Anesot was the first warlock who broke my hands in a rosarium box. He almost did the same to someone I love. He is dead, but he remains my enemy. Always." He pauses again, and I wait. "Accra told Helisent that Pel was the degivampire who drank her blood. He's the one who escaped. He's in Ezit now. I'd also wager he was the one who broke her hands given he's her familiar."

Pel.

It's a relief to hear his name. Before, he was a wraith who bit my witch and broke her hands. Now, he has a name, an identity, a form that I can punish.

"Pel works for House of Col. When Pel and Jen sailed together, one knew the way to Silt and the other to Pit." Halcyon leans closer to me. "I heard Pel knows the way to Pit."

He looks at me with wrath pitting his dark eyes.

I stare down, caught in their indigo threads.

Would I let Pel live for a chance to find Pit? Would I really be willing to defend another vile being who has hurt the witch for a chance to find Imperatriz?

Doubt takes root in me.

I made that choice once before—but I'm not sure if I'd make it again.

With another sigh, Halcyon turns and steps into the tunnel.

My shoulders lift as I catch a strange, terrible ala on the breeze. I recognize the twang from Helisent's necklace north of Cadmium. From the first vampire I ever scented.

It's different now because there are quite a few.

At least ten.

I freeze, hand braced on the rock.

They smell like *blood*; iron, salt, and protein. It's not fresh blood, either... it's thicker, more potent, and filled with testosterone and endorphins.

I smell hair next; their own hair, as well as fox furs, alpaca furs, raccoon furs, badger furs, and two other mammals I've never smelled before.

I smell caked dirt—but I can tell by the scent of the hides and furs that they're kept rigorously clean.

And feathers.

I smell a *lot* of feathers.

Halcyon scans me, then looks into the shadowy forest behind me.

A flock of white birds shoots into the sky, screeching as they flee. Then comes the sound of drumming and singing. It's so faint that I wonder if I'm imagining it; the drumming is quick, the chanting less distinct.

"Helisent said the wolves can smell everything," Halcyon murmurs. "Do you smell feathers or copper? Let's hope for feathers. Copper comes from Ezit."

I stare into the forest as the drumming and singing get louder, as the shadows of night deepen and pool along the ground. "Feathers." I step away from the tunnel. I set the jug down and square up in the direction they advance.

I remind myself that I would recognize Pel's ala—and I can tell with certainty it's not amid the pack that approaches us.

Halcyon sighs with relief. "Good. Only the free vampires wear feathers. They must have come as soon as Accra sent word."

The warlock levels his gaze where the vampires' alas and noise come into sharper focus. He steps in front of me, then looks back. "Wolf—are you listening to me?"

I focus on the testosterone that flushes into my system. Though I continue to calm my mind by taking large breaths, my body is on alert.

I can tell by their alas that they're physically large and brawny.

With the doublemoon on the horizon, Samsonfang's voice is clearer than usual.

He reminds, **They bite.**

"I'm friends with the vampires. You have no reason to fear them." Halcyon waves a hand near my face, but I don't look away from the forest, eyes shifting across its shadows. "They're going to come into Hella whether we invite them or not, so relax. They're like nymphs, Samson. They're friends. And it's alpaca season. They follow the herds. They're nomads."

Though a well-built warlock, Halcyon isn't a giant. Like Absalom, he stands only to my chin. I stare over him as he pits himself between me and the incoming pack, scanning each shadow for movement.

And while the warlock may be speaking the truth, I won't relax until I get eyes on the encroachers.

Halcyon tsks as he studies me over his shoulder. "You look like you're preparing for a fight. *Do not* fight the vampires."

Past Halcyon's horns, I make out red feathers bobbing amid the foliage. Though tall and broad, the feathers are soft and wavering— not rigid like all the others I've ever seen. They flutter back and forth with each step. The drumbeats and singing grow louder.

The drums give off a deep boom, like those in Velm. The chanting is comparably slow and rhythmic.

Halcyon waves another hand near my face. "I'm sure it's Vic's den. Let me handle this. Her people don't speak Mieiran."

I swat his hand away. "Don't touch me."

"*Then relax,*" he hisses.

Halcyon turns around, then he glances back, expression tense.

On a single note, the drums and singing halt.

The shadows of dusk have tripled since the sun slipped past the horizon; I can't quite make out what's stalking toward us. All I hear are shifting leaves and needles, scraping branches. I see a few flashes of reddish orbs, which glow for a second before disappearing.

My nose twitches.

I count eleven vampires slinking through the darkness. The youngest is an adolescent. The oldest is nearing his one-hundredth birthday.

They huddle amid the dark treeline, ten feet away from us. I track their alas as they spread out, as though surrounding us.

Halcyon raises his hands, gesturing as he addresses the vampires in Zarzyd.

My senses strain. The burgeoning night cloaks the world in darkness, and the vampires move like they're part of it; like they followed the frontier of night straight to Hella.

A voice responds to Halcyon. I track it to a general area, then study the ala of the assumed speaker. She is female, the largest and healthiest in the group. Her tone is drawling, indolent, and curious— and it seems to be coming from above.

When she's done speaking, Halcyon concedes a half step back toward me.

He jabs a thumb over his shoulder. "Samson."

The female repeats my name. It rolls off her tongue like she's tasting it. And then the vampire descends from the canopy of the gum tree. Though I'd smelled her ala and gauged her place imprecisely, I hadn't heard the vampire climb the tree, hadn't noticed a flash of her eyes from its canopy, or heard the croaking of its branches under her weight.

Her ala washes like a wave through the air as she stares from ten feet away.

She's in her fifties, in her prime.

And I have no idea what I expected a vampire to look like, but it's not... this.

Her skin is pale and red-tinted. In Mieira, the cool, near-black skin of the okeanids is contrasted against the pale, milky tone of the wolves—but the vampires redefine that scale.

The vampires are pale in a way that makes me feel just as brown-skinned as Helisent.

I could count the blue-green veins under her skin, tangled like tree roots. Her reddish-golden hair dangles to her hips, a glittering hue I've never seen in my life. It's like a young flame that just caught the kindling, like the warmth of the robin's bellies.

Her eyes are slender and angled upward, more so than the hooded eyes common to the hesperides of Gamma. And the pupils within them are slitted vertically, like a snake's.

She's tall and brawny, like her ala hinted. She stands a few inches below me and, much like a female wolf or a gorgon like Accra, I would have to put considerable force behind any move meant to fall her.

She stands like she knows it, too.

The vampire shifts her weight onto her back foot. My eyes flash to her full lips, which pull back to show a normal-looking set of front teeth. A sliver of clean white fur dangles from her hips, cutting diagonally from one side to the other. She wears nothing beneath, leaving half of her pubic region visible.

A metallic diadem wraps around her forehead, where tall and soft feathers bob a foot above her head. Aside from the diadem and its feathers, she wears no top; her small and pointed breasts are bare. She wears two chunky bracelets of knuckle bones that jangle at her ankles.

She reminds me of an unnumbered wolf.

Undisciplined, lawless, untrustworthy.

Halcyon glances over his shoulder. He gestures from me to the vampire. "This is Vic the Chosen, Queen of Night."

Queen of Night?

He clears his throat. "What's your *official* title, again? I can't remember. Klopsy-boy of Velm?"

I ignore the warlock. I stare past him and tell the vampire, "I am Samson 714 Afador, son and Kulapsifang of Imperatriz 713 Afador, heir of Velm, of Night, of Hetnazzar."

The vampire strides toward us. With each decisive step, her feathers and breasts bounce.

Halcyon holds his position as the vampire stops in front of him. Like me, she stares past his horns, red-gold eyes leaping across my features. Her flat, wide nose twitches as she takes in my scent. All the while, the warlock stares ahead at her chest; Vic doesn't seem to mind.

Until she lifts a hand and palms Halcyon's cheek. It's not a strike, but once her palm is flat on his cheek, she shoves him out of her path.

Halcyon falls to the side, double-stepping to catch himself. He doesn't bark anything at Vic or look particularly shocked or embarrassed; he just fixes his hair as he stares at us, eyes wide.

I study Vic's face and try to decide on the wisest course of action if she tries to manhandle me in a similar fashion.

To be fair, Halcyon has explained that, similar to nymphs, vampires don't believe in personal property or personal space. They're apt to touch and taste their way through the world with the same emphasis on sensory investigation.

And though Halcyon explained that they bite for sustenance, not pleasure or dominance, the hairs on my arms and neck stand up in anticipation of a fight.

I don't want to fight a woman—but I refuse to be bitten.

Give me a third option, Vic.

My gut steels as Vic reaches for my right arm.

She speaks in Zarzyd as she prods my golden torc. She grabs my tunic near my solar plexus, pinching the fabric between her fingers. She does the same for my pants near my thigh, then she sidesteps to look behind me.

I half-turn to follow her, unenthused by the idea of her getting behind me; there are still ten vampires in front of me, and I'm not quite sure *where*. Plus the warlock.

Vic reaches up toward my bun at the nape of my neck. I draw the line there, taking her wrist with a gentle but firm grip.

I look at Halcyon. "Tell her that's enough with the touching."

For a second, he looks like he might try to talk me out of the statement.

Then he translates with a sheepish tone.

Vic the Chosen's features pinch with displeasure. She yanks her wrist out of my hand; I don't resist. She gestures toward the final sliver of orange light that dies in the west above the tall canopy.

Then she barks a sentence at me, loud enough that her veins bulge. Her mouth finally opens wide enough for me to make out the sharp points on her upper and lower incisors.

Then she steps toward me—

She stops less than a foot in front of me; Halcyon doesn't stand between us this time.

She will challenge you, Samsonfang says. **Take her to the Vexen.**

Halcyon translates, "She says that it is night, and she is the Queen of Night. You can't give her orders during this time. This is the right of the vampires. They don't claim a territory, only a time. The night."

I take my eyes off Vic's slitted pupils to glance at the thick jugular vein that runs up her pale neck. I gesture eastward, in the opposite direction, where the moons will soon rise. "Tell her that I am the Kulapsifang of Velm. I reign under the moons. The only orders I obey are those given by my demigod or my Alphas."

Or Helisent, now that I'm in Vex.

Mirth lingers behind Halcyon's eye roll before he translates.

To my great surprise, my announcement doesn't instigate more posturing from Vic. Instead, she takes a step back. Her eyes flash to my neck.

She speaks again, this time with a more measured and curious tone. She slides her eyes from me to the warlock, waiting.

Halcyon tilts his head. "She asks if you drink blood. You don't, right?"

I try not to look disgusted. "No."

Halcyon translates; Vic responds with quick, agitated words.

He takes a sip from his jug of liquor, then asks, "She wants to know why you're looking at her neck."

Before I can respond, Vic steps forward again. With a wide and sultry smile, she angles her jaw to reveal her neck. She presents the stretch of pale skin to me, eyes glittering with mischief.

I fall still, utterly stunned.

Vic raises a hand and taps a finger against her jugular, beckoning. She purrs a word, stepping forward so our abdomens nearly graze.

I've never considered what might make me or Samsonfang back down from a potential fight; this might be the only gesture that could leave me totally off-guard.

Someone *offering* their neck to me.

It's... unfathomable.

She will want the same from you, Samsonfang tuts. **Take her to the Vexen. Now.**

I'm just as confused by Samsonfang's sudden interest in Helisent—

referred to as *the Vexen*. Never before has he acknowledged the power or authority of another being—not even Clearbold. Now, he seems apt to defer this issue to Helisent.

And why bring Vic to the witch?

Because the Female Alpha rules the women. This is not your battle.

Because...

Because... *what?*

A low sigh escapes me.

I stare ahead into the vampire's slitted eyes, then I glance at her pale neck, at her tangled red hair, at her pale nipples. My mind is far away, attempting to juggle everything I've uncovered since following Halcyon outside.

There's too much going on right now.

Vic is a vampire and she wants me to bite her; Samsonfang thinks Helisent is his Female Alpha; Pel might be the only way to find Imperatriz; Halcyon is infertile.

Behind it all is the ongoing knowledge that I may never make it home to fulfill my role as the Kulapsifang.

With another sigh, I remember the jug of vodka at my feet.

I stoop to pick it up and then take a hefty drink.

I ignore Vic, who watches me with a bunched brow, sidled up and waiting.

I look at Halcyon. "If they're going to enter Hella whether we let them or not, then we're wasting our time right now."

I step out of Vic's way, then glance into the shadowy forest. With only a sliver of dusk remaining, we're losing light by the second. I gesture toward Hella's shadowy portal in invitation.

Halcyon seizes his two jugs of vodka, then rushes past my opened hand. Vic rushes forward to seize one of Halcyon's horns with a wild cackle, and the warlock responds with a few curses as they disappear into the darkness like long-lost friends.

The rest of Vic's pack filters from the trees.

Their eyes flash with distended glimmers of reddish light.

Each wears similarly insufficient strips of suede leather and fur that barely cover their groins, along with plenty of ornamental feathers on their upper bodies and bone jewelry on their lower halves.

Feathers dangle from the ends of their hair, fixed with strips of thin leather; they tower and dance from diadems similar to Vic's; they hang from necklaces over their chests and backs. Most of the vampires are large and powerful like Vic, but some are smaller and lankier, similar to wielders or nymphs.

Each smells like blood.

Old blood; fresh blood; their own blood; mammal blood; bird blood; fish blood; menstrual blood; clotted blood; mixes of all these types of blood. One even has dark stains around his lips, as though he didn't bother cleaning up after his last meal.

Dirt coats their bare feet, but there's not a speck on their clean white furs.

I count eleven as they pass, just like I'd estimated.

I turn and follow them into the portal. I trail their alas through the millisecond of infrasound and then pass into Hella's tepid tunnel room. The vampires are already ahead of me, bounding with large strides toward the central fountain.

Samsonfang's statement drifts through my mind as I follow the group.

Because the Female Alpha rules the women.

Close to one year ago, in the jungle of Rhotidom on the triple-moon, Samsonfang had found Helisent fascinating and powerful. He was obsessed with tangling our alas, which he hinted would someday mix. Given this, his positing from earlier isn't *that* unexpected.

Unless I start to pair it with other Helisent-related mysteries.

In Alita, Vex cast a spell that saved me from the brink of death. Before that, I'd been exposed to Helisent's magic through a seething. Through her sexual ala alone, her magic took root in my mind and connected me to the witch through our dreams.

Which means the dreams might not be dreams.

They might be spells.

And the red threads—*what are those?*

I rub my face with a sigh.

For now, the only question that matters is how I get to Pit.

CHAPTER 9

I'M NOT SO SMALL IF YOU COUNT MY MAGIC

HELISENT

Honey Baby,
Your mother and sister are dead; you've never stopped mourning this. But you have suffered more in this life than either of them ever did. I hope you realize that.
Papa P.

Deep in the night, I sit before the Hellastone.

I lean forward and pinch another bloodred thread that drifts from the stone. It hangs in the air, catching on a breeze like it really is a filament of cotton or flax. Vex's raw dove cranes toward me like a seedling toward the sun.

I pinch the string-like thread and pull it toward one of my horns. With a few quick loops, the string fastens to my horn and begins to dissolve. I still have a limited understanding of how it works—just that it fills my mind and the backs of my eyes with a peaceful humming.

After each session with the Hellastone, my horns grow heavier. I crawl into my bed and sleep; when I wake, there are new spells in my repertoire. Intuition tells me which spells I've absorbed in the night; how to use them.

Last week, I woke up with the ability to jump through shadows.

Halcyon calls it shadowing. He says he's never heard of it done outside Ezit.

Still, learning how to use the spells I'm inheriting isn't nearly as intuitive as I'd hoped. The first time I shadowed, I was caught in the darkness for thirty long seconds before I realized I needed to keep walking through it.

I study the dark Hellastone, waiting for more strings to drift loose. In the dead of night, a dove-filled cylinder lights the long hall. I stretch my neck, my body exhausted from hours of work.

"Honey Baby," Parsifal calls from behind me.

I turn with a jump—no one follows me to this part of the cave. Based on the hushed questions the others have asked me, they're suspicious and slightly haunted by my descriptions of the Hellastone.

My papa stares at me from the threshold. His wide eyes dart from where I sit to the Hellastone, then to the large figure looming at his side.

With so little light in this part of the cave, I can't make out who the being is. But they look large enough to be a wolf, naked enough to be a nymph. I stagger to my feet and step toward them. My head feels disproportionately heavy, like Vex's dove is sloshing around in my skull and horns.

"The vampires are here," Parsifal explains, tugging his cloak tight around him. "They drank our vodka and now they're touching everything. This one laid down in Samson's bed, and he didn't like it. There's another lady vampire who has Halcyon cornered. She keeps talking about his hands. Oh, and Aura and Eos have taken one of the vampires hostage—I don't think he minds. It's hard to tell. There's a lot going on."

As I leave the long hall, my form fizzles out of being. Quickly, I step between my papa and the vampire.

She's taller and broader than I'd originally realized; my neck bends like it does to stare up at a wolf. She wears nothing but a diadem of feathers, a necklace of feathers, and a strip of white fur that barely covers half of her groin.

My attention goes to her hair next. It drifts to her hips in tangled heaps, red-orange like a bird of paradise. Her eyes are narrower than any hesperide I've ever seen; her pupils also look to be slitted like a snake's, catching the light and glinting.

The vampire takes a step back to study me. Her chunky white anklets jangle—bones, I realize.

She leans forward to swipe one of her massive hands over my head. "Where is the rest of you?" she asks in Zarzyd. "And why did you let a degi bite you? Explain yourself."

I blink at her. "Can I get a fucking name first? Who are you?"

The vampire tuts. "What sort of leader introduces herself? You know who I am. And if you did not, then you will soon."

We stare at one another. I shift from being too tired to care, enamored by her boldness, and annoyed with the prospect of navigating what seems to be a dangerously sized ego.

Parsifal leans toward me and whispers, "This is Vic, by the way. Vic the Chosen, Queen of Night. Halcyon introduced them before he was sequestered. What is she saying?"

"Just posturing to look tough." I take a deep breath; I'm tired, hungry, and cold from hours of sitting with the Hellastone. I switch back to Zarzyd and address the vampire. "My name is Helisent West of Jaws. Who invited you into my cave?"

"Night fell in your cave; I followed it inside. Before that, the gorgons sent me a letter. You need my help. You're going to wage war on Ezit."

I sling my arm through Parsifal's and guide us back toward the central fountain in Hella's center. Vic follows without a word. She walks a few feet parallel to us, using the distance to study me. With each step, she looks confused, then intrigued, and then disappointed.

I feel similarly about her.

I knew the vampires would be wild based on Halcyon's description, but he had promised Vic would be a diplomat. *If this is diplomacy, then what am I in store for with Zeu the Chosen?*

"I'm not waging war. It's going to be a modest invasion. We get in, then we get out." I throw my most intimidating look at Vic. "And I heard you don't like rules, so you can just think of these as suggestions. First, no sleeping in the wolves' beds. They hate touching. Second, no cornering Halcyon. He's already doing more than what he signed up for." I scratch my chin, trying to keep up with the vampire. She's now leading us back to camp with long strides of her powerful legs. "And why did the okeanids take one of your vampires hostage?"

Vic hisses, unamused. "Ret was degi. They have questions about life in Ezit."

My gut braces.

Though we'll need someone with inside experience of Ezit, I haven't been honest with myself about what it will feel like to confront Zarzynn's evil again.

Hella is... nourishing. Here in this cave, in my House, I'm surrounded by my power. It cradles me while I absorb all I can from the Hellastone.

I glance at Parsifal. His arm clings tight, keeping me at his side.

To soothe him and myself, I say, "Don't worry. We'll get everything sorted out tonight."

His features strain. "They won't go to sleep till morning, Honey. No one has slept since they got here. Or breathed deeply."

"I'll handle it quickly. I need rest, papa. It feels like there's a moon growing inside my head. Every spell I absorb..."

I trail off as we reach the plaza surrounding the fountain in Hella's center. Usually, our provisions sit in neat piles atop the fountain's wide lip. It's a communal area where we keep our supplies for cooking, cleaning, storing, and repairing—jugs of fresh water, extra leather and linen, utensils, and other tools.

It was never glamorous, but everything sat either near the fountain or the fire pit I built from spare limestone. In the past weeks, we've even grown accustomed to sitting in a particular order while we handle various mundane tasks.

That could have been years ago based on the scene now.

I count nine vampires. I recount based on the level of noise, but the original count stands.

Our fire is three times its normal size. Firelight reflects around the limestone buildings chaotically. I keep an eye on a second fire lit nearby; though Hella is built of limestone, the flames look prone to spreading.

Our cooking, cleaning, storing, and repairing supplies are strewn across the plaza. Vampires huddle over the piles, holding pieces up to the light and then passing them around.

One group strikes a pair of hand drums with our wooden spoons. Another duo fit their hips with the alpaca hides the wolves tanned.

Another twirls with Absalom's clean white cloak slung around his shoulders; Absalom stares in livid disbelief a few feet away.

The rest of the Mieirans stand in their doorways, as though physically blocking their rooms from being ransacked. Samson stands with his arms crossed and nose curled. Rex and Berevald peek over his shoulders, eyes tracking the mayhem.

Kiekerline and Hemlock occupy another doorway. Both look slightly more accepting of the situation; their arms are crossed, but they look more curious than indignant.

A long sigh escapes me.

To my right, Vic also sighs; hers doesn't sound exhausted as much as pleased. At home.

I turn to Parsifal. "Where's Halcyon?"

"I told you, he's being accosted." My papa points to our shared room.

I look over to see a female vampire, just as brawny as Vic, exit the room. She drags Halcyon by the wrist, eyes fixed on me. She stalks toward us with beating strides.

Halcyon shuffles at her side, muttering under his breath.

Just like the Queen of Night, this vampire wears a pristine white pelt around her hips. A metallic diadem wraps around her scalp and temple; four white feathers jut upward, shifting with each of her steps. She wears a strap of leather around her upper chest—it looks like it's just for decoration, as it doesn't cover her tiny breasts.

"Which one is this?" I ask Parsifal.

The vampire stops before us. Halcyon answers instead, boring his eyes into mine, "This would be Tol. We met a few years ago. I think she misses me—"

"*I'll be taking the warlock for the night,*" Tol growls. Firelight catches on her teeth as she bares them. Her incisors are slender and sharp, like tiny ivory blades. "And why are you so small?"

What the fuck is wrong with my height?

Tol tsks, standing at her full height, then looks at Vic the Chosen. The pair share the same flat nose and prominent brow—I wonder if they're related. Only Tol's youth differentiates them, her lips and cheeks slightly plumper.

I glance at the hold Tol keeps on Halcyon's wrist. "Halcyon, is this about the finger trick?"

Tol's grip tightens as though prepared to rip his hand off and run away with it. I can't tell if I pity the warlock's uncertain expression or find it hilarious; the finger trick is certainly worth getting a little fussy over.

"It is a gift and a curse," Halcyon explains. "Please don't let her take me. Also, do you remember what I said about the vampires? About what you should do if they came to Hella and started making a mess and—"

"I remember," I cut in.

Since I declared my intentions to go to Ezit and free the okeanids, Halcyon and I have drifted apart. Though we're still bound, and remind each other often, the flame in our love has extinguished like someone threw water on it. We still cuddle, we kiss, we make love— but now with a distance natural to those who don't know where life is heading.

Assuming we make it out of this alive, of course.

Halcyon looks across the madness. "Well, whenever you're ready..."

I stare across the scene, deep in thought.

I could overpower the vampires easily, but I don't know what scope of violence or coercion is acceptable. The expanding, almost unlimited, repertoire of spells lingering in my mind also doesn't help. It's *too* vast, too unexplored, too crushing with the options it gives.

Blinding them would certainly get their attention, but I don't know that I can undo such a powerful spell—even with healing magic.

Detaining them in a single room would give us all peace and quiet, but that's a temporary solution.

Humoring them would set the stage for a partnership, but I doubt that's the way to earn the respect of leaders like Vic and Tol.

I feel like I had a trick for this...

I snap my fingers, then point at Vic and Tol. The vampires whip their heads toward me, reddish hair bouncing and lips pulling back from their teeth—they must hate snapping. *Good.* Before either can open their mouths, I use smothering magic to block their voices.

Tol gurgles as she attempts to speak around my magic. Vic manages a hiss, eyes widening as her slitted pupils fix on me and expand with hunger.

I look at Parsifal and Halcyon, then gesture them toward the row of buildings. "Scurry on, boys. I've got this."

The warlocks look at one another before walking away. I don't watch them go; I hover in the air so I'm at eye-level with the vampires, staring at them while I maintain my smothering spell.

Behind them, the pack of vampires freezes.

Two of the largest vampires set down their drums and makeshift sticks; another male slings off Absalom's cloak and faces me.

I maintain my smothering spells while sending the rest of the pack to their knees with force magic. I target the force around their ankles and calves, gentle enough that the limestone won't break their skin but potent enough that they can't rise.

Their reddish eyes cling to me. They shimmer in the firelight.

But they don't shout a word. They don't widen their eyes with fear. They wait, chins lowered.

I switch my eyes back to Vic and Tol. "I'm not so small if you count my magic, ladies."

I focus on Vic first. "Vic the Chosen, it's nice to meet you. You are welcome in Hella, but you will respect the city and its residents. What you are doing now is not respectful—and I think you know that. I think you like that. When I release you from my magic, you will take your pack and find somewhere to sleep for the day. Tomorrow, I will speak with Ret. The degi. And then we'll figure out how to live together until it's time to go to Ezit."

I turn to Tol. Her shoulders shake as she squares up to me. Unlike the rest of the vampires, she's not handling my power move well. I try to ignore the ferocity in her eyes. "You can't have the warlock for the night. Not because I don't like to share, but because you didn't offer me anything in exchange. I don't have any handouts for you. Also, your feathers look *stupid*."

With a happy sigh, I float back to the ground.

I meet the gazes of the pack, who watch us with tensed jaws. Frozen in place, they're easier to study. Not all are sized like Vic and Tol; in fact, the women are the largest in the group. An older male also looks powerful in both bearing and cunning. Another large specimen looks too handsome to be particularly useful.

I look back up at Vic and lift the smothering spell.

At her side, Tol's face reddens and tightens with rage; I haven't lifted the spell on her yet.

I raise my chin. "Well, Vic the Chosen—are we squared?"

She takes a deep breath and stares across the group of silenced, kneeling vampires. The fires crackle and rage. The Mieirans stare on from their dwellings.

"You shouldn't insult a vampire's feathers," Vic says without looking at me. "Or our furs."

I almost roll my eyes; *how is that what stood out about my little speech?* "Then don't come into my home and make my people nervous."

Vic yawns. "It's almost dawn."

Is she posturing so she doesn't lose face?

Maybe we don't understand each other yet.

"The southern part of the cave gets the least sunlight," I offer.

"Accra likes you." Vic says it like it comes with a second, hidden statement. *'Accra likes you, but I don't.'* Something like that.

She looks at me. Despite her devious enthrallment and her annoyance at my stature before, Vic now looks calm. She looks accepting—like maybe there wasn't a hidden statement in her last comment.

I don't know what to say. How to look. "I like Accra, too."

"Good." She steps away from me, dragging Tol by the arm.

I take it as a cue to release Tol from my smothering spell, along with the rest of the vampires from their stationary positions.

Tol follows, looking back once to hiss at me. The men and women rise and dust themselves clean. Only the two larger males spare longer looks in my direction, their reddish eyes darting as they take me in. I wait until they slink behind Vic, who heads toward the cave's southernmost streets.

Then I stare at our strewn supplies with another sigh.

The wolves step forward to help me. The rest of the group soon follows, stooping to collect our items and then setting them back into order.

With dawn brightening the sky, I put out the fire. Well and truly exhausted, I tote a spare mug of vodka back to my room.

I pass Samson on the way.

For a second, he blocks out the fragile light and I fall into his shadow.

My thoughts whir, then go quiet with the realization that the Kulapsifang resembles the large, breathing thing that I clung to in the dark room of lost memories. The warm, alive thing that I turned to for comfort when I was dying on the ship.

The thought is so alarming that I rush back to my room.

There's no way it could have been Samson.

I repeat that thought again and again as I sip the liquor and Halcyon catches me up on the day's events.

But even when I close my eyes to sleep, I see the shape of his shadow, cast against the limestone around me.

I know that shape. I know its size. I know what it felt like to cling to it in a blackened room of lost memories.

What I don't know is what the fuck to do with that information.

I spend the next day avoiding the Hellastone and its trance.

As though well aware I plan on freeing the okeanids from Ezit, Vex urges me toward the hall.

The empty bottle of brandy angles its opened top toward it often. Anytime I have a spare moment, the image floods my mind; light glints off the glass bottle, foam froths near its top, it rattles against the wooden floor.

I ignore the image.

I need a break—especially if I'm going to speak with Ret the Degi tonight.

And none of us are rested after the debacle with Vic's den last night. The group hangs around the city center in the late afternoon, waiting for the vampires to wake while maintaining a tight formation around our tidied supplies.

In the meantime, Halcyon answers a few pressing questions.

"You said there are two packs in Vex. Where is the other one?" Samson asks.

"They're called dens," Halcyon replies. "And there are three. One is kept hidden—that's the den that raises their young. Vic's den preserves culture. They have a library hidden somewhere in Vex. And Zeu the Chosen leads the last den. He's a bit more combative—his den stays near Ezit. They do what they can to disrupt life there and help any escaped degis and okeanids."

"And what's going on with the other woman?" Parsifal asks. "The one who seemed to like you a lot?"

I pinch my lips to hide my smile. Halcyon doesn't like to talk about sex in public. He stares at the limestone, picking at it as though hoping to uncover a neutral response—but Aura and Eos interrupt with a few salacious giggles.

"Ret said Tol is obsessed with Halcyon," Aura says, straightening her turquoise-laden diadem.

"They met in Plet," Eos goes on, eyes wild. "Tol and Vic were taking a group of okeanids to New Hypnos, and—"

"Thank you," Halcyon interrupts loudly. "That is enough."

To his great luck, the vampire's cacophony echoes out to us a second later. I glance overhead, surprised—there's still light in the sky. Though the sun has set and dusk has arrived, I'd figured that even a graze of non-direct sunlight could hurt the vampires.

Apparently not.

First comes the sound of conversation and singing. Then footsteps.

Vic leads the den into the light of our (single) fire.

The others wear similar combinations of leather, fur, and feathers. For how meager the pieces look, each appears to be expertly crafted and clean.

Aura and Eos rush forward to meet the group's smallest member. Aura takes one of his arms and Eos claims the other. The vampire freezes at their touch, but seems to relax in the next breath.

The den glances across us, and we glance across them.

As though bored, the vampires begin to fan out.

I step forward to meet Vic. She wears the same pelt and feathers as yesterday, but her hair is now collected into a single braid. It dangles to her butt, as thick as a sailor's rope.

I offer her a smile. "Hi, my dear vampire—"

"We're going hunting," she barks, stalking past me.

I turn around and set my hands on my hips. Rather than chase Vic, I yell, "We're taking Ret for the night."

She doesn't turn her head to shout back, "Who gives a fuck about the degi?"

I tsk, discouraged by her attitude.

I turn and find Aura and Eos standing in front of me.

The vampire squished between them stands at my height—which may be the most pleasant surprise I've encountered on the mainland. A normal-sized being.

His red-gold hair hangs just past his shoulders, short feathers tied to a few strands. Rather than wear a pelt around his hips, the loose linen of Dexerxes clings tight. Compared to the rest of the den, Ret has little ornamentation.

He clears his throat. He meets my eyes, then looks at the ground. "Ret the *Once*-degi. Or just Ret."

Halcyon had mentioned the term degi is derogatory. "Right. Sorry. Ret works."

Aura and Eos watch him with gentle smiles, but Ret keeps staring at the ground like he's expecting a quick movement.

He murmurs, "And you are Helisent West of Jaws, the last living Vexen and familiar of Pel the Degi."

I flinch a smile at him. "Helisent works. And I'm not Pel's *familiar*. I didn't tell the motherfucker he could drink my blood."

His hands twitch at his sides. "Yes. Of course."

I glance over my shoulder. The den stalks toward one of Hella's tunnels; I'm guessing it's where they entered yesterday.

I turn in the other direction. "Let's go, then, Ret."

I guide us to the windowless hall where I took the group after my meeting with the gorgons. The group shuffles to take their seats on the tiered benches. Magical oil casts light from sconces on the walls, peachy like the orange of sunset.

I tug on Ret's wrist so he knows to stand by me rather than sit. He flinches at the touch, he dropping his shoulder and looking at my hand. His eyes flash to mine, back foot shifting like he's ready to flee.

We both freeze.

My gut clenches. "Sorry."

Ret shakes his head and looks at the ground—

And my heart starts to pump.

I hate standing next to the once-degi vampire.

Next to a being who would have broken my hands in a rosarium box on behalf of his House.

To know that he would have had no choice in doing that but to face similar violence himself.

To know the kind of fear that such violence leaves in your mind, in your nerves, in your psyche.

I survived a few weeks on that ship.

And how long did Ret survive in Ezit?

Nausea weakens my legs. I can sense the Mieirans watching me; it's like the heat from a fire. I don't want them to see me like this—

Halcyon stands up and steps toward me.

Ret takes two broad steps away, eyes burning on the warlock. But Halcyon doesn't spare him a look. He stands before me and whispers, "Ret can tell his story alone." My throat goes dry. I can't believe how strongly I'm reacting to a single touch. "If it's too much, then we can leave. I'll tell you where the red moon Wanda came from. Okay?"

I nod, trapped in a numb state. It all came on so quickly.

Halcyon shuffles me toward the bench where my papa sits. I settle in and Parsifal scoots close enough that our legs touch. He reaches over and smooths my hair, then pinches my cheek.

I stare at my hands.

I can't tell if it's helping ground me, reminding me I'm safe, or catapulting me into an outer space of awful things.

With my mind elsewhere, Kierkeline addresses the vampire. "Ret, welcome to Hella. We would love to hear the story you told Aura and Eos yesterday. As you know, we've traveled very far to take our okeanids home. Anything you can tell us about Ezit will be a great help."

Ret runs his hands through his hair, reddish eyes on Aura and Eos. With a long sigh, his shoulders hunch. "I wasn't born in Ezit. I wasn't born degi. My mother was taken by the House of Serac when I was a child. So, I was raised in Ezit as a degi. But I was born free." He runs his hands through his hair again. "Maybe some of you remember an okeanid named Vili. She was born in Hypnos."

To my surprise, Hemlock leans toward the vampire, causing his jacaranda necklaces to swing forward. His bushy eyebrows bunch together. "Vili? She was taken two years ago. She was slated to be a Queen—the demigods whispered about her in dreams. Can you take us to Vili?"

Ret's shoulders slump further. "Vili was my friend."

I sit back when he uses the past tense. I look away from my hands and the group, toward the wall.

"Vili is the reason I escaped degi-life." Ret takes a huge breath. It's large enough to raise his shoulders. After that, he doesn't slump again. He lifts his chin and tells the story like he's driving a sickness out of him, word by word.

"Vili did not accept life in Ezit.

"That is what the Houses want. They want us to *accept* what they offer. They want us to enjoy our underground chambers. After that, they expect *anticipation*. They want okeanids and vampires to predict what they want. They want us to come up with ideas that serve them. Only then can you be *invisible*. Acceptance, anticipation—and then invisibility.

"Invisibility is as close as we come to freedom. You can move between a House's underground tunnels. You can... spend time with other degis. The harder you work for them, the more invisible you are.

"Only invisible degis are given an okeanid and a rosarium necklace. The rosarium can subdue magic—even great magic if the stones are potent enough. But they're only given to degis who first accept their position, then anticipate what their House wants. Only to the invisible degis who do not cry, who do not argue, who do not fight."

Ret looks at Halcyon, and Halcyon stares back at him. "You killed Jen. You almost killed Pel. These are Ezit's most invisible degis. Jen had his own clothes. And Pel knew the way to the islands where the Houses hide their wealth from one another. Clothing and knowledge are high forms of power."

I clench my eyes shut as I teeter back toward the black room where my memories lurk.

Pit. Pel. Rosarium.

The words are like physical blows; my heart rate continues to increase, my palms dampen.

This room feels very small.

"The House of Serac deemed me invisible. They deemed Vili invisible, too. They paired us together and we lived in a large room underground. We were violent in quiet ways. Our first act of violence was this language. Mieiran. It was our weapon. Our second act of violence was magic.

"I could always hear the ocean in Vili's eyes. It was her lullaby. I had never seen the ocean when we met. And then we started our work —to make Vili a necromancer. It starts with trading blood. She drank mine, I drank hers. Then she slept on the mirror. That's how they do it—wielders make the okeanids sleep on mirrors lined with rosarium during the day."

Each word is more unfathomable than the last.

Parsifal weaves our arms together. Halcyon sets a hand on my leg, stroking lightly.

You survived already, Helisent.

"A vampire can't withstand sunlight. And with our blood, neither can the okeanids. Half of them goes into the mirror to escape the sun. With my blood, Vili lived half in the mirror. That's how they speak with the deathlings—they find them inside the mirror. They bring them to the mirror's glass. They present them. Vili said death was almost like an ocean. Something she could swim through inside the mirror.

"This is the first step to becoming a necromancer: the ability to pass into the mirror where deathlings wait.

"It took us almost one year."

Half of me wants to know more. *What's a deathling? How are death and mirrors related? How large must an ocean of the dead be?*

Could I bring back Milisent? Andromeda? Part of me doesn't want to know if magic is capable of defying the bounds of death. Part of me likes knowing that there is something greater than dove and ejima and wielders.

Ret shakes his head. His words drop to a whisper, "But if Vili became a fully-fledged necromancer, we would be separated. Vili would be sold to another House to commune with the dead for those who paid a high price. And I would stay with the House of Serac to create more necromancers from the okeanids Pel and Jen kidnapped from Mieira.

"So, we planned to escape. But Ezit is... layered with magic. Hosts cast complex spells and pay great wages to wielders to maintain these spells. It makes escape nearly impossible. Our rooms are underground. Degis and okeanids don't really know what the city looks like. How can we escape a place we cannot see?

"Our best chance was the water system. All okeanids are pith by distance by the time they arrive in Ezit. Vili was pith aside from the lullabies in her eyes. Still, we thought the canals that brought water in and out would be familiar.

"The canals... the water system... their noise sort of sounded like Vili's eyes.

"We were wrong. It was too dark. The water was too quick. It wasn't ocean water, either. Vili had no power over this water. None of the canals led out like we thought they would—it was a maze. Then we were found... and I... couldn't think. Fear is... fear makes everything more complicated. I was holding Vili... and I freed us... but I couldn't keep her head above. And Vili drowned."

I close my eyes—

And Vili drowned.

Like me, Halcyon tenses. He shifts closer to me, as does Parsifal. Their warmth guards me, surrounds me.

I keep my eyes closed until I can't feel the cold water burying me. Until I can't feel and taste the salt water in my throat, my nose. Can't feel it sting in my eyes. Can't feel it's weight surging toward my lungs.

"It's cruel to be born degi," Ret continues. "And it's worse to be *made* degi. But vampires only believe it's immoral to die degi." His voice shakes. "Vili didn't die degi. Vili died free, with me, escaping Ezit. Zeu the Chosen found us a few weeks later and took me to Vic's den in Vex. The den helped me take Vili to the ocean. I sent her back to Mieira on the waves."

With a long sigh, Ret glances around the tiled walls.

Silence fizzles and crackles through the room. I can hear my heart pumping in my ears.

"You honored Vili," Hemlock says eventually, voice thick. "Thank you for sharing your story, Ret. Thank you for helping Vili."

Ret's jaw clenches. "The necromancers are magically powerful, but they're physically weak. And they're mostly pith, Vili said. The Houses make the vampires weak, too. Not enough food, never enough sleep, little concept of time. That's why I couldn't save Vili. Why she couldn't save herself."

"And Vili was taken by the House of Serac?" Aura asks.

Ret casts his eyes down. "Yes. House of Serac. I know where the Houses of Col, Argot, and Serac keep their degis, okeanids, and necromancers." The vampire looks up, studying Halcyon once again. "The Male Host of Serac looks like *you*. His sons, too."

Halcyon arches one of his eyebrows. "Interesting."

I jump in to switch Ret's attention away from Halcyon—my own, too. I know his father is a monster, and likely his brothers, but confronting the fact that Halcyon has such deep ties to evil bothers me—especially when it's a blood tie.

Like what binds me to Axerxa.

"Can you draw a map of the city?" I ask.

Ret studies me with flitting eyes. "Aura and Eos told me your plan to free the okeanids. I wasn't sure if that was the truth. If it is, I will give you everything I know. I will draw a map as best as I can. I know the underground chambers well. Zeu showed me maps of the city above, too." He shakes his head. "But I will not go back to Ezit with you."

I nod. "I understand."

Ret sighs, as though relieved. "The center of Ezit is called Ezitlos. Only the Hosts can access Ezitlos; they concentrate their most important businesses around the city center. Some believe that's where they keep the remnants of their Landmarks. They hide their most important resources nearby. Their necromancers, too.

"Newly arrived okeanids are isolated for long periods of time to confuse them, on the edges of Ezit. There's another location where the degis are paired with okeanids to begin the necromancy rituals."

For the first time since meeting Ret, my anxiety soothes. "Three locations? That's manageable."

"Three locations *per House*," Ret clarifies. "Houses don't keep their assets together; the Houses are enemies amongst themselves. So, there's a total of fifteen locations. And I only know where those of Serac, Col, and Argot are."

My stomach drops. "Well, nothing's perfect."

"What else can you tell us about Ezit?" Hemlock goes on. "About the necromancers?"

Ret rubs the back of his neck. "As Aura and Eos know, an okeanid's power is strongest when the moons are all full. On a three-moon night, a necromancer can work for longer without getting tired. The Houses organize festivals on these nights. They let their poor visit the necromancers since many wielders can't afford their services.

"The Houses line the streets with mirrors—mirrors as large as ponds. The deathlings come at their own leisure. If a wielder is lucky, they see someone they recognize."

A three-moon night?

The triplemoon?

When I turn to look at Samson, he's already staring at me with his eyebrows raised. Rex watches me with a remarkably similar expression. Berevald offers a quick smile; of the three, he's the easiest to read. Right now, his eyes tell me, '*I told you so.*'

A curse bubbles in my throat. I don't trust phased wolves and nothing will change that.

Still... Ezit should have little to no understanding of what a werewolf is, and that it can't be touched by magic under the light of the full moons.

At least, not in theory.

(I will never underestimate Zarzynn again.)

Just to make sure, I ask Ret, "And what does Ezit do with the wolves they kidnap?"

"A wolf...?" Ret slides his eyes to Samson and his pack. "Like them?"

"Yes. Where does Ezit keep them?" I go on.

Ret shakes his head. "I have never seen a wolf before. But Pel and Jen know about the wolves. Before Jen was sold to Col, he worked in Serac. Jen knew the wolves from the House of Serac."

I narrow my eyes. "Tell me the extent of Ezit's knowledge of Velm. Please, every detail helps, Ret."

The vampire spares another hard look at Halcyon. "All I know is that the House of Serac knows of Velm—and chooses to avoid it." He shifts his gaze to Samson and his pack once again, eyes flitting. " The Houses are well aware of the wielders in Mieira. Of the five types of nymph, too. And the Houses don't do anything without motivation. So, what do I know about the wolves? Nothing."

Once again, a brittle silence fills the room.

Interesting...

For now, I'm relieved it seems like the Houses know little of the wolves. And even if they do know more, a wolf in its form is immune to magic whether they know it is or not.

I offer Ret a shrug. "The wolves are notoriously cloistered."

I unhook my arm from Parsifal's and stand. I ignore the whirling of fear and anticipation in my head. The weakness of my knees and stomach as I walk to Ret's side.

I try for a smile and tell him, "That's all for tonight, Ret. I'll prepare supplies for you to start drawing a map of Ezit… and Ezitlos. I promise to free all the degivampires that we can. If they're held near the okeanids, we can kill two birds with one stone."

Ret glances at the doorway, at the quiet street beyond. "Okay." He inches toward it, glancing back at us.

"Thank you, Ret," Eos calls from her seat. Like Ret's hair, a soft feather is tied to the end of one of her black locks.

Aura nods, tears framing her blue eyes. "Thank you."

"Of course." At the entrance, the vampire turns back. He raises a hand toward Aura and Eos, then waves it with an awkward, tense jerk. Baffled, the okeanids wave back. Ret waits in the threshold, wagging his hand until the rest of us raise ours in response. Only Halcyon looks around as though confused.

Ret lowers his hand with a ghostlike smile. "Vili said that, in Mieira, a whole group would wave back to me if I did that. I never believed her."

The vampire turns and leaves, shuffling into the darkness while the rest of us hang behind in another loaded silence.

Hemlock sits back, hand on his heart. "This place hurts me."

At his side, Kierkeline sinks into herself. She sets her head in her hands and sucks in deep breaths. When she looks up at me, her brow puckers. "You really don't remember anything about what they did with Butter? She's not an okeanid, Helisent. Not entirely."

Descending like a ten-foot wave, dark water floods my mind.

It drags in nonsensical memories.

I squeeze my eyes shut to try to push them out.

I shove the memory of Butter as hard as I can…

But I remember her if I really try…

A man is grunting.

A man drags her body away from me.

The ship rocks gently.

I am covered in filth.

They're leaving me on the ship—

Halcyon whispers in my ear, "Vexen, would you like to know how the moons were made?"

They're leaving me on the ship—

I try to move.

I can't.

Grunt by grunt, her body shifts across the wooden floorboards—

Butter's face is angled toward me; she is sleeping; she does not know we're dying. Her eyes are closed. Her lips are chapped. Her tunic is caught on her shoulder.

Her bare feet disappear...

I push the memory into the dark room.

(I think I'm also pushing Halcyon away from me.)

(I might also be clinging to him.)

Because the door to that room is open...

I drag in a huge breath.

'There's one for each of you.'

Someone whispers in my ear, "And the last moon, the red moon known as Wanda, was a large apple. A red apple. It was so beautiful that the wielders who lived in Vex refused to eat it. The vampires came to marvel at its bloody hue. It grew and grew and grew."

Slowly, the memory of Butter disintegrates...

"A young warlock dreamed of eating the apple and woke with his teeth against its skin. But he never broke the red flesh. He was sitting by the apple the day it grew too heavy for its branch. The moment he heard the stem break, he threw out his magic to save it from falling and bruising on the ground."

Slowly, the door to the black room swings shut...

"But it happened so quickly that the only spell he could think of was weightlessness. The apple stopped midair, then began to float. Up and up and up it went, growing all the while, becoming redder and redder. This is where the red moon Wanda comes from. An apple tree in Vex."

Slowly, I open my eyes.

Halcyon's face is close to mine. I study his features, finding comfort in their familiarity. After a few more steadying breaths, I realize we're alone in the room aside from Parsifal, who stands beside us.

It sounds like the group is ambling back toward the city center—

I clear my throat, embarrassed by my reaction.

I tell them, "I don't want to talk about Butter. They took her away. I... I... I..."

They nod, waiting.

"I couldn't stop them," I admit.

Halcyon whispers back, "Of course not, Helisent. No one could have."

"Come here," my papa says, opening his arms to me.

Parsifal floats so I can rest my head on his shoulder. I fold my arms and lay against his chest while he cradles me. Halcyon strokes my hair, my arm, as I suck in soothing breaths.

My papa says, "Maybe the memories are ready to come out. If they aren't, that's okay. But if they come back, it will be okay, too, Helisent."

"What if I remember something worse than what I thought I would remember?" I don't even know if that makes sense, but I can name about ten things that could have happened to me on that ship that I would prefer to leave in oblivion.

"Nothing has ever broken me, Vexen," Halcyon murmurs. "And you are much wiser and cunning than me. If I survived, then you will."

"And I know you hate to think about your mother," Parsifal says, "but there is more stubborn power in your blood than you know. I don't think any of it has to do with magic."

I smash my face into the soft fabric of my papa's peridot cloak. I listen to the thud of his heart in his chest. "Okay."

We stand there for a while, then slowly disengage. With a few shushes, Parsifal wipes my cheeks clean.

Halcyon peeks out the door, then turns back. "Someone wants to speak with you. I think it's about the triplemoon. How do you feel?"

I roll my eyes as I set my layers back in order. I can already picture Samson lurking somewhere, toiling over the great burden of being so important.

To be honest, I'd love a distraction from the wolf.

"I'm okay." I glance between the warlocks, thankful for their warmth and confidence. "I'll speak to him. If we're going to go to Ezit with the wolves, we need to use the doublemoon wisely. I think it's coming up soon."

Halcyon makes a measured sound of displeasure as we head for the door.

But Parsifal smiles, patting me on my back. "Good thinking, Honey Baby."

Outside the long hall, the night has left a humid chill in the air. Rather than ask to borrow Halcyon's cloak, I use warming magic to get comfortable. He and my papa head toward the fountain, where chatter and laughter pick up around the fire.

I amble toward Samson, who leans against a building across the avenue. His hair is messy tonight, dangling to his chest in wavy tufts. After a glance at the warlocks, he heads toward me.

We meet in the middle of the street and he hands me a wooden cup. I sniff its contents, then freeze with shock. "You brought me vodka?"

Samson nods. "Are you okay?"

I sip from the cup. "Sure. No. Whatever." He stares at me as I drink. In his silence, I go on. "I'm guessing you want to talk about the triplemoon. What are you thinking, Kulapsi?"

For a second, it looks like he's going to smile. Instead, he says, "I'm thinking the wolves have a lot of experience killing wielders, and this is the only appropriate time that knowledge will come in handy."

I take another drink. "Yeah, I guess all that child-killing might be useful after all. So, how far away is the triplemoon? We can use the doublemoon as a trial run. I can't take you, Rex, and Berevald with us if you can't figure out who you're supposed to be eating. They'll phase, right? All of you will phase on the doublemoon?"

Samson tsks lightly. "The moon cycles are close this time of year. The doublemoon is in eleven days—yes, we'll all phase. After that, we only have four weeks until the triplemoon."

"Sounds good." I tilt my head. "It's kind of weird you didn't bring up the child-killing. I was waiting for you to deny it."

Samson nods, as though commiserating.

I nod back, waiting for him to explain himself.

"A wielder's power doesn't travel back up their family line," he explains. "Child-killing negates a large portion of magic from a lineage. And it forces the adults to grieve. Emotional pain, much like physical pain, distracts a wielder. It weakens their ability to command powerful spells."

We stare at each other.

My mouth actually falls open; I'm shocked, disgusted, and relieved not to be waging war against Velm. "Right. Okay." I try to focus on what's actually important. "If you and I are going to invade Ezit together, there's one other thing you should know..."

"Something *I* should know. I see." He raises his eyebrows, dead-pan. "And what's that?"

I hover into the air so that Samson and I are at eye level. I study his features; the deep-set and almond shape of his eyes, the straight nose, the calm set of his lips. "I *hate* your father. I do not trust your father. And I will *never* recognize his authority."

I wait for him to object; he doesn't.

I go on, "And I still expect you to lift my banishment. If you can't swing it with Clearbold in charge, that's fine. It's not like I give a fuck about Velm. But when it's your turn on the marble throne, Kulapsi-fang... You will restore my honor and speak the truth of my virtue."

He crosses his arms. "You will *give a fuck about Velm* before then, Helisent West of Jaws. Aside from that, we're in agreement."

I huff. "Clearbold has ruined Velm for most of—"

"Imperatriz 713 Afador is the rightful Alpha of Velm," Samson cuts in, words burning. "*She* is the rightful leader—not Clearbold. *Imperatriz.*"

I flinch as the door to the black room springs open—

Another wave of dark water buries me—

I'm alone on the ship again.

Butter is gone; I'm dying.

My tongue is swollen. My head and body ache.

Every breath is my last; again and again and again.

Death smells like salt water and damp wood.

Someone is touching me—cleaning me—

"Be still."

Everything hurts. The boat rocks gently.

The being feeds me, but I do not want to eat; I want to die.

"Don't forget me."

"Helisent," Samson murmurs, snapping me back to reality.

I clear my throat, then float back to the ground.

I close my eyes.

Everything whirls in my head. I can't hold onto anything—

I don't remember what we were talking about.

I think we were bickering.

I just want to be alone now. I don't want anyone to look at me.

"Come on. You should rest." Samson takes my hand and guides me back to the fountain.

I take deep breaths and keep my eyes closed. I shuffle next to him and try to ignore how weird all of this must seem to someone as unflinching as him.

He passes me off; someone else takes my hand. There's someone soothing me with a back rub. Then Parsifal starts chattering in a quiet voice.

I listen to his stories and scratch my arms and neck.

It's like I can feel something tied around them, itching.

CHAPTER 10

I SEE A RED AX

SAMSON

My grandson,
Your mother loved Hypnos. She stayed there for six months before her wedding.
She said she dreamt of the Northing as she lay on the beach. That's where I
found her when Silent City called: asleep near the water, covered in sand.

The next week is a war unto itself.

After their hunting excursion, Vic's den returns with blood on their skin, on their lips, on their weapons—everything aside from the fur articles that dangle from their hips.

As the nights pass and the vampires get more comfortable in Hella, Rex, Berevald, and I struggle to define them. Whatever they do —whether exploring the cave, making love, singing, dancing, arguing, dreaming, challenging Helisent's authority—they do with an unrepentant passion.

The first few nights, my packmates and I twitch on our bed mats at every sound. We spy from the window by the door when conspicuous silence falls.

By the sixth night, their raucous hustle feels normal—and welcome.

Vic treats our nightly festivities like a throne. She drums, she drinks, she dances, she sings. And she's the best at many of those things; members of her den whirl around her in perfect tandem. Tol, her apprentice, watches Vic without blinking.

The women welcome us into the den's madness. They teach us the steps of their dances, then watch and laugh as we fail to replicate their movements. But they don't let us join their singing; the den spends at least one hour of darkness each night belting melodies into Hella's highest arches, layering them over one another so the noise never ends.

Pulled nearer by their disruptive presence and the nearing doubloon, Samsonfang's tangible presence in my psyche mounts.

Before I sleep, he whispers brief and elusive messages.

First, ***I see a red axe.***

The next night, ***Axerxa is watching.***

And tonight, the strangest of all...

Wake gently.

I wake to a noisy commotion.

Rich sunlight fills my shared room; the ruckus isn't from the vampires. Shouting drifts in from the door and window as I rub the sleep from my eyes.

"Honey Baby!" Parsifal hollers. "There's an evil child here."

Kierkeline is close behind. "Kill it, Helisent! We can't show Zarzynn weakness and the child comes from Ezit."

Then Halcyon, "The child poses no threat. It's just—"

"Helisent!" Hemlock bellows from the apartment next to ours. "There's a child out here! And it looks dangerous!"

Last is Absalom, who stays one door past Hemlock. "Who's fucking littleling is this?"

"Helisent, it has strange horns!" Hemlock goes on.

I sit up and reach for my tunic. I shift two inches before I feel something hard and sharp between my legs. I freeze as the piece knicks my thigh, then rip up my sheet.

A bloodred axe lays flat between my legs.

"What the fuck...?"

The axe isn't *just* an ax—it's Velmic. Just like the weapon that lays at my bedside, this axe has a sturdy wooden shaft, wound leather cords for gripping, and another set of twine that binds a razor-sharp blade to its head.

I look from the Velmic axe at my bedside to the red one.

Though similarly built, the red axe looks... coarser. And red.

Every single piece of the ax, leather and handle and blade, is *red*. The color looks like fresh blood, almost glossy—but it's not dyed or painted. The axe looks like it was built of bloodred leather, bloodred wood, bloodred carbon steel.

"You okay?" Bere asks.

He smiles at me, eyebrows raised. Rex also looks amused and puzzled as I stare beneath the sheet.

I pull up the red ax, letting the sheet fall.

Bere and Rex study the axe. Like me, they look suspicious and awe-struck.

Bere lifts his sheet. "Where's mine?"

Rex asks, "Where the fuck did that come from?"

I turn my hand to take a closer look at the weapon. The axe looks like it was just sharpened, a bright glean gilding the blade's edge. "I don't know... but I think Samsonfang knew. He's been telling me things as I go to sleep. The other night, he said something about a red axe. Last night, he told me to wake gently."

"And... what does that mean?" Rex goes on.

Bere looks at Rex, deadpan. "That he was going to wake up with an axe between his legs."

Rex rolls his eyes. "I'm talking about where the axe came from. Is it... magical?"

Last week, I came clean to Berevald about my relationship with Helisent. Rather than badger me with questions, my packmate nodded. When the nodding ended, he directed his gaze at Tol, who was sharpening one of her fangs with a coin-sized whetstone. With a thoughtful and appraising sigh, he said, "It's a big world outside Velm."

Though encouraged by his response, I didn't tell him about the spell Vex cast to save me in Alita. I wear my tunic at almost all times since it's hard to predict when the scar will turn red.

I have a pretty solid guess at who made the axe and put it here; Vex. I have little to no idea *how* that actually happened. (Red strings? A dream? A spell? ...Helisent?)

Helisent shrieks outside, near the fountain—

I'd forgotten about the littleling with strange horns.

I frown as I study the red ax; an intruder and a weapon show up on the same morning... *what are the odds?* Uncertain of what to do, I set the axe near the original at my bedside. I stand up and pull on my shirt; Rex and Bere do the same, pausing to study the red ax, then follow me outside.

Our group forms a half-circle twenty feet away from the fountain. Kierkeline and Absalom's hands are flexed at their sides, ready.

My blood stills.

On the fountain's far lip stands a witchling aged around sixteen or seventeen years old. One hand clings to a pale envelope. The other is hidden inside a plain white cloak that hangs from her shoulders to her toes, hiding her within.

Her skin is pale green, like the chute of a vine. The whites of her eyes glow faintly, as do her horns. Unlike Helisent's and Halcyon's, her jade horns don't curve back and around. All four jut upward in straight, clean lines. They almost look like weapons, sharpened and smoothed just like Halcyon's.

Bere growls at my left side. Rex shifts to my other flank, a low noise in his throat.

A jade witchling.

House of Col.

Which one of your people did this—which elder demanded my witch be brought to Ezit?

And did your people collude in my mother's disappearance?

It is too late to save Helisent torment.

But I will make the world regret harming my witch—

And taking my Alpha.

Vengeance is honor.

The witchling will grow into a witch, and who will she hurt then?

I suck in a deep breath as my mind boils with wrath.

Lesser instincts like rage and bloodlust fill me with the impulse to kill. To slink back into my room, seize the bloodred axe at my bedside, then find the right moment to send it careening toward the witchling's jugular.

I am in a blood feud with this witchling. With her people. With every single Col wielder who I lay eyes on. Not killing the Col wielders risks my own survival. It risks the well-being of my pack; my territory; the things that I rely on for survival in that territory; the legacy of my bloodline; the safety of all those born into its future.

It is a foul thing to consider killing a child.

Unless, of course, this child threatens my pups.

My future *Afadors*.

My eyes lock with the witchling. Hers widen as she takes a step back.

Kill her.

My nostrils flare as I study the witchling's ala; I can sense her heart pounding in her chest as my senses heighten, can smell the testosterone in her bloodstream.

Berevald grips my bicep. Rex takes the other as I turn back toward our room. My chest rises and falls as I suck in huge breaths; adrenaline rushes into my system with each.

As soon as I step into our room, Berevald and Rex shove me further inside. I catch myself from stumbling to the ground, then turn back.

Berevald rushes toward the axes at my bedside and huddles over them with a defensive stance. "You don't have the authority to kill in Hella. This isn't Velm. It belongs to Helisent."

Rex broadens his stance, blocking the doorframe. He swivels and yells to the group, "Get the witchling out of here. *Now*."

My body fizzles, ready for a fight. I look from Berevald to Rex, figuring I should go to Rex first since he doesn't have any weapons; but I'll need a weapon to kill the witchling. I study the axes below Berevald's guarded pose.

My hands twitch.

The next breath, I don't scent the witchling.

It helps lessen my rage—barely. I heave in breaths while I try to smooth my frayed thoughts.

I experienced the urge to child-kill; all of my companions saw me fail to hide that impulse; only wolves understand the nature of blood feuds and their violent implications; I'm supposed to be one of Mieira's foremost leaders.

Outside, the Mieirans chatter too calmly. Aura brings up the weather, Eos brings up the alpacas. Hemlock peppers in a few allegories.

Rex and Berevald hold their positions.

Their blue-black eyes track me as I pace the room. As my shoulders drop with relaxation, theirs do, too. But Rex doesn't move out of the entrance; Berevald stays primed above the axes.

I run my hands through my hair with one last sigh. I show my palms to both men. "I'm okay."

They slide their eyes toward one another. Rex glances over his shoulder to study the scene outside. Berevald takes a step back from the axes, though he stays close enough to intercept me.

Then Helisent shrieks from outside. "Where the fuck is the boy-wolf?"

"*Lekeli Kelnazzar,*" I groan. She'd just started calling me Kulpsifang. Even during our warmest weeks of love last year, she only used the term sparingly. Now, she's back to *boy-wolf.*

With another sigh, I drag my feet toward the door. Even Rex looks a bit sheepish as he stands aside to let me exit.

I step onto the street, unsure of what to do with my face.

Try for a smile? Stare at the ground? Start with an explanation?

The Mieirans sit around a spread of breakfast snacks; dried fruit, nuts, millet cakes, and honey. Only Hemlock looks truly aghast, a dribble of honey caught on his emerald beard beneath a chastising frown. And Halcyon, who stares at me with his arms crossed and one leg hiked over the other.

There's no sign of the witchling or hint at where she went.

Helisent stalks toward me with her hands on her hips. Like me, she hasn't had the chance to fully wake up. Her hair is out of sorts, half pulled back. Her linen layers are skewed around her chest, drifting around her hips.

I clear my throat. I have *no* idea what to say. "You look healthy."

Her eyes are wild—and her irises are red, I realize. I study the bloodred bands, interwoven with scarlet and vermillion threads. "Try again."

I still don't know what to say. "Good morning."

She waves a hand like she's swatting away my words. "What?" She glances around, stepping forward to peek into my room where Rex and Berevald exit. "Are you fine now... or?"

I nod as a blush warms my cheeks. "I was... a bit surprised."

"Like in the wolf way? I know you're weird about territorial stuff."

I tilt my head, surprised that she's trying to understand me. Especially at this moment. "The witchling wasn't invited into the cave. And... her bloodline. House of Col kidnapped you, Helisent. They've taken hundreds of okeanids. One day, she will be a witch. She will pose a threat to you. To Mieira. To Velm." I shrug a shoulder. "And why would she be here other than to hurt us?"

I don't mention the red axe.

Should I?

I need a cigarette.

Helisent holds up a square sheet of paper. "She was dropping off a letter. Halcyon says Ezit sends littlelings to discourage others from killing the messenger. And you know what—you probably don't want to hear this—she seemed kind of cool. Her name is Nineveh. Definitely a cool name. *Nineveh.*

"I guess word has spread that a Vexen is back. She wanted to see me in the flesh. I'm a *celebrity*." She wags her head back and forth, like she's not sure if she's happy about that. "Anyway, she's gone—so I'd like to formally invite you to *calm the fuck down*."

She raises her eyebrows, hammering home her point.

A spark of infrasound fizzles around us. I don't see anything, but I'd guess she's blocking out our conversation from the eavesdropping group of Mieirans.

"I'm calm," I say.

"Fine. And thanks."

Thanks? "For what?"

"Never mind." She turns back and lifts the smothering spell. She walks over to the group and I trail her, wondering what she meant.

Thankfully, it seems the group interpreted our chat as a conclusion to my episode. No one brings it up—not even Hemlock or Halcyon. The group sticks to their meals, glancing at Helisent as she takes a seat and unfolds the white paper.

Her eyebrows bunch. She flips the paper, then hands it off to Halcyon.

He also flips the paper and reads it with a sigh. He looks at Helisent, who goads him with her elbow. Then he reads it aloud to all of us, rotating the paper to follow its curving script.

To Helisent West of Jaws

The Last Vexen
The degis Pel and Jen wrongfully kidnapped you on the coast of Hypnos. House of Col extends its fullest apologies. This mistake has cost us greatly. We eat, drink, and speak in shame.

To offer compensation, we invite you to Ezitlos. There, we will present you with our finest necromancer and our largest mirror. The dead will be at your disposal. We await your arrival with this and many more gifts.

House of Col, House of Cliffs, & its Hosts

Halcyon hands the paper back to Helisent. He lowers his chin to level a knowing look at Parsifal.

Parsifal shifts his gaze to his daughter. His expression darkens. "Honey Baby—we agreed to go to Ezit *together* on the triplemoon. With a small army."

Hemlock nods. "This letter sounds like a nicely worded trap."

"What do you think, Halcyon?" Kierkeline asks. "You understand Ezit more than any of us."

"What do *I* think?" The warlock bends at the waist and buries his head in his hands. He raises his head, eyes wild. "The killing magic that I'm teaching you—the spells I've shared are only a *shred* of the spellwork they wield in Ezit. They've had thousands of years to create deadly spells, cruel tricks. So... that's what I think when I think of Ezit. Of death. Slow, painful death."

"Accra said they'd try to woo me before getting violent," Helisent says. The group pivots toward her; a few even gasp. She goes on quickly, "I'm not saying I should accept the invitation. I'm just saying I could learn something valuable by paying Ezitlos a little visit before the triplemoon."

Halcyon speaks as soon as she finishes. "Pel will have told them that you can't wield your magic—"

"I can wield my fucking magic now, Halcyon."

"Against *how many?*" he counters, pressing his palms together. "Only the elite know killing spells, but the rest of the city isn't going to *roll over. Tens of thousands* of wielders live in Ezit."

"And they're all *sharing* magic from their Houses," Helisent goes on. "I'm the only one not sharing. *I'm* a fucking Vexen."

"Are you quoting Axerxa on that one?" Halcyon raises his eyebrows.

Axerxa? That's the name Samsonfang whispered into my mind the past few nights.

Halcyon knows Axerxa?

Helisent's face contorts with rage; I prepare myself happily for the insult she's building for the warlock.

Parsifal reaches over to pat her leg before she can reply. "Honey Baby, would you mind waiting? Halcyon still has a few more lessons to teach us—Absalom isn't even close to being ready to face Ezit. And we need to see how the vampires do with the wolves on the doublemoon."

She looks at her father, face twitching. Then she blinks, setting her features into a calm mask of thoughtfulness.

She even nods, patting the top of Parsifal's hand. "Fine. We'll stick to the original plan."

It's a wholly convincing statement based on the relieved nods from the rest of the group.

But I watch the witch a moment longer.

In fact, I watch her throughout the day.

She stares into the distance often.

She glares into the distance, she twists the ends of her hair, she gets lost in conversation.

I know the signs well; the witch is scheming.

Lya scratches his belly and watches me like he's waiting for an explanation.

I look from the red axe in my hand to the gulf of shadows nearby. I've been standing in front of Hella's southern portal for twenty minutes, trying to talk myself out of following the witch. I have no proof that Helisent plans on going to Ezit tonight. I also have no idea when or how she'll travel to the city; I may have already missed her.

And now, there's a witness to my actions.

Lya hasn't said a word, just stood on the threshold of the hall that leads to the portal. With little light left from the bonfire near the fountain, orange traces his arms, his stomach, his bundle of feathers, the tip of his dick where it dangles past his pelt. His ala is thick with the scent of badger blood, dry bone, and what seems to be Tol's sexual ala.

Wonderful.

I have no idea what the vampire is doing. Part of me wonders if he's responsible for keeping tabs on the wolves if we wake in the night. Another part of me thinks he's interested in my brightly colored weapon.

I adjust my grip on the axe. If it's a gift from Vex, then it might be foolish to leave it behind. Even more foolish than leaving the safety of Hella in the dead of night.

I step forward and look back once at Lya, then turn and stride into the portal. The shadow engulfs me like a heavy cloak, infused with a graze of tickling infrasound. Now that the bass of magic makes me less nervous, I've started to understand how it moves through me. It alights in my veins, spreading similar to adrenaline, like a flood crashing through my circulation.

I step into the pebbled grass before the pine barren.

With the doublemoon only three days away, the lights of Vicente and Abdecalas are bright. Their silver, green, and pink hues turn the forest into a slightly more colorful place. Still, below the barren's thick canopy, there's little light.

I study the branches overhead in search of Helisent. Though I haven't seen one of her nests in over a year, it's a habit to look up anytime I'm searching for her in a forest.

Nothing.

Insects buzz lazily amid the branches; an owl hoots someplace out of sight.

I adjust my grip on the ax, holding it up. "Vex, if you want something from me, now is the time for a sign."

I sigh, resigning myself to the idea that this has more to do with my obsession with the witch than her plans to go to Ezitlos.

Then comes a soft grunt and a vivid curse. I step aside to make way for another being who passes through the portal. I try to figure out what to do with Lya, then realize the vampire didn't follow me.

Helisent staggers forward with a long gray cape over her shoulders; she doesn't notice me as she looks back at the portal. The fabric clinches in the front to hide her layers. Her hair is pulled back tight against her scalp in the Velmic style, causing her round eyes to stand out. They glitter, red and alluring.

She's been hiding her irises less and less lately. The sight of their bloodred hue makes me hungrier to see her horns, to see her skin painted bright red.

Helisent watches the portal. From the outside, it looks like a forgotten pile of limestone boulders and shadow. She creeps backward from it, as though afraid of making too much noise.

With a satisfied huff, she turns around and lifts her chin to waltz away.

She notices me with a gasp. "Why—" The witch looks at the red axe.

For the second time today, I'm well and truly at a loss for words. I clear my throat. "I am here."

She gives me the once over. "Yeah, no shit. Are you lost?"

"You're going to Ezitlos."

Helisent adjusts her cloak with a few proud jerks of her hand. It must be Halcyon's—I've yet to see her wear anything except the linen layers. "Unless I'm just taking a midnight jaunt." She glances again at the axe in my hand. "Are you hunting?"

With the dim light, the weapon is a deep crimson. "I... no. I'm not hunting. I woke up this morning and it was in my bed."

Her features bunch. "What? Why? What'd you do?"

"Me? Nothing." I hold out my leg. "It cut my thigh."

Helisent doesn't look at my leg; even if she did, my pants cover the nick. She rubs her temples, glancing toward the forest. "I don't have time for this right now. Look, I need—"

"We traveled together for five months last year," I interrupt before she can dismiss me. "We went from Tet to the Deltas to Rhotidom. I like to think we travel well together. If you insist on going to Ezitlos, then you shouldn't go alone."

I don't mention that I think it's idiotic to go. That I kind of admire that idiotic bravery. That I judge myself for following her idiocy without a second thought.

Helisent makes a pensive sound as she considers my words. Then she pulls a dark sock from her cloak. I blink at the soft fabric, baffled when she sticks her hand into it. With a few jerks and curses, the witch starts to pull a woven blanket from the sock. The narrow piece rips a few times to make way for the bundled rug.

I bite back my smile as relief floods me; she's making a lilith. I was right; she's going to Ezitlos. She might even let me go, too.

She shakes out the rug, then tucks away the ripped sock. Helisent wiggles her fingers and sends the blanket folding into a comfortable size. It lowers toward her hip, waiting for her to take a seat.

She tosses her hair over her shoulder once she's settled on the lilith. She sits at the same height she did last year, which lets us travel at eye level.

Then she gives me the once-over. "Accra said Ezit is two weeks walking from here. I'm sure Vex will show us a shortcut... unless we see it coming first. Halcyon says it's the size of an island."

I'm not sure what to think. Every comment I've heard about the city changes its shape into something even more unfathomable. *It's the size of an island?* Sure, why not.

"So, here's the part where you start walking if you really want to do this."

With that, the lilith takes off. We head northeasterly, quickly passing into the pine barren's heavy shadows. The witch's cape floats behind her; I wish it didn't carry traces of Halcyon's ala.

For a long time, we amble in silence. Above us, creatures flit through the canopy, snapping twigs, rustling leaves, scratching branches.

It feels peaceful and familiar, reminiscent of the months we spent crisscrossing through Mieira.

I wonder what it feels like for Helisent.

From her perspective, she's waltzing into danger with a stranger.

(Her papa says people never change.)

Eventually, she shifts her focus away from the horizon of dark forest and onto the red axe in my hand. "You didn't have to paint it red. I don't care what color your axe is, Samson."

"I didn't. I told you, I woke up and it was in my bed."

"Interesting."

Sensing she doesn't believe me, I offer, "Last year, you said your magic was like a twin. Maybe your twin put it there."

She looks at me, head tilting. "And what is my twin doing giving you an ax?"

I choose my words carefully, then turn my gaze forward. "I think it's from someone named Axerxa."

"*Right.* Axerxa gave *you* an axe." She snorts indignantly. "Are you in cahoots with Halcyon?"

I focus on Axerxa instead of the warlock. "Samsonfang brought up Axerxa. So... who is he?"

She grins, small and snide. "Why don't you ask Samsonfang?"

I look at her, nostrils flaring.

She holds her back straight on the lilith, her feet dangling from it. Moonslight grazes her white hair. At night, deep in the quiet forest and away from everyone else, my curiosity unleashes.

Everything I've successfully buried since coming to Zarzynn rushes to the surface with unfettered urgency.

"Fine. I'll ask Samsonfang."

I stare at her, waiting for a comeback.

With a delicate little *hmph*, she raises her chin and redirects her gaze straight ahead.

I keep watching her. "Why did you thank me earlier? I thought you'd be angry about the... incident with the witchling. But you thanked me."

A long sigh is her only response.

I order my thoughts into a neat series of questions and pray she's not going to ignore me the whole night. I *should* be focusing on Ezit—not mining the witch's feelings toward me. But I can't help it—

I want her to remember me.

Even if she hates me.

I can't deal with this dance anymore. Wolves don't lie. And even then, I've never been one for zhuzhing.

I need her to know that we were in love and that our love hasn't ended for me. That I betrayed our love and want to repent however she'll let me. That I'm bound to Vex, to her magic, and I need to know why Vex wants me alive.

Helisent murmurs, "I guess it felt nice."

Now, it's my turn for a beat of silence. Shame from this morning warms my gut and my cheeks. I won't be living that down for years to come, especially considering I lost control in front of a Rhotidic King, a GhostEater, and an almost-member of the Class.

"My reaction *felt nice* to you?" I whisper back.

"Yeah." Helisent shrugs, keeping her gaze directed away from me. "It felt nice that someone stood up for me. That someone would do something so ugly for me."

"Oh." I don't know what to say.

See? Samsonfang's tail thumps against the ground where he lounges in my psyche.

I blush again. I don't know why, but it feels...

Like maybe I'm still kneeling in that plaza and Helisent is looking down at me and I'm looking up at her, waiting for approval.

"I mean, don't kill any children, Samson," she goes on quickly.

"I *won't*, Helisent. It was just a surprise."

We stare away from each other. I can't tell if our silence is any more relaxed than before.

After a long moment, she taps my arm. She blinks at me, looking uncertain, "When we first spoke, you said we'd become friends."

I nod, waiting for her to go on. She shakes her head, like that was the question.

"It's the truth," I say.

"I can sense a cave—one that will lead us to Ezit. We're almost there." She sighs, pressing her hands against her scalp as though checking for stray hairs. "And I'd really like to trust you before waltzing into Ezit. So..."

She raises her eyebrows.

I inhale deeply. The blush in my cheeks renews.

As the night deepens, so does its hush. Aside from my boots scraping the pine needles and limestone, it's almost silent.

What do I say? I need to prove that we were close, but I don't want to say anything too intimate; she might not believe we were in love— or that we were lovers at all.

So, I keep it simple. Profoundly simple.

I look at the witch, staring into her red eyes. "You have seven horns, Helisent West of Jaws. Not six."

Her mouth falls open.

I smile. "The seventh is your tail horn."

I swear, I can hear her heart thump once in her chest—thudding like a fruit that falls from a tree and hits the dirt.

She clamps her mouth shut. Her eyes widen, wild and red.

Satisfaction clangs through me. "You kept them coarse. Not like Halcyon's."

"*Samson!*" she bellows.

I look forward and try to get rid of my smile. "Yes?"

Samsonfang howls in the back of my mind. (We're both *huge* fans of Helisent screaming my name.)

"I didn't think I would have shown them to you." Her eyes dart toward me then shift away. I can't tell if she's feeling shy, surprised, or shocked. Maybe all three; Helisent's horns were the only thing that ever made her timid.

"You didn't show them to me." I try not to sound too smug. "You let me feel them. And then you stuck your tail horn in my mouth."

She clears her throat. "Stuck my tail horn in the Kulapsifang's mouth…"

Another stretch of silence. This time, it feels loaded.

"Was I… happier?" she asks. "Happier than I am now?"

The question surprises me; I hadn't thought she'd ask something so subjective. Something laced with at least a modicum of trust in me.

"I think you were hopeful about what would come after you avenged Milisent. And I'm sorry you haven't been able to explore that."

I rub my arms as the night's chill creeps in.

The air eddies from my lungs with a long sigh.

I *have* to tell her.

Don't overthink it—just do it—just say it—

"What happened in Alita was my fault."

She doesn't dwell on my confession for long. "I have no doubt you'll make up for whatever happened in Alita." She pats me, fingers brushing the same spot where she held my arm during our traveling last year. "Maybe that's why Vex gave you the axe. They're for fighting, I'm led to believe. Maybe Vex knows you'll be useful to me."

I set my hand over her fingers before she moves them. "I will, Helisent. I'll fight for you and Vex."

She blinks, expressionless. She slides her hand away from mine. "Well, I should hope so. You're stuck here like the rest of us."

I ignore the rib. "It's more than that. I only told you the bare facts. What happened in Alita… there's a lot you still don't know." I stare at the ground, too nervous to look at her. "I was wounded very badly, and you saved me. But you didn't know healing magic, so your panic magic took over. Your ejima. And now that we know... what Vex is, and what ejima is..."

I take a breath and try to formulate my words.

Helisent cuts in, "Oh, I get it. Do you think Vex wants something in exchange for saving you?"

I adjust the axe in my grip, studying its weight and feel. "Maybe. But that's not what I was implying. Helisent... what if my injury was more than a serious wound?"

I remember seeing the yew tree— the same sight I'd beheld right before Hetnazzar saved me from being mauled by a wooly at age twelve. And I'd felt the same unyielding calm in Alita as I did outside Bellator. The same acceptance of my life, and my fate, and all that I had done. All that I would never do.

I go on, "What if I was... dead, or nearing death, or at the precipice of death, and the only way to save me was with a powerful spell. Not a one-and-done healing spell, but something more... permanent."

The lilith slows to a stop.

Helisent's expression breaks as she stares ahead.

She whips her head toward me. "*What?*" Her breath stutters. "Like Vex is... like *you* have the rest of my...? *You're* the other...?"

I wait for her to finish the question, but she doesn't.

Like Vex is... what? The rest of her... what?

The other... what?

I lick my lips, then force the words out. "Sometimes, the scar on my chest turns bright red. Red like your magic. Halcyon thinks it's because the spell is still active."

"*Let me see.* Let me see your chest."

Afraid of startling her, I gingerly shrug my tunic up and over my head. Her features bunch even more as she studies the dark mark on my pale skin, almost colorless in the muted night.

I go on, "I had chest pain when you were held in the rosarium. It stopped suddenly—I'm guessing when Halcyon freed you."

She closes her eyes. She exhales, long and low.

Then her round, red eyes pop open. She raises her hand and straightens it—only inches away from my face, as though leveling a spell at me from point-blank range.

Her jaw clenches as she stares into my eyes.

Oh, shit.

I hold my breath as I wait to find out if Helisent still loves me.

If she can wield magic against me as a centerheart.

She's certainly trying—certainly testing her magic and what it's willing to do to me. Her fingers twitch. Her nose curls.

After a long stretch of nothing, I raise my eyebrows in silent question.

(What I would do for a hug right now.)

Helisent lifts her hand and clears her throat. "It seems my magic *is* keeping you alive."

It also seems like she still can't wield against me. That she's very surprised by this discovery. I hear her heart thump in her chest again.

I shrug my shirt back on and try to sound casual. "So... Vex wants me alive?"

"Yes," she says curtly.

Our next stretch of silence is the toughest. I fill it with imagined confessions.

Helisent, we were in love. True love. Pure love.

Too basic.

Helisent, I'm centerheart for you, too.

But I'm not a wielder, so that's impossible.

Helisent, I need you how Velm needs the moons, so have mercy on my soul or cut me loose.

Way too stressful and loaded. Also slightly threatening.

A clearing comes into view before I can stick my foot in my mouth again.

Beyond the shadowy pine barren, moonslight fills a rocky field with a pale light, similar to the clearing above Hella.

But the dell doesn't end in another stretch of towering and lonely forest. Instead, a cluster of red rocks pile into the air, like a fragile and impromptu hillock. Like my scar, like my ax, like Helisent's eyes, the red color is faded to crimson in the heavy night. Moonslight casts off its uneven surface, littered with crumbling gaps and jutting slabs. The rubble extends twenty feet in either direction before sloping back toward the ground.

I fall still at the tree line as Helisent's lilith slows to a stop. Her eyes glow—not just her irises, but also the whites of her eyes. Their shimmering looks like the magical oil that fills the glass cylinders in Mieira.

Helisent rubs her face with a sigh.

I blurt, "I felt like I had to tell you."

She keeps rubbing her cheeks and temples like she's questioning every single decision that led to this moment. To me. To us. To what happened.

She slides off her lilith. She heads toward the rock formation and I follow. As we near it, I make out an entrance tucked into the boulder's meeting angles. Instead of a shadowy entrance, like Hella, peach-colored light beckons into the cave.

From my vantage, it looks like a portico to a staircase that leads below.

"Well, if we're being honest with one another now," Helisent murmurs, baring her bright eyes at me, "then you should know I lied about my magic being a twin. It's really like a demigod. Maybe several demigods."

I blink at her, blood stilling.

Part of me thinks she's trying to scare me. The rest of me realizes this is probably the truth. Especially if Vex is responsible for pulling me back from the precipice of death—and keeping me from dying for almost a year.

Helisent clears her throat. "Accra said my ancestors chose annihilation before they accepted coercion." She gives me the one over. "I control the future of Vex. And if what comes next destroys me, Samson 714 Afador, Kulapsifang of Velm, then you will be the last living being with any tie to Vex. Swear to me you won't let it die."

She blinks her red eyes. I've never seen Helisent look so... neutral.

I want to hold her hand. I want her to make me beg. I want to carve her name into a bloodred column of marble.

Something *more* than this. She deserves *more* than promises at highmoons.

I shift, squaring up so that we're facing one another. "I swear to take care of Vex if you die." *But I won't let you die, little bird.* "And if I die, Helisent West of Jaws, then you need to find Imperatriz 713 Afador. Find my mother and return her to Velm. And once Imperatriz is back home, you can kill Clearbold 554 Leofsige."

Her eyes shoot to mine. She scans me from head to toe again. A smile pulls at her lips.

"In that *exact order*," I clarify.

She smoothes her hair. "I didn't realize you... weren't a fan of Clearbold."

I probably shouldn't have told her that. "I told you we'd become friends."

The faint smile grows on her lips, but she doesn't bother with a response.

(I'm still hoping for a hug.)

Helisent tugs at her cloak. The fabric slips from her shoulders as she slings it off. Beneath, she wears a plain dress, similar to the beige piece she wore beneath her velvet peach robe last year. This one is sandalwood brown, fuzzy and soft. On either side, a steep slit reaches her hips from the dress's end.

She looks... so warm. So soft. Her ala soaks the thick fibers of the alpaca wool; I want to steal the dress and sleep with it wrapped around my head.

She catches me staring before I do, rolling her eyes once.

Then infrasound reels from her body, rushing outward. It passes through my body with booming bass, not nearly as subtle as Hella's portal tunnels or Helisent's spellwork.

I drop the axe and bend at the waist as soon as the infrasound passes, holding my balls as agony shoots into my stomach. My gut clenches, preparing to heave.

I sink onto my butt, sucking in deep breaths and trying not to vomit. I roll onto my back a second later, flattening myself to the ground.

Helisent never saw me throw up last year. I don't want this to be the first time.

"Oops," the witch croons, someplace above me. "I must have forgotten that infrasound bothers you. Just give me a second. I can't always control my magic in Vex..."

My face starts to sweat. I clamp my eyes shut and cradle my balls.

My poor, poor Afadors.

"There we are. It's time to go, boy-wolf," Helisent says. "I dampened my power. You won't feel it anymore."

Then something warm leans against my chest.

I can smell her ala in its form; bitter, overpowering. It reminds me precisely of the limestone common in Vex, of Hella's tepid and ancient scent.

I open my eyes, forgetting about the pain when I realize how close she is.

I flinch when I see her, inhaling a gasp.

It's Helisent *in her form*.

She looms over me only a hand's length away.

I stare at her face, which she bares at me like a bloodred weapon.

Her eyes glow with an almost blinding hue of deep red. I narrow my eyes so I can study the exact vermillion shade of her skin. It's dewy, soft and poisonous like the carnivorous flowers of Rhotidom. Silvery moonslight traces her round cheekbone, her curved lips, the tall arch of her nose.

My eyes flash to her horns, desperate to soak up every detail before she moves. They span much of her scalp, the largest as thick as my forearm. Tufts of hair grow between, catching on the horns' rough surface. They're larger than Halcyon's—and he doesn't have a hint of the thickest, coarsest horns that curve back around her ears like a ram's.

Like her eyes, the horns shimmer with pulsing, living magic that burns red. Like her eyes, they seem pitted with light that glows and glows.

And they're just as coarse as when I first touched them.

My lips twitch with a smile.

She is everything.

She really is.

I drink in her ala, savor her nearness. My hands shift on my balls, yearning to caress Helisent's shoulder, back, arm.

But the witch tsks as soon as I smile, then she lurches backward and stands. "Gross. I thought you'd be scared."

Helisent stomps toward the cave's entrance. Still nauseous, I roll onto my side and watch her go. Then I rise with a grunt, grabbing the red axe with one hand.

With another groan, I follow the witch.

She looks back from the portico.

Her twisted horns look like the white-hot of raw iron being beaten into shape by a blacksmith. Her seventh horn flicks behind her, its flat spade bone aglow like those on her head.

It's like I'm in a dream.

Like I've found the entrance to another world, and in this world, I'm bound to a red-hot witch and all of her bad ideas. In this world, I have no choice but to follow her to horrible places.

First, Skull. Second, the phoenix's nest. Third, Zarzynn. Fourth, Ezit.

"Stop fucking smiling." Then she scampers below, boots scraping against the limestone stairs.

I rub my face once she disappears. I slap my cheeks twice. "Stop fucking smiling." And then I follow the witch into darkness. Again.

CHAPTER 11

DEGIHOUSE (GOOSEWORLD)
HELISENT

Honey Baby,
Milisent built Gooseworld's palaces from loose cotton and set them in the
treetops. You were focused on secret passages—you said nobody would bother
moving in if they didn't have somewhere safe to hoard their treasure.
Papa P.

I rush down the stairs as fast as I can, spiraling into the cave.

I need a moment away from the Kulapsifang.

As I hustle below, sconces light up with magical oil. With each step, another one pops to life. They burn with the peach of sunset, casting off the bloodred walls and filling the cave with warm light.

I'll only have seconds of privacy before Samson catches up, and I can't deal with him walking toward me with a stupid lovestruck smile while holding his balls with one hand and a razor-sharp axe with the other.

How did this happen?

Mentally, I've been re-approaching a state of normalcy.

Now, everything is shifting out of place with the realization that I must have partnered with Samson last year to find Anesot, fallen in love with him along the way, and survived an extreme mishap in Alita. From his perspective, our love also survived that mishap. Based on my inability to wield against him, Vex agrees.

Halfway down the stairs, I close my eyes and take a deep breath.

I'd already suspected we may have been closer than I'd originally thought. *Closer*, as in *friends*, possibly *best friends*.

Not... lovers.

At least this explains why Samson seems in cahoots with my father. Why he begged on his knees without that much pushing on my part, and why he's in a blood feud with the House of Col, and why he wants me to give a fuck about Velm.

Why he looked at my form with rapture, not dread.

But doesn't Samson have a wife—and a proper *wife, not like a Halcyon-wife?*

And since when is he okay with me killing Clearbold?

I slap myself on the cheeks. "Get it together, Helisent. *Focus on Ezit.*"

It does little to help.

From out of sight above, Samson calls down, "Helisent?"

"What?" I snap. "Do you need a map to go downstairs?"

I clamp my lips shut; I hadn't meant to sound so harsh.

Samson ambles into view. He's not smiling anymore. Without the distracting grin, I focus on the rest of him.

Did we...?

I look at his hands, then his crotch, then his feet, then his face.

There's no way. We're not anatomically compatible.

He shifts, as though uncomfortable, then glances over my shoulder. "Should we...?"

I turn around and descend the spiraling stairs two at a time.

I try not to feel self-conscious about my form. I'd wanted to scare him because, just like my form reveals itself near the Hellastone, I have no control in this cave. Vex lends its magic to me, so it has the final say in what spells I cast. I've come to realize this is the nature of being centerheart; with so few wielders at its disposal, Vex wants allies —not enemies.

And right now, I can feel Vex's magic concentrate within the primordial limestone around us. Bass lurks in the stone like a growl in a beast.

The spiral staircase empties onto a flat mezzanine. Its curved walls seal us into a rounded, tunnel-like vestibule. Several passages branch out, leading into utter darkness and whispers of infrasound; only one tunnel is lit by triangular sconces.

I guess it's straightforward enough.

Still, I wait one moment, wondering if I'll see any images of empty brandy bottles.

Nothing.

I head down the lit hallway, away from the staircase. Unlike Hella, the cave is plain—aside from its color. A bloodred hue soaks every single pebble and nook, every uneven gap in the walls. But the stone looks naturally vibrant, not painted or blanketed with crimson tiles.

The tunnel almost vibrates with bass.

Not just *any* bass. Now, I recognize it as the latent form of my magic. A hint that it's in use or wants to be.

I pause, glancing at Samson. He doesn't seem to be in physical discomfort like he was outside. "You can feel it, right?"

He raises his eyebrows in response. "Of course. It's your magic. I know its sound."

"And it doesn't hurt you now?"

He studies the arched ceiling. "No. It's more like a tickle down here."

The hallway curves as we wander onward. The sconces flicker to life in tandem with my steps, illuminating the tunnel twenty feet ahead of us. It's colder and damper than even the darkest streets in Hella.

I glance back and realize the lights are blinking out behind us, leaving only a gulf of darkness in our wake.

My feet shuffle to a stop, as do Samson's.

The same way I once sensed Hella's location through intuition, I can now sense something in the earth, surrounding us. Watching us.

Or maybe not watching. It's more like singing.

From deep within the rock, I start to make out different sounds. Not *infra*sound, because not all of them are low-pitched.

My head tilts as my ears prick up—

First, I hear the highest pitch. It's easiest to make out because it's so contrary to my bass—more like an endless female screech. It rattles my ears, my bones, the tiny hairs on my neck—

I hear a second pitch, layered deeper than the highest. Then a third, and a fourth, and a fifth. The last pitch, nearly as deep as mine, is farthest away—as though it's singing at a great distance. So similar to Vex, and also faint, it's the hardest to pick out.

I close my eyes and try to concentrate.

I open my eyes; Samson is already staring at me.

"How many do you hear?" I ask.

"Five. Five others. They're all higher-pitched."

I clear my throat. "I think they're the other Houses."

One, two, three, four, and five.

Lahar, Talos, Col, Serac, and Argot.

I strain, listening closely. One pitch, the second-highest, is familiar. But I'm not sure which House correlates to which pitch of magic. And that's just the start of my ignorance.

I stare ahead where the tunnel ends in darkness. Another shiver shoots up my spine.

I look up at Samson; half of me hopes he'll convince me to back out of this idea. *What can I really hope to learn from a visit to Ezit?* I'm not sure—all I know is that Halcyon and Ret's knowledge can only take me so far. And I don't want my first time seeing Ezit to be the night of the invasion.

I clear my throat again. "Are you scared?"

He balks, glancing further into the tunnel and then back to me. "Not of this." Then he keeps moving.

But my feet won't let me follow. Samson looks back from a few strides ahead, then offers his hand. I stare at it for a second, wondering what he's trying to hand me.

I glance at his face—*is he serious?*

He is. He wants to hold hands.

I slide my hand into his, happy for the warm touch and the reassurance from such a large being. I'm less welcoming to how his hand readjusts, folding our fingers together like its muscle memory.

I start marching down the hall before I get in my head.

I squeeze his hand for comfort as the journey goes on.

And on.

Eventually, a cool patch of moonslight comes into view at the end of the warmly lit tunnel.

I stare at the circle of light, hand tightening on Samson's. My heart starts to ratchet, my palms sweating. It's intense enough that I freeze again, worried the door to the black room of dead memories will swing open.

I wish Halcyon were here; he knows how to snap me out of this.

"It's okay, Helisent," Samson says quietly.

I release a shaky breath. "I know I made a big fuss about me and you being the last beings with ties to Vex's magic, but... what do you want me to do if this goes tits-up?"

Samson watches me with his eyebrows tugged together.

I clarify, "They won't take me alive again."

He makes a low sound. "I see." He studies the patch of moonslight, then looks at the red axe in his free hand. "Why don't you let me fight our way out if it comes to that?"

I wait for him to produce a more coherent thought; he doesn't. "You and an axe versus Ezit?"

With an impatient sigh, he squats. He looks up at me, evil glittering in his pupils. "Zarzynn participated in my mother's disappearance eighteen years ago. And then they took *you*. I've spent my life accessing levelheadedness, so I understand you question my ability to rampage, but... it's in there. I still have access to that part of myself."

"Your pretty little axe won't stop a spell, Samson 714 Afador."

"No, but it should give you time to come up with something."

His features don't deviate. He actually meant that.

I snort. "Was I really that quick on my feet last year?"

"No," he says with a sigh. "But you didn't know then what you do now. I trust you."

I stare into his blue-black eyes. Once again, his features don't deviate.

After a long sigh, I guide us into the circle of moonslight. We lean back to squint up into the watery light; I can't see anything but the night sky, faded by peripheral light.

I nod at Samson. He nods back, and then we start floating.

He doesn't look uncomfortable as his feet lift from the ground—just curious. For a second, I think he's looking around in wonder as we float into the narrow tunnel that leads above. Then I realize he's following my tail's spade end as it undulates.

"Stop staring."

Samson looks at the cave's rocky wall, but his eyes flicker back to me a second later. He murmurs, "You're the most beautiful thing—"

"Holy shit, get it together."

I push off Samson's shoulder as we near the exit.

I pretend not to notice his warm fingertips skimming my calf as I pass him.

I reach for the lip of the tunnel, just as bloodred as the limestone below, and then propel myself upward.

I glance at the city around us, decide what I'm seeing is unfathomable, and then turn back to help Samson rise from the tunnel. He steps onto the red rock, closing the distance between us so that our arms touch.

We stand in a hexagonal area penned in by obsidian walls. And past the thirty-foot walls sits an unfathomable city. What I think is a city but could easily be something far more nefarious, possibly even alive.

My head tilts back as I attempt to take in the scene.

Cities are...

If cities are sables, then this is a wooly mammoth.

Ezit expands beyond the obsidian walls around us, on and on and on, layered with rooftops and multistory buildings. Dotted with fluffy canopies, the cityscape doesn't look too unfamiliar—except it doesn't expand horizontally. Ezit is shaped like a bowl. Maybe a box.

At its border far in the distance, the buildings don't dwindle into countryside. Instead, walls extend high into the sky. Stone and wooden buildings line them; roads and streets rise upward and weave between the structures like vines along a tree trunk. Windows line the buildings stacked on the vertical walls, lit warmly from within. Even trees and bushes crane along Ezit's walled border, shivering in the wind.

The walls curve inward near the top, as though sealing the city into itself. Trees and houses also droop from these tilted, upside-down portions. A circular gap in the middle reveals the night sky, directly above where we stand in Ezitlos.

I can sense magic upholding it all. Magic that buzzes and gathers with the force of an ocean. Magic that is differentiated by pitches that are coming into clearer focus.

Only Vex lies empty behind us, an expanse of shadowy pine barrens. The city almost reminds me of a pie—and Vex is a slice that's missing, left abandoned.

Compared to the city beyond, the dirt-floored hexagon of Ezitlos doesn't seem too intimidating. The straight and thick obsidian walls that pen it in look like quaint giants.

Within, the unpaved ground in each section is colored—only faded, muted. My eyes jump from one section to the next: a ruddy gold, an almost-black indigo, a misty portion of beige, a bright smear of red-orange, and another almost-black shade of jade.

Only the orange hue is nearly as bright as Vex.

The colorful stretches of dirt meet in the center, where each area narrows to a point. They widen outward toward the thirty-foot walls of obsidian.

The glossy black stones tilt slightly inward, casting seams of shadows to the ground.

And there, sat between the walls and the center point where each House meets, wait Landmarks. Or what's left of them.

A few damp rocks sit in a pile to my left, pale golden in color. Tired droplets of water rise from the rocks, like a waterfall trapped in reverse. The droplets rise a foot, then fall back toward the rocks. *House of Talos; waterfalls.*

Past the waterfall sits a jagged slice of white-blue ice, cool air wafting from it like fog. Though glowing brightly, the Landmark can't be larger than my forearm. It sits alone in the dirt. *House of Serac; glaciers.*

Next is a fragile rainbow that glimmers and disappears amid ghost-like mist. Water gurgles inside a pale cluster of fist-sized rocks. Every few seconds, hot condensation sparks with high-pitched magic. *House of Argot; geysers.*

Next is the largest and brightest Landmark. The ground is broken into jagged, burnt-orange pieces. Lava gurgles in a deep rut, curdling onto the rocks before bubbling and melting again. The seam of broken ground stretches from the center point of Ezitlos to the obsidian walls, spewing a deep and palpable hum of magic. *House of Lahar; volcanoes.*

Last is a dark jade section. I don't see any remnant of a Landmark —only the wind remains, whipping through the air like a gale storm and whistling a weak hum of magic. *House of Col; cliffs.*

"This must be Ezitlos," Samson says. "The city inside the city, like Ret said."

Slowly, he turns. Behind us, Vex's red limestone expands into a shadowy tangle of pine barren. There's no obsidian wall, no hint of Ezit's urban sprawl. The borders with Talos, to the north, and Col, to the southeast, are defined by more towering obsidian slabs. They divide the city from Vex.

Samson and I turn back around to face Ezitlos.

I hadn't thought of what to do once we arrived—in the dead of night, no less.

Before either of us can come up with a plan, the shadows hugging the walls start to shiver.

I take a step back and Samson takes a step toward me; we ram into each other as figures emerge from the shadows hugging the obsidian slabs.

In quick succession, wielders shadow into Ezitlos. Distinct pitches of infra and ultrasound fizzle outward with each arrival.

The wielders are obscured with long, transparent veils. The veils block their faces, and their bodies, shifting amorphously.

My eyes flit around the hexagon.

Beneath the veils, the wielders wear opaque robes, which cover their arms, their necks, their legs. Lavish amounts of jewelry sparkle amid the layers; drooping necklaces, diadems, bracelets, brooches, rings, headbands. Though their layers are muted in color, it seems each House prefers a specific type of gem.

They catch the light from Ezit's bright streetlights, visible above the walls, glimmering like their eyes and horns. Col wears moonstone, Talos garnet, Serac amethyst, and Argot pearls. And like my horns, theirs also glow, curling with deadly luminosity. Thankfully, only the Col Hosts groom their horns to grow straight up.

My eyes leap around the hexagon.

I try not to stare at the Serac Hosts.

At the precise tint of indigo eyes that fix on me. I can tell the Male Host from the Female Host only by his slightly broader frame.

Suleiman.

Dread kindles in my gut.

Halcyon didn't want me to do this.

More appropriately, he begged me not to come here.

I filter over the rest of the Hosts. I pause at Argot; their skin, visible from their naked hands, is powdery and lifeless. Their eyes glow like white-hot suns, white-hot moons beneath their thin veils.

Only Lahar remains empty, its lava gurgling noisily as it bubbles from the burnt-orange ground.

No one speaks. The Hosts venture a few steps toward Ezitlos's center point, then stop with their eyes fixed on me. They're like glowing wraiths beneath half-real fabric, half-real nightmares I've known better than to dream up.

I take a deep breath, relieved to sense Samson looming behind me, close enough that my horns are poking his abdomen.

"We were going to send our own invitation to Hella tomorrow," says the Male Host of Argot, speaking in accented Zarzyd. A rainbow catches the misty light as he angles his head. A distracting array of colors flutter above his veiled horns. "How is the Kulapsifang?"

I try not to look as surprised as I feel. Ret mentioned that some wielders knew about Velm—but knowing of a *Kulapsifang* is quite advanced for those claiming to have a *basic* awareness of wolves.

Rather than turn my back to the Hosts, I reach up and tap Samson's chest blindly.

He bends and whispers into my ear, "Yes?"

"He asked how the Kulapsifang is. Any idea why an Argot Host knows about you?"

He pauses. "I'm one of three living Kulpasifangs right now. And I'd remember meeting these wielders."

"Interesting." I suck on my teeth while I stare at the Argot Host. Switching to Zarzyd, I ask, "Which Kulapsifang?"

The rainbow fizzles out above the Host's head. It's accompanied by a high-pitched clang, like two glasses being tapped together. It's hard to differentiate between his layers and his horns and his hair and his pearl jewelry; everything is stark white, edgeless like a dream.

He says, "The reigning Kulapsifang, Clearbold 554 Leofsige."

A low growl emanates from Samson behind me; I don't bother asking if he understood the comment.

The Male Host of Argot continues, "You are wise to seek help from Velm. You have no control of your ejima, Helisent West of Jaws."

I blink at him, translating his words again and again.

Control my ejima? He sounds like Halcyon.

The more I learn in Hella, the more I realize how inappropriate this idea is. Vex's ejima has outlived me for thousands of years. It has been cast into thousands of spells thanks to the ingenuity of thousands of wielders.

I look from the Host to his fragile, ailing geyser.

These wielders play a game of control.

They seek total authority over their magic based on the idea that Landmarks are wild, savage, untamed...

I raise my hand to beckon Samson back down.

When he leans toward me, I say, "I think they made their Houses degi. *Degihouses*, Samson."

For a second, I study the bowl-shaped city beyond Ezitlos's obsidian walls. Things start to click into place, one thought leading to a realization, and then another...

To control their Landmarks and wield the raw magic dwelling within the earth, the Hosts whittled their Houses down into fragments—the same fragments we see here in Ezitlos. They took away the physical place where the magic lived so they could wield it in larger portions.

Which means the Hosts didn't build Ezit solely to centralize their greed.

When their homelands were divested of magic, the land would have withered, and without fertile land, all those who lived there suffered—

Their greed made them refugees. And with fewer resources, fighting became inevitable. Along the way, its residents forgot what peace was. Once peace was gone, the next generations lost happiness. And once both were artifacts of an ancient history, there was no hope to reclaim either.

How a language is lost, how a talisman is misplaced—slowly, over time, with incremental missteps—

Samson straightens again.

Uncertain of what to do but positive I should remain as tight-lipped as possible, I look away from the Argot Host and his silent partner.

As though reading my disinterest with Argot, another Host addresses me; the Female Host of Col. "Greetings, Helisent West of Jaws. As offered in our letter, you and your guest may speak with the dead as you please. For as long as you please. There is no question you may not ask. Let me offer you a necromancer now."

I study the Host. She seems to be smiling, her teeth catching the light through the veil.

Like her partner at her side, she's tall and slender. Her nose must end in a point; it pokes from her veil below her straightened horns.

She pivots to turn back to the obsidian wall. Her veil doesn't slip as she walks, fixed to the tips of her horns.

Before she reaches the obsidian wall, I tell her, "I have no use in speaking with the dead."

The Host turns back to stare at me, angling her head. Another gust of wind rattles through Col, shaking her and her partner's veils. For a second, they press against their bodies, revealing sturdy and muscular builds.

I go on, "But I will take the necromancer. All the okeanids, actually." A false bravado fills me. I'm sure Samson can feel my body trembling with each breath, can hear my heart thumping and smell the sweat in my palms. But my voice doesn't shake as I look around Ezitlos and repeat loudly, "I will not leave Zarzynn until I have every single Mieiran in my company."

The Col Hosts slide a glance at one another.

With a tsk, the Male Host speaks, "The five Houses of Ezit have agreed not to forfeit our okeanids and necromancers. If you like, we can discuss payment for them. We can also discuss *bartering*—we understand Mieirans prefer candles to coins."

With each second I spend in this place, wrath replaces my uncertainty.

I raise my chin. "Their lives are owed to their demigods. Their lives are not to be bartered or sold. Give them back."

"The last time Vex stood against Zarzynn's Houses," Col's Female Host says, laughter in her throat, "you *lost*."

"Let's not become combative with a lost Vexen," calls a voice from the other side of Ezitlos. "We're happy to know the spirit of Vex remains unchanged, Helisent West of Jaws. And you can't fathom the beauty of necromancy until you've experienced it yourself. Please, let us share this gift with you."

I turn to see the Male Host in Serac bow his head, the Female Host close at his side. Their indigo capes form long trains that extend five feet behind them, perfectly resting on the ground below their veils.

Suleiman spreads his hand over his chest. "I offer a warm welcome to you and your guest. His presence honors us. We send our goodwill to both of you, and to the Kulapsifang Clearbold."

Samson releases another low growl while I try not to look as livid as I feel.

Ret was right—Serac knows a lot more about Velm than we thought possible.

Maybe Argot, too.

And it's abundantly obvious who Velm's ambassador was.

The Female Host adds, "You have already received one gift from Serac. Let our House offer you a second now."

'One gift from Serac.'

My mind jumps from Clearbold to Halcyon immediately.

I can't fathom what that would be aside from Halcyon, which means they know he saved me—they may even know he's in Vex as we speak.

A flush of adrenaline tells me to leave this place. To return to Halcyon and make sure he's safe, that his wives and sons are safe.

I do a double take as something crosses the wall's shadowy barrier in Serac. Samson makes sense of it before I do. He tugs on the back of my dress as I wander closer to investigate.

It looks like a broad, oval mirror with legs. I count ten fingers gripping the bottom of the mirror's curved wooden frame. The oval mirror hides the carrier's upper half; I can't see anything other than skinny legs in fitted pants and clean leather boots.

For a second, I wonder why the wielder doesn't use magic to lift and carry the mirror. Then my mouth goes dry.

The mirror. A necromancer.

They hustle toward Serac's Hosts from the obsidian wall, a dark cloak flaring behind them.

Samson tugs on my dress again. I finally yield, feet planting into the ground while my thoughts spiral.

Is it Butter?

Who is that?

How long have they lived here—far from their demigod, their people, their home?

The necromancer stops between the Male and Female Host. They adjust their grip, causing the mirror to tilt back and reflect Ezit's upper walls.

"Helisent West of Jaws." A muffled female voice speaks Zarzyd behind the mirror. "There are three deathlings who want to speak with you."

I'm both relieved and enraged her voice isn't Butter's.

The Female Host of Serac reaches over to lay her hand on the necromancer's back, stroking lightly.

Rage washes through me, then disgust, then terror; it loops again and again.

I address the necromancer in Mieiran, "I don't want to see the dead. I want to see your face, my dear okeanid."

In the same cadence and tone, the okeanid repeats her original statement.

Vex's low bass thrums in the ground below my feet. I can feel it spiral around my horns, my hands.

I take a step forward, eyes fixing on the slab of glacier in Serac—

Then a red-fleshed figure shifts into the mirror's frame.

I stop when I recognize the warlock's broad face and full cheekbones, his large eyes and the unending fierceness in his pupils. Of the three faces Vex showed me when the gorgons told their stories, Axerxa's was the most alive.

He glances over me once, then looks around, as though making sense of his surroundings.

I clamp my mouth shut, hoping I don't look as surprised as I feel.

Axerxa makes a long noise as he settles back into the center of the frame, staring at me.

With a flicker of a smile, he glances over my shoulders to Samson. In Zarzyd, he says, "Good choice. Your littlelings will be strong. Does he like the ax? Ask him if he likes the axe. I will send more weapons."

My mouth falls open. I'm not sure which thought to follow—

First, Axerxa thinks I brought Samson here as my Male Host. But this isn't possible—there will never be a red wielder at my side.

Second, I'm face-to-face with one of my ancestors. And he has a voice. And many opinions, it seems.

I close my mouth and open it again before finding a response.

My eyes dart around Ezitlos; the Hosts watch me with unmitigated curiosity.

I clear my throat and go with, "He's not my Host. The axe is fine, thank you."

Axerxa tsks, studying Samson again. "You didn't ask him if he liked it. Ask him."

"Axerxa, I'm sure you realize where we are right now." As much as I'd love a casual chat with the warlock, this is not the time or place. "Why don't we have this conversation later? I want to return my people to Mieira. Any advice you have to offer on Ezit would be appreciated."

A few of the Hosts shift in my periphery.

I'm not sure what help Axerxa can offer and whether it's wise to ask right now, but I'd be stupid not to take the chance. And I'd love to use the gifts of a necromancer against the Houses in any way possible. Even better if that's in front of them.

"Ezit was much larger when I saw it last. A lot cleaner, too." Axerxa jerks his chin toward the House of Argot, then the House of Lahar. "Argot and Lahar hold the most power. They kill their brothers, sisters, and families like a sport, so each has more magic to wield. Tread lightly in dealings with either."

The Argot Hosts lower their chins, glaring at Axerxa. Samson adjusts behind me in response, boots scraping the limestone. My dress shifts as he takes a handful of its fabric between his fingers.

Axerxa turns and scoffs at the Talosen Hosts. Both remain at the edge of their wall's shadow, as though planning to make a quick getaway. "Talos is useless. They are cowards. But I'm sure you've already figured that out."

I make a mental note to correct him on that later; House of Talos has helped keep Vexen magic alive in Mieira.

Axerxa squints toward the opposite side of Ezitlos. Both Colyd Hosts stand near the obsidian wall's seam of darkness, just like the Talosen Hosts.

The Male Host slides his pale green eyes toward Talos; I swear I see his head angle as though signaling. The moment ends as quickly as it began—and I'm too focused on Axerxa to spare any more attention toward either House.

"If I'm staring at Col, then I must be in Serac right now," Axerxa reasons. With a huff, he raises his eyebrows and tells me, "Serac and Col will do anything to undermine the other. They control the clouded islands of Stretch. They raid Plet. They want to find land across the sea to—"

With a loud crack, the mirror shatters and the necromancer holding it crumbles to the ground. Shards break across her body, some as large as a femur bone. Axerxa's features splinter, breaking across shards of glass before disappearing entirely.

The Seracyd Hosts level their glowing eyes on me.

They want to find land across the sea to—

To what?

I blink at the broken glass and the unmoving necromancer beneath.

My hands start to shake.

I spent eight months rotting in Jaws for killing Anesot and Oko—two wielders who deserved a cruel death for what they did to my sister.

And... this?

This is a different type of evil. Of entitlement.

I stare at the corpse and the shards burying her.

'What comes next will destroy you.'

The longer I survive in Zarzynn, the more I wonder what Accra meant by that. *Destroy my body, my magic—or my soul?*

I look at the Female Host. My voice shakes, "Give her to me."

She doesn't shift an inch. "Helisent West of—"

"Give me my okeanid." I hadn't meant to shout, but my words echo around Ezitlos, trapped between the obsidian walls. A stubbornness I know will see me die before I capitulate starts to seep into my mind, my body.

The Seracyd Host raises her chin. "They enjoy death. They speak with the deathlings often. Now, she will be with those she loves."

My head tilts as my vision careens with red rage.

They enjoy death?

The Female Host tilts her head, violet eyes shifting place beneath her veil. "I suppose if you want her so badly, you could come and take her."

Something inside me snaps.

I raise a hand and tap Samson's chest; he bends down so I can whisper in his ear again. "Did you mean what you said earlier? About trusting me?"

"Yes."

"And did I also trust you last year? Yes or no—no zhuzhing."

He doesn't hesitate. "Yes."

I lean further against him for a moment, letting my back rest against his abdomen. In the back of my mind, deep in my heart, I trust that he's the looming, calm being from the dark room. I know he is safe.

I clear my throat. "Okay. Look alive, then."

"Be brave." He straightens to his full height, hand tightening on his bloodred axe.

The only thing standing between me and the dead necromancer is the House of Talos.

I glance at the golden Hosts, who are now nearly crouching by the obsidian wall. I study the listless little waterfall near Ezitlos's center point. I lock my eyes on the Landmark and go straight for it. Samson follows me with quick steps.

I don't hesitate when I cross from Vex's red limestone onto Talos's gold-tinted dirt. I glance at the waterfall; the droplets fall and splatter, almost silent.

I can sense the Landmark straining, can hear an echo of thunder that seems to stir only in my mind. And then I sense its pitch—not just palpitating through the air but interacting with Vex's deep bass. The pitches meet and layer once I enter the House; a two-note song.

Interesting.

I pause in the House of Talos near the waterfall. Samson stays close to my back. The only sign that the wolf is uneasy with my decision is that he now holds my upper arm instead of my dress, prepared to haul me away.

I trust that he's watching the rest of the Hosts while I concentrate on Talos's threadbare waterfall.

The symphonic sounds are oddly calming.

They cut straight through my racing thoughts to soothe me.

Though these wielders may despise me, their Landmarks are demigods. Though their magic can be weaponized, they aren't weapons by nature. Their desires are much broader, much simpler.

Wielders make enemies—but not Landmarks.

Safe in Talos, I fix my gaze on the jagged chunk of glacier in House of Serac. At the unmoving body under the mirror's broken glass.

Both Hosts stand flanked around the fallen necromancer and the shattered mirror.

I focus on the indigo glacier rather than the wielders. The icy slab shivers with light, pitted within with magic. Cool mist wafts from the slanted piece, fizzling with weak veins of lightning—

'Be brave.'

I lunge forward and plant my right foot in Serac, then take a step onto the black-purple dirt. I face the Hosts, whose cloaks and veils stir behind them, raising as their magic gathers at the ready.

I can hear its high pitch, can sense my magic as it grazes this new sound. It isn't totally unfamiliar. It reminds me of Halcyon. Of Anesot, too.

Like in the House of Talos, Vex and Serac hum together, layering into a two-pitch symphony. One that doesn't seem to reflect the animosity between the Hosts and I.

My heart thumps in my chest as I meet their gleaming indigo eyes.

I look from one to the other, waiting for their move.

But neither shift. They stare—and with the veils in place, I can't read their expressions. Whether I'm playing into a trap right now.

Suleiman's bearing reminds me of Halcyon; how he stands, how he shifts his weight.

His glowing eyes switch from me to Samson.

Staring at the wolf, he says, "I wonder if the Kulapsifang knows what you are doing right now."

Rather than explain that Samson can't understand him and that he's been sorely misled by Clearbold, I take a step toward the necromancer. Let them wonder if we're stubborn or ignorant or mute.

Their cloaks continue to undulate, flapping faster and faster, like birds taking flight—

I take another step, and a quicker one after that—

The Hosts yield two steps away from the necromancer.

I still can't tell what their play is—whether the Female Host was taunting me, whether I'm stupid or daring for this response.

I lunge forward one last time, rounding the necromancer to one side and hoping Samson realizes he needs to pick her up. I wave my hand toward her body in case he doesn't.

I sense Samson in my periphery. He kneels and reaches forward, axe tucked between his arm and side.

My eyes whip around Ezitlos once. Given the stringent division between the Houses, I'm wagering that none of the other Hosts in Ezitlos, who have all fallen silent, would overstep into Serac—physically or magically.

But I spare a few glances just in case while Samson's hands fit around the necromancer. Broken shards tumble off her as he jostles her into place against his chest and stands. A few fall and shatter, while others settle into place over the necromancer. Without a spare hand or attention to spare, we don't remove the glass.

I watch Serac's Hosts as Samson backtracks toward Vex. We stay near the Landmarks around Ezitlos's center point, re-entering Vex with only a few strides.

My eyes linger on the Female Host's shimmering eyes a moment longer.

'They enjoy death.'

I will make her eat those words someday.

For now, I will take this necromancer's body back to Vex and, one day, back to Hypnos. I will whisper over her grave all the vengeance I took.

Samson stops near the tunnel that leads to Vex's labyrinth of caves below. I stand beside him, then raise my chin and announce, "I want the okeanids. I want the necromancers." I save my most withering look for Col's Hosts. "I want Pel, too."

I don't wait for a response. My body is heavy from exertion, my mind fragmenting with a thousand different thoughts.

I've learned a lot more than I bargained for.

I'm even leaving with a necromancer.

One last time, I study Ezitlos and the city beyond it.

When I was a little girl, Milisent and I dreamt up an imaginary world. We named it Gooseworld after the tiny red gooseberries that fell from the scraggly trees on our homestead; the color of our magic.

In Gooseworld, wielders did incredible things with our magic; Mili dreamed up a palace built in the clouds, while I made beautiful and tiny closets for hoarding treasures. I built each in the crook of a fruit tree, fit with thimble-sized windows.

Gooseworld has always lived on in my heart.

Not as *Gooseworld*, home of cloudy palaces and lairs for looting, but as the hope that I would someday live in a world where wielders were kinder than those in Mieira; that this kindness would make wielders heroes and protectors and innovators to the nymphs and wolves—not beings to be feared, descended from the War Years' bloodthirsty mercenaries.

I understand myself now.

That Gooseworld was how I protected myself from *this* truth.

That one day, my power might grant me a great capacity for evil.

Gooseworld dies in my heart, wilting like a flower in a bud that never bloomed.

Part of me is glad Milisent didn't live to see it die. Part of me thinks this is actually the moment she dies; with Gooseworld.

With a sigh, I turn back to join Samson and descend the tunnel.

As soon as I turn around, he lunges for me.

Time slows down.

At first, I almost laugh—Samson's facial features break into a mask of panic. His eyes widen and his lips part. "Heli—" The necromancer and the shards balanced on her free fall as the wolf's arms extend toward me. One knee bends as he jolts forward.

Time slows down, giving me just enough time for three realizations.

One, the wolf is attempting to shield me.

Two, because one of the Hosts cast a spell.

Three, they waited until I turned my back to do so.

One second, I'm watching Samson drop the necromancer and reach for me; the next, I sense a wave of crushing magic descending from behind me.

Then Vex's ejima responds.

Vex's blunting spell only has enough time to shelter us. It surrounds me, Samson, and the necromancer, spanning a few feet. As the spell cradles us, the wolf falls over me; I barrel into his stomach, crashing into glass fragments and the necromancer's slack body.

The crushing spell rumbles over the protective shield around us.

Past Samson's arm, I watch the spell decimate Vex's towering pine barren.

The trees flatten beneath a piercingly high pitch of ultrasound, kicking up dirt and sending needles and leaves and twigs high into the air. On and on the crushing spell rushes like a tsunami—far enough that I can't see how far its destruction reaches.

I hear the echoes of the high-pitched magic, the tear of breaking trunks, the rumble of limestone boulders.

I'm screaming before it ends.

But I can't break loose from the tangle of limbs. A skinny set of cool arms weigh me down, trapped within Samson's protective hold. Glass shards topple against my arms and back.

"Are you okay?" he asks, breathless.

I pull away with a growl, using floating magic to manage the glass. I ignore the wolf and flail back onto my feet.

Another shriek peals from my lips as I turn back to Ezitlos.

I heard the spell—I heard Argot's magic as it battered through Vex—after the *fucking cowards waited until I turned my back*—

Ezitlos sits empty.

My hands ball into fists. Tears clog my eyes before my anger fizzles out.

They almost had me.

Again.

"Helisent," Samson says.

My jaw clenches, nose curling—

I study the shadows hugging the obsidian walls.

One of them will be stupid enough to come back.

And I will not lose again.

"Helisent."

I whirl back to the wolf and the necromancer, prepared to scream again. Past the wolf and the dead necromancer spans a stretch of destroyed forest. Reddish trunks stick up at odd angles, while dirt fills the sky like clouds. On and on and on, deep into Vex, as far as I can see—

Destruction.

Ezit is already winning.

"Helisent, we need to leave. She's alive—but she needs help." Samson stands back up, jostling the necromancer into place against his chest. Dark blood speckles his arms and tunic, dripping from a few straight cuts from the shards. "Kierkeline might be able to heal her. We need to get her back to Hella."

Slowly, I regain control.

A few tears slip from my cheeks.

I wait a few more seconds, focused on the shadows of the obsidian walls; nothing.

He's right—we need to leave. Now.

I look at the wolf, scanning him from head to toe. Aside from the shallow cuts, he looks okay. "Are you hurt?" When he shakes his head, I reach forward, setting a hand over the necromancer's heart. "Let me see what I can do for her before we leave."

Warmth clings to her body, her blood.

My hand fills with heat; the first sign of healing magic. It floods the body to identify which processes are working and which aren't. With a deep breath, I shift my hands so they hover over the necromancer. I work my fingers to help open her lungs; her blood needs oxygen.

I don't have time to heal her fully.

Halcyon's wives and sons don't know I've just insulted Serac.

The full gravity of that sinks in, slamming into my gut like a punch.

I try to focus on the task at hand—

Which is getting the necromancer back to Hella where Kierkeline can save her, then shadowing Halcyon to Plet so I can bring his family to safety in Vex.

(And then taking Kierkeline's potion and handling whatever memories come back to me, and then rebuilding the trust I just broke with Halcyon, and then figuring out how to free the okeanids and necromancers from Ezit, and then getting all of us back to Mieira.)

Fuck. Fuck, fuck, fuck.

I guide us into the tunnel that leads below.

Without sparing any more words, I guide us back through the tunnels to Hella. Like they did on the way to Ezitlos, sconces light up to guide us down a separate cave-like tunnel.

Samson's boots scuff the limestone as he follows me. To my chagrin, my breathing doesn't become easier as we hustle. It hiccups until it turns into panting, which makes my vision stir.

I start to panic somewhere in the first half-hour.

Dawn is breaking beyond this cave.

I start to babble, "When we get back to Hella, take the necromancer to Kierkeline. Then I need you to look after things—with the vampires, especially. Keep the group from falling apart until I get back. I need to leave for a day or two. Can you do that?"

He keeps marching behind me and I keep scurrying to stay ahead of him. I don't want to see his face and deal with what we confronted on the way here. What happened in Ezit. What's going to happen now.

"Of course," he says softly. "And where are you going?"

I can't stand the thought of Halcyon waking up and realizing I went to Ezit. He's going to think he means nothing to me; that his family means nothing to me; that I've been using him without any real consideration for what he's risking for me.

And now that I know what sorts of spells the Hosts are capable of and that they aren't concerned with honor...

My voice shrinks. "I owe Halcyon a favor."

"I see. And... does this have anything to do with the Male Host of Serac?"

A fresh wave of panic descends. I look over my shoulder, shocked by Samson's discovery.

He explains, "Wolves have a strong sense of smell—and nobody was blocking their scents in Ezitlos. The Male Host of Serac is Halcyon's biological father. But the Female Host isn't his mother."

Holy fucking moons. I didn't realize wolves could smell *that* well.

Excuse me—I must have *forgotten* they can smell that well.

I face forward and clear my throat. "Don't tell anyone. You swear?"

"I won't. I swear."

After an hour of walking, a narrow staircase comes into sight. It spirals upward and into the pale morning light. I follow the stairs toward the singing birds.

I bolt from the cave, then pause below a familiar stretch of pine barren. I tilt my neck back, studying the canopy and footpaths below. All looks normal as far as I can see, all the way toward Hella's subterranean passage in the distance.

At least Argot's spell didn't carry this far.

At least I can hope the display of power was just for show.

I turn back to Samson. He adjusts his arms, as though exhausted from carrying the necromancer. He looks me up and down, then studies the forest. "What happened?"

I want to trust Samson; he was a worthy partner to have by my side in Ezit.

And I'll need another ally if I just obliterated Halcyon's good faith.

I raise my eyebrows. "You said there was a lot I didn't know about Alita. So? What am I missing?"

Samson lowers his eyes. He studies the necromancer's face, then looks up at me with a morose expression. Dark smudges ring his eyes, a red axe tucked under his arm.

"I betrayed you," he says. "In the end. In Alita."

I flinch, taking a step back in the rocky grass.

I force myself to look back at him, wishing I hadn't asked. The rest of me is slightly relieved by his response. I'm very good at handling fucked up things. It hurts—it always hurts—but it does feel normal.

Something in my gut knows that dawn is always pain.

He kneels and sets the necromancer on the ground. He cradles her head, gently setting it atop pine needles.

I begin, "You betrayed—"

"*Vexen!*"

I turn, gut clenching when I hear Halcyon. He hustles between the trees from Hella's portal, eyes brighter than usual. Like Samson, Halcyon looks disheveled—like he's been up and searching for me.

His eyebrows bunch together, his jaw clenched. His wrath trips me up; I've never made anyone so angry unintentionally.

I address him in Zarzyd. "I know—"

"No, *you don't know.*" Halcyon's words are rushed, like he doesn't have enough air to speak them. "We're leaving—we're *leaving.*" He doesn't spare a glance at Samson or the necromancer laid on the ground. "*Now!*"

"I'm sorry, Halcyon." I glance at a pine tree to my right, its rigid shadow. I turn toward it, prepared to shadow into Hella. "I'll meet you at the fountain in ten minutes."

"*Two minutes,*" he growls.

I don't look at Samson.

It all goes quickly after that.

I shadow from the pine tree to Hella's central plaza. I ignore the swarm of worried Mieirans who rush after me. I tell them we brought back one of the necromancers and that I have to leave for a day or two; Parsifal trails me, gripping my arm without asking any questions.

I'm guessing Halcyon already clued him into this next part. That we're going to Plet. That Halcyon will never forgive me. That his wives and sons won't, either.

With a bag of bare necessities, I turn back for one last item. I clear my throat, then lean down to whisper into my papa's ear, "Kierkeline has the potion?"

He shakes his head, then takes my hand and sets a glass vial in my palm. "It's time, Honey."

The vial is warm, as though he's been clutching it for some time. He closes my hand around it, then raises it to kiss my fingers.

I tuck it away, then stare at the ground and wait for Halcyon to come back.

Parsifal doesn't say anything. He leaves my side to bring over a few extra millet cakes and a sack of dried berries, then tucks them into my bag.

My mind keeps snapping between Samson's words and those from Serac's Female Host.

'I betrayed you.'

'They like death.'

CHAPTER 12

AMARO (GOOSEWORLD)

SAMSON

My grandson,
On one triplemoon, a witch found your mother. She threw gooseberries at
Imperatrizfang all night; she waited for her to change forms at dawn. She told
crude jokes and offered her brandy. Despite her best efforts, your mother drank
and laughed with the red witch.

I stare at the shadow of a nearby pine.

With the witch gone, I direct my glare at Halcyon.

The warlock looks back at me, features bent with anger.

My control snaps—

Maybe Halcyon can lead me to Pit or knows someone who can. Maybe Halcyon is the only reason Helisent is alive. Maybe he'll be invaluable to her success in the future.

And maybe not.

I've been exceedingly lenient with the warlock. I've been handling this whole fucking experience with aplomb. No more.

My fingers tighten on the red axe. I lower my chin to scowl at Halcyon. "Watch your fucking mouth when you speak to Helisent West of Jaws."

Adrenaline, cortisol, and testosterone shiver around the warlock, pooling and intensifying like my own.

"You put the witch in danger, Samson." Halcyon studies the axe in my hand, then tallies the rest of me like he's preparing for a fight. (He fucking should be.) "You put *me* in danger. You put those *I love* in danger."

I don't know what he said to Helisent because they were speaking Zarzyd. I also don't know why Halcyon is reacting like this, but I know there was a better way to speak to Helisent. Especially when he could see that she was already rattled.

I raise my eyebrows. "*You fucking heard me.*"

My mood spirals—

I won't stand here and be spoken down to by a warlock who makes Helisent feel insecure and then *thinks he gets to command me*—

"Helisent and I are bound." The warlock pivots on his heels after he says it. He backtracks toward Hella without another glance at me. "*Stay out of it,* Samson."

He stomps across the dried pine needles, cracking between his boots.

My body shivers with rage as I adjust the axe again.

I square up to Halcyon as he stalks away from me, then relax my body with a long breath. The breath doesn't calm me; it helps me focus on my target.

I take one step forward—

And send the axe cruising with all my might.

It sails past Halcyon, close enough to his head that the blade nicks the hood of his cloak before it sinks into the pine tree inches from his head.

He whips around, glowing eyes fixed on me. His gray cloak rises into the air as he studies the red axe sunken into the trunk. Slowly, he turns to square up with me from fifteen feet away.

My gut steels, preparing for his magic. Without Helisent at my side and without the triple or doublemoon to call on, I have no way to defend against magic.

Which is a lesson I should have learned with Oko.

(Wolves don't hate wielders because they are lawless; wolves hate wielders because we are helpless against their magic.)

"Are we playing games now, Samson 714 Afador?" His voice is deep and low. "I love to play games, wolf."

"I would *love* to, Halcyon." I take off with a roll of my shoulders, eager to get within reaching distance. Maybe he knows little of wolves

—maybe he'll make the mistake of letting me closer. "Let's start with the Male Host of Serac. What happened? You lost your father's favor in Ezit and now you want the Vexen to take you to Mieira?"

Halcyon heads back toward me. With each step, his expression of rage lifts. It's replaced by cunning and unhinged mirth. A smile toys at his lips. "Try again."

Indigo light fizzles in his eyes, then guilds his horns. They glow from within like Helisent's.

I keep walking toward him, knowing I will lose this encounter without magical aid.

But even if my instincts let me back down, I don't think my pride would.

Halcyon's vile smile turns into a full grin. "I said—*try again.*"

In the last second, I pray Vex will protect me from Halcyon's magic.

It doesn't.

Even if it did, I wouldn't deserve it.

The warlock raises his hand and straightens his fingers toward me. A note of ultrasound batters through the forest, higher-pitched than Vex's magic. Then comes a pinch in my skull, like my consciousness is a candle being blown out.

I fall backward, legs folding just enough to prevent me from hitting the ground flat. The air knocks from my lungs, my vision black. I smell the pine trees and the needles, the warlock and his horns, the limestone layered with moss, the birds and their oily feathers.

Then there's nothing at all.

Vaguely, I can feel someone shaking my body.

Something slams into my cheek.

I open my eyes and my fuzzy vision returns gradually. I'm staring into the canopy of Vex's sparse pine barren. Moss dangles from the branches overhead. I smell pine needles, flaky limestone—and the Mieirans.

My face tilts as someone holds my cheeks. "Samson—Samson, can you hear me? Your eyes are open, but you look dead."

My nose twitches; Berevald.

I blink, meeting his eyes. A groan is my only response.

He twists to tell someone, "He's up. I'll stay with him until he's ready to walk. Take the necromancer back to Hella. We'll be back soon."

Rex starts, "Are you sure—"

"He's fine," Bere continues. "Get a meal ready, though, would you?"

Rex agrees, then footsteps drift away from us. I turn my head to see my packmate carrying the necromancer's tiny frame. Beside him, Aura and Eos reach up to keep hold of the fallen okeanid; Aura sets a hand on her shoulder, Eos on one of her booted feet. Kierkeline also hustles at Rex's side. She cups the okeanid's shaved head, fingers spread wide.

Berevald shifts into a cross-legged position at my side. His hair dangles to his hips in untidy heaps, his harem pants hung low on his hips.

He pats my chest. "You okay?" He turns to look over his shoulder at the group; they're almost out of earshot. "What the *fuck* happened last night? We felt something—some kind of magic. It didn't sound like Helisent's. Then Halcyon woke everyone up and said you two were gone. Did she take the potion? Did you two abscond on a lovers' retreat? He thinks you went to Ezit."

I feel my cheek. It aches from my cheekbone to my jaw. "Did you slap me?"

"Yeah. Pretty hard." He leans forward to look at my face. "Not much swelling." He sits back with a sigh. "You looked like you were having a nightmare. Also, your axe seems to be lodged in a tree at what looks to be Halcyon's height. Don't worry—I didn't share that observation with anyone. What the fuck happened?"

I sit up with a groan. I can't tell if my body is more exhausted after a sleepless night or from hitting the ground.

Berevald rises, then stoops to grab my hands and help me up. My head spins once I'm on my feet. I set my hands on my hips as my stomach flips.

He studies me. "So?"

Rather than explain, I push the last twelve hours away—starting with sneaking out of Hella and ending with Halcyon's knockout magic —I can't begin to parse out everything into manageable segments—

Like a rush of infrasound, it passes through me.

I bend forward and vomit across the limestone. Berevald takes a step back with a curse. I squat as my stomach hurls again and again.

I fold my hands over my face when I steady myself.

All the anger I felt at Halcyon splinters into self-loathing

I mishandled things. Badly.

It was selfish to tell Helisent about our love when we were walking into danger. It was foolish to let her waltz into Ezit without more concern for her safety. And it was maddening to follow her as she panicked about upsetting another man.

One who I now realize she must love.

And why would I tell her that I betrayed her like that—when she was already upset?

Why didn't I wait for a better time?

These feelings teeter like fields of fresh snow, primed for an avalanche. I breathe in and out, hoping it will take a more stable form.

Bere lowers his chin and grips my shoulder with a strong hand. "I'm guessing the lover's retreat didn't pan out. You'll feel better after you eat and sleep. Come on. Let's go back. Oh! And I know what will cheer you up." He claps me on my back, baring a roguish smile at me. "While you were off... in Ezit, I'm guessing... I was having the time of my life."

As we amble back toward Hella, we stop for my bloodred axe. Berevald watches as I yank it from the soft wood, then clean its blade with my tunic.

He stares at me expectantly.

I bite. "The time of your life—in Zarzynn? Let me guess—"

"No, don't guess. You'll ruin it." He slings his arm over my shoulder, then retracts it immediately. "*Lekeli Kelnazzar*, you reek." He takes a step away from me to put an arm's length between us. "A few hours ago, I woke up. It was still dark. Tol was in your bed—"

"The younger one?" I tsk. "Vic's apprentice?"

"Yeah, that one. So, she—"

"What the *fuck* is she doing in my bed?" What's worse than one vampire leaving their ala in my sheets? Two.

"Probably looking for you—stop interrupting. You weren't there, so I stood up to shoo Tol. And I may or may not have... been a little aroused. You know how it is if it's close enough to morning. Anyway,

Tol noticed and got a little curious. And she was already half-naked. She *lives* half-naked. We're all mammals, Samson, and—"

"And you took Tol to bed with Rex sleeping next to you?" My mood is lightening already.

"No—I told you to stop interrupting." Bere throws me an annoyed glance. "Things got a little hot and heavy with me and Tol. Then Vic showed up. And Vic *was not happy* that I was with the apprentice—I think Vic technically gets first dibs on everything. Men included. But instead of kicking Tol out, she started to—I don't even know how to explain this, Samson, but—Vic started to *demonstrate* to Tol that *she* knows all the secrets of pleasing men."

With each step on the coarse limestone and each detail from Bere, I return to my body.

It's like waking up from a nightmare and being pleasantly surprised by reality. The birds sing happily in the pine trees. The breeze is still kissed with night's coolness. Somewhere in Hella, Rex is preparing a meal for me.

There are small signs that things are okay.

"Then Rex woke up," Bere goes on. "He realized what was happening, freaked out, tried to lecture me, and then went back to sleep.

"After that, Tol and Vic took me to the fountain. All the vampires knew what was up. I'm pretty sure they can smell like us. Lya tried to join—I told him to go check on Rex instead. Then Vic and Tol took me to their den. Let me tell you, Samson, I know how the lambs feel when they're led to slaughter."

I doubt the lambs feel jack horny when they're led to slaughter, but I'm happy for a reason to laugh. By the time Hella's portal comes into view between the trees and outcroppings, the weight of my brutal sadness and self-hatred has dwindled.

"Well," I offer, "you definitely had a better night than I did."

He runs a hand through his hair. Now that I'm more cognizant, I can smell Vic and Tol's alas wafting from his locks. Even his chest hair and arm hair seem coated.

His eyes light up as he turns to me, grin wild. "Samson, there are things they did with my body... it's like, together, we form a triangle of—"

"Wonderful, Bere. I'm happy for you."

"If it weren't for their positions here, I'd take them back to Velm and marry them." He sighs, features pinched like he's actually weighing the possibility. "I've never met a wolf with two wives, but if you really want to support the Northing, my dear Kulapsifang, you'll let me push the frontiers a little."

"This might be considered Northwesting since vampires come from Zarzynn. What about their fangs? And don't you like the daylight?"

"The fangs are a unique challenge… something about the danger… and there's so much *Night* to share with them in Velm. They could live normally throughout Night—so long as they like the cold."

"They dress like they don't mind it."

We keep chattering, even once we pass through the portal. Inside the limestone cave, I focus on the large meal Rex hands to me, then I crawl into my bed.

It smells like vampires.

And when I close my eyes, all I see are Ezit's Hosts; the gentle sway of their transparent veils, the abstract shape of the fabric, the lethal glow of their eyes and horns.

I feel saner when I wake.

Not *fully* sane, but after more than a month in Hella, the cave's scents and sounds are familiar. I'm used to sleeping on the limestone, used to the way the light filters in from above at certain times of the day. Based on the optimistic chatter and laughter that echoes from the fountain and the bright, warm light, it's midday.

I sit up with a groan, rubbing my face and dreaming of a bath with warm and soapy water.

The vampires' scents have lingered. So have the memories of Ezit's Hosts. Neither is as potent as the shame of losing a fight with a fucking warlock.

I'm still on the bed when Rex passes the door later. He does a double take, then heads to my bedside.

"What the fuck happened?" Rex's blue-black eyes study my face urgently. He kneels. "Start with last night."

I take a deep breath, then recount last night's adventure and how it ended this morning.

Rex nods, staring blankly at the wall. His lips purse, then part;

stress. When his eyes flash to mine, he asks, "And? What do you think happens on the triplemoon?"

Do we survive?

That's what he wants to know.

I'd love to have a surer answer. "The other Houses don't have nearly as much magic at their disposal as Helisent. But it's like Halcyon said—having an untapped source of magic isn't nearly as important as knowing how to wield it."

Rex looks at the wall again. His full lips purse once more.

"How's the necromancer?" I ask before he can lapse into more anxiety.

My nose twitches as I pick out her scent from the communal space outside. It's tangled with the cold and foul twang of death. The only difference between her ala and a corpse is the iron in her blood.

Rex sinks from his haunches onto his butt. "Well, she's alive. Her name is Meres. It seems like her life is... tied to the mirror. After an hour of working on her, Kierkeline told Absalom to put the mirror back in order." He scratches his chin, glancing over his shoulder out the front door. "She got better once they did that, but it's hard to tell how... how she is.

"We still aren't sure if she can walk in direct sunlight. Ret says the okeanids drink vampire blood at the start of the necromancy rituals— but it doesn't necessarily mean the necromancers remain creatures of the night, like them. He said he thinks the okeanids in New Hypnos have developed a few techniques to undo the process. For some, at least."

"Meres wasn't attacked in Ezitlos," I explain. "The Host broke her mirror, then she collapsed."

He nods. "Meres said they're vulnerable when they're speaking with the deathlings. When they... go into the mirror."

I keep drinking in her scent, combing through it for some stronger sign of *life*. On the way back from Ezit, I was convinced she was dying in my arms—and her ala hasn't changed much since then.

Bere comes padding into the room, holding two jugs. He offers me a quick smile as he takes a seat next to Rex. "I thought I heard you. How do you feel? Here, take one. There's berry liquor and water."

I accept the water first, downing the mug with a few gulps. "I'm better. Thanks." I take the liquor next. My stomach is empty and growling; I'll take a quick buzz. "And what's a deathling?"

Rex goes on, "I'm not sure—she just woke up. I heard her telling Eos that the dead aren't actually dead. Or not all of them. There are the true dead, and then deathlings. She says deathlings wait on the border of our world. They stay close to life because they have a message they want to send or a being they want to watch over. She can find them in the mirror."

Beres nods. "Meres is with Aura and Eos now. I think they're chatting with some of the okeanids who didn't survive the... transition."

The pair look at one another. Bere's eyebrows raise slightly, Rex's chin dips almost imperceptibly.

Before I can ask what they're debating, Rex says, "Meres just checked for Imperatriz, but she couldn't find her. Even if a soul doesn't remain a deathling, a necromancer can still sense them in death."

Berevald reaches forward to shake my leg, a grin on his lips. "She's alive, Samson—like Anesot said. And if we can get Pel, then we can force him to take us to Pit. Maybe before we return to Mieira, if we're lucky."

Rex leans closer to me. "Or we call in a favor from Halcyon. He said he knows plenty of sailors in Plet—all we have to do is think of a good barter to offer or get some of these coins."

I say, "About that..."

I elaborate on what I heard in Ezitlos: two mentions of the Kulapsifang, both times with Clearbold's name attached—not mine, not Imperatriz's, not my grandmother Sutnazzar's.

I rub my face with a sigh. "Clearbold has some connection to Pit —and if the Houses are working in his favor, then we can't mention Imperatriz. If we ask Halcyon to bribe someone in Plet, then word will spread. Even if we don't use her name, it wouldn't be hard to figure out. And I don't want anyone in the city to turn their attention toward Pit. Or Imperatriz."

Both of my packmates stare at me, as though waiting for me to go on.

"If they know we're looking for her," I reason, "they will use it against us. They will hold it over our heads."

Rex shakes his head, rebutting my argument.

Berevald groans, unconvinced.

Rex clenches his jaw. "We can't…"

I know what he's thinking. *We can't have come this far and not push for more. We must find Imperatriz.*

"We can trust Halcyon," he goes on. "I know you don't like him—"

"I trust him," I counter. "It's the wielders and vampires in Plet who I don't trust. I can't risk them learning that someone important lives on Pit. We will be blackmailed with her life—*at best*."

Berevald looks from my face to Rex's, but he doesn't step in. Rex shakes his head again, letting me know that he disagrees. I stay quiet in case he wants to air out any other points.

But I know that I hate my argument more than he ever could.

"If that's really what you believe." Rex stares at me, raising his eyebrows.

I stare back. "It is."

"Fine. And speaking of the warlock…" Rex glances over his shoulder once again. "Halcyon told us he and Helisent would be back soon—do you know where they went? Parsifal knows and he won't tell anyone. And… tensions are a little high since everyone knows you went to Ezit. You know, after we agreed we'd wait for the triplemoon."

Bere nods. "Hemlock says he can feel a large portion of forest rotting in Vex. He's a big fan of trees, so he's pretty riled up. Kept going on and on about how killing a forest is like killing a demigod."

I slump in my bed. "I don't know where they went. All she said was that she owes him a favor. But it was bad—whatever happened between them. I'm guessing he didn't want her in Ezit. I'm guessing it has to do with his father's role there.

"And Helisent didn't level the forest. The House of Argot did that. I have no idea what kind of spell it was."

Once again, my packmates slide their eyes toward the other.

"He says it's *a lot* of death," Beres says evenly.

"And that it almost reached Hella," Rex adds.

"Well, I told you—we thought Meres was dead, so we… trespassed into the other Houses. And I don't know what Helisent was saying in Zarzyd, but I sincerely doubt she was offering any of the Hosts compliments. They were either testing her or trying to kill us both. That much was clear."

Rex narrows his eyes. "And she didn't take the potion? It was all business between you two?"

The pair bare their eyes into me.

I can sense their silent question—

It's something like, *You followed the witch into Ezit? Without any promise of rekindling things? Without telling us?*

Nausea starts to curdle in my gut again. "No. She didn't take the potion." I suck in a huge breath, wishing I wouldn't have shot the liquor. "But she figured it out on the way there. Just the basics. Just that we were in love. That she can't wield against me." I swallow the lump in my throat. "She tried."

I don't tell them that I made myself look like an asshole; I figure it's implied.

Rex nudges my chin. "Stop it with this face."

"Yeah, what's going on?" Berevald shoves my leg. "Tell us."

They wait, watching me with equal measures of curiosity and apprehension.

I need Helisent how Velm needs the moons; what the fuck is Velm without the moons?

Way too profound.

None of this is worth it if I can't have the witch.

Way too pathetic.

Sometimes, I don't feel real.

Way too... I don't even know what to do with that thought. It's probably best to ignore it entirely.

"I'm feeling..." I don't think I'm allowed to feel what I'm feeling. At least, not in my position. So, I shake my head. "I just need a cigarette. I'll be fine in—"

Rex nudges my chin again, this time with more force. Berevald raises his hand to slap my thigh. I'd rather be beaten than admit what I'm feeling right now, but I know I wouldn't win that fight.

I clear my throat. "I don't feel very... confident... right now."

They nod, bearing neutral expressions.

Rex asks, "About what, exactly?"

"You always seem *abundantly* confident," Bere adds.

"Maybe... about who I am." After that first admission, the words start to flow more easily. "I'm not sure if I'm living up to my name. I lost my mother. Then I lost my witch. I found the witch again, but

I'm putting all of us in danger to be here. *And* I'm fucking things up with her, and making her life harder when—"

"We know that Imperatriz is alive," Rex cuts in.

"And we have an idea of where she is because of you," Berevald says.

It's not enough.

I shake my head. "I could be losing Velm as we speak. I see the Leofsige symbol all the fucking time—I have nightmares of it, I think about it in the mornings and at night. And how many villages South of Gamma are removing their nymphs and wielders? How many unnumbered wolves will die before they escape Velm?"

I don't bring up how deeply fucked my future is if Clearbold really has endeared himself toward Ezit's Hosts.

(And *why* would he do that?)

It grates on my mind and body and instinct to be so far from my realm. From Bellator and Rouz and Mort and Wrenweary. From Night. From my wife. My throne.

This time, Rex and Bere take longer to respond.

Berevald offers, "What if we make a pact to kill Malachai when we're back? That will solve the Leofsige problem."

Rex ignores him. He leans toward me, his words harsh and deep, "It was never going to be easy, Samson. We've known that since you were twelve. Clearbold has raised you with no plan of letting you take the throne.

"He *does not want you there*—that's why you feel a lack of confidence. Because it was *the Kulapsifang's* job to teach you to inherit her place, and Imperatriz isn't here to do that.

"Clearbold *wants* you to feel this. This is his goal—to put a seed of doubt in you so that when push comes to shove, you will question your own claim. There's no fucking way I'm following Clearbold. Or Malachai. *You* are our Kulapsifang. There is no question of whether or not you *should* be because you *already are*.

"You have your Female Alpha waiting for you in Velm, and I trust her, too. Together, you will steer Velm back north, like Imperatriz wanted. Don't doubt yourself now, Samson. You are closer than you think. We all are."

Berevald looks from Rex to me, nodding. "And our packmates, Riordon and Pietrangelo, trust you. Plus, it seems like all the Mieirans here are getting closer. They trust you. They believe in you. It's not for nothing."

I take a deep breath.

Rex and Berevald stand, helping me to my feet. They linger close, waiting for me to initiate an embrace. I lean forward, and they lean toward me. Our heads touch and our hair falls and brushes together. We breathe deeply, guarded by the familiarity of our alas, of how they layer together.

When I pull back, we part ways with a few rugged pats.

I head to the washroom and sigh my way through a cold bucket bath. With all the angst gone, I take the moment of privacy to revisit Helisent's form; her jagged and rough horns, the way they pressed into my stomach, the hue of her dewy skin, how soft it is, the glow of her power, the ala of her bitter magic.

"You're the most beautiful thing—"

"Holy shit, get it together."

All the while, I can feel Sennen in the sky, hidden within the daylight as it waxes and waxes and waxes toward its full glory.

After another long nap, I meet the Mieirans who gather around the fountain.

In the last twenty-four hours, they've seen me show extreme aggression toward an innocent child, then waltz into Ezit against their wishes.

Still, I consider their measured gazes reasonable. Once again, the only being to look truly angry is Hemlock. He crosses his arms and raises his chin like he's waiting for me to beg for forgiveness.

I like to think Meres's presence has calmed them. After all, the ill-advised trip wasn't a total bust.

Aura and Eos guide Meres away from the group, toward their dwelling. Without the threat of Ezit looming and the heavy blanket of night, I study her closer.

She looks larger, her legs stronger and her cheeks fuller. Aura has passed off the turquoise-laden diadem, which sits proudly atop Meres's shaved head.

For a brief second, she looks like any other okeanid living in Hypnos or the Deltas—except the whites of her eyes are streaked with cerulean. Her irises don't have a distinct outline. They bleed into the rest of her eyes like ink in water.

She cradles the remnants of the oval mirror against her abdomen. Absalom must have melded the remaining shards together; this oval mirror is one-third the size of the original.

I ignore my reflection in its glass and force a smile.

Meres stops before me and offers one back. Aura and Eos also smile—unlike the group at the fountain, they look supremely pleased to see me.

"We got one back." Aura looks from me to Meres.

Eos raises her chin. "And it's always the first step that's the hardest."

Meres watches me, optimism and exhaustion in her gaze. "You carried me home."

Like her appearance, her voice relieves me. In Ezitlos, she spoke without weight or cadence or life. Now, her tone is deeper, more complex.

I bow my head. "I'm sorry for all that has happened in Zarzynn."

Meres's small smile doesn't falter. "One day, when I go home to Hypnos, I will tell all who will listen that the Kulapsifang of Velm carried me to freedom. Someday, you will come to Hypnos and tell my people I'm not lying."

I smile back, desperate for how hopelessly normal that sounds. "I'll come. I promise."

"Good. I need to rest now; the sunlight is draining. When I wake up, I will take Parsifal to the mirror first. Andromeda North of Skull is staying close to me. She wanted to speak with Helisent in Ezitlos, but Axerxa is more powerful." Meres takes a step toward the dwellings, Aura and Eos sticking to either side. The necromancer shifts her head to watch me as they walk on. "When Andromeda North of Skull is done, you will come to see me. There is a deathling waiting for you, Samson 714 Afador. He's worried about Velm."

He?

I'm not sure which thread to follow first—the fact that a deathling fears for Velm or the idea that Andromeda North of Skull is waiting for Parsifal as a deathling. The question of whether Milisent is with her.

(I'm also curious about whether the red warlock who showed up in

Meres's mirror in Ezitlos was Axerxa. He seemed to be addressing me, but Helisent never elaborated on what he said.)

I head toward the group once the okeanids have passed.

Meres's approval has at least lifted Hemlock's sour mood. Hoping to keep his favor, I tuck my hands behind my back and recount last night's adventure to the group, sparing no detail. Given I couldn't understand the words spoken between the Hosts and Helisent, there's not much to share.

When I finish, the group sits back, visibly dissatisfied.

Absalom crosses his arms. "So, you have no idea where Helisent and Halcyon went? Parsifal knows, but he's refusing to tell us."

The nymphs and wielders shift to look at Parsifal.

The warlock noisily sips from his cup of tinted liquor, glancing around the cave like he's lost in thought. Droplets cover his peridot cloak, crumbs from lunch in his beard. His eyes are muddied with red.

My gut sinks.

I've upset the only warlock who ever cared about me.

With a start, Parsifal turns to meet our expectant stares. "What? Why is everyone looking at me?"

"We would *love* to know where Helisent and Halcyon went. And when they'll be back," Absalom says. "And what they're doing."

Parsifal nods. "Yes, Absalom, you want many things in this life."

Absalom raises a hand for emphasis. "Give us *something*. We're sitting ducks in this cave without Helisent—and without the witch here to tell us what was *said* in Ezitlos, all we have is Samson's speculation."

"I think what he's asking is... should we set up defensive spells?" Kierkeline pushes. Unlike Absalom, her tone isn't contrite—but her gaze is direct as it lands on me. "We felt the spell cast into Vex. It was the single largest spell I've ever felt, my dear wolf. By a long shot."

I agree. It was like the light of the sun, speeding everywhere all at once, driving into every nook, battering through every surface.

The best I can offer is, "The caves are sentient. They led us to Ezitlos last night and then back again this morning. And the attack was a retaliation against us for taking Meres. I think Argot made its point. For now, at least."

"You know where she is," Absalom concludes flatly.

I raise my eyebrows. "She wouldn't tell me where they were going, just that she owed Halcyon a favor."

Absalom looks away from me, back to Parsifal—questions burn in his eyes.

Parsifal doesn't notice. He sighs loudly and glances around, nursing his drink.

Kierkeline gets my attention with a wave of her hand. She jerks her chin toward Parsifal and mouths the words, *Ask him. Alone.*

I'm done pushing for more information about Helisent or Halcyon, or both of them together, but I don't tell her that.

I nod knowingly, then head toward Parsifal. In a false show of privacy, the rest of the group pivots away from us and chatters loudly about the upcoming doublemoon.

I tap Parsifal on the shoulder, then gesture toward the meeting hall down the street. "Can I speak with you?"

To my relief, he doesn't bark a refusal at me.

Parsifal shuffles to his feet, sloshing more liquor onto his cloak. He follows me on teetering legs.

He grunts, "I'm not telling you shit, Samson. Don't ask."

I glance over my shoulder to make sure we're out of earshot. "I'm not going to ask where they are."

"Good." He straightens his cloak with a few tugs. "It'll make sense soon—just keep a cool head in the meantime."

I hear my axe sink into the pine tree near Halcyon's head for a second time today. "Sure."

I guide us into the meeting room. We pass the mosaics of red-tiled clouds that fill the walls, heading for the tiered benches.

I take a seat on the limestone bench and Parsifal does the same.

I take a deep breath. "I'm sorry that I didn't try to stop her from going to Ezit. It was irresponsible to put her in danger."

Parsifal leans back. "What?" His massive eyes are glassy, incredulous.

I clear my throat. "I'm sorry..."

He waves a hand to cut me off. "Helisent would have gone whether you were at her side or not. You didn't put her in danger, my dear wolf. She does that to herself all the time. She's been that way since Milisent died."

I sit back.

Parsifal isn't angry with me?

Tears well in his eyes. He pulls his legs onto the bench and crosses them, staring at the space between us. He slumps, shoulders sagging. "I think it's good you went with her. The warlock wouldn't have. He has... tight boundaries."

Relief courses through me.

He wipes his cheeks as his tears fall. His words are ragged whispers. "You understand her more than most, Samson. You're both motherless. You're both alone in the demands of your power. And you're both going to be leaders whether that's what you wanted for your lives or not." He reaches forward and pats my hand. "You're a good boy, Samson. A very good boy."

I bite my lip and ignore the lump in my throat. The tears that sting my eyes.

He thinks I'm... a good boy?

Parsifal squeezes my hand, then lets it go. "I just wish you could have known her before—before—" He exhales, long and calming. "I wish you could have known my witches as they were. I kept them west of Jaws for a reason. They were free—free from anything that could hurt them. They made up this little world. Gooseworld. Milisent and Helisent wanted to change life for wielders. Did she ever tell you about Gooseworld?"

He raises his chin, waiting for an answer.

"No. She didn't."

"I thought the banishment would be okay. I thought it would give Helisent time to heal from what happened with Anesot and Oko. That's why I didn't fight it as much as I should have. But this world wants to teach my daughter evil." His voice breaks, lips quivering. "And now she'll never have the chance to create Gooseworld. There was a place... a place for every little bird..."

Parsifal's shoulders buckle as he weeps. I lean forward to offer him a comforting pat.

I don't really know what to do or say.

Just in case Parsifal cares about me as much as I care about him, I offer him the same reassurance he gave me. "You're a good papa. A *very* good papa."

For a second, I wonder who I would be if I'd had a father like Parsifal. If I'd known that kind of love as a child, as a young man. I can almost feel this ghost of myself, watching from the past, clinging to this moment—

To a future that involves love.

Parsifal bares his wet eyes at me, golden irises shimmering. He squirms toward me on the bench.

The movement reminds me so much of Helisent that I immediately know what the warlock wants: a hug. I scoot forward to envelop Parsifal in my arms and he leans against my chest. It's almost exactly how his daughter falls into an embrace—except his gut presses against me rather than a large chest.

Sheltered between my chest and arms, Parsifal whimpers, "She's going to curse me when she sees me."

I almost ask him what he means—then I realize he's talking about Andromeda. He's not morose because me and Helisent went to Ezit last night. He's morose because we brought back Meres, and the necromancer says that Andromeda is waiting in her mirror.

Parsifal goes on, "And what will Mili say? Her papa wasn't there to protect her, Samson. No one was with her when she... when Oko..."

My arms tighten around him. I pat his back gently, but I'm not sure how to cheer him up. "What if we get you ready to see Andromeda? Come with my pack. I'll fix your hair and Bere will wash your cloak. Rex will get you a glass of water." I pull back to see how he's taking the suggestion. He sniffles as he dries his eyes with my tunic. "I'm sure she'd like to see you all gussied up. Witches like fancy warlocks, don't they?"

He straightens, staring past my shoulder like he's deep in thought. "Yes... gussied up... I was still handsome when she died." He switches his eyes to me. "Will you stay close? When Meres brings her into the mirror? Just in case..."

My heart stops at the idea.

I absolutely *do not* want to meet Helisent's mother right now—especially when Helisent has yet to meet Andromeda.

(Especially when I have a growing fear that she might be the faceless witch from my seething dreams. The one yanking angrily on the red strings entombing me.)

"Just in case what?"

"In case I need to distract her with something," he goes on. "In case she figures out how to come back to life and tries to kill me. In case she hates me—someone will have to carry me home if that's the case. And possibly put me out of my misery."

Wet streaks trail his eyes and cheeks and nostrils.

"Fine. I'll stay close—but I'm not sitting within earshot." I stand up and take Parsifal's cup with me. "Let's go get you cleaned up."

I head for the door, hoping he follows.

"Samson!" he barks.

I turn back to find him searching for something, flaring his cloak's layers and glancing along the bench.

He turns toward me, eyes locking on the mug in my hand. *"Give me that."*

Parsifal drinks himself into oblivion shortly after our conversation.

We watch him from the window as he snores loudly on his back in the plain bed. When he's been out for ten minutes, Bere and Rex trail me into the room. We hover over him to brush his hair and trim his beard. We even tug off his cloak and wash it thoroughly, then ask Kierkeline to dry it with a spell.

By the time he snorts himself awake, he looks more put together than I've ever seen him. Aside from the bags under his eyes, he looks prepared for a trip to a palace.

Parsifal doesn't put this together.

He sits up, looking from me to Rex to Berevald with a groan. "What the fuck are you three doing?" He tugs the lapels of his cloak shut. "Waiting for a peep and a squeeze?"

Slowly but surely, we guide Parsifal toward a small meal at the fountain, then on to the meeting room where Meres waits with Aura, Eos, and her mirror.

The necromancer sits on the ground next to the wall opposite the benches. Rather than hold the mirror, it sits on the floor atop a cushioned stand, propped against the red-tiled clouds. Meres sits beside it, one hand resting on the mirror's back—almost like a hand drum.

Aura and Eos drift away from Meres to stand next to me.

Parsifal takes one step into the room, then looks back.

After convincing him that I'll stay close enough to hear his shouting but not close enough to follow his conversation, and after an encouraging speech from the okeanids, the warlock finally steps into view of the mirror.

With a gulp, he tidies his cloaks and his beard, then nods at Meres. "I'm ready, my dear okeanid."

"I'm a necromancer now," she replies. "It is acceptable to address me as such."

With that, I trek back toward the fountain with Aura and Eos. Overhead, the sky sours into night and the cave glitters with golden light.

Soon, the vampires slink from their den; someone needs to occupy the vacuum left by Helisent's leadership—or allow Vic and Tol to enjoy free reign.

I take my seat on the lip of the fountain alongside Hemlock and Kierkeline as the nightly chorus of activity begins.

I loiter between the group and the meeting hall as the night drags on.

I decide to check in when the Mieirans start drifting off to bed.

A few feet from the door, I hear Meres. "Samson 714 Afador— come for the warlock. It's time for him to say goodbye."

I head into the room, lit with peachy light from the sconces lining the walls. Instead of sitting in the center of the room where I left him, Parsifal now kneels in front of the mirror by the wall.

He stares, eyes wide with absorption.

Meres smiles at me from her seat on the floor, seemingly undisturbed by the warlock's silent fixation.

I take a step toward the pair, ready to help him stand.

I flinch when I realize a witch stares at Parsifal from inside the mirror. Her chin is lowered, her eyes fixed on the warlock. Her irises twinkle like freshly drawn blood. She has her hands raised to the mirror; her skin is paler than Parsifal's deep olive tone.

Parsifal reaches out; their fingertips press together from opposite sides of the glass.

The witch notices me, shifting her gaze away from Parsifal.

My heart thumps in my chest when our eyes meet.

At first, I assume the witch is Milisent because she looks so young.

I drop that idea in the next second—

Her expression brings to mind what Parsifal has shared about his witch: Andromeda was nothing like her daughters, Honey and Mint. Andromeda was bitter enough that anyone who loved her called her Amaro.

Maybe she doesn't look *bitter*—

But the witch's eyes twinkle like she knows a thousand things that I don't, and she can sense that I am young and untested and unworthy. Her lips part like she's preparing an insult about me to whisper into a friend's ear.

Her white hair is messy and long, tucked behind her ears. Unlike Helisent, she doesn't have a round face and massive eyes. Her face is slender, her jaw stronger—like Yngvi and Yves. But her presence feels similar to Helisent's, especially the way she scans me.

Shameless, curious, demanding.

But certainly not the witch I've been seeing in the seething dreams.

Parsifal doesn't turn; I don't think he's registered my presence. He traces Andromeda's cheek. She looks away from me, back to the warlock. Her eyes shimmer like tilted jewels, like she's trying to lure him into the mirror.

"This one, Parsi?" Andromeda North of Skull asks.

Her voice is deeper than I would have thought and very direct. Almost... Velmic.

"Which one, Medi?" Parsifal whispers, breath fogging the mirror.

Andromeda lifts her finger to tap on the glass in my direction. "That one."

"Which one?" Parsifal repeats without looking away.

I look at Meres, confused by Parsifal's trance-like state. With an understated grin, she says, "Death is more alluring than we like to believe. Samson 714 Afador, a deathling is still waiting for you."

I clear my throat, uncomfortable with the idea. "Thank you, Meres."

I squat beside Parsifal, trying not to look at Andromeda or acknowledge how piercing her stare is. It leaves my skin ablaze where she watches me. She's beautiful; her features look hand-sculpted, from her button nose to her arched eyebrows.

Helisent inherited her lips.

I set my hand on Parsifal's back. "Are you ready to go?"

The warlock doesn't spare a glance at me.

Andromeda keeps watching me. "Tell your mother I'm still waiting for my kalimba, Samson."

I force myself to look at her; she doesn't know that Imperatriz is gone, that she hasn't played a kalimba in almost eighteen years.

Rather than explain that the Female Alpha is missing, I nod. With each glance, I feel like I'm overstepping my bounds with Helisent—she has never seen her mother before. She has never heard this witch's voice or looked into her eyes.

I wrap my hand around Parsifal's upper arm and tug lightly. "It's time to go. Meres will keep her mirror with her—I'm sure you can visit Andromeda again. But she's had a very long day. We should let her rest."

In response, Parsifal lunges toward the mirror. His hands flatten against it, then his fingertips curl, like he's trying to reach into the glass.

Andromeda taps her fingertips against the mirror, teasing him with a sultry laugh. "Parsi, darling, there's a wolf here to take you away. I'll be waiting for Helisent. Come back with my lastborn. Milisent wants to speak with her. And with you."

The warlock drifts closer to the mirror. "Medi... wait..."

Andromeda huffs, satisfied with his desperation. Then her eyes flash to me. "Take him now. Make sure he rests. He is old, after all."

I pull on Parsifal's arm—tugging once as a warning. He barely notices, jerking his arm back to his side.

"Parsifal, say goodbye. It's time to go."

I step behind him and haul him upward beneath his armpits. I groan with a curse—he's a lot heavier than he looks, and the warlock doesn't attempt to manage his weight to help me.

He bucks his legs as I drag him away from the mirror, shouting a few times. While I struggle with the warlock, Meres bids farewell to Andromeda. I don't see where the witch goes—whether she fades to nothing in the mirror or exits to one side.

I pin Parsifal to my chest and back toward the door. Meres kneels to lift her mirror from its curved stand. By the time I set Parsifal on his feet outside, the necromancer is striding back toward the fountain. Only Aura and Eos remain, sitting on the fountain's lip and staring expectantly at us.

Parsifal stares at Meres, taking one step toward her.

I stay at his side, prepared to grab him if he tries to follow.

Aura and Eos hop from the fountain and loop their arms through Meres's. Already, the trio's alas are tangling.

As though snapping out of the trance, Parsifal whirls around. He startles when he sees me, scanning me once. "Where'd you come from? Is Helisent back yet?"

"No. You were with Meres." I shake my head. "Were you really that out of it?"

With a long sigh, he raises his hands and smooths his hair. As though he didn't hear me, he looks up at me with a wistful smile. "Well, she doesn't hate me. Looks like I still have my charm. Thank the *moons*."

In a remarkable turn of mood, he takes off. "Let's go get the boys. We need to celebrate with a drink."

He even skips, double stepping once to clack his heels together.

A slight weight eases from my chest as I watch him go.

The day is at least ending better than it began.

CHAPTER 13

RANTING AT THE CHILDREN
HELISENT

Honey Baby,
It's okay to change. People never do, but it's fine to try.
Papa P.

I sit alone in the bedroom and stew.

I've laid in the bed and paced the nook since Halcyon and I shadowed to Cleo's apartment this morning. There are only so many details that I didn't notice during my first visit; all the tiny tchotchkes lining the room's dozens of shelves, the array of wielders visible from the window, the stacked buildings and their tattered flags. I can even eavesdrop on the conversations from neighboring apartments now that I speak Zarzyd.

Unlike the last time I woke in this room, I have my wits about me. For the most part.

The longer I wait for Halcyon to round up his brood and bring them back here, the more I revisit the last insult he hurled at me.

I'd asked him how long he would be gone, where his wives and sons were hiding, whether he wanted help finding them.

Halcyon said that he didn't know where they were. That they'd hidden so thoroughly that not even he knew where they were. So that if he was caught and tortured by Ezit's forces, he couldn't give up their location.

Which was already upsetting enough.

Then he opened the front door and turned back. "I had planned it, Vexen. I had planned for you to go to Ezit against my wishes. You never swore you wouldn't. What you *did* swear was not to tell anyone about my father."

Then Halcyon slammed the door as hard as he could.

I'd never been slapped with a sound before, but that's how it felt.

I've been sitting in his youngest son's bed since then, formulating the perfect comebacks for the warlock.

I know I fucked up, but I'm more likely to argue with Halcyon now than apologize; I didn't tell Samson about Halcyon's father being the Male Host of Serac—he smelled it for himself.

Then there's Samson's confession.

I stare at my hands as I lay back with a huff. My square palm and short fingers wouldn't release a single strand of magic against the wolf on the way to Ezit—even though I was only attempting to cast a pinching spell.

I think next of the leveling spell Argot unleashed into Vex.

How hands as small as mine are supposed to wield magic that will contend with spells that powerful.

I'm in over my head again.

At least Halcyon's cupboards were full—wine included.

I hiccup, then lean to reach for the bottle at my bedside.

It sits on a stool by a bowl of pears and Kierkeline's tiny vial.

I lift the dark bottle, then realize it's empty. With a curse, I set it down and then hold Kierkeline's vial up to the light.

Clear liquid fills half the narrow container, sloshing back and forth.

Is it wise to bother with these memories now? Will they help me in the coming weeks?

Probably not. And I should at least wait for Halcyon to get back.

But...

It's not *just* about our alleged affair. In the forest, Samson had told me, *'Sometimes, the scar on my chest turns bright red. Red like your magic.'*

And I need to know if Samson, not Pel, has access to Vex's missing magic.

My fingers tighten around the vial. I pop open its top, then lean forward to sniff.

I reel back with a gag; it smells like sour blueberries and feet.

I stare at the vial. I glance at the dark, empty bottle with a groan.

I guess this is the room where crazy shit happens. Where I get in over my head.

I wait a few more minutes, hoping to hear Halcyon open the door and hear his family shuffle into the apartment after him. Below, the neighbors chatter and laugh drunkenly. Outside the window, the birds with massive orange beaks caw and swoop from the sky.

I put the vial to my lips and clench my eyes shut. I throw my head back and swallow its contents.

I slap the blanket to coax the bitter liquid down. "Oh, for fuck's sake, Kierkeline."

I swear the flavor sinks into my teeth and my gums and my throat. It follows my nose up into my brain. I try to stand up, prepared to get a glass of water, but I slump against the comforter as my vision cuts.

I try to call for help or at least shift myself into a more comfortable position, but my body sinks against the blanket and relaxes. The blackness in my vision starts to shake and shake and shake.

I see something taking shape in my mind's eye. It's a plain and sturdy door. It starts to swing open slowly, hinges creaking loudly. Inside the dark room, light starts to bloom.

"Oh, shit." I'm not sure if I'm speaking or not; it's too late to back out of this. "Oh, no."

I see Halcyon, glimpses of his horns and his eyes and his cropped white hair.

I'm in this room, Halcyon is hovering over me; there is discord; there are two Colyd witches near the door who are wiping their eyes and rushing toward me with clean linens and rags. Someone is crying —maybe shouting—I'm not sure.

It only gets worse from there.

With a gargled shout, I sit up on the white bed.

I try to catch my breath as my head reels.

There are a lot of memories in my mind. There are too many thoughts—too many demanding realizations—

I feel like a bird soaring through the air, trying to catch its own shadow.

I look around and realize I'm not alone anymore; two warlocks watch me from the other side of the small room, in front of the sliding door.

One is a fucking full-grown adult, hands tucked behind his back and chin raised. This must be Vulcan, the eldest. Though a young man, his posture is reserved. His features closely mirror Halcyon's, but his frame is broader. He looks taller, too. His white hair is carefully pulled back between his horns, tied into a tight bun.

The warlockling at his side looks terrified. This is Memphis, then. A decade or so younger, he stands to his brother's chest. His upper lip is large, like Halcyon's, stuck in a pout. Unlike his brother, he keeps his messy hair short—aside from two thin braids that fall near his left ear. He backs up a step when our eyes meet, bumping into the door.

The three of us look around at one another. My panting slowly calms as I sit in the middle of the bed.

"You pissed yourself," Vulcan offers.

"In my bed," Memphis adds.

I stare at the warlocks; they stare back at me.

I don't know where to start. The last thing I'm worried about are these warlocks and where they sleep and whether or not it's covered in piss. "Look, I don't have the *wherewithal* for your..."

I don't even have the wherewithal to finish that sentence.

I stand up, balancing on the soft mattress and blankets. My body refuses to handle its new memories with grace. Adrenaline rockets through me, demanding that I go back to Hella—

That I find the wolf—

I open my hands to the heavens and bellow, "He got *married!*" I look from Vulcan to Memphis, whose eyes widen. "He fucking married *Brutatalika!* My primary *lover* is *married!*"

I open my hands to the warlocks, but they can't appreciate how fucking terrible this is.

Do I have a thing for men with wives? And daddy issues?

I'll deal with that later.

I throw my hands up again. "And someone *took my fucking robe.*" I bare down to scream with all my might, "My precious garment! The world will not know peace—"

I fall onto my knees onto the mattress. The warlocks were right; cold pee stains my dress, along with the sheets and blanket. I'm very close to caring about that—

I just need to make sure all these memories are back where they're supposed to be.

I bury my face in my hands. A lump creeps up my throat.

Samson is married.

The Class took my dignity and possibly my velvet peach robe.

And...

"Simmy is never going to forgive me." I'd sworn to him that I wouldn't abandon my banishment without telling him first. And then I did just that—even though he sacrificed a lot to take care of me in Jaws's loneliest little outpost.

Esclamonde, too.

"The fucking degi..." I don't have the strength for another scream. All the energy drains from me as I remember meeting Pel in Cadmium, him sinking his teeth into my neck, and then meeting him for a second time in Hypnos.

My hands clench as I try and fail to block out the memories of the ship.

Nestled like a jewel in a field of rubble, I see another memory from the ship...

With another flurry of movement, I leap from the bed.

I look from Vulcan to Memphis. "Where is my shit—everything your moms took from me on the ship?" My breaths come so fast and hard that I feel like I'll pass out. "Imperatriz... Imperatriz 713 Afador..."

That was really, really, really not how I wanted to confirm Imperatriz's existence.

I'd planned to impress her someday—

Vulcan and Memphis look at me.

Vulcan slides his eyes toward Memphis, then back to me. His eyebrows pucker. "Sorry? Are you okay?"

"Where's my fucking shit?" I go on. "Where's Halcyon?"

I need to know if whatever Imperatriz tied around my arms and neck survived the trip to Plet. I need to take whatever it was to Samson as proof that his mother is alive.

(Then I need to maybe strangle the wolf for defending Anesot, maybe make him fuck the anger out of me, maybe need to strangle him while he does that.)

"Your fucking shit?" Vulcan asks. "What is a fucking shit?"

"You do not seem okay," Memphis goes on.

I look down at the piss-stained dress woven from alpaca wool. I can't believe the state of my dress since being kidnapped.

I try to start somewhere simple for them. "I need a dress."

The warlocks back up until they're pressed against the sliding door. Memphis glances back like he's considering opening it and slipping away to freedom.

I go on carefully, "I need a *clean* set of clothes. As you pointed out, I pissed myself."

Vulcan reaches to slide open the door. He looks at the floor and says, "I will bring you fresh clothes—"

"*No pants.*" I shuffle past the pair and head into the hallway. "I remember where the washroom is."

Uncertainly, Vulcan calls after me, "So... just a shirt?"

I pass the empty salon on the way to the washroom. "A *dress*. I want a *dress*. It's a shirt that goes past your butt."

Part of me wonders what Halcyon is doing if his sons are here—still, I trust the children would be weeping if something were amiss.

I shut the door to the washroom and heat the water before I sink into the tub. The warmth comforts me, helps me sort through everything that's welling in my brain.

I go through it all—

Simmy and I getting closer in Alita where we formed our first warren. Adding Pen and Zopyros to that warren when we moved to Luz, then slowly welcoming more nymphs. I remember years of fruitless tips about Oko, collected from Itzifone in Solace.

I remember the morning Ninigone, Head Witch of Luz, saddled me with the mentee, Esclamonde Black Rock Antigone. I remember that same evening when I met Samson 714 Afador in Solace.

My life in the last four years is beyond anything I'd hoped for myself during my banishment in Jaws.

Most of it, at least.

Like he'd once done to me, Anesot got his hooks into Samson. And when it mattered most, Samson stood in front of the warlock who killed my sister and begged me to spare him. All for a chance to find his mother.

It takes a lot of hot water to get through that last day in Alita.

I blame Samson, I blame Anesot, I blame myself.

But the truth...

I would have done the same, would have betrayed Samson for a chance to save Milisent.

The truth...

Maybe I could have handled things better when I realized Oko knew something about Imperatriz's disappearance.

I should have methodically and carefully explained to Samson what I had intuited about his father, his mother, Oko, and Anesot—maybe made a graph or a chart or something Velmic. Instead, I mixed the revelation in with a series of insults.

I don't know that I'll ever admit that to Samson, but it helps ease the rage I feel toward him.

And he did follow me here.

And he has lived in a cave where I imagine he can smell all sorts of disappointing things wafting from the room I share with Halcyon.

By the time the dirty water swirls down the drain, I feel like a proper being again—one who is capable of interacting with Halcyon's sons in a more appropriate manner.

After I dry myself, someone knocks. From the other side of the door, Vulcan says, "I have a very large shirt."

I open the door and grab the shirt. Judging by the way Vulcan flinches and turns around, he hasn't seen many naked women in his life. I shut the door, shrug it on, and then look down at the massive and unshapely garment with a tsk.

"Vexen," Vulcan goes on from the hallway.

I get to work drying and untangling my hair. "I'll clean the bed in a minute. Relax."

"I cleaned the bed. I want to ask something else."

"Oh?"

"My father made a deal with you to take our family to Mieira, correct?"

I snort. "Yeah, he did. No telling where we stand on that agreement, though. He's very angry with me. I don't know if you noticed."

"I am angry with him, too."

My ears perk up. "You don't say...?"

"No, I *do* say. When you met, I wanted him to make a deal for one more witch," Vulcan starts. "But he did not ask you to take this witch to Mieira with us."

I clamp my mouth shut, delighted by the fact that Vulcan is defying Halcyon right now. So far, the warlock has kept mum about his approach to fatherhood and his relationship with his children. I've wondered what it would be like—especially with an adult son.

Very duplicitous, it seems.

"Her name is Vega," Vulcan goes on. "She is my age. We are bound for years now."

I gasp. "Halcyon didn't say anything about being a grandfather..."

"He is not a grandfather. We are not bound by a child. We are bound by love."

I roll my eyes. "I see. And you want me to take Vega with us?"

"Yes. She is from the House of Argot. She is a fourth-generation Pleten. She has no ties to Ezit."

"Look, I'm on your dad's shit list right now, so... I'm not sure if I can get away with pissing him off more than I already have. Also, *fuck* Argot."

"I see."

I cross my arms. "What does your mom say? She's Cleo, right?"

"My mother is Ceyx," he says. *Fuck.* "And she also thinks it is a bad idea."

"So, what? They don't like Vega, and you think they're wrong about her?"

"No." He pauses. "I think they are wrong about *you*."

I rip the door open. Vulcan staggers back, like he was leaning against it. "Wrong about me? Why? What are they saying?" I roll my eyes again. "I only went to Ezit because I was *invited*. Oh, and by the way, I have since figured out how to bring *Ezit to its knees.*"

(Theoretically.)

His mouth falls open. "What? You went to Ezit?"

"That's why your dad is so mad at me." I set my hands on my hips. "Did he not say anything?"

"No, he took me and Memphis from the safe house and told us to stay with you." Vulcan lowers his head toward me, eyes wide. "Did you really go to Ezit?"

"Yeah. Really. Now, why don't your parents trust me to take Vega?" I turn around and send my wool dress into flames—I could have cleaned it, but the *real* Helisent would never be caught dead in such a stupid dress. I need something with *color.* "I'm basically a full-blown master now. I've been spending months absorbing my Landmark's magic. It's not been for nothing."

Vulcan clears his throat, staring as the flames raze the dress. Ash drifts around the square washroom, along with the scent of burned wool. I flutter my fingers to get rid of the ash, which soars down the drain in a tidy line.

Vulcan goes on, "They said it was a lot to ask for passage for *five* beings. They did not want to offend you by asking too much."

I tap my fingers against the doorframe. "Oh." I can't tell if that decision was based on fear or respect, but after knowing Halcyon for a season, I can appreciate fear and respect are intertwined here in Zarzynn. "It's not a problem. Vega can come with us. Just let me figure things out with your dad before we tell him. Speaking of which..." I twist to face the front door "Where are they?"

"They went to check on the ships," Vulcan explains. "They are sending word to some friends in New Hypnos, too. They don't want anyone to connect the ships to you. There have been a few rumors in Plet that some are going to leave for Mieira. People are looking out for firebirds—they are waiting for a chance to stow away."

Memphis leans into view from behind Vulcan. I jolt; I hadn't noticed he was in proximity to us.

The gangly warlockling studies me with tense features. "Can you tell them to come back? You can send a message if you have something of Halcyon's."

Down the hall, past the bedroom and the salon, the front door's knob shifts. Memphis takes off toward the door, but Vulcan grabs his tunic and pulls him back to his side. I shove past both of them, raising a hand and preparing to meet the intruder.

The door opens a sliver and Halcyon slides into view.

I drop my hand with relief. Vulcan releases the adolescent, then the brothers shuffle past me to greet the warlock.

Halcyon scans Memphis, Vulcan, then me. His eyes gutter when we lock eyes, features twitching with anger.

Rather than address me, he holds the door open. Cleo and Ceyx walk in with quick steps. I don't know which is which, but my eyes dart from one face to the next, trying to figure out which is more beautiful.

They have square jaws and pointed noses, their faces so symmetrical they look unreal. Their cheekbones are perfectly sculpted, while their horns are smoothed and shined like jade ornaments. They step into the room, graceful, effervescent, and a dozen other adjectives I'd never use to describe myself.

It wouldn't hurt so much to be presented with their loveliness if I hadn't just dealt with the realization that Samson is with Brutatalika.

And if they weren't from the House of Col.

Before I killed her in Alita, I tortured Oko. And her eyes turned from gold to green in those moments. Anesot was Seracyd, but Oko was Colyd. The same house that sent Pel overseas and funded my trip to Zarzynn.

I blink at the witches.

(I will never trust them.)

Memphis hustles toward the trio. One of the witches reaches for him, tugging him to her side; she must be Cleo. Vulcan ambles over a moment later. He takes his place beside Memphis. Seeing them flush in a line, I realize Vulcan is taller than Halcyon by at least an inch. I can see why; like Halcyon, his wives are tall and well-built.

I'm not sure what to do.

Wave? Smile? Cross my arms?

Halcyon tucks his hands behind his back and bares a neutral expression at me. "Helisent West of Jaws, I see you met my sons."

I glance across their ranks. "Vulcan wants me to take Vega to Mieira."

In perfect unison, Ceyx, Cleo, and Halcyon turn toward Vulcan. Halcyon and Cleo glare vividly, while Ceyx hisses something. To his credit, the young warlock stares back evenly.

"I said I'd do it, no need to be angry." Now that they're slightly distracted, I approach the family and offer a plain smile.

"I see." Halcyon sighs, eyeing me with suspicion. "Then let me introduce my wives. This is Cleo, and this is Ceyx."

The women offer weak smiles, but I can't tell what's behind the lackluster greeting. Possibly my closeness with Halcyon, my trip to Ezit, the fact that they're now bound to me and my bad decisions.

A balance of fear and respect. And a dash of mistrust.

I stop before them and study the witches. "Hello, Ceyx. Hello, Cleo. Where are my things? Everything you took off me from the ship —I'd like to see what survived."

The witches glance at Halcyon, who looks down the hall. With that, the family starts moving. Cleo guides Memphis back toward his room. She turns at the last moment to grab Vulcan's sleeve; he begrudgingly follows.

Then Ceyx lifts a small bag that's slung around her body. It's a simple clamping purse, like the starter bottomless bags handed off to Mieiran littlelings.

Like Halcyon, she sticks to fitted gray clothes. Pants hug her hips, while a fuzzy tunic frames her shoulders, chest, and waist perfectly.

I watch her reach into the bottomless bag and ignore Halcyon's frigid stare.

Ceyx pulls out a bundle of dark fabric and hands it to me. "This is all there was." Her voice is delicate, like a songbird. "It was tied around your neck."

The fabric encases a soft but semi-rigid shape. My breath catches as I peel back the fabric and see a long, straight braid of dark gray hair. The strands sit loose in the fabric, tangled and dirty.

Tears sting my eyes.

I feel... really embarrassed.

It's hard knowing that Halcyon and his wives found me in the state they did. Knowing that Samson's *mother*, the Female Alpha and Kulap-sifang of her generation, also saw me in such a pitiful state...

And she *cleaned* me...

(What's the only thing worse than my lover's mother getting a full view of my undercarriage? Being covered in my own mess when she does.)

"Whose hair is it?" Ceyx asks.

I look up at her and lose my train of thought; she's so beautiful that it's distracting. She reminds me of sunrise, of freshly baked goods, of the quiet only found in peaceful groves.

"It's a long story," I say with a sigh.

I seal the fabric with a containing spell with the hopes the wolves will still be able to smell Imperatriz. I remember a lot of salt water at the very end.

The floorboards creak as Cleo leaves the bedroom. She looks at her sister first, then at Halcyon, as she joins us near the front door. Cleo is a bit smaller than her older sister in terms of height; her eyes are rounder and her lips fuller. But just like with me and Mint, it's easy to tell that they're sisters.

I thought our first meeting would be a lot more fun. I'd even scripted a few casual jokes. Now, it feels like standing in front of the Class.

Except...

I was foolish to ever let the Class rule me. And I won't make that mistake again.

I look at Halcyon and raise my chin. "I didn't tell Samson who your father is. Wolves can smell—*really well*. When we get to Hella, the wolves will know exactly how all five of you fit together. Figure out how you want to handle that before we go to Vex."

Halcyon's expression doesn't soften, but he at least looks away from me, as though calculating the statement.

I turn toward Ceyx and Cleo. I wish I didn't feel so jealous and insignificant; *why the fuck are women in Zarzynn so tall?*

"Please decide if coming to Hella is really what you want. Halcyon has been a great help to me..." I'm not sure how to say this next part. "He says we're bound. But being bound to Halcyon also means being bound to both of you. And to Vulcan and Memphis.

"The truth is that I can't be bound to any of you. Not that it wouldn't be nice... but my purpose in life is to keep Vex alive. I assume this will involve more trips to Ezit, if not other dangerous adventures. I don't plan on *apologizing* for having these responsibilities. Halcyon saved my life and brought me to Hella. For that, I'll take your family to Mieira."

The words hurt, but I don't feel shocked speaking them.

I feel relieved.

Part of me has known this would happen since I announced my plans to attack Ezit. I knew my predisposition to danger would make me incompatible with someone who values caution and safety.

Halcyon had predicted I would go to Ezit. He'd begged me not to. And I had gone only to find Samson waiting for me.

Samson didn't try to talk me out of the idea. He stood at my side with nothing more than an axe to defend against Ezit's Hosts. And when Argot cast that spell, he ran toward the danger; toward me.

He did that knowing that if I died, so would he. He didn't think twice even though he's the only Afador who can lead Velm.

What Halcyon and I have is a strong partnership.

But what Samson showed me in Ezitlos is true devotion.

I look from Ceyx to Cleo to Halcyon. "If you come to Hella, come with the understanding that I will invade Ezit on the triplemoon."

Cleo looks at the other two, as though she's about to interject.

I keep going, "If you come to Hella, you must do so with faith in me. Or, at least, with faith in the future I promised you. The ships will sail whether or not we come back on the triplemoon." I toss my hair over my shoulder and turn to Halcyon. "Which I *will*, by the way. I know how to handle Ezit—they're just like you, my dear warlock. Worried about *controlling* ejima. About wielding great spells as though their power is devoid of a source. But I know something none of them have realized: the Landmarks are demigods. They know more than I ever will—all I have to do is not think too much. Vex will do the hard work."

Halcyon's expression breaks—I can't tell if he's curious or aghast. "*What?*"

"You know how I got the necromancer back, Halcyon? I just *walked into Serac and picked her up*." I raise my eyebrows. "Ezit's greatest weapon is its reputation—not its actual skill. I mean, they haven't fought a Vexen in centuries. They're rusty. They doubt me. It's perfect.

"Oh, and I figured out who's working together during my little trip. Col and Talos are allies—I mean, I don't have *proof*, but they were trading little glances. Then there's Serac and Argot. They're allies, too. Lahar—well, Lahar scares me a little." I shrug a shoulder, so they know I'm being reasonable. "But I'll deal with that when the time comes."

Halcyon glances at his wives before sliding his eyes back to me. Slowly, like it will deter me, he says, "Serac and Argot are mortal enemies."

"There are at least thirty square miles of destroyed pine barren that would beg to differ," I counter. "After I took the necromancer, Argot cast that spell you felt in Vex. Not Serac. *Argot.*

"Look—I don't need you to believe me. I just need you to under-stand what coming to Hella means. Argot made their first move. I don't think anyone will send me any more gifts or invitations before the triplemoon. It might be safer here in Plet."

Halcyon flinches, along with his wives. Each of them glances at the door to Memphis's room.

I take a step back, clenching the braid and letting it fill me with conviction. Imperatriz has survived on Pit this long. It gives me hope that Accra was wrong. That what comes next doesn't destroy me or, at least, not all the way.

Ceyx takes a deep breath. "Serac knows, then?"

I nod. "Like I told Halcyon, the Seracyd Hosts made it clear they knew who saved me from the ship."

Cleo sighs. "Then we have no choice. We will go with you to Hella. It will be safer than Plet. The Houses have spies throughout the city."

I wait for Ceyx or Halcyon to disagree; nothing. "I can take us back to Hella when you're ready. Also, I probably scared the little one. Memphis." I glance at Halcyon. "I drank Kierkeline's potion."

He raises his eyebrows. "I see. And how did that go?"

"I pissed the bed."

He lets out a long sigh.

I go on, "Also, we should probably talk before we go back. In private." I gesture to the front door behind the Pletens. "Shall we?"

"Helisent West of Jaws, we can give you pants," Cleo suggests in a small voice.

I look down at the large t-shirt, then back up at the witch. "Are *you* the one who put me in pants last time?"

Cleo nods. "Yes. I'll find you some—"

"I don't want pants. *Ever.*" I glance at the door, waiting for Halcyon to open it. "We won't be long."

Ceyx steps in front of the door, hands wrought together. "What about a cloak? We have a floor-length cover somewhere..." Like Ceyx, Cleo turns to search the cramped salon and kitchen.

I'm not sure what the fuss is about, but start tugging the large shirt over my head. "Is this one of your shirts? I didn't take it. Vulcan gave it to me..."

Four hands clamp down across me, holding the t-shirt in place before it can rise above my thighs. I blink into the fabric, caught over my face.

"For your modesty, Helisent West of Jaws," Ceyx whispers from outside the fabric.

My what?

"You have no undergarments on," Cleo continues.

Have they never seen a naked woman before? No wonder Vulcan tried to physically escape my breasts.

With a shuffle, I tug the shirt back down over me. For the first time in days, Halcyon's tense expression lifts. He almost looks close to smiling.

I bare my hands to Ceyx and Cleo. "Slow down. *Undergarments?*" I'd rather be banished again. "Those are for periods, and I'm not bleeding."

I glance at the loose layers the witches wear. Though the tailored pants and tunics look semi-tight, they end at their wrists and ankles. The witches also wear long and flowing cloaks as an outer layer.

"Or..." I pray they disagree with me. "Do witches in Plet *always* wear undergarments?"

Ceyx and Cleo give me the one-over. They make a series of inconclusive and high-pitched noises as they glance at each other.

Eventually, Ceyx says, "We weren't sure if witches behaved like the nymphs in New Hypnos."

Cleo goes on, "The okeanids don't wear undergarments."

"You are free to do as you like," Ceyx adds.

"Yes, of course." Cleo offers me a confused smile.

"Right... thanks..." I pivot toward Halcyon before angling back to the witches. "Actually, I have some questions—what about the *breeze?* And if you want to fuck, you have to like... *fully* disrobe? Doesn't it feel stuffy down there, too? Let me see. I want to see one. An *undergarment.*"

With feline amusement, Cleo and Ceyx slide their eyes toward Halcyon.

Ceyx says, "I suppose Halcyon has been enjoying his time in Zarzynn after all."

Cleo says, "We will show you an undergarment another time, Helisent West of Jaws."

I wave a hand at them. "Just call me Helisent." With a grand gesture, I present Halcyon with the front door once again. "Do you not want to talk before we go back to Hella?"

Still wearing his almost-smile, Halcyon explains, "The undergarment talk started because you wanted to speak in private. You were hinting we could speak outside, but that would cause a stir. We cover ourselves in Plet. Not even children wear as little as you are right now."

I stare ahead at Halcyon, then backtrack through my time here.

During my week of spying on Plet through Memphis's window, I never caught sight of a normally dressed wielder. In fact, everyone I saw wore sleeves to their wrists and flowing layers to their ankles.

Which means I'm the one who isn't normally dressed here.

I glare at the massive shirt. It dangles to just above my knees. "If it made Halcyon so uncomfortable, he could have said something." I roll my eyes and stomp down the hall. "Why don't we go to the bedroom?"

I slide the door open.

Memphis and Vulcan lounge on the bed, avoiding the spot where I left my puddle even though it's cleaned. Memphis scurries past me; he seems just as skittish as his mother. Vulcan also rises and leaves quickly, keeping his eyes down.

I pace a few steps and ignore the whispers that drift in from the salon. All I pick up is something about a meal, a bottomless bag, and a piece of jewelry. With each passing second, I'm desperate to return to Hella. My hand starts to sweat from gripping the wrapped braid so tightly.

With a long sigh, Halcyon steps into the room and slides the door shut.

Alone with him, it's hard to regulate my emotions. I'm *livid* about his reaction to me going to Ezit, about the fact that I actually felt bad —but I'm also aware that a few days ago, I might have admitted that I loved him.

I guess that's the basis of our relationship—

A mix of desperation and hope and danger.

We stare at one another.

I guess I'll start. "I don't know you how I think I do." The bold statement falls flat between us. Halcyon blinks at me, as though uncertain how to handle it. "Or... I don't know you how I wish I did. How I think you *deserve* to be known, Halcyon. Since I woke up in this room, we've had to think about survival. Now, I can see that you've had to think of that your whole life. I hadn't realized that at first. Or maybe not the gravity of it..."

I raise my chin and wait for him to respond.

He rubs his face with his hands. "You met my father. You went to

Ezit. I know you don't fear it, but please understand that I *do*." He steps forward, angling his head away from me to whisper, "Seven years ago, my brothers found Cleo, okay? I used to be more lenient."

It's a vague enough explanation that I don't push for more details.

For a second, he breathes unsteadily. I drift closer, wanting to offer him comfort.

"I know that you think I'm acting ridiculously," he goes on, "but you must understand that I'm..."

Terrified?

Unwilling to endure more pain?

Uncertain of who he really is beyond fear?

"I should have been more careful. Throughout my whole life. Now, I'm making up for lost time. And when you first woke up... you needed that. Safety. But maybe not anymore. And if that is true, and you don't need safety, then what can I offer you, Vexen?"

Slowly, he turns his face toward me. Tears fill his eyes, but they don't fall. His jaw and mouth are locked, waiting.

I pinch his chin. "You have given me more than most others, Halcyon."

His eyes study mine. I brush my thumb against the star-shaped scar near his left eye.

With a long sigh, he straightens his shoulders. "So, what happens with the wolf now?"

I narrow my eyes—*does he know about Samson?* "What do you mean? Which wolf?"

He arches an eyebrow. "The Kulapsi-boy."

I put my hands on my hips. "I *did not* tell him about your father, Halcyon."

He rolls his eyes. "Please, Helisent. I'm asking because you drank the memory potion, not because he figured out who my father is."

It seems like Halcyon knows about my affair with Samson—just in case he doesn't, I play dumb. "And?"

"You remember Samson. You *and* Samson."

I make a long and uncertain sound. "Who told you about that?"

Halcyon rolls his eyes again. "There were a few signs. Did Samson show you his scar from Alita? It's *red*."

The blood drains from my face. I wave a hand. "Stop worrying about the wolf. I'll handle it."

"You need to figure out how to introduce my family to him."

I tsk. "The child thing was a one-off. It's just because she's..." Halcyon nods while I put it together—Ceyx and Cleo are both Colyd, like the child-messenger. "I'll explain that Ceyx and Cleo were marooned here like everyone else in Plet. That will help."

"Are you sure? He threw his axe at me this morning."

I make another involuntary noise, then scan Halcyon in search of injuries. "What? Where? Why?"

He shakes his head indignantly. "He didn't hit me. We were having a... lively discussion."

I blink at him. "Don't do that. He's the future Alpha of Velm. You don't need to make enemies in Mieira before you get there. I'll go back and do damage control with the wolves—"

"Wolves? I have a good relationship with Rex and Berevald."

"They're a *pack*. If Samson has an issue with you, they'll both take that to the grave. Good fucking moons, Halcyon—has no one explained what a blood feud is? They're treated like artforms in Velm. Just—let me deal with it." I rub my temples. Things are quickly piling up in this room. "Are you *sure* you'll actually feel safer in Hella with me and the Mieirans? And the vampires? And the gorgons, if they come back?"

"I'll feel safe in Hella." He nods, then glances at the door. "Did you actually tell Vulcan you'd bring Vega?"

I try to assuage him with a broad smile. "It's young love, Halcyon. Their names match, for fuck's sake. How could I—"

"Thank you. It will mean a lot to him. Vega deserves a good life."

The words are genuine and tender enough to make me pause. I hadn't realized how doting Halcyon had been with me until returning from Ezit. I'm happy to understand him better in all of his moods, but I prefer soft Halcyon. Safe Halcyon.

I reach over and take his hand. His fingers hook through mine and he yields a step, letting me drag him closer. I sigh, smoothing out his already-tidy tunic with my free hand. "I can't believe you've been letting me walk around half-naked."

He responds with a low, happy chuckle.

"And what I said earlier about us not being bound... maybe we can be bound in the future." I creep closer to him, twining our free hands together. "Would you be... open to that?"

He drifts closer. "You mean when Samson goes back to his wife?"

"Yes." With a sigh, I let my head fall against his chest. "That's if you're also done going back to your wives. *Plural.*"

"I guess we'll have to see." His chest hums as he speaks, filling my ear.

I untwine our hands to wrap my arms around him. "I'm sorry for ranting at the children when I woke up. And pissing on the bed. It was really disorienting."

His arms fold over me, holding me against him. "Don't worry about it. They're young and resilient."

"Let's fucking hope so. If they can't deal with me, they'll never make it in Mieira."

His chest shivers with another happy chuckle. He leans down, stroking my hair and pressing his lips against my scalp. I pull back, staring up at him and blinking my lashes. I'd like one more kiss. For now, at least.

Halcyon obliges, leaning down to peck me once, warm and relaxed.

"Will you still teach me how to do the hand trick?" I ask.

His warm breath fans across my face. "Get us to Mieira like you promised and I'll teach you everything I know."

"Deal."

Then I smile, and he smiles, and we kiss one last time, warm and fleeting and devilish.

CHAPTER 14

FIVE-MOON WOLF

SAMSON

My grandson,
Your mother spent months in Mieira with the red witch. I went north to take
her back to Velm. Do you understand what I'm telling you, Samson? Your
mother kept going north, and I kept dragging her back south.

Meres fills the forest with the stench of death.

It's hard to ignore—especially at night. Above the canopy of thin pines, Abdecalas and Vicente are nearing full. They beam green and pink light through the branches and bundled needles. Trailing both is a waxing Sennen, almost impossible to see given the moon's tiny size and dimmed color.

Beneath their light and amid the familiar scent of the pine trees and limestone, I'm almost fully comfortable in Vex.

But Meres's ala catches in the slight breeze and sends the tart odor of death across me—through my hair, through my clothes.

She sits beside a thick trunk a few feet ahead of me. Her mirror sits on its padded frame, propped against the tree. To our right, a small fire flickers. Meres's cerulean eyes flash, half-aglow like the reddish gleam of a vampire.

Her head tilts as she bares one of her vague smiles at me. Her turquoise diadem glints with light. "You're nervous. It's normal."

She's right. Every time my eyes shift toward the mirror where my reflection waits, they jump back to the necromancer. To the quiet forest behind her. To the healthy fire to our right. Anywhere but the glass.

"I'll feel better when I know who wants to speak to me." I clear my throat, then shift to sit cross-legged. "The doublemoon will be here soon... it doesn't really help any wolf relax."

Meres nods, her passive smile growing. "All of us will rest easier once Helisent and Halcyon return."

Before I can second that sentiment, the mirror buzzes, its surface trembling with the familiar infrasound of magic. The glass sounds like it might break for a split second, which is followed by tense silence.

"Wonderful," Meres purrs. "Here he is."

A male wolf slowly comes into view. Like Andromeda North of Skull, only his face and shoulders are shown in the frame. And just like Axerxa in Ezitlos, the wolf looks around, as though getting his bearings. Like he can see me sitting in the dark forest, cloaked in night and firelight, and wants to know more.

My nostrils flare, but I can't smell him to identify his lineage or generational count. His silver hair and features hint that he died well into his 100s. His broad shoulders and strong jaw look vaguely familiar—but wolves have homogenous features more than any other being. His thick eyebrows and strong nose are a composite blend of familiar Velmic traits.

How he holds his gaze is more pronounced.

The way he scans my features makes my gut drop.

It's how Clearbold studies me.

How he looks for weakness.

"I am Samson 714 Afador. Who are you, deathling?"

His blue-black eyes jump to meet mine. "Samson 714 Afador... I am Malasuntra 711 Afador."

I blink dumbly, sitting back as my features slacken. I scan his face, searching for traces of my grandmother, Sutnazzar 712 Afador. My mother inherited her Kulapsifang's features—but it doesn't look like Sutnazzar took after her father, Malasuntra.

"How is my daughter?" Malasuntra asks. With each second, his features soften. He seems to relax, shoulders slumping. "How is my granddaughter? And how are you, Samson 714 Afador?"

I glance once at Meres. She dragged me away from Rex and

Berevald, who had set up camp outside of Hella to ride out the incoming doublemoon's high tensions. She said that the deathling would wait no longer; neither would she.

She tilts her head as she meets my gaze now, as though waiting for a question.

I address her in Velmic, "Tell me now if you can understand us, Meres Hypnos."

As kind as it is for her to bring this deathling to me, I'm not keen on chatting with Malasuntra in front of an audience.

She raises her eyebrows, deadpan. "You'll have to repeat that in Mieiran or Zarzyd if you want a response, my dear wolf."

I nod. "I hope you don't mind—I'd rather speak with the deathling in Velmic."

"I do enjoy the eavesdropping." Meres winks at me. "But you carried me from Ezit. Speak in any language that pleases you, Kulapsifang."

She flashes me one of her smiles, and I offer one back.

She says that deathlings wait for their loved ones on the precipice of death; she also clarified that they aren't connected to our lives. They don't know what they've missed while they've waited to retrieve their loved ones.

I study Malasuntra's sturdy features.

On the ship to Zarzynn, Rex, Parsifal, and I outlined the events of the last year in a letter sent to my Rouzen bedroom. I have the information neatly arranged in my mind in a chronological line. But the pit in my stomach deepens as I stare at my ancestor; it's the same sinking feeling I had when Sutnazzar 712 Afador officiated my wedding to Brutatalika.

A feeling that I'm an imposter.

That nobody knows how weak I am, and this weakness will someday see me die a coward's death after losing control of my realm.

Malasuntra glances around the forest, over my shoulders. Quietly, he asks, "Are you in danger, Samson 714 Afador?"

"No." I remind myself that he's an ally; that even if he isn't an ally, he can't return to life to interrupt my future. "Well, not immediately. It's a passive sort of danger. I'm... far from Velm."

Like I did a moment before, Malasuntra sits back, as though

presented with something that must be delicately handled. He raises his chin. "Do the Kulapsifangs mince words with one another now?"

I understand what he really means. He wants to know why I'm speaking cryptically.

The first few words I manage are awkward—they almost sound like make-believe.

"I am looking for my mother, your granddaughter."

How many times have I said that? How many more times will I tell this story?

Malasuntra doesn't interrupt as I file through the bare facts, then pepper in some of my own theories about everything Helisent and I learned last year. I end with my marriage to Brutatalika, then catch him up on the trip to Zarzynn. The possibility of finding Imperatriz on Pit and our refusal to alert Zarzynn to her existence. The possibility of returning to Velm only to find it parsed out between Clearbold and Malachai. The possibility of nymphs and wielders facing violence in Velm in my absence.

I describe Helisent West of Jaws only as it relates to my life and role in Velm—not my personal feelings. I glance at Meres throughout my explanation, waiting for her features to deviate and reveal that she speaks Velmic and is planning to leverage this information against me someday. But she watches the fire, and me, and the forest beyond with such a relaxed expression that I begin to feel more comfortable.

When I finish, Malasuntra reaches up to rub his face. He asks, "Have they been going south? Your father and his false pup."

I shake my head. "No. The Leofsige line comes from Mort. Most of their activity is concentrated in the southeast."

Malasuntra's brow puckers. "Nothing south of Rouz? No talk of Southies?"

Southies. It's a diminutive term for wolves who live in the sparse villages further into the mountains. Survival is hard throughout my territory, but Night lasts even longer in the southern region. Those who survive there have earned a reputation for being callous and artful in equal measure; their accents are as strong as their moonshine, their wooden halls filled often for dancing and revelry that the rest of Velm finds nymph-like. They call it survival—dancing warms the hall through winter's iciest stretches.

Still, I haven't heard the word *Southie* since I was a boy. Even then, the term was so outdated that even Clearbold turned his head at its use.

I shake my head. "No—and we don't call them Southies anymore. Clearbold has never seemed interested in Rouz. Imperatriz enjoyed Rouz. I spent a lot of time with her there growing up. I don't remember any talk of southerners."

Finally, Malasuntra's face darkens with anger. His jaw clenches, eyes narrowing. "So, Clearbold bartered with Anesot to remove Imperatriz purely of his own plotting?"

"As far as I know, yes. It seems he may have also been looking to build an alliance with Anesot, if not the Houses of Serac and Argot, too. The Hosts in both Houses seemed to believe *Clearbold* is his generation's Kulapsifang."

"Well... it's possible I didn't make a mistake after all." Malasuntra rubs his face again, then watches me with a wary and guarded expression. "You're married now, so I'm sure you understand just how deeply the Kulapsifang's life belongs to Velm. I didn't smile when I married Sutnazzar to Ilias, and I doubt my daughter smiled when she married you to Brutatalika."

She hadn't.

My grandmother had overseen the ceremony with an unyielding expression of frost. She spoke only to offer her blessing to me and Brutatalika. Even her interactions with Clearbold were sparring. I'd chalked it up to her age and the great distance she had traveled from her home to join us in Silent City. I'd secretly wondered if she blamed my weakness for her daughter's disappearance, how I sensed others doing.

Part of me had accepted her reticence without a second thought.

Since then, I've started to read more of the letters Sutnazzar wrote me.

Like this meeting with Malasuntra, I've been surprised by her words.

They are so opposite to her pensive silence.

"Marriage is the end of our freedom," Malasuntra goes on. "I knew that my marriage was *correct*... but that didn't make me love my wife. Not how she deserved to be loved as the Female Alpha of Velm. When I married Sutnazzar to the Male Alpha of Velm, I thanked my daughter. She chose to stand in Silent City. She chose that over whatever other pursuit she knew would bring her happiness.

"I had failed Sutnazzar already." Malasuntra clears his throat. "You see, Samson 714 Afador, I'd met a Southie long before I married the Female Alpha of Velm." He *really* shouldn't be saying Southie. "One autumn, I stumbled upon a little village south of Lake Rouz. A Southie named Aithe lived there and there was nothing... nothing particularly spectacular about her. She had a low generational count. She lived with her parents even as an adult. She enjoyed baking; villagers brought her wood throughout Night in exchange for pies and loaves.

"I fell in love with her without understanding how deep love could run.

"Wolves are sparing with our love. We treat it like a finite resource that might not last through Night if mismanaged. So, I never... noticed... how I *really* felt about Aithe. Every time I left her village, I told myself it was the last time. I told myself that my presence would prevent Aithe from finding a suitable partner; she would never travel north for the waricon series that would decide the Female Alpha. And if she did, she would never make it past the first round.

"I judged myself for loving someone who wasn't my Alpha.

"And I denied the truth... a truth that didn't seem to fit in with what I knew about myself and life in Velm. We weigh life on a scale; warmth versus Night, order versus chaos, growth versus preservation. And, without meaning to, I had discovered the scale on which love balances. Do you know what its polar opposite is, Samson? Power.

"My inability to realize this earlier was my failure as the Kulapsi-fang of Velm."

Malasuntra pauses, studying my face as though waiting for an interruption, or a curse, or a question. I gulp once, wishing I would have confided in him my relationship with Helisent.

It sounds like he might understand me more than I'd thought another wolf could.

But I wait for the end of the story.

He goes on, "When my thirtieth approached, I went south once more. I told myself it was to say *one last* goodbye to Aithe, but she wasn't there. I slept next to her oven for a week and received no word.

The villagers asked me to leave. They knew I should have been heading to Silent City for my wedding.

"But this was not the truth. And I would not know the truth for many more years.

"I went north to Silent City and I was married. I toured Velm and then Mieira with my newly formed pack. My wife did the same with her own hand-selected pack. And twenty years later, we conceived Sutz. Holding Sutnazzar was another moment that made me understand the distinction between power and love.

"As Sutnazzar's father, I would love her forever. As her Kulapsifang, I would mourn all she would never have the freedom to do as my heir. And as her Male Alpha, I knew that I would steer her toward her own future in Silent City. I knew that Sutnazzar would say goodbye to her own Aithe someday.

"We all do, Samson." Malasuntra pauses, raising his eyebrows.

It's a follow-up to his first cryptic question; *what secret are you keeping, Samson?*

Tell him, Samsonfang urges. **Tell him the witch is the Female Alpha.**

But he doesn't wait for a reply. "I'd sworn never to return to her village, but I broke that promise." Malasuntra sighs, closing his eyes for a moment. "And when I went south of Rouz to Aithe's village, she was there. She was baking in her oven like she always had. She had a young man at her side. A young man in his early twenties."

Malasuntra stares at me with an unflinching gaze.

The sounds of the forest dwindle. The crackling fire, the skittish things in the underbrush, the wind in the leaves all fade into a loud ringing sound.

"I told myself another Afador had to have compromised the lineage at some point. One of the male Kulapsifangs—a female Kulapsifang couldn't hide a pregnancy.

"That's what had happened south of Rouz. Aithe had left the village, and she only returned after her parents convinced the village to keep her secret—*our* secret. The village was home to around eighty wolves, and they ran in a pack under the triplemoon. Southies are like that. Bonded. So, Aithe and our son were safe there. She named him Love." For the first time, Malasuntra smiles. He stares emptily at the ground, lost in a memory. "That tells you what you need to know about Aithe."

Panic starts to set in as I study Malasuntra's intoxicated smile.

Does Clearbold know there's a second line of Afadors? He's never given me any indication, but I can't help but wonder...

The ringing in my ears fades. I feel Samsonfang in my mind, pacing like a caged beast. He's baffled. He's distraught.

Which of Velm's traditions are real?

Or are they just stories we tell?

Rage sparks in me.

"And was it worth it?" I ask. "Was Love worth setting a precedent that Clearbold used to destabilize Velm?" I lean forward, words clipped. "They kidnapped my mother and took her to an island where things are left to rot. When they kidnap the okeanids and take them to this place, they bind them with magical stones. They broke the witch's hands to take her here. I hope that paints a better picture of Zarzynn. Of what's happening right now."

Malasuntra shakes his head. "Love was not a choice—"

"What about every other Kulapsifang who stands in Silent City like they're supposed to?" With each word, my wrath spirals.

I hate that Malasuntra is right. I hate that I'd also stood next to Brutatalika with a sense of duty—not devotion. That had changed and tilted more toward love in the next months we spent together, but at that moment, the marble of Silent City was cold. The columns reached into the gray sky while I stood surrounded by more enemies than supporters.

It had been a display of power; not love.

"What is it you're counseling me to do right now, Malasuntra 711 Afador?"

He leans closer to the mirror, jaw clenching. "I was planning to confess that Aithe and I created a secondary line of Afadors. Love bore a son; his son bore another son. Right now, you are not my only great-grandson. One more survives in the far south. His name is Hadadrimmon. And now that we've spoken, I wonder if I didn't make a mistake.

"Find the Aithessons, Samson. Find Hadadrimmon 342 Aithesson. He is your blood. You'll need numbers if you're going to eliminate the

Leofsige threat, and Love said that Hadadrimmon was a strong pup. He held him before he died."

I cross my arms.

Hadadrimmon 342 Aithesson.

I speak clearly so my great-grandfather might understand. "Malachai is also my blood. So is Clearbold. I don't think it makes anyone particularly relevant to me on principle. And it's possible the Leofsige line will *partner* with the Aithessons to dethrone me." I lean forward like he did, beseeching, "What I *need* to do is find Imperatriz. Only she can *prove* that Clearbold plotted against the Afador line. Without Imperatriz, I'll be starting a civil war in Velm with no proof of my father's wrongdoing."

"What you *need* to do, Samson 714 Afador, is focus your energy where it is needed most. *You* are the sole heir of the Kulapsifang and the Male Alpha. You need to keep Velm together—whether or not Imperatriz returns. She gave Velm a Kulapsifang, did she not?" He lets that sink in. "Now, tell me what powerful allies you've made."

Whether or not Imperatriz returns.

This is the first moment I've ever deeply considered that reality.

That she survived the journey to Pit... and that's the end of my good fortune.

I run a hand through my hair. I try to calm myself, to clear my thoughts.

Tell me what powerful allies you've made.

With each passing second, my anger for Malasuntra shifts. I hate him because he did something I won't have the boldness to do. I hate him because Aithe could hide in the deep south, but my lover can't be hidden away.

Helisent will never bear me a son named Love.

Helisent will never have a village to help her keep a secret; even if she did, that's not the life she'd want.

"I have the confidence of the world's most powerful witch," I offer quietly. "Probably."

Malasuntra's gaze shifts at that. He angles his head, studying me quickly. "Well, that's quite a coup. Well done. Now all you have to do is convince her to find Imperatriz."

I huff. "That's—"

"What does she want? The witch. What does she want above all else?"

My mind goes blank. I can't fathom what Helisent might want above all else. Last year, it was Anesot and Oko's deaths. Now, it might just be to return to Mieira.

To survive the triplemoon in Ezit and free the okeanids.

Malasuntra raises his eyebrows. "Figure that out, then give it to her. While she sorts out Imperatriz, you stay in Velm. Stay close to Brutatalika. And find the Aithessons. I can't speak to Hadadrimmon's character... but if he's anything like Love, he will be wise beyond his years."

After a long sigh, I nod, numbly waiting for Malasuntra to toss me another uninvited confession. I should have trusted the feeling I had in the pit in my stomach as soon as Meres said a deathling waited for me.

I study Malasuntra's features, wishing he'd been stolid like Sutnazzar or wise like my mother. But maybe my grandmother isn't stolid. Maybe my mother wasn't wise.

Maybe we're all just pretending.

Maybe we're all imposters.

That's the first realization born of this conversation that makes me feel better.

"Straighten your back," Malasuntra says. "Sit up straight."

I do as he says, almost on muscle memory.

My mind is elsewhere. My anger has given way to confusion, distress, uncertainty.

Things aren't the way I was raised to think they would be. I've known that since I drank Kierkeline's potion in Hypnos, but it's like I keep finding new branches of a maze when I think I'm striding toward an exit.

"You aren't expected to handle this alone," he goes on. "Think of the Leofsige conflict like a season of Night; only those who prepare will survive. And now you have all the pieces. Clearbold doesn't know that you're a step ahead of him. You have a powerful witch on your side, along with your wife. And somewhere south of Rouz, you have Hadadrimmon. Surely, he can handle Malachai while you get rid of Clearbold. Chin up, Samson. This is your fate. Accept it."

Malasuntra is right; this is my fate whether or not I accept it. But part of me wishes I didn't know about Hadadrimmon. That I didn't have to factor another huge unknown into my decision-making.

"Imperatriz disappeared when you were twelve, correct?" Malasuntra asks.

I feel suddenly exhausted, my limbs and eyelids heavy. "Yes. Twelve."

"Then I guess you wouldn't know how Kulapsifangs speak to each other. I argued with my father a lot, and Sutnazzar argued with me. Your mother was particularly unruly—she decided to boss me around as soon as she could talk. She took food off my plate well into her adolescence just to test me. She challenged Sutnazzar to a waricon once—Sutnazzar declined."

We stare at one another for a long moment.

I'm not sure what point he's trying to make until he concludes, "But you are very quiet. What are your opinions, Samson? Kulapsifangs raise Kulapsifangs; this is our tradition. I'll come back for you. I will help you find your voice."

I'm too dazed and suspicious for a long-winded answer. I settle for a head nod. I don't tell him I'm not interested in finding my voice—not as much as I'm interested in finding Imperatriz, in helping Helisent survive our attack on Ezit, in keeping Velm unified.

I look at Meres and switch back to Mieiran. "I think that's all for now."

Malasuntra watches me evenly while Meres shifts.

She scoots toward the mirror's face, holding it in place with one hand and waving to Malasuntra. The former Kulapsifang shifts once, glancing at the hand, and then his image starts to disappear. Like a stone sinking into a lake, he fades out of view gradually.

I see myself in the mirror once his image is gone.

The fire crackles to my right, sending bright light across my features.

I stare ahead, realizing how old I look. Lines around my eyes and forehead are becoming more prominent, but I don't feel more mature inside.

The necromancer shifts to stand up, and I help her rise. She stoops to lift the mirror; I would offer to help her, but she refused twice on the way here. Now, she eyes the path back to Hella.

"You didn't like what the deathling had to say," she murmurs, almost apologetically. She adjusts her grip on the mirror, going on before I can thank her. "Would Rex and Berevald like to speak with anyone? I don't quite remember where they are..." The necromancer twists back and forth, doing a full circle with the mirror balanced against her collar. "I haven't been in a forest in years... and even before I was kidnapped, I grew up on the beach. So many trees... such a crowded place..."

"I'll take you back to Hella. We'll pass Berevald and Rex on the way."

I stoop to dismantle the small fire. I use a hollow goat horn to collect a piece of the kindling. It drops to the horn's narrow end, simmering and sheltered for transportation. I stomp out the embers next; though unlikely to spread given all the limestone, the pine trees are dry and brittle, thirsty for a wildfire.

We take off toward the camp where I left my packmates. "You can rest tonight, Meres. There's no need to introduce us to each deathling right away."

The necromancer nods. She takes a few steps closer to me as the firelight dwindles and we're left in darkness. I set my hand on her upper back to guide us.

Soon, another fire comes into view between the trees. Rex and Berevald are silent, which is suspicious given I left them with a half-full jug of vodka and a hand drum.

I inhale deeply, relieved not to smell any vampires.

Tomorrow is the doublemoon. With tensions high, we'd begged them to stay inside Hella and let our fangselves, closer to our conscious minds, get accustomed to their presence. It will be our only chance to meet the den in our forms before invading Ezit—and any rough starts will be hard to forget on the triplemoon.

As we round a midden of boulders, Rex and Berevald come into view. They sit side by side, hands folded in their laps. *And why are they on their best behavior?*

Then I see Helisent pacing on the opposite side of the fire. Her hair shifts as she turns on her heels, lips pinched into a pout. She must be cloaking her scent; I can't smell her ala at all, even though she's only wearing what looks like an oversized shirt. The paltry linen dangles just above her knees, shapeless and drifting in the breeze.

The witch looks from me to the necromancer with flitting eyes. "Hello, my dear okeanid. I need to speak with the wolves alone. Do you mind?"

The witch smiles politely, then gestures back toward one of Hella's tunnels.

I glance at Rex and Berevald. Both watch Helisent, as though prepared to stand and flee.

What the fuck happened here? Did Halcyon tell her about the ax?

Meres steps forward. "Andromeda North of Skull and Milisent West of Jaws are waiting for you. Axerxa would also like to speak with you under calmer circumstances. They're all quite combative."

Helisent snorts. "Tell them we'll have plenty of time to catch up when I die."

Meres stops, then backs up a step.

The witch's smile turns from polite to crude. "Thank you. That will be all for now."

The witch gestures once again toward Hella's tunnel. This time, a dancing light simmers a foot in front of Meres. It flutters, like a butterfly pitted with Helisent's reddish glow, drifting ahead of the necromancer.

I offer the necromancer a bow of my head. "Thank you, Meres."

This time, Meres doesn't smile—she winks again, like we're long-lost friends, then scampers forward to follow the light. As she passes Helisent, she murmurs, "They have waited many years, Helisent West of Jaws."

Helisent looks over her shoulder, watching Meres pass her. The necromancer ambles forward with a steady pace, following the fluttering red light with her mirror held against her abdomen.

When Helisent turns back, I'm not sure where to go or who to look at.

The witch raises her eyebrows at me and points to the patch of dirt beside Rex and Berevald. "Sit down."

I take a seat as she starts to pace again. Malasuntra and Aithe and Love and Hadadrimmon drift from my mind as I focus on Helisent and realize she's holding something. She clutches a narrow bundle to her chest, knuckles white.

She rounds to where we sit on the opposite side of the fire and hands me the bundle, then backtracks to pace again.

I pull the fabric back gently, confused; the salt-and-pepper braid inside doesn't smell like anything. Rex and Berevald lean closer to study it.

After a buzz of infrasound, an ala drifts from the strands.

My heart thumps in my throat.

My head goes light.

I pull the braid to my nose and inhale as deeply as I can.

I exhale through my mouth, then pull in smaller breaths—

I smell my mother.

I smell Imperatriz 713 Afador.

Unlike the hair tie Anesot dangled in front of me last year in Alita, Imperatriz's ala has changed. Though her ala isn't potent, as though faded by water or oil, her vitals are far more encouraging than the hair tie. I can tell that she's eating well, that she hasn't been sick in a season, that she's past her fertile years and into some of her strongest decades.

Much like wielders and their magical repertoires, a wolf's peak physical form is usually in their seventies and eighties before ailing in their mid to late nineties. Imperatriz, wherever she is, is enjoying the power of her golden years.

I sit back, focused on the braid.

Rex and Berevald also stare at it in stunned silence. Rex cranes over to smell it, as does Berevald. Neither touch the fabric or hair, afraid of contaminating her ala; it's already weak enough that I wonder how much longer her scent will endure. Given it's her hair, her scent will always be palpable—at least, for wolves with higher generational counts.

It has to survive the trip back to Velm.

To Bellator.

I look across the fire at the witch. "Where is she?"

Helisent crosses her arms. "Pit."

I shake my head, confused and desperate. Adrenaline fires through my veins, begging me to jump into action. "How—how do you—"

"The ship docked in Pit," she explains. "That's where Pel and Jen sold the okeanids. They kept me on board. I remember the vampires saying something about a wolf—a wolf that lived near the docks. They didn't want her to interfere. They spoke of wolfbane. And then they left.

"While they were gone, Imperatriz came onto the boat. I don't remember a lot. But she... she tied things around my arms and neck. That's all that was left—the braid you're holding. She told me..."

Helisent sighs, staring emptily into the canopy. "She told me to take the braid to you, Samson. I think she's been trying to stow away on the ships. Whatever Pel and Jen were using—wolfbane—that's how they keep her from stowing away."

Helisent remembers her time on the ship—

And what else does she remember? Did she take Kierkeline's potion?

"What's wolfbane?" Rex asks.

"How does she look?" Berevald asks. "Is she well?"

Helisent looks at Rex first. "I don't know what wolfbane is. I can't even guess what it is, but she said that the vampires had put it on... the box. That's why she couldn't free me." She pivots toward Berevald. "And I don't know how she looked. I was tired by then. Really tired. She sounded... okay. Strong, I guess. She knew my mother. She gave me food and water."

"But you didn't communicate?" Rex pushes.

Helisent shakes her head. "That was the worst stretch. Pit. She was nice to me. She was trying to help me."

"And she couldn't... stay on the ship when it left?" Berevald clarifies. "Because of the wolfbane?"

"Exactly. It sounded like Pel and Jen feared her. I think they mentioned something about the House of Serac, too."

I stare at the braid in my hand.

This was what I'd wanted back in Alita—wasn't it?

To trade Helisent's safety and sanity for my mother.

I run my thumb along the braid. I never forgot how it felt to tangle my hands in my mother's hair. How thick and strong her strands were; how it felt to be bathed in her ala—everything I loved in her ala, its strength and the safety it brought, comes back now.

I bring it to my nose and close my eyes.

"How long were you together?" Rex continues.

"I don't know. Time wasn't real. Not for me." Helisent clears her throat. "It could have been days or twenty minutes."

I can sense Rex and Berevald staring at me, waiting for me to ask questions. But my mind has switched to Malasuntra's proposition—

that I offer Helisent a trade in exchange for her searching for Impera-triz. He was right—her magic is a much more efficient option than attempting to bribe someone into taking us to Pit or finding it ourselves. Much safer, too.

I open my eyes and look from the braid to Helisent. "Can you track her with this? You said your magic is stronger than ever before. Is there a way for you to take us to Pit?"

Had we spoken about our motivations to find Oko last year, I would have asked Helisent this question already.

She rubs her temples, glaring at me. "I have to get us back to Mieira, Samson. I don't have the time or energy for a fucking side quest right now. And maybe if you hadn't *thrown an axe at Halcyon*, he'd be more willing to help. He knows a lot of people on Plet. At least one has to know the way to Pit."

I groan, covering my face.

Still, Rex growls, "*Lekeli Kelnazzar*, Samson."

Berevald sighs. "Fuck."

I glance at my packmates, then at the witch. "We decided against looking for help in Plet. Even with the benefit of Halcyon's judgment, it's better that no one realize we're looking for someone on Pit."

Helisent tosses her hair over her shoulder. "I see. And speaking of Halcyon, he's back in Hella. You three need to play nice because I brought back his wives and his sons. Well, they aren't really wives how you guys think of them—but they're all bound together. Also, the witches are from Col."

I'm thankful Rex and Berevald also physically react to that state-ment. Rex curses again, while Berevald actually gasps. Another stran-gled groan escapes me.

I switch my gaze toward the path that leads to Hella.

His wives and his sons?

"His wives are *Colyd*. That means they're green wielders. I don't know if you heard that." Helisent keeps her attention fixed on me. I try to control my facial expression—I can't tell if I'm relieved that Halcyon is tied up with responsibilities beyond Helisent or outright shocked. Once again, I realize I know very little about the warlock. "Oh, and thanks for threatening him with his father after you swore not to. *Smooth*, Samson. Really fucking *smooth*."

Like Helisent, my packmates watch me with unpleasant surprise.

I strive for my most reasonable tone, gesturing with my hands. "I will try to be more—"

"No, no, no." Helisent chuckles with dark mirth. "I wasn't *asking* you to *try* to do anything. I'm *commanding* you to play nice. Be kind to his wives—they're the ones who saved the braid Imperatriz tied around my neck. And be nice to his sons. Oh—one brought his girlfriend. She's Argyd. Be nice to her, too."

I stare into the fire as I struggle to process the information.

Halcyon has *two* wives and *two* sons, and one of those sons is old enough to have a lover. *How fucking old is the warlock?* He doesn't smell older than his early forties, which seems too young for littlelings. For *two* littlelings. With *two* separate wives.

Helisent looks at me while she points to Rex and Berevald. "And how does this work? Do I command them, too, or do you do that?"

I try not to sound too compromising, afraid that Rex and Berevald might realize I'm actually very comfortable begging Helisent for things. "We recognize that you are the leader of Vex."

Helisent directs her poisonous glare at Rex. "Does this one understand that? Because the last time we spoke—"

"I already apologized—" Rex cuts in.

"—he was a real fucking asshole," Helisent barrels on, voice rising with each word.

Holy shit.

She remembers, Samsonfang chimes in.

I can't think straight.

I blurt out, "That's just his personality."

Rex points his glare at me next.

Berevald confirms, "It's true, Helisent."

"Fine." The witch crosses her arms. "I need to speak with Samson alone. You can return to Hella, but keep in mind there are two Colyd witches inside—and that they're *very welcome*."

Rex and Berevald shift toward me. Neither budges an inch, glancing from my face to the braid in my hand to Helisent.

Before Helisent can order them to leave, which they'd loathe, I explain, "We need to spend the night outside of Hella. The double-moon is tomorrow, so we're a bit... on edge. It would be best not to chance any conflict with the vampires. Rex and Berevald will set up camp at another location."

Desperate to be alone with Helisent, I stand up and dust myself clean with my free hand. Rex and Bere mirror me, eyes still caught on the braid. They bend their heads to smell it one last time, then round the fire to split our supplies.

Thankfully, they leave the jug of vodka behind, toting away a portion of our food and water. Berevald grabs the buckhorn where the ember from my fire with Meres kindles. He looks back at me once, bearing an understated smile before following Rex into the night.

While I wait for them to drift out of earshot, I ask Helisent, "Can you protect the braid? Her ala is faint. I'm afraid it will..."

Disappear.

The soft fabric tightens around the braid, sealing it within as her ala vanishes. I hold it tight; I know it will be safer with Helisent in one of her bottomless bags, but I can't stand to part with it quite yet.

It comforts me.

And I need comfort right now.

Helisent paces like a wildcat on the opposite side of the fire.

I remain on my feet, wondering if I should sit back down. Just to make sure we're on the same page, I ask, "You remember?"

She drops her chin to leer at me. "*Everything.*"

My body starts to shiver—from nerves or apprehension or relief, I can't tell.

For over a month, I've dutifully repeated my mantra: *Helisent does not remember you, but one day she will. It is possible she will still love you when that day comes, so keep hope until then.*

I've kept hope... until this very moment.

I brace myself, body locking like I'm anticipating a blow.

Helisent throws her hands out wildly, frozen in place. "Well, what the fuck were you thinking?"

I hang my head. "Anesot kidnapped Imperatriz. He worked with Clearbold to do it, just like you had suspected. He wanted me to stand in front of him while he convinced you to forgive him. He was planning to bring you a necromancer so you could see Milisent again. After he convinced you to forgive him, he said he'd take me to Pit. To Imperatriz."

Her features tighten; she starts to pace again.

I gulp. "And then I tried to get a few answers out of Oko. That didn't go very well."

She nods like a madwoman. "And why not, Samson?"

"Because I don't have magic to call on."

"*Wrong.* Try again."

I narrow my eyes. I'm not sure what she wants to hear. "Because Oko is dangerous?"

"No."

Lekeli Kelnazzar. "Because I don't know anything about wielders?"

"No."

"Because... I'm a big dumb wolf?"

"No." She rolls her eyes. "Fuck, you're bad at this. Try one last time. Dig deep."

I take a deep breath. I go through our last moments in Alita, starting with our fight in the hostel that morning.

Or I guess it wasn't a fight. That wasn't what had happened in that room.

Helisent had told me what she suspected, and I'd taken her words as a threat, an insult, an impossible thought from a raving witch.

With a shame that touches my core, I tell her, "Because I didn't listen to you when you told me what was at play."

Even after I'd sworn to teach her the value of trust.

She nods one last time, then she screams, "Because *you* said that you *loved* me, but you still thought I was *stupid Helisent* in the end. I was just another *foolish wielder* when it really came down to it." She approaches me, staying on her side of the fire. The orange light lashes over her features as she whispers, "*Asshole.*"

The word is fragile, almost inaudible.

Alit with the flames, I can see the silvery tears rimming her eyes.

My eyes sting, too.

"And now what?" Tears slip down her cheeks as she throws her hands out again. "You'll just keep following me until I find Imperatriz? Is that what we're doing? Caught in a game of cat and mouse and wolf and witch and wolf's mother?"

Before my talk with Malasuntra, I had a strong grasp on who I was supposed to be.

Maybe not on who I *actually was*, but who the world expected me to be. That, at least, was a solid compass to point me in the right direction. But knowing that Malasuntra had Aithe... it undoes my conviction to be the Kulapsifang everyone expects me to be.

And if I could be anyone...

If I could do anything...

Then this is all profoundly simple.

I clear my throat. "I need you."

She snorts. "Obviously—"

"Not to find my mother. I need you because I love you. If I weren't the Kulapsifang of Velm, you would be my pack. Just me and you. Helisent West of Jaws and Samson 714 Afador."

Forever.

That last word is too intense.

Wielders don't understand monogamy. They don't recognize marriage.

But things have never been clearer to me than they are at this moment.

I belong to Helisent how Velm belongs to the moons.

And if I had it my way, she and I would be our own Alphas, and our children would be our pack, and on the triplemoons the witch would sit with Samsonfang and our pith puplings, bathed in the glory of the moons.

My wife's eyes would be the second and third sennens.

She would make me a five-moon wolf.

But this will never happen.

There are layers to reveries, ranging from the semi-possible to deeply unfathomable; wolves keep their dreams balled up like this, contained and ordered.

So, I opt for a more palpable fantasy. "I would take you south to Velm with Night on the horizon. We would go into the forest when I smelled snow in the sky. I would cover the windows of our cottage at night while the snow fell so you'd be surprised to see it in the morning." She watches me, expression falling. Her tensed hands relax, falling to her sides. "And then I'd carry you into the piles. You would cling to me because it's cold, and it's wet, and you would hate the snow as soon as you touched it. Inside the cottage, it would be warm. It would smell like us—so much so that even you could smell our alas mixed together."

Helisent wipes her cheeks Quietly, she asks, "Really?"

I nod, then round the fire pit. I'm desperate to be near her, but I'm still nervous she doesn't feel safe around me. That she hates me for what I did in Alita.

I meet her halfway, hoping she'll close the distance.

She doesn't. Helisent keeps watching me, face wet with tears and gleaming under the firelight.

I take one more step toward her so she knows I'm edging closer for a touch. (I'll even take a slap—just *any* touch.)

She crosses her arms. "What is this—you want a hug?" She scans me from head to toe. Her breathless voice shakes. "You're *married*, Samson. Things are different."

I did my duty marrying Brutatalika. Someday, our partnership will bare the next Kulapsifang. All of that exists like an abstract cloud on the horizon, slowly taking shape in a future I can't quite fathom yet.

For now... for now, I'm still free enough.

"I know." I clear my throat. "But if you feel comfortable... then..."

She scans me again. I prepare a better invitation—something firmer, something that would acknowledge my wife and our marriage, while also indicating that I want Helisent however I can have her.

Then the witch shifts toward me, lunging a step before launching herself with her arms outstretched.

I meet her on the next stride—

And for the first time in months, it feels like I finally *relax*.

My arms wrap around Helisent's soft body and hold her to my chest. Helisent clings to me, setting her head on my collar so I can bury my nose in her hair behind her ear and take in her ala. I sink onto my knees and shift my other arm below her butt, helping support her as her legs wrap around me.

Our breaths meet and sync, and then we're just how we should be; a single being intertwined, warmed by the fire beneath the light of near-full moons.

The tears that stung my eyes now wet my cheeks and slide into Helisent's white hair. The witch starts to cry loudly, fingers balling in my shirt as she shakes. And I weep quietly, stroking her back and her hair.

I catch my breath before she does. Helisent cries and hiccups and gets out half-sentences like 'this fucking place' and 'I don't get it' and 'the whole world', but none of it adds up. Just a storm of panic unleashed in hindsight.

I hold her. I listen. I try to take it away, like I could absorb it straight from her body. And when she finally quiets, she raises her hands to wipe my cheeks dry. I do the same for her, keeping one hand under her so she doesn't shift out of place.

She sniffles as she stares at me, a hand's length away. "What now?"

I'm not sure what she means—*about us, about Ezit, about Imperatriz?*

I go with the first option, focusing on her body. On its weight and how full her hip feels beneath my hand, the way her ala drifts around me. I study the curve of her lips. "Kiss me."

Her fingers trace my cheeks, a smile playing at her lips. "It's annoying that everyone would assume I seduced you. But you and I will always know the truth, Samson—the Kulapsifang of Velm begged me to kiss him. Twice."

I raise my eyebrows, waiting.

She raises her eyebrows, staring back.

"Well—are you going to or not?" I'm happier than I've been since waking in Alita with no memory. It feels like everything that has transpired since then sits behind a veil—on the other side of a barrier or maybe hidden in the shadow of our love.

Just for a moment.

Her fingers trace my features. She bites her lip. "I always want to kiss you. I just want to make sure we aren't doing something unwise... *again*."

"I understand." I nod, trying to process her concern while my entire being focuses on her lips, and how they move in tandem with her teeth and tongue while she speaks. "But I think I'm... really unwise for you."

No, Samsonfang growls. ***It is always wise to be devoted to the Alpha.***

I still don't know how to unpack that statement. But, the sensation of simplicity that washed over me a moment before expands. So I offer another explanation as Helisent holds my face, tracing my jaw and then my brow with her tiny fingers. "I'd like to be with you however I can. Whenever I can. But if you aren't comfortable, then I don't want to... beg you for kisses. Repeatedly."

(I think I kind of do, though. And I have no idea where this little impulse comes from—*why do I want her to make me beg?*)

I stare at Helisent while she chews on my words.

Then she raises my chin with her hand, leaning down to press her soft lips against mine. And I watch, waiting until her eyes close and our lips melt together before shutting my own.

The kiss is nothing like what I've experienced before—not the clumsiness I felt with my first partner, Maia, or the posturing I always fell into with Rex, or the cautious exploration Brutatalika and I experienced.

The kiss is also nothing like the maddening passion of my first meeting with Helisent in the Luzian Estate.

When we kiss in Vex, I swear I feel magic for the first time in my life.

It's not an aggressive bass that rattles all it touches, but a sensation that buzzes around my core, fizzing light and almost tickling. It wraps around my heart first, filling my chest with gentle infrasound. Then, like the adrenaline of a scare, it soars through my veins, filling me with such a lightheaded rush that I open my eyes—half-expecting to see Helisent floating us into a nest.

I'm still kneeling on the ground, clutching the witch near the fire.

Her wide eyes are fixed on me; she must have felt it, too. Her hand tightens on my jaw. "What'd you do?"

I shake my head. "Nothing—what'd *you* do?"

Her hand shifts to my collar, then she pulls my shirt away from my chest. She leans forward to stare into the gap between my skin and the fabric, eyes locking on the bright red mark over my chest.

She reaches to graze the bright scar with a fingertip.

Then she extracts her hand and stares at me. I stare back, equally uncertain about what I just felt, how it relates to the mark of Vex, and why kissing spurred it on.

I drift closer to Helisent and kiss her again when I can't think of an explanation.

I don't care; I'm so fucking unwise for this witch.

(Forever.)

Helisent kisses me back—this time without another graze of magic.

We sit by the fire, kissing and touching and running our hands through each other's hair. I have no idea how much time passes. I fall into a daze, transfixed by her ala, desperate for her warmth, hanging on every breath I feel expand her chest.

She hasn't forgiven me, but this is a beautiful start.

Eventually, Helisent pulls away and points at a towering pine tree. "Should we sleep in my nest? For old time's sake?"

I nod with a smile.

But in the next second, I'm craning toward her lips and she's tangling her hands in my hair. Someplace nearby, the pine tree waits.

CHAPTER 15

MORNING CREATURES

HELISENT

Honey Baby,
I kept you west of Jaws so you would know joy. I grew you soft, just like
Andromeda and I always planned. Looking back, this is either my greatest
accomplishment or an unforgivable disservice.
Papa P.

I wake up with a small gasp.

I'm a hand's length away from Samson's face—

I'd forgotten, and now I'm treated to the surprise all over again.

With a smile, I curl against his chest. He lays on his side, facing me and head resting on a folded arm. His other drapes over me to seal me against him. Normally, it would be too much touching and body heat and scratchy chest hair.

Right now, it's perfect.

A painless dawn.

I stare at his features, slack with sleep. His lips are fuller, a light pink that reflects his pale skin, prone to rouging. I reach out to poke his straight and semi-flat nose as it snores and snores. His full lashes twitch as he dreams, asleep in my nest for the first time in almost a year.

He's so perfect. Even his little nose hairs and the soft lines taking form on his forehead.

It took us a while to situate ourselves last night. Unlike our stints nest-dwelling on the way to Alita, I don't have my usual suite of supplies. No birch twigs, no blankets, no pillows, no balms and creams; all we have are Samson's camping supplies, which is little more than a blanket. It drapes over his torso where he cradles me.

I lift the blanket to stare where we lay intertwined. He must be close to waking; his dick is hard, bowed up toward his belly.

I smile, shimmying closer.

Despite extensive cuddling and kissing last night, I wasn't horny.

I didn't even try to make out the outline of his dick through his pants—and that's second nature. I just dragged him into my nest and tucked us under the blanket and curled into the smallest shape I could and started crying again.

I wept for all I relived in that memory potion; the hardest memories weren't all from the ship. Four years is a long time.

At one point, I think I was crying because I *wasn't* horny.

But, like my papa says, people never change.

And Horny Helisent is back.

Warmth seeps into my body the longer I lay against him. For now, I keep my hands to myself.

Just like I didn't start exploring last night, neither did Samson.

I snuggle closer, pressing our abdomens together. I take a deep breath to gently heave my chest against him.

With a long breath, he stirs. His eyes slide half-open; he studies me for a long moment with a sigh, pulling me closer. His hand slides up my back, then sweeps down lower, past my hips and my butt. He grips my calf to pull my leg over his hip, and I scoot closer to half-straddle him as we lay on our sides.

He nuzzles his face toward mine, burying his nose into the crook of my neck and into my hair. I giggle as his tadmazzar kicks up, sending a deep rumble from his chest.

This feels very familiar.

A sleepy and half-awake Samson stirs to find me at his side, setting off tadmazzar while his hands roam across me, soothing and squeezing. And I fall pliant in his gentle hands, shifting back and forth so he has access to whichever part of me he likes.

We are morning creatures again; half-awake, fully aroused.

I shift closer with each stroke of his hands. I angle my body, using the leg that's hooked over his hip to rub my sex against his. His tadmazzar deepens as his tongue runs along my jaw, toward my ear. I tangle my hands in his hair, tugging lightly as I grind myself against him.

His hand slides under my shirt-dress and I arch to extend the touch, desperate to feel more of his coarse fingers against me. His breath catches when he grabs my ass, shaking his hand to feel me jiggle.

(If I had to guess whether he prefers a butt to a pair of breasts, I'd say he wants whichever jiggles more.)

My skin trembles and tingles where he touches me. He keeps his face buried between my collar and hair, planting kisses on my neck, on my shoulder, behind my ear. I try not to angle my head too much, knowing he likes to be surrounded by my hair, my ala.

I use magic to tug the hem of his pants down, lifting the fabric so it doesn't catch on his cock. Samson obliges me, shifting his hips so they slip down past his knees. He fits his hand around my hip to help angle me toward him.

I yelp with the giggly joy of knowing what comes next. With my shirt-dress bunched at my hips, I reach down to guide his sex toward mine.

We're both so warm—

He moans into my hair as I stroke myself with his head. I douse him with my wetness, then slide it across my clit again and again. He doesn't nudge into me, letting me move my hips down across him.

I tease him while I coax out my pleasure, slowly and without hurry. Samson twitches like he's trying not to move; I cradle his face with my free hand. With a groan, he pulls away from my neck. Our hair tangles, falling over our faces as he kisses me. His tongue meets mine, his hand slides into my messy hair.

He pulls back and looks at my lips.

I use magic to brush our hair from our eyes. I stare at Samson and he stares at me. He looks so different now that I remember him; his bold and unfamiliar features are idyllic, and comforting, and...

"I can smell you," I blurt.

His expression loosens, like he might smile. Then he starts to move his hips, gently thrusting into me. "What do I smell like?"

"You smell like musk." I fight for the words as he slowly nudges further. "You smell like leather and cedar."

He smiles while he kisses me. "You smell like limestone. You smell bitter and sweet at the same time."

My eyelids flutter as pleasure starts to mount throughout my body. Given last night's weeping and the stress of the last year, I hadn't expected an orgasm. But I can already feel one concentrating in the soles of my feet; that's where they build, like storms offshore.

"Bitter?" How unexciting.

He stares dreamily at me, his rhythm slow, thorough, teasing. "Bitter."

He curls toward me, shifting to be fully inside me, and I crane up toward him. For how anatomically incompatible I had once thought we were, we can still kiss like this.

Intertwined, he whispers into my lips, "You've always smelled like Vex. Like Hella's limestone."

I've heard better; I've also heard worse.

I concentrate on the orgasm in my soles instead.

I shift to push Samson's shoulder. He follows my momentum and moves onto his back, holding me against him so our bodies stay flushed. I straddle him, hands flat against his chest and knees against the sticky pine-twig nest. The tension in my body, and all the wild energy bundled in the soles of my feet, begs for release.

Samson curses something as he watches me wind over him, brow furrowed and red warmth filling his cheeks. That's familiar, too—I never got around to asking him last year whether he was grunting wordlessly or speaking Velmic.

My hands clench, propping me against his chest; my right hand spreads over his heart, over the bundle of red scar tissue. My toes curl as an orgasm explodes through my body, oozing and lingering between my legs.

I clench my eyes, then fall against his chest in a shivering heap.

He strokes my back with a warm hand.

I lift my knees to shift our position, but he slides out of me, softening. I look down; pale cum slides down my inner thigh.

I look up at Samson. "You came, too?"

He nods as another wave of tadmazzar kicks up. His smile is understated, gleaming mostly in his blue-black eyes.

I inch closer to his face so our noses touch. "Really? Samson—we *never* did that before."

His smile grows. "I guess we're all grown up now, Helisent."

"That's cute." I sit back and pat his belly with a happy sigh.

I glance around the canopy, body alight with energy and optimism. Still, bereft of my usual supplies, the nest looks hopelessly bare. Without my birch twigs to call on, I wove the nest of pine. It's sticky and coarse, not smooth and pale.

Samson shifts into a sitting position with his back against the nest's rim. Droplets of cum dot his belly near his relaxed cock. His pants remain tangled around his calves.

I try to tame my grin. "I like how undignified you are with me."

He studies himself with a sigh. "Good. It's your fault."

Slowly, our former routines start to come back to me. This is usually when he'd roll a cigarette and I would light it. Instead, I get to work clearing our scents from both of us, along with our clothes.

"Oh, shit—pitroot. Do you have any with you?" I ask. "I obviously don't have vagueroot, but I can ask Ceyx and Cleo for suggestions."

I don't mention that Halcyon can't have children, so we haven't had to worry about birth control. (Terrified of baring more sons, he paid a warlock to snip a special vein in his grundle—and now his cum is just for show. Something like that.)

"Ask who?" Samson asks.

I really don't want to say the name *Halcyon* in this nest. "The witches from Col. In Zarzynn. They probably know what a witch should take to avoid pregnancy."

"Right." Based on Samson's dramatic frown, he's now thinking about Halcyon and his wives. "I have pitroot in my bag. I'll start taking it immediately."

I almost joke about him bringing pitroot—he must have been really convinced I would forgive him if he brought it along. Then I remember he married Brutatalika a few months ago and was probably taking pitroot to avoid knocking up his wife when his hot cum runs down her inner thighs after they—

"Helisent?"

I blink, realizing there's red light beaming from my eyes.

I straighten my hair and clear my throat, shoving the Female

Alpha out of my mind. "I was just remembering... this one time... it's a long story." I ignore the red light until it dwindles. "So, who knows about us? It seems like Berevald knows."

Samson sits up further. Now that I've cleaned him, he shimmies his pants back on. "Berevald knows. Obviously, Parsifal and Rex know. I think Kierkeline and Absalom both suspect, but neither has pushed me on it."

The sky brightens beyond the canopy and the air starts to warm. Birds chirp and soar through the branches; the underbrush below shifts with movement.

I move onto the nest's ledge, then turn back to help Samson float below.

He peaks over the ledge at the ground, thirty feet away. With an unhappy sigh, he holds my waist while I guide us into the air with a floating spell. His eyes flit through the canopy as we slowly descend.

When we land, he heads toward the camp's dead fire to collect his supplies while I dismantle the nest. When it's done, we meet on the narrow path that leads back to Hella, alit with golden light.

Samson clears his throat. "Where will you sleep from now on?"

I look down at the cluster of pine twigs in my hand. "I haven't really thought about it."

He glances down the trail that leads to Hella. "Is it like a warren, then?"

It takes me a second to understand what Samson means. "No. Not even a little bit. Ceyx and Cleo wear *undergarments*." He doesn't put that together; I'm also not totally sure about the implications of undergarments. "Right... so me and Halcyon..."

I have no idea how much to tell him about me and the warlock—how much Samson deserves or wants to know, what I feel comfortable sharing, what Halcyon would also feel comfortable with me sharing.

I go with, "Me and Halcyon are in this nebulous thing and I'd say only five to ten percent of that is romantic."

(For now.)

Samson nods. "He said you two were bound."

"We're bound by the agreement we made." I choose my words carefully. "I'm taking his family to Mieira because he took me to Vex. Pletens value being bound. It's how they... make family, make alliances.

But his family needs peace and safety, and I don't think my future will be especially peaceful in the coming years. So..."

Samson stares emptily at the ground, as though deep in thought.

I clear my throat and wait for him to bring up Brutatalika.

I still have no idea how he feels about his wife. Whether she makes him feel safe or uncertain. Whether she trusts Clearbold. Whether she trusts Samson.

We stand in silence for a while.

I watch the flitting dragonflies, the chirping flycatchers as they sail through the air.

Eventually, he says, "Clearbold wants to divide Velm. And... he's succeeding. Malachai and his pack are carving a new symbol throughout Mort. And Invidio, the pack leader who challenged me to a waricon last year, removed all the nymphs and wielders from his village. It's been happening more and more often—and the regional pack leaders aren't fighting it."

For a moment, he stares at me like I'm not here. Like he's a thousand miles away from where he stands.

"I can't lose control of my territory, Helisent. What I said last night... I meant it. I meant that if I had real freedom in my life, I would choose you. I would choose us."

His voice lowers, head tilted with something that looks like regret. "But that isn't my fate. My fate is to be a loyal Kulapsifang to Velm, to be devoted to the Female Alpha, and to make sure that my mother's legacy isn't compromised."

Suddenly, Accra's words flood my mind. The gorgon had mentioned there were two types of fate—but I'd been too overwhelmed to ask for more.

Could Samson have two fates, too?

His shoulders slump and he sinks onto his knees. I flinch at the movement, concerned by his dead expression, the way his eyes scan me. "Can we make a promise to each other?"

I hate that we have these conversations after we've already climaxed.

It spoils the uplifting mood.

But with a long sigh, I nod. "And what are we promising each other?"

"I want you to promise me that you won't compromise my

marriage with Brutatalika. No matter what. And... if something happens to me, then know that you can trust her. That she can be trusted to lead Velm.

"From my part, I promise that I'll never interfere with your relationships again. I won't throw any more axes. And I won't stand in your way when it's time for you to..." He sighs, air emptying from his lungs. He clenches his jaw, staring past me. "When it's time for you to continue the Vexen line."

He must be talking about babies. About the red witches I'll someday birth.

(Part of me is relieved there's no chance of baring a wielder with a wolf. If I thought there was a possibility of Samson giving me a litteling, I'd never let that go. Ever.)

I shove it from my mind. "Fine. I promise. You have my word—and I have yours." I'm glad he had the courage to propose this compromise. But... "Then what?"

"What do you mean?"

"When we get back to Mieira... what happens between us?"

"Well, we aren't promising we won't see each other anymore." He sets his hands on his chest. "I mean, that's not a promise I want to make. I want to see you when I can. I will always want to be near you, Helisent."

I arch an eyebrow; if he hadn't been so devoted to me while sharing a cave with my warlock lover, I might doubt that statement.

"Fine then." I step forward to run my hand along his cheek. On his knees, his head is perfectly aligned with my chest, but he doesn't crane forward to nuzzle me. He looks up at me with begging eyes. "What's with all the kneeling?"

"You still haven't forgiven me for Alita." He blinks, eyebrows puckered.

I step forward and crush his face into my chest. "I forgive you this time. Don't expect a lot more of it, though. It's not in my nature."

My breasts muffle his words. "I won't. I promise."

I pull back and head down the path before he can wrap his arms around me; it's getting late. "Now go find Rex and Berevald and meet us in the cave." I look over my shoulder. "Be ready for the Colyd witches, okay? They're really nice."

He stands with a long groan. "I will be *very* nice. You have my word."

I head toward a broad shadow just off the path. I look back at Samson; he looks back at me. We stare for a moment.

I feel like me again.

Unfortunately, I have little time to transition from Samson's indolent lover to the leader of Vex.

When I shadow back into Hella, I realize half the group is already sitting near the fountain.

Parsifal sits between Ceyx and Cleo with a wide smile and a cajoling glint in his eyes. Vega sits beside Ceyx; I try not to jump when the Argyd wielder directs her gaze at me. My brief stint in Ezit did little to endear me to the white wielders... but I think we'd all struggle anyway.

Vega's skin is powder-white, just like her irises—not the sunless pale of the vampires or the pink-beige tint of the wolves. I can make out where her irises end based on the whites of her eyes—which are off-white compared to the rest of her. The two-horned witch has a narrow, hand-sized pair of horns jutting from her forehead. Wildflowers dot her braided hair and curl around her horns.

The pink and blue blossoms do help...

But I'm happy she has Vulcan's love.

I can't imagine a warm welcome awaits her in Mieira.

"Honey Baby." Parsifal smiles when he sees me. He leans forward to pick up a mug of steaming tea, then hands it off to Ceyx. He does the same for Cleo and then Vega. The witches hold their mugs with both hands, staring at Parsifal as though waiting for him to drink from his.

I'd forgotten about the sharing thing. How stringent Halcyon was about doing things in tandem with me. As my papa, it seems the Pletens are extending this courtesy to Parsifal.

"I can't believe Halcyon has been hiding these witches all this time," he goes on, eyes wide.

"And their sons." Vulcan leans over his plate to glare at Parsifal.

Halcyon raises his eyebrows at me, ignoring them. "And where are the wolves? I'm guessing you found them last night?"

With a loud yawn, Hemlock heads toward the group from his

dwelling. A few seconds later, Aura, Eos, and Meres poke their heads from a window, as though checking to see if they've missed anything in the early morning.

I tuck my hands behind my back. "They'll be back soon. And they'll be on their best behavior."

Hemlock takes a seat near the millet cakes. He offers a brief smile to the Pletens, then faces me. "And what about when they phase tonight?" He takes a bite of the flaky, golden cake. "I didn't sleep well last night. I had a nightmare the pretty one ate me. But that wasn't the worst part—I mean, you know what happens after something gets eaten, right?"

I slide my gaze toward the Pletens, who go still at Hemlock's words. I hiss at the king, "I'm sure they'll be happy for the vote of confidence. And stop being so nasty over breakfast."

I haven't considered how nerve-wracking the idea of mingling with phased wolves would be.

Things I've *actually* thought about in the last day: upsetting Halcyon, meeting Halcyon's family, Samson's face, his cock, his emotional well-being, his wife, his future, his hair, his dreams, etc.

Absalom strides from the dwellings near the fountain next. He folds his hands together, a patient gaze set on me. "Helisent, can I speak with you? Alone?"

I study the warlock in the spotless white cloak. My attitude towards him hasn't warmed since I drank the potion and realized he was one of many fruitless conquests from Luz. Worst of all, he turned his knowledge of me into a bargaining chip with the Class... after once pouring honey into my ear about how his influence in the elite group would benefit me.

My blood boils as I stare at him.

Absalom stops near the seated group. "I brought—"

"I want to strangle you and drown you at the same time," I snap.

Absalom doesn't bat a lash. "Why don't we talk about it later, then?"

Like Hemlock, he sits near the millet cakes and starts filling his plate.

I glance at the Pletens to see if my threat made them uncomfortable. Vulcan and Memphis watch Halcyon, waiting for his response, but the warlock continues to eat as though accustomed to our bickering. He leans forward to scoop a nub of honeycomb atop his millet cake.

On either side of Parsifal, the witches hold their mugs. Their steam lessens by the minute as Parsifal digs into his plate with gusto. They glance at Halcyon, then Absalom, then me.

I explain, "Papa—you have to drink your tea with them since you gave it to them. It's polite."

"It's okay," Cleo cuts in with a winced smile. "We can drink our tea by ourselves. Parsifal doesn't need to change for us."

Ceyx nods in agreement, and then the witches pick up their mugs, glancing at the other as they take timid little sips. I'm not sure they drank any tea, but I figure they'll be even more uncomfortable if I call them on it.

The okeanids wander over a second later, followed by Kierkeline.

I munch on breakfast and try not to think about the scent of cedar or the blue-black of night or the low rumble of tadmazzar that sometimes feels like infrasound.

Until I hear the low conversation of wolves drifting from the southwest. I try to remember what it was like not to remember Samson; I remind myself that the group still thinks I'm involved with Halcyon.

A preternatural silence falls over the group as Samson, Rex, and Berevald step into view. Each looks primly dressed and groomed, leaving no hint they roughed it outdoors. Or in a pine nest.

Halcyon and Vulcan crane to watch the wolves, then they scoot slightly closer to the Colyd witches and Vega. Ceyx and Cleo shrink, as though trying to make themselves smaller. Still, neither hides their gleaming jade horns or dims the ripe yellow-green of their eyes.

As the wolves drift closer, they study the Pletens, eyes moving quickly and nostrils twitching.

They walk slower than usual and stay on the far side of the street. Keeping their steady pace, they round the group and then squat to pick up a plate and fill it with food.

I try to keep things casual. "Samson, Rex, Berevald—this is Ceyx, Cleo, Vulcan, Memphis, and Vega."

I point each out with a quick gesture, ignoring how tense the Pletens are; the unmistakable glimmer of violence waiting in Vulcan's black pupils, the way his hands are relaxed in a semi-flexed position on his thighs. (Halcyon hides his nerves better than his son.)

The wolves take their seats near Hemlock and the okeanids. They seem to be politely ignoring the fixed stares from the Pletens, which even my papa notices.

Parsifal elbows Ceyx. He whispers, "See? I told you it would be okay."

Ceyx ducks her head toward him to respond in Zarzyd, "They're large like gorgons... but they look violent."

Parsifal flashes a smile. "I only speak Mieiran."

I explain to Ceyx in Zarzyd, "The wolves can hear everything, so don't repeat that in Mieiran." Her eyes widen, so I soften my tone and switch back to Mieiran. "How was your first night in Hella, my dear Pletens? Did you sleep well?"

When I left Halcyon and his brood last night, they were moving into a two-story building. Though Zarzynnian wielders don't hover and fly like Mieiran wielders, the group clearly prefers a bird's eye view. Each chose a second-floor room. I haven't peeked into my own dwelling to see whether Halcyon moved in with them or stayed in our shared room.

"It was a little cold," Ceyx admits, then looks at Cleo.

Cleo offers a shy smile. "Only at night, though."

Vega adds, "This is my first time on the mainland."

I don't know what to do with any of that information. I glance at Vulcan and Memphis, waiting for their conclusions.

Vulcan shrugs. "It's a cave."

Memphis mirrors his brother. "We have caves on Plet."

Parsifal smiles at the warlockling. "We have them in Mieira, too."

"Yes, I know." Memphis scratches his chin. Every time I see the adolescent, he looks ganglier. Thinner and taller, like a sprouting seed. Unlike Vulcan, he takes after his mother, his features softer and broader. "They're in a place called Tet. That's where the fog lives—and ghosts. Something lives in the caves, but no one knows what it is. Many think it's a city called Skull."

The warlockling gnashes into his millet cake, unaware that the group now watches him.

Halcyon notices. He quickly explains, "The nymphs in New

Hypnos like to keep Mieira alive through storytelling. Memphis likes to listen."

Hemlock puffs out his chest and straightens his back, looking entirely regal aside from the string of honey on his emerald beard. "Memphis Plet, tell me what you know of a place called *Rhotidom*."

Memphis studies the dryad with glittering eyes. "Rhotidom is a jungle home to dryads and their demigods. The trees are so tall that they block out the sun. The dryads spoil the sables. You wear the lilac of the jacaranda tree. Some sables also wear the same color because they're spoiled. Dryads weave them vests and hats. They live like tiny kings."

Hemlock shifts his head, eyes narrowing. "I see. And what else do you know about Rhotidom? Something not about sables?"

Memphis chews on his lip as he thinks. "The nymphs say that you can find anything in Rhotidom. Incense and silk—but I don't know what those are. And medicine and flowers and... well, they talk about the sables a lot. If enough sables form a pack, they can wield significant influence in the smaller villages. And even in a city called Alita."

Hemlock sighs. "Memphis Plet, I will tell you better stories. I will tell you why the lilac of the jacaranda tree is the color of life. I will tell you how we make silk from worms. Which roots you should use for medicine and which ones for incense." He raises a finger as he expounds, "And in honoring the sables, we honor the forest and its demigods. That's why they're spoiled, if you must know."

Memphis's back straightens as he focuses on Hemlock.

"That's enough about the jungle," Kierkeline barks. The Ghost-Eater bares her crooked smile at Memphis next. "Tell me, warlockling, what you know about a city called Ultramarine."

As Kierkeline focuses her smile on Memphis, Ceyx and Cleo also grin—not timidly or politically, but genuinely. The Pletens relax, beginning with the witches.

It's the start of a round circle; we test what Memphis knows, endeared by the matter-of-fact way he speaks and the stories the okeanids in New Hypnos have passed on about our world. He knows the legends of Hypnos best of all, then a smattering of general stereotypes about the rest of the cities and regions.

Most amusing of all is Memphis's description of Luz. "That's where people go to do nothing, but everyone who lives in Luz thinks that they're changing the world. They say life is peaceful, but it's really just *hedonism*."

I almost choke on my millet cake. "Who the *fuck* said that?"

Memphis blinks at me. "An okeanid."

I throw my hair over my shoulder. "I see."

Then comes a quiet question from the wolves. Samson asks, "Memphis Plet, what do you know about Velm?"

If Memphis notices the tense silence that precedes his answer, he doesn't let on. He sighs thoughtfully, staring at the fountain's trickling display. "Velm is the land of wolves. Wolves turn into beasts on the triplemoon and the doublemoon. And not even all of Ezit's magic can stop them. That's all they say about Velm. Sometimes they talk about the queen of Velm—or she isn't a queen. She's a…"

Memphis glances at Cleo, his mother, as though looking for a hint. Rather than answer, Cleo looks to me for help.

"A *Kulapsifang*," Berevald offers with a small smile.

Memphis's eyes light up. "Yes. A Kulapsifang. They like the Queen Kulapsifang of Velm." Grins kick up around the circle as the words *Queen Kulapsifang*. Samson's is smallest but warmest of all. "She said that all beings want safety, love, and possibility—and the rest is just details. But the Queen Kulapsifang is gone. She left. A long time ago."

"She didn't leave," Samson explains quietly. "She was taken away on a ship, like Meres and Helisent. And we don't turn into *beasts* when the moons are full. We turn into wolves. Do you know what a coyote looks like, Memphis Plet?"

This is the first time I've seen Samson mid-political maneuvering; he does it well.

Establishing a connection to Halcyon or his Colyd wives would be difficult. But establishing his goodwill with Memphis, the most vulnerable Pleten, is a sign of robust peace-building.

And as Samson begins his explanation of what the others will see this doublemoon, what a wolf is when it's turned skin, and what it wants, and why it wants those things, I can see the glint of distrust lessen in Halcyon's eyes.

At one point, the warlock's lips part, fully engrossed in Samson's story. (It's the part where he explains how detailed alas are and how wolf alas sometimes *mix*.)

When Samson is finished, we're more relaxed.

It's the best moment I can find to catch them up on what happened in Ezit. The group asks a few questions about Landmarks, about ejima, about the veils, about the spell Argot unleashed across Vex.

About why we need to be on high alert for an attack from Serac. I skate around the topic of Halcyon's parentage, but no one pushes for more.

No one even looks mildly surprised by another threat of death.

Berevald even chuckles with dark humor. "Well, if Serac is going to attack, they could at least come to Hella. We've come a long way from home. Ezit should meet us halfway at some point."

Samson won over Memphis with his storytelling. Berevald wins over Vulcan with that comment; the young warlock cackles roguishly, then stops suddenly, as though surprised by himself.

Later, I return to my room and find Halcyon's things exactly where they sat a few days ago; mine, too.

I step inside and glance around. When we first arrived in Hella, the room was our candlelit sanctuary against the unknown. Now, the tidy bed looks cold, as do the stacks of supplies lining the wall. It doesn't smell lived in either—just like dusty stone.

Halcyon leans on the doorframe beside me. "That went better than I expected." He studies the room with a sigh, tapping on the stone frame. "I didn't know what to do about all of this. What do you want to do?"

I set a hand on my hip. "What's your ideal setup?"

He purses his lips while he thinks, glancing over his shoulder toward where the Pletens sleep across the street. "Somewhere close to my family, just in case they need me. But I don't want to leave you alone. Or will you...?"

He looks at me, indigo eyes glowing as they take me in.

Will I find a way to share my nights with Samson?

In a perfect world, I could make a permanent nest in the forest above and return there nightly with the wolf. In a perfect world, Halcyon would also be waiting for me in this room just in case.

"Let's keep our things here. That would be helpful for... appearances. For my sake, at least. But you don't have to sleep here." I offer a smile. I'm nervous to push for more. He already agreed not to tell a soul about Samson and me.

"Why don't we use it as a backup?" He steps past me, heading for one of the piles of clothes. "Have you seen my gray cloak, Vexen? The one you wore to Ezit?"

It's the start of multiple domestic arguments—first about the cloak, then about me washing my feet before bed to keep the bottom half of the sheets clean, and finally about Halcyon leaving half-drank cups of liquor around the room (I finish them and accidentally get drunk).

When we're done, we lounge across the bed and chatter.

Halcyon tells me the key to dealing with Vega is looking at the place between her eyebrows; she won't realize I'm not making eye contact with her. And I tell him why Luz is the best place in Mieira; it's true that we do nothing and yet still accomplish everything.

"Also," I add, "hedonism is the fucking best."

I smile, imagining Luz's temple district with its columns extending into the cloudless sky. The rolling hills of Gamma that we watched from the rooftops. The arts district and its noisy, feckless inhabitants; my neighbors. The market district where Itzifone hawks half-truths in a seedy tavern, where Boonmasent breastfeeds a littleling, where Gautselin and Elvira and Chariovalda make people cum with enough gusto that stars fly out of their eyes.

"You're going to love it, my dear warlock."

And I'm going to love it all over again.

So long as I don't think too long about whether my warren still exists.

Where Onesimos and Esclamonde live now.

I wake early the next afternoon, long after collapsing into my bed at dawn following a long doublemoon night.

The meeting between the phased wolves and the rest of our ragtag group went reasonably well.

Especially when we learned that the wolves can travel via magical portals. Though *immune* to magic, this seems to apply to direct spells. I attempted to cast against Samsonfang twice—but he didn't respond to either spell. However, when I led the Kulapsifang to a shadowy portal, he followed me to a neighboring fruit grove.

Though he had to hunker down to fit into the shadow, Samsonfang was able to pass through the portal both ways.

Like the gorgons, it seems they have selective immunity.

Which means I'll be able to transport the wolves to Ezit on the triplemoon.

Still, the meeting didn't go without a hitch.

First, Vic and Tol wanted to get touchy with Berevaldfang. And Berevaldfang, to be fair, may have allowed some petting—but Samsonfang didn't. I trailed the women, shouting, "Not his neck!" and "Too close to his neck!" every time their pale, reaching fingers drifted past his cheeks. I was too late to stop them from shearing a tuft of hair from his right paw; I'll let Berevald deal with that on his own time.

The den took off after that, which Berevaldfang watched with a whine. But the wolf stayed put at Samsonfang's side. After introducing the vampires, being by being, I guided our group toward the trio of wolves. Though they stayed on their bellies to lessen their bearing, even the okeanids approached them with wide eyes and stuttering steps.

Even I'd forgotten just how massive a phased wolf is. Standing at their full height, the wolves reached the pine barren's towering canopy.

I waited as long as I could, fighting exhaustion, to introduce Halcyon to Samsonfang. The Pletens aren't joining the invasion—but the wolves still want to plan for a worst-case scenario.

Still, though I hadn't expected the meeting to go *great,* I hadn't expected Samsonfang's growl to scare me, too.

The wolf unleashed a low sound as the warlock approached my side. My blood ran cold as the limestone beneath my feet shivered, and Samsonfang's lips pulled back to reveal his clean, white fangs.

I scanned my options in a split second. I could either jump in between them and hope Samsonfang wouldn't kill me or use my magic to fling Halcyon out of the wolf's reach—possibly straight up into the air.

But he didn't pounce at the warlock.

And, to his credit, Halcyon didn't scream. He took one large stride back, jaw clenched and indigo eyes fixed on the wolf's maw.

I winced a laugh, patting Samsonfang on the nose and hoping he could feel me shaking and felt bad about scaring me. I didn't reprimand him for the growl—the only words that came out were, "*Oopsie boopsie!*"

(I have never been so scared I couldn't insult someone.)

I threw one last glare at Samsonfang, then guided the group back into Hella and collapsed on my bed in a dead sleep.

Hours later, I sit up with a groan; I still feel possessed by that dead sleep.

I rub my eyes, then realize someone is staring from the doorway.

"Sorry, my dear witch," Hemlock says. "We didn't want to wake you, but you just kept *sleeping* and *sleeping* and *sleeping*."

I grunt in response. It feels like I could sleep for days more.

But I dutifully pull my blanket off, expecting an emergency. "What happened?"

When I look up, Hemock is gone. Now, Eos and Aura poke their heads in. A second later, Meres joins them. Like me, the women are wrapped in the gorgon's beige layers; they drift to the floor where they stand together.

Aura stands tallest, her turquoise earrings and necklace twinkling proudly; below her is Eos, whose narrow locks are pulled back with a turquoise clip; last is Meres with her wide, blue-white eyes. They play off the turquoise diadem, a gift from Aura that she wears at all times.

Eos says, "We need to talk."

Aura clarifies, "No—we need to *show* you something."

Meres nods. "You won't believe it until you see it. Or feel it."

As though they rehearsed, all three bare smiles at me.

I rub my face to avoid sinking back into bed. "I'm not *super* into surprises these days."

"Can you take us to the beach?" Aura goes on.

"The *beach?*" I flutter my fingers to set my magic in motion, tending my hair, lifting the grime from my face, and smoothing my clothes so it doesn't look like I slept in them. "There's no beach around here."

"We understand that," Eos explains slowly. "We're asking you to *take* us to one."

I blink at the nymphs. Someone is being stupid right now and I can't tell if it's them or me. "Do you want to swim? Is it the freshwater fish we've been eating? The saltwater fish don't taste that different. Or is it the mollusks? Halcyon said nymphs liked them more than anyone else. I can get you some tomorrow."

Aura arches an eyebrow at me, "Why don't we talk about this *at the beach*?"

I study Meres last. "You want to see the ocean, then?" I stand up when I realize she probably hasn't seen it since she was kidnapped—which was three years ago. "Sorry, Meres. I didn't think to offer earlier."

They shuffle away wordlessly. One of them giggles conspiratorially.

I dress quickly, eager for a snack before we leave. While I scarf down a few pieces of fruit, the nymphs stand in a flush line and watch me. Hemlock strokes his beard, tending to it while he arches his neck and jaw. It's grown considerably since arriving.

As soon as I finish my meal, Aura raises her eyebrows. "Any beach will work. So long as it's in Vex, you should be able to take us there... with a... shadow. However that works."

I lick my sticky fingers clean. "Well, let's find out." I do a full circle, looking for a large patch of shade.

While I'm uncertain how shadowing will work when I leave Vex, I have full trust in the process so long as I reside in my House; the land is connected to my body through residual magic. (I never doubt where my fingers are. Whether my toes will wiggle when I move them.)

Overhead, the sun tilts toward the west. The shadows in Hella lengthen, leaving whole streets entombed in shadow. I head for the closest side street that branches off from the central plaza.

"This way," I call to the nymphs. I wait until they fall in step behind me, then stride toward the darkness. Unlike the portals that lead in and out of Hella, tucked into spacious nooks, those I create often linger along a wall. It's hard not to brace for impact. "Don't think about it."

I turn back when I hear their footsteps stop.

The nymphs look from me to the shadow. Though the black gulf is intact, perfect for shadowing, its darkest stretch clings to a limestone wall.

"Don't think about the wall?" Aura squeaks.

"How does this work, exactly?" Hemlock bends his neck to study the shadow from different angles. "The portals leading into Hella aren't just shadows. They feel fuzzy. Fuzzy with magic. This... does not feel fuzzy."

I'm shit at explaining all I've learned from the Hellastone. Still, I try, "Well, shadowing works because the world's natural state is darkness. If it weren't for the sun, we would live in perpetual night. So, think about it like wielding darkness... or accessing a sunless state." I gesture grandly to the shadow. "Just hold on to each other and close your eyes if you don't trust me."

I step forward, ignoring the hand that clamps to my forearm.

At some point, the Mieirans need to trust me.

Not just trust me in theory, but actively have faith in me when I walk into a shadow—or Ezit on the triplemoon.

I step into the shadow and my magic reaches for me, alighting the darkness with bass.

My next step lands on an uneven and damp portion of limestone. Past a barnacled stretch of rock spans the ocean, calm and unending and deep blue. Night blooms like a black flower in the sky.

The others shuffle onto the rocks behind me. We shadowed from a crevice between a few bent and craning trees. They're wider than they are tall, their pinecones and needles shivering in the faint breeze. Past the trees are stretches of limestone, sand, and soil, which slowly recede into a pine barren.

I've never been here before—

I glance at the okeanids and Hemlock, who also look around at the beach and forest.

"So, how'd I do?" I ask.

Hemlock smiles, setting his hands on his hips. He faces the pine barren, studying the trees like dryads are wont to do when presented with a new stretch of forest.

The okeanids turn to face the ocean.

Salt water sprays against the mossy and barnacled limestone as waves hit the shore.

Meres makes a low sound, then tilts her head as she steps toward the waves. Aura and Eos glance at one another, then weave their hands together; they hang back to watch Meres wander toward the water.

The necromancer's shoulders raise as she draws in a huge breath. Her empty hands flex at her side.

Hemlock babbles about a grove behind me, about a rare type of flower and what color it might be.

Meres takes another step, almost a leap. At the shore's rocky ledge, she squats and waits. Her dark skin and gray cloak blend with the pale rocks, the navy ocean, like the okeanid is a piece of it cast into flesh.

My heart thumps in my chest, body alighting with goosebumps.

I'm not sure what I sense—

Or I do—

I know what I sense. I've sensed it many times before.

I just don't believe it.

Meres shifts suddenly, reaching forward as another wave slaps the rocky shore.

Like she's catching something midair, she swipes at the foam that sprays upward.

In response, the ocean gutters within a fifty-foot radius. The surface of the water jerks to the left, following the momentum of Meres's hand. The milky sunlight that glows from the west fragments, breaking like glass on the ocean's surface as the tide shifts under the necromancer's command.

Meres rises to her feet.

She looks over her shoulder, eyes glittering with a blue pulled from the simmering ocean. "I haven't wielded in years. Three long years."

Aura and Eos step forward to meet Meres, and the trio bends their necks to press their foreheads together. Devilish whispers drift toward me, as though they're plotting.

There's no way...

I look at the Rhotidic King, mind emptying with shock.

He watches the exchange, lilac robe kicked up by the breeze. His jaw is tensed, but his brow is smooth; he accepts this, whatever the women are doing, whatever is happening in the ocean.

"Are they talking about the demigod?" I stagger toward him. "The one that saved your ship?"

"Yes. It's here—just off the coast." Hemlock spares a glance at me. "I was wondering... since we arrived... I'm far from home, but I can feel my demigod lounging just north of Alita right now. The hawk-moths are crawling out of their cocoons. They're very uncoordinated in their first hours—the demigod is laughing as they find leaves suitable for fanning out their wings.

"And if I can sense *that* from here, I'm sure the Hypnotic Demigod can sense its okeanids in Ezit."

Six hands spread around my back and arms as the okeanids turn me around and guide me toward the ocean. My shoes slip on the slick limestone and I pull back, nervous of the shadowy water and how endless it looks and how often the women whisper.

The necromancer fixes her blue eyes on me, a wicked smile hanging from her lips. "I could feel my demigod as soon as the Kulapsifang carried me out of Ezit. Aura and Eos thought they could feel it offshore.

"They thought the demigod had followed them here. They were right. It has stayed on these shores. Do you understand? It wasn't following the Mieirans. It wasn't saving them, either. It was *taking* them here. To me. To us. To Ezit."

I've been focused on Vex and Ezit since I arrived—not the demigod that saved the Mieirans from a shipwreck.

I stare into Meres's eyes as the pieces fit into place.

If the demigod *took* the Mieirans here instead of Plet... and if almost-queens like Vili and realized queens like Otrera have been here for years... and if they're all committing violence in subtle ways...

My gut drops.

I whisper the question, "You've been calling a demigod to Ezit, haven't you?"

"Not just me." Meres lowers her chin to seethe, "Every single okeanid in Ezit. Every single day. For years. We have prayed for its arrival. For it to find us. For it to free us."

I shake my head. Though relieved to have the attention of a demigod, I don't understand what it changes right now—aside from safe passage home.

A demigod wouldn't wage war in Ezit. They prefer desita and similar joy-brewed sentiments.

Meres turns away from me, whipping her head toward the darkening ocean. Aura and Eos trail her toward the limestone's slippery edge. Their hands link, shoulders pressed together, as a pit of blue light sparkles and grows offshore.

My heart leaps in my chest as I watch the unmistakable blue glow of a demigod take shape.

It rises twenty feet from the okeanids, cresting the surface first with its well-groomed and symmetrical afro. Then comes a male face with familiar, composite okeanid features—a broad pair of shoulders is next, then a flat chest.

It rises to its abdomen, jutting from the waves like it's part of the ocean made animate. Its full lips part with a broad smile as it angles its head toward us, catching sight of its okeanids.

Aura jumps on the balls of her feet excitedly; Eos and Meres stare with their necks bent.

The goosebumps on my arms and the back of my neck press against my skin urgently.

Once my disbelief passes, I feel relief—blinding relief. I could use the help of a demigod. It might not battle Ezit like the rest of us, but it should be able to offer some sort of help in the mega-city.

In the next second, my gut clenches.

This is an *okeanid* demigod, which is tied to salt water, specifically. There's no inlet that leads to Ezit, a land-locked city—only freshwater rivers. And only a naiad demigod would travel by fresh water; only a dryad demigod would travel by a pine barren.

I glance at Hemlock. He understands the nature, power, and will of demigods more than any of us. He paces a foot away, tugging at his beard and glancing at the demigod now and then.

Blue light glows brighter as the sun's light disappears.

I look up when I sense the demigod staring at me.

I walk a few steps closer, ignoring the insistent and desita-filled smiles of Aura, Eos, and Meres. I clear my throat, prepared to welcome the demigod to Vex—

That's when I see a familiar bottle in my mind.

Vex's bottle lays empty on the floor on its side. I wait for it to spin, to fill up—something. If I'm seeing the bottle, it means that Vex is communicating with me directly.

And, much like a nymph demigod, Vex is also wordless.

I stare into the demigod's eyes while holding the vision of the bottle in my mind. I wait for something to make sense, for the bottle to reveal something.

Someone grabs the bottle by its neck, raises it high, and then shatters it against the floor. Green shards clatter against the wood, liquid caught between them.

I jolt back, startled by the sudden violence.

This—again?

I've happily ignored this vision of destruction since Vex first whispered it into my mind after finding Hella. It's replayed in my head over the last months, and I've dutifully buried it each time.

It rattles my mind now.

It brings to mind Accra's cruel prophecy.

'*What comes next destroys you.*'

Fuck.

My fists clench as I stare into the demigod's eyes. I wait for another vision—for some insight from the demigod—maybe this one will actually speak, unlike its counterparts.

Once again, I see my small hands seize the bottle's neck on the floor, then shatter it with a decisive swing.

Rage swirls in my gut.

I hate this vision; I don't understand what it means. I can't believe I'm in this overwhelmingly fucked up position. And now there's a demigod in the mix.

Meres faces me, backlit by the glowing shape of her demigod. Their eyes are the same; glowing, fixed on me, unyielding. "You saw what Argot was capable of—and that's just *one* of four enemies you've made in Ezit. You can't do everything alone, Helisent. Bring my demigod into that city, and you will not need to set the okeanids free. *We will do it ourselves.* With a demigod that close, even the weakest okeanids will be able to wield salt water. Water isn't infallible, but we know how to use it. We know—we've never forgotten."

I shake my head.

I've never been more conflicted to see a demigod.

Terror whirls through me in a deluge.

"No," I tell Meres, tone biting. I look at the demigod next, trembling with fear and wrath and stubbornness as I meet its eyes. "No," I repeat.

This is Vex.

This is my Landmark.

And, "I'm risking enough to save your okeanids. And it will all be for nothing if our ships sink on the way home." I raise my chin. I ignore the loop that replays in my head—a vision of a shattered green bottle. "We will sail from New Hypnos on the morning after the triplemoon. If you found your way here, you can find your way to the village. Rally the okeanids there. Then guide us home."

I turn my back on the demigod.

I ignore the sound of glass breaking, the soft grunt as I lift the bottle and slam it downward. The urge to count the number of broken shards.

To my great surprise, Hemlock doesn't balk as I turn toward him and lead us back toward the shadowy portal. In fact, he dips his chin, as though in silent agreement with my response.

I wish it made me feel better.

CHAPTER 16

GET HIM, SAMSON

SAMSON

My grandson,
The mind speaks in thoughts, the body in instincts. Both are convinced of their
authority, but neither speaks the truth.

I scan the dark forest, searching the canopy for Helisent.

Above, the narrow branches fan out like fingers—none look sturdy or thick enough to support a nest. Still, I keep squinting overhead as I wander.

Deep in the night, there's little light for me to follow.

There's also no ala for me to trail. She's cloaking it so any vampires who wander out of Hella won't find her. Or us, assuming I can locate the witch without a scent to track.

I switch my focus to the footpath and the sparse bushes that line the ground, searching the shadows for some sign of Helisent's white hair or bright eyes.

With each step, my body grows light with expectation.

Since our reunion last week, we've only spent three nights together —all outside the cave. With each that passes, I dwell on her more. Helisent's ala fills my mind while I grind the millet into flour; the tone of her moans and high keens drown out the nightly symphony of vampire yowling; the sensation of her fingertips roaming my arms, my chest, my face consumes me as I sharpen my bloodred axe.

I pause when I hear a familiar buzzing—

Not of infrasound, but a beehive.

Fifteen feet overhead, a sliver of moonslight curls along an oblong hive twice the size of my head. I squint, wondering if Helisent wouldn't mind slicing a piece of honeycomb off for me...

Then I hear a long and sultry giggle.

Ten feet into a dense portion of barren, I see a witch.

Helisent lounges atop a mossy boulder with a dark bowl in her lap. As I approach, she lifts the spell hiding her scent; her ala and the scent of honey drift out toward me in a tantalizing cloud.

"If I remember correctly," Helisent sticks a finger into the bowl and draws out a string of golden honey, "wolves have a sweet tooth."

The witch's hair dangles to her waist, soft and brushed. She wears the same large t-shirt she brought back from Plet, which hikes up along her thighs.

I wander closer, legs moving of their own volition.

She dips her honey-covered finger into her mouth, then leans forward to grab my tunic. I follow her, hunching over where she sits on the boulder and taking her chin. She blinks, white eyelashes dancing, and waits for me to kiss her.

Honey coats her tongue, her lips, her teeth.

The entire world disappears around me—the moons, the forest, the buzzing beehive.

I focus on the mix of Helisent's bitter ala and sweet honey.

I sigh, lost in a haze.

Helisent clings to my tunic as my tongue dips into her mouth. I reach to cradle her lower back, dragging her closer. Helisent follows my movement, using floating magic to hover against my chest and abdomen.

I stand up straight and close my eyes, pulling away from her lips to savor the thick honey, layered with Helisent's taste.

She laughs, long and happy. "I remembered correctly, then."

I glance away from her sticky lips long enough to find the bowl, now balanced atop the boulder. Chunks of pale honeycomb sit amid the amber goop.

"Is it enough?" she asks.

I raise my eyebrows. "For me? It's plenty." Enough to give me a stomachache later.

She pulls away from me to sit back on the boulder again. I tug my tunic over my head. I glance behind me, studying the quiet, shadowy forest.

I ignore the instinct the mark this area—we're not quite close enough for that yet.

"You protected this area?" I confirm. "No one will smell us or hear us?"

I bend at the waist to unlace my boots, then set them near the boulder and stack my folded tunic on top.

"Yep. Unless they want to watch."

"Shouldn't you..." I trail off when I straighten and realize Helisent has slipped down her tunic-dress. It bunches at her tummy, leaving her chest bare. Lines of glistening honey cross her breasts, dripping down along their soft curves, catching on her perked nipples, oozing toward her belly.

I blink dumbly.

I think it might be the most beautiful thing I've ever seen.

I look at her face to see if this is a game or a test—no words come out, but I think she understands.

Helisent throws her head back to giggle more.

Her breasts jostle as she laughs, honey beckoning me.

Without any objection from the witch, I bend toward her chest. Her back bows as I run my tongue across the first drizzle of honey, following it across her breast and down her nipple. She moans as I pause, sucking to make sure I clean her skin before working my way to another string of sweet honey.

Goosebumps line her body, her breaths fragile and ragged.

I shift a knee onto the boulder, reaching to cradle her upper back. I quickly make a mess of the honey, smearing it across her with my free hand and then running my tongue over her. The honey coats my chin, my fingers, the tip of my nose.

Helisent moans and laughs intermittently, grabbing my hair with a familiar passion and then digging her nails into my shoulder, my arm. Soon, I start to chuckle along with her, until I'm horny, amused, desperate to see what happens next.

The witch drives me crazy.

She is everything, Samsonfang tuts.

Quiet, Samsonfang.

This should be yours, he goes on.

I pause to repeat a mantra I created last year: *No possessing the witch*.

But it's hard not to want this forever. It's hard to keep convincing Samsonfang he's wrong about Helisent being my Female Alpha.

What's worse is that the feeling doesn't leave after I cum. It intensifies when we lay tangled afterward. (It's like having a limb taken away. I can physically feel its absence, and it alarms me.)

I don't think twice about being a wolf covered in sticky honey in a dark forest with a devious witch. I shift again, moving my knee back toward the ground. Helisent squeals when I tug on her legs and gently place them over my shoulders. I pause so she can situate herself on her back. Once she's propped up on her elbows, she shimmies toward me vulva-first—an offering.

I look around for the wooden bowl of honey, then dip my thumb into the bowl. With just a dab, I reach to rub circles onto her clit. She twitches at the contact, then moans, low and growling. I pause, enjoying the weight of her legs on my shoulders, the intoxicating scent of her intimate ala, heavy with honey, and the sight of her dark-rose vulva, splayed like dewy petals.

I sigh through my tadmazzar.

Nothing else exists right now.

I draw in one last breath, then lean forward to run my tongue across her. Worried about getting honey inside of her, I don't take any more from the bowl—but I'd be at it for hours if I knew it wouldn't bother her health.

I tease her with my fingers, with my tongue, with both at the same time.

Helisent squirms and twitches and whimpers—and then she sits up. Her mischievous smile grows as she looks at my crotch and reaches for the bowl of honey. "My turn, boy-wolf."

I happily comply, taking off my pants and then cradling my erection as the night's chill hits. I stand, humming with tadmazzar as I wait to see how Helisent wants to arrange us; she beckons me forward with a curled finger, and I follow my hard cock straight to the witch.

Her breasts are still covered in streaks of honey and my saliva when she dips a finger into the honey and then draws it along my shaft.

She leans forward and takes me with one hand, running her tongue and her wet lips across me to collect the honey. She dips forward to take my head into her warm mouth, sucking and swirling her tongue.

I look up into the canopy—

Nasty, smelly badgers.

Sour milk.

Don't cum, don't cum, don't cum—

She licks and sucks me clean, hand pumping now and then until I'm covered in Helisent's spit and honey. When I look down, it lines her lips, spreading onto her cheeks and chin and fingers.

Just as I get ready to ask Helisent to clean us both so I can be inside of her, and maybe lay down her large shirt so we can get more comfortable, she gasps.

She jolts back, landing on her butt atop the mossy boulder.

I freeze, but don't see anything that would indicate danger. The forest is quiet aside from the buzzing hive—

Helisent's eyes fix on something behind me. "What the *fuck*—"

"I'm waiting my turn."

I flinch at the sound of a deep and amused voice.

I turn around and see a male vampire leering at us from ten feet away.

He's in peak physical form, maybe a decade older than me. Like Vic and Tol, his brawn consists of finely worked muscles that wrap around his arms, his torso, his legs. He wears a pristine white fur pelt around his hips and a feather dangles from his loose necklace, hanging down to his belly button.

His body is hairless, like the rest of the vampires. But instead of a long and bushy mane, this vampire keeps his hair tied into four braids at the nape of his neck.

He leans against a tree, features too shadowy to make out.

But I can see his eyes, pitted with reddish light like a nocturnal predator.

They don't study me, but leer at the witch behind me.

My vision shakes as adrenaline flushes through my body.

I hate that other men get to be with Helisent. I can't stand the thought of her bringing a bowl of honey when she meets them at night. But if there's one thing I *absolutely will not abide by*, it's another male cutting into *my* time with the witch. Watching me and the witch in some of the few moments of sanctuary we're granted.

And then thinking he gets a *turn with her*.

Get him, Samson, Samsonfang growls.

I can feel my heart race in my throat, in my fingertips, in the soles of my feet.

The vampire pushes off the tree. He finally shifts his eyes to me. And then he smiles.

"My turn?" he repeats.

Get him, Samson.

I have spent my life crafting arguments to talk Samsonfang down from that impulse, just like any respectable wolf.

I have never lost this fight against Samsonfang.

Not until now.

I take a step away from Helisent; she says something to me before I take off. Something about magic. Something about this vampire. I don't know what she says, even though it sounds urgent. I don't even notice that I'm still ass naked, that my dick is way too hard to be involved in a physical altercation, that I'm covered in honey and Helisent.

Get him, Samson.

The vampire rolls his shoulders, picking up his pace to meet me.

Helisent is still screeching from the boulder.

But I'm now focused on the broad-shouldered vampire. We approach the other with our arms raised; he stands almost as tall as me, his thick muscles compensating for his lack of brawn.

Rather than tackle me straight on, he shifts his body at the last moment to meet me at an angle.

My momentum slows—wolves attack head-on after squaring up.

With a shuffle of his feet, the vampire jolts to the right, then twists. In the limited moonslight, driven mad with rage, I'm not quite sure what happens... just that the vampire rises into the air and twists his soaring body downward.

A foot flies toward my head.

It sails into my temple, knocking me to the side.

I stagger, sidestepping as black dots careen through my vision.

What the fuck?

I turn to find the vampire a few feet to my left. I square up again, studying him and wondering what just happened. I've never seen anyone jump that high or spin that much, and then land a brutal *kick* with so much showmanship.

The vampire glances across me. His head tilts like he's also confused.

We step toward the other again. When the vampire angles his body this time, I'm not so clueless. I take a quick step back, dodging another imaginative kick. When he prepares a third, I lunge forward, raising my hands to throw him off-balance.

I catch his thigh on the way down, sending my weight over him. We grapple as we land on the limestone—and then the fight pans out more like a waricon. My comfort zone.

Rather than meet me with force, the vampire tries to writhe free. I bear down with every movement to prevent him from wriggling loose.

Now, there's nowhere to run.

No beautiful spinning kicks to set him free.

To be fair, the vampire batters me multiple times; once in the jaw, twice in the ribs, a few times straight to the gut. But as soon as he's on his back and I'm straddling his abdomen, there's nothing to save him.

I put my weight into my fist, grunting with each strike until the vampire stops shifting beneath me. I pant as I loom over him and wait for him to rouse.

Satisfied with his swollen cheeks and eyes, his busted lip, his slack features, I shift my weight onto a knee. I tug on the vampire's shoulder to angle his head to the side and expose his neck.

His jugular pumps in tune with his heartbeat.

I lean down, vision shaking with the urge to end this fight—

"Samson—*no, no, no!*" Helisent shouts.

I freeze for a split-second, my body taut. My lips pull back from my teeth as I focus on the vampire's smooth neck.

"There's something wrong with his blood—I think it's rosfrost," Helisent goes on, voice shaking. "Remember, Samson? Vic said that Zeu's den finds the rosarium, grinds them to dust, and drinks the slurry. I can't wield against him—and if rosfrost is in his blood, it could hurt you."

My body trembles as I hold the vampire.

Rosfrost.

I should listen to Helisent—

But the urge to bite is strong. It holds my mind and body in a vice.

I can hear my mother's voice.

Kill him, Samson.

Helisent hunches on the ground at eye level, a few feet away, eyes wide. "I know you want to bite him. Please don't do it. Vex's magic can't do anything against rosarium. Okay?"

Her eyes switch to my chest.

To the scar of Vex.

"I don't want it to hurt you." She reaches toward me, extending her fingers. "Samson. Sweet wolf. Please. He's knocked out. It's okay."

I stare at the vampire's swollen face. Both of his eyes are fully shut, his breaths noisy as they suck in and out.

It would be easy to end this now—

Helisent gestures to me again, beckoning me away from the vampire, but I don't take her hand—

She shouldn't be so close. It could be dangerous for her. She could be caught in the crossfire—even I could hurt her if she tried to break up a fight like this.

But she isn't a wolf.

And she doesn't know this.

She drops her hand and pulls her legs to her chest, curled up. She doesn't say anything else; her eyes flash from him to me and then back again.

Slowly, I regain my composure.

I notice small details first; Helisent's ala is gone, as is mine—it's not mixed with the honey in the bowl, or lingering on her breasts, or smeared across my crotch. Then I realize the witch is fully clothed, and she's holding my articles. Finally, the forest's peaceful sounds start to filter back in.

I slide off the vampire, sinking onto a hip on the cold ground.

I feel my eye, swollen to triple its size thanks to the roundhouse kick. Then I tally the vampire's bruises; none look particularly threatening, though they'll take a week or so to heal.

With a sigh, I look at Helisent. She's still curled up, watching me like a nervous child.

"Are you okay?" she whispers.

I nod. Despite a slight headache and fatigue and blue balls, I feel fine. "I'm more worried about whoever this is. Any ideas?"

Helisent pinches her lips together. "I think it's Zeu the Chosen. Halcyon says he always wears four braids. Only him and his warriors drink the rosfrost. Vic's den avoids it."

Fuck. "The King of Night? The one who wages war against Ezit?"

At least I mostly patched things up with Halcyon before making another enemy.

"Remember?" Helisent asks. "That's why he drinks the rosfrost. So they can invade any time they feel like it. It feels... weird. Bad weird."

That's why Helisent didn't want me to bite him. If Vex's magic keeps me alive, then ingesting something that negates magic could kill me. Quickly.

This time, I reach toward Helisent, extending my fingers. "Thank you."

She shuffles forward and takes my hand, still hunched small. I pull my hand back to draw her to me, to see if she's willing to be near me.

She is; she lifts her chin to peck me once on the cheek, then leans against my side.

It feels strange to be so close to someone after a vicious fight. Wolves organize our violence into waricons to prevent it from bleeding into other areas of life. Still, thinking Helisent might need comfort, and acknowledging that I do, I wrap an arm around her. She shuffles closer, then we stare down at the unconscious vampire.

His mouth hangs open; if it weren't for his bruises, I'd think he was sleeping peacefully.

Helisent clears her throat. "So... what do we do?" She reaches out and pokes his ribs.

I have a few spare ideas, but I go with, "I'll carry him back to Hella. I'll tell everyone we met unexpectedly and didn't get along. Now that I can smell him better, I can tell he's been drinking. We'll chalk it up to that. And when he's awake... let's pray he doesn't remember and bribe him if he does."

She raises her eyebrows. "I think we know what bribe he's going to ask for, Samson."

My gut clenches. What a foul, horrible creature; I should have bitten him. "Tell him I'll suck his dick if he's so worried about it."

Helisent opens her mouth to respond, then closes it. She blinks, looking from the vampire to me. Amusement dances in her eyes. "Would you really?"

I level my scowl at her. "No."

She leans in front of me, blocking my view of the vampire to study my face. "Fine, not with Zeu. But now I'm interested—in general, when you and Rex…"

I stand up and the witch rises with me. She hands me my pants first.

I tug them on with a shuffle. "You want to know if I've ever given a blow job?"

"Yes." She hovers in the air to stay at eye-level with me, watching each of my movements with wide and ravenous eyes. She forgets about my shirt as she does so, and it brushes against the prone vampire like she's forgotten his presence. "Samson? Yes or no?"

Once my boots and shirt are back on, I fix my hair. As though wholly scandalized, she keeps hovering, staring at my face from a hand's length away.

Does she think I'm a selfish lover with men? In Velm, there's nothing more masculine than two men in bed together, nothing more feminine than two women in bed together. *And aren't I masculine?*

Maybe she's too straight to understand. Either way, I don't mind letting her wonder.

I kneel once I'm fully clothed, shifting back and forth to get a strong grip on the vampire. He must weigh nearly as much as I do. With a grunt, I roll his weight toward my chest and then stand up.

Helisent keeps hovering, waiting for her answer. "Samson, my lover—please. Just a hint. I want to know what sorts of fantasies to entertain later."

I keep ignoring her, half out of amusement and half because I'm now concentrating on hauling the supposed King of Night to Hella.

"Can we deal with the unconscious vampire first? Meet me back in Hella. I'll explain what happened to the others."

She makes a long and frustrated sound, then turns to scamper into the nearest shadow.

With each step, I struggle to manage his dead weight; it shifts back and forth, his legs and arms akimbo.

Now that the witch is gone, I study his face with tsk. "Who the fuck taught you how to speak to women?"

I wake the next morning and wonder if Zeu the Chosen has regained consciousness.

After waltzing into Hella with the unconscious vampire in my arms, things went surprisingly smoothly. Vic and the rest of the den were suitably aghast and suspicious. They took his body and laid it by their massive fires, then examined each of his injuries.

Like me, Vic could smell the alcohol in Zeu's blood.

Rather sheepishly, she asked Helisent to translate an explanation. And Helisent, who was pretending to have been woken and in a bad mood, faked a yawn before turning toward me.

She said, "Vic says Zeu is a bit of a drinker. Sometimes he says things he doesn't mean, which I'm guessing means she believes your story. She'll introduce both of you tomorrow night."

And then Vic rejoined the vampires who gathered around Zeu's unconscious form. I still can't understand much Zarzyd, but it sounded like they were fawning over him. Even Ret paid close attention to the King of Night, helping take down his hair, brush it out, and then rebraid it.

Only Tol was missing.

She and Berevald showed up around dawn; Berevald dirty and exhausted, Tol smiling and purring. She left him quickly to head toward Zeu, then helped carry him back to their den for the morning.

I grabbed Berevald by the forearm and dragged him back to our room instead.

I told him what happened, desperate to explain the spinning kick. That left Berevald in stitches for a while. Breathless, he said, "Someone gave you a black eye with their *foot*. Maybe it's an insult. Like you're not worth hitting with a hand. Could you see which part of his foot he was using—it wasn't his big toe, was it?"

I wasn't sure whether to laugh or brush him off. "Ask him to fucking show you when he wakes up, Bere."

After a few hours of sleep, I have the whole day to wonder how Zeu will handle our second encounter.

Like me, Helisent seems to nervously pace when sundown comes. She rearranges her place at dinner three times, moving from Halcyon's side to Parsifal's to Memphis's. Like me, she goes still when we hear the grinding of the rock—a mammoth slab of limestone the den slides in and out of place to block their lair.

The booming chatter that echoes over next is reassuring. There's too much jovial shouting and laughter to precede a brawl.

I casually stretch in case I'm wrong.

The group rounds the corner and Zeu shuffles at their center, looking half-asleep. His face is a mosaic of bruising, mostly concentrated around his eyes and jaw. Their purple and green coloration is stark against his pale skin. Given the swelling, it barely looks like the vampire's eyes are open.

On one side, Tol drives him forward, their arms latched. On the other, Vic walks with one hand against Zeu's back, guiding him.

Zeu's veins aren't the same shade as the other vampires. They're darker—almost black—tangling just beneath his skin like rivers of blood. I follow them across his arms, his abdomen, to his thighs.

Rosfrost has a color, then.

In silence, our group watches the den approach.

The vampires sit down a few feet away from where we dine, like usual. Zeu stays front and center while the others linger; the group looks from us to him with wide grins, as though presenting a fantastic surprise.

Zeu yawns, then grunts something in Zarzyd.

I try to quiet my adrenaline, but smelling his ala sets off another instinct to fight. He's in his late thirties, he's full of testosterone, and now I can smell the twang of rosfrost in his veins—

It's hyper sweet, like rotted honey.

And...

It's not totally unfamiliar; my fangself knows this scent.

Where have I smelled rosarium before?

Zeu doesn't seem to notice everyone watching him with bated breath. He reaches for the jug of fig wine, but Tol slaps his hand. Vic leans toward him, straightening her arm and shoving it toward his lips.

Zeu looks down, then takes Vic's arm by the elbow and the wrist. He bends his neck to fix his mouth around her forearm.

I flinch as he sinks his teeth into her skin. They break into her flesh with a light pop, and then he shifts her arm, widening his mouth to collect her blood.

Halcyon groans loudly, then barks something in Zarzyd. Vulcan echoes him a second later. The warlocks turn their backs to the vampires, shielding their plates; the rest of the Pletens follow suit.

Parsifal stands up and sprints away. "I'm going to be sick."

Helisent scampers after him. "My fucking *moons*..." She dry heaves as she runs.

The rest of us sit through Zeu's noisy gulping and Vic's quiet hissing. When he releases her arm, she sits back at his side, licking her wound and studying his face.

Zeu takes a deep breath; he doesn't bother wiping the bright blood that slips down his chin and neck.

Then he leans forward to take the fig wine. Hemlock reaches after the jug, but all he gets out is a shocked squeak before Zeu tilts his head back to drink.

And drink.

And drink.

"He's finishing it," Aura whispers.

Zeu slams the empty jug down. He finally wipes his mouth, smearing the blood and wine across his chin. Then he looks across our ranks like he's just now noticing the group of nymphs, wolves, and wielders watching him in aghast silence. His eyes shift beneath their swollen lids.

Zeu stops when he notices me. "My den told me I got into a fight last night," he says in lightly accented Mieiran. He reels back with a hiccup, then a smile edges onto his lips. "They didn't say I lost."

I look for the right words to diffuse the tension. "You got in a solid kick."

He crosses his arms, and his genuine smile grows. "Yes, it always starts in my favor." He glances over me, then studies Rex and Berevald. "And where's the other one? There were two of you last night."

I return his smile and hope the vampire was as drunk as he smelled. "You wouldn't have survived two of me, Zeu the Chosen."

He leans back with laughter. It sends adrenaline into my veins; I don't trust this vampire even when he's laughing. "What is your name? Sam-sam?"

For a second, he reminds me of Helisent.

For a brief flash, I realize he might not be trying to piss me off.

Maybe this is actually him trying his best, and his best is deeply affected by the amount of alcohol in his system, along with a string of unknown traumas.

I take a deep breath. "I am Samson 714 Afador, son and Kulapsi-fang of Imperatriz 713 Afador, heir of Velm, of Night, of Hetnazzar."

"Sam-sam 714 Afador," he announces loudly, "I am Zeu the Chosen, King of Night."

Sam-sam.

King of Night.

I try to remember how I handled Helisent when we first left Luz —but even then, I was more suspicious of her than annoyed or insulted.

I stare at Zeu. Eventually, I force out the words, "It's nice to meet you, Zeu."

He continues to bare his smile at me like a weapon. "Yes, it is."

With an impudent sigh, he looks around. He grunts something at Vic, and the Queen of Night jerks her chin toward the streets where Parsifal and Helisent disappeared. Though Helisent sounds to have gained her composure, Parsifal still heaves urgently.

Zeu's flat, wide nostrils twitch as he stares in their direction.

Vic murmurs something into Zeu's ear. He looks away from the side street with a tsk and focuses his attention on Halcyon's back; like the rest of the Pletens, he hasn't turned back around to face the den.

"*Halcyon?*" Zeu makes a long sound of disgust. "You have *two* wives. Now, you want the Vexen. You want too much. Warlocks take too much. Look—your son takes a wife already. Tell me how you do it, Halcyon. Is it the finger trick? You make the *Vexen* accept third place—"

"The *Vexen* will be back in a *moment*," Helisent screams from out of sight.

Zeu turns at the sound of her shouting, angling his head to hear it better. Then the corners of his lips tug upward.

He knew she was listening.

He's trying to piss her off.

Last night, I hadn't realized that Zeu might actually be interested in Helisent. *What kind of man kicks off a courtship with a sexual threat?*

My gaze shifts from the vampire to the warlock. *And what the fuck is the finger trick?*

A moment later, Helisent and Parsifal round the corner and stride toward us. Helisent tugs her father by his wrist, and Parsifal shuffles along with wan cheeks. The witch's hand tightens on Parsifal as she studies Zeu.

She drags her papa to his seat, then sits down between him and Halcyon. Like the rest of the Pletens, her papa faces away from the den. But Helisent looks over her shoulder to half-face the King of Night with a violent frown.

Zeu smiles as he studies her. His eyes glitter with mischief, with impulse.

"You will welcome me to your cave," he says. "We will drink tonight."

Helisent starts, "Zeu—"

"My mother's name was Heb. Did Accra tell you about Bathsheba yet? It's a common name—*Heb*. We remember your people. I like *Eli* for Helisent. Vic likes *Sen*. Assuming you're worth making a name of." Zeu crosses his arms and leans back like he has many great things to consider. "I will help you, of course. My den wages war on Ezit—I have many caches of rosfrost. Different kinds, which we use for different types of battles.

"And, most importantly, I have many warriors—their pelts are spotless, their fangs are sharp. Vic says you need maps, too. Those are much harder to come by than warriors and rosfrost—but you will have what you need. First, you will welcome me to your cave, and then we will drink."

Helisent stares at him for a long time. Her frown slowly disappears into an unreadable expression. Her silence is lethal; after all, it only takes one tiny spell to cloak the sharpening of knives.

Eventually, she says, "I think I'll finish my meal first."

Then the witch smiles at Zeu the Chosen before turning around to face her plate.

Zeu stares at her for a moment longer. The rest of us go back to our meals as the tense silence gives way to something slightly calmer.

We finish dinner with minimal chatter. Once it's done, Helisent carries on with her night without a second glance at our newest guest. He doesn't follow her, which relieves me. Still, I don't sleep that night.

I lay on my side, staring at the door, listening for Zeu's low voice, attempting to track his ala as it shifts on the breeze.

CHAPTER 17

I WILL NEVER RUN (WAR ZEU ISN'T NORMAL)

HELISENT

Honey Baby,
You never laughed around Anesot. He didn't like to laugh, so you thought you
shouldn't either. Part of me wondered if this was an act of rebellion against me.
Papa P.

The triplemoon waits two and a half weeks away.

My tiny army grows.

While we wait for Zeu's den to arrive, a gorgon shows up on behalf of Dexerxes. I recognize the gorgon as the youngest Accra, with glossy dark hair and only a whisper of black freckles on her cheeks and shoulders.

We speak near the fountain when she arrives. "Accra sends me, along with an apology. We cannot spare more. Ezit has sent messengers—they're monitoring our village. They're counting the able-bodied who leave."

I shrug. "Zeu says we'll have twenty vampires willing to fight and die showing up any day." The young gorgon bows her head, but I take her hand before the okeanids could guide her to a dwelling. "Accra told me that there are two kinds of fate. What are they? Do you know?"

She bows her head further. "I have maps. Dexerxes know the House of Argot well."

"No, no. Fate. Not maps. I need to know what Accra says about fate."

"It is our fate to learn this lesson alone." Then she pulls parchment maps from the bag slung beneath her drifting linen layers.

The maps are more helpful, I suppose.

Between Accra-Four, Ret, and Zeu, our understanding of Ezit expands. We focus on the underground chambers where the necromancers, degis, and okeanids are kept. The trio helps create a plan of attack—which groups target which cells, where the wolves will be able to level the most damage, how we can weaponize the okeanids' ability to wield salt water.

Our hesitant invasion plan evolves into a complex rescue mission.

One that depends increasingly on the experience and animosity of Zeu and his warmongers.

I know the King of Night is an ally—and a valuable one at that—but every time I'm near the vampire, I try to wield against him.

First, it was to look for a weak spot—maybe I could target some part of his body where the rosfrost doesn't reach, like his fingernails, his hair, his teeth; no dice. Then it was to sense how the rosfrost absorbs my magic. It's like picking at a scab, investigating my own weakness in the hopes of avoiding being compromised by the pink stones again.

He notices.

To curb my unease, he shows me three different types of rosfrost. On the triplemoon, he explains that his den will use a temporary version of rosfrost, which their metabolism will burn before sunrise and allow them to travel via magical portals.

The second form of rosfrost is meant for longer stints of protection; the last is its raw form, mined from the ground in massive pink chunks.

It doesn't feel any different than the other rosfrost I've come across.

Meres has also become a nuisance. If she's not hounding me for another trip to the beach so she can collude with her demigod, or bring back buckets of salt water, then she's chasing me with her mirror, blathering about my dead mother and sister.

I've taken to fleeing to the Hellastone once again.

This morning, I kneel in front of the jagged, bloodred stone.

Crimson tiles glisten on the walls around me, reflecting the milky light into a kaleidoscope of red and marigold. I sit in peaceful silence as I pull threads of spells from the Hellastone.

I imagine my ancestors doing the same; Axerxa, Bathsheba, Dexa. All of us sit in a line in my imagined memory, whole, vibrant, alive.

I stare at the string tangled in my fingers.

Each is smaller than the previous, less concentrated with bass. Either Vex knows the triplemoon and my departure are imminent; or I've absorbed all the spellwork my horns can hold.

With a sigh, I pull the red thread free and wrap it around my horn. Before I set my hand on the stone for another, I hear footsteps.

I tilt my head to make sure I'm not mistaken, then stand and back away from the Hellastone. I leave the hall and prepare to intercept the encroacher.

Whoever it is, they should know better.

One block from the entrance, I round a corner and jump when I see Absalom.

Our eyes meet and he stops mid-stride, his white robe flaring around him. His straight hair is longer than I've ever seen it, dangling to his chin. His pout doesn't look nearly as boyish anymore—his cheeks are less full, too.

"What the *fuck* are you doing here?"

"I have your robe," he says quickly.

I stop in my tracks. "What? *You*—"

"Stop cursing me for five seconds." He reaches into the bottomless bag strung across his chest. "*I'm on your side.*"

I'd love to believe him—I could use an ally in the Class, a patsy to wield.

Still...

I set my hands on my hips, stopping in front of him. "Well, explain yourself, Absalom. And give me my fucking robe."

With one hand, he delves deeper into his bag. With the other, he extends his pointer finger to emphasize his words. "I was on your side last year. After Esclamonde's mother went looking for you, Ethsevere Black Rock Antigone showed up. He's the—"

"I know who Esclamonde's uncle is. Old as dirt, leads the Class." I shrug a shoulder. "So, how are you on my side? Tell me what makes you better than a fucking spy. As far as I can tell, you left your post in Luz to report back to the Class after I was banished. You know what would have been *actually* helpful? You sticking up for me. You telling the Class that you knew Samson and I were *working together*—"

"The Class is fucked. Really, really *fucked.*" He stops searching in the bag, baring his eyes into mine. "It's better if they don't know you're allied with the Kulapsifang."

I cross my arms. "See—now that's interesting. Run with that, Absalom."

"Fine, then. We'll cut the niceties." He nods, as though convincing himself of something. "Anesot had four members of the Class in the palm of his hand—that's why nobody planned on seeking justice for Milisent. It was four versus two, Helisent. Ethsevere and another witch, Cosisent Septegeur, fought for you and your sister after her death.

"After you were banished last year, the best Ethsevere and Cosisent could manage was moving me from Luz to keep an eye on you. He decided to send Esclamonde to watch over you—and I tipped Onesimos off that she was leaving."

I take a deep breath.

It's hard to believe him—the only warlocks I *actually* trust are my father, brothers, and Pen. (Sweet Pen. I wonder how he's doing.)

"That was how I kept an eye on you," he goes on. "Onesimos and Esclamonde would tell me what to report back."

I take another deep breath.

Was Onesimos betraying me? Was the fucking mentee in on it?

And, most of all, "Then why didn't you do anything?"

Absalom shakes his head. "What do you mean?"

"If you were in touch with Onesimos and Esclamonde, and you're *on my side,* they must have told you that I wasn't doing well. So, why didn't you do anything?" My body tenses, arms clasping tight. I don't know why this stings so bad. No part of me actually thought Absalom or Ethsevere (or Cosisent) *cared* about my well-being.

He clears his throat, avoiding my eyes. "The Class wanted you to fear being an outlier. Solitude was the only punishment they could level against you. I had to play their game or lose my position."

I suck in a breath.

I will make them pay.

I will make them need me, and then I will give them what they wanted.

Solitude.

Absalom's voice lowers. "Helisent West of Jaws, I need you to let that go. Just for now, just for a second." My eyes flash to his, mouth twisting as a response forms—but he doesn't give me the chance to interrupt. "The Class's loyalty to Anesot... I'm worried it was actually loyalty to Zarzynn."

My mouth actually falls open.

Once again, he barrels on before I can respond.

"Before Meres was a necromancer for Serac, she was kept in Col. She says that Col's Hosts are aware of Mieira. She doesn't know the extent of their knowledge, but they'd consulted with her to learn more about life in Mieira. They know about the Class in Septegeur and the wolves in Velm, about the demigods, about Gammafaces, about where the phoenixes live."

He leans closer to me, beseeching, "The four wielders in the Class who refused to hold Anesot and Oko accountable—they're still holding out, Helisent. Those two have been dead for almost a year, and they're still loyal to Anesot and Oko. Oko came from House of Col. Do you understand? If not all of Ezit, then at least Col, and possibly Serac, have sunk their teeth into the Class."

I want to disagree. Want to fight the nausea and doom that curdles in my stomach at the thought of finding Zarzynn's fangs not only sunken into Velm, but also Mieira.

Unfortunately, it doesn't look like Absalom is spinning lies.

He stares at me, waiting. I stare back, heart pumping in my chest.

I still don't know how deeply I trust Absalom. Or maybe I trust his motives, just not his conviction to handle what he knows well.

Regardless, he may be my future patsy.

So, I confide, "Col and Serac are enemies. So, I'd barter it's Col that's influencing the Class."

Absalom straightens, eyebrows bunching. "That makes sense. You said that Serac and Argot are allied. So, either Col is working alone or they're working with Talos."

House of Talos; golden wielders.

I blink into Absalom's wide, golden eyes. "Well, that would make sense. Talos stands the best chance of any House in gaining a foothold in Mieira. We wouldn't even know."

Which could be the case with any wielder so long as they're capable of hiding their form.

For a moment, neither of us speaks. We stare at the limestone sidewalk, lost in thought.

My stomach flips and twists. "Fuck!" I bellow.

Out of words, out of hope, out of patience, I growl another string of curses. I brush past Absalom, forgetting that he's still searching for my velvet robe, and head down the avenue that leads back to the fountain. I don't have the time or energy or wherewithal to handle this last surprise.

I don't plan on handling it when I get back to Mieira, either.

"This is your problem, Absalom Metamor," I call over my shoulder.

After a sigh, he says, "You are still selfish, Helisent West of Jaws."

I turn back at his solemn, cold words. He tugs my robe from his bottomless bag and it slips free like a liquid starlight.

It's like seeing an image of myself from the past.

Like seeing a perfect representation of the witch I used to be, distilled into a texture.

Absalom shoves the cloak toward me. "And what a shame that you are, because the world needs you. If we survive the triplemoon, it will only be the start. I hope you realize that. I hope you realize what you're doing here."

He stalks past me, leaving me with the velvet robe. It sags onto the limestone; I'd forgotten how heavy it is. I stare down at the fabric, bunching it between my fingers and then bringing it to my nose to inhale the stale scent of long-lost perfumes.

Maybe I haven't admitted just how different everything will be until now.

Holding the peach robe, I realize I'll never be that witch again.

The one who drinks and riots to avoid the pain of dawn. The one who looks for warmth and love in fleeting surges instead of stability. The one who can't stare herself in the mirror without hearing a witch screaming.

I sling on the robe.

I adjust the drooping sleeves and then tug my hair free from the collar.

I stare down at myself; it still fits in that comfy, too-large way.

Absalom stalks back toward the city center. His white robe sways with each stride of his long legs. He runs his hands through his hair, scoffing and murmuring under his breath.

"Thanks for the robe," I yell after him.

I meant it to be a sort of apology, but as soon as the words leave my lips, I realize I'm not done being angry with him or the Class.

So I add, "*Asshole.*"

Later that afternoon, Aura and Eos pound their hand drums for the Pletens.

I sit next to my papa, who gushes over the display. The string of six Pletens moves in a single-file line behind Memphis to showcase a traditional dance. They copy each of his moves as he dances at a measured pace. It creates a wave-like effect; by the time the sixth wielder, Vega, mimes Memphis's dance move, he's already two steps ahead.

Unlike Halcyon, who began the dance, Memphis likes to tease the Pletens with silly moves. They look ridiculous trying to wave their arms and sidestep like him. And once there's one error, the rest of the Pletens struggle to follow the sequence.

Even Vulcan, the stoniest of the group, chuckles as he falls off-kilter. Only Cleo and Ceyx manage to look graceful, keeping pace with the other easily.

When Memphis moves to the back of the line, he waves at me. "Vexen, you are bound with us. You can come."

I snigger, falling against my papa. "Memphis Baby, I can't even dance when I'm leading. I'll join next time."

Parsifal immediately pushes my arm, insisting I join. The okeanids join in next—even Berevald claps loudly, goading me toward the line of Pletens.

I'm about to give in, feeling confident with my velvet robe slung over me, when I see a bottle in my mind.

I stop mid-stride, focused on the vision.

The bottle doesn't spin or rattle against the ground. To my relief, nobody picks it up and shatters it.

I look to the north where the Hellastone sits—

I turn, studying the streets and the circular pit leading into Hella from above. I don't see anything out of place or warranting a message.

Silence hangs in the air.

Then a large hand comes down on the bottle, grabbing it by its thick center. The hand is male, the hand is in its form, and that form belongs to a Seracyd wielder.

"*Shit.*"

The Pletens move into action, reading my gaze and the sudden change in mood. Then the Mieirans scramble to their feet.

"Serac." It's the only word I manage—shouted toward Halcyon and his brood.

I'm still not even sure if what I sense is correct, if what I've concluded from the vision makes sense.

Halcyon, Ceyx, and Cleo lunge for Memphis. They sandwich him between their bodies, half-dragging and half-carrying him toward the two-story building the clan shares. Vega and Vulcan fall into line with the Pletens after taking the other's hand.

Their formation is tight; Halcyon leads and Vulcan trails, while the witches surround their youngest with their hands raised at the ready.

Halcyon looks back to shout, "Can you sense where they are? How many they are?"

"No." I can barely think around my shock and adrenaline. I wait to see what the indigo wielder does with the bottle. Like every other vision, all I see is the bottle—everything else is out of frame.

"I don't know," I call back. "I feel..."

I keep spinning and looking for a hint. With the afternoon dwindling, shadows expand and deepen beyond the glowing lights set up around the fountain. Half of Hella sits in darkness.

Samson grunts something in Velmic, then Rex and Berevald take off toward the okeanids. They herd Aura, Eos, and Meres toward their dwelling, arms spread to encircle the women.

Like me, Samson, Absalom, Kierkeline, Parsifal, and Hemlock do a full circle.

My body quivers with fear, but my mind focuses.

I refuse to fail the Pletens.

I hear the first intruder before I see him. He growls like an animal, throaty and visceral, as he steps out of a shadow in front of the rushing Pletens. The Seracyd warlock meets the group head-on, blocking their entrance to their dwelling. A black cloak flares at his heels as he bares his hands forward—

In a split-second, a lash of ultrasound lifts from his fingertips, directed at Halcyon.

My fingers twitch as I prepare a sheltering spell—

But a split-second moves very quickly.

They pile and pile and pile into a single unfathomable second.

Before I can wield, another figure steps out of the narrow shadow cast by the fountain's central pillar to my right. I turn just in time to face the second intruder; my eyes meet those of Halcyon's second brother, his eyes spewing violet light.

My breath catches in my throat as I count his features—

A straight nose, full upper lip, strong jaw—

One split-second, two split-second—

Then he pivots, twisting his hips and grunting as he shoves a blade toward my stomach—

I flinch as something red and hot sprays across my face and chest and arms.

I open my eyes, expecting to feel the dagger's pain.

Three split-second, four split-second—

Instead, a bright red axe juts from the second intruder's neck, rigid and proud.

I blink to clear my vision. A splatter of blood warms my chest and face.

The warlock sinks to his knees with a wet rasp, eyes rolling back into his head as the violet light fades from them.

Everything slows as adrenaline courses through my veins.

Samson stands ten feet away, an empty hand extended toward me.

Our eyes meet; I don't register my near-death, or the fact that Axerxa's axe saved me, or that Samson must not have lifted his eyes from me since this conflict began.

I turn back toward the Pletens.

All I see is an empty street and a two-story building where shouting and ultrasound echo from the windows.

Absalom, Kierkeline, and Hemlock sprint toward the racket.

An explosion batters through the building. Someone staggers away from the door, clutching their chest as they fall; a second figure rams into the first, sending them both onto the ground. The first has purple horns, the second jade.

I make it two steps before I realize both Halcyon and Ceyx are knocked out cold on the limestone, toppled over one another. I don't have time to react before three figures fall from the second-floor window.

Think, Helisent.

Concentrate.

The falling trio is intertwined in a struggle. I make out the first intruder, Memphis, and Cleo. Their cloaks wrap around them, tangled, while Memphis's arms lift slackly, as though unconscious.

Cleo's visceral and wordless cry weaves through those precious split-seconds, distracting me—

The falling wielders sail toward a bank of shadows. The warlock clings to Memphis—

The shadows start to overtake them as they fall.

The second brother wanted to kill me, but this warlock wants to kidnap Memphis.

I pivot and turn into the shadow cast by the fountain where the second intruder emerged. Samson rushes after me, lunging with wide eyes.

Too slow.

The darkness and magic overtake me and, in that split-second, I focus on Cleo, Memphis, and the intruder. I don't know where the Seracyd wielder is going to shadow them, but so long as I reside in my House, the land is connected to me.

The air. The shadows.

In the next split-second, I barrel into their warm bodies. I can't see anything—I don't know where we are—just that I chased them through a shadow, and it was black, and then I ran into something.

And now we're falling.

I hug the first body I hit, dragging myself into the cluster of frantic wielders. I look past our plummeting bodies; we're still inside Hella, sailing through the air twenty feet below its pitted entrance.

That's all I put together in a single split-second—

I open my eyes long enough to figure out which body belongs to my enemy. There's so much fabric—and Memphis's dead weight is hard to work around—

I hate the feeling of falling.

I don't know what's happening.

But I know there could be another blade heading for my belly, that Memphis is bound for Ezit if I don't save him now—

Cleo takes hold of the intruder's collar with one hand and presses her thumb into one of his eye sockets with the other.

In my desperation, cutting magic comes to mind first. I shift to grab the intruder's leg, using his black pants and cloak as a guide, and send the spell down his spine, eviscerating him with a single motion.

Combined with Cleo's gouging, it's a supremely unpleasant death. His gargled scream says as much.

The world flies by as relief hits me; he's dead, and so is the other one.

We're safe.

And then we hit the ground.

Thankfully, the intruder takes most of the brunt. Cleo lands on his chest and head, thumb slamming further into his eye socket. She jolts backward with a cry, then her free hand finds Memphis and clutches his tunic. The warlockling lays flat across the dead man's lower abdomen and legs. Memphis's limbs are splayed—but they're seemingly unbroken.

With a shaky grunt, I try to move.

I mostly landed on the warlock's shoulder—and my own.

I roll off him and onto the limestone.

Adrenaline keeps pumping through my veins; each split-second tells me something different, pulling things into a more fathomable order.

I glance up. We landed a street away from the fountain, where there's more commotion.

Behind me, Cleo groans in pain as she shifts to check Memphis.

With another grunt, I shuffle to my feet. My right arm hurts at the elbow. I keep it tucked against my chest as I turn away and move as quickly as I can toward the city center.

Vega rushes around the corner, catches sight of us, then breaks into a dead sprint.

As she passes me, she says, "Argot—*witches*—*hurry*—"

I ignore the pain exploding in my body—my elbow, my ankle, my ribs. I round the corner and go straight toward the fountain. Spells clang, each sound more jarring than the last as they echo between Hella's walls. I hear the magical pitches of Argot, Serac, and Talos, layered and tangled and warring.

I don't know where to look first.

The only chaos I've ever been deeply involved in was at afters parties.

This is... markedly different.

Near their dwelling, Halcyon and Ceyx remain prone on the ground. Vulcan kneels, craning over their piled bodies with one of his hands raised. Five feet away, an Argot witch bends at the waist, hands clutching her throat and mouth. Like the Seracyd invaders, she's unveiled; her curved horns are blindingly white.

But I don't think Vulcan is wielding against the witch. Instead, Aura and Eos raise their hands toward the intruder, only half-visible where they stand on her far side. Near the nymphs, a bucket full of salt water sloshes, spilling its content onto the ground. A watery trail runs from the bucket and nymphs to the bent witch.

Her hair and face and upper cloak are soaked. The witch claws at her face and nose as droplets fall. She raises one of her hands for a split-second, directing it at the okeanids; nothing happens.

It must be difficult to wield while drowning.

Meres stalks toward the distracted witch with one of the wolves' axes. It's disproportionately massive for the small nymph. She uses both hands to raise it above her head before, with a wild scream, she brings it down onto the witch's head.

I look away—there's another Argot witch outside the wolves' shared room.

She raises both of her hands and directs her long fingers toward the doorless entrance. Her four horns spark with light; she shrieks wildly as ear-splitting ultrasound unleashes from her hands. It batters through the doorway, into the room. It's repelled in the next second by a powerful shielding spell, which absorbs the witch's magic with a loud *boom*.

Dust emanates from the empty doorway—

Then a throwing axe careens from the clouds of dust billowing from the room. The Argyd witch deflects its momentum, casting a spell with a flick of her fingers. The axe lands on the ground with a loud clatter, sliding toward me. The witch turns to watch it go, then meets my eyes—and sees my raised hands.

A second axe soars from the clouded doorway. It sinks into the side of the witch's head with a loud *thunk* before either of us has time to cast. The witch blinks at me as crimson blood spurts outward and slides down her face, staining her high collar. She even staggers a step, features bunching like she's confused.

I keep my hands raised in case she's not dead.

Her eyes roll back, then I let myself look away.

I take a breath in—

I spin to find the next threat, but there's a moment of reprieve from ultra and infrasound.

In it, I hear breathing and shouting and boots scraping on stone.

I close my eyes.

In my mind, I see a glass bottle. It lays on the wooden floor—a female hand takes hold of the bottle this time. Her skin is white as milk, her nails long and thick.

I open my eyes—

The scene at the fountain remains calm. I don't see or hear a threat of magic, nor an Argyd witch.

Like I did when chasing Memphis, I trust my magic to shadow me to wherever the witch hides in Hella. I turn toward the nearest shadow.

Kierkeline pivots where she stands a foot away from me. With a snarl, the GhostEater digs her fingernails into my forearm. "Zeu said to capture one if they came to Hella. Let's go."

She follows me into the shadow.

We rush from the darkness onto a shadowy street. The fountain must be at least ten blocks away—only distended sunlight from above and the pale blush of street lamps reach us.

It makes the scene almost impossible to read.

Absalom sits on the ground with his back against a wall, head sagging as he clutches his gut. The wound gushes blood, lapping over his hands and pooling on his robe, on the ground beneath him.

Accra-Four is draped over him, one hand on his collar and another raised toward the Argot witch who stalks toward them. The gorgon clenches her eyes shut as she faces the witch; her bared hand isn't wielding, it's begging.

The Argot witch flicks her head to toss her long braids over her shoulder. They fall between her four full horns, speckled with red blood. Then she raises her hand, directing her fingers at Absalom and Accra-Four.

The witch turns at the last second, breath catching in her throat as she notices our arrival and pivots to face us.

In the same second, Accra-Four opens her eyes.

I see it happen—see the gorgon lift her chin and widen her eyes as the Argyd witch shifts out of her line of focus. I see the gorgon's body turn to follow the witch's pivot, toward me and Kierkeline—

I flinch, turning my head and shutting my eyes.

Then I hear something like frost on a lake. Something that sounds like ice taking hold of formless water. It crackles to my right where the GhostEater stands, where the GhostEater gasps and gargles a half-curse.

I don't look; I keep my eyes clenched shut.

Accra-Four starts screaming, but I ignore her. I send a wild crushing spell toward where I think the Argyd witch is standing. Past the gorgon's bellowing comes the sound of cracking bones. Beneath it all, I hear the GhostEater's fragile voice.

I think Kierkeline says, "I'll tell her."

My heart plummets to my feet.

A cry lodges in my throat—all that comes out is a strange wheeze as I try to find my words.

I keep my eyes on the ground, too nervous to look up as Accra-Four screams the word *no* over and over.

Fuck. Fuck, fuck, fuck.

I reach out in search of Kierkeline. My hand knocks into something hard—I look down and see a solid boot and skirt. They aren't made of faded leather and cerulean fabric. Both are rigid and gray, as though carved from a slab of granite.

Oh, no.

I look from the boots to the skirt. I make it as far as a gnarled and granite hand, half-outstretched toward me, before I turn away from Kierkeline's stone form.

I lick my lips and try not to heave.

Focus, Helisent.

Absalom is bleeding out; I will need my little patsy someday.

"Is the witch dead?" I force my shaking voice to a higher volume. "Accra? Can you see?"

The gorgon doesn't hear; she's still screaming.

"Absalom—Absalom—" I wander closer to the pair, arms outstretched and eyes closed.

The warlock doesn't respond, but it's easy enough to follow the gorgon's howling.

I reach her legs first. I act without thinking, first ripping a strip of her linen clothes free and then shoving it toward her chest. It's awkward madness. I can't tell where she is in relation to Absalom, whether she's still crouching over him or if she's sitting at his side.

All the while, Accra-Four begs forgiveness, begs me to kill her, and I beg her to put on the blindfold, to let us get up and make sure the invasion is over.

Eventually, she shuffles out of the way.

I turn my back to her and open my eyes. Absalom's head hangs against his chest, eyes shut and mouth bloody. I press my hand to his abdomen and use healing magic to gauge his injury; it's a deep gash but there's nothing lodged inside him. I concentrate first on stopping the bleeding, then focus on his stomach lining. Warmth kicks up quickly, spreading from my body to his.

Don't think about Kierkeline.

Just save the patsy.

Accra's shouting dwindles into bereft sobbing.

I let my body relax as I work on Absalom, desperate for a second of peace.

My arm must be broken—the pain is unnatural, centered around my elbow's joint. I think one of my ribs must also be broken. Each breath sears like something is pushing against my lungs. My left ankle swells as I squat over Absalom.

"Honey! Honey Baby!" my papa screams from another street. "Where are you?"

Samson is close behind. "*Helisent?*"

In a voice that doesn't sound like my own, I call back, "I'm here. Wait—wait—just wait—"

I hazard a glance to my right where Accra sits, keeping my eyes down. I see a few of her pale linen layers, then a bare foot. I realize she's curled over herself, bent over her thighs with her head in her hands.

Parsifal's voice is closer. "Why? What's going on?"

"Accra... Accra..." That's as far as I get before my papa and Samson round the corner.

Both pause, looking from me and Absalom and Accra-Four to Kierkeline's stony, upright form to the Argyd witch splayed on the ground five feet away.

Parsifal nods solemnly before he approaches me. Samson eyes the Argyd witch, then Accra-Four for a moment longer. While I put Absalom under a restful sleep, Samson coaxes the gorgon onto her feet, then helps her tie on her blindfold. My papa goes to Kierkeline. He murmurs a few things over her, but I don't have the heart to watch.

I don't want to remember her like this.

I don't want to have an answer for Butter if she asks me someday.

Rex and Berevald show up shortly after. Samson helps me stand so that Rex can carry Absalom back to the fountain. Berevald takes Accra-Four by the hand and follows them.

I finally glance down and realize I'm still caked in blood. Coagulated drips mark my arms and chest; I can feel it drying on my cheeks and neck.

I hazard a glance at my arm. A bone juts out of place at my elbow, bulging out like it's trying to break my skin. My nausea and lightheadedness double. My whole body goes loose while my heart rate ratchets in my chest.

"Oh *shit*."

It feels like I just jumped into icy water after days without sleep.

My vision starts to fade suddenly. A large hand grips my shoulder, then Samson scoops me into his arms. I fall against his chest, breaths coming faster and shallower.

"Take her back, my boy," Parsifal says quietly. "I'll take care of our dear GhostEater."

When I wake up from an achy oblivion, I smell blood.

It takes a while to put everything together. I'm in my bed; it's night; there's a bonfire near the fountain; nobody is screaming.

My velvet robe hangs on the wall near the door, covered in flecks of blood. They dot the chest and sleeves, concentrated into a pool of maroon goo around the collar.

I stare at the robe for a long time.

When it's too much to take, I go to the fountain and join the silent Meirans, the silent Pletens, the raucous noise of the elated vampires. I track the scent of blood to the fountain, which is filled a few feet with maroon liquid. I stand for a long time, staring down at the rich blood, the pale stone. Debris catches on its glittering crimson surface, reflecting firelight in oozing shapes.

Someone tells me the vampires drained the intruders and have been feasting on their blood.

Someone puts a plate of food in my lap and makes sure I eat it all.

I don't know how long I slept.

Where Absalom is and whether someone finished healing his wound. What my papa did with Kierkeline's corpse. Who calmed Accra-Four.

Halcyon kneels before me later. "Thank you, Vexen. Thank you." He licks his lips as he stares up at me, hands on my knees and eyebrows bunched together. "You still have time. You still have time to change your mind."

I wonder if he's right.

If I've fucked us all with the delusional thought that I can save the okeanids and necromancers from Ezit. If I've let my own foolish stubbornness replace rational thought.

He whispers, "I'm going to stay with my family tonight. You're welcome, too."

I pat his hand, then he stands and leaves with a sigh.

Meres sits by my side afterward. By now, most of the vampires have returned to their den and the Mieirans have dragged their feet to bed. My papa is the exception; he's sleeping near my feet on a mat beside the leftovers from dinner.

With a sigh, the necromancer sets her hands on her thighs. But she doesn't speak.

Eventually, I clear my throat. "I'll start taking barrels of salt water to Ezitlos. I'll hide them in the debris. You'll have all you need to wield during the triplemoon."

She doesn't look at me. She stares up at Hella's entrance, and sighs. "It won't be enough. You know that."

I clench my jaw. I stare into the fire's brightest, lashing flames and try to shove away the teetering doubt in me—

'If we survive the triplemoon, it will only be the start.'

"I can't do everything," I admit.

"No one expects that. All it needs is a canal. A way to follow the salt water into Ezit. An okeanid demigod can't travel via fresh water."

"Carving a canal through Vex would compromise my Landmark." I slide my eyes toward the necromancer.

I've never been more desperate for her demigod's help. In the last hour, I've at least admitted that my stupidity might mean my death—and that simple truth is what it is.

But I won't put my papa at risk.

I won't lead Samson into that city, either.

Not without more certainty.

Meres shrugs as she stares into the dwindling fire. "If you say your Landmark is like a demigod, then you should have more faith it in. A little *canal* never hurt a demigod, as far as I know."

"My demigod isn't like yours. It's only magic, and magic is form-less. It needs these caves, Meres. And any path I carve from the shore into Ezit will cut through Vex's cave systems. I can't compromise my own demigod to cater to yours."

"But you'll abandon it. You'll sail us all home and never return to Vex." She raises her eyebrows, turning toward me. "How is aban-doning your Landmark so much better than destroying it?"

With a sigh, she pats her thighs again and stands up. She steps around my papa, who snorts once where he sleeps near the fire.

I watch her walk away.

I chew on that question for a while.

Eventually, exhaustion resettles. I tug my papa's cloak over him so he doesn't catch a chill, then drag my feet back to my bedroom.

I stop at the door; the room isn't empty.

Zeu sits in the center of my bed with his legs folded.

My gut clenches.

Though dawn approaches, it hasn't grazed the sky yet. With only lamplight in the bedroom and a meager fire outside, Zeu's eyes are pitted with orbs of iridescent red.

His braids sit neatly over his shoulders, hanging down his hairless chest alongside the single, dark feather that dangles from his leather string necklace. Thankfully, his white pelt covers most of his groin; I can only see a few red-gold hairs trailing below his belly button.

I study his features, finally healed from Samson's beating. Like Vic, he has hooded eyes that gracefully angle upwards at their ends. They pair well with his high cheekbones and his sculpted jaw. In the dim lighting, I can't make out so many of the dark veins beneath his pale skin.

He looks... otherworldly. Which I guess he is. He's of the night world; I'm a daylight creature.

And though I've been in close proximity to Vic's den, I've yet to share any intimate moments with a vampire.

"I'm not dangerous," Zeu says quietly. He leans forward to pat the bed in invitation. "I was an asshole. It was unfair."

I'm too numb to fear him right now. Too on edge from the invasion and full of doubt.

"I was angry with you, Vexen," Zeu goes on calmly. "That's all."

He leans forward to pat the bed again.

I cross my arms and lean against the doorframe. "Go on, then. I'm listening."

"My den stays close to Ezit. The caves there are too complex for wielders to track us. They fear the darkness and the dead ends. They prefer sunlight and plans. We were preparing for a raid when Vic's letter came. She wrote that Accra told her Hella was occupied again."

Zeu scratches his chin. He glances from me to the bed again, as though hoping I'll sit down.

Though I can't see it, I can sense the rosfrost in his veins. It feels heavy and lulling, like the goading whisper from a lover that's actually a scorpion.

"Vic wrote that you were going to wage war against Ezit. And I was *happy*. This is what my den does, Vexen. We wage war. We refuse to let Ezit know peace. We know that we will not win—how Axerxa knew he would die when he stayed to defend Hella.

"I already told you when we met. My mother was named Heb, after Bathsheba. We grow up hearing stories about Bathsheba and how she was raised. We grow up hearing about Axerxa and the wives he sent to Plet, then to Mieira.

"So, I packed my things. I was happy to hear I wouldn't be waging war against Ezit alone anymore. After five hundred years of silence in Vex, its Vexen had finally returned."

For a long time, the King of Night stares at me from the bed.

I stare back. My gut is still clenched, my stance light in case I need to run.

"Then I finished the letter." Zeu tuts and scans me, jaw clenching. "You will not wage *war* against Ezit. You will launch *one* attack. And then you will abandon this place."

Is he in fucking cahoots with Meres?

And who would choose a life of fighting over returning home?

Slowly, I relax against the cool doorframe. This time, I scan Zeu. "And what? You hate me for it?"

"I will never run," he seethes from the bed, crossing his arms. "Running is for prey. For cowards."

I roll my eyes. "So, you think I'm a coward who's *running* from Ezit?"

"I did. Yes." He wags his head, considering. "But I woke up and saw you covered in Seracyd blood. You and your Mieirans killed and we filled the fountain with blood. So, maybe I was wrong."

I narrow my eyes. I have no idea where he's going with this. "Is that an apology?"

"No. I'm not sorry about that. You may still be a coward."

"What do you want, Zeu?" More exasperated than on edge now, I charge into the room. I head to the far wall and squat to sort through my pile of clothes, picking out something warmer for sleep. I try to ignore the goosebumps that rise on my skin as I pass Zeu. "I'm tired, so if you have something to say, then say it."

I look over my shoulder as his silence continues.

When our eyes meet, he says, "I'm not sorry for thinking you're a coward. But I am sorry about how we met. In the forest."

My blood freezes. He hasn't acted like he remembers interrupting me and Samson outside Hella the night we met. And I've been thankful.

I may be a shameless witch who prefers the warren life, but I like to know when I'm being watched in a sexual manner. Even the freest nymphs I've ever met would find Zeu's actions and words vile.

Possibly even punishable.

"Sorry about what?" I ignore the blood that rushes to my cheeks.

Zeu raises his eyebrows. "For saying it was my turn." Then his features break, lips pinching. "I was angry with you again. First, because Vic told me you weren't going to stay in Zarzynn and reclaim Vex. Second, because you were with—well, I didn't know what a wolf was, but I didn't like that. Bathsheba chose the vampires, Vexen. I thought you would, too."

My heart thumps in my chest.

I ignore the fact that he must have felt *entitled* to my attention and skip over to the fact that he knows about me and Samson.

Fuck.

Zeu shrugs. He glances around the room, craning his head toward the door as though checking for spies. Then he turns back to me, eyebrows raised. "Why do you pretend to be with the warlock? These sheets don't smell like sex. You and the wolf hide from one another. Why? You are the Vexen. What you want is yours."

I drop my clothes, then stand up. "What I want is not automatically mine, Zeu. And it's none of your business." I also glance at the door, happy that I don't see anyone lingering within earshot. I look at the vampire, raising my eyebrows. "What do you want?"

He angles his chin; it looks like he's close to smiling. "That's a complicated question."

"I mean for keeping my secret. Mine and Samson's secret."

Please don't say what I think you're going to say.

Zeu holds my eyes for a long time. I can't tell if he wants me to guess. Eventually, he says, "I want your trust, Helisent West of Jaws." He leans forward, eyes carving into me. "Didn't you ever make a bad introduction? One that you wish you could change?"

Yes.

Hundreds of times.

Maybe a thousand.

With a long sigh, Zeu stretches out to lay across the bed. He props his head in his palm, getting comfortable as he studies where I linger on the far side of the room. Away from the door. "Vic's den keeps our culture alive. Her people live freely. But my den... we wage war on Ezit. Often. My harem keeps me soft. It's easy to go crazy with anger. And without Ell, Ria, Sol, Tos, Niq, and Iop... I get a bit..." He sighs again, flicking something off the sheet. "I'm not *me* without all of them. Just War Zeu. And War Zeu isn't normal."

I sit down again near my stack of clothes. There's no way I'm joining him on the bed, but I'm interested in hearing him out. Each word is softer than the last, leading someplace I hadn't expected.

"You're welcome to invite your harem to Hella, Zeu," I reason. "Especially if they're responsible for managing you."

"Maybe I will." He sighs. "I wanted to meet Ret first. Alone."

I tilt my head. Since proving his usefulness in translating for the groups, Vic has started regarding the once-degi with more respect. Sort of. "Ret? Why?"

Zeu's eyebrows bunch. "I wanted to see if he was normal yet. He is doing much better than I was a year out."

The room's cold touches my core.

I clear my throat, wishing I had a drink with me. "You're once-degi?"

He flinches with a loud tsk, sitting up and crossing his legs. "*I am Zeu*. The same as my mother named me. I was not once-degi. I was always a vampire. *I was always Zeu*"."

War Zeu.

I want your trust.

Waiting my turn.

You may still be a coward.

An oddly comfortable silence fills the room. It's still cold, and I'm still uncertain, and Zeu's eyes are still pitted with flashing red—but I'm no longer actively afraid.

I stare at the vampire, happy to understand him better.

With a profoundly simple smile, he says, "I will never stop fighting. They will never know my peace. Not until they kill me, Vexen."

His words make my heart thump. Not out of fear for my safety, but out of fear that he and I may be more alike than I care to admit.

I think I understand him.

And I hate that.

CHAPTER 18

VIEIRA

SAMSON

My grandson,
You were a silent child. You clung to your mother; your father pulled you away
from her so you wouldn't become soft. You raged when he did. Now, I wonder if
you knew before the rest of us. (Do you, my Kulapsifang?)

I keep my eye on the single-story building where Hella's portal waits.

Hemlock shuffles between me and Helisent. The dryad glances over his shoulder with every other step.

"Hemlock, chill out." Helisent elbows him. "Meres doesn't want to come."

I hazard a look back at the fountain. The necromancer doesn't stare in our direction; she's bent over her plate as she converses with Vulcan. The warlock says something with a shrug, which sends Meres reeling back with laughter.

Half the group collects the empty plates from dinner, while others lounge and chat. It's a normal evening—even with Accra-Four and well over a dozen vampires spread around the fountain.

I don't know that I'll miss this place, but I'll remember Hella's central plaza fondly.

Hemlock slows down for a third time. "She might change her mind."

I press a hand to his upper back.

I'm desperate to reach the portal where Helisent will transport us to New Hypnos before any more beings join our trio. Only an hour ago, the group decided Helisent, Hemlock, and I would travel to New Hypnos to bear the good news of the impending triplemoon. After months of secret ship-building and plotting against Ezit, it's time for the okeanids in New Hypnos to pack their bags.

Vicente and Abdecalas are nearly full; Sennen bloats with reflections of light.

Seven more days.

Still, I'm more focused on finding alone time with Helisent. In the week since we slaughtered Ezit's Seracyd and Argyd invaders, we've yet to carve out more than a few hours of solitude. And when we did, we didn't waste time with words. We kissed until our bodies were flushed, then started yawning and fell asleep half-undressed.

More of Zeu's retinue filter in nightly; we adjust our plans with each new brawny and sharp-toothed vampire. But we can only coordinate with the vampires by night, which means sleep is hard to come by. Rejuvenating rest is almost nonexistent.

And Hemlock keeps looking back like he's going to shout another invitation to Meres.

Thankfully, we turn left onto the narrow street where the portal's vestibule awaits. Hemlock follows as we shuffle into the cold room and move toward the threshold of shadows that boils with magic.

With a grumble, he steps into the portal with us.

On my next step, I flinch from the light. After spending months in a cave, direct sunlight feels like an assault. Based on the screeched curse from Helisent, she agrees.

Hemlock strolls forward with a long sigh, opening his arms to the golden beams of light at dusk's end.

The sun sinks into the ocean, a burning speck. A sprawling green hill spans before us. Wind whips over the land, shaking the wild grass and lifting the sleeves of Hemlock's cloak.

Like me, Helisent turns to study the spread of treeless, rolling hills. The ocean sits far to the west, a seam of dark blue. To the north, I make out the faded outline of a strange city. It looks taller than it is wide, precariously stacked along a dark cliffside.

Helisent nods toward the city. "That's Plet." She swivels and squints to the southeast. "Which means New Hypnos must be that way."

The only signs of life past the next hill are narrow trails of smoke that crawl skyward, along with the faint hint of civilization on the breeze. From the distance, I smell large fires, smoked fish, limestone, and ground flax seeds. As the sun dips below the horizon, a cloak of darkness falls over the island, peaceful and dim.

The scents intensify and then disappear as we traverse the hills that lead to New Hypnos. I realize why once the village comes into sight; it's hidden in a broad valley. From Plet, the vast knolls must hide the settlement entirely.

It reminds me of Mid City—if a bit sturdier. The thatched walls aren't eroded, while its main dirt road is bordered by pale rocks. A cluster of thatched and planked dwellings sit connected by footpaths along the valley. The streets funnel out to the ocean—but like in Vex, there's no beach. Just a gradual drop-off that ends in restless waves and a barnacled stretch of rock.

A small crowd gathers before we're in earshot. They surround the large cisterns near the village entrance.

The okeanids look familiar—and hopelessly strange. Their ocean-blue eyes pop like pockets of sky, their thick hair neatly arranged into shingles, afros, and locks.

But they don't watch us with the warm welcome common in Mieira. None wear the lapis lazuli or the turquoise common in Hypnos.

They stand with their arms crossed. They don't hold hands. They watch us like we're ghosts, like they're prepared to send us back to where we came from. And they wear the fitted layers common to the Pletens, shorn off at their triceps and knees to keep their arms and feet free.

I glance at Helisent and Hemlock. Even the king looks uncertain as we approach; his smile widens, then disappears, and then he clears his throat.

We stop before a crowd of around fifteen. Behind them, okeanids flood onto the village's main street, leaping from doorways and stopping as they catch sight of us. In their ranks, I count one Argyd witch, one Colyd witch, and one Lasan warlock. I count their offspring, too; their alas are blended with bitter magic and briny salt water.

Within a few minutes, the crowd of fifteen balloons into a group of fifty.

I catch a few whispers as more villagers wander over.

"Did someone already tell her?" an adolescent male asks.

"She's coming out," whispers back a middle-aged woman.

"I didn't believe it until now," the adolescent goes on.

Eventually, a matriarch steps forward from the mob, striking the ground with her walking stick. The group parts to let her pass.

Cataracts fill her large eyes. She fixes them on Helisent, mashing her lips together like she's preparing a curse. "Why did it take you months to visit?"

Helisent looks at me and Hemlock, as though waiting for one of us to explain. Hemlock tucks his hands behind his back and takes a half-step back. I do the same, hoping Helisent gets the message.

Helisent's eyes narrow on the okeanid. "I've been busy."

The matriarch raises a hand and points at an okeanid who stands to her left. The man crosses his arms as he studies Helisent. "Zephyr North of Hypnos was in Plet three and a half months ago. He was staying with a friend in one of the residential buildings. He heard the voice of one of the Sisters West of Jaws not *once*, not *twice*, but three times."

The matriarch nods at the okeanid.

Zephyr raises his chin at Helisent. "You were arguing with a warlock named Halcyon Plet. I heard his voice, too."

"You've been in Zarzynn for months and have made no contact with your own people." The matriarch's condemnation is quiet, cast mostly through her burning, hazy eyes. "Tell me, is Zarzynn offering you glory and wealth? Do you enjoy collecting the coins they make in Ezit? Did they offer you a tour of the city?"

Then comes a long silence.

I don't hazard a glance at Helisent. I clench my stomach and stare ahead, waiting.

You can do this, little bird.

"See—I knew you'd say something fucked up like that," Helisent coos, leaning toward the matriarch.

Lekeli Kelnazzar...

"Which is *good*," the witch goes on. "Because if I hadn't thought of that first, I'd probably be angry right now. But since *I did* think of it, I can tell you that Zarzynn offered me nothing but a rosarium box. And the only tour of Ezit I'll be going on is on the triplemoon. I'll be joined by the Kulapsifang of Velm and his boy-pack, along with a dozen vampires—*Zeu's* vampires—and a few Pletens. I even got a fucking gorgon. One of the *Accras*.

"So, did you want to invite me into your village and then apologize over what I'm hoping is a *very* boozy booze? I mean, you like the *original* Hypnos, right?"

The corners of the matriarch's lips twitch, like she's close to smiling. But she doesn't trade her bitter expression for a kinder one. She just raises her eyebrows. "And the demigod? We're wielding again. It must be near."

Helisent crosses her arms. "It's close. That's all I'm at liberty to say about that for now." She studies the group, then pivots toward Hemlock and me. "That's Samson 714 Afador. He's the Kulapsifang of Velm. And this is Hemlock East of Alita, King of Rhotidom and all its sables. So, can we come in?" She claps her hands together, then points her joined fingers at the matriarch. "Right, sorry—what's your name?"

The matriarch sighs, then she turns back. She leaves out her left arm without another glance in our direction. The witch steps forward and links their arms together, following the okeanid onto the village's main street.

"My name is Ledo South of Hypnos," she says. "And which Sister West of Jaws are you?"

Helisent snorts. "How long have you been here, my dear Ledo? I'm Helisent West of Jaws. A warlock killed my sister almost seven years ago. He came from Ezit, you know."

The group trails the women in a vague blob. Before we get left behind, Hemlock and I follow. He seems focused on the okeanids, their lack of welcome, and the doorless, threadbare buildings around us.

But I keep sight of Helisent.

Her steps are confident, her shoulders relaxed and her chin raised.

She looks like a leader.

And one who's been at it for a while.

She even brought up her sister and Anesot in the same sentence.

'A warlock killed my sister almost seven years ago.'

When I first met her, those words would have been preceded by hours of hard drinking and a tear-fueled meltdown—if at all. And now...

Hemlock sends an elbow into my ribs. "You're going to need to hide that smile better when we're back in Mieira. You're not fooling anyone in Hella. Just so you know."

I pinch my lips together. I hadn't realized I was smiling.

Hemlock goes on, grooming his beard with a few strokes, "I'm going to request a separate room tonight. It's for my sake, not yours."

I glance at the lilac-cloaked dryad, but he stares ahead evenly. Another smile tugs at my lips. "As you wish, my dear king."

What follows is an hours-long ordeal in the village center.

First, we attempt to get a head count on the villagers to divide their numbers evenly between our ships. This is complicated by the fact that many okeanids have started families with Pleten wielders—and some live in Plet.

As descendants of Mieira, they're all welcome aboard.

But that raises questions for the Pletens whose only tie to Mieira is their okeanid lover and their shared offspring.

And what about extended family? Aunts and uncles may have no direct ties to Mieira, but they desperately want to leave the island for a brighter future.

In Velm, the answer would be simple: we can only take those who belong in Mieira by right of blood. In Antigone, I imagine the response would be even less inclusive.

Thankfully, Hemlock steps in to diffuse the mounting uncertainty. He tells Ledo, "We've already agreed to allow passage to part of Vic the Chosen's den, including the Queen of Night.

"This is your village. These okeanids are under your care. You will decide who boards the ships, my great Ledo. We will respect your decision."

After a quick nod from Helisent and I, Ledo moves on to another topic: the demigod.

The matriarch wants to know if the demigod will enter Ezit with us.

Helisent raises her eyebrows. "If it can get to Ezit, it can do whatever it likes. I certainly wouldn't say no to help from a demigod."

Ledo raises her chin, studying the witch. "Even if you save the okeanids one by one and free them all from Ezit, they will return home and worship their demigods. Not you, Vexen."

I sit back at the statement, surprised by Ledo's implication.

She thinks Helisent wants to save the okeanids for glory?

Helisent snorts. "Do you know what I want more than the worship of okeanids? More than the attention of demigods?" She pauses. "To be left the fuck alone, my dear Ledo."

I file that answer away, thinking of Malasuntra's question. *Helisent West of Jaws wants to be left alone more than she wants anything in the world.*

(I like to think I'm a close second.)

After a moment of eye contact, the women nod at one another, and Ledo leads us to a dining hall. We sit on the ground beside the matriarch while the villagers pack around us, warming the hut as they watch us and whisper to each other.

The meal is meager but delicious. While we eat, I answer a few questions about Velm. The okeanids want to know how the wolves are; we're mostly fine. Whether my father replaced a problematic pack leader in Lampades; he didn't. Whether I married the Female Alpha; I did. Whether the Northing is underway; it's not.

At highmoons, we're shuffled off to a cramped hut on the village's outskirts. Ledo thanks us for visiting, then gestures to the hut's creaking doors with an unreadable smile. Its wooden walls are slightly concave, though its pitched roof looks sturdy enough. Inside, cobwebs dangle from the rafters. Grass and twigs litter the ground below.

I catch a whiff of the stale scent from the doorway; hay and goats, plus a dizzying series of related scents. Thankfully, they're relatively mild, hinting the storage shack hasn't been used in a season or two.

Hemlock and Helisent poke their heads inside, then we all glance at each other.

I raise my eyebrows at the king; I remember a promise of privacy.

He leans out of the threshold and sets his hands on his hips. "I'll be looking for a warm bed tonight, thank you."

Helisent whips around at his words, eyes alight with mischief. "A *warm bed?* With *whom?*"

Hemlock wags his eyebrows. "A king doesn't kiss and tell." He runs his hands through his hair quickly. "But a king *does* like to look his best, my dear witch." He spins in a circle, then bares a smile at Helisent. "If you don't mind..."

With a giggle, Helisent raises her hand and flutters her fingers at the king. He shivers as a brush of bass echoes around us. Under an invisible touch, his hair and beard rustle as they're groomed into perfection. His cloak sleeves roll, then his tunic unravels slightly at the collar to reveal a few perfectly curled tufts of emerald chest hair.

He thrashes for a few seconds, kicking his feet and jumping as though pinched on the butt. Then he glances across his tidy layers, feeling at his face.

Helisent crosses her arms with a smile. "You've never looked more handsome, my king."

Hemlock touches his face with a pout. "It was very invasive. Did you..." He wriggles his boots. "Did you cut my toenails?"

"It's called a pedicure, you wild animal." She flings a hand toward the village's main street. "Now go find a warm bed."

Hemlock doesn't spare a look at the village. He looks at his hands then he brings them close to his face. "Am I..."

"Covered in an appropriate amount of hazelnut oil? Yes. You are." Helisent throws a glance at me, as though confused by his reaction. "Did you want to look good or not?"

Hemlock stares at Helisent uncertainly. "I feel like a baby seal."

She emphatically gestures to the village's main street again. "You're welcome."

Half a dozen okeanids loiter around our storage hut, eavesdropping. Hemlock strides onto the dirt road with a smile when he notices them. To my pleasant surprise, the okeanids immediately approach the dryad king—not eavesdropping, then, but awaiting an audience.

When they're gone, Helisent turns into the dark storage hut.

Inside, it's almost totally black. "Whatever treatment you just gave Hemlock... can you do that to this hut?" I ask.

The witch steps inside with a sigh. "Just give me a minute. Can you fill the water jug?"

I head to the cistern and fill a jug for us. When I head back, I find a few pups lingering near the rickety door, craning their necks for a look inside. Now, it's warmly lit from within. They scatter when they see me, squealing with laughter as they race back toward the main road.

I open the door and sigh with relief.

Inside, magical oil casts light from the rafters. The scents of lavender and wild grass drift from the wooden panels. Helisent sits on a broad and soft bed in the center of the room, surrounded by blankets and a few square pillows. Though not nearly as luxurious as her bedding from last year, it's a reasonable spread compared to our pine nests in Vex.

The witch brushes her hair, head tilted. Golden light dances off the straight white strands with each stroke. Her heavy robe hangs from the wall nearby; Helisent wears only the loose and soft tunic dress. She smiles when I enter, patting the space beside her.

I set down the jug of water, slip off my boots, then get comfortable. For a few moments, we fall back into a mundane routine of bedtime rituals. I finish brushing her hair, and then she brushes mine. She cleans our hands and our feet, and then we fall back into bed.

I lay on my side and prop my head on my hand, staring at her.

Rather than scoot closer, Helisent turns to pull out a torn piece of parchment from her bag. She glances at me, eyes dancing with nervousness. "I know it's not sexy to bring paperwork into bed, but we keep falling asleep or fucking as soon as we get a moment alone. And not that we can't sleep and fuck, but..." With a sigh, she watches me with wary eyes. "I need to tell you about a conversation I had with Zeu the other night."

I used to fear she'd say Halcyon's name in bed. Now, I'd rather her shout Halcyon's name ten times than utter Zeu's once.

I take a deep breath and sit through her recollection of Zeu's apology and his promise to keep our secret—in exchange for her trust. I swallow every word and try to hide the anger that boils in me.

Here's what I conclude from that interaction:

First, Zeu wants the witch.

Second, he knows he fucked up his first meeting with Helisent in an irreparable way.

Third, he's playing a long game to win her affection, and that long game has no rules—certainly no sense of trust.

But I don't say that; I don't want Helisent to think I'm acting out of jealousy or that I don't trust her judgment.

It takes me a moment to find the right words. "Trust means something different to every being, Helisent."

I reach over and stroke her cheek. A pit of doom rekindles in my stomach; I recognize it from our time traveling through Rhotidom on the way to Alita. Then, I'd sensed our imminent doom in every touch—just like I sense it now, as my thumb runs down Helisent's soft cheek and along her jawline.

"Please make sure you know what it means to him before you decide to trust Zeu."

Her crimson irises shoot to mine. "I don't trust him, Samson. I never will."

My heart wants to believe that.

But fear prevents me. Fear asks me... *what happens if I'm not there next time?*

Rather than answer that question, I switch my attention away from the vampire. "I also have a few things I need to tell you... one is about Malasuntra 711 Afador. He's a deathling. I spoke with him the night you came to our camp and told me you drank the potion."

My gut clenches. "And the other *thing* that happened... I met— well, not really *met*, because I was just helping Parsifal—"

"You met Andromeda," Helisent interrupts. "My papa told me. He said she likes you. Did you know she was friends with Imperatriz? Parsifal said she visited our homestead a few times."

I study her expression for a hint of displeasure. But Helisent stares at me openly as she awaits a response.

She snorts a second later. "Look, I know everyone thinks I'm crazy for not taking up Meres's offer to speak with my mother or sister, but... Well, you won't like this, but I think it's kind of pointless in Vex. Either I die in Ezit and see them quicker than I thought, or I survive the trip back to Mieira and reward myself with a little reunion."

She leans forward and kisses the tip of my nose like she didn't just outline a horrific scenario. "Now, tell me about Malasuntra. I hope he's better than Clearbold."

As I recount the tale, Helisent nods, eyes widening during the most shocking portions and brow furrowing during the most intense.

She doesn't ask many questions. When I'm finished, she chews her lip and then concludes, "Malasuntra was right—you need to focus on keeping Velm together. On getting rid of Clearbold and Malachai. In the meantime, I'll send dove to Imperatriz."

Relief floods me. I've thought of asking the same, but I haven't known how to ask Helisent to spare the time and energy with so much going on.

"Maybe after the triplemoon—"

"No. Now." Helisent sits up and reaches for her bottomless bag. The tattered cloth pouch barely looks capable of withstanding a strong headwind—nonetheless carrying copious amounts of material goods. The witch sticks her hand into its fold, calls up my mother's braid, and then sets it between us. "Do you think she's going to be scared of magic like you were?"

My head goes light as I sit up. I stare at the bundle, running my fingers along the sturdy braid folded inside the fabric. I try to be rational. "Helisent, you need access to *all* of your dove on the triplemoon. We can send it after—"

"If I die, what happens?" She leans toward me, eyes blazing. "Who sends her dove, Samson?"

I sit back, heart thumping as that statement washes over me.

She's right.

I see a warlock leap from a shadow next to my witch; I see the copper blade in his hand before my witch does; I throw the red axe just in time.

I see my witch falling through the air; I hear her hit the ground with three others; I see her round the corner with a broken arm cradled against her chest—

"Don't make that face." Helisent pinches my cheeks with a hand. "Both of us could die. I'm just stating facts. And I'd hate for your mother to be left high and dry after all she did for me. Now—do you think she's scared of magic how you were? Should we write her a note to send with the dove? Will she know how to use it?"

Helisent gathers more materials from her bottomless bag.

I fight nausea, bouncing between two awful realizations.

The first is that Helisent really might die in Ezit, and I might not be able to stop that. (I've already grazed this reality multiple times in Zarzynn, and it's not getting any easier.)

Second is the realization that I don't know my mother. Whether she'd be afraid of magic or know how to use dove. Whether she'd judge me for being involved with a powerful wielder.

'All beings want peace, safety, and love. The rest is just details.'

Or was she pretending like Malasuntra when she said that?

Helisent sets a piece of paper, a small vial of ink, and a tattered quill before me. "Write her a letter. Maybe you don't need to mention what's happening with Velm... I think she'd like to hear about you more." She reaches forward to drag my hand toward the quill. "You write. I'll package the dove."

Just like I struggled to pen a letter to Brutatalika on our journey to Zarzynn, I struggle to do the same with my mother.

Summarizing the recent drama in Velm is easy enough—but doing as Helisent suggests, writing about myself, leaves me baffled and silent.

I hear Malasuntra's words echo in my mind.

'But you are very quiet.'

I take a deep breath, quill primed against the paper.

'I will help you find your voice.'

Helisent studies my hand as I hold the quill. A cylinder filled with maroon, almost black, dove sits in her palm. It takes me a moment to understand that her dove is darker because it's highly concentrated; she's sending a *lot* of amorphous magic.

"Just write one sentence if you're overthinking it." She clears her throat, then murmurs, "You could say you got married. I'm sure that would make her happy."

I nod, but quickly drop that idea. In the end, I write a few fragile sentences. They summarize the truest things I know about myself. Maybe the words don't communicate much about my personality, but it's a start.

'Clearbold sent me to fell the wooly when Night came after your disappearance. Hetnazzar came and killed the wooly on my behalf. I didn't tell anyone. I should have. A good Alpha should know his flaws; Malasuntra says mine is having no voice.'

I hand Helisent the parchment and she wraps it around the cylindrical tube. The maroon dove leaves the paper coated in a heavy red light.

She brings the pieces to her lips with one hand and holds my mother's braid with the other. She closes her eyes and says, "Imperatriz 713 Afador resides on the island Pit. She came onto the ship to offer me food and water when I lay dying. Vex, I ask you to give the appropriate honor to Imperatriz 713 Afador for saving my life. Our glory is owed to her."

Goosebumps line my skin. For a moment, this rickety hovel is a palace of hope.

"Take this offering of dove and this note, written by Samson 714 Afador, to Imperatriz 713 Afador. Use this braid to find her. First, you are to put this offering in a place where she will see it. Second, you are to help her use this dove to achieve her will. Third, you are to refill this cylinder with more dove if Imperatriz requests or needs more magic."

Helisent takes another long breath. The cylinder sits balanced in her small hands like a blood-filled rod. I can sense her magic within it; dense and roiling, like the ocean during a storm.

With a sigh, the witch lifts our blanket, sets the parchment-wrapped-cylinder into its shadows, then flattens the fabric. In a matter of seconds and with a few motions, the cylinder disappears.

A dusky village on a forgotten island isn't a place for conjuring miracles, but I'm still hopeful. For all my doubt, I trust Helisent's power. Vex's power.

She offers me a fleeting smile. "I hope it works—and half of magic is just wishing, so... cross your fingers."

I try to smile back, though I'm uncertain of how to feel. I'm hopeful and doomed; optimistic and unyielding.

Helisent sighs. "I wish I could hold you."

I raise my eyebrows. "I'm very open to being held right now." Anything to calm the tides of hope, doom, and uncertainty.

The witch leans onto her hands and knees to close the space between us. We shift into a familiar shape; Helisent sits in my lap, butt on one of my thighs and legs hiked onto the other. I wrap my arms around her, folding her against my chest. Her head falls against my collar, near my neck, and I bend to bury my nose into her hair.

"I mean hold you like this," she says quietly. "Where I'm the big one and you're the little one. I wish I could make you feel safe how you make me feel safe."

She angles her neck to stare up at me.

I look into her red eyes. I wish she was the big one and I was the little one, too. At least for a day or two. "You make me feel safe. Just because I can't fit into a little ball like you doesn't mean you don't comfort me."

Her fingertips trace my features, starting with my lips and then moving up my nose. "Remember when you said that if you could pick any future for yourself, you'd pick me? That me and you would be together, and you would throw me into the snow?"

Every morning, every night.

Too needy.

One day, I'll write it all down just to have a private fantasy of my own.

Too fanatical.

Tell me you think of it, too. Tell me you need me how I need you, Vexen.

...And if she doesn't?

Afraid that if I open my mouth, all three of those thoughts will spew out, I nod in response.

Helisent straightens, half-rising onto her knees so we're at eye level. I could count her white eyelashes, the streaks of crimson and vermillion woven in her pupils. Her eyes are landscapes. Like a part of Velm that I know instinctually.

"I want that, too," the witch whispers. "I'd even let you throw me into the snow. Just once—don't be fucking stupid, Samson. But I'd like that. You taking me to Velm. You showing me the snow. I want to smell it."

She clears her throat.

Her voice lowers even further—not for fear of being heard, as I'm certain Helisent cast a smothering spell around the hut, but out of something... something like respect.

Maybe it hurts her to feed this impossible dream of ours. Maybe it hurts her to keep this love alive with tiny morsels of affection and freedom knowing we have to hide it again someday in darkness, in lies, in self-control.

(It hurts me.)

She says, "Sometimes... sometimes I do this crazy thing. This *unwise* thing."

A lump forms in my throat. I try to swallow it away. "Tell me."

She closes her eyes and leans forward to press our cheeks together. Her breath is warm when she whispers into my ear, "There's this imaginary world in my head. I made one with Milisent when we were little. We called it Gooseworld. But this one... this one I make with you."

My hands spread across her upper back and her hip. The lump in my throat aches and aches. "Tell me everything."

I close my eyes, holding Helisent and pretending we're already there. Whatever place she makes for us in her head.

"I call it Vieira. It's all the best things about Mieira and Velm. There are snow-capped mountains for you. Like Rouz. The place you like. We live in a long hall of marble. The mountains are for you, but the valleys are for me—there are many hot springs to keep me happy, and plenty of dancehalls, and a bloodred marble column in my honor.

"In Vieira, I can always smell you how I do now." Her nose skates the tender skin behind my ear. I can't tell if she's miming the way I smell her or if she's really able to smell me better there. "My robe is white. White like snow, because you love snow, and it matches my hair."

Her warm hand spreads across my cheek, cradling me while we breathe entangled.

So long as I don't open my eyes, I believe in that place whole-heartedly.

Vieira.

"Do you want to live there with me?" Helisent asks.

"Yes. I do." *Forever.* I clear my throat, tightening my arms when she tries to pull back. "You're not the only one who has a special place for us."

She nuzzles into me with a low giggle. "Really?"

"Really." My heart skips a beat. For a split second, I try to turn away from this conversation, knowing it will hurt me. But... "You didn't mention pups in Vieira. Ours would be pith, you know."

Helisent giggles again. Her hand shifts from my cheek to my chest. "Well, they would be *puplings,* since they're half-witch, Samson. And our greatest gift to them would be that they're pith. They wouldn't be like us. They would be useless and *free.* Nobody asks anything of the magicless."

That's not exactly how I would phrase it, but warmth spreads from my gut throughout my body. She actively thinks of a future with *me.* Of a pupling with *me.*

I don't want to let go.

Vieira is real so long as I don't open my eyes.

So long as I ignore this stupid hut and this moons-awful continent.

I press farther into the darkness, into the imaginary place where

Vieira's snow-capped mountains cradle a valley with enough hot springs to keep the Vexen warm through Night.

"And what about our pith puplings?" I go on. "When I imagine Vieira, I see daughters with red horns."

(They won't have horns. They won't ever be born. Vieira will never exist. But this is my imaginary sanctuary. And in it, my daughters take after their mother. No more half-brothers. No more legacies of fathers and sons. Just giggling and screaming and being small enough to hold in my arms. I'd probably be able to hold all of them at once. I would be the night sky and they would be my moons.)

"And they'd have hair white like snow."

Helisent makes a long and happy sound. "How does two sound? I only need two to make up for the Vexen I've taken from this world. All the rest will just be extras."

It's easier to see with each word. "Then we'll need two more red marble columns."

"Here's the thing, my Kulapsifang—I want your marble column to be black, not white. Blackish blue like your hair. Like the night sky where all the moons and stars are."

Sometimes, it feels like we share the same thoughts. Like there's a thread that connects my mind to hers and, along that thread, our thoughts are whispered to one another.

With a long sigh, Helisent pulls back. She snorts, tugging on my tunic. "Open your eyes, Samson."

"Not yet." I shake my head. "It's too real. I can almost smell it. If I open my eyes, it'll disappear."

She falls against me with a sultry laugh. She kisses me, lips soft and warm. "Fine, then. If we're continuing with this fantasy, then I think you know what comes next."

I'm very hopeful I do. Still, I raise my eyebrows. "What's that?"

She kisses me again. "Making *tons* of fuck."

I open my eyes at the awful phrase; Vieira scatters like a series of broken memories in my head, replaced by Helisent's image. She sits in front of me with a wide smile and a ratcheting cackle.

"I didn't realize you hated the phrase *that* much." She leans forward and kisses me, still laughing. "I'll be more mindful."

Then she perches in my lap again, her warm curves draped across me. Our hands roam the other; she tangles her hands in my hair, runs her nails lightly over my arms and chest. I kiss her neck, burying myself in her ala while I hold her against me.

It's the only way to conclude a dream of Vieira. The only way to soften the blow of waking up.

Helisent uses magic to undress me, starting with my tunic and pants and ending with hers. The night's chill fills the hut; I tug one of the blankets over us as we lay down. I drape it over my back as I angle toward the witch.

I keep the blanket over my shoulders, sealing us beneath.

I want to be entirely separate from the world right now.

I lean down to kiss her and she rises to meet me. Our alas pool between the blanket's fragile bounds and the sheets below. Without rushing, we kiss, our bodies growing warm and our alas layering. We crane against one another, the witch's hands stroking me as I grip her ass and her hips. I lean down to kiss her breasts, to kiss her belly, to run my cheek across its soft ridge. But she doesn't let me drift farther down; she pinches my hair, then guides me back toward her lips.

"I want you closer," she murmurs. "Inside of me."

She shimmies down toward my cock. I shift onto my knees, then lean my weight onto my hands near her head. She watches me; I can feel her eyes searching me for something.

She reaches up to hold my chin as I nudge into her, eyes delving into mine. I see the poisonous berries of the yew tree in them; the fresh blood spilled from my prey; the split cherries that fall in Velmic groves.

She holds my chin; she wants me to stare back at her. For a second, I feel bare, stripped inside and self-conscious of how I must look when under her spell. She fits around me so perfectly, wet and hot and comforting; it's hard not to groan, not to grind my teeth, not to curse and forget what my face looks like.

Her eyelids droop while she watches me work over her. She raises her hands and runs her nails across my chest and my arms, not so gently this time. The pain of her scratching distracts me sometimes; the first time she did it, I thought she was reacting out of pain. Now, it's a sign of pleasure that hints she's enjoying herself.

I please her for as long as I can, claiming one orgasm, then two, as I shift from long and deep strokes to more shallow teases. I pause when her hips shift and her legs shiver—

I lean down to kiss her neck, her lips, and then look into her eyes. "What do you call me in Vieira?"

"You are my Kulapsifang," she whispers into my lips, "no matter where we go."

"And you are my Vexen," I whisper into hers. "You are my witch."

Forever.

"Who lives in Vieira with us?" I ask.

Helisent's eyes clench shut. She bites her lip, moaning, and I kiss her chin, her cheeks. "Only happy beings," she says breathlessly. "We're all happy in Vieira."

"I will always make you happy, Vexen."

Forever.

"And how do we get there?" I ask.

My body trembles, gut clenching with the urge to lift Helisent's hips and drive deeper into her.

The witch stares up at me, cheeks flushed with red and breasts shaking with each panted breath. "I'll take us." She arches her back and moans, raising her hips in time to meet mine. "I'll do it all, Samson. Just don't stop."

My breath catches as I see her breathing stutter. I lift a hand and grip the pillow near her head as red-hot pleasure breaks through me.

Helisent runs her hands over me gently, calming me as I shift onto my side and tug her close to me.

She huffs and sighs and cuddles in; I like having her sticky body so close to mine, pasting her ala across me. I start to fall asleep within a few minutes, exhausted from the day and our dreaming and our love-making. I wait for Helisent to break away like she usually does, to sprawl across the bed. (She complains that I run too hot, that my chest hair scratches her delicate skin, that I snore how boulders fall down mountainsides.)

Tonight, she doesn't.

Helisent's head falls slack against my chest. Her breaths come heavy and long. And then she starts to snore.

That night, I dream of Helisent.

She's not climbing through the yew tree as a child. Instead, she's an adult, wearing the same shirt-dress that she does in Hella. We're standing side by side on a small hillock, staring down at a massive yew tree.

Its thickest branches bow back toward the earth. They touch the ground before rising again, creating a thick seam of shadow around the yew's trunk. Heavy red berries dot the shaggy emerald needles.

A few of the branches shift, trembling from their base to their fluttering ends. I squint, then glance at Helisent. "It looks like something's down there."

She gasps. Her eyes widen as they fix on me; it doesn't look like she notices the yew tree at all. "Samson... Samson, what happened?"

I look down. Red strings tangle around my limbs. They remain loose rather than pulled tight; this tells me the faceless witch isn't lingering.

So why is Helisent so nervous?

"What do you mean?" I ask.

She reaches out, gulping down a breath, then touches one of the strings. She pulls on it; it goes slack, hanging from my arm. "When... how?"

Before I can answer, something shifts below the yew tree, causing its branches to rustle.

I squint; I can make out strings weaving through the branches, taut and bright. They droop from the tallest branches, collecting on the ground and disappearing amid the grass.

Something shuffles below the yew's broad canopy. The red strings and the branches they're tied to shift again, going taut, as something that looks like a shadow huffs along the ground.

The dark shape slowly comes into focus.

Helisent presses against my side. "Samson, what is that?"

I know what I will see this time.

I'm not afraid.

Hetnazzar's perked ears and its blue-black fur come into focus. The great wolf sits on its belly, head raised and paws crossed. Its head angles as we watch, shifting down toward something trapped between its paws.

Helisent's nails dig into my arm, past the light strings. "Is it... Is it...?"

"It's Hetnazzar."

"Not that," she gasps. "It's holding..."

Hetnazzar shifts again, exposing more of itself from the yew's branch-laden shadows. I make out more of the demigod's features; its gleaming nose and the cold, white fangs poking past its maw. The jagged black nails of its massive paws—

And the thing between those paws—

It's a jagged cut of bloodred limestone, half as tall as the witch.

"The Hellastone," she murmurs.

Hetnazzar shifts its head again; I recognize the angle the great demigod seeks. It's the same I use in my form when biting into a bone.

Like me, Helisent jolts forward, hands raised as the demigod gnashes into the limestone.

And then the piece cracks, breaking in two with a vicious sound.

I shout at the same time Helisent screams—

We stagger forward and the dream gutters. It shifts from a mountainside to something dark and enclosed.

I study the jagged rock that surrounds us above and below—black and tepid and addled with rot. I inhale deeply. It's not totally unfamiliar.

I've seen shale like this before.

Tet?

Helisent whips her head toward me, as though wondering the same thing.

Why are we in Tet?

I wake, sitting up so fast my head spins. I take a deep breath to get my bearing in the rickety shack in New Hypnos.

Helisent also stares ahead at the wall, eyes wide as she pants for breath.

She turns toward me, jaw tense. "I had the craziest dream."

My mind goes still. My body goes still. "You saw it, too?"

She nods, blinking quickly.

Neither of us say the words yew tree, or Hetnazzar, or Hellastone.

I rub my face.

Then I ask the question I should have a long time ago, "Helisent... the strings. The red strings. They're—that's your dove, isn't it?"

She nods, cheeks pale. "Not just dove, but spells. Dove is... amorphous. Spells are strings."

"Spells? What kind of spells?"

"I don't know," she whispers.

"And dreams? Are dreams a type of magic? They changed after Alita, Helisent. The seething dreams."

She looks away from me, voice dropping. "I don't know, Samson. Like you said, Vex cast the spell in Alita. Not me." She rubs her shoulder with a sigh. "And what about your demigod?"

I don't dream of my demigod. Before these recent dreams, I hadn't seen the great wolf since I was twelve years old and waiting for death with a wooly mammoth before me.

"I don't know."

She nods. "So, we don't know."

I nod back.

CHAPTER 19

LIKE AN EIGHTH HORN

HELISENT

Honey Baby,
I was always going to fail you. That's why me and the Boys liked Samson when
we met him in Alita. He taught you how to breathe. Isn't that crazy? I never
taught you how to breathe. It never even crossed my mind.
Papa P.

From Hella's northernmost streets, I look down upon my city. It slopes down from where I stand toward the fountain at its center. Gentle golden light surrounds the plaza below. Overhead, light from Marama, Laline, and Cap flood in, tracing the rooftops and their spires with silver and pink and greenish hues.

The triplemoon.

Three phased wolves await my tiny army outside of Hella, dressed in fur and fangs.

A few hundred miles east, Ezit lies unsuspecting.

I stare across the city, trying to memorize how the tile mosaics catch the light as they blanket the curved buildings. How the streets tangle and untangle in perfect chaos.

I sigh, emptying my lungs.

There's just one last place to say goodbye to.

I cross the street toward the Hellastone's empty hall.

I haven't had the nerve to venture here since Samson and I

returned from New Hypnos. I still see his demigod breaking the Hellastone. I still hear that awful *crack* echoing in my mind. But I've been too much of a coward to see if a dream might be more than a dream.

My fists clench as I wander closer.

From far below, chatter and hooting echo from my tiny army.

I step into the doorless threshold, into the silence that pools between its tiled walls.

I freeze, gut clenching.

In the center of the hall, remnants of the Hellastone lay scattered across the floor, shattered into dozens of pieces. The wasted limestone shards are pale and grayish; lifeless, magicless.

"Fuck." I clench my jaw to keep from screaming the word.

I wander toward the stone as dread washes through me.

I can't say I'm surprised, but I'd hoped the dream was only a dream.

I kneel before the shards, studying the limestone chunks.

'What comes next destroys you.'

I've run from that prophecy, pretending it's not my destination.

But here I am.

Standing before my Landmark's broken core.

Before I stand, a bloodred sliver catches my eye. I pick up a plain stone, turning it over. Gray pebbles flake away, revealing a bright and rod-like red piece lodged into the stone.

I pinch the bloodred stick by one end and pull it free.

The straight rod is as long as my hand and as narrow as a finger, rounded at either end. I hold it up, studying it in the dim light. It's disproportionately heavy for being so small, like a bottomless bag.

The vision of the bottle pops into my head—

I clench the rod as I see a small and familiar hand pick up the bottle in my mind's eye. It lifts it overhead, then brings it down with a grunt.

I wait for the vision to dissipate, then steel myself for what comes next.

It's too late to back out.

I stand, tallying the shards of gray rock and then glancing at the red-tiled walls. It feels like any other empty room; I can't remember if it always felt this way. If the hall changed or if I have. I back away to the entrance, uncertain of what to do—with the rod, with the realization that dreams might not just be dreams, with the shattered bottle in my mind.

I wait a moment longer in hopes of a positive omen.

Nothing.

I turn and leave the hall.

For the last time.

Ezit looks larger the second time around.

I wander toward it with my tiny army at my back.

We pass through the remains of the pine barren, toward Ezitlos and the mammoth city beyond. We walk silently, my papa at my side.

The first time I came, I'd been more focused on Ezitlos's thirty-foot walls than those looming miles in the distance, where the city's streets rise toward its upside-down, hanging avenues. And even then, I didn't have much time to gaze in wonder.

The Hosts had arrived and I'd turn my attention to their glowing horns and ailing Landmarks.

I never had the chance to appreciate how massive Ezit is.

In my memory, it seemed smaller.

I take a few steps toward Vex's red limestone portion of Ezitlos. My neck bends as my head tilts back and I study the city again.

My only comfort is that I can now distinguish five neighborhoods. Each is differentiated by architecture and colorful accents. They branch out from Ezitlos like spokes on a wheel, broadening as they expand toward the vertical portions. Houses and trees hang from the walls, gridded into neat streets with accents that look like lampposts and sculptures.

Structures descend from above, hanging from the inverted walls.

Many are multilevel. Squinting, I can make out at least six floors on one narrow tower in the House of Argot.

Combined with multistory buildings on the ground level, the city almost looks like the jaws of a great beast.

I clutch the rod on reflex.

So far, the limestone piece has done little but warm in my sweaty palm. Still, I'm hopeful that it's capable of something great. Something like a miracle.

I glance over my shoulder.

The vampires don't spare a glance at the city. Around forty formidable warriors stretch and converse in a loose group. For the first time since Vic wandered into Hella, her den wears a semblance of clothes. They aren't *clothes,* per se—but each wears enough leather sheaths to pass briefly like layers.

Some sheaths hold curved blades no longer than my palm, while others shelter straight daggers as long as my arm. The shined leather straps glisten beneath the golden streetlights of Ezit and the silver glow of the moons overhead.

Near the vampires stand the Mieirans, huddled and silent. They press their shoulders together as they study Ezit's walls and inverted tiers. Aura and Eos look feverishly from Meres, then to the city, and then to Hemlock.

The phased wolves lurk behind both groups, raising their noses to inhale loudly. Samsonfang glances my way cyclically, shifting around the Mieirans to move in tandem with me. At either flank, Rexfang and Berevaldfang stay close enough to graze his shoulders. Rexfang hasn't shifted his gaze from the city, while Berevaldfang whines every time the vampires wander into new formations.

Vulcan and Vega stand to the side, clutching the other's hands. Like the Mieirans, their eyes rove over the cityscape, soaking up every detail. "That must be Argot," Vulcan tells her, gesturing eastward. "Directly across from Vex. See the tower overhead? I've heard about that. It's their guild."

Vega doesn't linger long on the hanging tower. Instead, she focuses on Argot's slice of Ezitlos. Her eyes glimmer as they fix on the ailing geyser, which sputters water and fragile rainbows.

Zeu walks over and plants himself between me and the white witch. From my periphery, I see Vic lead the dens toward the obsidian wall that borders the House of Talos. The shimmering black stone goes on and on and on, disappearing into the night.

The King of Night shifts to block my view of the wall. "Not yet."

I roll my eyes. "I wasn't going to knock it down. I'm here waiting dutifully for the signal."

Rather than snide smiling or glimmering eyes, Zeu looks calm— almost lethally at peace. "Good. And what else did we agree on?"

I should have saved my eye roll. Dutifully, I tally off Zeu and Vic's list of rules. "I won't go into the city. I'll be here in Ezitlos with Parsifal like a sitting duck to draw in the Hosts. You and your little warmongers will have all the time in the world to find the underground chambers and free the okeanids and degis."

His features don't deviate. It's hard not to study his bulky muscles; they seem firmer and larger. His veins are nearly black with rosfrost, a stark contrast to his milky skin. The longer I stand in his shadow, the more nervous I become.

His icy tone doesn't help. "Say it again—*you will not go into the city*."

My features pinch. "You fucking heard me, Zeu."

"You *cannot* handle close-quarters combat. You saw what happened in Hella. You *are not ready*. We need you here to handle the offensive spells—remember, they'll come from above. And you will—"

"Respond *defensively*." I roll my eyes again. It might be my last chance, after all. "We've gone over this for weeks. Do you think I'm stupid?"

"I think you have a head full of dangerous ideas and little to no discipline." His pessimistic tone bothers me; I'm not sure where all the doubt has suddenly come from. Up until now, he hasn't seemed worried about my resolve. "Do not deviate from the plan. Everything relies *on the plan*."

I set my hands on my hips. "So, you uphold your half and I'll uphold mine."

He nods. "Very good."

"Can I help you with anything else? You're hovering." *Also, you infuriate me.*

Zeu glances over his shoulder. The vampires shift into five distinct formations along the border to Talos. The Mieirans drift into place behind them, including Rexfang and Berevaldfang.

Only Samsonfang hangs back, sitting resolutely with his eyes glued to my exchange with the vampire.

He and his packmates haven't had enough time to acclimate to the vampires' presence. They did well with Vic's den on the doublemoon —but Zeu's retinue arrived after. Now, it's up to the wolves sterling self-control to separate allies from enemies. To trust the decisions of Zeu and Vic's denmates when the action starts.

But a wolf in its form is the most capricious creature in the world —and I say that as the last Vexen. Stood in front of the King of Night.

Zeu spares a glance at the wolves. He doesn't seem worried by their proximity to his warriors or the murky unknowns pooling in their blue-black eyes.

He turns back to me. "We're ready. Once the wall is down, you will stay here in Ezitlos with Parsifal and watch the skies to..."

I direct my fingers toward the glittering obsidian that pens in Talos, cutting the vampire off with a destroying spell. I do it partly to shut him up—and partly to convince myself I'm ready for this and partly to end this terrible, awful tension.

My magic soars from my fingertips and crashes into the wall. A single seam of broken obsidian expands into vein-like ravines. Starting from the point of impact near Ezitlos, the stone crumbles into massive shards.

Some buckle toward us, spilling onto Vex's red limestone and sending the vampires scattering. Others buckle inward, crushing onto the rooftops and roads of Talos's outermost streets. They settle into place, kicking up fragile dust.

My papa comes to my side as the Mieirans close the distance between the vampires and skulk toward the city. The groups wait at its crumbling border, primed for action.

Zeu and Vic step into place leading them. Vic throws her arm into the air, then she leaps over the obsidian chunks and lands inside the House of Talos.

The rest of the vampires slip between the gaps in the dark stone like pale droplets. Mieirans follow them, along with Vulcan and Vega. Samsonfang spares one last glance before he leads his pack into the fray.

Within minutes, shouting echoes from the streets. The loud warning cries turn into crazed screaming; mindless, wordless, panicked.

They're quickly followed by vibrations of ultrasound and the wolves' vicious growling. Penned in from the rest of the city, the terrible sounds echo around Ezitlos. Though we had discussed tipping the slabs penning in Ezitlos, I didn't want to risk harming the Landmarks.

My papa's hand encircles my wrist, his shoulder warm against mine.

I glance around Ezitlos every few seconds, waiting. I look at the shadows that hug the obsidian, then to the Landmarks. I lean my head back to study Ezit's uppermost tiers—Zeu and Vic have been adamant that it's where I'll face the most action.

But for what seems like an endless period, all me and my papa hear is the slow and methodical slaughter of Talos.

Breaking glass, fire-laced explosions, growling and barking, booms of ultra and infrasound.

I ignore the cries of the children. The desperate pleas of the adults.

I can't make out their words but it doesn't help lessen how awful this feels.

"Why hasn't anyone showed up yet?" I clear my throat, eyes jumping around Ezitlos. "I think they're trying to psyche us out, papa."

"That's okay. I'm not scared."

Even my voice is shaking. "And why not?"

"If I die, I get to see Andromeda and Milisent. If I live, I get to stay with you. The same is true for you, Honey Baby." He gasps, raising a stubby finger skyward. "Look—did you see that?"

High above, three piercing lights flicker. They gather and flare in the central circle of open air pitting Ezit's upside-down streets. I squint, trying to piece together what kind of spell the Hosts will attempt first.

I shake out my shoulders and my hands, preparing to cast swiftly.

While I do, the rod thrums in my left hand.

I lift it—I'd nearly forgotten about the red piece, having used it largely as a worry stone in the last hours.

"Vex," I whisper toward it. "I don't know what this means."

Parsifal leans over and looks away from the sky. "What's that?"

Before I can respond, the light overhead bursts like a flash of lightning. I flinch, looking away, as the magic gathers and thunders like a monsoon, roiling and growing.

Then the shadow hugging Argot's obsidian wall shivers with ultrasound. A wielder with a swaying white cloak and white boots steps into Ezitlos. Four large horns glow like the white-hot magic gathering above.

My eyes dart from the lights to the Host—

I can't focus on both threats.

My mind splinters—

I choose.

I raise my hand toward the Argyd Host. The last time I came here, the Host leveled Vex's pine barren. Compared to that, Parsifal can't be a difficult target.

But my split-second window to defend my papa ends when the blinding spell tilts overhead and then spills down toward us. Within it are multiple pitches of magic, blended from multiple Houses.

I shift my gaze upward, eyes widening.

It's not a monsoon at all—this spell is shaped like a cannonball and it's filled with blazing, fiery magic.

It sails toward us, now incomprehensibly silent and unfathomably colossal.

I stare stupidly overhead. Every spell I envisioned disappears amid my dumbstruck terror.

The rod buzzes in my left hand again.

On instinct, I raise the limestone piece toward the incoming attack. At the same time, Parsifal steps in front of me to focus on the Host.

That's all I see from my periphery as a spell gathers in the tiny red rod.

Magic careens from its rounded tip. I lower my stance, bending my legs to steady myself as bass shakes the ground beneath me. It soars up through my body and out of the rod.

I gasp as it passes through me.

I can feel magic in my eyelashes, in my breath, in my joints. Everywhere in that split-second.

The spell takes shape as it flies from the rod, ripping into the air and spanning wide to form a blunted shield. It meets the fiery cannonball mid-air, unleashing a storm of bass and sparks as the spells collide.

Fire and wind ricochet outward, racing toward Ezit's walls and tearing homes and trees from their sideways foundations. Others catch on fire, sending more golden light wheeling throughout the city.

The sound alone is enough to stun me.

I stagger back a step, blinking overhead.

The magic dissipates into the air. My ears ring from the sound, heartbeat pounding.

With a jolt, I come back into my body. Parsifal lies on the ground a

few feet away, clutching his knee. Blood pours from his arm, seeping
into his cloak. He jerks his hand toward the Argyd Host on the other
side of Ezitlos, his cheeks red and features bent.

Papa.

The rod vibrates in my left hand again.

I can feel Vex's limestone beneath me, the power of the full moons
above me.

Red fills my body, my soul.

Red fills my horns as my form spreads across my body.

I don't feel bad about the screaming children anymore.

I will never feel bad about anything ever again.

This city tried to capture me. This city produced Anesot. This city
now wants to kill my papa.

Papa.

I direct the rod toward the Argyd Host, who stands a few feet
behind the geyser that sputters mist and rainbows. All I see are two
glowing white eyes beneath four glowing white horns, half-obscured
behind a transparent veil. Two nails press through the veil, pointed at
the warlock on the ground at my side.

Those glowing eyes fix on me. Their hand shifts, too.

I think one word.

One word—again and again and again.

Destroy.

A scream rips from my lungs as infrasound breaks the air around
me and another spell shoots from the rod.

Once again, I'm not sure what type of magic it is—just that Vex is
wielding itself now between my flesh and this rod, and I'm fine with
that so long as this city suffers.

The spell hits the Argyd Host first. The wielder staggers backward, as though rammed straight in the chest. Then they float upward
ten feet into the air, robes and limbs hovering weightlessly.

Stunned, the Host attempts to break free, bucking and jerking
with their glowing white eyes fixed on me—

But my spell is not finished.

It barrels on, obliterating the obsidian wall so that Ezitlos looks
like its missing a tooth. The battering spell gains speed and power as
it lays waste to Argot's neighborhood and sails toward Ezit's outer
wall—

On and on and on in a straight path from the poised rod in my left hand—

Vex's magic levels the neighborhood.

Like the floating Host, the remnants of Argot float aloft ten feet into the air.

Glass shards hover amid shattered windowframes, salons and kitchens float away from their foundations. Half-finished meals amid displaced plates, flowers and dirt rising from broken pots. Books, shoes, birds, lampposts, cups. There are wielders, too, tangled amid their cloaks and the debris of everything they ever knew and loved.

I swear I could count it all, every shattered piece of Argot.

Doors float free of their frames, carts of their produce.

I can feel every dark memory that had been stacked in the room of lost memories clatter back into the light.

I am suddenly whole again.

And I'm livid.

My papa?

Destroy.

I scream again.

With another bass-filled boom, magic spews from the rod. Every floating item slams onto the ground; whatever survived the first wave of destruction isn't so lucky this time.

Dust billows into the air. The fires taking hold of Ezit's vertical and upside-down streets spread, sending smoke and embers into the air. The air boils with heat and light and infrasound.

I stare ahead, waiting for the dust to calm so I can search Argot for survivors.

Destroy.

My papa stares at me from the ground, eyes wide and glassy. With a shuffle, he holds his bloody arm and sits up, careful with his knee.

I rush to his side. He's wounded above his elbow and his knee is dislocated, but neither injury is life-threatening. I get to work on the flesh wound first, pressing my free hand to his broken skin.

He stares ahead at what remains of the House of Argot, throat bobbing. A few feet away from the sputtering geyser, the Host lays still.

I move on to Parsifal's knee. He jolts when my magic shoves it back into place. He licks his lips and clutches my shoulder as I help him to his feet.

I dust off his cloak, then glance overhead; no more flashing lights. "Are you okay?"

"Right as rain, Honey Baby." He scans me next, taking my arm. "Are *you?*"

I almost roll my eyes, but I'm cut off by a wave of nausea.

I buckle at the waist and spit as saliva fills my mouth. I shiver, trying to shake it off. I don't make it far before I hurl onto the ground where I stand.

My papa pats my back as I clear my mouth and spit. "Why don't you try pacing yourself from here on out?" I wait for him to lecture me on my cruelty and inefficiency, but he gasps in the next second. "Oh, look! They're here! That was faster than I thought it'd be. *Ha!*"

Without letting go of my arm, he shouts over my curled form, "Welcome, my dear okeanids! Wait over there—yes, by the shadows. I'll be there in a moment. This is Helisent, by the way. Don't mind the horns. She's on your side. You don't have a drink with you? Not water —booze. Actually, some water would be nice. Neither? Oh. That's okay. Welcome to Vex!"

The invasion of Ezit passes both quickly and endlessly in a series of split-seconds, strung together in an awful tapestry.

The invasion of Talos leads to the House of Serac. Within hours, both Houses have fallen. Alone with Parsifal, I'm only certain of our progress based on the gradual shift of terrified screaming; it moves clockwise incrementally.

All the while, Hosts and powerful wielders work together to conjure monstrous attacks. They descend every twenty minutes. Once Talos and Serac fall, the violent assaults from Argot and Col double in power.

They rain down on me as my papa ferries the freed captives to safety further in Vex.

I think we're winning.

It's only because of the rod.

And, despite my hopes at the night's start, it isn't a lasting solution.

My instincts are tied to Vex's power—and both seem to pool and coalesce inside the rod. But I've been leeching energy since I obliterated Argot; my fatigue only spirals from there. My body can only contain and direct so much dove. Flesh isn't nearly as enduring as limestone.

As the terrified screams shift toward the already-leveled House of Argot, my body grows heavy. My quick breaths burn.

I keep looking east, hoping for a trace of dawn.

Please. Please let this end before my strength gives out.

I don't care if it destroys me—I just have to last until I can shadow us to New Hypnos.

A while later, my tiny army races back through the crumbled obsidian wall from the House of Col. I curse with relief; I hadn't noticed the groups enter the House of Lahar or advance into Col.

My papa rushes over to receive the group.

Argumentative shouting drifts over. I do a double take as I monitor the sky, but I don't recognize anyone as they mill around and shout. Almost everyone is covered in ash and debris, limping and hunched over, wide-eyed and shaking.

My papa drags one of them toward me, supporting him by the arm.

I squint at the man, confused. A tattered lilac robe hangs from his body. Soot covers his beard, which is half singed off.

Hemlock.

He shouts, "Helisent—Col set their captives loose. It's down to Lahar. We couldn't get into the chambers. They're fortified. Butter— we have Butter—Butter is free—we're halfway through—all of us— Lahar will hold—Lahar—we will come back..."

I glance at my papa; he looks just as concerned by Hemlock's monologue.

My exhaustion isn't helping.

An okeanid rushes toward us next. She seizes Hemlock's free arm, stepping in front of him. "*No*—Otrera is in Lahar—we will not leave without our queen."

She lets go of Hemlock to seize my arm.

I shove her out of my way when I see flashing lights gathering above. They're harder to make out now that fire is gnawing through half the city.

I step away from the frantic trio and raise the rod. A shielding spell mushrooms from the stone, spanning across the city to shelter us. Hundreds wait behind me. They scream and flinch at each attack, as though fully prepared for a sudden and fiery end.

I lunge back a step.

This spell isn't the patchwork effort from Zarzynnian wielders who have survived our invasion. It's a pointed explosion that gains momentum with every second. It batters into Vex's shielding spell, cracking it like an eggshell.

Its momentum is narrowed to a single point—and it's aimed directly at me.

I stagger back another step but manage to keep my hand raised and the rod pointed overhead.

Icy air shivers around its rounded end, like a breath of winter. Then Vex's spell explodes like a beast from a cage, unhinging its jaws to consume Lahar's infrasound. It rattles through my body, shaking the ground.

Lahar's spell extinguishes fifty feet above Ezitlos like a fiery arrow shot into an avalanche. Steam gurgles above our heads as magical fire and frost meet.

I sag with fatigue.

Half-crouched, I squint to study Ezit's upside-down streets, focusing on Lahar's portion.

Fuck.

I suddenly understand why Lahar has been silent until this point. They've been letting the rest of the Houses drain their power. They've been letting me do the same.

Fuck, fuck, fuck.

Panic rushes through my body.

It hits a wall of utter exhaustion.

My legs want to buckle. I think if I laid down and closed my eyes, I could fall asleep on the limestone.

How many more spells can Lahar conjure like that—and how many can I deflect?

And most importantly...

How much energy do I need to spare to shadow our group to New Hypnos?

The okeanid rushes back toward me. My papa grabs her by the

arm, pulling her away. Then Hemlock grabs my father's cloak, entangling the trio.

I ignore the tussle. Hemlock and the okeanid are crazed, waving their arms around.

I need to focus.

I comb through the ranks of my tiny army, searching for the missing parties.

Time to cut our losses.

Time to get me out of here—un-destroyed.

I'm sorry, Otrera.

I can't do everything.

I do a full circle, making sure I haven't missed anything.

I turn toward the bickering trio and shout, "Where are the wolves?" I glance across our numbers again. "And where are the vampires? You were supposed to stay together!"

"*Lahar!*" screams the okeanid—who I suddenly realize is Meres. She seizes me by the arm again. Like Hemlock, soot covers her face, causing her blue-bled eyes to stick out. "They're in *Lahar!* We *cannot* leave Otrera!"

I look away from Meres, scanning the group once more.

No blue-black wolves blending with the night. No pale vampires covered in holstered daggers.

My heart leaps into my throat; a fresh wave of adrenaline gives me the strength to grab Hemlock and roar, "Where the fuck are the wolves?"

Where is Samsonfang?

Where is Samsonfang?

Where—where—where—

"They're on a fucking rampage, Helisent!" the king bellows back.

"They're in Lahar!" Meres cries, taking hold of my lapels with both hands.

"They're tearing the city apart!" Hemlock goes on.

"Back off her!" My papa seizes Meres's forearm and drags her away. She kicks and screams nonsense, flailing.

Hemlock steps in front of me and grabs my shoulders. "We need to *go*. We have done what we could—good *fucking moons*—"

With a growl, I swat at his hands. I look from him to Meres. "You're fucking idiots!" I reach into my bottomless bag, hands shaking. I watch Ezit's upside-down streets with wide eyes while I call up Samson's snowflake. "I told you not to leave the wolves!"

The king gestures into the city and then to the skies. "They're on a tour de carnage—they're *wolves*—and the *moons*—"

Okay, so we've all lost it.

I don't have the energy to brainstorm a solution right now.

I don't have the wherewithal to lead for much longer.

Samsonfang is in Lahar with his packmates.

This House has held out to the very end.

This House will wield its full force against me soon.

And I...

Halcyon was right.

Accra, too.

Don't think about that. Find Samsonfang. Save his pack. Find the vampires, if you can.

I look at my papa. He clutches Hemlock by his tattered robe, knuckles white. With the other, he holds Meres by the wrist.

His face contorts with a scream as I sprint toward the nearest shadow. "*No!*"

In one hand, I clench the snowflake; in the other, I clench Vex's rod.

The shadow beckons me, my magic reaching toward me—

I use tracking and shadowing magic in the hopes of finding the wolf quickly.

But as soon as I fall into the shadow, I sense an immediate change.

It doesn't thrum with Vex's pitch of infrasound.

Instead, the pitch raises slightly.

Lahar.

It's too late to back out, too late to rehash the shadowing spell—

With a gasp, I step into a dimly lit and vast chamber. Square stones line the ground and the ceiling—even the archways circling the open floor. It almost looks like a ballroom, it's wide clearing empty and clean, its walls layered with colorful tapestries. Firelight and moonslight pour in from a round stained-glass window that takes up most of one wall. The rest of the room sits in shadows, its thick walls insulating from the bedlam outside.

I step out of the shadow.

I try to move silently, but there's nowhere to hide.

In the room's center, four figures stand hunched over, their skin burnt orange and their horns savagely aglow. They flinch, looking at me with unpleasant surprise.

I take them in quickly—

They don't wear long cloaks or veils. They wear pants and short-sleeved shirts made of modest fabric.

The smallest wielder is no more than two or three years old. The child clings to a woman with a full bosom, their cheeks wet with tears and snot. The woman kneels on the floor, arms wrapped around the littleling. A third figure looms over both, his head angled toward the witch's ear, as though whispering something to her.

The fourth wielder takes a step toward me, pitting himself between me and the family of three.

Our eyes meet—

On instinct, I raise my hand when he does.

Six horns jut from his head, including a thick, curved set curling around his ears, nearly as large as my own fifth and sixth horns.

Six horns?

It's enough to make me hesitate—

To make me wonder whether Lasan wielders are truly my enemy—

The warlock doesn't balk.

With a tremble of bass, something moves in the shadows on the room's far wall and then slams into my gut. I cry out as I stagger backward, my back hitting the shadowy wall where I entered. I barely register the pain as the rod slips from my hand and clatters onto the stone floor.

Hot blood oozes onto my dress and robe as panic magic takes over; without the rod, it comes straight from my weakened body.

Several square stones drop from the ceiling and slam onto the ground. A few more rip upward from the floor. The square blocks soar into place around me, blocking the next objects the warlock fires at me.

The stones cobble into a lightless chamber and fix to the wall at my back, sheltering me from all sides. As soon as the last stone shifts into place, darkness falls and the pain hits.

I crumble to the ground with a rasp, clutching my side. Outside, the wielders start to shout and debate. A few grazes of infrasound rattle against the stone chamber.

I curse and groan, trying to catch my breath.

Gritting my teeth, I manage to locate whatever sank into my lower right abdomen. I cry out as soon as I touch it. Pain shoots through my abdomen, down into my legs.

Whatever it is, it's as sharp as a shard of glass, as thick as a dagger. I try to grip it, but there's no hilt—the entire object seems to be a double-sided blade. I feel at its edges as my body shakes with anguish and shock.

I leave the weapon lodged inside of me to look for the rod.

I can't summon any more magic from my form. I can't even think around my pain. Worse, Lasan magic shivers around my chamber. Within seconds, the stones begin to warm uncomfortably. Though not as direct as an attack, the stones heat more with each passing second, the air boiling within.

Gasping, I run my hand along the ground, using the glow of my horns for guidance.

I find the rod just in time to save myself from being scalded by heated stones. With a growl, I direct it toward the stones and let cooling ice magic surround me.

After a minute, the magical heat lifts—but I don't know if it changes my fate.

I'm losing blood.

I'm not sure I'm seeing straight at this point.

And even if I manage to get back to Vex, I won't have the strength to take us to New Hypnos.

I scream as loudly as I can. My wound crackles with sharp pain, blood pooling on the stone beneath me. "No, no, no!"

My self-hatred at least gives me the stubborn strength to rip the object out of my abdomen, then press my hand against the wound. I grit my teeth, grinding them together. I clench my eyes in the darkness and press the rod to the lesion.

Soon, the healing magic takes hold.

Without the urgent strain of a life-ending injury, it gives me a moment's reprieve.

A single moment in which I pant in the darkness, my mind racing.

Here's the cold truth: I'm out of magic and answers.

But before I can weep from my own stupidity, a vision flickers in my head.

In my mind's eye, I see myself taking an empty bottle of brandy by its neck. This time, when I slam it onto the wooden floor and watch it shatter, I'm not dismayed and frightened.

I open my eyes and study the rod as it shines and hums, pitted with pure red infrasound and radiance.

In a deluge, it all fits together. Words and visions soar through my mind, one after the other—

'*What comes next destroys you,*' Accra tells me.

I hear the crack of the Hellastone as Hetnazzar gnashes into the Landmark in a dream.

'*A little canal never hurt a demigod, as far as I know,*' Meres says.

I see the blue of the okeanid demigod as it stares at me from the dark ocean.

I see myself take the empty green bottle and batter it against the wooden floorboards.

'*And then you will abandon this place,*' Zeu says.

I think... I think I understand...

'*What comes next destroys you.*'

'*But you'll abandon it.*'

The rod's bass-filled growl doubles, then triples. My body shivers in response.

'*What comes next destroys you.*'

It sounds bad... unless destruction isn't the end.

Accra's prophecy doesn't mention death.

'*You must already know there are two types of fate,*' Accra says.

Huddled in darkness, I have no idea where the ocean lies.

But I know that, hundreds of miles away, an okeanid demigod is waiting.

The rod guides my hand westward.

I can feel Vex's magic pool inside the smooth stone.

Limestone is much denser than flesh. Much stronger than bones or sinew.

This body has no more dove or energy within it, but this tiny rod is all that remains of the Hellastone.

And it's not so small if you count its magic.

It shivers in my shaking hand.

I think... I think I understand...

My legs wobble as I haul myself to my feet, half-bent to compensate for my half-healed wound.

In the darkness, the rod glows like an eighth horn.

Don't do it, Helisent.

There's a lot to lose if you're wrong.

I have no other option now.

I sigh, long and shaking, as I tighten my grip on the bloodred piece.

"What comes next destroys me," I whisper.

To become a fulfilled Vexen, Helisent must be reborn.

To be freed from Zarzynn, Vex's current form must be destroyed.

To spare us from annihilation, the okeanid demigod must walk into this city.

I suck down another breath.

"I am wicked and foolish," I remind myself, "and I won't ever change."

One more breath.

Warm tears slip from my eyes, down my cheeks.

I close my eyes and surrender to this.

To whatever happens after destruction.

I can sense an invisible cord running in a straight, taut line from the coastline where the demigod waits to where I stand now in the House of Lahar. I can feel it run all the way to the ocean's salty, cold water.

I can sense the demigod there, waiting, floating, envisioning.

I send whispering magic to its ear, "Follow the canal, my dear demigod. Save your okeanids—but don't forget the rest of us. Don't you dare forget Samsonfang or Parsifal South of Jaws."

One more breath.

"Vex, I'm ready."

Just one more breath—just in case it's my last—

Then, in a trembling voice, I growl, "*Destroy.*"

I feel a tremble far away, like a distant boom of thunder.

The cord spanning from me to demigod shivers, then the pressure explodes, as though snipped in half.

Magic careens from the rod and shoots westward. Deep curdles of bass reverberate through my body, through the stone chamber sheltering me.

In a shockwave, my Landmark breaks and my magic soars free. I feel it unleash as the limestone caves split open like a fruit and the seed of Vex explodes, rushing into me, into the rod—

I feel it sink into my bones, into my hair, into the breath cradled inside my lungs.

But I can only hold so much.

I fall to the ground in the darkness, terrified and panting.

I feel my dove flounder in the air, outside my body and this land.

The cavernous seam in Vex deepens, plunging westward.

I can't see it as I curl against the wall, but I can feel it, can envision it in my mind; the gulf widens and consumes the pine barrens, limestone caves bury themselves as the brittle cracks expand.

A canal takes shape, vast and deep.

Enough for a demigod to walk through.

That's the last thing I sense before silence falls; the ocean rushing toward Ezit.

For a long time, nothing happens.

My breaths grow ragged and weak as fatigue and pain overcome me.

I close my eyes. I try to stay conscious in hopes of a miracle, but my eyes drift shut. My breaths lengthen and relax.

Then a cool droplet falls onto my scalp and cheek.

I reach up. My fingers hit slimy, wet stone. I rub the substance between my fingers, then bring it to my nose.

My lips part with a relieved smile.

Salt water.

CHAPTER 20

THE TRIPLEMOON, SAMSONFANG PART III

SAMSON

My grandson,
Your mother birthed you on the triplemoon in the dead of Night; I was with
her. She wanted to tell you this after you killed the wooly and became a man. I
wanted to wait for her return so she could tell you herself. But you should know
the truth. Samson was born second, Samsonfang first.

I keep my nose low to the ground as my pack pushes further into the House of Lahar.

I pick up my pace.

Something happened in Vex—

I can't sense what changed, only that Vex's distinct infrasound just broke through the air in a tsunami of sound. It split the air and dimmed the world for a split-second. Whatever windows survived the other spells exploded this time.

Now, magic drives into my ears, my fur, my nails, my vision, my soul.

Red fills my mind.

Red fills my body.

Infrasound, too.

What has my witch done?

She must be very angry.

I keep my head low. My nose runs along piles of stone and wooden rubble. Embers burn within and smoke spews out gently. My nose runs along the corpses of the horned wielders, the coagulated blood that clogs the veins of the vampires' corpses. They lay in piles of pale limbs and tangled cloaks. I search them for survivors.

For Pel.

Down one street, then back up its far side.

Deep into Lahar.

I ignore the explosions of infrasound and ultrasound.

Flames and thick smoke and twisted lights pool overhead in a wounded night sky.

I search for Pel.

Rexfang flanks me to the left. His nose runs along the ground, too.

Berevaldfang flanks my right. An echo sounds from a narrow alley; his lips pull back from his teeth as he faces the noise.

A middle-aged warlock backs toward the shadows, twenty feet away. He hunches down in a shadow and presses his back to the wall. He hopes we won't see him.

Wolves see comfortably in moonslight-filled darkness.

Berevaldfang's tongue runs along his bloody teeth.

The warlock gasps. He stands and runs.

His feet slip on the shattered glass layering the ground.

A huff from Berevaldfang, a growl-filled snap, then a crunch of bones.

My packmate rejoins us on the street. He shakes his head; I understand the movement.

His jaw is sore. So is mine.

We keep moving down the broad avenue.

Compared to the obliterated Argot, the House of Lahar feels sentient. Like its wielders remain. Like they're spying from the blown-out windows.

My paws crunch through the rubble with each step. The sky overhead boils with sound and magic and smoke. Dawn hides behind it all; a whisper that grows in volume. I feel it on my spine.

I'm running out of time to find Pel.

I've killed dozens, maybe hundreds tonight.

It will mean nothing without Pel's death.

You bit my witch—

You bit my witch—

You bit my witch—

Near the center of Lahar, I stop.

I strain my ears.

The Houses of Talos and Serac fell first after a violent bedlam. We entered Argot to find it leveled. We crept from one underground chamber to the next, following the maps Zeu and Vic brought.

We lost the Queen and King of Night after freeing the largest underground chamber in Argot.

I had waited amid the pale flood of vampires.

I had plucked the violent degis from the ground like mites. I had snapped their spines and limbs with single nips. Their blood soaked into my gums. Their weapons sank into my paws and legs.

All this vengeance does nothing for my witch; I still have not found Pel.

He must be in Lahar.

And if not in Lahar, then in Col.

I will move methodically. I will find him.

I hurry down one street and turn down the next. Lahar's dim streets aren't destroyed; they're abandoned. It makes it easier to comb through the air for an ala—

But I don't catch the scent of another okeanid-filled, subterranean chamber.

Or Pel.

Rain begins to patter against my fur and the street. With a huff, I tilt my head back. The droplets burn my eyes and wounds; salt water, I realize. Overhead, nothing looks out of place. I glance toward Vex, miles away. Still nothing.

My head tilts. In the distance, I hear the roar of rushing water.

It sounds like an unfathomable flood, of pounding, expanding infrasound.

Take the pack back to Vex, Samson warns. **Don't be caught here when the sun rises.**

I growl. I turn away and stick my nose back to the damp street.

I have not given her vengeance, I scold.

Tonight is mine.

Pel, too.

I turn from the avenue onto a crooked lane. Rexfang turns left at the same crossroads, then Berevaldfang continues straight. So long as we revolve around one another within a close radius, our alas will carry. I will search for Pel, my packmates will search for the King and Queen of Night. Without the dens to lead us to the underground chambers, we're guided only by our noses and ears.

The former is quickly becoming less reliable as the saltwater drizzle intensifies.

It clogs my nose, soaks my fur.

I raise my head, tilting my nose skyward.

The droplets are briny—and they're steeped with okeanid magic.

With the hypnotic ala of their demigod.

As the droplets grow heavier, they start to shimmer, as though pitted with blue light.

And how did the okeanid demigod get here?

I huff to clear my nose, then continue down the alley. I make it one more block when a gust of rainswept wind carries a familiar ala.

Not Pel—

I smell Helisent West of Jaws.

Here, in Lahar.

Her ala is blurred with cortisol and the foul twang of iron— blood. A lot of blood.

My nails scratch against the stone street as I take off, legs pumping as my nose twitches—

Find her—find her—find her—Samson hisses.

Adrenaline soars through my body as I race through the streets.

Where is my witch?

She was not supposed to leave Vex.

She was not supposed to lose this much blood.

I follow her ala deep into the House of Lahar, away from my packmates.

Red fills my mind, red fills my body.

I follow her scent to a five-story clock tower. Rain patters against the street and cobbled stone edifice. With each passing minute, the deluge picks up. The rain glows brighter. It slaps the buildings as it falls slanted from the sky.

I shake it from my fur. I follow her scent to the base of the clock tower. It leads between two arched, wooden doors.

The King of Night kneels before them. Tol stands at his side. She takes a step back when she sees me. She throws a hand toward the door and shouts angrily in Zarzyd.

Her livid tone bothers me. Zeu's presence bothers me. Helisent is in trouble—

I do not trust the King of Night. He wants to manipulate and possess my witch.

I do not trust Tol. She is an outsider with whom I have made no connection.

My lips pull back from my teeth. I storm the door. Tol backs up, dragging Zeu by the arm.

The King of Night shouts at me in Mieiran. "The doors and walls are covered in rosarium and wolfbane. We need to find a window higher up or a..."

I claw at the entry. I reel back in the next second; we've encountered plenty of wolfsbane tonight. Its putrid scent shoots straight from my nostrils into my brain. My eyes clench as the scent explodes through my senses, stinging and confusing.

When I come to, Helisent's ala hits me again, leeching from the shut doors.

I claw at the doors on instinct, then reel back.

I smell four other wielders inside the clock tower.

I smell Helisent's iron-scented blood in a large puddle.

Find her—find her—find her—

The rain heightens to a downpour. The slanted droplets make it almost impossible to see.

I step back, a wrathful whine in my throat.

Helisent is inside this clock tower losing strength and blood.

Along with four other powerful wielders.

Something very intense happened in Vex, possibly to Vex.

There's a downpour that smells strongly of okeanid demigod magic.

Tol and Zeu are both irate.

I don't know where Rexfang and Berevaldfang are.

And dawn is coming.

Think, think, think.

I step back and look above. I raise my nose toward a narrow window on the clock tower's second floor. The glass is shattered, allowing me a clearer picture of what's happening within.

I was right—there are three powerful Lasan wielders and one wielderling. Each is whole and healthy.

Then there's Helisent. She already lost the fight.

When I turn back, Zeu and Tol follow my gaze. They study the window. They debate in Zarzyd, then scramble into action. Zeu locks his hands together, then lowers them between his knees and squats. Tol steps into his hands, then he hauls her upwards with a grunt. Tol leaps with a victorious shout, clawing at the stones and clambering toward the window.

One of her hands reaches its sill. She clings on tight with her fingertips, body swinging.

I step closer. I push against her foot with my nose; she pushes off with another optimistic shout. She hauls herself into the opening, then disappears inside.

I lift my nose, sniffing at the window.

"She wasn't supposed to leave Vex," Zeu shouts from the ground. "Is there a fucking reason the witch is so unmanageable? She's fucked it all up. Every single..."

I turn and growl. I lick my exposed fangs, hoping he understands.

Rosarium protects him against wielders—not wolves.

The thought spirals as I lock eyes with Zeu.

Salt water pours from the sky. It batters against us and the stone street and the abandoned buildings.

He is waiting his turn, Samson reminds me.

The King of Night angles his body—just like he did when we first met in the forest outside Hella.

I take a step away from the clock tower, skulking toward the vampire.

He draws a curved, sickle-like blade from its holster on his back.

Adorable.

Then a long and pained scream echoes from the clock tower's second-floor window. Though female, it isn't Helisent. It's followed by a powerful gust of infrasound that shakes the wooden doors. The pitch contains both Lasan and Vexen magic.

I rush back to the doors. This time, when I claw at them, the potency of the wolfbane has lessened. It pools on the ground, washed away by the downpour.

Red fills my mind.

Red fills my body.

I gnash against the doors. With a broken creak, they buckle inward. I rush forward, but the archway is too low. My snout makes it inside, but my forehead presses against the archway's keystone, trapped.

With a keen, I back out, then try again.

Helisent's ala drifts from the opened doors. She's losing strength and blood. I smell an open wound and bile—symptoms of a grave internal injury.

Before I can shove my head back through the doors, Zeu rushes past me.

I nip after him, enraged. But the archway is too low.

I growl and bark, desperate for entry.

Rain pounds against my fur, against the stones. Water gurgles up from a nearby drain. It floods into the street and laps against the walls.

My witch—my witch—my witch—

Helisent—Helisent—Helisent—

From the darkness inside, a bellow echoes, *"Move, you idiot!"*

Zeu rushes from the building. He hauls a bundled Helisent against his chest. Her horns are on full display, aglow with magic. Her tail is curled in her lap, its spade bone aglow like the rest. Even her red skin seems to glow from within, like she swallowed the sun. Her robe is torn and dirty, her eyes closed and her mouth agape.

I lunge toward the pair as Zeu sinks to his knees. He sets her on the ground, rolling back onto his haunches. My nose hits his abdomen in the next second. He flounders onto his back. I glare at him, pinning his chest as I bare my teeth.

I lick my fangs clean; they're ready to sink into his hips and rip him in half.

He grits his teeth as he glares back at me. His chest heaves.

I huff again, growling once and nudging him with my nose—

Just so he knows.

Just so he knows the witch is mine, and I could have his death if I wanted that, too, and he will never be stronger than me in any of his forms, and I will always take what I want before he does—

Because I am the King of Night.

Not this pale blood-drinker.

Not now. Later.

"Tol," Zeu says.

Begrudgingly, I release him. He scrambles onto his feet and rushes back into the clock tower.

Helisent groans and props herself up on an elbow. In one hand, she grips a glowing red rod. She presses the other to the wound near her appendix.

Her features bend with pain. Her red eyes narrow. "Samsonfang," she gasps. "That's you, right?"

I clack my teeth in confirmation. I lower my head to her side and angle my nose toward her wound. Though the lesion is largely healed, I smell an abscess from her appendix and intestines. And she's still bleeding internally.

She's losing strength and warmth.

Get her out of here, Samson shouts.

With a groan, my witch sags back toward the street. Salt water spews from the grates lining the street. It soaks Helisent's robe and washes away the blood and bile from her wound.

I set my snout next to her—

She needs to stand up.

She seems to understand. Helisent curses as she pulls herself off the ground with handfuls of my fur. She sinks back onto her butt in the next second.

Her blood sugar plummets.

She can't stand—she can barely lift herself into a sitting position.

With a pained grunt, she leans against my maw. Her eyelids flutter as she looks at me.

Her lips move but she doesn't say anything.

Panic fills my mind; my witch is never silent.

I lay on my belly, then set my muzzle on the ground again.

Helisent needs to hoist herself onto my snout. She needs to climb onto my head and hold on so I can carry her to safety.

There is no other way.

I growl. I snap my teeth together.

She stares at me. Her head sags against my fur. Her shaking hands pat my muzzle. "You go. I'll meet you there. The demigod... the demigod will know what to do."

I growl. I clack my teeth again.

Get her out of here. Please, please, please—

She shakes her head. White hair sticks to her cheeks, her neck, her blazing horns.

I nuzzle her. I cross my eyes to look up toward my head. I whine, then repeat the movement.

Helisent huffs into my fur. "You want me to get up—like on you?"

I clack my teeth together.

Before she tries, Zeu and Tol rush out of the clock tower. The latter sinks to the ground and rolls using his shoulder. He plants his foot onto the flooded street and reaches for one of his throwing stars. He unleashes three iron stars from a holster. They sing through the rain with vicious whistles, then disappear into the clock tower's shadowy precipice.

There, a six-horned wielder plants himself in the archway.

His horns glow brightly like my witch's. A tattered robe sways where it's torn from his shoulder. His molten eyes glance at me, then shoot back to the vampires.

They lock on Helisent, half-hidden behind my maw.

My witch—my witch—my witch—

I leap toward the warlock and open wide.

Rather than flee, the warlock raises his hand toward Helisent.

A spell soars from his fingertips as I sink my teeth into his shoulder and thigh. I snap my jaw shut. It aches after hours of biting and tearing, but the wielder's bones and flesh yield. With a few cracks, his body slackens atop my tongue. His blood seeps toward my throat, into my gums.

I rip my head to the side to send his body skipping over the flooded street. It falls into a dead heap forty feet away.

Behind me, Zeu pulls Tol off of Helisent. I nearly lunge and bite again—then I realize Tol was shielding Helisent.

Zeu straightens her body on the ground. He touches her face, but Tol stares upward. Raindrops hit her open, unflinching eyes.

Zeu touches and lifts her, as though searching for a wound. He bellows her name. He presses his fingers to her jugular, then lowers his head to bite her. When he pulls back, blood stains his lips and chin. His eyes are wide, unbelieving. He screams her name again.

Within a few moments, her warm blood starts to cool. Its scent of rosfrost is fading. The doses were only meant to last the night—

And dawn is coming.

Zeu bellows one last time at her corpse.

The rising water buoys the dead vampire aloft.

"Give her..." Helisent leans toward Tol. "Let me try..."

Her shaking hands settle on Tol's chest.

Zeu pushes them away.

I round Tol's corpse. Helisent leans against my paw while I crane over her. I shield her from Zeu's hands and the rain.

He leans over Tol. He touches her cheeks, the bite mark on her neck, the holsters hugging her body.

"Just let me try," Helisent says again, voice small and weak. "If your rosfrost is wearing off, then I can use magic to heal her. I can—"

"Bring someone back from the dead?" Zeu snaps.

Helisent sobs once, weak and fragile. "Zeu... we need to go back. The demigod... I don't know what it did. What I did."

And I need to find Rexfang and Berevaldfang.

Zeu leans over and pulls Tol against his chest. With a grunt, he stands and adjusts his grip. He tells Helisent, "Get us to New Hypnos like you promised. I'm taking her back to Vex. Get there. Get our dens to New Hypnos."

He turns and takes off to the northwest. Each step sloshes as the water rises and he disappears. Above, misty clouds of pale light have eaten away the red-orange of the fires. They block the brightness of the full moons, turning the sky into a glowing mirage.

I position my muzzle on the ground again.

Helisent needs to climb up.

Currents whorl through the rising tide, awash with sharp debris.

I will never question you again if you get her out of here. Samson beats at my mind like a caged beast. *Save the witch—save the witch—save the witch—*

Quiet. I'm concentrating.

I set my snout against her side. She takes a fistful of my fur with each hand, then heaves herself toward my muzzle. She sags against me, too weak to pull herself up. I tilt my head slightly, hoping to give her a better angle.

With an exhausted moan, Helisent half-rolls into place.

I fall still as her weight shifts back and forth.

The floodwaters glow brighter and brighter with each passing second.

The hypnotic scent of demigod magic heightens.

In theory, I trust the demigod.

In reality, I don't want to find out what its planning while lost in Lahar.

My witch shifts and swings a leg over my snout. She straddles me, hands clenching the fur between my eyes. She looks from one of my eyes to the next. Her body shakes, frigid and lacking sugars; shock and exhaustion.

She tugs her sopping robe into place. "Go slow. Please."

I rise slowly and keep my head steady. Helisent lurches from one side to the other, but doesn't fall. Her legs squeeze either side of my snout.

I head to the northwest. In the distance, bright mist blankets Vex. I see a blue-glowing demigod as tall as the clock tower standing within. It's proportioned like an okeanid with a halo-like afro. Its hands extend toward the city, ten long fingers splayed wide.

Like a wielder, almost.

With each second, the demigod comes into starker focus.

The mist condenses to form its glowing limbs.

With each second, the floodwaters rise higher. Water washes into the windows, inundating the homes around us.

The frigid tide reaches my chest as we near Ezitlos. My claws lift from the stone. My legs kick, paddling on instinct as a blue-glowing flood buries the city. Littered with glass and torn wood and powerful tide pools, I struggle in the water.

Helisent's legs loosen their hold.

Keep her above.

Floodwaters bury the rooftops of the single-story buildings, then ease up toward the second-story windows. I kick off walls and rooftops, attempting to buoy us aloft without dropping Helisent.

My witch starts groaning nonsense. All I make out is, "Death... familiar... you know?"

Then I run out of surfaces to push off.

The water rises to my neck. I splutter, exhaling through my nose as I swim. I widen my paws to paddle more efficiently.

My limbs ache and burn, my neck strains.

With a whine, I sink, the water rising to my neck and toward my ears.

I tilt my nose upward. It should give Helisent a few more seconds to help herself.

She throws herself against me, almost ripping the fur from my forehead.

Keep her above.

I clench my eyes shut.

Water floods into my nose, down my throat.

Then my body lifts suddenly, as though weightless.

I open my eyes as I crest the water and hover aloft.

The water below whorls with shadows and blue light.

I wait for Helisent's magic to steer us toward Vex.

Then I realize we're floating in a blue-tinted, phantom-like orb. All around us are twinkling droplets tinged with black shadows and blue magic.

We aren't alone. Dozens of other orbs rise into the air above Ezit's flooded streets.

This is familiar. Just like the shipwreck.

Nearby, I see Berevaldfang and Rexfang in a shared orb. Like me, they paddle into the air on instinct, four legs kicking. Smaller spheres linger nearby, sheltering individuals and small groups.

Helisent's tiny hands cling to me. They hold her in place while her robe floats aloft.

I swim through the night sky with a delirious red witch plastered to my face.

Thank you.

She's mine.

The orbs sail toward the glowing demigod where it stands in Vex amid raging floodwaters. As we near, the great being's form doubles in brightness. It seems to clench a shadow between its hands like bundled black fabric. Its fingers glow and fizzle with lashes of blue lightning.

I keep my eyes on Rexfang and Berevaldfang. They reach the shadow before me and my witch and disappear into its dark precipice.

Before we follow them, Helisent leans back to look up at the demigod. But it doesn't spare us a glance. It stares at Ezit, nose curled with distaste and eyes half-closed with merciless, detached resolution.

We disappear into the pulsing shadow held between its hands. The portal feels heavy—like a passage through icy water rather than buzzing infrasound.

We emerge someplace spacious. My paws hit the dry, rocky grass. Then I smell thatched huts and caches of dried fish.

New Hypnos sits in the valley before us. Over a hill, pale light grows in the east. Indirect sunlight fills the air and grazes my fur. A whorl of hormones flushes into my blood.

I round the okeanids and wielders and vampires. They gasp and chatter in wonder. Then they stagger toward the docks; a few begin to weep. Four ships bob on the water with white sails. Already, two look fully packed with exhausted, wide-eyed beings.

Parsifal beelines for us, shoving others out of his way. "Honey Baby!" He waves his hands in the air, eyes wide. "Samson—Samson! My dear Afador, put her down! *Down, boy, down!*"

I lower onto my belly, then set my head flat on the grass.

Helisent shifts with a grunt. She looks toward her papa. "Healer. I need a healer."

Parsifal waves to Ceyx and Cleo. Cleo leaves her sister, who directs the freed beings onward. She rushes toward Helisent but stops ten feet away.

She looks from my bloody fangs to Helisent, then shakes her head.

Parsifal rushes forward and reaches up to help Helisent down. His gut presses into my whiskers, his groin dangerously close to my incisor. With a quick spell, he collects his daughter against his chest, then rushes her toward Ceyx.

The pair gently set Helisent on the ground. Ceyx rips aside her clothes. She presses her hand to the wound with an unhappy sound.

After a moment, she looks at Parsifal. "She'll be okay. It feels like she did a rush job of healing herself. I'll help her now, then work on her more after she's had time to rest."

The warlock strokes his daughter's face. He dries his cheeks with a shoulder. "Okay. Thank you, Cleo." He looks over his shoulder at me. "Go on, Samsonfang. Take Rexfang and Berevald-fang someplace discreet. The ships will sail as soon as you're onboard."

I watch until her blood sugar rises and the stench of her abscess lifts. Even her molten glow seems to purify, deepening into a crimson hue. Helisent, as though in a deep sleep, keeps her eyes closed. Her lips twitch now and then.

Satisfied with Ceyx's healing, I turn away.

I round the massive group. At the rear are Rexfang and Berevald-fang. They meet my eyes, then disappear over the hill's crest.

I look back at my witch just one last time.

Parsifal and Ceyx help Helisent sit up. My witch takes a deep and steadying breath.

As though she can sense me, she looks up. Her features smooth with a small smile.

I throw my head back and howl. The sound catches my throat at the perfect angle. It spreads my sound through the sky, drifting up toward the moons.

She winks once.

Then she gestures toward the hill where my packmates wait.

I hustle away.

I stagger to my feet before my vision fully returns.

Which is a bad idea—I'm on an incline and start tumbling down-hill before I can figure out which way is up.

Someone grabs me by the arm. "Let's go, let's go, let's go." I smell Rex before I register his voice or the cool air hitting my naked body or the rocky grass beneath me.

I follow his momentum blindly.

My vision returns as we scale the hill. Berevald hustles a few feet away from me, attempting to sling his legs through a pair of pants as he walks.

He falls onto his hip as his ankle catches in the fabric. "Shit!"

Rex shoves a bundle against my chest. "Here."

As I tug my pants on, I realize there's a fourth figure looming nearby on the hill's crest. It's Vulcan. Whatever's happening, it can't be that dire; the warlock stares down at us with an impish half-smile. He holds a few spare layers in one hand and a jug of water in the other.

A bloody cut oozes near his chin—he looks whole aside from that.

"They're still digging the graves." Vulcan glances over his shoulder toward New Hypnos. "You have a few more minutes."

Digging the graves?

I comb my mind for memories, but the fog of last night is still heavy in my head. My aching body does little to help.

"Where are our torcs?" Rex asks.

Vulcan reaches into a bottomless bag strung across his chest. He pulls out our torcs, which were mixed together. Rex smells each, sorting them before passing them out. Bere and I pull our shirts on, then our torcs, then hold Rex's as he does the same.

By the time I'm dressed and cognizant, my entire being aches.

I spit when I realize my mouth is coated with sticky blood.

Like a battering ram, memories of the rampage rush through my head.

It's a catastrophic deluge that ends with an image of a dead vampire staring up at the sky.

Tol...

Like me, Rex and Berevald have bloody mouths and jaws and necks. Bruises and cuts pepper their pale skin, concentrated around their hands and forearms, their feet and calves.

I reach up, feeling at my bruised and cut gums. Blood coats my fingertips when I look down.

Berevald curses as he starts to investigate his own injuries. He prods his gums with his fingers, then bends forward. He vomits into the grass, a mix of blood and bile.

I reach for the jug that Vulcan holds, but the warlock backs up a step. "He needs to see a healer if he's vomiting blood. He likely has an internal injury, and—"

"It's not his blood," I explain, taking the jug from his hand.

I can feel my own stomach turn.

It's full of blood, of sinew, of other non-edibles.

The real danger is bones, which could splinter and puncture an organ—but that's a fun surprise that would come later in the week. Not now.

When Berevald finishes vomiting, I hand him the jug. He doesn't drink the water, just sloshes it around his mouth. Rex and I do the same, then start to scrub the blood and entrails from our jaws, our necks, our chests.

Vulcan waits, watching us and glancing over his shoulder now and then.

When we're cleaner and the jug is empty, we follow him toward New Hypnos.

With each step, I realize we're going to need that healer.

My ears are still ringing. The world sounds fuzzy; it feels far away. There's an open wound on my thigh, another just below my butt—it sends lashing pain through my leg with each step. Several of my ribs ache like they're broken, while two of Rex's fingers look sprained. Berevald fared best of all aside from a deep gash near his shin and a swollen wrist.

The memories of the rampage will take longer to heal.

I don't think I'll ever let them go—I certainly can't handle them now.

I'm too exhausted. Too jarred from the cruelty we unleashed last night. Too stunned by the presence of the demigod and the endless bounds of Vex's magical power. Too focused on the hopeful white sails that catch the wind atop the ships' decks.

Vulcan leads us toward them.

We limp through the abandoned village.

The only beings not waiting onboard or ferrying packages up and down the gangplanks are Zeu and Vic. The vampires stand as dawn warms the sky at our backs. They pay no attention to the light, to the fact that the sun will peek over the horizon any second. They stare into three deep graves with their hands tucked behind their backs.

I smell Tol's corpse and two others, but the shock still doesn't land.

I feel nothing as we walk past the burials. If there's any one dominant emotion, it's disappointment.

I'd hoped...

Hoped to find Pel last night.

Imperatriz, too. No matter how improbable.

I have my witch—

But I have failed Velm in leaving Zarzynn without our Female Alpha.

I have failed myself in leaving Zarzynn without my mother.

Vic and Zeu don't look up as we pass, as though equally numb. I pause, staring at the three graves. Berevald and Rex fall still at my side.

Cold dirt layers the scent of the corpses.

Then Vulcan guides us toward a gangplank and we follow him aboard. Ceyx waits for us on the ship's upper deck. She rushes forward, scanning me, Rex, and Berevald.

I tell her, "Nothing life-threatening. We need food and rest. How is Helisent?"

"She's well enough. I'll take another look tomorrow." Ceyx ushers us toward her perch near the boat's highest deck. "Aura told me Berevald doesn't do well with the waves. Let me treat him before we leave. Hopefully, I can prevent a similar bout of seasickness."

As soon as we board, okeanids haul the ship's gangplank onto the deck. Others shout as they work the ropes and sails hanging from the masts. Footsteps pound against the wood.

We follow Vulcan and Ceyx to a sitting area on the weather deck.

I sit down and stare across the three ships that neighbor ours.

Helisent and Parsifal sit on the deck of the ship beside ours. They're speaking with Halcyon, who nods quickly and intently.

Helisent hunches against the railing, covered with her papa's peridot cloak. I can trace her glowing form beneath it; the curve of her horns, her nose, her shoulders. I study the brightness of that vermillion glow, lifting my chin to search for her ala. It doesn't carry the hypnotic twang of a demigod's ala... but...

But all of her is alight.

I try not to gape.

I've seen her aglow at night, but during the day she looks ethereal. A walking Sennen. The daylit moon.

She raises a hand, which slips free of the cloak. She holds the small rod, which glows in the exact hue as her skin.

Her papa and Halcyon stare at the piece as though transfixed.

I stare at the witch, who sits no more than forty feet away. Right now, that distance might as well stretch from Bellator to Antigone.

A rut opens in my stomach.

This is the start of another goodbye.

The rut deepens when I realize all the ships have been boarded—and it's not Vic who joins Helisent's retinue. Zeu hustles for the stairs that lead below deck. My heart hardens as I watch the King of Night disappear into the stairwell's shadows.

As I watch Parsifal guide his daughter toward the same passage.

They disappear into its shadows, leaving Halcyon aboard the weather deck.

The ships cast off from the shore where Vic stands above three freshly turned graves.

The Queen of Night stares down with a morose expression.

For a while, we sit wordlessly as the ship barrels into the waves. The sun rises and its light washes over us.

After a while, Vulcan asks, "That was a demigod right? The blue thing?"

I nod. "An okeanid demigod from Hypnos. It followed us here."

Vulcan stares into the distance, eyes narrowing. "Then why did it break Vex? We were helping the okeanids."

Break Vex?

Is that what I felt?

I blink at the warlock. "What makes you think the demigod *broke* Vex?"

Vulcan shrugs a shoulder. "That's what it looked like—like the demigod tore Vex in half. It flooded the entire House. I'd never felt a spell that massive. It... it split the House down the middle." He jerks his chin toward the neighboring ship where Helisent and her papa just disappeared below deck. "And how else would she have gotten the wand?"

"Vulcan," Ceyx hisses. "Let the Vexen speak for herself—and the same for the demigods. You don't know what you're talking about."

"A *wand?*" Aside from the piece's glowing color, it hadn't seemed special.

"According to legend, it's for casting powerful spells." Vulcan glances at his mother, waiting for another objection. In her silence, he goes on, "In Plet, we revere the Vexen because they fought Ezit to the very end.

"The last Vexen who lived in Hella was named Axerxa. He sent his wives to Mieira so he could prepare for one last stand against Ezit. He knew he would die, but he refused to leave. To give Ezit what it wanted.

"His wives prepared a gift before they left. Unlike a body made of flesh, a piece of limestone... a piece of *Vex*, can store great quantities of magic. They gave him the wand to help him wield against Ezit, and

Axerxa died doing just that. Ezit's armies left his corpse in Hella, and him and the cave and the wand were forgotten over time. We kept the wand and Axerxa alive through stories… but nobody knew if it actually existed. Theoretically, creating a wand from any Landmark should be possible.

"We named Vex's after the red moon. Wanda."

Helisent mentioned that Axerxa was one of her male ancestors. He'd gifted me the red axe in Hella before visiting in a mirror Helisent during our first trip to Ezitlos.

She hadn't mentioned that he was a folk hero.

That he'd once called Hella home.

I can still hear Samsonfang whispering his name into my mind…

Axerxa is watching.

Rex asks, "What does the wand have to do with the demigod?"

"We'll let the Vexen explain when she's ready," Ceyx cuts in. "She knows better than anyone what happened last night."

I ignore the witch, fixing my gaze on Vulcan. "What do you think happened?"

The warlock looks at Rex, then at me. "I told you—I don't know what else aside from a demigod could have broken a Landmark. The Houses of Ezit have tried to do what Helisent just did for centuries— free their magic from their Landmarks. And if that's really what happened, then it means we're staring at the House of Vex as it exists now: through the witch and the wand. Hers is the first to leave Zarzynn for good."

Vulcan's eyes shift toward my chest, then back up to my face.

For a second, I assume Halcyon shared his theories about my scar with his son. Then I realize I hadn't been wearing a tunic when Vulcan guided me and my naked pack up a hill thirty minutes ago.

My scar had been pulsing bright red—he saw it, and he's not an idiot.

"Unless, of course," the warlock goes on casually, "Vex's magic has found other places to hide, too."

Ceyx looks at me, eyes wide. She hisses, "*Vulcan*," then tears into a string of livid Zarzyd.

Rex bores his eyes into mine, begging for a response. Berevald twists toward me, away from where Ceyx gently cradles his wrist.

The Pletens understand that Vex is responsible for keeping me alive—and it's clear they have a few other theories about my relationship to the House's magic.

I'd love to dive into those theories. I'd love to explain all the possibilities to my packmates, then extrapolate.

But the seed of magic Vex placed in my heart belongs in a place called Vieira, far from reality.

Too tired for sense or rationality, I take a deep breath and look at Vulcan. "When I return home, I'm going south to assume control of my territory. Velm. I will depose my father and reinstate my mother's rule. The journey will be difficult, but I have my pack on my side. I also have my wife and Female Alpha, Brutatalika 567 Sigivald. Together, we will set the stage for a new reality in Velm. A better one.

"While I do this, Helisent West of Jaws will travel across Mieira to instate her own authority. She will search for a warlock to carry on the Vexen line with her. Along the way, I imagine Vex's magic will find *many* places to hide. I'm sure it knows what to look for, as does the witch."

Vulcan's brow bunches. He glances at his mother. "But—"

"What I'm saying is... Vex is *one* being who's making decisions. Helisent is the second. I'm the third." I lower my chin to stare at the warlock. He looks older than he ever has, heavy rings underneath his eye and dirt smeared along his jaw, near his cut. "I like to think we all want the same thing—me and Vex and Helisent. But please understand me, Vulcan... I'm not stupid enough to think I'll get it."

Vulcan sits back, brow smoothing like he understands.

Just to make sure he does, I add, "So don't bring it up so lightly, my dear warlock."

I sit leaning against the wall, staring at the note in my hand.

'I'll visit tomorrow night. Find us a place to be alone.'

I glance around the cramped room. It's located on the ship's lowermost deck, the only portion dark and undesirable enough to guarantee us privacy. Though these ships are at least five times the size of the one we sailed to Zarzynn, they're packed.

Candlelight shivers against the vestibule's four walls. The room, which includes little more than a narrow bed with no mattress and a bare shelf, is dim and scented of salt water and wood.

I'm worried the witch will have a panic attack as soon as she arrives. But the more candles I light, the more the shadows shrink—and Helisent needs one large enough to use as a portal.

I look back and forth, from the candles to the shadows.

I sit up to leave in search of an extra candle, then sit back down when I sense infrasound in the room. I can't tell if it's from the time I spent in Vex or the seed of Vex within me, but the bass doesn't disturb me—doesn't set my senses on fire or cause any physical discomfort.

Magic pools in the shadow near the door, boiling like water before Helisent steps through.

Her hands enter the room first, then her face. Her hair falls around her features, soft and brushed. She wears a beige linen dress, which reminds me of the old layers she wore in Hella.

She rushes toward me, knocking me back onto the bed. We encircle the other; within a few breaths, her body relaxes in my lap. Her weight is a comfort, like a woven winter blanket.

For a long time, we don't speak.

I stroke her hair and shoulders and back. Her hands ball around my shirt, arms tugging me close.

Eventually, we loosen our grips to lean back.

Helisent stares into my eyes, eyebrows bunched. "I didn't... I didn't stick to the plan. I'm sorry."

I cup her cheek. My thumb grazes her lips, her chin. "Only those who didn't know you thought you'd stick to the plan." I tuck her hair behind her ear. "Are you okay? How do you feel?"

Before sleeping, Rex, Berevald, and I attempted to come to terms with the level of carnage we created. We estimated our kill count someplace in the high hundreds. We estimated the number of beings saved was close to that, but that was just a lullaby designed to comfort us.

We know what we did to that city.

The issue isn't whether it was justified—

The issue is knowing how Velm would respond if Bellator faced that level of violence.

And that our destruction still didn't yield any solution to return Imperatriz to Mieira. That we came this far and trespassed such great violence without meeting our goal. A goal that feels more like a curse, an impossible task, a mountain that I'll never traverse.

Berevald has been coping with Tol's death on top of that.

I close my eyes and sigh.

It's a lot easier to manage with Helisent in my lap.

Especially as she nods like she understands, red eyes studying my features. "I killed a lot of people, Samson." She scratches her nose, glancing at the wall. "And I can't tell if I feel bad. I think I should. Maybe I'm in shock."

"I'm in shock, too. Maybe we all are." I pinch her chin, guiding her to look at me. "Are you okay? You didn't answer."

Is your wound healed?

What is the rod, Helisent?

And did you really destroy your Landmark?

I sink back against the wall. Helisent wags her head back and forth, as though formulating an answer. "Better than I should be, I think."

We go through the basics.

Like I do for her, Helisent seems to spare me from the gruesome details. She says that she found the wand laying amid a broken Hellastone; she doesn't bring up my demigod or the dream in New Hypnos, and neither do I.

I don't bring it up because I don't know what to do with it.

Because I don't understand what it changes.

Like Vulcan theorized, Helisent says she destroyed Vex to pave the way for the Hypnotic Demigod. She says that Vex is free of Zarzynn... unless, of course, it's dying without a physical Landmark to cling to.

She says she doesn't know where, exactly, her dove is. Just that most of it is attempting to cling to her and the wand.

"What happened to Tol..."

I set my thumb over her lips, stopping her there. I've had a few days to quantify the vampire's death. "She knew what she was doing. She chose to defend you."

Her throat bobs. "But I didn't... I didn't stick to the plan."

"That's how these things go—rarely according to the plan. If you had stuck to the plan, we would have left without freeing those kept in the House of Lahar. The okeanids were able to free themselves using the demigod's magic—and they wouldn't have had access to that without you."

She blinks at me, head tilting.

Hoping I've found a strong appeal, I go on, "Queen Otrera is freed because of your decisions. She's going home thanks to you. Should I mention that the demigod is probably going to owe you a few favors? Witches love debts from powerful beings, don't they?"

She chews her lip, nodding absentmindedly. "Yes... we do." Her expression lightens further. "Queen Otera asked me to send a letter to Cadmium on her behalf yesterday. That's where the ships will dock. She asked them to prepare a festival in our honor.

"But... she's half in the mirror. That's how they describe it. Her and a degi—sorry, a vampire—are still rooming together. They became friends, I think how Ret and Vili were friends.

"Cleo and Ceyx think the necromancers can transition back into a more normal state with a few techniques developed in New Hypnos. They've worked with Pleten healers there before. So... the okeanids will have a choice whether to keep their mirrors as necromancers or not."

"I'm relieved to hear that." I stroke Helisent's arm, eased by her optimistic tone. I'm not sure how to ask, but... "And what about Butter? Have you seen her?"

"Yeah." Her smile disappears. "Since she's part witch, and that witch is from Kierkeline's line, she's... a bit different than the other necromancers. She killed both vampires that tried to... change her." Each word comes quieter and slower. Tears rim her large eyes. "I don't know if she wants to keep her necromancy powers. I guess we'll see. She needs more time to rest."

I wipe the tears that slip down her cheeks. "What happened to her wasn't your fault."

She doesn't respond, staring at her hands. "Three months, Samson. She was held in Argot for three months. Some of them were there for *years*." She slumps forward and rests her forehead against my collar. "But you know what the *really* fucked up part is? If Pel hadn't have bitten me in Cadmium last year, then he wouldn't have kidnapped me in Hypnos. That means I never would have gone to Plet, and we never would have saved the okeanids."

I stroke her back, hating her argument but unable to disagree.

Helisent straightens. Her eyes widen, fixed on me. "Holy fucking moons, Samson. That reminds me. What did that one whore tell us?"

"What?" I shake my head, trying to keep up. Even for Helisent, it's a quick shift in topic. "A whore?"

"The selkie whore. What did she say that one time?"

I blank for a second, reaching back toward a memory of a muddy cove in the South Deltas. What I remember most isn't the selkie's prophecies but getting close to a soaking-wet Helisent for the first time.

"Let's see... she said you were a red witch. She said we'd encounter the fifth scent soon, which was Pel. She said his kind were taking okeanids across the ocean, and that Clearbold wasn't doing anything to help."

Helisent nods with each of my recollections, as though tallying them. When I finish, she says, "Not that. It was something different. What else did she tell us?"

I shake my head again. "Something about magic. I think she wanted us... to be of service to her."

"Not that. Something else." Helisent looms over me. "*Think*, Samson."

Slowly, the memory comes back into focus. A warm and flailing Helisent; a tiny and muddy cove; a pink-and-pale river selkie.

"She said my magic was waiting near Rouz, I think. That it would come up on the Irme River."

For a split-second, I wonder if she could have been talking about Hadadrimmon 342 Aithesson, my distant relative—I'd assumed she was talking about Hetnazzar.

Helisent pushes against my chest. "No. Something that started with an 'S'."

An 'S'?

"A Sennenwolf?" I ask. "I hadn't heard of one before. Why? Do you know what it is?"

"The *Sennenwolf*... that's it..." Helisent stares blankly at the wall. Then she snaps her gaze to me. "In Ultramarine, I found Kiekerline and traded with her for information on the other GhostEater. I brought up what the selkie had mentioned, including the Sennenwolf.

"Kierkeline told me it was a weapon that made Bloody Betty look like child's play. It belonged to Velm. Are you sure you haven't heard of it?" Helisent closes her eyes, nose crinkling like she's deep in thought. I let her take her time, uncertain what point she's trying to make about the selkie. "She said the Sennenwolf was a weapon used before the War Years. Whatever it was, it was enough to keep the wielders at bay. To keep them out of Velm."

With a sigh, she opens her eyes.

I pat her hip. "And what made you think of our run-in with the selkie? Pel?"

She seizes my tunic with her hands. "Because she predicted this! She said we'd figure out what the fifth scent was and that it was taking the okeanids to a place across the sea. She was right about that—which means all the other shit she said wasn't just the foolish rambling of a water-bound whore." She starts to tick off more points with her finger. "First, she said we'd be of service to her. Second, she said you'd rule the wolves soon. Third, she said *the Sennenwolf is coming...* or something like that."

Her argument makes sense—but I have *no* energy to handle another round of destiny with a selkie. To figure out what a Sennenwolf is and where it's hidden.

"What if we deal with one thing at a time?" I propose. "Whatever the Sennenwolf is, I'm sure we'll find out eventually."

She tosses her hair over her shoulder. "Samson, my sweet wolf, I'm not even sure what bullshit we're supposed to be worried about at the moment."

I pat her hip again. "I think we should worry about getting back to Mieira—either with the help of a demigod or a phoenix. A few of the okeanids on our ship think the demigod is resting. They're worried it won't wake up if a storm comes."

She nods. "Right. Perfect. I'll worry about that for now."

"And there is a silver lining..." I strain forward to run my nose along her neck.

"What's that?" she asks.

I kiss the tender spot on her neck. "We're alone."

She shifts, angling her head to bear a devilish grin at me. "You mean you didn't lose your penis in the battle? There's a rumor going around some of the ships..."

"What? Which ship?" I sit up further. "Was it Zeu?"

She reels back with a cackle. "I was *joking*, Samson. Nobody has breathed a word about your penis. Not around me, at least." She pinches her lips as she giggles again, then hooks a finger through the hem of my pants. She tugs it back, peeking at my groin. "There you are." She looks up at me, pinching her lips again. "I saw Samsonfang's balls."

"Really?" I swat her hand away. "And to think I'd been worried you were on the cusp of death."

"Very fuzzy! The cutest."

I hope the room's dim light hides my blush. "Wow. That's great. Thank you."

She throws her head back with more laughter. Then she rights herself, purring insolent nothings into my ear and pressing her warm curves against me. I play like I'm offended, resisting her touches and trying not to laugh. I let her bully me across the hard bed, knowing that, eventually, our playtime ends.

If not in this room after I bathe myself in her ala, then later.

When the ship docks.

CHAPTER 21

THE EYES OF A WHORE
HELISENT

Honey Baby,
For how much you avoid acknowledging Andromeda North of Skull, she was
walking the same path as you are now. That path is the Northing. And she
walked it with the Kulapsifang of Velm.
Papa P.

A group of forty lingers on the ship's weather deck.

They crowd around its pointed bow.

They stare ahead at Cadmium, which comes into clearer focus with each wave we topple over. The city's white walls and orange-gold accents glitter in the sunlight.

A few okeanids chant a city anthem into the wind, arms slung around one another.

The Pletens stand to one side silently, watching the city twinkle like a gilded jewel.

I can't believe this awful adventure is coming to an end.

I don't think I could survive another week at sea—even if I've spent most of my nights with Samson below deck on his ship. We're running out of edible food, the wine has been gone for a fortnight, and heavy rainstorms have left mold everywhere.

I stare from the ship's railing, desperate for land.

I shift when I notice something out of the corner of my eye. Amid the blue water and white foam swims a spotted gray seal, keeping pace with the ship.

It twirls along the surface, its belly and fins cresting the twinkling water.

It looks very familiar, even though I haven't seen many seals in my life.

This one blinks its massive, wet eyes at me. I stare into them—they look dark magenta, not black. A swimming thing with pink eyes...

I turn around and shout, "Papa! Come here."

Parsifal sidles over, a wide smile on his cheeks. "Honey Baby, we can hear the drums and cheering already. Come up to the front of the ship, you'll—"

"No, no." I grab his arm and drag him toward the ship's railing. I point at the seal. "Is it just me or does this seal have the eyes of a whore?"

Though he looks baffled, Parsifal eagerly leans over the railing to take a look.

The seal twists and soars through the water, graceful and agile. It even raises one of its fins as it skims along the surface, either waving or luring us below.

"What the fuck is that all about?" I ask Parsifal. "It's obviously trying to tell me something."

"Helisent, it's an animal." Parsifal turns back to the festivities at the front of the boat. The chanting has heightened to a fever pitch. "Come on. There's a festival waiting and you're the guest of honor. Leave the seal."

I shoo him away without taking my eyes from the water.

Since shattering Vex to set my magic free, I've started to feel... differently about life. I feel power in inanimate things; the ocean, first and foremost. It feels like a spell unto itself, like a tangle of bass that sits in the earth's core, far below where everyone imagines the ocean ends. I can sense similar magic in temporal elements like wind, and starlight, and laughter.

The latter is the strangest of all.

As the necromancers regained their health on our journey home, there's been more mirth on the ship. I don't just feel the haze of desita or the slight exhaustion after it; instead, desita feels like the first whisper of infrasound that composes a spell.

And in sensing how *alive* the world is on a fundamental level, I've grown more convinced that things can be *sentient* in a way they weren't before.

Which means the seal could be more than a seal. Possibly even a whore.

I shout at the mammal, "I don't know what you're trying to tell me!"

Anything could be a demigod, full of life and utterly wordless.

The seal disappears, submerging far below. I set my hand on my hips, then head to the group of noisy nymphs and wielders.

More okeanids and necromancers sprint onto the upper deck. They leave pounding in their wake; though shadow-bound below, the vampires must be awake and sensing a literal change in the tides.

I stand near the Pletens and study Cadmium's white-walled buildings. The city was built on an incline, making it look taller and grander than a tangle of skinny streets.

I pick at the wooden railing.

My heart thumps when I consider all those who might await me. What do I say to Simmy? To Brutatalika—or *Clearbold?*

And what the *fuck* do I do with Zeu? Tol's first decision as the Queen of Night was to stay in Zarzynn and take control of Zeu's warrior den. Which means I'm now responsible for the King of Night as he leads Vic's former den.

I don't know what's worse—his shameless flirting from before or his cold reticence now.

"How are you?"

I jump when Halcyon grazes my arm. I almost jump again when I meet his eyes. Last night, I convinced the Pletens to hide their forms in Mieira—at least, for the time being.

His cropped hair looks a lot better without his indigo horns taking up so much space. The rest of him looks a bit plainer—his indigo eyes don't burn as brightly and his brown skin reveals more of his age. Still, he's as sturdy and handsome as ever.

He rolls his eyes. "Don't look at me like that."

I pinch his arm. "Relax, Halcyon. You look good."

I glance at the rest of the Pletens gathered around him. Without his form, Vulcan doesn't look as much like Halcyon; his features are softer, his nose more pointed, like his mother.

Without the haunting hue of blinding white skin and irises and horns, Vega's round face comes into focus. She has a darling cleft in her chin that I never noticed before. Her eyebrows look thicker, her gaze more piercing.

Ceyx and Cleo stand nervously, hands behind their backs. Rouge fills their broad cheeks, delicate tendons line their long necks.

Memphis stands between them. He notices me staring, then winks; it's become our signature.

I wink back.

"Someone is flying," Halcyon says. "Oh, wait—there are two of them."

I head to the railing to search the skies. Sure enough, two wielders soar through the air, bright red cloaks catching in the wind. They move horizontally, arms raised for balance as they move from ship to ship.

My papa puts it together before I do.

"My boys!" he barks, scrambling onto the railing and then falling off it. He quickly catches himself in a hover, caught in his now-threadbare peridot cloak. "*Boys! Boys! Boys!*"

I climb onto the railing and use steadying magic to keep myself upright. I squint, using my hand to block the early summer sunlight.

Ynvgi and Yves find us. They beeline for our ship, their eyes wide as they careen downward at an angle. I open my arms, too excited to manage a word in my wild bellowing.

The crowd makes room for the pair.

It hits me as soon as I make eye contact with Yves, then Yngvi—

I did it.

I survived.

I brought everyone home.

(Almost.)

Parsifal shouts, "I got her!"

Yngvi crashes into me, and Yves is right behind him, and then our papa adds to the pile. We're a group of clutching limbs, shaking and smiling. I can only tell the twins from my papa based on their height and lack of round bellies.

We stay like that for a long time.

Yves tries to say something but starts crying instead. Then Parsifal starts with the waterworks. I angle my chin upward for air; I'm surrounded on all sides. I can barely breathe, especially with Yves and Yngvi looming.

Yngvi steps back, wiping his eyes, and stares at me. Yves does the same on my other side, which leaves Parsifal to stagger back. He looks between the three of us, sniffling and stuttering and smiling.

"Did you get shorter?" Yngvi steps forward and measures my height with a hand.

I tsk.

The Pletens watch us, frozen in place with shock. The nymphs around them look far less confused. One of them even shouts a greeting to my brothers, which the pair heartily return.

I straighten my dress and then my hair. I prepare an insult, but the twins have already moved on.

Yngvi jabs his thumb toward the Pletens. "What's this? Why do they look so nervous?"

I shuffle toward the Pletens and smile wide. "They're from *Zarzynn*. That's where we were, by the way. Zarzynn."

The twins immediately focus on Ceyx and Cleo, raising their chins as though pleasantly surprised.

Yngvi bows at the waist with a flourish. He bares a smile at Ceyx as he straightens. "I can think of a thousand ways to welcome you to Mieira."

Yves runs his hands through his hair, smoothing his untidy updo as he directs his attention to Cleo. "Do you know what they say about life in Mieira, my dear witch?"

"*Not now.*" I bare an apologetic smile at Halcyon. "See, I told you everyone here is super nice."

Then I introduce the Pletens and my brothers before the latter can do any more shameless flirting. Each offers a short head bow; I'd mentioned that they could either wave, smile, or bow their heads when greeting new beings. It seems they're opting for formality.

I set my hands on my hips with a happy smile. "I'm going to take them to Luz once all the festivities in Cadmium die down. The vampires, too."

"Who's Thevampires?" Yngvi asks.

I narrow my eyes. "You'll find out at sundown. You guys are staying in Cadmium for a bit, right?"

"Helisent, they're preparing the party of the century," Yngvi explains. "There's enough wine, brandy, and ale to get a whole village drunk."

"Kiki Red Tier couldn't make it," Yves explains with a vibrant smile. "We've been staying with your warren—"

"My warren?" I shout, whipping my head toward the piers. "My warren came?"

In the last ten minutes, we've converged on Cadmium. Thousands of wolves, nymphs, and wielders await us, packed together and shouting.

I press against the railing, scanning the crowd for a familiar face.

My warren... remembers me? Fondly...?

My chest starts to shake; excitement, apprehension, and a blinding sense of relief fill me. The idea that anyone who knew me in the last few years decided to hold out hope for my fate is... shocking, to say the least.

Especially all those I left behind or used in pursuit of vengeance and oblivion.

I start to pick out faces from the crowd.

First are dryads from my warren, Makarios and Melita. Their mouths are opened wide, their faces scrunched as they lean over the metal railing on the far side of the pier. Emerald hair falls to their waists, tangled in braids. Ten feet away is Aleixo, a naiad, and then Evgenia, a speckled-skinned hesperide.

Nearby, I find Pen and Zopyros with their arms hooked together. Pen wears a red cape like my brothers, his white hair pinned back. Zopyros, another hesperide, smiles so wide her cheeks dimple.

My warren pulls away from the railing, racing and weaving through the packed bodies toward one of the long docks. They follow the ship, as though preparing to meet me.

Elvira Ultramarine is the first wolf I notice—and that's because I can't believe she's smiling. I can't believe she's also screaming joyfully alongside Gautselin Mort and Chariovalda South Bend Gamma— owners of Luz's finest pleasure house.

And there's fucking Itzifone Bugs Alita in his emerald cape—

And his withered old mother, Mieira's only GhostEater, Draginine West of Jaws, seated on her lilac lilith and drowning in silver jewelry—

And Boonmasent Luz with a hideous baby in her arms—

And Ninigone Luz, her eyes wide and her cheeks red—

They're screaming my name, I realize.

Hel-i-sent! Hel-i-sent! Hel-i-sent!

I've heard my name shouted thousands of times, but this is... different.

I stare across the crowd, condensing more with each second. The piers are packed, as are the neighboring streets that lead into the city. They chant my name and they seem happy about it.

Yngvi pats my back. Yves props me up onto the railing so everyone can see me. My papa keeps shouting and shouting and shouting.

For the first time in my life, I fall truly silent as I stare across the packed city.

Not the angry kind of silent where I'm cursing people in my mind, or contemplative silent where I'm plotting the future, or sneaking silent where I'm waiting to pounce.

This is a silence that touches my core.

Tears sting my eyes.

In that innermost silence, I buckle with relief.

I destroyed Vex to let the okeanid demigod take its reign... and maybe it really was the first step to renewal.

The ships slow down as they angle toward the docks. A few officials hold the line at the pier, preventing the crowd from spilling onto the piers. Waves slosh onto the wood as the ship comes to a slow halt and ropes are thrown overboard.

Huddled on the railing, I see two figures break past the line and rush onto the dock.

I make out a streak of red cloak and a vermillion afro—

"Simmy!" I scream the name before I've confirmed it's him. Instinct leads me over the ship's railing, sends me hovering down its curved side. "Esteban!"

I sprint onto the wooden planks, almost falling over after weeks of teetering ship-living. The pair rush toward me, arms outstretched.

The first thing I notice is how skinny and bird-like my mentee is;

Esclamonde hasn't filled out her bony frame in the months I've been gone, nor has she opted for a smaller cloak. And Simmy looks disproportionately older, streaks of gray hair peppered among his red-orange tufts.

His eyes open, wide as saucers, when he meets my eyes.

I barrel into the pair just like I did with my brothers. We wrap our arms around each other, hunkering down on the wooden planks like we're trying to disappear. We press our heads together, forming a perfect and endless circle.

Like me, Simmy's weeping is more existential. Esclamonde wails and pants like she's going to pass out. It's alarming enough that Simmy and I part to stroke her back.

"I'm fine," she gasps, head hanging as her body shivers.

As we comfort her, Simmy and I look at one another.

A lump grows in my throat as his eyes churn with warmth. I can see the dimple marks on his cheeks, the precise curve of his full lips.

He runs a hand down my back.

I'm not sure what to say. "Are you mad at me?"

Are you mad at me for running? For being broken? For hurting you by hurting myself?

"*Mad?*" Tears rim Simmy's eyes. He clears his throat. With all the shouting and madness, he practically has to yell, "Have I ever been an angry nymph?"

I shake my head.

He smiles, setting his tears loose. "And doesn't your papa say people never change?"

I nod, body shivering with a few latent sobs.

Onesimos goes on, "When the festival ends, let's go home. To Luz." He cranes toward me and I close the distance, pressing my lips to his. Such safety. Such warmth. Such unbelievable normalcy.

Then gangplanks start hitting the dock around us. Okeanids and necromancers rush past us, into the city. My warren comes straight towards us, fighting the tide of rushing beings.

Parsifal and my brothers lead the Pletens from the ship, forming a chain with their hands.

We stand in a large group to make introductions. For how tense the Pletens looked when meeting my brothers, they're no longer glassy-eyed and submissive. Memphis's mouth hangs open as he studies the ecstatic crowd, the white city strung with cadmium accents. Cleo looks from him to the city, pinching her lips; they seem to be quivering. At her side, Ceyx wipes her eyes. The sisters stand side by side, Memphis right in front of them. Two feet away are Vega and Vulcan, hand in hand and just as awestruck. Halcyon slings an arm around his eldest's shoulders, shaking him once and smiling.

Out of the corner of my eye, and maybe because part of me is always searching for him, I see the dark hair of wolves. I see their golden torcs catch the light like crystals, and I turn my head.

Samson, Rex, and Berevald walk swiftly down the dock beside ours; two wolves await them. The first female has thick gray hair, pulled back into a familiar bun. A black cape hangs from her back; the Alpha's cape.

The other wolf is female and close to my age.

And she's beautiful enough that my features fall, that a pit in my stomach lurches toward the center of the earth. Privately, I've consoled my jealousy with the idea that Brutatalika would be as broad-shouldered and block-jawed as the males. She is. But I hadn't fathomed that someone would make it look *good*, and feminine, and somehow both refined and deadly like the tip of a golden dagger.

I feel like the most wretched and lonely thing that has ever existed, surrounded by a screaming crowd.

I look across the nameless faces of the Mieirans as they barrel into hugs, cry and hold one another, toast to the future.

I did it.

I survived.

I have the adoration and acceptance of Mieira, but it isn't *actually* what I want or hope for anymore. I know what I want as I watch the wolves. And it makes me feel dumb for hoping and wishing in the first place. That's the *true* problem; not my inability to get what I want, but the inability to stop fucking wanting things.

I shove that away.

I paste a smile to my face, then turn to the Pletens.

I open my arms wide to gesture to the madness that awaits us in Cadmium's streets.

Nearby, a warlock holds a bucket and a donkey leans into it, guzzling ale; a trio of naiads lead a chant about a place across the sea;

two okeanids sprawl on the ground as they enjoy a passionate and horizontal reunion.

I scream, "Welcome home!"

I look into the mirror and hiss at my reflection.

My lips are too curved. My cheeks are too plump, my face too round. The arch of my nose is too tall. My eyes practically bulge out of my head. And none of this fucking jewelry is hiding it—not the colorful and layered necklaces, not the dangling and jangling earrings, not the tiny beads tucked into my braided hair.

Not even my brand new velvet robe, red as my eyes and blood and magic, helps.

Butter leans against me and gazes into the mirror. "You look beautiful, Helisent."

Under the golden light of magical oil, I'm almost apt to believe her. But it doesn't help that I'm nursing a hangover from our week-long festivities in Cadmium. (Though designed to celebrate our survival and the return of the okeanids, I fear the parties in Cadmium might kill me.)

"I mean it." Butter slaps my wrist as I start fussing with my hair again.

Since landing in Cadmium, we've stayed together in the same flat as my warren, which borders the apartments where the Pletens live and where Zeu's den sleeps through the days.

"You look like a little piece of moonslight." Butter smiles, but it only makes me feel worse.

She's very beautiful, with cool brown skin, plump lips that are the right shape and the color of dark roses. Her long eyelashes were designed to lure in lovers; I've seen them in action. Her soft curls hang around her face, effortless and fragrant.

She slides a mug of steaming tea toward me. "Drink some. You'll feel better."

With a sigh, I take a sip.

Someone knocks at our door.

Zeu enters before anyone lets him in. Despite being in Cadmium for over a week, he hasn't taken to Mieiran norms of privacy; even the nymphs find him and his den forward.

The King of Night wears a white pelt around his hips like always.

Tonight, he also wears a thin strip of magenta fabric beneath the pelt —a gift from some thoughtful nymph. It helps cover up more of his groin, along with his hips. The color matches one of his latest acquisitions: a second feather, short and rigid, that dangles from his plain necklace. This one is purple-pink, belonging to the canaries that live throughout Mieira.

Like me, he must have dressed up for the occasion.

A chance to sit in a formal meeting with some of Mieira's most important leadership: members of the Class, Velm's Kulapsifang, and multiple nymph monarchs.

We've barely spoken since the triplemoon. Our interactions have been polite and strained. I'm hopeful things will smooth over, but it won't matter once his den is settled in Luz.

(I know he blames me for Tol's death. I know it's my fault, too.)

He leans against the wall and crosses his arms, staring into space.

I turn back to face the mirror. My mind has switched away from Zeu and onto the incoming meeting; I study my features once more with the urge to cry.

Another knock at the door saves us from any more awkward silence.

Halcyon opens the door a crack and calls in happily, "The Pletens are ready for our debut." He opens it further to poke his head in. A relaxed smile hangs from his lips. "Are you—"

"We're leaving." I slide off the chair and grab my bottomless bag. I sling my velvet robe across my shoulders, then glance at the mirror one last time.

I look like a child playing dress up.

Halcyon holds the door as I stalk toward him. His eyebrows bunch as he studies me. "Alright, then." Vulcan and Vega stand in the hallway; they also stand aside so I can pass.

I like to think Zeu's exit from the apartment explains my bad mood, but I don't turn around to find out.

I keep striding down the hallway toward the staircase; it's only a five-minute walk to the Cadmium Estate from the residential building where I live with the remnants of my tiny army.

Butter calls after me, "Simmy and Esclamonde are coming home soon. We'll be here when you get back."

To pick up the pieces, she means.

I don't respond. I keep stalking forward; I take the stairs with Zeu on my heels, then turn onto the busy street. I don't check behind me to see if the Pletens keep pace. Zeu certainly does, bumping into my elbow as we delve into the night.

Outside, Cadmium's feverish festivities continue. One week in, the number of impromptu beds increases, along with the number of beings sleeping on them. Otrera's note called for a large celebration—but Mieirans only had two and a half weeks to arrive in Cadmium and set up shop.

With so much effort expended, the parties will continue for another week or so. Each day, more exhausted troops arrive from distant places; Septegeur, Metamor, west of Luz. It would be wrong to send them on their way so quickly.

But the madness makes the streets difficult to navigate—many visitors brought tradable goods and even livestock. I count sables and goats in the narrow streets, along with stalls hawking bright skirts and sparkling beads.

Eventually, the clean marble walls of the Cadmium Estate come into view. They catch and reflect the streetlights in whorls. Navy tapestries hang over the estate's walls and its gate; a towering wolf stands before it, hands tucked behind his back.

I walk faster, hopeful I'll recognize Rex or Berevald. But it's a stranger, at least ten years older than either of Samson's packmates.

With a sigh, I stop short of the gate—hopefully out of earshot.

I face the King of Night and smooth my robe. "Zeu, what did we talk about yesterday?"

He stops, glancing at the passersby. "We spoke about the names of the moons and why the nymphs don't like hoarding. In Velm, they're called Sennen, Abdecalas, and Vicente. In Mieira, they're called Cap, Laline, and Marama. And the nymphs don't like hoarding because... it's offensive. And they're very easily *offended*."

I roll my eyes. "I meant about this meeting." I make a mental note to follow up on the hoarding topic later.

Halcyon, Vulcan, and Vega huddle around us, pressed close to avoid being separated by a rushing nymph or a shouting wielder.

I stay focused on Zeu. "What did I tell you?"

He fusses with one of his braids. "I will behave. I will speak thoughtfully. I will not interrupt anyone who is speaking." His eyebrows bunch. "What else? I won't... I won't..."

Zeu gestures to Halcyon, like he's asking for a hint.

Halcyon says, "No physical intimidation."

Zeu nods. "Yes—no physical intimidation." He straightens his white pelt and the magenta fabric beneath it. "I will sit quietly next to the Vexen. I will not threaten to bite with words, physical posture, or eye contact."

Last week, I would have been surprised the vampire could remember that much. One week into Zeu's antics in Cadmium and I appreciate his intelligence more than ever before. What's under it is a thick layer of anarchy, which is harder to predict. Especially now that we're on uncertain terms.

I press my hands together and level my gaze at the vampire. "And what's the *last rule*, Zeu? The most important one of all?"

He raises his eyebrows. "Aside from your secret?"

My nose curls. "*Yes, aside from that.*"

"I will not upset the Kulapsifang of Velm," he says, straightening to his full height. "Or his wife."

"Very good." I smooth my hair one last time, then head to the gate. The guard bows his head, then swings open the door and leads us past a square garden toward the main door.

I wrap a spell around myself, which lessens the potency of my ala and also prevents others from hearing things like my racing heart. It speeds already, thumping in my chest as the guard slides open the estate's door.

Inside is a familiar stretch of lifeless and pale and sparkling marble. The foyer walls extend upward—at least twice as tall as the room is wide. Every step and breath sound in the empty corridor.

We pass a few rooms with navy curtains pulled tight over the doorways. We follow the gentle sounds of a meeting as it beckons from a room at the end of the foyer; low voices, glasses clanking. I don't pause to think about what we're going to find past the thick, navy blue curtain where another straight-faced wolf awaits us.

He holds a thick curtain aside so we can pass through.

Without a second thought, I step into the large room. I don't look up as I beeline for the empty cushions laid out in a spacious circle. In my periphery, I tally the group imprecisely; three wolves sit near the entrance, then two white-cloaked wielders, then a few colorful nymphs.

I waltz to the five places left for me and my retinue. I prepare to sit down in the middle cushion but do a double take when I realize only Halcyon, Vulcan, and Vega have followed.

I try not to curse out loud when I realize we lost Zeu.

I gesture for the Pletens to sit, then backtrack.

The wolf holds the curtain open for me. Back in the foyer, I find Zeu leaving one of the curtained rooms we passed.

He raises his eyebrows when he sees me, bare feet heavy on the marble. "All of the rooms are empty. Are they going to war? They must expect to bring home loot, an incredible amount of—"

"Not now." I grab his forearm, digging my nails into his skin and tugging him toward the meeting room.

All I get is an annoyed little noise as he jerks his arm free.

I gesture toward the curtain. "*Get inside.*"

Zeu ducks past the curtain as the wolf holds it aside.

I follow him and, once again, focus solely on the two empty cushions that await us.

I realize one of them is next to Hemlock. The king's face crinkles with a broad smile when he sees me, and that helps soften my clenched stomach. Zeu takes the seat next to the lilac-cloaked dryad, leaving me to take the cushion between him and Halcyon.

And then, with a sigh that I hope sounds casual, I sit down and straighten out my robe and look around the circle.

Next to Hemlock, Queen Otrera sits with her back straight. She looks healthier than she did on the ship. Her cheeks are fuller, her eyes brighter. Lapiz lazuli hangs from her ears, her wrists, her neck, glistening like droplets of the deep ocean.

On her far side sits a hesperide queen—her broad, unlined face is familiar, but I can't remember where I've seen her before. She wears the dusky gold of Gamma and a crown of woven grains atop her thin brown hair.

The Gammic Queen and Zeu eye one another for a moment. I've noticed the same happen at night as more vampires and hesperides interact.

Both have graceful, hooded eyes. The nymphs have round faces and eyes shaped like almonds, usually the color of amber; the vampires have sharp jaws and high cheekbones with narrow eyes that curve upward. Their irises and pupils glow with a red-gold iridescence.

I look from the queen to Zeu, then back again. From a distance, it's uncanny. Up close, their features are much more distinct.

Then I force myself to keep looking around the circle.

I swallow Brutatalika's appearance like food that's too hot.

I've been hopeful I'd wrongfully assumed she was beautiful, born from a great distance and my slowly ailing vision and all of the ruckus. But I was wrong. She's like Halcyon's wives—not nearly as delicate or refined, but still a type of stunning that I physically react to.

Her lips are light pink, her eyes deep-set and crushing. Her cheekbones are high, casting her jaw in an effortless angle of strength and health.

My only comfort is the shock of moving on to the next woman.

She's the other wolf I spotted during our arrival. The black cape hangs from her shoulders, tapering along the ground. It contrasts her gray hair—not born from magic, but age.

As soon as our eyes meet, I see Hetnazzar in my mind—

I see the demigod tangled amid red strings.

I hear it bite into my Landmark with a loud crack.

I'm too afraid to meet Samson's eyes before I move on to Absalom and Ethsevere. The warlocks sit in prim white cloaks, pooled around them like liquid. Absalom offers me a small smile, but Ethsevere studies me with a bent brow.

Rather than start with the Class, Queen Otrera begins. "Helisent West of Jaws, please try your drink."

I lean toward the goblet set before me. The Pletens and Zeu have their own set before their cushions. I lift the cup and sniff once; it smells like acidic brandy. I take a sip, then smack my lips together; the others also test their drinks.

I take another sip—

It's tart and bitter. Bitter... so bitter...

My sip becomes a gulp.

Zeu sets his goblet down with a clatter. A long sound of disgust peels from his lips. Vega also seems to be quietly coughing next to Vulcan; the warlock reaches over to pat her back.

Queen Otrera smiles at me. She reaches into her cerulean cloak and pulls out a massive, light-pink fruit. It has the skin of an orange, only softer and paler—and at least three times the size.

"It's a grapefruit." Otrera directs her smile toward the Pletens. "It's disgustingly bitter. We will drink it in Helisent's honor."

She hands the fruit to Hemlock, who passes it off to Zeu. Rather than hand it to me, he investigates the fruit; he squeezes it, he sniffs it, he wedges one of his incisors into the fruit. My body locks as he shifts his jaw to collect its juice.

Zeu flinches again, making another long noise of dissatisfaction. He shivers, mouth pinched, then passes the fruit to me.

I'm not sure what to do with it. I smile at Otrera, then I stare into the hole Zeu bit into the fruit. It has pink insides. "Thank you." I pass the fruit to Halcyon, who doesn't actually take it. He smiles and nods, like he's not sure what to do.

I set the fruit next to my goblet.

If I wasn't reminding myself not to look up at Samson every other second, I'd probably feel true appreciation for the drink. It's disgustingly bitter like Otrera said; this honors me deeply.

"Helisent West of Jaws," Ethsevere says.

His voice sends rage into my veins; I remember it from my months of banishment.

I clench my jaw while I study him. He has the narrow face and bulging eyes of his niece, Esclamonde; it helps me endure his stare.

"The Class would like to beg your forgiveness," he says, chin raised and voice neutral.

My mouth actually falls open.

Zeu's warm breath grazes my shoulder. He whispers, "What is the Class?"

I shush him, jerking away as I focus on Ethsevere.

A satisfied smile spreads across my face. I take a large drink from my goblet and sit back, relaxing my body so I can savor this moment. "Okay. I'm ready, Ethsevere. *Beg me*, my dear warlock."

Ethsevere gestures to his compatriot. "Absalom will read a statement on behalf of the Class."

I roll my eyes. "Absalom begs me for shit all the time. How is that special?"

Ethsevere ignores me as Absalom pulls a rolled piece of parchment from his sleeve.

Absalom clears his throat as he straightens the paper, then reads, "'The Class is powerless against Helisent West of Jaws. The Class lifts her banishment and apologizes for leveling a banishment to begin with. It is clear that grave mistakes were made.'"

My mood lifts with each word.

I'm still not sure what the future holds with the Class. Four members were loyal to Anesot and Oko; according to Absalom, some may still be in cahoots with the Houses of Col and/or Talos. Whatever comes next with the Class won't be nearly as pleasant as Ethsevere's statement suggests.

Still, it's the *Class*.

An apology is incredible, bordering on unbelievable.

And highly suspicious.

I toss my hair over my shoulders. "And how much dove does the Class need?"

Ethsevere's jaw clicks as he stares at me, but Absalom smiles.

Eventually, the elder says, "Whatever you are willing to spare. And however quickly. The priorities are Antigone, Perpetua, Eupheme, and Alita."

I offer them a demure shrug. "I'm taking the Pletens and Zeu's den to Luz once the festivities are over. I'll begin packaging my dove then. You can come and get in line. I'll expect more begging."

Absalom's subtle smile spreads to Ethsevere. I sit back, happy to know that both wielders aren't just willing to play nice with me... but play, in general.

Still, I want to end this meeting—and if Otrera was representing the nymphs and Ethsevere the Class, then this is almost done.

I take another drink and look at the elder wolf.

She watches me for a moment, like she's weighing my gaze. "My name is Sutnazzar 712 Afador." Her voice is deep. The longer I hold her eyes, the more I'm convinced she can read my mind. "It is nice to meet you, Helisent West of Jaws."

My spine locks, body fizzing with nervousness. "Hello, Sutnazzar 712 Afador."

Sutnazzar gestures to her right; I meet Brutatalika's eyes and have never felt smaller. "This is the Female Alpha of Velm, Brutatalika 567 Sigivald. I don't believe you've met." Before I can panic about what to say to Samson's wife, and how to make my voice sound, and how long to hold her gaze for, Sutnazzar goes on, "You remain banished from Velm."

My heart skips a beat.

My eyes flash to Samson.

He stares at me like we've never met. This room might as well be Solace sometime last spring.

I shift, uncertain of what to do.

I set my goblet down and cross my arms. "Where is Clearbold?"

Sutnazzar says, "Bellator."

"I see." My mood spirals quickly.

A series of thoughts batter through my mind—Clearbold should have come here to receive Samson. Sutnazzar should be thanking me for sending dove to Imperatriz. And *someone* should acknowledge that Samson's life is owed to me after Alita.

Owed to Vex.

Sutnazzar goes on, "The Pletens and vampires are also unwelcome."

One of the nymphs sighs loudly, but I'm not sure if it's Otrera or Hemlock. Even Ethsevere looks uncertain by Sutnazzar's words. He whips his head toward her, eyebrows bunching.

I clench my jaw; instead of nervousness, I now feel anger.

But I'm trying—

I'm trying *really* hard.

"Who rules Velm?" I ask. "You or Clearbold?"

"The Male Alpha of Velm," Sutnazzar says. "My rule came to an end when my grandson was born to Imperatriz 713 Afador."

I stare into her eyes, begging for more. *Does that mean Clearbold told her to say these things? And is he not here himself as a final insult to me?*

Here's the truth: it's not my place to worry about Velm.

About Clearbold's latest manipulations and plots.

I have no right to meddle.

"I guess we'll move on, then." I shrug; I'm not sure what else to do. No response fits—they're all too threatening or vague. With a sigh, I turn toward the Pletens. "For those who don't know, this is Vega. Vega is a *white* wielder. Vulcan is an *indigo* wielder, like his father, Halcyon." The trio don't look happy to be labeled with a color, but they agreed to live free of Houses in Mieira. "They prefer to live in their forms, but they've agreed to hide them for a while longer. Like I said earlier, they'll be coming to Luz with me. So will Zeu and his den."

Ethsevere crosses his arms as he studies the King of Night. "And are you taking responsibility for Zeu and his pack?"

"Absolutely not." I snort. "Zeu takes responsibility for himself."

Zeu nods. "I lead my den. We will follow the Vexen west."

"Helisent," I correct him. "Just Helisent."

He hisses quietly; he hates Zarzynn, but not Vex.

Hemlock leans over to pat Zeu's leg. "And you agree to drink blood *only* from those willing to share it?"

Zeu goes silent. He sets his hand on his chest delicately. "I am not a *predator*."

"Of course not." Hemlock smiles. "But we approach life a bit differently here. The animals are *also* free—"

"Is this about the goat?" Zeu throws his hands up. He reaches toward me, grabbing my arm to direct me to the king. "Tell him I must eat."

I jerk my arm loose, then offer the Rhotidic King a pliant smile. "It was just a little goat, Hemlock."

Queen Otrera leans past Hemlock to offer delicately, "She was the largest goat in Cadmium. Pippo provided milk for dozens."

"What?" Zeu snaps. "Should I milk the goats before I kill them?"

Hemlock shouts, "She was wearing a *scarf* when you bit her! She was not chattel up for the kill!"

Zeu turns to grab my arm again; he tugs me toward the nymphs more gently, and I follow his momentum this time. He explains, "I saw the scarf. I thought it had fallen off a clothing line and gotten wrapped around the goat's neck." He urgently asks me, *"They dress the livestock?"*

I pull my arm free again, then study the Rhotidic King. "Hemlock, if I promise to keep Zeu out of Rhotidom and away from your precious sables, can we let Pippo rest in peace?"

The dryad's eyes widen. "The sables..."

I offer him a consolatory nod. "Have no fear. Zeu and his den will stay with me—at least until they get the hang of life in Mieira."

The hesperide queen raises her chin—I finally realize why I recognize her. She's the Gammic Queen who was crowned in Luz's temple district right before Samson and I left the city last year. Her demigod had waved to me and Simmy like it could sense a change in the wind.

She tells the vampire, "Zeu, King of Night, Gamma's plains are home to many animals. We have enough to spare. You are welcome in Gamma when you need blood. I reside two days east of Luz."

Zeu sits back and grumbles something inaudible. It takes me a second to realize he's probably shocked and suspicious by the offer; like me, I don't know if Zeu has known many warm receptions.

"Our goats are fat and slow and naked," the hesperide queen goes on.

Zeu flashes her a smile. "Well, I don't mind running. A chase helps build the appetite."

"As you prefer," says the queen with a quiet laugh. "My people will be intrigued by your kind. When you come for food, we will ask something in return. A bargain is a way of bonding in Mieira. But send word before you arrive. I understand that sunlight poisons you, and Gamma is half sky. We will make preparations to welcome you."

Zeu shifts again. "Okay. I will be in Luz with the Vexen—with Helisent. Me and my den."

A beat of peaceful silence fills the room.

Good enough for me.

I clap my hands together. "Now... if that's all..."

I need to leave this room where Samson sits with his wife.

I need to escape the gaze of his Kulapsi grandmother.

I need to find another goblet of this grapefruit brandy and drown myself in it.

I stand up with my drink and no one stops me.

I waltz back toward the curtain; footsteps follow me. The wolf pulls aside the heavy fabric and I slowly lose my composure after that. With each step into the foyer, my expression falls; tiny sniffles mount in my chest before the second wolf opens the gate for us.

I drink in the cool air once we're free of the marble hall and its awful silence.

With a long sigh, I dive into the packed street and turn toward my residential building.

Halcyon's warm hand takes mine, twining our fingers together. We weave through the bodies.

Vulcan and Vega branch off with a wave. Zeu has disappeared entirely.

So I walk with Halcyon, hand in hand, while Cadmium's madness reels around us.

He brings my fingers to his lips and kisses them. "If you're up for it, I could teach you the finger trick tonight."

I don't think it will save me now.

But it would be stupid not to try.

The finger trick lifts my mood for a few hours.

First, Halcyon demonstrates how the spell works. Then Butter waltzes in and asks how the meeting went; I tell her about the finger trick instead. Halcyon, who's been quietly stealing glances at Butter all week, lets us scoot closer to him on the bed. His hesitancy soon turns into smiling and whispering and gentle kissing. He's a very passive lover, which means Butter and I quickly take control.

The finger trick isn't actually that hard to learn. And once I get the hang of it, I prefer to do it to myself.

Luckily for the warlock, Butter is happy to pass off the reins to a professional.

They romp around in the center of the mattress. I scoot onto the mound of blankets at the edge of the bed and figure out just how many times I'm capable of coming. (Halcyon assures me it's never hurt anyone before.)

But someplace between my seventh orgasm and sunrise, I slip into a subterfuge. I stare at the wall as sunlight starts to filter in from the window. The mattress shifts as the warlock and okeanid-witch chatter and laugh.

Onesimos wanders in, which sends Halcyon into a fit of huffing and staring. He pouts at the oread, blanket tangled around his hips.

The oread ignores him. He takes a seat at my side and faces the wall. For now, he's playing like he doesn't want to be involved with Butter and Halcyon, but I know he'll ease his way over in a moment.

Onesimos kisses my shoulder, voice soft. "How did the meeting go?"

"Fine." But it didn't go fine.

The more I think about Sutnazzar's words and the cold thrum of her blue-black eyes, the more I get the feeling something is wrong. Very wrong. I also know that I'm not welcome amongst the wolves in Velm...

"Tell me what you're thinking." Simmy wraps an arm around me, fitting himself against my side. I lean against his warm, silky skin.

Behind us, Butter giggles her way into a moan and Halcyon whispers something about ice.

"I'm still banished from Velm, but I think I need to... I need to see him. And Sutnazzar and Brutatalika." I clear my throat, too afraid to look at the oread. He knows about me and Samson—I shared every last detail with him, Butter, and Esclamonde when we spent our first night in this room. "Is that crazy? I'm worried, Simmy. About Velm. About why Clearbold didn't show up."

With a sigh, he sets his cheek against my shoulder. "I understand." His head is heavy, his body relaxed where it presses against mine. "What would you tell them? How would you help?"

I open my hand. I've spent the last thirty minutes folding three pieces of bloodred paper into four-pointed stars. "I want to give them these—so they can find me if they need me. In case there's an emergency."

Nobody came to Cadmium to receive Samson.

Not his Alpha, not the rest of his packmates—only his grandmother and his wife.

Simmy lifts his head and meets my eyes. "You're a leader, Helisent. Mieira needs your foresight and wisdom—Velm included. I don't think it's out of the question that Samson and his wife might need your help in the coming months.

"But remember that the wolves deal in genders. They will expect you to speak with Brutatalika and Sutnazzar. So brace yourself—and then go, before you overthink it."

I close my hand around the paper stars. I stand up, grabbing my cloak and slinging it over my shoulders. I take my bottomless bag from the table and make for the shadow in the room's corner. I glance back once; Halcyon and Butter are a tangle of limbs and whispers beneath the thin sheet.

Simmy nods at me once in encouragement, then glances back at the lovers.

I pull Samson's white snowflake from my bag.

I exhale, then use following magic to locate the wolf via the carved snowflake. I step through the shadow toward him. Though it took me a while to get used to shadowing outside of Vex, I had plenty of practice on the ship.

It's entirely possible to shadow places I've never been.

But it's a bad idea if I don't have some type of psychic connection to that place—whether a person, a distant memory, or even a belonging.

In that single step, I recalibrate, asking my magic to take me someplace *near* him. It's early morning, and I don't know when wolves prefer to make fuck, and I will blind myself if I accidentally catch him and Brutatalika in a lover's embrace.

I clench my eyes shut, clench my hands closed around the snowflake and stars.

My next step is onto cold marble.

I keep my eyes on the glossy floor and tuck the snowflake away, too nervous to lift my chin and find out which room I'm in. I catch movement to my left; I'm back inside the Cadmium Estate's largest room. Rather than a circle of cushions, there's a small table near the doorway to the interior garden. As dawn breaks, pale light filters into the hall. It reflects off the walls and floor and ceiling, filling the room with hazy light.

Samson, Brutatalika, and Sutnazzar sit near the garden. A spread of breakfast foods sits between them on the table. Sutnazzar sits alone on one side of the table, while the married Alphas occupy the other. They sit cross-legged, knees almost touching.

Samson's eyes widen and his jaw clenches when he sees me.

Sutnazzar and Brutatalika take my entrance less in stride.

Brutatalika's features quickly pinch, a mix of wrath and shock. Sutnazzar sets her hands on her knees, like she's prepared to stand up and charge me.

And because I'm a foolish witch who didn't prepare what to say, or how to handle my intrusion, I start talking without thinking, "I have gifts. Really good gifts. You'll thank me later."

I hold up my hand, pinching the red stars so the wolves can see them.

I focus on Sutnazzar, taking a few steps toward the table now that the trio have acclimated to my presence. "You were very rude to me last night, my dear Afador. I couldn't tell *why...*" I focus on Samson's grandmother, determined not to acknowledge the married Alphas any more than is necessary. "After all, the wolf's life is owed to me."

Sutnazzar arches an eyebrow; it reminds me so much of Samson that I want to point it out to him. "Would you like to sit and eat with us, Helisent West of Jaws?" She gestures to the open place next to her, across from Brutatalika. "You smell like you haven't eaten or slept in days. Or is it sex and brandy that feeds you?"

Fuuuuuuuuuuck.

I hide my scent without breaking eye contact with Sutnazzar.

I smooth my hair and try to remember the last time I bathed.

Then I offer a smile to Samson's grandmother. "I enjoy a varied diet, thank you." I study the spread of food on the table—there's more meat than bread or fruit. "And do you always offer food to those you banish?"

Sutnazzar snorts lightly. One corner of her mouth tugs upward. "I'm shocked you don't understand Velmic politics better. You have been a friend of my grandson for a long time now."

I narrow my eyes. "I don't speak in zhuzhing. You'll have to be clearer, Sutnazzar."

"Zhuzhing, my dear witch—not *zhazhing*." Sutnazzar raises her eyebrows, like she's making sure I'm listening.

Once again, it's hard not to point out how much she sounds like Samson.

It's also hard to tell what Sutnazzar's play is right now. She seems to like me fine despite Clearbold's ongoing reticence.

"Whatever you say, my dear Afador." I take another step toward the table. I still haven't switched my gaze away from Sutnazzar. I open my hand to her, offering the small stars. "Take one. Throw it into the air if you need me—throw it as far as you can and tell it to find me. I'll know that you're in need of help."

Sutnazzar takes one of the stars, studying it between her pinched fingers.

I was right that something is wrong—she wouldn't take the stars unless it was necessary.

I brace my stomach, then pivot toward Samson and Brutatalika. I offer the remaining pieces to them. "Only use them in case of emergency. If I receive one of these, I'm going to assume you're in *dire* need of help."

Samson reaches forward and takes one. I don't meet his eyes—I barely look at his fingers as they take the paper star.

Brutatalika mirrors him, studying my face. "Thank you for saving Samson in Alita, Helisent West of Jaws."

The air empties from my lungs as I meet her eyes. I hate what I see in them, which is calm and genuine focus. It's the same focus I see in Samson's eyes, and it tells me they'll make a good match, and that the next Kulapsifang they birth will be just as powerful and composed and visionary.

(This is *good* for Samson, the man I love.)

(This is *good,* Helisent.)

(SO FUCKING *GOOD.* WOW, I'M SO *HAPPY.*)

I clear my throat. "Well, he looked very helpless bleeding out on the dirt floor."

I stand and turn away from the table in the next breath, stalking toward the shadow where I first entered the hall.

Sutnazzar calls after me, "And thank you for sending dove to my daughter, Helisent West of Jaws. It was a gracious offer considering your history with Velm. Her braid gives me great comfort."

My temper spirals—I know it's about being in proximity to Brutatalika and also the latent danger brewing in Velm. I don't trust wolves. I trust *Samson,* and *Samson* alone—not his grandmother, not his wife, not his capital. Maybe Rex and Berevald. That's it.

I whip around.

My hands clench as I look at Sutnazzar. "Do you know what you're doing?"

My question is loud, echoing across the walls angrily.

Do you know what Clearbold did to Imperatriz? What he accomplished in Ezit?

What he wants to do to your grandson, Sutnazzar?

Will you protect him when I'm not there?

Will you use that red star to find me when he needs me?

I can't tell if I've overstepped with the volume and sass behind that question.

Sutnazzar looks at me like she's waiting for me to answer instead.

I turn around and stalk into the shadow.

I waltz back into the room where Halcyon and Butter are now on top of the sheets. Halcyon lays on his back, ass naked and sprawled out like a corpse. Butter lays curled against his side, head on his chest. Neither notices my entrance—

But Simmy does.

He turns where he remains sitting on the edge of the bed, waiting for my return.

He raises his arm so I can curl against his side. He pats my head, shushing me calmly as my sniffles turn into sobs. "That's okay, my little witch. Everything will be better in Luz. Okay?"

I don't really have a choice but to believe him.

CHAPTER 22

ON THE WAY TO BELLATOR

SAMSON

Dawn beckons in the east.

I stare past Brutatalika and Sutnazzar, into the misty light that breaks over the rolling hills south of Gamma.

Mort waits a few weeks to the east, into that light. Unlike my wife, my grandmother looks prepared for the journey to the coastal city. Her hair is tidy, her chin is high; she stands with her hands tucked behind her back.

Brutatalika hasn't brushed her hair. It dangles to her hips in fragrant tangles. Cortisol hangs like lead in her ala—it's grown stronger over the last two days, while the black rings around her eyes have deepened.

Her eyes flit from me to my grandmother. She's losing this argument.

"You didn't listen to me in Cadmium," my wife whispers. She shakes her head, jaw gritted. "You left, and Malachai spread his influence. Now, you want to waltz into Bellator *without me* at your side?"

Since I left Cadmium one month ago with my grandmother, wife, Rex, and Berevald, we've traveled nearly halfway to Bellator. Things get bleaker with each week.

Returning to Cadmium without finding Pietrangelo or Riordon waiting for us was enough. So was being met with cold regard by the Cadmium pack. But I can't fathom the ongoing reticence from the villages we've passed since then.

Only a handful have recognized my rule.

The female pack leaders have stepped forward with meat, ale, bedding, and fresh clothing for Brutatalika and Sutnazzar, but the men haven't offered the same to me, Berevald, or Rex. Unwilling to ask my wife and grandmother to rough it, the three of us have taken to setting up camp on the village borders.

Which is a humiliation I hadn't seen coming.

And before I respond with the violence and wrath I feel churning in my gut, I need to go to Bellator.

Alone.

"Your pack is in Mort, Tali," I reason. "Rally them and keep the city strong. I'll worry about Bellator. First, I need to find Pietrangelo and Riordon. Then, I'll focus on Clearbold." I look at Sutnazzar next, "And you go home. Stay out of the cities."

"The Leofsiges aren't targeting the women." Brutatalika takes a step toward me. Her chin lowers, eyes beseeching me. "You can't go to Bellator alone, Samson. You cannot fight a waricon against Clearbold without *all of us* there in support. *We are a pack now.*"

Just out of earshot, Rex and Berevald pack their bags to prepare for another day of hiking. The plains are giving way to the hilly, forested mountains that precede the towering giants cradling Bellator and Rouz. The mornings grow brisker each day we push south, even with Night months away.

I take Brutatalika's hand, folding her fingers beneath mine. I hope she believes me when I say, "I will face him alone and I will kill him alone."

Or I will die trying.

There is no other option.

Not after I spent the first months of my reign in Zarzynn while Malachai and Clearbold began a campaign to defame me. Not after I returned home *without* Imperatriz.

(They whispered my ignorance before. Now, I've found two packets outlining my failures as Velm's Kulapsifang and Clearbold's potential as a new heir of Hetnazzar.)

Brutatalika pulls her hand away from mine. She grabs a fistful of my tunic, jerking once to get my attention. "We work *together*. We make decisions *together*."

She turns toward Sutnazzar.

Before she can continue her appeal, my grandmother tells her, "And, by that logic, you die together, Brutatalika. But first, I'd suggest surviving." Sutnazzar looks between me and my wife. "Regardless of what happens in Bellator, Velm needs you. You keep my daughter's rule alive. You will represent her interests in the future."

Regardless of what happens in Bellator.

To me.

"Then I will go north." My wife releases my shirt and steps away from me to face my grandmother. "I will find the red witch. Together, we will search for Imperatriz. I have her braid. We'll prove to Mieira's packs that she's alive. Me and the witch will start laying out the proof."

In the last month, I haven't had the time or strength to miss my witch.

But she's come up in conversation often. Like Sutnazzar, Brutatalika has pulled every last detail about Helisent West of Jaws from me, Rex, and Berevald. The questions aren't designed with any notion of uncovering an affair (thank the fucking moons)—they're crafted to understand whether the witch can be trusted, what sort of violence she's capable of, how I ended up with a bloodred ax, and just how long it would take for her to show up if one of us threw the red stars into the air.

Neither me nor my wife nor my grandmother have tucked away the red stars. We keep them in reaching distance in our satchels.

And I live with the constant desire to throw the paper star into the air and wait for my red witch to come and save us. I live with the constant anguish of knowing I *shouldn't*.

(I *shouldn't* think about her as often as I do; I *shouldn't* wonder where she is, and whether she's luring men into the forest with a bowl of honey; I *shouldn't* feel her absence like a limb ripped from my body.)

"Regardless of whether my daughter returns, you must rule Velm." Sutnazzar strokes Brutatalika's arm, eyebrows bunched. "Go to Mort. Tell stories of Samson's glory in Zarzynn. Set the foundation for destroying the Leofsige line. How many can wield an axe at once, Bruatalika? One. Samson wields the axe first in Bellator, while you rest. And when he is tired from his efforts, he will rest and you will wield the axe. Do you understand?"

Brutatalika slides her eyes from Sutnazzar to me.

Rage boils in them; I wait for her to curse me, my grandmother, the Afador line. But she gestures listlessly toward Rex and Berevald. "If you're all waiting for a goodbye, then you won't have one." She turns her back to us and stalks into the dawn. Mist hangs over the hilly plains, blurring the horizon. Without turning back, she calls out, "I'll see you in Mort, my Kulapsifang."

Sutnazzar doesn't follow my wife.

She watches me with a tranquility I can't fathom. She reaches up to touch my cheek. She holds my chin and tells me, "Bite him three times, Samson. Once for your mother and again for me. Bite him a third time for yourself, my Kulapsifang, and don't let go until you're the Alpha of Velm."

She smiles, then she lets me go.

CHAPTER 23

ON THE WAY TO LUZ

HELISENT

I wake up with cramps.

I groan into my pillow, turning onto my side in my nest.

At least we only have one more week of travel to Luz—then I can rejoin my warren, which has already reached the city. I imagine they're preparing my bed and telling Boonmasent Luz I'll be heading straight for the spa.

Soon, I'll restart my life as a leader in a red velvet robe. I won't have to listen to the vampires drain the livestock with noisy gulps every other morning.

"Good morning, witch."

I also won't have to wake up to Zeu's breathy whispers at the first graze of dawn.

Over the last month, we've repaired our fledgling friendship; I have Mieirans to thank. The wielders, nymphs, and a few wolves have shown kindness and curiosity to Zeu's den. They also like saiga blood, which is a relief.

But a friendship with the King of Night is trying.

Without opening my eyes, I shove him away from me. "Why the fuck are you up here, Zeu? Leave me alone. I have cramps." My hand hits his firm chest; he doesn't budge.

His warm breath grazes my ear. "I'm sure you do. I can smell blood between your legs. It's full of magic."

I open my eyes. Zeu's face is close enough that my nose grazes his cheek when I flinch, jolting backward. He wears a small smile, studying my features.

I tug my blanket over me, wrathful about being woken, about my cramps, about the fact that the vampire can smell my menstruation and finds it appealing. (There's also the gnawing agony of Samson's absence, which has made me a *significantly* less pleasant person.)

"No drinking my blood—no matter where it comes from." I find it unfathomable that I actually have to say that out loud. "And get out of my nest. I'm sleeping. It's dawn—shouldn't you be hiding underground somewhere?"

Once a week, my tiny army takes a day off from our nocturnal journeying—which means I should be able to sleep through the worst of my cramps today.

"I'll leave in a second," Zeu promises. "I just want to know what the green thing is. You never said there were green beings in Mieira—and this doesn't look like a Colyd warlock."

"There aren't green things here."

"Yes, there are." He almost sounds offended. "There's a green thing in your nest right now. It looks like an adult baby—it's the ugliest thing I've ever seen. I've spent the last hour trying to kill it, but it's not corporal. Such a tease, this fat little baby."

"What does that mean? *Corporal?*" Zeu's tightening friendship with Memphis has led to a surprising amount of vocabulary acquisition. Both know more Mieiran than I do at this point.

"It doesn't have a body. I think it's a trick of the light. Just look to your left—it's *right here*, Helisent."

With a growl, I sit up and shove the vampire from my side with a grunt. He rolls to one side of my nest, mostly out of respect.

I don't see anything out of place. Zeu points at the other side of the nest.

With dawn barely grazing the sky, the stars continue to twinkle overhead. The new Marama moon leaves only Cap and Laline shining. The limited light makes it difficult to see where my birch twig nest ends and the night begins—

But I quickly lock eyes with a green thing.

A toddler cast in bright green light sits on my nest's ledge with one leg hiked over the other. At first, I assume it's a lost child—its eyes are round, its cheeks chubby and soft. Even its belly protrudes like it just ate a full meal.

Then I meet its stewing gaze and note the faint lines on its forehead and cheeks. The spikey stubble that dots the being's chin.

Oh no.

In a deep, gravelly voice, Creepy Baby asks, "How ya doing, sweetheart?"

A scream lodges in my throat. A gag is all that comes out, followed by the word, "Why?"

"So you *do* know this thing?" Zeu sits up. "What is it?"

I ignore the vampire and level my gaze on the awful little ghost. "Who the fuck let you out of Tet? And when did you start speaking?"

Creepy Baby's cheeks crinkle as it smiles. "You don't remember our agreement?"

"I didn't agree to shit. My deal was with the other ghost." I glance at Zeu. "This is Creepy Baby. He's a ghost. Are you sure you can't kill him?"

Zeu opens his mouth to respond, but Creepy Baby cuts in, "I'm *quoting* you, witch: 'Take me to Oko right now, my dear Creepy Baby, and I will give you anything you want.'"

I blink at the ghost as it raises its bushy eyebrows at me.

Fuuuuuuuuck.

The more innocent the cover, the more sinister the trick.

This is what happens when I don't listen to my own advice.

I could cry right now; the cramps aren't helping. (And Samson would know how to handle this.)

I ignore the vampire again, controlling my urge to cast a spell on the ghost—just to see what I'm capable of. The other half of me acknowledges that Creepy Baby brought me to Oko, who brought me to Anesot. Without the meddling of this beastling, I may not have had my vengeance in Alita.

"What do you want?" I bark.

"I want to rule Skull." The ghost raises his hands as he elaborates, like he's planning something fantastic. "I want to be the King of Tet and all its ghosts."

I snort. "And how the fuck can I help you with that? I'm not going back to Tet anytime soon, Creepy Baby."

"And why not?" He crosses his arms and shifts his legs, as though catching a chill. "The tunnels are changing. The rocks are turning red in some caves. Rumor has it you're the only red witch left in existence. Red rocks, red witch—you see the connection I'm making?"

My magic is in Tet?

"What's Skull?" Zeu asks. "Tet is farther west, right?"

"I heard your little caravan is going to Luz," the ghost continues. "Come to Tet after you're all settled. I'll take you to the rocks. Then you and I are going to make a deal, Helisent West of Jaws."

I blink at the ghost.

A thousand insults flood my mind, then disappear into whispers.

It's too early, and I'm too crampy, and my brain doesn't work before dawn turns into morning. "Both of you need to get the fuck out of my nest before I start having coherent thoughts." I pull the blanket over my head and fall back against my pillow. I don't bother to check if they're listening.

Just in case they aren't, I shout, "Now!"

WANT TO KEEP READING?

Here's a little sneak peek at what's to come in the next book of the Sennenwolf Series, *White Night*.

(WHAT MUST BE DONE)

My nose twitches.

Adrenaline wakes me from a shallow sleep.

My mind latches onto the ala of a stranger.

Someone is here.

I sit up on my bed mat and pivot toward the scent.

A stranger crouches on the far side of our quiet camp, across the fire pit's dead coals.

Mist obscures his shadowy shape and the thin forest around us. Berevald sleeps to my left, Rex to my right; each snores lightly, still asleep.

I squint at the stranger, braced to find out if he's a friend or foe.

His eyes widen as we lock gazes, their whites stark. Dawn barely warms the sky or the chilly fog. But I can see the stranger, the whites of his eyes, and the white-wrapped bundle that sits near his feet.

I rip off my blanket and prepare to stand.

There must be an axe tucked inside the bundle. Maybe a vial of poison that's been masked with pungent oil.

We're nearing Bellator; tensions are rising.

The stranger doesn't shift, tracking my movements as I rise. I stare back, half awake and unsure how harshly to handle his intrusion.

I inhale deeply to study his ala. The stranger is in his sixties with a low generational count; less than 300, maybe less than 250. His musk is as potent as the muddy grass lining our camp.

Alone, he's not a threat.

I take a calming breath. "Who are you?" Then I inhale another, nostrils flaring as I search for more strangers within the mist.

The wolf keeps his hands in his lap, away from the bundle sitting in the dirt. A lock of blue-black hair slips past his ear, obscuring his narrow features. "They're offerings, Kulapsifang."

The bundle's lumps are soft, not rigid and tracing sharpened metal. In the next breath, I register the scent of red meat and sourdough bread.

The wolf explains in a low voice, "I trespassed because you've been avoiding the villages. I caught your scent two days ago. I've walked through the nights to offer you sustenance. Bellator knows you're near —the packs are sending word ahead of you. You shouldn't arrive unprepared, Kulapsifang."

I force the sleepiness from my mind.

Sending word ahead of us?

I could give a shit what Clearbold does.

I know too much to be swayed by fear. I know where Imperatriz is. I know that Clearbold worked with Anesot to strand her on Pit. I know that two Hosts in Ezit think my father is the Kulapsifang.

It won't matter soon.

I glance around our temporary camp just to be sure; nothing looks out of order, and the wolf's ala is musky but not heavy, hinting he hasn't lingered here long.

He isn't the first wolf to seek us out discreetly, far off the beaten path.

Last year, I would have treated this trespassing as a threat—even with a bundle of offerings. But this isn't the same Velm. Back then, he could have approached me in the daylight. He could have found me lounging in a village estate surrounded by gifts and pack leaders.

"I will leave now." He rises and his eyes lower, scanning me quickly. The man's frame is thinner than I'd originally thought.

The two-day trek must have taken a toll—especially considering how heavy the bundle is.

In my silence, he continues, "My village is two days west of Wartooth. We are only a few dozen wolves, but we hang the black banners of the Afadors. Every single home."

He bows his head and takes a step back. Mist shrouds half of him.

I come to my senses before he can disappear. "Wolf, what is your name?"

"Ebeneezer 231 Ronin."

I step past Rex, who is rising from a heavy sleep, and round the fire pit.

Ebeneezer takes a half-step back.

I stop in front of him. "Hello, Ebenezer. I'm happy to hear about the black banners hung in your village."

I haven't seen a black banner in weeks. When I left Velm for Zarzynn, they dangled from poles, from windowsills, from balconies.

But they've been replaced with the white flags of the Leofsige line, a foreign symbol scribbled at their ends.

"As you know, I've been gone for months. Your offerings are welcome, but my pack needs information, too. Whatever you know will help us, Ebeneezer."

I study the wolf's watery, blue-black eyes.

They reflect the pale mist like white clouds.

He tells me, "Spring was a time of great divide. High-ranking packs wandered into villages and handed out white flags. They told... they told many stories...

"That the 714th Kulapsifang did not kill the wooly.

"That the 713th Kulapsifang made deals with wielders who will threaten Velm.

"That the 712th Kulapsifang keeps a grave secret deep in the south.

"The pack leaders returned at midsummer leading the herbal caravans. And they only traded turmeric, feverfew, echinacea, and peppermint to those who had hung the white flags.

"My village has no stores for Night, my great Kulapsifang." His voice wavers. "We lost our healer and our hesperides to a violent exit. But we still wave the black flags, Kulapsifang."

Rage flickers through my body.

I've heard similar accounts from other wolves who have risked much to help me and my pack. Tales of exits in which non-wolves are forced out of villages, rumors about the failures of the Kulapsifangs, and troubling updates about the herbal caravans.

It's late summer, which means the caravans are making their way across my territory, depositing stores and providing small settlements with resources for the coming Night.

I meet Ebeneezer's eyes and nod.

Half of me wants to tell him—

I will walk into Bellator and challenge my father to a waricon. I will kill him, and take the throne. Then—stability, peace, hope.

But words mean little in times like these.

This wolf needs action.

I tell him, "Ebeneezer 231 Ronin. Return home with my blessing and the blessings of Hetnazzar. Your village's offering honors us both."

His lips tremble with a smile.

I tell him, *"De segen it tauma-kuro Kelnazzar."*

Ebeneezer's jaw clenches with conviction. He straightens his back, rising to his full height to reply, "De segen it tauma-kuro Kelnazzar, Kulapsifang."

Bless the black Night.

I glance around for the nearest blade. Rex's throwing axe is within reaching distance from his bed mat. Wearily, my packmate watches me pick it up and turn back toward the stranger.

I lift the axe toward my neck and sheer away a few strands of hair. Since nearing Bellator, we've taken to avoiding the cold gaze of village leaders and their packmates, their meager offerings, and the possibility of a dangerous run-in. I've even taken to soaking my hair with cedar oil and other herbs, hoping to dim the spread of my ala.

I need to enter the city in good shape, as do Rex and Berevald.

Still, I'd like Ebeneezer to know my scent. To take it back to his village.

He looks from the axe to where I clutch the loose strands, then carefully takes them.

I tell him, "Flags don't lessen the cold of Night. Your village should do what it must to build your stores. I will pray that Hetnazzar leads healthy prey into your territory." I raise my eyebrows, hoping he understands. "Return home and sleep well. When you wake up, know this: I will do what must be done in Bellator, Ebeneezer. And I will try to end this before Night comes."

He staggers a step backward, sparing a cautious glance at Rex. "Thank you." He turns and hustles away, glancing back once before the mist swallows him whole. "Goodbye, Kulapsifang."

"De segen it tauma-kuro Kelnazzar," I whisper in his wake.

Bless the black Night.

(PAY ATTENTION, DON'T JOKE)

I hiccup where I lay between my brothers.

I settle into my pillow and tug my blanket up to my chin.

Yves is sprawled across the living room floor to my left, Yngvi squished toward the wall to my right. The light from the kitchen window casts a gentle glow from the street. Outside, Luz has finally quieted, its residents waiting for dawn or fast asleep.

My brothers have stayed close in my orbit since we reunited in Cadmium and marched back to Luz.

Tomorrow, they'll leave to accompany Parsifal back to Antigone. Our papa is sleeping in the other room, his snoring echoing through the small apartment with gusto.

Then, theoretically, life will move on as usual, letting Zarzynn's memory fade like a distant nightmare. I'll settle into this quaint, two-bedroom apartment with my new warren: Esclamonde, Onesimos, and Butter. Downstairs are the Pletens—aside from Vulcan and Vega, who insisted on finding their own place.

It's a good setup.

So long as I don't wonder about Samson too much.

(I do.)

I hiccup again, then look around for my cup; it's out of reach near the window. "Yves, can you hand me—"

"Actually..." Yves sits up, rubbing his face sleepily. He twists to reach toward the pile of cushions—not to grab my drink, but the bottomless bag he shares with Yngvi. He drags it into his lap, shoves his hand inside, and starts looking for something. "We should probably do this now. There's going to be no waking you up once you fall asleep."

I yawn, eyeing his bag. "Well, hurry up. You're running out of time."

On my other side, Yngvi drags himself into a sitting position. With half-closed eyes, he watches Yves search the bottomless bag.

Yves finds what he's looking for. From what I can see in the dim light, it's a rectangular lump. Quickly, he lobs the soft-ish rectangle over me toward Yngvi. The bundle hits the side of his head with a gentle rustle.

Yngvi cries out dramatically.

I reach for the blockish item that landed near my shoulder. I squint, realizing it's a series of tightly tied letters jammed into a brick-like shape.

"We wrote them for you," Yves explains.

Yngvi has also switched his attention to the bundle. "Papa wrote you a lot of notes last year."

"We wrote some for you, too."

"You know, since we were the ones..." Yngvi glances at Yves. "In the first years of your life."

I look between them, too exhausted to read between their cryptic words. "What...?"

"Parsifal was barely there when we were growing up." Yves clears his throat, trying to sound sober. "I mean, he was physically there but mentally very far gone. We've never talked about that. We've never talked about a lot of things..."

"Oh, not this," I groan. "I'm way too fucked up for a heart-to-heart." I hiccup loudly, reeling where I lay. "See?" But they're both sitting up, looking from the other to me. The solemn mood is a shock at the end of a raucous, pleasant night—which has come at the tail end of a long and happy return to Luz. "Why are you two doing this?"

"Because you're turning into Parsifal," Yves says bluntly.

I gasp, causing Yngvi to quickly amend, "Not that that's bad."

"Parsifal is an admirable warlock," Yves confirms. "What I meant is that... you can turn into him, but don't stop there. Be... more, Helisent."

GLOSSARY & WORLD

The * symbol marks terms that are newly introduced in Book 2, *Seed of Vex*. Keep flipping for a character guide, followed by a visual guide to Ezitlos.

- <u>Ala</u>: A wolf's scent. Alas are highly unique. They carry information on gender, health, generational count, family ties, and more. Only wolves can smell alas.
- <u>Bitterroot</u>: A bitter flavor preferred by wielders.
- <u>Centerheart</u>: A wielder who is unable to cast magic against those they love.
- <u>Demigod</u>: A very large and blue-glowing magical being that is tied to a specific geographic region in Mieira. Demigods are the source of elemental power that nymphs who are born in their domain can draw on. Demigods appoint kings and queens to help them with custodial duties related land-based resources. The only non-nymph demigod is Hetnazzar, who roams Velm.
- <u>Desita</u>: a state of ecstasy that the demigods and nymphs can energetically absorb. Wolves and wielders can feel desita, though it doesn't boost their physical and emotional health, as it does with nymphs.
- <u>Dextro</u>: Cocaine.
- <u>Driproot</u>: A sleep aid.

- <u>Dove</u>: A type of wild magic that wielders can store in order for other beings to use. Nymphs and wolves, though largely non-magical, can apply dove from a wielder for almost any purpose.
- *<u>Ejima</u>: The intelligence and consciousness of a House and Landmark, which are enacted through magic. In other words, it's willpower.
- <u>Fangself</u>: A wolf's form, which is imbued with a secondary set of instincts and desires.
- <u>Form</u>: A true physical appearance. A wolf will phase into their form, a giant wolf, on the triple- or doublemoon. A wielder will use magic to hide their form so others can't see their horns or tails.
- <u>Highmoons</u>: Midnight.
- *<u>House</u>: A region in Zarzynn that is supported by the magic of a Landmark and its wielders. Zarzynn is home to six Houses, each of which draws its magic from a distinct Landmark.
- <u>Kulapsifang</u>: A title for the inborn Alpha of Velm, who is born from the previous generation's Male and Female Alpha. Often abbreviated as "Kulapsi."
- *<u>Landmark</u>: An ecological and magical core of a House, which generates and stores magic through natural phenomena.
- <u>Lilith</u>: A cushion used by wielders for floating.
- <u>Mixed</u>: A wolf couple whose alas merge to form a separate third ala, mixed from their original alas.
- <u>Northing</u>: To move North into Mieira from Velm.
- <u>Pith</u>: To be magically powerless. Nymphs born far from their homelands and demigods are pith by distance. Some beings, like the offspring of wolves and wielders, are born pith.
- <u>Pitroot</u>: A contraceptive for male wolves.
- <u>Seething</u>: To be compromised magically by a witch's sexual ala. This occurs only between male wolves and witches. Seethings cause a wolf to dream of the witch in question.
- *<u>Rosarium</u>: A calcified stone that is mined from Zarzynn's dead Landmarks. Rosarium can be used to nullify magical

power, including that of nymphs and wielders. It has no effect on vampires or gorgons.

- *<u>Rosfrost</u>: A liquid potion made of water and powdered rosarium. It provides the drinker with magical immunity.
- *<u>Stretch</u> (Plet, Pit, & Silt): A chain of islands that sit between mainland Zarzynn and northeastern Mieira. Plet is the largest and most populous. Silt and Pit are hidden amid clouds of fog; only a select few know how to find them.
- <u>Southing</u>: To move South into Velm from Mieira.
- <u>Torc</u>: A piece of jewelry that wraps around the necks and upper arms of wolves.
- <u>Unnumbered</u>: To live as a wolf without a generational count or pack.
- <u>Vagueroot</u>: A contraceptive for witches.
- <u>Waricon</u>: A wrestling match common to wolves. Waricons are designed for friendly competition, entertainment, and to resolve disputes of leadership.
- <u>Zhuzh</u>: A way wolves will finesse the truth without technically lying.

Words I Didn't Actually Make Up

- <u>Ala</u>: "Wing" in Spanish.
- <u>Saiga</u>: A species of antelope indigenous to the Eurasian Steppe; they are critically endangered.
- <u>Zhuzh</u>: This doesn't necessarily mean *to lie*, just to "fancy" something up. Some linguists think this word came from Yiddish. Others think it might be Romani.
- <u>Laline</u>: "Moon" in Haitian Creole.
- <u>Cap</u>: "Moon" in Mongolian.
- <u>Marama</u>: "Moon" in Maori.
- <u>Rosarium</u>: "Rose garden" in Latin.
- *The heartbeat as the first drum*: This is a concept Capes has only seen discussed in relation to Native American powwows and culture. If you want to do more research, look for Native sources.

CHARACTER GUIDE

The first portion of this list covers characters newly introduced in Book 2, *Seed of Vex*. The second portion covers characters from Book 1, *West of Jaws*.

From Book 2, *Seed of Vex*

- <u>Accra</u>: The eldest gorgon and matriarch of Dexerxes. She is aged nearly 250 years.
- <u>The Accras</u>: A collective term used by the Mieirans for Accra and the three matriarchs who trail her at all times. When Accra dies, the next-eldest Accra will assume leadership of the female gorgons in Dexerxes.
- <u>Accra-Four</u>: The youngest of The Accras of Dexerxes who comes to invade Ezit alongside the Mieirans.
- <u>Aura Hypnos</u>: A hypnotic okeanid with powerful water-based magic. She's one of the leaders of her warren, which is based in Mid City-Sunrise.
- <u>Berevald 522 Firstin</u>: Samson's third packmate, known for his long hair, open heart, and interest in vampires.
- <u>Ceyx</u> (Plet, Col): Halcyon's first wife. Vulcan's mother and Cleo's sister.
- <u>Cleo</u> (Plet, Col): Halcyon's second wife. Memphis's mother and Ceyx's little sister.

- <u>Eos Hypnos</u>: A hypnotic okeanid with water-based magic and an interest in leading okeanids. She's one of the leaders of her warren, which is based in Mid City-Sunrise.
- <u>Halcyon</u> (Plet, Serac): A four-horn wielder residing in Plet. He was raised by an evil warlock after his mother's death.
- <u>Hemlock East of Alita</u>: A Rhotidic King who rules over parts of Mieira's Rhotidom Jungle. He's known for his jacaranda jewelry and lilac-colored cloak.
- <u>Jen</u>: A degivampire taken captive by House of Serac. Pel works with Jen to kidnap okeanids from Mieira's coasts and deposit them in Ezit.
- <u>Memphis</u> (Plet, Serac): Halcyon's teenage son.
- <u>Ortera Hypnos</u>: The last Hypnotic Queen to be appointed by the demigod of Hypnos. She was kidnapped alongside Helisent West of Jaws and Butter Ultramarine.
- <u>Pel</u>: A degivampire taken captive by House of Col. Pel is the same vampire who drank Helisent's blood in Cadmium after biting her neck. This makes him Helisent's vampire familiar.
- <u>Ret</u>: A once-degi vampire who is part of Vic's den.
- <u>Suleiman</u> (Ezit, Serac): The Male Host of Serac and Halcyon's biological father.
- <u>Tol, Princess of Night</u>: Second-in-command to Vic and part of her den.
- <u>Vega</u> (Plet, Argot): Vulcan's girlfriend.
- <u>Vic the Chosen, Queen of Night</u>: Leader of Zarzynn's second-largest vampire den. Her den is responsible for transporting free degis to Plet, amongst other cultural activities.
- <u>Vulcan</u> (Plet, Serac): Halcyon's adult son.
- <u>Zeu the Chosen, King of Night</u>: Leader of Zarzynn's largest vampire den. His den is responsible for aiding the escape of degis from Ezit through guerrilla warfare.

Vexen Ghosts

- <u>Dexa</u>: A male Vexen who helped found the gorgon village of Dexerxes centuries ago.

- <u>Bathsheba</u>: A female Vexen who joined forces with the vampires of Zarzynn to free their kind from Ezit.
- <u>Axerxa</u>: A male Vexen who died fighting the unified Houses of Ezit during their last campaign in Vex. He was the last Vexen to live inside Hella.

⁂

From Book 1, West of Jaws

- <u>Absalom Metamor</u>: Sniveling warlock with an interest in Helisent and becoming a member of the Class; possibly a spy.
- <u>Boonmasent Luz</u>: Owner of Luz's finest witches-only spa. Mother-to-be.
- <u>Calypso 'Butter' Ultramarine</u>: Okeanid-witch from Ultramarine.
- <u>Chariovalda South Bend Gamma</u>: Hesperide, co-founder of Coil, and better half of Gautselin Mort.
- <u>Clearbold 554 Leofsige</u>: Samson's father and the Male Alpha of Velm by right of waricon and marriage to Imeperatriz 713 Afador.
- <u>Draginine West of Jaws</u>: Mother to Itzifone Bugs Alita and also Mieira's oldest GhostEater. Manipulative, shrewd, covered in silver jewelry.
- <u>Elvira Ultramarine</u>: Unnumbered wolf who is Coil's most popular resident. A bit of a maneater. Hates Helisent.
- <u>Esclamonde Black Rock Antigone</u>: Witchling from Antigone and Helisent's mentee. Still uses a fucking lilith.
- <u>Gautselin Mort</u>: Unnumbered wolf and co-owner of Coil, Luz's sexiest pleasure house.
- <u>GhostEater (Kierkeline Ultramarine)</u>: Mieira's youngest GhostEater and a powerful witch. Lives in Ultramarine. Grandmother to Butter.
- <u>Invidio 499 Kelberg</u>: Pack leader of a small village South of Gamma. Not a fan of the Afadors.
- <u>Itzifone Bugs Alita</u>: Bartender of Luz's seediest tavern, Solace/Soulless.

- <u>Imperatriz 713 Afador</u>: Reigning Kulapsifang of Velm. Disappeared seventeen years ago.
- <u>Malachai 555 Leofsige</u>: Clearbold's second heir to the throne. Not an Afador.
- <u>Onesimos Eupheme Jaws</u>: Helisent's favorite lover and oread. Co-founder of her warren.
- <u>Parsifal South of Jaws</u>: Helisent's papa. Big gut, bigger heart.
- <u>Pen South of Alita</u>: The only warlock in Helisent's Luzian warren. Trustworthy, horny.
- <u>Rex 507 Kaneling</u>: Right-hand, best friend, and former lover of Samson 714 Afador. Doesn't hate Helisent but is suspicious of her. Maybe he also hates her. Who knows?
- <u>Yngvi West of Jaws</u>: Helisent's probably-oldest brother. Yves' twin.
- <u>Yves West of Jaws</u>: Helisent's second-oldest brother. Yngvi's twin. Insists he's the oldest.
- <u>Zopyros Gamma</u>: Hesperide, Helisent's warrenmate.

WIELDERS

Witches and warlocks descended from magical Landmarks in Zarzynn, also known as Houses.

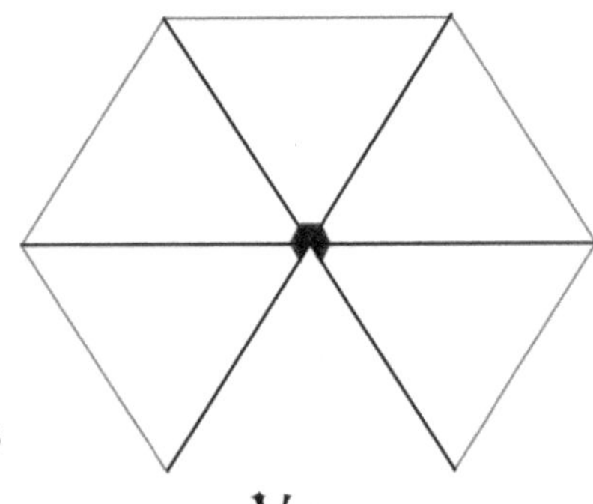

HUNDREDS OF YEARS AGO...

As bloody conflicts worsened in Ezit, the Houses of Talos and Vex were forced toward the coasts by the armies of Serac, Argot, Col, and Lahar. Thousands of wielders fled from Zarzynn toward the islands of Stretch. Some even ventured onward to Mieira...

EVENTUALLY...

To save their people, the House of Talos capitulated to the will of Ezit. However, the House of Vex refused to admit defeat. The last Vexen sailed from the shores of Vex around five hundred years ago, coinciding with the War Years in Mieira.

WELCOME TO ZARZYNN

MAP

NYMPHS

Mieirans born to demigods that rule unique ecologies.

Dryads

Born with forest-based magic, native to the jungle of Rhotidom and the forest of Septegeur.

Hesperides

Born with wind and seedling magic, native to the plains of Gamma.

Naiads

Born with freshwater magic, native to the rivers, lakes, and swamps of Mieira.

Okeanids

Born with tidal and moon magic, native to the shores of Hypnos and the Deltas.

Oreads

Born with fire and mineral magic, native to the volcanic cones of Jaws.

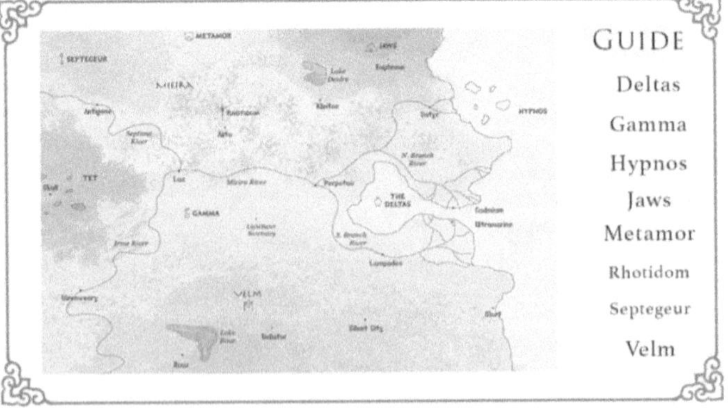

GUIDE

Deltas

Gamma

Hypnos

Jaws

Metamor

Rhotidom

Septegeur

Velm

WOLVES

Shifters from Velm who are ruled by a single demigod, Hetnazzar.

Long ago, Hetnazzar selected the Afadors to rule and protect Velm. For 714 generations, the Afador line has continued unbroken.

• THE WAR YEARS •

Though centuries have passed since the bloody War Years, its ghosts linger close in the wasteland of Tet. Some wolves still claim this region as part of Velm. Others fear the ghosts of Tet and the city of Skull.

THE AFADORS

Samson
714

Imperatriz
713

Sutnazzar
712

Malasuntra
711

OTHER BEINGS
Found in Zarzynn, Mieira, and Velm.

Vampires

Night-dwellers from Zarzynn. They spend their days in hidden dens, then emerge at night to hunt. For centuries, Zarzynn's free dens have sought sanctuary from Ezit in the empty House of Vex.

Selkies

Pinkish fish-beings who reside in Mieira's freshwater channels. Selkie are known for prophesizing. Okeanids and other coastal inhabitants believe selkies turn into seals when they enter the ocean's saltwater.

Gorgons

Peaceful and long-lived beings from Zarzynn. Eye contact with a gorgon is deadly. Gorgons live in cloistered villages that are walled off from the outside world. Outside of their villages, gorgons wear blindfolds to protect others.

Ghosts(?)

Mostly-alive beings native to Tet. Many claim they appeared after the War Years. Others insist they're nothing but an illusion created by Tet's heavy fog and distended sunlight.

The LightEater

A mysterious being located in Gamma who attracts massive bolts of lightning. The LightEater does not move, speak, or act. Despite this, worshipping nymphs dote on the LightEater from a nearby temple.

ACKNOWLEDGMENTS

This book is also dedicated to the Rat King. (Yes, again. Maybe many more agains, too.)

It's Homosapien time again—

Tiny Dancers, aka the Blue Jean Babies: I can't believe anyone follows me in any capacity. I'm thankful that you're on this journey with me! I hope we have many years together to spend counting head-lights on the (fantasy-romance) highway. Thank you for your support. Every little comment means a lot.

Cory Apple-Head: Thank you for investing your time, care, and energy into my dreams. I'm so sorry that I will never reciprocate by dunking myself into a bath of ice water. Never. Ever. (I will find other ways to help you achieve all your heart's desires!)

EV: Thank you for holding Samson accountable for his behavior and for always wanting the best for Helisent. And also for doing the same things for me as a real-life human.

Brandon: They say the devil works hard... but you battled through COVID to proof this book, which is really astounding. Thank you so much for all of your hard work and care <3

Mr. Capes: Thank you for helping me accomplish my many sordid goals even though I'm usually stumbling around drunk like Jim Lahey and shouting half-thoughts like Ozzy Osbourne. You are my Randy And my Sharon.

ABOUT THE AUTHOR

Capes is the pseudonym for author TL Adamms. She likes romance, fantasy, things with metaphysical ends, nature, the color red, and slow fashion. She writes to make sense of the world; she reads to forget it. She's very happy you've found her work. Please, indulge yourself!

Capes's stand-alone fantasy, *The Unburied Queen,* was shortlisted for the 2022 Foreword INDIES.

Website:

WWW.CAPESCREATES.COM

Instagram:

CAPES.AUTHOR

Facebook:

AUTHOR.CAPES

Peace, Love, Unity, Respect... and Fantasy Fiction.

www.ingramcontent.com/pod-product-compliance
Lightning Source LLC
Chambersburg PA
CBHW061032310726
48969CB00004B/931